THE LOST CITY

BOOKS BY JOHN GUNTHER

THE LOST CITY

a novel by

JOHN GUNTHER

Harper & Row, Publishers

New York, Evanston, and London

Dedicated to
all the friends and comrades
of old Vienna days,
with a particular bow to several,
and to
the memory of Dr. Wilhelm Stekel
with his gift for repairing
broken wings

CONTENTS

Author's Note

Most of the action of this novel takes place in Vienna in the early nineteen-thirties. I have taken several liberties with places, names, and dates; certain Vienna streets are invented, and there are a few anachronisms. As an example radio broadcasting across the Atlantic did not begin in a serious way as early as I indicate, and I have shifted some elements in political chronology.

The story is based in part on an actual event, but the characters are drawn largely from the imagination. I have had to include a few minor characters who are counterparts of men in official or semi-official life at the time—e.g., the American minister, the British chargé d'affaires, the chief of the Austrian Press Department, and the presidents of the various press organizations. These, as they appear in the book, are entirely invented, and bear no resemblance whatever to the persons who actually held these positions in Vienna a quarter of a century ago.

I myself lived in Vienna in the period covered by *The Lost City*, and although I draw on much that I saw and learned there the book is a novel, a work of the imagination, not a reminiscence or disguised autobiography. For instance I never once entered the premises of any such bank as the A.O.G. or met anybody connected with it, I was never blown up by a Nazi bomb, I never met an Archduke, I never lived in a *Gemeindehaus*, I never trained with the Schutzbund, I never took part in the fighting of February, 1934, and I never flew over Vienna or participated in any air raid. The personnel of the bank are totally invented, and I never had any confrontations with anybody like Count Diederbach or Herr Generaldirektor Dostal.

But as to the background of Vienna itself—the sights and sounds of the old lilac city, its mood and beguiling temperament—all that is real.

J. G.

New York
April, 1964

ix

BOOK ONE

A Call from Strothness

I. THE FÖHN

Mason Jarrett, a large man with bright black hair, brown eyes which had a tendency to become bloodshot, and a clement disposition, approached the spiked iron gates at the entrance of the Döbling villa. In later years he remembered that gusty March afternoon quite well, even after climbing a long way up the stepladder of time. If he could fix any date for the beginning of it all, this would be it. Mason was returning home from a stag lunch at the Czechoslovak Legation (they didn't have embassies in those days); he was drowsy and no wonder. They had had roast goose and those dumplings with caraway seeds and all that Pilsner, liquid amber with only the thinnest line of foam on it. Moreover a *Föhn* was blowing, the sultry, insidious wind off the Styrian Alps which turns the mountains purple and the human spine to butter. He looked up at the sky—piebald between sunny patches and curds of cloud. When a really big *Föhn* blew in Vienna almost all work stopped.

Mason did, however, have that series of mailers about Hungary to finish and, if possible, to get off to his newspaper on the night train. He opened the gates of the villa, crossing the lawn on the moist pebbled walk which crunched under his tread. He was trying to work out a lead for Article III but, before he reached the front door, he dissolved into a fantasy about a short story he wanted to write. He wondered if Paula would be home, and thought about what would be going on at the café tonight. It promised to be a lively night.

The Jarretts' villa stood on the northern rim of Vienna, with the profile of the Wienerwald hills clearly visible on a good day. Nearby were the Grinzing vineyards, where Beethoven had stonily walked

3

in dour majesty. The building itself, which seemed Italianate, had peach-colored stone walls and broad pillared windows, and rose handsomely, squarely, in the center of an acre or two of foaming garden. It belonged to the Wallenstein-Blohr family, and Mason and Paula occupied the whole of the second floor—six or seven sunny rooms, and, miracle of miracles, no fewer than two baths.

"Paula," Mason Jarrett began to say, entering the hall, "Darling, I picked up an item or two at lunch." No matter when or where, Mason always worked. Even his fantasies, his dreams, were work. "There were a couple of bankers there, types I don't like much, you know, so smooth that you felt oil running out of them. And one tough old buzzard—he'd put gooseflesh on a statue. But they had some interesting things to say. German banks in rotten shape. There's been a lot of new investment in Czechoslovak industry by the A.O.G."

The A.O.G., Allgemeine Österreichische Gesellschaft, was the largest, most powerful bank in Austria.

Paula did not answer, for the good reason that she was not in the room. "She ought to be home pretty soon," Mason muttered to himself. She was spending the afternoon with Kitty Jameson, who was passing through Vienna on the way to Greece; Paula and Kitty had been close since they went to Vassar together, but nowadays seldom had a chance to meet.

Mason thought back to more of the talk at lunch.

"What about your local political situation? What about the Nazis here?" a British visitor to Vienna had asked him. On this kind of thing he was always crisp.

"They have no power at all right now," Mason had replied. "They didn't win a single seat in the elections last November. But there's a strong pan-German sentiment here and conceivably they could become a third force if things break up."

"Any Communist threat to speak of?"

"There aren't more than two hundred authentic Communists in the whole of Austria. However, some extreme left-wing Social Democrats may be Communist-inclined. It's the old, old question—what influences a person most, stomach or head?"

The Englishman looked puzzled.

"If you're hungry enough the stomach overrules the head. Then people get radical and go Communist. That's the theory—I'm not sure I altogether believe it. Maybe communism comes from the head first, no matter what."

Still groggy from the combination of lunch and *Föhn*, Mason walked from the hall to the living room. An observer, if percipient, might have learned a good deal about him from the way he walked. This was one of his signatures, like the blue Pelikan typewriter ribbon he always used. It was a kind of lope, both dogged and springy, casual but spirited. Swift, silent, he padded on the balls of his feet, scarcely seeming to raise them from floor or pavement, and conveying a buoyant smack of the American west, of open spaces: so a friendly frontiersman might have walked.

This, at least, was the way Mason Jarrett walked after a certain hour in the morning, say eleven. Until then he shuffled. It took him an abnormally long time to wake up in the morning. He crept around in battered slippers, and sat interminably at the breakfast table wrapped in an ancient bathrobe, scarcely alive, until Paula sometimes thought she would scream. Then without transition he would become fresh, brisk, and full of bounce.

An observer might also have learned something from the way he carried his clothes—appalling! Two hours after getting into a new suit he looked as if he were dressed in a baked-potato skin.

Mason glanced at the clock, yawning. Paula should be home in a minute. He ought to put in a hard hour on Hungary, but let it wait. He sank down on the big white sofa and picked up the last copies to reach Vienna of *Time* and the *New Yorker*, which were striplings then, three weeks late. Dozing, he yawned again, then thought of the color of Paula's eyes and hair.

He woke up, startled. The telephone was ringing in his office down the corridor with the high triple note which, in the Vienna of that day, signified an international call—sharp, commanding. Jarred but alert, he moved to answer. International calls were a dime a dozen, and the mere fact that somebody was telephoning him from abroad had no significance at all. Yet he had a surprising reaction, that of disturbance, even of foreboding. His muscles tightened. He felt an almost sinister premonition about it. This was no ordinary call. What pebble was about to drop into what pond?

On the line was Jarrett's colleague Strothness, the Berlin correspondent of the *Star*.

"Hi, Harry, what's up?"

Strothness—taut, tense, intolerant, and a fiery zealot; a believer, pure, courageous; his eyes were so blue that they seemed to cast blue shadows on a tablecloth.

His voice was hurried, but with every word molded carefully, as if he were kissing each onto a sheet of paper. "Listen, I have a tip on a whale of a story—really big. It's very much up your street too. Germany and Austria are going to make a Customs Union."

A pebble? No—a rock!

Strothness continued: "It's not official, it's not even admitted—that's the point. Nobody will say a word. What I need is confirmation. Vienna is full of leaks, more so than we are, check with your friends, see what you can get. Big story? I should say so. Union of Germany and Austria is forbidden by the peace treaties, although the jurists here contend that it's quite legal. This will knock the French into a brace of fits. But listen—not a word please, not a word to anybody, not even Sandor—this could be a nice clean beat."

"Right. I'll call you back."

Mason Jarrett liked and respected Strothness, but he was not altogether sure that Strothness liked him in return. Probably he disapproved of Mason's deplorable—as he put it—lack of deep inner conviction about politics. Then too their professional relationship held curiosities. Strothness was a veteran, ten years older, at a period when ten years made a lot of difference, and he had had prolonged experience in Berlin. But Jarrett was a newcomer to Vienna, comparatively speaking, and this was his first independent post. Besides, since Vienna was closely related to Berlin, he probably should have asked for counsel from Strothness more often than he did, and Strothness perhaps disliked it that the younger man did not defer to him. Strothness had never quite made Jarrett out; that was the long and short of it.

Strothness said, "Damn nice little story—your situationer about Carol from Bucharest last week. I wish I had your facility, Mason."

"I worked my head off on that story."

"Oh, I know you're a dutiful, conscientious boy under the skin."

Mason smiled. At the beginning his senior colleagues had used words for him like "avid" and "reckless," not being aware of other facets in his character, like intense self-consciousness and self-division. Strothness concluded: "See if you can get anything on the Customs Union and let me know, as soon as possible. Best to Paula."

Mason had been waiting for that. Strothness liked Paula and had an eye for her. Once, though, Mason heard from a friend that he had referred to her as "that fancy bitch." Strothness, a bachelor and a puritan, knew little about women. Fancy Paula certainly was, but a bitch, no.

Mason put down the phone. The Customs Union project would knock his whole area into a cocked hat, he knew. This was not merely the German reply to Briand's plan for a United States of Europe; it was the first attempt by Germany to break the shackles of the peace treaties. It would destroy the Little Entente, eliminate Austria as a buffer state between Germany and Italy, and ruin the French position everywhere. The old German dream of penetration into Mitteleuropa was revived. Germany was on the march.

For this was 1931, long before Europe exploded and went to pieces. This was the early spring of 1931, when most people had never heard of Hitler, or thought that he was a bad Austrian joke. This was March, 1931, and no one had ever seen a ballpoint pen, stiletto heels, or frozen food. Lucky Strikes were still packaged in green, and nobody had ever listened to a Geiger counter, hired an organization man, or bought a dacron suit.

2

Mason sought to think out what his first step should be on the Strothness story. His face lost its usual air of confidence and took on what Paula called his baffled look. He groped. He was still inexperienced in handling stories on the highest political level. Besides, this was a tricky situation. He was being asked to get information on a story without tipping his hand on it. Paula always said, "Darling, you must learn to think things *through!*" Well, that was easy enough for Paula, the only woman he had ever met who actually liked logic— a realist. She had no fear of facts at all and was inveterately logical. He himself operated largely by feeling his way around roomily or acting on impulse or by obscure processes of intuition.

He walked back to the living quarters of their villa, which he and Paula both loved with fervor, to ask Frau Gertrude for a cup of coffee. Get to work, he told himself. That's a damned hot story.

The Jarrett accouterments, within the sumptuous outer shell of the villa, were modest but had a certain style; they were comfortable, but chic. The living room gave the taste, Paula's taste, of young people in whose lives periods of rapture and despair alternated, or were commingled, and who did not, like their elders, have to be guarded about time. Large white chairs with harlequin silk cushions; the big squashy sofa, its slip covers tattered; a table or two of Spanish walnut with a deep velvetlike patina; broad taffeta curtains the color of burnt orange. Mason glanced at a bowl of slightly threadbare roses on the hall table, and at the somewhat untidy pile of gramophone records nearby, sloping like a broad Leaning Tower of Pisa.

Stifled by the *Föhn,* Mason pulled the corner window open—a curved double sheet of glass with a space between; it even had a *Furteshka,* or sliding panel which could be opened independently, and which the Viennese, in their odd way, called a *Was-ist-das.* A big black ant, shaped like a dumbbell, waded across the stone sill of the window. He could not resist peering out into the garden where pyramids of green bushes and small trees were being shaken by the wind; moist leaves piled up along the walks lined with a few early snowdrops and crocuses. Except for the swish of the wind, the silence was intense. He heard then the peculiarly liquid, sloshing sound of horses' hoofs on cobbles, and, down their street, a fiacre passed. Who might be within? His imagination raced. The woman, straight out of Schnitzler, would have coral lips and topaz-colored eyes; the man, in a tie as white as halibut, wore a short, brisk, black-pointed beard. He leaned close to her bare shoulder and, with a flourish, took off his mask. . . . Her first words would be remonstrative. . . . The man would lean back with cynical laughter. This fantasy, this vision, became completely real to Mason. The fiacre went plop-plop and disappeared, and abruptly he turned the dream off.

Get to work, for God's sake! What held him back? Did he secretly, inexplicably, resent having to work with Strothness on a story? Did he fear its implications? Oh, *Quatsch!*

Mason saw the Frau Dozent, their landlady, strolling in the garden. She paused for a moment by the large fruit tree with its fantastically twisted double trunk, the bark looking braided, and heart-shaped leaves. He waved; she saluted in return, then pointed up and made a downward cupping motion with her hands which said, as clearly as words, "Soon it will rain." Mason replied with a thumbs-up gesture; communication between them was complete. A cat screamed. No: not a cat, but the screech of a taxi taking the Mozartgasse turn too fast.

Mason turned back to his office. Surely the first thing was to call the Czechs and the Poles, since they were the people most likely to talk, to leak, if they knew anything about this Customs Union thing. Prague and Warsaw were the capitals which would gain most by letting the facts be known, on the assumption that any premature announcement would kick up such a fuss that it would kill the project. Mason could not reach anybody at the Czechoslovak Legation. Everybody must have gone home to sleep off that monumental goose and the Pilsner. Nor did he have any luck with the Poles. His best Polish source, Dr. Wiskiewicz, the press attaché, was out. Mason had a high regard for Dr. Wiskiewicz, who had a head shaped strangely like a football. The secretary said that Dr. Wiskiewicz would call him back.

What next? No use going after the Bundeskanzleramt, the Austrian Chancellery. The Austrians would be quitting work for the day and were mostly useless anyway. Herr Gesandter Dr. Emmerich Wimpassing, the chief of the press bureau, would lie softly right into his face no matter what he knew or did not know. As to the American Legation, it was pitiably uninformed and the minister, a short good-natured man with a long neck and a head like a taffy apple, jutting out from a shiny stiff white collar two sizes too large, the neck never touching the collar, so that he always seemed to be preening, had no political sense at all; he did little but play around with the local—to use a humorous term—aristocracy. As for the British, they were smart and right on the ball, charming too, but inclined to be aloof, except for Yancey. He called Yancey—he was out. He might go after the local Yugoslavs, and then the French, but they never talked to anybody. Who else?

The telephone rang and Mason Jarrett jumped to pick it up, hoping that Dr. Wiskiewicz might be on the wire. But the accent was American. "Jarrett? Mason Jarrett?"

"Hello? Yes. Who is it?" His voice was a light tenor, not the voice one would normally expect from so big a man.

"Mark Thorne. I got in on the Orient this morning. How are you, Mason? Like to see you."

Thorne was not one of Jarrett's favorite people, but it was a convention to be agreeable to all visiting firemen. Thorne was crude, aggressive, and a chaser. He had good qualities too, and as a matter of fact was not a bad sort at all, but Mason did not trust him. Stationed in London, he was European manager of the news agency that Dr. Karl Tetzel, one of Mason's good friends, represented in Vienna. But I don't really hate him, Mason said to himself. If you hate, you lose.

"Nothing on my mind," Thorne went on. His voice was virile, easy. "Just want to say hello and chew the fat."

Mason loathed phrases like "chew the fat." "I'm sort of tied up at the moment, Mark."

"Well, I'm only here for a day or two. Gotta chase down to Istanbul, my man there seems to have tapped the till. I have to fire him, and find somebody else."

"I'll be coming down to the Weissenhof around nine-thirty tonight—why not meet me there?" Mason said.

"Okay."

Calls from visitors like Thorne were not a novelty to Mason, and reflected the widened horizons of his life these days. Dozens of people passing through Vienna came to see him and Paula: magazine editors from New York, youthful British dons on holiday, psychoanalysts restoring themselves at the central fount, mountain climbers, and an intermittent stream of fat cats with letters of

introduction from Chicago. Then too there were newspaper friends
from Paris en route to assignments or heading for vacations in
Dalmatia or the isles of Greece. Vienna was a crossroads, and the
Jarrett establishment had already become a crossroads within a
crossroads. Mason knew what was going on in Central Europe; to
an inner circle, he was beginning to symbolize Vienna almost as
Strothness symbolized Berlin, or colleagues on other papers symbolized other cities, like Marmaduke Haven in Moscow, with his
agile tongue and wooden leg, or Leighton J. Cooke, so knowledgeable, so indomitably spirited, in Madrid. Added to the factor of
professional interchange was a personal element. He and Paula liked
people and were therefore liked; they gave and therefore received;
they conveyed the impression of having established a strong, stable
relationship, and this drew to them those less fortunate; they were
happy, and so unhappy people, the waifs and strays, clung to them,
seeking to absorb something of their own vitality and fresh joy in
living.

Thorne, talkative, was gossiping. His voice had power. Mason
wanted to get him off the phone, but Thorne acted as if he had
all the time in the world.

"No chance of a drink right now?" Thorne said.

"Sorry, no. I'm in a jam on a story. Let's meet tonight."

"Right, but I'll probably have to be with the Tetzels."

"Sure—why not?"

Thorne paused. With a slight edge in his voice, he asked, "How's
Paula?"

"Fine." Mason did not mention that she was going to the Opera
this evening with Kitty, to hear Mayr and Lehmann in a standard
Viennese gala, *Rosenkavalier*, or Thorne might conceivably contrive
to be hanging around there. The son of a bitch, handsome, bold,
always grabbing off other people's women.

"Give her my best."

"You bet."

Mason still felt torpid, almost comatose. Must freshen up. He
rose from his desk (they had bought it in the Dorotheergasse auction
rooms for ten dollars) and splashed water on his face from the bronze-
bound washbowl (gold taps) set in the ornately papered wall,

then squeezed out a white caterpillar of toothpaste on a brush and scrubbed his teeth. His office was a converted bedroom. It was also a shambles. Disorderly sheaves of paper lay strewn on the floor. What now? He wanted to talk to Dr. Laszlo Sandor, his best friend in Vienna, who was omniscient and with whom he worked hand in glove on almost everything. But Strothness had specifically counter-manded this, for the obvious reason that he didn't want to risk giving anybody the story.

What the hell was a Customs Union, anyway? Did it necessarily mean political amalgamation? Fishing in a grim confusion of papers interspersed with everything from ancient menus to out-of-date time-tables, he looked up the relevant clauses in the St-Germain Treaty and the Austrian constitution, ran through recent speeches by pan-German politicians, and, feeling like a man digging in a mine, but enjoying it, collected some statistics on trade in the Danube Valley. Once, when he was second man in Paris a couple of years before, his boss Philip Hazelwood had come across him in the library sim-ilarly attacking the background of a story through documents. Hazel-wood, who had more than a slight touch of ego, tapped him on the shoulder. "Delighted, Mason, to see you go after something just the way I'd go after it!" He spoke in commendation, with his intensely shy, fastidious smile, but then his eyes fell to Jarrett's feet. A puzzled look became one of disapproval. Mason followed his eyes to the floor and discovered that he, Mason, was wearing one black shoe, one brown. Maybe he had a hangover when he was getting dressed. Hazelwood marched out of the room.

Mason looked at his watch—*dreiviertel sechs*, or three quarters after five. Well, if the Viennese chose to express time in such absurd terms it was their own business. Of course it was far too late for Strothness to file now. The *Star* was an afternoon paper, and even allowing for the difference in time between Europe and Chicago, the paper could take nothing after four in the afternoon European time except in the most pressing emergencies. In fact Mason and his colleagues usually filed at about one-thirty in the afternoon in order to catch the syndicate wire in New York early in the morning.

He glanced at his watch again. Where was Paula? Really, she ought to be home by now. He thought that he might as well get on with the work he had to do anyway, Customs Union or not, and dutifully assembled his notes for Article III in the Hungary series. The stories Mason liked to do best described the way people lived. He was primarily a writing man rather than a news man. He liked to prowl about in a new country and do a group of mailers discussing not merely the policies of the Prime Minister and who ran the place but what the streetcar conductor ate for breakfast and how he amused himself Saturday night. These stories were clever and had a nice human touch and the *Star* liked them.

What picturesque points of interest could he use in the Hungary story? The fantastic castle in Sarospatak. How Szeged became the paprika city. Origin of painted furniture. He needed verification of some figures on the land reform, and put in a call for his stringer in Budapest. Then he telephoned the Poles again, hoping that Dr. Wiskiewicz had returned. No.

3

As Vienna correspondent of the Chicago *Star* Mason Jarrett had an enormous territory to cover—all of Central Europe, the Danube Basin, the succession states, everything from Prague to Istanbul. It was part of his job to visit intermittently each of the nine countries for which he was responsible, in addition to Austria, and he had spot news to handle in Vienna day by day. Frequently too there came emergencies—a coup d'état here, an attempt at revolution there—which would send him hurriedly out of town. Almost the most incredible, idiotic thing about American journalism in Europe was that a man arriving in Belgrade or Warsaw, say, highly difficult and secretive capitals, where a story complex in the extreme had just broken, was expected to file an accurate interpretive dispatch about it within an hour or two of his arrival. Well, kept you on your toes. His temperament was calm, his manner fresh and open, but sometimes the strain of his daily routine came close to making him explode.

Erji Sandor, wife of the estimable Dr. Sandor, once said to him in her remarkable English, "Wiz you I feel I sit on Vulcan." It took him a second to realize she meant "volcano."

The office telephone rang again, and Mason heard the bulbous voice of James N. Drew.

"Coming down to the café tonight, Jarrett?"

"Yes." Mason as a rule was laconic on the telephone. He was one of those who believed that this hateful instrument, without which he could not exist, was designed for brief communication rather than prolonged conversation.

"Good. Something I want to ask you about. In fact you could do me a big favor."

Immediately Mason thought that Drew, who was at once bashful, boyish, and portentous, must also have had a tip on the Customs Union story. Drew was a stout man in his middle thirties, with a heavy long face and an extraordinarily sweet—that was the only word for it—smile. He blinked when he talked. He was a mess, but, God damn it, he did have that sweetness. Drew was Vienna correspondent of an important American agency, International Press, and strictly speaking he and Mason were not competitors, since the Chicago *Star* took the service of Drew's agency, and they were even expected to cooperate to an extent. But Strothness had told him to say nothing to any other correspondent. Of course sometimes a man worked even with his most direct competitors. He and John Dixon of the Chicago *Daily News* often traded news, or saved time by dividing up a story they were chasing together, but this was on the understanding, strict if unspoken, that neither ever interfered with the other if he was at work on something exclusive. Such a lot of journalism was a reciprocal process of barter, picking your friends' brains. Who cared? After all, the friends picked back, and you gave value for value received. Even so, Mason liked nothing better than to be on a story on his own.

Drew, who had been born in backwoods Tennessee, put up a front of formality even with his friends, and seldom used Christian names. Breaking this rule he went on, "Mason, I need your help. Something nasty is in the works. I've been insulted, and I think we'll have to call an *Ehrengericht*."

"A what?" He was relieved—Drew's call had nothing to do with the Customs Union.

"*Ehrengericht*—Court of Honor. We'll institute formal proceedings just as soon as I clear it with you."

"Me?" But he was the man everybody always turned to.

"Seen tonight's Abend? There's a story, page three, full of filthy innuendoes, dirty lies, saying that the Weissenhof is a nest of conspirators, spies, and that we're all a lot of crooks."

Mason's black eyebrows became sharp peaks. "Are we?"

If Mason knew anything at all about Vienna it was that Drew was perpetually surrounded by hangers-on and parasites, who used the Weissenhof as a rendezvous. He was deeply involved in all the shadowy submovements of Viennese political and journalistic life. Every evening two or three tipsters would come respectfully to the café and whisper to him confidentially. This gave Drew a great sense of power. It also helped to make him a target for all the shysters, crooks, and political confidence men in town.

"My dear sir, this is a serious matter. Besides, Emilie is involved."

"Right, tell me more."

"I'll tell you when I see you. Too busy to talk now. And there's another thing I want to ask you about. Jove!"

He rang off. "Jove" was a strong word for James N. Drew, and Mason knew that he must be passionately upset.

There was nothing much Mason could do on the Customs Union story now. He would have to wait for the evening. He was determined to keep busy on it all night if necessary. He must not let Strothness down.

"Entschuldigen, bitte," he said to their cook, Frau Gertrude, as he prowled into the kitchen. He opened the icebox, one of the few electric refrigerators in the whole of Vienna of that day, and pulled out a tray of ice cubes. Partially opaque, lightly dusted with a powder of frost, faintly sticky, they resembled Turkish Delight. He poured himself a Scotch from a bottle a third empty which would have to last them a week longer. Usually they drank a local vermouth or slivovitz, because they could not afford Scotch often.

One pleasant thing about Vienna was that people with modest incomes could eat better here than in any other city in the world, Paris excepted. He hadn't had a new suit for more than a year, but, by heaven, Frau Gertrude was under instructions to buy nothing but the best and use butter by the ton if necessary. In his execrable German he talked with her for a moment; that is, he asked her

about the state of her husband's health, agreed with her that they
needed a new corkscrew, and promised to take up again with the
authorities the complicated matter of her social insurance.

He went on: "I hope your daughter is all right now."

"When excited, she still cannot hold her food." Frau Gertrude
was not a cheerful woman, but neither Mason nor Paula had ever
seen her out of temper.

"I know." They had asked her to bring Rosa to the villa on her
birthday, and gave her a doll's house and a harmonica. The little
girl almost fainted with pleasure, then threw up.

"The doctor says that she will outgrow the state of nerves, but
wishes soon to give her an elaborate examination."

"Would you like the gnädige Frau to take her to our own doctor,
Dr. Antioch?"

"Perhaps. Excuse me, it is now necessary to make ready sauce for
the Mehlspeise."

Frau Gertrude lived on the other side of town, and it took her
a full forty minutes on the cold, clanging tram to reach the Döbling
villa, where she arrived six days a week at seven-twenty in the
morning. She cooked three meals a day, scrubbed, washed, did the
ironing, and made the beds, which was no small job in Vienna,
where all mattresses were, like Gaul, divided into three parts. She
had precisely the same responsibilities in her own small household
in the Second Bezirk, which she had to attend to before six-thirty
in the morning or after nine at night. Her wages were one hundred
Schillings per month, or fourteen dollars. This was high. Erji Sandor
was able to pay their cook only eighty Schillings, about eleven-
fifty. But in addition to fourteen dollars a month and her meals
Frau Gertrude had her social security, her health insurance, a
month's holiday, and thirteen months' pay for a year, the invariable
Vienna custom. Her face was pale, her manner dignified, and no
one would ever dream of addressing her without the prefix "Frau."

Mason sniffed good kitchen smells, and dipped his finger in the
sauce. Paula, now. He doubled up, slapped his thighs, and began
to laugh—Frau Gertrude looked startled—at the thought of Paula
in the kitchen. Paula knew practically everything there was to know
about Bach, Fischer von Erlach, Baudelaire, and Puvis de Chavannes,

all this without fakery, without a trace of pretension, but she couldn't sew a button or grill a steak. She had all the classical virtues, she was intensely superior, she was the personification of the intellectualized youthful American, elite of the elite, educated to her fingertips, strong, but it was totally beyond her to fry an egg.

In the living room Mason said "Mousie" aloud, and stretched his large hand with the heavy blunt fingers toward the floor as if to fondle the silverish tawny small cat that was not there. Mason had grown up among animals, loved them, and had always had pets around, but Paula could not endure animals and would not have one in the house, not even a tiny dog or a kitten, because they gave her a violent rash, irritated the flawless skin that was her best feature. So, when they married, Mason gave Mousie, whose original name had been Geraldine, to the Hazelwoods, and had felt the loss severely ever since. He could see her now, curled in a corner like a macaroon.

He said to himself, I think I'll have a second volume, and made himself another drink. Now thoughts of Mark Thorne and James N. Drew teased him. What kind of crisis was this *Abend* thing involving Drew? Of one thing Mason was certain: it would have to do with money and, after that, sex. Maybe Vienna had too little of the first commodity, too much of the second. His mind roamed among his colleagues stationed in Vienna: mostly they were a hard-working, respectable lot, with children growing up and never enough money to go around, who did not resemble at all the type of newspaperman made familiar by the movies. The foreign correspondent who talked out of the side of his mouth, cigarette dangling, his feet on a desk, about to rush off by chartered plane to cover a romantic crisis in Siam, and who had never read a book, was, even then, largely an artifice of some outsider's imagination. One of Mason's closest friends in Vienna played the viola in a string quartet; another worshiped at Quaker meetings; still another had a considerable reputation as an expert on Chinese ceramics.

Three of the agency men in Vienna were, however, genuinely hard-boiled—newshawks in the old tradition, tough as blue jeans, named Wolfe (broken nose, pot belly), Bass (wore a green eyeshade in the café), and Clippert (high singsong voice). Hot competitors, they ran in a pack—forever at each other's heels. If one appeared anywhere, the other two invariably trotted on to the scene at once, red-faced, panting.

The phone rang: long distance. Mason jumped. A month ago he had asked their Rome man, Elliott, to try to find him a good small marble copy of the Venus of Cyrene, something hard to come by; now he had found one and was calling to say that he had shipped it up.

Elliott was a youngster, the junior man on the *Star* foreign staff after Jarrett, full of sass and savvy.

"Any news, Rob? What's going on?"

"Not a thing. Our Mr. Big is rolling his white eyes and munching his thin, steely lips at nothing what-so-ever. I haven't filed a line in a week. As to the situation in general, fascism is still an attempt to make Romans out of Italians."

They both snickered.

"How's your weather?"

"Fine."

In his atrocious German Mason whispered conspiratorially, *Kennst du das Land, wo die Zitronen blüh'n, Im dunkeln Laub die Gold-Orangen glüh'n.* He couldn't remember the next two lines and skipped over to *"Kennst du es wohl?—Dahin! Dahin!"*

"What's that?"

"One of the most luscious, sublime lyrics ever written in any language, even if it's by a German."

"Oh, sure, of course, Goethe. But I'm not a nature lover."

Mason had a sudden flash, thinking of Strothness and the Customs Union. "Even in those days the Germans liked to kick around in other people's countries—damned expansionists!"

"Wotcha driving at, Mace?"

"Not a thing."

"Well, you must have meant *something*, but never mind." Elliott chatted for a moment. "Well, *ciao.*"

Mason remembered the week Elliott had spent with them in Vienna last year. He was crazy about girls. As a matter of fact practically every visitor to Vienna was crazy about girls, a commodity that Vienna and its suburb Budapest were, more than any cities in the world, amply and deliciously equipped to provide. Members of the resident colony itself might be respectable, but, my God, thought Mason, the visitors really did go wild. Vienna liberated something in them. They were ravenous and insatiable—woman-struck. They became competitive, acquisitive, possessive, about girls off the streets whom anybody could have for ten Schillings. Their first destination, if they could afford it, was usually the Grand Bar, where lovely, lissome creatures abounded but where it was often necessary to pay court, a process which could be slow and very, very expensive. If the Grand Bar failed, night clubs like the Koenigen or the Mariposa were available a few minutes away, and as a last resort there was always Kärntnerstrasse.

Bluitt! Remember Bluitt! He was Drew's boss in Paris—jaunty, mean, squeaky voice, wise guy, know-it-all. A month or two before, visiting Vienna, he took Drew to lunch at Sacher's, the most celebrated of the classic hotels. They were well into their *Tafelspitz*, boiled beef, when a girl alone at another table, wearing a scarf like crushed tinfoil and with nails the shape of pistachio nuts painted silver, who in every feature expressed the absolute essence of deluxe pouledom, the real thing, gave Bluitt, who had three sons at a good school in England, the eye. In an instant, he was out of his chair: without so much as a growl of apology to Drew, off he went; he plucked the girl from her table like a doll, and, with one hand flat against the middle of her back, between the shoulder blades, propelled her right out of the restaurant. Drew's mouth fell open; morosely he finished lunch alone. Jove!

And remember Abercrombie, the chief correspondent in Berlin of an extremely distinguished British newspaper. Arriving in Vienna last winter he telephoned Mason at midnight and asked him to rush over to the Majestic at once—an emergency. There Mason found him stark naked with his Vienna string man and three girls they had just picked up. "Now, Mason," boomed Abercrombie cheerfully, "we're a man shy, and take your pick." Mason looked alarmed. "Help yourself," Abercrombie persisted. He was so drunk he could scarcely stand. The telephone rang; London calling. Abercrombie listened carefully, grumbled, but then said placidly, "London has a flap on about Hindenburg. Must send a story right now, from here." He

typed it out, called London back, and telephoned it in, drunk as he
was. It ran six hundred words or so, and not a word was blurred.
Lucidly, comprehensively, with perfect balance, airtight, it explained
the intricacies of Hindenburg's position in the light of the German
political situation of the moment. Abercrombie, regrettably, came to
his end a few months later. Roaming through a Berlin suburb after
midnight during a thick, greasy snowstorm and dead drunk, he
slipped, fell, and passed out in an icy ditch. He had been sweating
profusely around the collar; his neck froze in a halter of ice before
he was picked up, and this brought on a pneumonia that killed him.

Men on Mason's own paper had a tradition of not drinking much.
Strothness did not drink at all, and Hazelwood little but wine. But
Mason had heard that Throckmorton, a tough egg, who had just
been assigned to Moscow and whom he had never met, had been
known to hoist a few.

Mason heard a key scratch in the front door—Paula at last. He
walked down the corridor trying to look calm, but his pleasure that
she was home could not be concealed. Yet a nervous pall overcame
him. His muscles tightened, and again he felt the curious sense of
foreboding, of apprehension, of the approach of something possibly
sinister, that had come to him earlier that afternoon with Strothness's call.

4

On seeing her his premonitions, such as they were, vanished. Bending
over and with his hand cupped like a trowel he lifted her chin,
scrutinizing her as she flung herself at him. Her body seemed heavy;
the little shelf of tilted flesh between nose and lip, with its soft V,
as if a kernel of corn candy had been pressed there, was grayish, not
rosy, and a tiny, almost imperceptible white line bound her big,
chubby lips—sure signs of fatigue.

She hung on his neck for a moment, then shook herself free with
a quick movement, so that her hair, in the shape of aprons, slid forward over her cheeks.

Mason said, "You're late, I was beginning to get worried. It's a
hell of a thing, leaving me alone all afternoon."

"Darling, I'll bet a million-a you didn't give me a single, solitary
thought."

Whenever she and Kitty Jameson spent an hour or two together Paula picked up one of her verbal mannerisms, the adding of an "a" to occasional nouns, like "thing-a" or "doctor-a." In fact even their voices became alike.

"Well, what were you doing?"

"Kitty had an introduction to a Count Something-or-other and we went to his house; he has the most beautiful Vermeer I ever saw. Apparently it's famous, but he seldom lets anybody see it. Subject conventional, the usual interior full of sunshine, with a girl who looks as if she were stuffed with frankfurters, but so lovely! Imagine being able to paint light in a room that way. Then—"

"I've been busy too. I think we have a story, and there were a lot of calls."

"Finished Hungary yet?"

"No."

"What's the story?"

"I'll tell you later. How's the Föhn?"

"Blowing hard. It plays hell with my hair."

"It's lovely hair."

"I think I'm going to dye it."

"What?" Her hair was light, wayward, hard to keep in order, and sometimes she put ironmongery in it at night: an offense, deplorable. He adored its color, pale auburn with a touch of gold. Of course it might grow darker in time. "Dye that hair and I'll cut your throat."

"It looks like butter with paprika in it."

She studied herself intently in the mirror, frowning. She primped often. No matter how avidly he admired her she always refused to take his word for it that she was attractive. One of her characteristics was a habit of self-depreciation, which did not, he thought, rise so much out of modesty as out of fear and perverse reaction to her own superiorities.

They strolled toward the bedroom. "Unhook me, please," Paula said.

"What color would you dye it?" Mason asked.

"Black, like yours—jet black. And I'd have a whorl cut into it, too."

Practically from the day they met she had been fascinated by an infinitesimal bald spot, no bigger than a pea, on the crown of his head where the hair made a small, stiff pinwheel.

"You couldn't manage that, I'm afraid." Mason laughed.

"I wish we were the same person."

"We pretty much are. Now, hurry up, run your bath."

His tone made her say cheerfully, "Oh, I know that you don't *like* me as well as I *like* you, but God will even it up some day."

"Sure, sure, but you ought to hurry if you're going to be on time for the opera."

"I've told Frau Gertrude to have dinner ready at seven, *pünktlich*."

"It's almost seven now. You always try to push time backward. Maybe that's why you get better looking every year."

She smiled with quick pleasure; her cheeks rose, and became two perfect eggs. Mason watched her slim, adroit fingers at the dressing table, and then she turned sharply.

"You have your purple suit on! Please, please, take it off." The whites of her eyes, curved arrowheads, flashed; tiny highlights shone near the pupils.

The suit wasn't purple at all but a dark, rather shiny shade of brown. But it had always been purple to her, and she hated it.

"It isn't purple," said Mason.

"It is so purple."

"Well, I'm damned if I'm going to change my clothes just because you're color-blind or have some idiotic resistance to the color purple."

"Please take it off."

"For God's sake, who the hell cares, even if it is purple."

Mason had scarcely looked into a mirror twice in his life; he did not even see himself when he shaved. Explaining this he would say lightly that he had so much ego that he could afford not to be vain.

"I care," Paula said with firmness.

"All right, okay, okay." He sighed leniently. As usual he was passive: she was the fighter. But he felt annoyed. Why did they get into such banal, trivial disagreements? Sometimes they became involved in emotional snarls so subtle, so abstruse, that it became impossible for either to resolve the difficulty by any simple statement. That usually happened if she became, as she sometimes did, too possessive, too demanding.

"Darling, you arc the apple of my you-know-what." She accepted his submission and slipped out of the room. In a moment he heard her bath running.

Under a foam of suds, Paula stretched. She felt a shade sheepish. What had provoked her to fly off the handle that way about anything so minor as a purple suit? Usually loss of temper, even if slight, over a trifle was symptomatic of a larger disturbance in another realm. Oh glory, she thought, with a little giggle of guilt. Truly she had little to complain about. Mustn't get so spoiled. Mason could certainly be a handful on occasion, and he was the maddest of contradictory creatures, but he was the best man she had ever met, and the miracle was how he put up with her, the way she couldn't help trying to dominate and would never give an inch.

Mason carried the remains of his drink back to the living room. He loved Paula, adored her, had faith in her, dependence on her, admired her, and knew fully what an asset she was and that, no matter what, she would always be on his side, which perhaps was the most important thing in any marriage. There were few incompatibilities between them and they laughed at the same things and made love pleasantly all the time as young people do, and their life together was signed, sealed, and delivered—for keeps—in a marriage that would go on forever, because it was by nature indissoluble, indestructible. But . . . but . . . after five or six years Mason felt that some of the bloom had worn off. Lately, he had been bored and irritated with her often.

Could it be possible that I'm no longer in love with her, he asked himself.

No, no! In terror he withdrew from the question, thinking instead, What is it that's lacking in me?

Feeling an unusual, sudden compulsion to do something unexpectedly positive, he strode toward the bathroom not knowing whether he wanted to whack her on the behind with a hot-water bottle, yank her out of the tub, or embrace her tenderly. He opened the door with a note of command; she looked surprised, then smiled radiantly. Slim, luminous, her body glistened from the sheen of warm water. But, even with tawny ovals of skin clouded by steam, she gave the impression of being crystalline—a dancer's body, carved from pink ice. She turned slightly and Mason saw her breasts in profile, delicate, slightly concave on the upper surface, convex on the lower. Her back was smoothly sloping, and her hips lean.

His heart missed a beat. "Hi, sweet," he said gently, "hi—" and, as she rose, grasped her slippery shoulder. Out of the tub with a splash, she pushed him away smiling and delighted, and said, "No—no—it must be seven already—really I *am* late." Then her face changed, it became very sober, and she murmured, "Hold me, hold me!" with desperate intensity. She could be one of the most intense girls anybody ever met, intense in moments of joy, confusion, disappointment, or distress, as Mason knew only too well. "Hold me!" In her tone were commingled love, worry, and desire for protection. One of Paula's puritan characteristics was her persistent fear, even when she was happiest, that all she had might be suddenly snatched away.

Several times he had tried to explain this by saying that an unreasonable fear of calamity usually indicated bad conscience or a sense of guilt about some dereliction, quite possibly imaginary, in times long past. She refused to be thus comforted. She adored pleasure, but she could not get over her feeling that she might be punished for achieving pleasure. She loved joy and found it in a wide range of experiences all the way from a phrase in a scherzo to the crinkled shape of a leaf, but she feared the experience of joy as well.

"Hold me!"

Now Mason would certainly have to change that purple suit, whether he wanted to or not, because it became soaking wet as she put her arms around him and hugged him close, then rushed off to dress.

5

"*Das Nachtmahl ist serviert*," announced Frau Gertrude. The dining room walls still had the softly luxurious paneling which the Blohrs and Wallensteins had installed a generation before; knots in the pale, highly rubbed wood looked like oysters, or human eyes. Sometimes when Mason had a drink or two they winked back at him.

Paula wore a dark green dress with big gold buttons, the skirt shaped like a tulip upside down (never in his life had he been able to describe women's clothes). Sitting down, they murmured "*Mahlzeit!*" to one another, lifting their glasses in the little ceremonial toast without which no meal could begin, even a meal of two people, husband and wife, in this ceremonial old city, any more than you could go to anybody's house for dinner without leaving a Schilling for the cook.

"*Mahlzeit!*" Paula repeated.

One of her most remarkable qualities was her capacity for renewal. An hour before she had looked a mess, pale and tired, her face a scandal. But now! In her hair he saw tints of copper, flame, and cinnamon. Her eyes were large, set rather widely apart over broad, high, almost Slavic cheeks. Forehead somewhat low, but pleasantly round at the temples; brows firmly arched. She had a decidedly snub nose, widening at the nostrils, and lips somewhat heavy; the upper had a forward slant, canting up. The first time he ever saw her he said, "You have clown's lips." Her teeth and gums were American— that is, perfect—and her skin would have given life to pearls if she had any.

Frau Gertrude, with her milk-white face and strained, anxious look, served a tart, faintly creamy fish soup, then a honeycomb of spinach in which square nuggets of ham were cunningly concealed, and *Palatschinken* for dessert. This, despite its name, had nothing to do with the flesh of the pig but consisted of two small fragile strawberry omelettes, bursting with warm juice and reposing placidly side by side. "My Lord, how good!" Mason muttered.

They had coffee in the living room. Paula told him about Kitty ("What a darling-a, but she's really too compliant, too willing to accept abuse") and he talked about the Czech lunch and the Customs Union story. "I haven't got a line of confirmation yet."

"You might call that German we met the other day—rather a striking type, what was his name, Von Traum."

"Paula, what would I do without you?" he exclaimed, and went straight to the telephone. Von Traum might well be the best possible man with whom to check on this story. Just like Paula to think of him! But Von Traum was out; Mason left word for him to call back. Then, once more, he tried the Poles. No luck. Paula, he saw, was shaking with mysterious laughter. He looked at her questioningly.

"Your fingertips are too big to get into the holes on the dial— it's such a delight," Paula said. Then, "I love to be around when you're working on a story. You're so earnest."

This nettled him slightly. "Earnest? I thought your present line was that I was too romantic."

"Oh, it's always earnest people, people who plow through to the happy ending, who are most romantic."

Look at him. Three sharp vertical lines formed on his forehead, and the rest of his face, usually so relaxed, became disturbed. He exploded tensely, "I've got to get something on that story! I should have been chasing around town all afternoon!"

"What good would that have done? You can't file anything till tomorrow anyway."

"I could have done something more than put in a couple of miserable phone calls."

"You had the Hungarian thing to finish."

"That's just mail stuff. And I didn't finish it. I'll break that Customs Union story open if I have to split a gut."

Paula marveled. Why should any old story matter so much? The Story, *Story*, STORY, dominated not only his life, but hers too and the lives of their whole colony. The Story, which could lie lurking behind any telephone call, which could be imprisoned inconspicuously in the dullest of dull speeches or the most banal of banal incidents, had to be dealt with, and dealt with promptly, efficiently, and made to come to life, once a clue to it appeared. Indeed the Story, compounded infinitely, was what made a newspaper, and history itself consisted of nothing more or less than an interlocked succession of stories day by day. The irony was that when the Story, to which every endeavor, every enjoyment, every preoccupation, had to be subordinate, finally reached London or Chicago or New York, the result of a vast subtle intricate web of human and mechanical effort, it might be chucked off the front page after an hour to make room for a baseball score, and was wastepaper the next day.

"You work harder than anybody in this city," Paula said. "You don't have to have a byline every day."

"I waste an awful lot of time."

"You're far too conscientious, too diligent. Oh, darling, I admire you for it! But I think we deserve a little time off every once in a while, so that we can do our own things, together, go to the movies, or pop into a museum on the spur of the moment. I've scarcely had an hour with you for weeks!"

"That really isn't true."

"Well, say to hell with a story every once in a while."

What a picture he continued to make! Heavy bulges rose over his brows, to intersect the vertical creases still on the forehead. Of course he was not merely industrious, but madly scrupulous about all his professional relationships. Paula grimaced at a sudden memory. Soon after taking over Vienna he set out to explore his new territory, and took her with him on a trip to Turkey and Greece. The Star, as a beau geste, paid her way. Nowadays, because he could not possibly afford to take her along, even if he cheated on his expense account which he would not do, he had to travel alone. Well, that time, after a heavenly week in Istanbul, they sailed homeward by way of the Aegean. Expense accounts had to be prepared and posted to the Star rigorously on the first day of every month. They passed through the Dardanelles on a day that happened to be the first, and Mason, the crazy man, sat all afternoon in the smoking room *doing his expense account*, thus never getting even one quick glimpse of one of the most glorious sights on earth, although he could not possibly *mail* the account until they arrived in Athens later in the week! Demented, Paula thought.

It was a desperate misery to her that he had to travel so much, and was away so often. Since their arrival in Vienna eight or nine months before, he had had to go to Bucharest twice, Warsaw once, Belgrade and Sofia once, Budapest three times. Of course all the correspondents in their circle, with such an immense territory to cover, were in the same predicament. Wives could be bereft for weeks, months, at a time. A standard joke concerned the Hearst man who, with his wife pregnant, left Vienna suddenly on a routine assignment; when he returned his child had already finished kindergarten. Paula knew, moreover, that in some peculiar, mushhead way several correspondents actively enjoyed their long unaccompanied journeys. What was even more ridiculous was that they assumed blandly that their frequent absences gave point to their masculine indispensability. They came back at last having flung themselves about in God knew what crazy indulgences, and expected dumbly that all the time their little Sophies would be waiting patiently, and alone, in bed, yearning like cows for their safe return.

Paula slipped back to thoughts about Mason's fussiness on expense accounts. One reason why money was often a worrying problem was not merely that he liked to spend it like a drunken sailor, as did she, if they had any, but because he positively would not, but would not, take advantage of the system whereby accredited correspondents in Austria received favors from the government like free railway fare, opera tickets, and so on. He was the only man, except Donald Bishopson of the New York *Register*, who had the best job in town, to make a principle of this. Maybe, Paula had suggested once, this was why that funny old stick, Minister Dr. Wimpassing, the head of the press department, disliked him so much, out of resentment that he would not be bribed even by accepting favors so minor, so exiguous, as a pass on the railroads, or, more significant, a slight, *ach*, *er*, kickback on his transmission tolls.

"In case you're interested," Mason Jarrett had written George Hilliard, his immediate boss in Chicago, after he had been in Vienna a few months, "my expenses are running maybe ten per cent higher than those of any other men here, except the people on the *Register*. This is because I don't want to take even nominal favors from the government. Even free tickets for the Salzburg Festival are a kind of bribe. I hope that the *Star* will agree that our independence (pardon, I don't mean to lay it on in such a stuffy way) is worth ten per cent."

A cable snapped back from Hilliard at once: YOUR VIEW CORRECT APPRECIATED ACCEPTED.

But Paula, on the other hand, although she was the most honest woman he had ever met, thought that Mason's scruples were exaggerated. She said, "For goodness' sake, darling, take their silly little bribes. They're just *tickets!*" fairly spitting out the word "tickets." Many women who pretend to be realists had one hell of a capacity for self-deception, Mason knew, but not Paula. She knew things exactly for what they were. Everybody else was being bribed;

why not they? It was the custom of the country.

They finished coffee.

"Seriously," Paula said, "have you thought of the implications of this Customs Union thing?"

"What do you mean, implications? Sure! I've been reading up on it—" His face darkened slightly. He knew that she meant more than the implications that came from mere research, and he made the gesture, in mock misery, of buttoning his collar against a possible small storm.

"If it goes through, would you be for it or against it?"

He hesitated. "There's a lot to be said either way."

Her voice could not have been friendlier, but it became a little tense. "In other words, you're on the fence, my darling of darlings, which I must say has happened before!"

"I'm not sitting on the fence at all. But I try to see both sides, like any good reporter."

"Well, which side do you like best?"

Truth to tell, not since the call from Strothncss had he given one second's thought to what he, Mason Jarrett, did think of the project.

"It's not my business to editorialize, but to report facts," he defended himself. "I write the news."

"Oh, I know you can't editorialize—that's your silly old rule. But anyway—"

"It isn't a silly rule at all. It's what makes American news reporting the best in the world. We have certain inhibitions, and they're good for us on the whole. Once you get reporters giving vent to their own opinions, their own prejudices, you lose the principle of objectivity altogether. Our papers would turn into *Pravda*, or, maybe worse, the *Völkischer Beobachter*. Sure, sure, I know that a lot of bias does creep into almost everything everybody writes, but still, even so, objectivity is a big strength and we ought to keep after it."

"Darling," said Paula, "I'm not talking about what you write, because you're always fair, no matter what. I'm asking what you yourself think, not as a reporter, but as you."

"Well, all right!" He hated abstract talk like this; his voice became defiant. "As to the Customs Union, well, we're so damned poor down here, in Austria I mean, we're not viable as a country, we're absolutely down and out—hitching up to the German economy would give things an enormous boost, improve conditions everywhere in the Danube Basin, stimulate trade, encourage business, give the average citizen a better break."

"But think of other factors. Make a Customs Union, and the next thing you know, bingo-bongo, there'll be *Anschluss*, formal union of Germany and Austria, which is what that crazy Hitler wants."

"Hitler isn't in power yet by any means. I hate the Nazis just as much as you do. But I'm trying to think of this whole problem from the point of view of the country I'm working in—from the local, Austrian point of view."

"And the local, Austrian point of view is what?"

"The great majority of people in this country *would* incontestably welcome a Customs Union if you could keep politics out of it. Actually the Austrian constitution describes Austria as a German state which should be incorporated into the Reich as soon as possible."

"There must be a catch in that. And you can't keep politics out of it."

"Even the Social Democrats want *Anschluss*—"

Paula interrupted firmly. "I'm against *anything* that would bring Germany and Austria closer together, and I know I'm right!"

"Don't be so darned cocksure."

"Oh, Mason," she wailed, "you ought to care more! Strothness cares. Hazelwood cares. Even Elliott cares. Why don't you care more?"

"Hazelwood, he's far and away the best of all of us, Hazelwood has said again and again that what he likes best about my work is that I always manage, in spite of everything, to be objective, detached, judicial."

"Pooh! The essence of being a judge is that, weighing both sides, he does make a verdict."

"Well, you have a point there, but—"

"A person must take sides as between good and evil, otherwise you find yourself on the side of evil."

"I do care—"

"Not enough." Again, her eyes glinted: light sparkled in the pupils, making the irises flash. "If you haven't got convictions, it means that you haven't lived."

He interrupted, but, high spirited, she cut him off. "Another thing—what financial interests are behind this whole business, who's going to gain most by promoting it? Could the A.O.G. be mixed up in it somehow? You know, biggest bank in Central Europe, interlocks with all the German banks, close alliance with all those Rhineland industrialists—oh, glory, I don't know. But it might be an interesting angle, don't you think? Goodness, look at the time, I must *tear!*"

He rose, and felt a variety of emotions: strong admiration for her, a touch of irritation (why do women have to get so damned intense?), a feeling that she was right, as usual, and he wrong, and, out of this, exasperation. She rose, and kissed him on the mouth.

They rocked together for a moment.

He whispered, "Why are your eyes shut so tight?"

"I can see you better that way."

He walked her toward the door, and the mood became businesslike. "When do you think the opera will be over?" Mason asked.

"Don't know. If we're out by eleven, I'll pick you up at the café."

"Bring Kitty along, of course."

Paula slipped into her old nutria coat, glancing at the mirror with a scowl ("I do have the worst luck with lipsticks!"), and asked, "Is my hair all right in the back?"

"Yes." He gave her shoulder a friendly squeeze, kissing her on the cheek. "So long, sweet."

"So long. Don't drink more than about twenty beers." She looked at the mirror again. "Oh, if only I were a pippin-a, like Kitty!"

She was gone. After a moment came a rap; he walked back to the door, and there she was again. In a voice at once commanding, humorous, and mock-deferential, she held out her hand.

"Twenty Schillings, please."

Mason searched in his wallet, handed her a bill, and watched her skid down the stairs.

6

Two or three minutes later the doorbell rang again, and there stood Dozent Dr. Wallenstein, their landlord.

"I intrude? No? Ah!"

"Hello! Come right in!" Mason greeted him with the utmost cordiality, adding, "A cognac, Herr Doktor? Or a taste of kirsch? Come now! Have a drink!" But he did not want the Dozent to stay long. It was getting late and he wore time like a hairshirt.

"Thank you, thank you! I stay not one second."

The Dozent, who had a cap of hair like steel wool and bright flushed cheeks, passed over an envelope of clippings. His manner was, as always, electric and emphatic. He spent every weekend in the mountains, and was deeply sunburned. The red in the cheeks rose from behind the brown.

"I thank you, thank you, for the privilege of reading these articles, your stories! With what subtlety, what discrimination, you have handled this very delicate situation. Ah, ah! If only the articles could be published in Vienna itself, what! That would stir up all the old roosters, eh?" Dr. Wallenstein, with full vigor, made a sawing motion with his hand. "And the portrait you give of His Magnificence, telling all that is necessary without offense! Capital, my dear Jarrett, truly capital! I congratulate you!"

He jabbed a friendly finger, the nail wide and fan-shaped, into Mason's breastbone.

Dr. Wallenstein had suffered a crushing blow a month or two before, a curt announcement from the Rector of the University (who bore the sumptuous title His Magnificence) to the effect that, although he was only fifty-six, he would be retired at the end of the current academic year. This was because, if not, he would necessarily, automatically, have to be promoted from Dozent to full professor, which could not be done because Dr. Wallenstein was Jewish. Vienna at that day derived most of its exquisitely edged cultivation, its prestige and intellectual distinction, from Jews—Freud, Alfred Adler, Stekel, Schnitzler, the Rothschilds, Felix Salten, Werfel, both Zweigs, Bruno Walter, Max Reinhardt, and a cornucopia of others—but because of the relentless anti-Semitic bigotry of the academic ruling class Dr. Ludwig Heinz Wallenstein, one of the best-known men in his field, ophthalmology, in all of Central Europe, could never, never be allowed to become a full professor.

Mason had told Paula about this and, outraged, she had replied, "Couldn't you write something about it? Something that might make the university ashamed of itself?"

"I don't see how. It's not what you would call news and I can't get the *Star* mixed up in a personal-grievance case. Besides, publicity would probably do more harm than good. Get people's backs up— you know how those things go."

"But why not write a mail series on anti-Semitism in Vienna in general?"

"Well, now!" Such a series would be difficult to do, touchy; it might get him into trouble, but it was just the kind of story he liked to handle. "You're a very useful wife—that's a good idea!"

Hilliard telegraphed him congratulations on the three articles on anti-Semitism he had proceeded to write, something that did not happen often with mailers. Now clipsheets had arrived and he had lent them to Dr. Wallenstein.

They talked about the cineraria in the greenhouse, the state of the powder snow still to be found near Kitzbühel, family matters, and the Dozent's plans. Dr. Wallenstein put out both hands, palms up, fingers spread, wagging them and shrugging his shoulders as he walked to the door and said good night. "I will try to resume fully my private practice. They cannot take that away from me. I will miss the podium, but perhaps it will be beneficial for me in the long run to start learning again, instead of teaching. Ha!"

Strolling back into the living room Mason took, as always, infinite delight in the villa's every inch. Damned expensive, though! For their spacious, sunswept, glossy sweep of rooms, as well as unlimited use of the garden, the Jarretts paid the Wallensteins a rent formidable for Vienna, indeed monstrous, seven hundred Schillings a month, or a hundred dollars. How, how, Mason sometimes asked himself in later years, *how* had they managed to live so well on what they had? His salary was average for the foreign correspondent of the period— that is to say it did not give them any margin at all. Paula found life unendurable if she did not have flowers and she could not resist giving gifts to friends, and Mason would have died, more or less, rather than be unable to buy new books. They didn't have a car, and never smoked American cigarettes, which cost sixty cents a pack in Vienna, but they entertained a good deal, spent weekends in the mountains, dined in pleasant restaurants, pubcrawled often, and went to the theater whenever they felt like it. How had they managed it?

The Jarretts had arrived in Vienna from Paris in June, 1930, nine months before. Mason remembered vividly the afternoon in Paris when Philip Hazelwood had taken him aside and, as casually as if he were mentioning the price of cabbages, announced that he had arranged with Chicago to have him transferred to Vienna. "You will have much better opportunity and range for writing your own special type of feature story," declared Hazelwood. This was a substantial promotion, since it meant that after several years of being Hazelwood's second man and a utility correspondent all over Europe, he would now have a bureau of his own, a bureau as attractive as Vienna and one with such a large, variegated back yard. But not for years did he know whether Hazelwood, a perceptive man who thought that feature stories were for children, had arranged the transfer out of genuine regard for his, Mason's, talents, and was thus giving him an opportunity, or wanted to get him out of Paris. Hazelwood, he thought, like Strothness, didn't really like him, and did not want anybody with such an easy, readable touch, so highly favored by Chicago, working in his own office. Anyway, the transfer to Vienna was a big boost up. Paula took a fleeting trip home to America to see her father, mother, and the most recent of her stepfathers, and Mason proceeded to Vienna to explore the ground.

He poured himself a cognac, and his thoughts shifted to the Wallensteins. Dr. Wallenstein, when he was a youthful doctor, had married into the Blohr family of engineers—prosperous, bourgeois, and impeccably established. Their handsome villa had stood on Mozartgasse for more than eighty years. Now, for the first time in its history, it held strangers, for the reason that the Wallensteins could no longer afford to keep it up. What a poignant hullabaloo there had been the day the Jarretts moved in! The grandmother, a widow, Frau Ingenieur Blohr, with a yellowish creased face and sharp half-closed eyes, saluted Mason at the threshold of what had been her own inviolate citadel, her domain, for two generations, like an antique queen, surrendering it on her own terms. "Circumstances . . . compel . . .

alterations. You vill kindly maintain these bremises vell!"

That whole day, having been evicted from her room, which was to become Mason's office, Frau Ingenieur Blohr sat behind a barred servant's window on the lower floor, immobile, rigidly intent, inscrutable, watching the Jarretts and appraising their accouterments as the movers brought them in—the books and files, the worn beds and tables and dilapidated furniture. Her nose made a spot of moisture on the pane, and from time to time her lips twitched, but she never uttered a word. Toward sundown Mason saw her rise stiffly, with a sigh; then she disappeared.

So the whole Blohr-Wallenstein family, with its unassailable correctness, its punctilious dignity ("Some of the old academic families here, damn decent people"), transferred itself to the floor downstairs—the Dozent and his wife, the grandmother, an uncle, a youthful niece (sand-colored hair, freckles, attractive, by name Nella), and two silent, excessively aged women, servants now retired with the position of family retainers, who, like very old women in Russian novels, did the darning and, before receptions, helped polish silver.

As the Jarretts' van from Paris, eviscerated, prepared to take off, Paula exclaimed ardently, "Oh, Mason, I can't bear it, I don't think it's right that we should dispossess these people—well, that's not quite the right word, I know—but we have all this space now, just the two of us, and they have so little! Can't we give the grandmother her room back, at least? I wouldn't mind if she lived with us."

"No. Eras end. Anyway, I have to have an office."

Relations between the Jarretts, Frau Ingenieur Blohr, and the Wallensteins became, before long, friendly and then intimate. The Jarretts liked the Wallensteins extremely, and were well liked in return. Moreover, with such a large augmentation in their income as was represented by the seven hundred Schillings a month that Mason paid, the Wallensteins could now maintain their station in society, take holidays in the Salzkammergut, continue to employ a cook and gardener in addition to the ancient retainers, go to concerts (they were vehemently musical), and complete the education of their son, Otto, who was at school in England, and would soon return.

7

Now Mason tidied up the living room and prepared to douse the
lights. He stood for a moment near Paula's desk. On slips of blue
paper were notes and shopping lists in her fashionable handwriting
done with a broad stubby pen in blue ink. For some reason these
notes and slips moved him profoundly. He remembered the first
time he had seen that uphill, square Vassar handwriting. The
letter to him had contained the sentence, "I love you very much,
which seems to be simple statement, but isn't." And then another
line: "Sometimes I am jealous of myself, because I know you."

Mason and Paula had met in Paris back in 1925, when he was
twenty-five or thereabouts, she two or three years younger. He had
been going around for several months with a girl with the improbable
name of Alice Purple. He had always been crazy about girls but, partly
because of his self-consciousness, had never been much of a success
with them. He paid court zealously, but with little result. He had
violent heartaches, which went unassuaged. He loved and suffered
to the hilt, but his love was unrequited. Of course he was too choosy,
too discriminating; he had to have somebody extremely special,
which made it the more difficult to find anybody. Perhaps subconsciously he wished this to be so, and thus had a tendency to pursue
girls impossible to attain. He retreated into a kind of invertebrate
romanticism. But Alice Purple liked him. She was British, loose as
tenpins and so beautiful she made your heart stop; she had ice-blue
eyes, set deep and almost colorless, and a waterfall of glossy sepia-
colored hair. She had an easy camaraderie and was pert and engaging and often, while sitting with a man, held her teeth slightly open
confidently and with the brightest good humor, and gave the impression that she had personally invented sexual intercourse.

The Hazelwoods asked Mason to a small evening party. He knew
well what it would be like—the guests carefully chosen, the atmosphere somewhat muted, the ensemble suave. Hazelwood did
not like Alice Purple and Mason came alone. What would his life
have been like, he sometimes wondered, if he had not been invited
to the Rue de Grenelle that evening? He separated himself from
the other guests, sipped champagne, and searched along the book-

shelves, studying them. Hazelwood had a magnificent library—divided between contemporary politics and works on his own private, almost secret passion, medieval France. As usual Hazelwood was shy, detached, and given to throwing off highly sophisticated aphorisms that might, or might not, hold up on close analysis. Mason overheard him say to the State Department man who was the guest of honor, "Beware always of a truly virtuous woman. They seek to convert to their own image, they emasculate, they destroy."

Mason became conscious of Paula in a flash. She was sitting in a circle with Ernesta Hazelwood, two or three embassy wives, and a Cuban painter. The first thing he noticed was her brilliant, flashing smile and lovely skin; gradually she came into full focus. He watched her for a moment with curiosity and then approached and hovered close; Ernesta, who did nothing in a hurry, introduced them at last. The girl's name was Miss Whipple. Quite clearly she was not only very special, but might even turn out to be attainable. Mason fluttered before her, despite his size, like some suspended object held by a ribbon attached to an electric fan. He walked with her to the buffet, talked clumsily for a moment, and asked her to lunch the next day. She looked delighted, but shook her head. His face fell. "Oh, but please, I have something on for tomorrow, and it's hard for me to break a date—I suppose the silly way I was brought up! Could we make it some other time? Would you call me up?"

"Why wait to call up? Friday?"

"Yes."

"Larue's at one."

"Good."

That was the end of Alice Purple.

Paula, who had a job on a fashion magazine, had been in Paris about six months, and lived in a tiny neat apartment near the Etoile. It seemed a million miles in space and spirit from Mason's unkempt hotel near the Dôme. One day they set out to window-shop along the Rue du Faubourg St. Honoré. Before long he had bought her an evening bag which obviously he could not afford. He always kept a few loose checks on his Chicago bank in his wallet and he fished one of these out. When he had paid the bill and they were out on the street again Paula said, "But don't you have a checkbook? You didn't fill out any stub." He replied, "Fill out a stub? No, why should I?" It dumbfounded her to find out that he seldom, if ever, filled out stubs. "But how do you know what your balance is?" she protested. He said, "I guess and if I guess wrong the bank writes me a letter." "But that's irresponsible!" she wailed. "Not at all. Why should I bother to write out a stub when I'll get the canceled check next month? Believe me, one thing I am *not* is irresponsible." Gripping herself, Paula asked, "What's your balance now?" Mason smiled, "Well, that bag was forty dollars, wasn't it, and I think that leaves me with about fifteen."

Then, at one of their early breakfasts, she saw him eat a fried egg for the first time. She was both repelled and entranced. It was his custom, for no particular reason except that he hated messy yolks, to trim a fried egg carefully with his fork, neatly separating every fragment and filament of white from yellow, and then pop the whole of the unbroken, quivering yolk into his mouth in one swift gulp. Paula cried, "Oh, have another egg! It's awful! Do it again!"

Paula had had an erratic childhood, with no fewer than three stepfathers before she was twenty, to one of whom (an explorer, who made mysterious journeys into the jungles of Surinam and New Caledonia) she had been romantically devoted; the others she detested. Her mother was, even today, a vital and commanding woman, also beautiful, who bossed the municipal council of her Boston suburb with a supple hand, still bullied her first husband (Paula's father) by correspondence although they had been divorced for many years, smoked cigars, passionately took up causes often sterile, and earned considerable sums as a merchandising adviser to a department store. Paula's father was altogether different—a professor of sociology, gentle, vague, withdrawn, a cherub. Sometimes when Paula was with him she had the feeling that he did not remember quite who she was.

In Paris Paula had, of course, any number of young men pursuing her; one, the leading contender, was a junior partner in an international law firm. At her very first lunch with Mason she described him fully, but did not tell him his name; this was not because she was secretive, but out of considerations of taste. Instantly Mason nicknamed him "Mr. Mysterious." It was clear from Paula's description that Mr. Mysterious would be rich in time, something that Mason knew he would never be. Never would Mr. Mysterious neglect to fill out his check stubs, and he would always know the balance of his bank account to the nickel. Mason also gathered, although she did not say so, that Mr. Mysterious was somewhat dull. It impressed and amused her without limit that in the following months Mason never once asked her what his name was, never expressed any curiosity about his person, and never admitted to a scintilla of jealousy about him or even conceded that he existed.

Mason asked her once, "And now will you kindly explain how you ever happened to fall in love with me?"

"Oh, that's easy! I fell in love with you first when I saw how deadly serious your face was looking at a wine list. Second, it dawned on me that I usually know what you're going to say before you say it but I want to hear you say it even so."

It did not take Mason long to realize that this girl, so marvelous in summer clothes, with her long legs and forward-canted chubby lips, was for him, irrevocably and forever. Not only was he mad about her but he recognized her quality. But for some months she resisted any talk of marriage. Paris was giving her a glorious whirl. Mason, on worldly terms, was not in the least a good match; besides, he lived totally outside her orbit. He was self-made, somewhat raw, and full of an inner life she was not at all sure she understood. Never before had she known well anybody outside the compound of the moderately well-to-do elite of the Atlantic seaboard. She had never had any experience except with well-educated men and women of good family, practically all of whom had known one another since childhood and who had gone to the same schools and colleges and weekend parties and who for the most part pursued academic or professional careers. Her milieu was not so much social or aristocratic as intellectual. And now here in hot chase of her was Mason Edwards Jarrett, who rose out of the wilderness of Montana, which was something more remote to her than Tibet. Besides he was, of all raffish things, a newspaperman—ye Gods! Yet this was the happiest period of her life, as it was of his. They might meet other people during the week, but they had every Saturday night together and then, after a lazy late breakfast in Mason's place or hers, took a walk or went to the movies and then made love during the long Sunday afternoons. "Incidentally I don't do this with every Tom, Dick, and Harry," she declared the first time, eyes flashing. In plain fact she had never done it with anybody before, but for months he teased her by signing letters or telegrams to her with "Tom Dick and Harry."

Mason became enlarged and liberated. Paula released him from his clumsinesses, his awkwardnesses and inhibitions. He had a new sense of pleasure in himself and utter fulfillment in life.

He knew that it was inevitable that they should marry, but he did not press her. He went on the assumption that when the right moment came marriage would happen almost automatically, and it did. After they had been together six or seven months, and when November cast a cold, dreary smear over the face of Paris, he felt that he needed a change, and, borrowing a week from his next year's holiday, went down to Antibes for a few days, alone. He wanted to write a short story. He had published several in the Left Bank magazines. He stayed longer than he intended, and, to explain the delay, telegraphed Paula to the effect that he was in the middle of something. Her reply was quick and, for a properly brought up girl, uncharacteristic. "Come back to the middle of me." Then the following week when he returned to Paris she went into one of her spells of outrage, saying that she simply had not been made for an illicit life, that she was not tough enough, irresponsible enough, confident enough, clever enough, unconventional enough, to live like the Alice Purples. A few weeks after their marriage she talked with the utmost fluid gaiety about the months before. "Of course it's the most lovely and fascinating period in a woman's life. The insecurity is so delicious. You *think* you're going to get him, but you can't be absolutely sure."

They found an apartment near the Boulevard St. Germain and batted around Europe on various assignments like happily crazed—but earnest—children. They both felt that they were in love not only with each other but with the whole wide dazzling world. She never saw Mr. Mysterious again. Many years later he became president of an important bank in Baltimore and died of an ulcer caused by overwork.

8

Mason put down his glass. Paula would have just about reached the
Opera by this time. One thing remained fixed, certain, and concrete:
how enormously she helped his work. There had been that bit of
conversation when he returned to Vienna from the trip to Budapest
and Bucharest the week before. He told her what the hall porter
at the Athena Palace had reported about one of the local princesses,
who had been found naked on the roof, and the anecdote about the
Archbishop in Sinaia and the girl sewn up in the monkey skin.

"Oh, Mason, you should write those stories!"

He was horrified. "Write them? I'm not a gossip columnist!"

"Well, clean them up a bit, and then write them. Anyway, why
not put in a lot of extra color in the next mailers, all the things you've
been telling me, like that bit about the Transylvanian strawberries
and what it means when a carriage on the boulevards has a yellow
flower pinned on the horse—all the little picturesque things you and
the other correspondents take for granted."

"Well, I cover a good deal of that sort of thing in news notes—"

"No. Your news notes are hinged to news. Do a couple of stories
without any reference to news at all, just convey mood, tone, atmosphere."

And this was exactly what he was doing in the new series about
Hungary.

She advanced on a new tack. "All of you sit on news far too
much, I think. There's too much taboo. I don't see why it can't be
printed that Pilsudski, for instance, has psychopathic rages, and that
Kemal Ataturk is a drunk."

"Well, for one thing, I wouldn't be allowed in Poland or Turkey
any longer, our territory would slowly, majestically, dwindle away,
and I'd lose my job."

"I'm not so sure. Take Hungary. If a cabinet minister is a crook,
say he's a crook!"

"And cost the Star a million dollars in a libel suit?" He repeated
a mild old joke, "You know perfectly well that no Hungarian is
happy unless he's suing somebody."

Later they were comfortable in bed, touching shoulders. It was difficult to trace back what happened next.

"What do you want most in life, Mason?"

"You. After that, to write a couple of books."

"What kind of books?" she asked sympathetically.

He became vague. "Oh, well, haven't quite decided—"

"Not journalism?"

"No."

"Good," Paula said.

"You remember those little Paris stories? Well, I might develop those—work them into a whole. But of course there's never any time—not a minute free here in Vienna."

She hoisted herself on an elbow.

"I think that would be simply wonderful. But I don't see how you'll ever get any private writing done while you're on a job like this. It consumes you day and night. I wish so much you would branch out more. Or maybe we could take a big chance and quit the *Star* altogether—"

"Paula, I couldn't ever quit the *Star*."

"Why not?"

Mason was aghast. He jumped as if stung. He became inarticulate. The *Star* was his home, his family, his father. He had a passionate devotion to it. He could no more think of leaving it than he could think of leaving her. What she said revolted him. A great deal of his youth was inextricably bound up with the *Star*, and the bondage carried right through to the present.

"Why not?" she repeated. "After all, it's just a Chicago newspaper!"

He sought to control himself. He felt that she was striking at the heart of his life. He said levelly, "For one thing, if you don't mind my being obvious, it's what we live on."

"If a man wants to write he writes. If you really want to write books outside journalism we ought to begin right now to adjust ourselves to a much lower standard of living, leave this villa—"

"Leave the *villa*?"

"—and set up life somewhere on a much simpler basis."

"We'd starve."

"Not necessarily. Haven't you belief enough in your own talent?

It seems to me that what you want is the best of both possible worlds—to continue to live as we're living now and have all the excitement and thrill of a career in journalism in this mad, wild Vienna world and at the same time write books on the side. The trouble with books written on the side is that they're never any good."

"Maybe I can disprove that statement!"

"Darling, all power to you if you can."

"Oh, shut up."

"Mason—"

"Shut up, I tell you!"

Paula had had no thought at all of hurting him or provoking him into losing his temper, something he seldom did. But the thought continued to prick her that if a person wanted everything it was probable, alas, that he, or she, would end up with nothing. Mason ought to face reality.

Obviously he was still bitterly hurt. She felt a tremor of fright. Often they had spats, but almost never a serious quarrel. He turned his back without saying good night or kissing her and she could feel by the lightest touch of his skin that he felt cold toward her.

Neither, troubled, could fall asleep. Mason tossed. She sought, curling in on herself, to make a nest on the far edge of the bed, but he thrashed about, bumping her with his heavy legs. After a while he fell into a nervous sleep and then woke and shook her by the shoulder and switched on the light. "God damn it, don't undermine me, Paula!"

She protested. Apparently she had committed some dreadful heresy by suggesting that he quit the Star, but on the other hand she had firmly supported him in his desire to write stories and had merely pointed out some of the difficulties that would have to be faced and surmounted.

"It's not just what you said about the Star. It's your general attitude. Somehow you always seem to be destroying my faith in an institution . . . or an ideal."

She stared at him. Really he was being unreasonable. How sensitive can a man get?

"You intellectualize too much! You're too goddamned sure that you're always right! You eat into my confidence! Don't take anything more away from me!"

"Take away anything? All I said was that you should *branch out.* I'm trying to build you up, not tear you down. I was trying to clarify a point or two—"

"Let me do my own clarifying hereafter!"

Paula became alarmed. She had never seen him so upset. She said, "Truly I didn't mean to be critical or . . . disillusioning. I think you're the most generally capable as well as decent man I've ever met, and you deserve any kind of life you want. Choose it and lead it and I'll be with you. And if we can manage to lead two lives at once so much the better."

"Oh, yes!" His irony was heavy, and he gave out a strange hollowish laugh. Once more they settled themselves for sleep. A silent moment passed. Each could hear the heartbeat of the other; the suspense became acute. She moved closer to him and held his back and he felt her hand soft and warm on his shoulder. "No," he muttered. She withdrew, hurt, and the silence became even more intense. A few minutes later, contrite, he twisted around to embrace her, but his body was still cold and when he made the beginnings of a caress his resentment was still so deep-seated that he remained inert. He could not express himself physically at all. Astounded, he said nothing. Paula became profoundly moved. When he still did not become active she bent her head, with the glorious hair, down and with quick deft fingers found her way to him and now was kissing him, overflowing with love for him, not aggressive but proud, pleased, triumphant, as he regained himself. Now she had him back.

Neither of them mentioned the quarrel the next day, but Mason knew that it sprang from deep roots. Indeed it struck at the very basis of their relationship—who was master?

❋

Now, tonight, this night, it was almost nine, and Mason burrowed in the closet for his Loden. The telephone rang—Von Traum, the German. Guardedly, he sounded him out on the Customs Union story without giving too much away. Von Traum seemed to be astonished. He spluttered, with the tone of a man caught off base, and said that, whereas an Austro-German Customs Union was of course inevitable in the future, like *Anschluss* itself, there was no immediate prospect of anything so beneficial coming to pass. He had no hard news at all. The story, if not downright false, was altogether premature. How Central Europeans loved that word "premature"! Von Traum concluded, in a brittle, metallic voice, "I hope to see you soon, Herr Jarrett. Greetings to the gracious lady."

As soon as Mason was off the wire Von Traum, eyes flashing, lips skinned back, hissed to himself, "So Jarrett knows! That means others know! I must call Munich at once!"

Mason was halfway out the front door when the phone rang again. Dr. Wiskiewicz was on the line at last. A good deal more candid with him than with Von Traum, Mason passed on to him, in strict confidence, what Strothness had said. The Pole responded with consternation. "Impossible, *unmöglich*, unheard of!" he snapped. "Such a project would be clearly illegal, as well as dangerous! A Reichsdeutsches plot—sinister in every implication! It would cost my country one hundred million dollars a year in trade with the succession states alone. The story cannot be true. If it is, the plan must be blocked, stopped. The French will withdraw credits from the Austrian banks, and so must the Czechs, with their heavy balances." But obviously Dr. Wiskiewicz had heard nothing whatever, not a whisper, about the story until Mason's call, and so Mason still did not have what he needed—confirmation. Dr. Wiskiewicz promised to get on to Warsaw in the morning and, without imperiling Mason's confidence, find out what was to be known.

What did Artur mean about withdrawing French credits from Austrian banks? He recollected some of the talk at the Czech lunch that day, and also Paula's suggestion about the A.O.G. Whom did he know in financial circles? Nobody except small fry like the A.O.G. clerk who soon after the first of every month received for deposit Mason's draft from Chicago, with gliding fingers, and said, "Ah, Herr Charrett! And vot is doing today your Volstreet? Comes yet new crash?"

Mason left the villa, crossed the garden, and turned toward the Hauptstrasse, with his soft, easy, frontiersman's walk. The *Föhn*, like a gray-green cat, licked him.

II. THREE FRIENDS

Early in the morning of that same day, several miles away in a different quarter of Vienna, Dr. Karl Tetzel had risen sleepily. He blinked to get the sleep out of his eyes. Dr. Tetzel, the resident correspondent of Mark Thorne's agency, was one of Mason Jarrett's colleagues. He leaned over Mia, his wife, lovingly, waking her but holding an invisible buffer between them so that he could recoil, seemingly unhurt, if she spoke sharply. Always these days he left a little space between them.

"Come," Karl declared after breakfast, "the buses will be slow today, because of the mist, and it is time to start for the station now."

"Very well. *Gleich fertig.*"

"It would make a bad impression if we were late," Karl continued, glancing toward the clock which had a broken hand. He looked dutiful and forlorn. "Herr Thorne is an impatient man."

"We will not be late, *Liebchen.*"

Indeed it was an important thing when Karl's boss, Marcus A. Thorne, came to Vienna. This did not happen often, because Thorne, a busy man, seldom had occasion to leave London. Vienna was small potatoes, even though the Balkans were supposed, as the adage had it, to begin at Landstrasse Hauptstrasse. Karl did not know Thorne well, except through curt service messages and the long distance telephone. He hated and feared him as a man may hate and fear an inanimate institution on which his whole life depends and which he cannot influence except by propitiation. Marcus A. Thorne was certainly an institution. Unfortunately, however, he was also a man.

47

Karl touched Mia's shoulder lightly, protectively, in the crowded oscillating bus. They lived in a poor quarter in Hietzing and it took them almost an hour to reach the station. They were greeted, as was usual at the Westbahn, by an aromatic, commingled odor of goulash, coffee, and steam.

"I will leave it to you to make the first mention of the money," Karl said.

"Perhaps he will bring it up himself," Mia replied. As always, the sight of a railway station made her tingle. She adored getting out of Vienna. What she loved best of all things, well, almost all things, was walking in the woods in spring, when the brooks overflowed with turbulent brown water and the sunshine never-endingly pulled wild flowers, pink and mauve and gold, into strong, stormy blossom.

Mason Jarrett once asked himself, Now, if I had Karl Tetzel to describe, what would I say? Well, he's graceful, slender, with pleasantly shaped hands. His eyes have a peculiar flutter. They dart. They are deer's eyes, frightened. What else? The mouth has a hard, arrogant arch, and other elements in his face are confused. Mason's thought had then turned to Mia, and the conception came to him: Karl has the look of a man who, every time he meets somebody, thinks that maybe the somebody has been sleeping with his wife.

Mia, a large young woman, was Scandinavian; some people thought that she was mildly crazy. Indeed her personality, unstable at best, seemed to have an eccentric, cyclical rhythm; she alternated unpredictably between phases of rhapsody and bleak despair. But she was wonderful to look at—lovely. Maybe she's a little sloppy, Mason had gone on thinking, but, my God, that mass of golden hair, the color of marigolds, those splendid hazel eyes, that majestic body. What would she look like in a shift of white gauze? She should have been an opera singer—what a Venus she would be in *Tannhäuser!* The way those breasts came out at you. They were solid, perfectly globular, and immense.

"The Karl," other journalists would sometimes say at the Weissenhof, "he is an honest fellow, and certainly he can beat all of us thumbs down at chess, but he lacks push. But Mia—ah! A sly one, too."

Inside the railway station, Mia gave Karl two coins, which he inserted into the slot machine for the tickets which were necessary before a person could proceed to meet a train. Mia always carried their money. When he left their flat in the morning, she gave him exactly what he would need, not a Groschen more or less, to cover his carfare and the cups of coffee he would need for the day's work. Karl was the son of a policeman, and, like most boys born in the Sixteenth Bezirk, he grew up to be an ardent Social Democrat. He planned to be a teacher, obtained a doctorate in political economy, and then drifted into journalism. Thorne's agency paid him a retainer of fifty dollars a month, and he and Mia could not have survived except for the stories he sold on space.

"On time the train is," Karl said in English.

The vaulted glass-bound barn filled up with puffs of white steam, porters shouted, men opened heavy doors lubricated with black grease, baggage trucks made a clatter, and the driver of the locomotive, which was still snorting and panting, as if exhausted by its run, leaned out of his cab with satisfaction and let his eyes rest proudly on its long steel flanks.

Mia pushed Karl ahead and he peered along the blue wall of train, with his dark, sensitive eyes alert. "Ah, I see him," Karl said.

A succession of memories shot through his troubled mind. First he had been secretary-translator to the correspondent of a Philadelphia newspaper. The Philadelphian lost his job when his publisher, four thousand miles away, dropped dead in a speakeasy and the paper was sold, like a ton of turnips, to an insurance company that did not believe in foreign correspondents. Next he was second man to a London agency man, an amiable drunkard who got fired for making passes at his boss's wife. Always he lost jobs through no fault of his own. For several years he was an assistant, quite well paid, in the bureau of a big Berlin newspaper, but a place had to be found suddenly for the brother of the mistress of the editor-in-chief. Then Karl lived, if you could call it living, by peddling tips to the exalted group of senior correspondents, Laszlo Sandor among them, who came to the Café Imperial every morning for their Gabelfrühstück, second breakfast. Through one of these, he finally landed the miserable job with Thorne.

"Hello," Thorne greeted them. Workmen in striped overalls ducked under the wheels of the carriages, tapping them with hammers. "Well, nice to see you folks!" He looked at Mia with some interest. "Heard your voice on the phone so often, pleased to meet you." He turned to Karl. "Where did you keep her hidden when I was down here a couple of years ago?" His smile was rich with bounce and cheer.

That was the time Mia had been away on a walking trip. For some reason Karl had not demanded that she give up her holiday and return to town to help him entertain Thorne. Perhaps he feared that she would hold him in contempt if he fawned on the American. Indeed, he stuck close to Thorne every moment, deferentially attending him. When Karl, after a crowded anxious day or two, saw him off with relief, Thorne said, "Well, thanks, I wish I'd had more time here. Didn't even get a lay!"

Now, collecting his bags, overtipping the porter, he was full of decisive, businesslike energy. He beckoned to a taxi with its long green hood and carapace of cracked black leather. Karl had made all the arrangements, but it was Thorne who said to the driver authoritatively, "Hotel Majestic!" The car with brittle tires rattled over the cobbles. "Well, well, good to be in Vienna again!" He rubbed his hands. "Hope your *Schlagobers* is as good as it used to be!"

Karl observed him warily. Vigorous, crude, and fresh, Thorne gave out a hearty sense of the physical. He had risen in his profession rapidly, and perhaps this was why he was inclined to hold in contempt colleagues who had been less successful. A fast, competent agency man, he kept his organization working at full speed with economy and efficiency. His bosses in New York admired him a good deal, but several thought that he would overreach himself one day, through ambition and overconfidence, and come to an indifferent end.

Thorne did not have an ounce of sensitiveness about the sensitiveness of others. When he had visited the Weissenhof that evening a couple of years before, the group was gossiping about Tom Cairn, who had gone into this comparatively new thing, radio, and had picked up what might turn out to be a wonderfully good job wandering all over Europe for N.B.S.

"Why," Thorne spoke with a certain indignation, "the thing about it is that they ought to have a young man for a job like that. Cairn must be almost forty."

He did not notice that several of the correspondents present, who were well past forty, flinched slightly—not so much to protect their own sensibilities but in reaction to his own glaring lack of tact. At this time Thorne himself must have been all of thirty-two.

Thorne went up to his room to wash while Karl and Mia waited in the Majestic lobby; then he took them to Schöner's for lunch. They had crayfish and *gebackenes Huhn*. Karl ate hungrily; it had been a long time since he had had a meal so sumptuous. Thorne kept up a running banter of questions and small talk, but his attention roamed. He would start a sentence and not finish it, and it seemed difficult for him to follow Karl's slow, carefully spaced English. Mia leaned over and touched his hand, smiling, murmuring lightly, "You should relax, Herr Thorne." He fixed her with a look of close, frank admiration and curiosity, and said, "You're certainly a gorgeous girl, Mia," jovially squeezing her arm.

"Help me do some shopping," he commanded them. He cashed a check at the branch office of the A.O.G. next door, and then bought a fitted case and two wallets at a shop nearby. Karl watched him closely as he paid out the money. Across the street he saw another fashionable shop, and here he promptly ordered three women's cashmere sweaters—one was of grayish rose, which Mia thought was the loveliest color she had ever seen, and then a pull-over for himself, of the new Vienna style, loosely knitted, gray on one side, black on the other. It cost a hundred and twenty Schillings. Karl and Mia became quite silent.

Out on the street, as if suddenly recollecting something, Thorne stopped and surveyed them squarely: "Say, about that letter of yours last month. Sorry I couldn't do anything about it, but you know what things are in New York since the crash. We've had a hell of a time. I've had half my budget lopped off."

Pushed by Mia, Karl had written him asking for a raise. Thorne had never answered the letter, and his robust, cheerful voice, so full of friendly vitality, had never given them an opening on the telephone.

"But as to the other point," Mia put in without hesitation now that the matter of money had at last been broached. "If we could have one hundred Schillings per month extra for expenses—surely—"

"New York hasn't made up its mind yet about that."

"Perfectly legitimate expenses," Karl explained hurriedly but with dignity. "Now, in an emergency, I do not even find myself able to take a taxi." He went on, with his voice apologetic, but now becoming sharper, "To buy a coffee, or even a drink of alcohol in one of the bars, is often of absolute necessity if I am to get the news."

"A hundred Schillings is only fourteen dollars," Mia stated.

Thorne looked pained and irritated. "I tell you I passed your letter on to New York. No answer yet." They both knew he was lying.

She stood with her heels hard on the pavement.

"Herr Thorne, perhaps you do not realize how it is with us here. We are near to starvation, the way genteel people starve."

Karl, frightened, receded. "Mia, do not bring up these matters now! Here, on the crowded street! Let us not annoy Herr Thorne, just after his arrival—"

She withdrew promptly, like a good European wife, but her large moist eyes were angry. "I am sorry, Karl. Please to forgive us, Herr Thorne."

"There now . . ." was all that Thorne could think of to say. Then his voice became conciliatory. "I'll see what I can do. I'll get in touch with New York again. You can trust me, absolutely."

Late that afternoon, after she left them, Thorne telephoned her at home. She was astonished, because Karl must surely be with him. He said in a quick voice, "I just wanted to say how charming I think you are, Mia—really gorgeous." He must have gotten rid of Karl for the moment. "We'll pick you up for dinner at about seven, and then go to the café. Maybe I'll have a chance to talk to you alone. Don't fail me! Please!" He rang off.

It was at about this time that he called Mason suggesting that they meet for a drink.

2

For James N. Drew too this had been an agitated day. With the Countess, as she was universally known, at his side, he walked that afternoon toward a lawyer's office near the Graben, through ancient squares like Am Hof, with its church and the unique, beautiful windows of its palaces. Even when he was most angry with the Countess his voice carried a note of amity, as if he were exercising the kind of protective benevolence that one might have for an errant child. But a moment before he had been bursting with outrage, shattered pride, and anger. "Emilie, for the last time, why did you borrow fifteen hundred Schillings from a Jew like Manfred Zapp—of all people! How *could* you do such a thing? Fifteen hundred Schillings!"

He made a clucking sound with his tongue, almost as if in admiration, dazed by the enormousness of the amount, and blinked.

"To invest in the Slovak iron shares, of course." Her voice, often so strident, so fierce, had become a frightened whimper. But she was an adhesively commanding woman, as everybody knew.

Drew went on: "You wheedled it out of him."

"He was very kind. I had good informations. I thought the shares would go up, up—I would make a surplus for you, a gift."

"So, they went down! That was six months ago and you never told me a word. Now Zapp, the damned Jew, wants his money back, and is threatening to sue!"

Even though Drew was fat, with greasy valleys in his long, heavy face, which looked as if the skin were lightly buttered, and his hair was spiky, bristly, black with the points tipped with premature silver, almost like porcupine quills, he had a certain attractiveness. His teeth were good, his blue eyes were bright, his manner boyish, except when, as at the moment, he was convulsed by crisis. Women liked him as a rule; particularly if they were newcomers to Vienna and heard soon enough that he was a nice southern boy caught in the toils of the wretched, vulpine Countess. "That poor fellow!" Sandor, who was devoted to him, must have said to Mason gloomily at least twenty times, "He is as one bewitched!"

Even more than Dr. Karl Tetzel, Jim Drew lived at the mercy of forces he could not control. He had an important job, and his dispatches reached newspapers all over the world, but the I.P. was the stingiest of all the great American news agencies. Twice in the last six weeks he had come to Mason with painful stories. He had been instructed to send some mailers to South America by a startlingly

novel route—air mail, no less, via the *Graf Zeppelin*—and then his
home office fairly blew him apart because the postage turned out to
be so expensive. "I ask you!" Drew exclaimed. For a long time he had,
like Tetzel, been paid partly on space. Well, last month he had had
a burst of industriousness and sent so many usable telegrams that
the I.P., to save money, suddenly shifted him to a straight-salary
basis, which might cost him dearly in the future. "Can you beat it,
the stingy bums!" Drew expostulated.

"Baires and Tokyo!" he snarled, blinking. The I.P. had close ties
with leading newspapers in Buenos Aires and Japan. The whim of
a man lazily enjoying himself on an Argentine *estancia*, or of a neat,
hissing little Tokyo industrialist, could send him chasing after any
kind of silly story. The Buenos Aires paper depended so much on the
I.P. that Drew, as a rule, like other I.P. correspondents in Europe,
filed direct to the Argentine; New York got nothing but a drop
copy of the dispatch sent to IPPICOM BAIRES. In effect, Drew
worked for a newspaper in South America, not an agency in New
York at all.

Thus Jim Drew had to work right around the clock, and, alone
among the Weissenhof group of correspondents, he almost never
left Vienna. Exactly once, seven years before, he had spent a weekend in Berlin. He had a marked admiration for the north Germans.
They had method, they had efficiency, they had bark and bite.
"Can't hold Germans down!" He clucked his tongue admiringly.
The fact that Drew, year after year, stayed immovably fixed in
Vienna helped him to augment his income. When Mason Jarrett
or John Dixon took holidays or left Vienna to survey their vast
territories or skipped off to Sofia or Prague when a big story
broke, Jim Drew filled in for them, acting as their substitutes and
filing for them under different names. For this he was paid five dollars
a day by each. When Drew was covering for his colleagues in this
manner, news stories from Central Europe had an astonishing
similarity in a considerable number of American newspapers, but
few editors knew that James N. Drew, under various pseudonyms,
was the author of them all.

Drew thought of Jarrett. Lucky dog, he said to himself. Good
job, good salary, wife like Paula, and that marvelous apartment out

in Döbling. Again he blinked and made a sound with his tongue, disapprovingly, but with a quick shake of his heavy head as well, as if to denote that he, James N. Drew, even if envious, even if conceding that some people have all the luck, nevertheless forgave the Jarretts for their good fortune—also to denote that he himself, although unfairly treated and harshly put upon, retained an immeasurable superiority over anybody else. By patronizing his friends, he became one with them.

Approaching the Graben, Drew patted the Countess on the shoulder. "Never mind, Emilie, we'll squeeze out of this somehow. Stiff upper lip, old girl." She had begun to cry. A note of command came into his voice; he was the hero unrecognized, the paladin still neglected, the underdog who would somehow, at the end, come out on top no matter what.

Here was their destination, Trattnerhof, a venerable office building. Drew said, "Stop crying, Emilie. We'll give 'em a piece of our mind!" Her chin rose, but quivered; she peered forward like a tattered eagle measuring a dim horizon.

Remarkable in Trattnerhof was its elevator. It was one of those really weird Central European contraptions, a chain of tall open boxes hung together vertically, each capable of holding one person, which rose like a dumbwaiter on an invisible endless chain. "Seven!" Drew barked to the Countess, shoving her into the first empty box as it appeared level with the ground. He hopped into the next box, and up he went—slowly, in the dark shaft, while the mechanism squeaked —watching the numbers painted on the sill of each floor. Emilie was directly above him, separated from him only by the piece of board that was at once her floor, his ceiling. There were no operators or attendants. Two . . . three . . . four . . . Drew hoped that Emilie would not forget to get out at seven. He sometimes wondered what would happen if you did not emerge with sufficient agility when the box reached the top floor, the eighth. Would you be carried around the wheel, crushed, and carried in your same box upside down in its descent on the other side of the shaft? No. This infernal machine jogged sideways when it reached its summit, and the chain of boxes reversed itself so that you could descend as you rose—all of a piece and right side up.

Correctly, the Countess leaped out at seven; Drew reached the same level an instant later and rejoined her.

Emilie Renate Gloriette Altmann, the Gräfin von Zwehl, was a good deal older than he. Under a chaplet of hair curled girlishly in methodical rings, like brownish yellow grapes, her eyes and mouth made a triangle of three black pits in a chalky face. She was seldom seen, even by intimate friends in Drew's own circle. The first time Mason Jarrett met her he noticed first of all the extraordinary quality of her eyes. The irises were of the palest gray, so pale that they could scarcely be differentiated from the whites; moreover, they seemed to have less than normal curvature. They resembled flat glass windows, which caught the light, and through which one could, by exercise of the imagination, look.

Otherwise, however, the appearance of the Countess von Zwehl was prosaic, trite. She did not look more romantic than a pin cushion. But her life had been neither prosaic nor trite. First there was the Constantinople period, and after that three husbands; all were still alive, on excellent terms with her and, what was more remarkable, with each other. The first was a Rumanian landowner who, gambling, would wager on a single card the whole of one of his family's villages; the second an optician in Budapest; the third, a penniless nobleman from the hunting country in Upper Austria, who, having got out of the Countess every cent she had, hit her in the mouth one day, knocking out her teeth, and then left her when his longtime mistress, who had been locked up in an asylum for a period, returned to him in good health. But Emilie still had the tenderest feeling for this man, Count Rudi. Perhaps she was still in love with him. It was for him, in any case, that she had borrowed the fifteen hundred Schillings from Herr Zapp. Of course, she grinned sardonically to herself, the story of the Slovak mine shares was a pure fabrication. The Herr Graf was being shaken down, or blackmailed, by a village girl whom he had got into trouble, and she had to help him. But why, why, she asked herself hysterically, was Zapp asking for his money back? That Zapp! This should teach her a lesson. A woman should never trust a man with such bushy, velvety eyebrows, such a luxuriously tended mustache. Such men were too vain. Probably Zapp had behaved as he did for the most obvious of

reasons—he was tired of her, and needed money for someone else.
Pfui!

The Countess was, all in her circle knew, capable of the most
astounding irregularities, which had become more pronounced in
the past few years. One of her paramount traits had always been a
passionate desire to gain attention. Behind her carefully composed
mask, she lived for one thing above all, sensation. Nobody who had
been there was ever likely to forget the scene at the Musikvereinssaal
the year before, with Fritz Kreisler playing the Beethoven Violin
Concerto, when she interrupted the Joachim cadenza by dropping
her opera glasses repeatedly with a loud bang on the floor of her box.
Then, looking prim, she let her beaded bag fall, as if by accident,
on the head of a bald man sitting in an orchestra seat below. Pandemonium followed; Kreisler had to stop playing; she came near to being
lynched.

Perhaps the Countess was disintegrating now, losing grip. Maybe
this was Drew's fault, and she treated him abominably. How she
hated him! He was too naïve, too coarse, too prejudiced (the childish
way he loathed Catholics, as well as Jews); he was intolerable, with
his eternal bright silly smile, his blink—an oaf! They had met when,
a youth on a scholarship, he lived in a students' hospice; she had
money then. She mothered him, cozened him, seduced him, and
supported him. Now of course it was he who supported her. Without Drew, the Countess was lost, finished, *erledigt*. Repellent scenes
were said to take place between them, and their neighbors reported
that their quarrels could be overheard from the street. Drew seldom
shaved more than once or twice a week, and the rumor was that the
Countess locked up his razor, only giving it to him under surveillance,
from time to time, out of fear of violence. Or perhaps (Erji Sandor's
theory) it was to keep him from being attractive to other women.
Most remarkable of all, Drew and the Countess kept moving. Every
few months, it seemed, they would give up one *Wohnung* for another—this in a city where living quarters were desperately hard to
find. Drew would stamp into the café, toss his big black hat on the
table, and say gruffly, without explanation, "New address, boys!"

Drew assisted the Countess, who now seemed dazed, along the
Trattnerhof corridor, and, in this labyrinth of narrow passages,

found at last the correct door. "It's going to be all right, Emilie," he muttered solicitously. "Bear up!" Warmly she clutched his hand.

After a moment's wait Zapp's lawyer, an unctuous little man, silken, by name Klengel, received them. He said "*Grüss Gott!*" to Drew and "I kiss the hand!" to the Countess.

Almost at once it became clear that it was not going to be all right. Wasting no time, Rechtsanwalt Dr. Klengel said that, unfortunately, Herr Zapp would be satisfied with nothing less than the full repayment of his fifteen hundred Schillings at once. Magnanimously, Herr Zapp would waive interest, but if the capital sum were not returned immediately, *sofort*, he would feel compelled, as a matter of self-protection, to inform Herr Drew's office in New York about the matter, which of course, most regrettably and deplorably, would result in the gravest embarrassment for Herr Drew, and possibly—who could tell?—mean the loss of Herr Drew's job.

Drew explained that he didn't have the money and that was that. He added, "How much time can you give me?"

Silence.

"Come now," said Drew with his arching smile. "This is Thursday afternoon, it's after banking hours, the A.O.G. is closed, and nobody has *that* much money in cash. Maybe I can raise it tomorrow, maybe not. If you don't give me a little time, you risk getting nothing at all. Let me have till Monday noon."

Rechtsanwalt Dr. Klengel nodded, and the Countess grimaced. They were saved—till Monday noon.

Then Drew asked, "What about the securities? I know they're down, but they may be worth something. The Frau Gräfin tells me that Herr Zapp has them in safekeeping for her."

"The what?"

"The securities—the shares in Slovak iron. You must have them."

The lawyer's unctuous face became bewildered. He was about to speak when the Countess seized his hand and, with a desperate, furious gesture, shook her head violently; a bolt out of her eyes struck him; he understood.

Blandly he turned to Drew. "Ah, yes . . . I will consult Herr Zapp. Ah . . . yes . . . the securities . . . Slovak iron, of course!"

Heavily, Drew led the Countess into the corridor. But now he had understood too, from watching the lawyer's face. Everything she had told him must be a lie. From beginning to end her story was a mass of lies. He grunted and slapped her in the face. She slid down on the floor; grabbing both her skinny wrists in one hand, he hauled her toward the elevator.

Inside his office Dr. Klengel sighed. The Countess had borrowed the money from Zapp, her former lover, on the pretext that Drew, critically ill, faced a major operation for an ailment which she could not describe but which she said was of an "indelicate" nature. Months later, Zapp had found out that this was totally untrue, and that Drew had not been ill at all. He had been politely dunning her ever since, and had only applied himself directly to Drew, through the lawyer, as a last resort.

❋

Drew reached his desk in the Journalistenzimmer, press room, of the telegraph office half an hour later, picked up the afternoon newspapers, and saw the story in the *Abend* describing the Weissenhof circle as a band of crooks, himself conspicuously among them. After a moment he telephoned Mason Jarrett, the only man in town he could think of who might help him.

3

Most of that same long afternoon, in spite of the *Föhn*, Dr. Laszlo Sandor, the veteran correspondent of the *Washington Sun*, worked with concentration on a complicated mail series about agricultural surpluses in the Danube Valley. His methods of work were well known. Seriously, almost pedantically, he assembled his material, his notes and statistics, from various folders, like a surgeon choosing his instruments. When actually writing he became agitated. Erji, his wife, had to be close to him in their apartment on top of the office building in the First Bezirk. She was the indispensable nurse in this operating theater. Sandor could not work unless she stayed in the same room, reading or doing what she called "fancy work" a few feet away; he went completely to pieces without her. Knowing this filled her with the utmost pride.

Mason Jarrett—now walking down the dark defile of Mozartgasse—

had often observed Sandor's working habits. Going after a story, he snapped up each item of news voraciously; he was interested in any detail, no matter how small. When he had enough details he proceeded to make what he called "combinations." He fitted bits of news together like pieces in a jigsaw puzzle. His whole soul went into these arrangements and combinations. What Sandor believed in most was the truth, together with the invincibility of virtue and the inevitability of progress. He could no more have twisted a story or given innuendoes to a dispatch than he could have cut off his son's hand. "My credo? You ask me that seriously?" he had said to Paula when the Jarretts arrived in Vienna. "My credo as a jo-arnalist? It is very simple. I am a liberal. Therefore I try to see both sides, exactly. I am a democrat, therefore I have standards. I am a spectator, therefore I try to see clearly. I am not a man of action. Therefore, I try to understand action. I am a writer. Therefore, I try to write well. I am a jo-arnalist. Therefore, I write the truth. But now"—his face crinkled into a characteristic ironic smile—"if you osk me how I know what the truth is, that I cannot tell!"

Like Balkan kings, Sandor spoke no language perfectly, not even his own. His English had a Hungarian accent, his Hungarian a French accent, his French a German accent, his German an Italian accent, his Italian an English accent, and so on around. His voice carried a chuckle, and his eyes, beyond heavy owl-like spectacles, held a friendly gleam. He loved to elucidate, to share his wisdom; he would say, "Now, it is something inter-est-ing that will happen. Let me tell you about." He seldom conceded the necessity of using pronouns at the end of sentences.

Panting, snorting, Sandor pulled the last page of copy from his typewriter. His hands trembled, and he sank back, weak, shaking, from the accumulated strain of his task and relief at having finished it. Dr. Sandor was an exceedingly emotional man. He wiped his glasses, and said aloud in English, "I am finished to the end, except to make the revisions whole. Erji, Erji!" he called out, although she was in the same room. "Another cup of coffee, please! And what is doing now our son?"

"He is with Fräulein in park."

Erji Sandor was a slim, youngish woman, seemingly as frail as a poppy, with dark brown hair, part of which was gray; the gray looked like a light lace handkerchief laid over the other part. Like Sandor, she spoke English with a syntax, as well as an accent, of her own invention and, unlike him, had nerves and sinews made of iron.

Erji was a Slovak, and probably had gypsy blood. Her father, of the most respectable class, had been an officer. Back in the forgotten year 1922, Sandor, at a loose end, sauntered one day into the old Hungarian Club in Vienna, part of which had been requisitioned as a records office. There he saw standing in line before a desk, a tall, willow-slim girl in a floppy wide straw hat; he could not see her face under the hat, but something in her figure stirred his interest. She caught him obviously staring at her and looked away embarrassed; Sandor turned and fled, and when he returned she had disappeared. He asked the secretary who the tall, handsome dark girl was; the secretary replied that she was getting her papers in order for a trip to America and would be back at the club the next day at three, by which time her birth certificate, which couldn't be found in the files, should have turned up. Sandor stood the next day beside the desk, and when Erji arrived the secretary provided an impeccably proper introduction.

"And why, may I ask, are you undertaking the long and difficult trip beyond the seas to America?" he demanded.

Erji said, "I am affianced to a young officer, but I have no dowry and I can only earn a dowry by going to America and working there for some little time."

"It is nonsense. In America you would get nothing but debts, and anyway you would not return."

The next day Sandor presented his compliments to Erji's father, and after some days of agitation the young officer was prevailed upon to withdraw his suit. Sandor and Erji became engaged. He had always had a slight nervous feeling of inferiority to the officer class; now he was marrying into it, and he became positively swollen with pride. He and Erji met daily, under careful chaperonage, but sometimes they managed to slip off to the nearest *Konditorei* and sip coffee and have a sweet alone. Erji wondered with incredulity in later years how she could ever have imagined herself to be in love with the youthful officer she had jilted—although his mustaches, she had to admit, were very fine. Sandor became the moving spirit of her being. Their courtship lasted the correct interval, and they were married the next year.

Nowadays there were no reservations betwen Erji and Laszlo and no distance. She asked nothing better of life than that she should run the household while he worked, sit quietly with him when he wrote his dispatches, and then go to a coffeehouse by his side in the evening. Laszlo asked for nothing more than what he had. She must always be close by, she could sing the old gypsy songs when they had a party, and she ought not to have more than three *Weisse Ohnes* in one sitting.

Albrecht, nicknamed Putzi, their six-year-old son, came in with Fräulein. He paid little attention to his parents, but casually sat on the floor of the room where Sandor worked and pulled a pile of toys from a bottom shelf. Laszlo beamed, and Erji dropped on her knees beside him, worshiping him with her eyes, adoring him. The child yanked at a tin locomotive.

"For my name day I want a new locomotive. This locomotive has only one smokestack. I want a locomotive with two, three, six smokestacks!"

"Locomotives do not come with six smokestacks."

"Oh, yes, they do. My locomotives do."

He sat with knees spread out, holding a picturebook with thin small hands.

"I think this is the picture of a rich man's house. No, it is the house of a king!"

"If it were the house of a king it would be called a palace and there would be much gold in it," Sandor said. Bending down he became bright red in the face; love for this child overwhelmed him.

"Do you know what I would do if I were a king?"

"No. What?"

"Buy a thousand yachts."

The Sandors chortled.

"Papa, what is the smallest thing in the world?"

"A germ."

"No—what the germ eats."

Rapt with pride at such brilliance, such precocity, the parents stared, beaming at one another. Sandor kept muttering, "The son! My son!"

The telephone rang, and Erji picked it up. "For you, Sandor."

Almost always she called him by his last name, for no reason that anybody could imagine, and sometimes in company she referred to him in the third person even when he was present. "Sandor thinks so-and-so," she would say.

His voice became startled. "Yes, Herr Hofrat, yes, yes, a pleasure, an honor, to be called by you. What? What? But of course I will come at once, thank you!" Globules of sweat broke out on his rosy sloping forehead. "I understand, absolutely confidential, off the record, from first to last! You can tell me nothing more over the phone? Ja, ja! The consequences can be unimaginable? But of course I understand that, Herr Hofrat. I come at once."

He turned to Erji, out of breath. His face had become deadly pale where it was not covered by a mat of short, soft, sparrow-colored beard, the same length all over. His nose, which protruded from this like a mound of strawberry marzipan, remained scarlet. He exclaimed in an awed whisper, "There are secret informations! Germany and Owstria are to make a Customs Union!"

He put on a coat in a rush, and raced heavily down the stairs.

4

Laszlo Sandor had not been born to be a journalist. He was supposed to follow his rich, eccentric father into the textile business, but of course he did nothing of the kind. By the time he was fourteen it was obvious to everyone in the household that he would never be a businessman. Calling him, even then, was the dangerous, enticing, never-to-be-forgotten world of ideas, of the satisfaction of intellectual curiosities and the exploration of philosophical fields of endeavor and the pursuit of truth.

The Sandors lived near Budapest, miles from the sea or any considerable body of water, but Laszlo's father was a passionate yachtsman. Holidays, when Laszlo was a child, were always spent on the bouncing waters of Lake Balaton, or even the Dalmatian coast. "Ffrrrr," the old man would growl. "Forward with that hawser. Forward, I say . . . watch your jib sheet. Imbecile! Idiot!" The boy would try to obey the peremptory and confused orders. "Frr-frr! I told you forward. No, aft with it now! Dolt! Imbecile!"

Laszlo grew up to be inveterately bookish, and, instead of playing football, pored over history books and made long lists of kings, battles, sieges; these he entered carefully in notebooks which he stowed away with unnatural neatness. He led a strange, secret life of the mind, which even now proved its value, because it accounted for his phenomenal erudition; his memory was faultless, and his industry immense.

At sixteen Laszlo went to Florence on a holiday, and returned knowing that he was destined thereafter to be a vagabond, a pariah. From the family point of view, that is. He did not consider himself to be a vagabond or pariah. He had discovered art. Then, at the University of Vienna, art and philosophy gave way to politics. He drank beer in student taverns, learned four languages, fought a duel, and won his Ph.D. with a thesis on the political ideas of Charles V. How his heart was churning!

"Fff-rrr!" barked his red-faced, angry, and yet proud old father. "What good to know the gist of every line Schiller ever wrote? You have chosen, you have only yourself to blame. I shall cut you off without a penny. Your brother Heinrich will take the business. Imbecile! Look sharp, don't miss that buoy!"

Came World War I. On a walking trip in the Auvergne, Laszlo did not see the newspapers and did not get out of France in time. Anyway he was youthful and singingly proud of his independence of the practical world and totally disinclined to take anything so stupid as a war seriously. The vital thing was to decide whether or not to apply for a scholarship at Oxford next year. He learned promptly to take war seriously. He was arrested by the French as an enemy alien and spent four brutal, interminable years in an internment camp. Yet he recovered from this black period of misery and despair in short order—because he loved life and was therefore an incorrigible optimist.

What a transformed world he found when, at last, he returned to

Central Europe in 1919! Almost everything he had known as a child had vanished utterly. The orderly world of the old Empire, so stately, so paternal; the comforting sense that things must always proceed as before, if only because tradition had decreed it so; the calm feeling of neighborly unity and satisfaction; the assumption that one is part of an organism, a minute fiber in a corporate body that has a real reason to work and therefore works; the twilight smoothness of a civilization that possessed every virtue but vitality—all this gone, ground to bits, torn apart by a tornado of insane and comprehensive violence.

"Do not assume to think, however," Sandor told Mason Jarrett, "that in the so-called estimable Empire all was ideal. By no means! The Empire was a monstrosity; it made ghastly mistakes, outlived its usefulness, and had to die. It deserved to die. Now it is common to ex-oggerate and believe that in the old days everyone lay down together, even as the lion and the lamb. All the minorities cheek to cheek, and the peasants and the landowners loving each other so sweetly . . . no! It was not like that! All was not ideal. On the farms, children of serfs were beaten like animals while the noblemen bought and sold their Titians. In the cities, nationalist students were daily subjected to brutal tortures by the police. But—dear me!—the distorted memory one has of the gentility of those days, the orderliness and companionship, the fondness of families, the long, quiet evenings and our high hopes . . ."

Laszlo, arriving in Budapest, prepared to meet his new relatives. His mother had died in the second year of the war, and his father promptly married again; all Laszlo knew of his stepmother was that she had been the housekeeper, no longer young, on a neighboring estate. His brother Heinrich, dull, methodical, was also married now.

His father had literally shrunk, and was perhaps two-thirds his former size; it seemed for a moment that he was pretending not to remember Laszlo, after waiting anxiously for him for years. He snapped, "Ah! You! Back again!" He drummed with his fingers on the desk with an extraordinary appearance of absent-mindedness and, in a voice that could be heard through the whole house, shrieked a sudden denunciation of his son for having deserted him. At the end he broke into harsh, childlike sobs and, wiping his eyes, confided that his new wife, Maria, had ruined him.

"Such a woman . . . a splendid figure of a woman. It was my error. You will see . . . she is handsome and imposing. She has a heart of flint. She has taken everything, and now mistreats me because there is nothing left."

The reunion at dinner was not jovial. The stepmother took Laszlo aside, whispering, "Your father is as a child. Everything has to be done for him. As if he were a child." Laszlo had a talk with Heinrich. They had never been fond of one another and it was difficult to establish contact now, to bridge the irrevocably lost years. Heinrich's wife was a pretty young woman, but harsh, who seemed suspicious of Laszlo and worried about his share of the estate.

Laszlo proceeded to Vienna soon thereafter and an event occurred that changed the course of his life. There seemed to be no openings for teachers at the university and he decided to enter some non-academic field. But what? He was still suffering acutely from a backwash of fatigue and shock at the changed circumstances of the world. One of his friends was the British consul, whom he met while doing some volunteer work for the Relief Administration.

"You're a useful citizen," the consul said. "Why aren't you busy at some job? There's Rappaport, the American journalist, just arrived, and totally without experience—he needs a translator if you wouldn't mind taking it on. He doesn't know a word of German himself. I say, what a lot of nerve those Americans have!"

Rather idly, not knowing if he really wanted this kind of work, Sandor dropped in to see Rappaport, the correspondent of the Washington Sun. The consul was supposed to have informed Rappaport about Sandor, but there had been some slip-up, and, unannounced, unknown, Laszlo found himself waiting with twenty others in a crowded reception room. One by one Rappaport called them in and interviewed them quickly—former officers, law students, middle-aged professors, young scholars, postwar flotsam. With amused but excited curiosity, wondering how Rappaport would greet him, pleased to be taking his chance without favoritism among these others, Sandor walked in to see a sharp, thin-shouldered, bespectacled young man who shot abrupt questions at him. After only five minutes Rappaport made up his mind. He walked briskly to the door and dismissed the other applicants. "Job's filled," he snapped.

So Laszlo Sandor became a journalist.

"Smart chap, Rappaport," murmured the British consul later. "Judgment of men, I say . . . picking Sandor out of all that mob."

Rappaport was assigned elsewhere two years later, and Sandor took over his Vienna job. It was at this time that he met Erji, courted her, and married her.

Sandor's father died that autumn, in 1922, as the inflation got under way. Laszlo had known for a long time that not much would remain in the estate, but the colorful range and diversity of his father's debts staggered him. It would have been easy to pay them off in cheap Kronen, but he thought that they should be liquidated in *valuta*, proper currency; he wanted every creditor to be paid off with a sum approximate in value to the debt when it was made. Heinrich thought that Laszlo's proposal was sheer madness, and they quarreled bitterly. Came the inflation, bursting on them like a geyser, sweeping almost everything away; at the end there was nothing left at all. "Ach," sighed Laszlo. "Dear me! What to do?"

Now he had a living to earn in earnest. Heinrich moved to Bohemia, carried off a lucky speculation, and bought into a successful wire-netting business.

❋

Tonight, this night, nine years later, Dr. Laszlo Sandor talked at length with the high official who had telephoned him about the Customs Union story. "What to do?" he kept muttering to himself. His agitation was profound. He returned home to find Erji kneeling beside Putzi's bed saying his good-night prayers with him. Sandor entered the darkened bedroom, looked lovingly at Putzi's face, and kissed the boy on the forehead. He left the room with Erji, and a long wail came from the boy—"*Mutti! Mutti!*" Erji was attempting to discipline him and she resisted this appeal to return to his room, as he always sought to entice her into doing. Sandor appealed to her, "Go to the son, please. Give him happiness now, at least." When she returned Putzi's face became sweet and sunny. She kissed him and said good night again, but he was determined to try to hold her longer and pleaded, "*Mutti*, excuse me, I have to tell you something, ask you something. Everything has to have a beginning, doesn't it?

What is at the beginning of God? The devil? And where does God end?"

Sandor ate a bite. Groaning aloud, he made further calculations about the Customs Union. "What to do?" he repeated to himself desperately. He put in several calls for Mason Jarrett, but Jarrett's line was busy.

5

Huge, with his swelling chest, but with his waistline well indented (in those days), Mason now approached the Hauptstrasse en route to his destination, the Café Weissenhof. A peculiar, almost sinister gloom had settled over the Döbling neighborhood. The trees sighed, the bushes drooped. This atmosphere of enervation, of apprehension, often accompanied the *Föhn*, which had several of the characteristics of Vienna itself—so seductive, so oppressive, but possessed of an enigmatic charm.

The yellowish streetlamps gave the plane trees lining the curbs the appearance of having been camouflaged in mottled ovals of yellow, brown, green. Overhead a full moon, swollen, slightly inflamed, with its man blurred, looked like an eye filmed over by a mist of cataract.

From the day Mason had first seen their villa he had been enchanted by the neighborhood, which was quite fashionable. It was also a slum. One segment, near the greenness of a shiny park, was bright with wooded paths and children in starched frocks accompanied by expensive governesses. Another, flanking an open market, was a plot of vegetable gardens, where the poorest of poor families lived in tar-paper shacks and grew carrots and cabbages.

Wrapped in his Loden he passed the Zuckerwaren, the Parfümerie, where he had his hair cut (when Paula thought that it needed cutting), the Elektrotechniker, and the Schuhmachermeister. The shopkeepers didn't know what to call him. Paula was, of course, the *gnädige Frau*, but what was he? For a time the proprietor of the Feinster Selcherei used Herr Redakteur, until Mason explained that he was not an editor, and the barber experimented with Herr Zeitungsdirektor, and then, when he returned from a trip to the Balkans wearing a shako, Herr Baron. It was unthinkable that he should not have a title. A person was undressed in Vienna if he, or she, did not have a title. Men had given him cards reading "D. Kfm. (merchant with diploma) Dr. Hans Pötzlein" and even "Direktor Ing. mont. h.c. (mining engineer honoris causa) Dr. Berthold Resch."

Mason reached the Grinzinger railway viaduct, and waited for the tram. Of course Paula, the extravagant girl, would have taken a taxi. "Come on, tram!" he said aloud. Here a small café-restaurant behind a green lattice gave forth a faint whiff of garlic and beer, which was sucked up by the Föhn and spread into the street. A group of young people came out; their laughter, their gestures as they talked, gave expression to a characteristic Viennese note of levity, helplessness, and hopelessness. "Come on, tram!" Mason repeated impatiently. He snapped his fingers, restless, as if the forces of the universe he was attempting to summon included even the transportation system of the Vienna municipality, the Gemeinde Wien.

In the group emerging from the café-restaurant was, he saw, Nella Blohr, the young pretty niece of the Wallensteins. They had met a few times casually, but had never had more than a minute of talk together. She looked scrubbed, pink, packed with quest, and appallingly young. Recognizing him, she flushed, tossing back her thick sand-colored hair with an impatient gesture. "Ah," she shrugged, "let me introduce . . . my friends. . . . Yes, yes, we have been in the café. . . . What do we talk about? . . . Of no importance!"

Her companions, loosely linked, drifted down the shadowy street heavy with the Föhn. Nella's attitude seemed to be that they were too young, too coltish, too undistinguished, for the attention of Mason Jarrett, whereas she, Nella Blohr, had the right to be regarded by him seriously. What a grown-up young woman she was trying to be, thought Mason—determined, too. How old was she—sixteen, seventeen? He said gravely, "Nella, you have practically the prettiest freckles I've ever seen."

Freckles, a symbol of extreme youth, of youth untried—an insult! But she looked pleased and Mason, not knowing quite why he did so, stared straight into her eyes and, leaning forward as if he were a mesmerist, chucked her lightly under her hard little ball of chin. She quivered and wriggled away. Again he was treating her like a child—another insult!

"Wait, stop!" He laughed. "I've just had a chat with the Dozent. He tells me you're going to be a mineralogist—the only girl to be studying mineralogy in the whole history of the university!"

"Ah, perhaps—yes!"

Proud little vixen, Mason thought.

"The Dozent says that your drawings of mineral sections are remarkable. I'd love to see them. Won't you come to tea some time, and show them to us?"

Us? She bridled with disdain. It was Mason who interested her, not his wife. But now she gave him an exploring, almost secret look. No longer was he some kind of unknown, unseizable creature from across the seas.

Mason's voice held a mixture of gravity and cheerfulness. "Also the Dozent mentioned that your cousin Otto is coming back from London soon. I'm eager to meet him."

Her face took on a superior look. An actress, too, he perceived. "Ah, Otto . . . you will find him . . . too intellectual perhaps, too smug! But he's quite, quite nice!"

Mason felt beyond his control a tingling desire to know this girl better. He wanted to touch her. It was ridiculous, but she aroused him, not so much in a direct amorous way, but with a desire to protect her and to fulfill his curiosities. Realizing that she grasped this, he became at once shy and withdrawn. For the first time, she smiled warmly, openly—she had penetrated to him—triumph! Mason did not know what traversed her thoughts next, but he himself went into a spiral of fantasy. She was pirouetting in the shadows of a dark stage, her face illuminated by a sudden glow as if the wavering shaft of a hidden spotlight had found her after a search. She whirled toward him, and he murmured, "Ah, but you're charming, charming!" Now she became a youthful grand duchess addressing a courtier; she made a gesture as if with a lorgnette, and then, reversing the role, curtsied. Her eyes became candid, confident. "Forgive me for having been so distant . . . things *throttle* me!" Her language as he imagined it took on an old-fashioned tone. "But now come to me if you dare . . . you do wisely to consider me. Ah, but I am full of wiles, what a race you will have to run!"

Mason, putting a brake on these absurd thoughts, said good-night. Nella muttered "Auf Wiedersehen," and with a flourish, skirt and hair flying, ducked down the street.

Mason's tram, the G-2, which the Viennese pronounced "Gay Zwo," not "Gay Zwei," carried him in twenty minutes to the Schottentor, where the university commanded a corner of the Ring. Incontrovertibly the Ring was the essence of Vienna. Mason surveyed it wondering what it must have been like in the old days. Even now it held more than a trace of imperial magnificence. After all it was only a street, a boulevard, somewhat shabby, encircling the Innere Stadt, but what an air it conveyed of former authority and nobility. First came the pavement for pedestrians, then the channel for automobiles and carriages, then a line of somewhat scratchy trees, then a gravel walk for the horsemen, then more trees shielding a lane of grass, with park benches, then the northbound tramline, and finally the broad river of the street itself. And all of this was duplicated for the southbound traffic on the other side of the heroic boulevard. What complacence it expressed! What extravagance!

Mason crossed the Ring and climbed the bump of hill near Haydnplatz. Here he paused for no particular reason before the square baroque building of the Allgemeine Österreichische Gesellschaft, the A.O.G., filling a whole block, impregnable, mysterious. By day, its windows shone with a peculiar violet glare, as if the glass were warped, or tinted by a distorted reflection of the sun. Tonight, lights were still flashing from windows above the great claws of the porte-cochere, giving evidence of activity that seemed open, but which, because it was so late, conveyed an impression of the surreptitious. Mason watched. Something special must be going on.

The Föhn had finally oozed into rain, but impulse made him wait and measure this somber fortress of a building, to look it over carefully and estimate its beam and bulk, for a further intent moment. Standing alone in the rain he gazed upward at the windows tier on tier, wondering what might be happening inside this inanimate colossus brazen with wealth and power. He felt frail, vulnerable, and alone.

The cobbles paving the streets here were shaped like loaves of bread, which glistened now with a light veneer of rain. Proceeding, Mason approached the Telegrafenamt a few hundred yards away, apricot-colored and carrying a giant grotesque statue, symbolizing communications, on its roof. He had been unable that afternoon to get his man in Budapest on the telephone and now must send him a telegram. His nostrils dilated as he entered. The building had the stale, sweaty odor of similar large public buildings all over the world: it might have been the City Hall in Chicago, or a big post office in the Bronx.

Having sent his telegram, he peeked into the Journalistenzimmer, the press room, where most of the foreign correspondents in Vienna worked, to see if any of his colleagues might be there. Rows of desks made a central parallelogram; a single lonely ticker chattered near the line of scuffed, splintered phone booths. Young Bleschke, Drew's assistant and the proprietor of an organization known high-soundingly as the Danubia Press Service, sat at a typewriter tap-tapping, pecking at it as if he were inventing a new language word by word. Bleschke was a man abnormally bland, considering all that he had gone through. The first day Mason met him the sole of one of his shoes had hung loose, flapping like a banana skin. Bleschke stopped pecking to look up, greeted him with "Not, uh, very much of news today, Mr. Yarrett," and went on typing. There were three ways to pronounce Mason's name in Vienna aside from the correct one—Charrett, Yarrett, Zharrett.

Outside, under shivering elms, Mason ran into the policeman, an old acquaintance, who patrolled this area. "*Feuer, bitte,*" asked the policeman, and Mason gave him a light—a courtesy which, by immutable Vienna tradition, could be refused to nobody. The policeman, in his flapping green cape, his shiny helmet, looked sodden and decayed. He thanked Mason with a broad leer and then unaccountably pointed up the street toward the Koenigen, a night club from which pungent, plangent *Wiener* songs could be heard, sweet-sour like the sauce on a Peking duck.

Outside Radio-Austria around the corner Mason collided with little old Dr. Heinrich Ritter. Some day he might meet a Viennese who was not a doctor.

"*Grüss Gott, Herr Charrett.*" Dr. Ritter, sprinkled by rain, grasped him. "I was hoping to see you in the café—"

"Let's get out of the rain." They walked back toward the

A.O.G., and took shelter on an arc of pavement under the porte-cochere.

"I have a certain, somewhat embarrassing request to make. . . ."

Dr. Ritter looked astonishingly like a sparrow. He was well over seventy now, but spry. Every evening he did his work in the Journalistenzimmer, took half an hour to verify fussily his names and dates, and then, invariably, day after day and year after year, showed his telegram to whatever British or American correspondent happened to be nearest to hand, to ask if his English were quite correct; and never had the English been other than quite correct.

Dr. Ritter's eyes were old, with the irises circled with a cloudy brown-white ring, but still sharp. His voice fluttered, and he spat as he talked; tiny bursts of spittle plopped toward Mason. Whenever Dr. Ritter passed a funeral, he rushed home at once to drink a bottle of garlic water, which he believed staved off hardening of the arteries.

"How are things going, Heinrich?"

"Not as well as one could wish, unfortunately."

For two decades Dr. Ritter had been foreign editor of the great *Wiener Sternblatt*. An office intrigue ousted him. He was only fifty then, at full development of his powers, but thereafter his course was down, down, down. He did translations for the Relief Administration for a time, worked in the Finanzministerium, and finally, by great good luck, got back into journalism as the correspondent of a minor British agency.

Something happened then that passed into Vienna legend. Dr. Ritter was a vehemently loyal and patriotic Austrian. In 1927 Vienna suffered grave riots, during which the Palace of Justice was burned down by an angry mob. On this day Dr. Ritter, lunching at a restaurant near the Ring, could actually see smoke jutting from the building, and he left the table to telephone his esteemed friend, Minister Dr. Wimpassing, the chief of the press department, to ask him what was going on. The minister assured him categorically that there was no truth whatever to the malicious rumors that riots had taken place, or that the Palace of Justice was in flames. "*Lieber Herr Kollege* (Colleague), I give you my word of honor that there are no casualties, none whatever. My dear friend, anything you may hear to the contrary . . . untrue—lies of the foreign press, enemies of our beloved Austria!" Dr. Ritter resumed his lunch, and by five o'clock there were sixty dead. So he lost *that* job.

"Herr Charrett, if you should have the goodness to lend me, as a matter of purely temporary convenience, the small sum of twenty Schillings, I would be infinitely obliged."

There were seven Schillings to the dollar at this time, a Schilling was worth fourteen cents, and so Ritter was asking for $2.80, just what Paula had taken. Mason pulled out his wallet; he was somewhat short, but could just manage it. "Glad to oblige, Heinrich," he said. "*Danke!*" Dr. Ritter replied fervently. "*Ich danke Ihnen vielmals. Danke, herzlichen Dank!*" He burbled, spitting.

They walked back into the rain, which was still painting a thin, transparent skin on the beveled loaves of stone bread.

"I will now be able to observe my daughter's birthday with a trinket of some sort," Dr. Ritter said, "or I can make a down payment for a new umbrella. *Ach*, Herr Charrett, you who are so strong, so youthful, you can afford to laugh, you can laugh at us who are over seventy."

"I'm not laughing, Heinrich."

"Well, some day you will be over seventy too. There are compensations. You watch all the rest die off."

6

Nine-twenty. Walking toward the Café Weissenhof, Mason, who was a prowler by nature as well as a stable citizen, came upon the prostitute with the wooden leg, a figure almost as familiar in the neighborhood as the decrepit policeman. Peculiarly enough, or perhaps not peculiarly, Luisa did a brisk business. There were men who liked novelties. Bobbing on her cane, she passed Mason with a smile; people said that she was a cheerful girl, eager, generous. Mason's thoughts turned to Berlin, a city he loathed. Vienna might be corrupt, but Berlin was worse—evil, sordid. There on the Kurfürstendamm a prostitute was made—for a few months anyway, positively made—if she got pregnant. It was the luckiest thing that could happen to a prostitute in Berlin. Men who had never had the experience of sleeping with a woman with a hard hill of belly flocked to those pregnant girls; it was something to smack the gross lips about.

As a matter of fact, Mason reflected suddenly, he had never slept with a pregnant woman himself.

On impulse, he turned abruptly and walked toward the Koenigen, the nearby Hungarian bar, really a small cabaret. He greeted the barman, Hugo, a friend of some months' standing.

"Good evening, Mr. Zharrett."

"Good evening, Hugo. How's business?"

"So-so."

"The *Föhn's* still with us," Mason said.

"Yes. I feel it in my feet," Hugo said.

"How?"

"They get swole."

Mason ordered a *Stock*, Austrian brandy, and hitched himself up on a stool. "Where's Trudi? She's still here, isn't she?"

"*Ja, ja.* Must have chust stepped out. Vill be right back."

Trudi assisted with the coats and hats at the *Garderobe* and sold cigarettes.

"Hilda?"

"*Ja, ja.*" Hugo gave him a look, as if to wonder how he could possibly ask such an unthinkable question. "Vidoud Hilda ve vud be nothing."

"You're right there, I guess, old chap."

Mason glanced around the establishment. Lights glittered behind the bottles on glass shelves at the bar; colored lanterns gave a soft illumination beyond, and clusters of large balloons, swaying fatly, hung squeezed together on beams overhead. Near the dance floor, in the middle of which was a revolving disk, six or seven well-dressed, solid-seeming men sat huddled at a conspicuous table. They were drinking *Sekt*, German champagne, and exchanging festive toasts, but even so they appeared to be inwardly guarded, cautious, as if they were not sure of their milieu. Mason, with his frank, easy, open expression, asked: "Who are those nabobs, Hugo?"

"From the Ah-Oh-Gay. All on the executif committee, if I mistake not myself. They came an hour ago, and are celebrating something."

Hackles of curiosity rose in Mason. He remembered Paula's talk, then the Pole.

Hugo looked envious, but his face also showed scorn, distaste. The men from the A.O.G., although rich as Rothschild, would leave exactly the proper tip, not a Groschen more. Tipping was a complicated process in Vienna. Even in a coffeehouse you had to tip three different waiters, dividing ten per cent between the Herr Ober, or Zahlkellner, to whom you paid the bill, the Kellner who did the actual work, and the Piccolo, or busboy. Those A.O.G. executives would calculate the percentages to the last Groschen. The medium people tip the best, thought Hugo, or Americans as generous as Herr Zharrett.

Reaching under the bar, Hugo passed over to Mason the plate of salted almonds, piping hot, slightly greasy, which were the invariable accompaniment to a drink in cabarets of this special kind, if the customer were favored. Delicious, they squeaked when you bit into them.

The orchestra moaned into a waltz, the lights were dimmed, and the girls, the *Animierdamen*, ladies who animate you, some sitting at the bar drinking water flavored with caramel so that it looked like whiskey, some paired off at otherwise disengaged tables, waited to be asked to dance. Most had taut, removed, sweet-sad faces. Some were outright prostitutes; some were not. Those virtuous had only one problem, which was to maintain their virtue.

Mason's eye darted around, while he watched unobtrusively the group from the A.O.G. The host at the banker's table, the obvious leader, was a tall man with deeply furrowed cheeks and thick hair of an unusual color: rich chocolate. Could he have dyed it? Was it a toupee?

The Koenigen, a small establishment, had a certain charm; it was not as brassy, as vulgarly commercialized, as the big night clubs near the Kärntnerstrasse, like the Wyoming, and it had the best czardas music in town. Strange, the way night clubs all over Central Europe were having a run on the names of western American states. There was an Arizona, a wonderful little joint, in Budapest, and a Montana in Prague. Montana!

Mason remembered the gray-greenish horizons of the ranch near

Great Falls, where he grew up as a boy, and the shriek of locomotive
whistles late at night, flinging their mournful anthems across the
prairie. That was music too.

Lonely, restless, he had wandered into the Koenigen for the first
time on a bland evening the summer before, shortly after his arrival
in Vienna and while Paula was still visiting her family in America.
For the next few weeks he took to the habit of dropping in briefly
after finishing work at the Journalistenzimmer or the Café Weissenhof a block away. The triangle represented by these establishments
made his circuit.

"Another *Stock*, Hugo."

He recollected now with amused, not-too-important relish the
evening he had first met Hilda and Trudi. Business was slack, and
Hilda, wearing that monocle—what an extraordinary affectation, how
attractive—sat alone at the bar, crisply cool. Obviously she was the
star, a personality, and she threw her weight around a bit. A hard
cookie, Mason had thought, but she's not coarse, not cheap. Basically,
she was probably as bourgeois as his laundrywoman. He took note
of her fine eyes first; then the big red sloppy rose of a mouth; her
shoulders, a trifle square, but white, white; her hands and in particular
the thumbs, which, as was so often the case with girls of this milieu,
were extravagantly long and slim, with nails sharp as talons. The
shafts between the knuckles of the thumbs were almost as slim as
pencils.

Hugo introduced them, and Mason felt a thrill as well as a tremor of
guilt. Paula would certainly not approve of this. He was shy, like
most romantics—as if fearful of giving way to his inner yearnings.

"You are here for the *Messe*?"

They always asked that, if it was the *Messe* season; the *Messe*
was Vienna's annual trade fair.

"No, no," Mason said. "I'm not a businessman, I'm a writer.
Besides I live here—beginning to live here, rather."

"You have not been in Vienna long?"

"Only a week or two, and I'd like to stay forever."

"American?" She already had him classified, so she thought.
Nervous; a goody-goody boy; not rich, but easy with money; wife
out of town.

"Of course. Can't you tell?"

"One cannot always be too sure, even from the clothes and most of all the shoes. You are not hurried in your movements, and most Americans forever make haste."

"About nothing, too, as a rule."

She appraised him through the monocle, appreciating this. "What do you write?"

"News, politics."

She wrinkled her nose with distaste and made a gesture of rejection. "Someday you will write something about me, which will be more amusing."

"I'd like to."

The headwaiter tapped her on the shoulder; it was time for her next number.

"You must, lacking me, console yourself now with my darling Trudi," the girl with the monocle said.

Trudi, summoned to the bar, shook hands. She was two or three years younger than Hilda, in her early twenties; she looked innocent and awkward. Mason led her to a table, and they drank Scotch, not Austrian Scotch but Scotch Scotch, which he could ill afford— a dollar a thimbleful in a place like this. Trudi had soft, white-blond hair brushed back from the forehead and held by a black ribbon, girlishly, and curious small teeth, which met with ever-so-slightly rippled edges; vaguely, he was reminded of kernels of corn, or even the side of a key. Her body was charming; she wore a black silk dress cut in a long Y, and her breasts, bobbing up and down, almost bouncing out of the dress, were small, round, and white.

They danced; and Mason had never had an experience quite like it. Her soft, sturdy body seemed to melt into him; yet she was feather-light, he had no sense that she had any weight at all. She floated, but was part of him. When the disk within the dance floor began to revolve Mason slipped and they made their way back to their table.

"I'm not a very good dancer," he apologized.

"Not bad. You are so very big, but not clumsy."

"I don't dance often—I'm too self-conscious." He leaned forward, smiling slightly. "I can't sing a tune, play a game, kiss a relative, imitate an accent, learn a language, or do a parlor trick."

He knew at once that he must be slightly drunk; otherwise he wouldn't talk this way.

"So?"

"It's the gospelth truth, *Kleines*."

His use of this term of endearment pleased her.

"And all out of self-consciousness?"

"Yes. You know, it's a very strange thing about me, but deep down I'm two people!" His voice became thicker, and his manner even more confidential. "Sometimes I'm thickth or seven people!"

She looked startled. The orchestra gave forth a raucous bang, and the room darkened.

"Sssh," Trudi hushed him. "Now she sings. The next number she dances, and later comes a sketch, in which she acts, but now it is the singing. Ssshh. Listen."

Hilda on the stage: astounding; a revelation; apocalyptic: Mason snapped to amazed attention. She had a deep rough furry voice which seemed to tear her slim, vibrating throat apart but which she could lower to an intoxicating whisper. There was power in it, passion, perfectly controlled. Her whole body rippled as the exploding force of her voice burst out. Singing Viennese and Hungarian songs, she chanted, brayed, moaned, murmured, for half an hour. Applause shook the room to its foundations: men shouted, almost screamed; women gasped; strangers clutched each other as they might at a bull-fight.

Mason came to know both girls quite well in the next week or two. Hilda's protectiveness to Trudi and Trudi's open adoration of Hilda were charming to watch. He did not pursue closely the details of the relationship between them, but could easily guess. One night a drunken German, really drunk, started to make advances to Trudi, and he heard Hilda say to him, in a tone he would not forget, "Leave this girl alone, or I'll cut you open with a pair of scissors."

Mason's own association with them could not have been more innocent. He sat around, joked, bought them drinks, horseplayed, and once or twice stayed up till four in the morning, until which hour they were obliged to remain in the Koenigen, and then strolled with them down the dark empty streets, so smooth and silent now, and bought them coffee and sausages at one of the all-night stalls on Rotenturmstrasse. He learned that Trudi lacked vitality and vivacity (well, Hilda had enough for two) and that Hilda was extravagantly ambitious.

Once on a Sunday the three went out to the Wienerwald and had a lazy picnic, full of white wine, untidy sandwiches, and foolishness. He listened to their banter and shoptalk, told them stories about the world outside their world, treated them always like perfect ladies, and never pried. Without effort, scarcely knowing it, they built up a close relationship.

He could not possibly have made love to them. They understood this perfectly. He had scarcely so much as kissed another girl since meeting Paula.

They lay full length in the Wienerwald grass, sunning themselves and nibbling cookies. Mason, in shorts, looked enormous. Hilda hummed, yawned, and, removing her monocle, played with it, seeking to deflect shafts of sunlight with it. Mason fondled impersonally Trudi's soft hair, which was now free of the black band, as if she were a kitten. "*Kleines*," he murmured. An impulse smote him. He grabbed Hilda's monocle and with a wild, indecent gesture made as if to plant it between Trudi's legs, twirling the glass vigorously with the motion of screwing a top on a bottle. Trudi grabbed at her skirt shrieking. Mason fell over on his back, grimacing crazily and yelling with laughter, and Hilda started to giggle uncontrollably, resting first one cheek on the grass, then the other, until tears spurted from her tight-shut eyes.

She pecked Mason on the cheek with a kiss.

"You need a woman," Hilda said.

"I have a wife."

He had not told them much about Paula, but they knew that she was absent in the United States.

"What good is a wife four thousand miles away?" Hilda asked.

Trudi looked sharply away. Her tact was marked and she knew at once that this was delicate, forbidden ground. She and Hilda did not belong to the world of wives and it was not wise to talk about them to a husband. Pensive, she plucked a blade of grass, sucking it. Wives lived in the safe, smug, conservative world across the big frontier. Wives were their enemies and they hated, feared, and envied them.

Hilda went right on treading forbidden ground. "Is your wife a cold woman?" she asked.

Mason was a little startled, but answered as matter-of-factly as if she had asked how old his sister was. "No, no—quite the contrary." Now he must be careful not to be too personal. "She's inhibited in some ways, just as I am. Of course her basic background is puritan, she derives from the puritan tradition, but that doesn't mean that she's full of a sense of sin so much as that she's a nonconformist."

"Nonconformist?"

"Somebody impatient about fixed rules."

The girls sought to digest this.

He wanted to add, but did not do so, "She has to take things through the head first." He remembered something she had said years before: "The rest of me closes up if my mind isn't open!" She had the occasional habit of seeming to be superior to the act of love, even amused by it, removed, detached.

Mason began to mention some of her other characteristics, like honesty and virtue, but broke off, not because he did not want to talk about her but because he knew that tribute to her too emphatic would make these girls feel inferior, or, at least, hurt their feelings. How could he say that Paula was, above all, a lady?

"I know of course that she is what you call a lady," Hilda said. "In that I am not interested. But what are her other qualities? Why do you love her? How can we know you unless we know her too?"

Mason said, "Well, she can be a little severe sometimes, because she has standards. In fact she's an exceptionally serious person."

"All women are serious—much more serious than men," Hilda said.

"Why?"

"Because few of a man's problems are altogether insoluble, which women's often are."

Mason squeezed a fist in a palm, rotating it. Right!

Trudi said, "You make her too ideal. She must have some blemish, some defect."

"Well, she's not domestic. She can't boil an egg."

"She should taste my *Sauerbraten*," Hilda said.

Mason proceeded. "Perhaps, like a lot of self-centered people, she lacks imagination. She's clever and intelligent, but not very intuitive about others."

"Do you carry with you, as do so many American husbands, pictures of her?"

"I'll say, sure."

Hilda and Trudi pored admiringly, but with reservations, over a set of shiny snapshots. Mason looked too.

"You really do love her, don't you?" Hilda said.

"Yes, I do."

"She loves you too." Hilda tapped one of the photographs. "I can tell from the expression."

Now, while still waiting for a glimpse of the two girls, Mason saw a tall, soldierly man with a russet hussar's mustache emerge from a back room of the Koenigen. One of the A.O.G men beckoned to him and he joined their table. He and chocolate hair bowed and shook hands and each deferred to the other politely, but with a sense of distance. Chocolate hair gave the impression of being harsher in temperament, heavier, but both were clearly gentlemen, and the man with the russet mustache was, obviously, somebody quite well known, whereas chocolate hair was new to this environment. Eyes around the room followed the mustached man, and Mason heard several excited whispers as he sipped his drink.

Now the Koenigen was filling up. Crowds surrounded the bar; waiters ducked and hustled; a spotlight caught the slightly corrugated, glistening skull of the leading czardas player. Mason heard the word "*Servus*," and there stood Trudi behind him. "*Servus*," a favorite and almost untranslatable Viennese term, could be taken to mean "At your disposal." She smiled and had the look of a girl who, approaching a man unseen, wanted to slip her palms over his eyes.

Mason greeted her warmly. "Trudi, I'm delighted to see you, I've been hoping you'd come in, I have to go in a minute, where have you *been*?"

"Where have you been? We have not seen you for some time, a matter perhaps of months."

"I've been out of town a lot, busy too. You're fine?"

"Yes?"

"Where's Hilda?"

Trudi pointed. She had at that moment entered the room, and was standing idly near the A.O.G. table. Russet mustache rose and bowed, kissing her hand.

"Hilda's okay?"

"Yes, oh yes." Her soft eyes shone.

"*Kleines*, dance with me."

They circled—again she gave forth her miraculous note of warmth, solidity, and, at the same time, utterly smooth weightlessness—near chocolate hair and russet mustache. Hilda saw Mason and hailed him with surprise and delight, slipping across the floor to greet him. For a moment he enveloped both Hilda and Trudi in his big arms and the three danced together while the A.O.G. men watched.

Now russet mustache beckoned to Hilda, whom he seemed to know well, and she joined him at a different table. Back at the bar with Trudi, Mason had a thought. "Listen, you could do me a big favor. Go over to the A.O.G. table, sell those men some cigarettes as slowly as you can, and try to find out what they're celebrating."

She returned in a moment. "Something about a reorganization at the Ah-Oh-Gay. One group, this group, has taken over from another group. But they converse in a low voice and it was difficult to hear." He felt excitement. But he must learn more.

Hilda caught a signal from Mason, and sauntered casually toward the bar. Russet mustache, blowing her a kiss, left the establishment.

Mason spoke carefully. "Hilda, *Liebste*, this could be important, very. Go back toward the A.O.G. table, please, get the man with chocolate hair to dance with you, and try to find out from him, now, or from his friends, what they're talking about. Don't come back here, that would be too obvious; but say that it's time for you to change into your costume. When you go backstage Trudi here will join you—understand, Trudi?—and you tell *her* what they're saying, if anything. Then Trudi will pass it on to me. Clear?"

That any conspiracy so childish, so brazenly improvised, could possibly turn out to be successful was, of course, impossible; but it did.

Hilda sat at the A.O.G. table for what seemed to be an interminable time, danced with chocolate hair, and took her leave from him and disappeared at last. Mason gave Trudi a covert shove. In five minutes she returned, joining him at the bar. "I did not quite understand everything," Trudi reported, "but Hilda said to tell you that something very large is going on behind the scenes. Arrangements have been made for some kind of secret agreement between Germany and Austria—what did she call it?—a union about something. Also she is very cross with you. What do you mean by staying away from us for so long and what is the reason for all this mysterious business tonight? She says you will have to do her a big favor soon, and now she is involved with the whole A.O.G. group and it is your fault if she cannot get rid of them."

"Trudi, darling, thank you, and thank Hilda very, very much, and I'll tell you everything about everything the first minute I reasonably can."

Mason asked Hugo for his bill and paid it. Out in the street, he walked swiftly back to the Journalistenzimmer, and put in a call for Strothness.

III. CAFÉ WEISSENHOF

Never as long as he lived would Mason Jarrett forget the Café Weissenhof. Shaped like an L, it had two long bays intersecting at right angles; guests in one bay could not see those in the other. Tall windows shaped like bullets rose over semicircular booths that, shoulder-high, were filled with circular tables topped with gray marble. The upholstery, in vertical stripes of black, buff, and orange, was renovated every year, but even so the moths got in. At the junction of the two bays stood the cashier's desk, and above this was a clock which told the correct time within about seven minutes.

Near the entrance a case contained newspapers, bound in rattan frames, from countries all over the world. You could sit in the Weissenhof, as in any other good Viennese café, all day for the price of a cup of coffee, and read newspapers in a dozen languages for hour after hour without being asked to order anything else—that is, for the first ten years or so, after which the Herr Ober might express mild impatience by not calling you by some title to which you were not entitled anyway, like Herr Direktor.

Financiers went to the Café Pucher in those days, stamp collectors to the Vindobona, and medical students to the Freyung; chess players favored the Herrenhof, and musicians (appropriately enough) the Schubert. The Weissenhof was the haunt of journalists, not of journalists in general, but of a particular group—the foreign correspondents resident in Vienna, together with political hangerson. Even the waiters serving the journalists' *Stammtisch* were politically minded. Herr Julius, the senior Zahlkellner, who had been at the Weissenhof for twenty-seven years, was a staunch Christian Socialist; he was fat, with a belly creased like a roll when he bent over, and

85

cheeks the color of dark brick, stained by a network of red capillaries. The junior headwaiter, Emil (not Herr Emil), tall and skinny, looked like an intellectual, with a slim pointed nose on the top of which pince-nez perched precariously. At Christmas he gave each correspondent a little gift, for instance a memorandum book of imitation leather, and on New Year's calmly asked for enough of a tip to pay for it; he was supposed to be a nephew of somebody important in the Heimwehr, the conservative private army. The swarthy young waiter who actually did most of the work, by name Josef, always needed a shave except on Sundays and was an ardent Social Democrat. His expression of greeting, with a bow, was invariably "*Empfehle mich*" (I recommend myself), and he said good-bye with the words "I have the honor!" The doorman, a woozy little man named Leo, was a Communist.

Mason, arriving from the Journalistenzimmer, squeezed himself into the booth where several tables touched like pennies in a row. He had not been able to reach Strothness in Berlin. His colleague had gone out for the evening, but the long-distance operator was going to track him down and call him back. "Make the call *dringend*," Mason had said.

He saluted Erji Sandor, patting her hand, with the words "How's my old gypsy girl?" a salutation she liked. She replied, "Very spiritful, zank you." She had already ordered her first *Weisse Ohne*, coffee with cream but not whipped cream, of the evening, and was sipping it. Mason asked for a *Lichtes*, and a stein of pale beer promptly appeared.

"Where's Sandor?"

"He come in *fünf* Minuten. He has finizzed his series of mail stories about agriculture, zanks God. Now in post office he puts in mailbox."

Erji, as usual, had a box of chocolates in one hand, a novel in the other. During long sessions at the coffeehouse, while Sandor talked or worked, she read, nibbled, and never missed, even by a nuance, anything that went on. Nor, despite the chocolates, did she ever gain an ounce. Mason's theory about this was that she was a true Slav, and therefore all the calories went into her soul. Seriously, he knew that the trait that distinguished her most was pride. She would cut off her hand for pride.

Mason continued to watch her with pleasure. Her face was narrow under tall brows and her teeth were white, square, and strong. One front tooth was short by a millimeter, leaving a tiny slit when her teeth closed; this added to her attractiveness.

Neither Drew nor Thorne, the men he had come to meet, had arrived. Across the room sat three excessively shady characters, toward whom Mason nodded vaguely. They were Dr. Zeissman, a Czech correspondent who took money from the Hungarians, Orlovsky, a White Russian who took money from the Czechs, and Reginald H. Tinkham, the venerable part-time representative of an Edinburgh newspaper, who took money from both—and from the Yugoslavs to boot.

Orlovsky was, as usual, tipsy—not drunk, just nicely tipsy. He liked Mason and moved toward him, wavering, with his glass of Schnapps aloft, and clinked glasses with him. "To my muzzer," said Orlovsky, raising his hand high for the toast. "To my muzzer . . . my dear muzzer Holly Rossiya!"

Conversation at the *Stammtisch* proceeded normally, that is to say it was about politics, but Erji Sandor and Mia Tetzel discussed rapturously the new Garbo film, *Romance*.

"Where's Karl?" Mason asked Mia, and she replied, "He has dinner tonight with Herr Thorne. I had a headache, but then decided to join them here." Mason, as always, admired her hair, the color of marigolds with its sculptured metallic sheen, to say nothing of her sumptuous body. In that era women with very large breasts dressed to conceal them rather than the reverse; even so, under Mia's bodice, impossible to hide, rose those solid mounds.

Mia called Josef, the junior waiter, and bought just two cigarettes, Egyptische Zweite Sorte, out of the orange-colored flat box. For these she paid ten Groschen, a cent and a half. Poverty. You certainly were poor when you bought cigarettes one by one.

Mason asked how Karl was getting on. Her eyes retreated, becoming opaque, like marbles; she disappeared into herself—a familiar phenomenon with Mia. Mason had the feeling that in spite of her bountiful appearance she was not at all strong; she was a large woman, but frail. She lit one of the cigarettes. When she opened her lips an infinitesimally thin thread of saliva was suspended between upper and lower for a fraction of a second.

John Dixon, the plump, blond, and somewhat callow correspondent of the Chicago *Daily News*, arrived with his wife, Dauphine, and two visitors named Henderson. Introductions were exchanged, and phrases like "*Ich küss' die Hand*" rang around the table. Mason and Dixon were intimate friends, even though their publishers, four thousand miles away, had a fierce rivalry and snapped at each other's throats, fire in livid eye. But it was a commonplace for American journalists in Europe to be fraternal no matter what kind of relationship their bosses had. The contempt most foreign correspondents (but not Dixon) had for their employers in those days was an enthralling phenomenon to observe.

"Anything hot going on?" Dixon asked Mason.

Mason certainly didn't want to talk about the Customs Union, but he didn't want to lie either and answered with a shrug.

Dixon looked lazy, but he had a bright, acquisitive mind and an enterprising nose for news. Sometimes Mason wondered if his life would be different if he could ever be as positive about anything as John Dixon was about everything.

"I think I've got that first act licked at last! Will you glance at it again, Mace?"

"Sure. Let's meet sometime tomorrow."

Most of John Dixon's energy went into writing plays. Perhaps this was one of the reasons Mason liked—and envied—him.

Dauphine Dixon, who was French, had hair the color of carrot juice; it took on the shape of a loose, lopsided beret no matter how she combed it. She was a tense young woman, zealous for her husband's career; her lips looked squashed together and her fingernails were bitten to the quick. She never left home without a notebook which she fished out of her bag with incredible speed and agility when she heard something that she thought was worth writing down as a source of future dialogue for one of Dixon's plays.

The boy came with the ten P.M. *Welt-Nachrichten* bulletins, which Drew and Sandor had delivered directly to the café. Mason's urgent thought was: Anything broken yet about the Customs Union? Nothing.

He gathered that Henderson, the man whom Dixon had brought with him, was a Congressman from Illinois. He had never heard of him before, or known that he was in Vienna. So Dixon was one up on him. Chicago papers made a considerable specialty at this time of printing brief reports about the activities of prominent local citizens, like Henderson, when they traveled abroad. Well, he belonged to Dixon. Mason wouldn't butt in. Besides, he had bigger fish to fry. But he set out to make himself agreeable to the Hendersons not only by reason of his good nature but because a Congressman from Illinois could, he knew, turn out to be useful some fine day.

Henderson, who had a figure which tailors call long-portly, said politely that he read Mason's dispatches regularly, and that the food in Vienna was far, far too rich for him. He was a dyspeptic, something rare in long-portlies. Mason began to talk to Mrs. Henderson, whose black hair was combed back from a widow's peak on her forehead. She used the locution "Is that right?" without end. It was Mason's business to observe everything, including even himself, and he put it into his mind that the widow's peak resembled the tip of a wet paintbrush.

Mrs. Henderson remarked to Mason Jarrett:

"We've just come from Paris. We're part of an official tour, but we managed to look around a little on our own. I suppose you people here are the equivalent of the Lost Generation at the Dôme. You know, that Left Bank café in Paris—full of poets, artists, Algerian rug vendors!"

"I've heard of it," Mason said dryly, reflecting that he had probably sat in the Dôme two hundred times.

"No, no, Mrs. Henderson," Dixon cut in attentively, "Vienna isn't Paris. We're very different here."

"How so?"

"We differ from the crowd at the Dôme in several ways, I should say. First, that's basically an art crowd, a literary crowd. Here, in contrast, we have music students, visitors being analyzed, and, of course, doctors. Incidentally, Mrs. Henderson, one of the reasons why

Vienna is such a Mecca for advanced medical students is that cadavers are more plentiful here than in any other city in the world. Yes, cadavers, bodies. Second, we're not expatriates. We live here because we're assigned here to do jobs. We work for a living. Third, there's a rather considerable difference in drinking habits. You know about Paris. But here the basic drinks are water, beer, and coffee. Of course you can get liquor in the bars, but it's rare in coffeehouses. If you asked for a Rob Roy here I doubt if Herr Julius would know what you were talking about."

"Is that right? You have a very systematic mind, Mr. Dixon." Indeed, Mason thought, he has.

"Now, as to our water," young John Dixon proceeded. "It's probably the best in the world. It comes straight from the mountains near Semmering, and it's ice-cold from the tap even on the warmest day. You've probably noticed one peculiar thing. With your coffee you always get two glasses of water, not just one. I think this derives from something in the days of the Turks, but, gee, I'm not quite sure. Of course you know that our *Kipfel*, the crescent-shaped breakfast roll, originated with the Turks when they were besieging Budapest. Vienna is full of odd quirks in the line of food. I suppose you know too that, when the Ober comes over to tote up your bill, it's up to you to tell him how many rolls or pieces of bread you've had."

Mrs. Henderson said again, "Really! Is that right?"

"Now, as to our beer. I don't think that any beer in the world excels it except perhaps Pilsner drunk actually in the cellars of the Brauhaus itself in Pilsen. Finally, consider our coffee. It's served here in at least fifty different forms." He paused. "Then I can think of several more differences. On the whole most of us here are more conventional than the boys in Paris, more bourgeois, though I don't think anybody would call us saints. Finally"—he laughed his somewhat self-satisfied laugh—"We have no Algerian rug vendors."

Erji Sandor dropped her novel and, to hide a giggle, with a knowing look took a big sip of her *Weisse Ohne*.

The junior headwaiter, Emil, tapped Mason on the shoulder. "Telephone, Herr Charrett." Mason walked to the booth at the rear of the bay. To operate the phone here you had to step on a wooden slat on the floor while taking the receiver off the hook.

Mason heard Strothness's taut voice, and the excitement that he had been carefully suppressing began to boil up.

"I'm at a dinner party," Strothness said. "Your call just came through. What's up?"

"I talked to my best Polish source, also a well-informed source from a country you know very, very well, and they had nothing, absolutely nothing. Then, by accident, I came across some people who belong to a big bank here—get it? I didn't talk to them myself, but . . ." Mason proceeded to tell him the gist of what had happened in the Koenigen.

"For God's sake, you don't expect me to take seriously something you hear from a night-club singer in a bar!" Strothness's voice was indignant.

"Well, I'm not so sure. It's interesting, and it could mean something."

"Are you drunk? Are you kidding me?"

"No. Mind you, that bank knows a lot."

"But you have no actual evidence?"

"None at all."

"Well!" Strothness appeared to be considering. "You certainly have news sources of a somewhat exotic nature, Mason!" His voice sank to a whisper. "Let me fill you in with what's happened here. I've kept right after the government, but they deny, deny, deny. Of course I could send a rumor story and you could follow. Just give voice to the rumors, with a lead like 'Well-informed sources say,' et cetera. But I'm so sure that the story is true that I'd rather risk waiting and break it open as a fact. Right after I talked to you this afternoon I called London. Oddly enough, Preble wasn't having tea with a member of the cabinet for a change, or splitting a magnum with an admiral of the fleet." Mason knew well the foibles of the *Star's* man in London, Rupert R. H. Preble, an old-timer, with his ginger-colored goatee and limitless social contacts.

Strothness went on: "Preble said that he'd get in touch with a member of the Labour Party Executive whom he knows well, and who has close connections with the trade unionists in the Rhineland. That could be a smart, productive angle. Of course I was astonished"—Strothness gave a somewhat pale laugh—"to learn that Rupert actually acknowledges the existence of the Labour Party. Well, anyway, he called back to say the Labour man was visiting his constituency up in Newcastle and couldn't be reached till tomorrow. Meantime, of course, I've been on to Hazelwood in Paris. He's working too." He took breath. "That's all. Good night, and let's talk early in the morning. I wouldn't risk using what you got from the night-club girls. There's a hell of a good piece about Kafka in the new *Querschnitt*. Read it." He rang off.

2

Presently Sandor arrived and sat down, creasing his belly against the coin of table; he had no need to order, everybody knew what he always had, and Herr Julius, bowing, brought him a *Nussbraun* at once. For the hundredth time Mason savored Sandor's essence—the warm welcoming grin, the hands rubbing together with a gesture of relish, the exuberance and spirit of generosity, the eyes twinkling behind the heavy spectacles, which, with the short beard high on his cheeks, made him look like an owl. Henderson, the Congressman, who had often read his dispatches, spoke up with respect, "Say, Dr. Sandor, give us a line on the political situation here. Back on the Hill, I want to be able to talk about what's going on in Central Europe. Lots of this, uh, stuff here seems kind of remote to us back home."

"I will explain you. In Owstria all is fantasy. The Heimwehr has taken arms from the Socialists and now Heimwehr men have entered into the government. The poor Owstrian government, it has all to contend with, and now, such luck, such terrible luck, it must have its own *allies*, the Heimwehr, into the government. It will be the doom on it, maybe." Sandor chuckled, but Mason detected an unusual note of strain in his voice. He must be seriously troubled about something; otherwise his English would not break down to this extent. "Have you alarmed yet about the Putsch plans? I know it for certain that the Heimwehr lads are arming in Bruck and Leoben, it will be like the crisis in Wiener Neustadt last year, at eleven A.M. on July seven, only this time they will come to Vienna and make their nonsense here!"

The Congressman said, "I'm afraid I didn't get all of that."

Immediately John Dixon came to Mr. Henderson's rescue, saying smoothly, "The whole situation can be put in two or three simple sentences. Austria is about equally balanced between the Christian Socials, or Clericals, who are strongest in the countryside, and the Social Democrats, Socialists, who hold Vienna. Each party has its own private army—the Heimwehr for the Clericals, the Schutzbund for the Socialists. They're at each other's throats, and the government, although supported by the Heimwehr now, has the responsibility for holding an even balance between the two, and keeping peace. Another point is that the Clerical army is illegal, the Socialist army legal. Clear? Next . . ."

Well said, Dixon, Mason thought. He wondered whether he could have given a summary so lucid, so concise. Meantime, what on earth was he going to do next on the Customs Union story?

Mrs. Henderson, who had been chatting with Dauphine Dixon, turned to Mason. "And all you journalists work right here in the café?"

"Well, if you can call it work," he replied. "Why not?"

"And how do you get your news?"

"We scrape for it."

"Is that right?"

There was a movement at the door, and Marcus Aurelius Thorne arrived with Tetzel. Mason greeted them. Thorne saw Mia and sat down next to her. His eyes became bright. Erji Sandor offered Mr. Henderson a chocolate, which he declined with thanks. "My dyspepsia. Say, do they have any sodium bicarbonate here?"

Again, there came a commotion at the door as Leo, the little Communist (sober tonight?), swung it open; Drew entered with the Countess. Paying no attention to her at all, he dumped her next to Erji and assumed his position at the head of the table, as leader of the group. The Countess looked pale; her lips were strips of heliotrope crepe. Erji was so fond of Jim Drew ("Zat is good boy, only so much in bondage!") that she tolerated the Countess; in fact, if pressed, she would have had to admit that she liked her, even though she was often shocked by her. She still blushed, lowering her eyes, at the memory of the time the Countess had said to her, in front of everybody, "You are curious why I stay with Drew?" Her voice became a coy hiss. "Because *fat men are so grateful!*"

John Dixon, for the benefit of the Hendersons, continued to talk about the Austrian political scene and gave forth the opinion that the only personage who really counted in the country was the ex-Chancellor, Monsignor Ignaz Seipel, with his Jesuit's intricate, sophisticated mind. Mason listened with half an ear. His own ideas about Austrian politics were simple enough. He had an instinctive aversion to the Clericals, most of whom were too rustic, too reactionary, for his taste. The Heimwehr was even worse—a *Lausebande*, boors, thugs. As to the Social Democrats, they were decent people for the most part, but fuzzy-minded and too theoretical and the taxes they imposed in Vienna were far too high.

Wondering now when Paula and Kitty would arrive, Mason sauntered to the washroom. Sandor intercepted him as he returned, steering him to an empty booth in the other bay. Sandor's face bore an anxious, appealing look.

"Mason, I am scarcely able to talk at the other table, but until now it is impossible to see you alone. I have something very big and I must tell you about. You must keep it all very, very quiet." He looked as if he were about to burst. "A story so big you cannot dream of, if confirmed. A story, I mean, I mean, it will tear all of Europe end from end!"

Mason became alert.

Sandor said, "About to be signed after secret negotiations is a Customs Union between Germany and Owstria!"

Mason thought fast. "I know."

Sandor looked at him in bewilderment. "You know? How?"

"I got a tip on the same story from Strothness in Berlin this afternoon, but he has no confirmation. I couldn't tell you about it, although I wanted to, because Harry specifically asked me not to, and it's his story, not mine. And now you're telling *me*! I feel like a dirty dog!"

Sandor waved his scruples aside. "Makes no matter."

Giving him a rapid sketch of what he knew, Mason asked, "Who's your source?"

"Hofrat Dr. Weissmuller." Weissmuller was chief of the foreign division of the Trade Ministerium.

"Well, that's about as high as you can get. I wouldn't give the matter of confirmation another thought." He realized that Strothness's beat was ruined, but this was not his fault and if they were going to be beaten by anybody he would prefer Sandor to anybody else. Now he had the confirmation he and Strothness had been searching for, but he did not see how he could possibly use it, since it belonged to Sandor. "Go ahead and file. Get over to the Journalistenzimmer and put it on the wire right now."

"No. Dr. Weissmuller swore me to secrecy, and said that I must get official confirmation elsewhere."

"Oh, nonsense, Laszlo, don't be so innocent. He swore you to secrecy to cover himself, but he wouldn't have told you about it unless he wanted you to break it. Besides, what Strothness has given me is confirmation enough for you."

"Perhaps. But I cannot break my word."

"We both have the story now, confirmed by each other," Mason summed up. "The question is who gets it into print first. I don't like to work against the interests of my own newspaper but clearly your tip from Weissmuller is better than anything we have, and so I think you should file first, right away." Mason smiled but his large brown eyes looked hurt.

What made this technical dilemma important was the fact that Mason's paper, the Chicago Star, was an afternoon paper; it was now far too late for any Star man in Europe to transmit anything in time for publication that day, in spite of the difference in time. But Sandor's paper, the Washington Sun, was a morning newspaper, and there was still plenty of time for Sandor to cable the story tonight for publication in America tomorrow morning, and this would give him a clean world beat. If Sandor waited, however, he would not be able to file until the next night, Vienna time, by which time, if Strothness and Mason filed tomorrow during the day, he would be beaten.

"What to do?" Sandor put his hands out helplessly. Mason knew that for Sandor to get this story first would be a big feather in his cap, bigger than for Strothness or himself.

"File now."

"No—I will avait tomorrow, when I am sure I can get correct official confirmations, as Weissmuller demands, probably from the Czechs."

"Strothness may have it all cleared up by noon tomorrow, and you'll be too late. You're being too damned noble, Laszlo."

"You are being noble too."

Indeed he wondered ruefully what he would say to Strothness when he called in the morning. If Strothness ever knew that he had confirmation tonight and had not told him he'd break his neck.

"I'll work it out," Mason said.

"Call Strothness again now and tell him that you have the confirmation from me."

"I can't steal your confirmation, Sandor!"

"Then what to do?"

"For Christ's sweet sake, let's have a drink." He summoned a waiter. His eyes were becoming bloodshot. Then, taking a line from Paula, he asked, "Story aside, what do you think of the implications of this thing?"

"If the French do not stop it, it will mean Germany rising again for the first time since the war in the basin of our so beautiful blue Danube, which is really a dirty yellow, opening the way even to Constantin-op-le and beyond. If it works, then will follow *Anschluss*, complete absorption by Germany of our poor, beloved, little Owstria!"

"That's what Paula says. Are you for it or against it?"

"It is not my business to be for or against. Owstria as today cannot live, there must, must, must be some solution to the Owstrian problem, or all Mitteleuropa will collapse. If we could be sure of the survival of a democratic Germany, then all would be well."

Mason said, "Germany democratic? Under Hindenburg and the Reichswehr? And with Hitler coming up? Sandor, I'm ashamed of you!"

They walked back to the *Stammtisch* together.

3

Thorne said cheerfully to Tetzel, "Got some business to talk about with your wife—do you mind?" Tetzel made a little bow of assent. Mia looked at Thorne carefully, and lit her second cigarette. Jovial, exuding energy, he led her to the other bay. He was bold and confidential. He told her what a wonderful city London was, boasted about his position there, told jokes about colleagues, and reminisced about his own first days in journalism, when he had been an aggressive cub reporter on a paper in Phoenix, Arizona. Then, "Say, be nice to me, Mia, and I think I can put through that raise for Karl."

Dumb with shock, almost paralyzed, she could scarcely believe her ears. She tried to gain time by looking away, but she could not keep from flushing. The blood rose in her creamy cheeks.

"What do you mean, Herr Thorne?"

"Call me Mark. You know perfectly well what I mean. I've felt it ever since we met this morning. I'm crazy about you. Tomorrow afternoon? Or evening?"

She said nothing. Maybe he was drunk.

"Or I could send Karl to Budapest for a day or two to look into that Bethlen story."

No, he was not drunk. His eyes were clear, his voice earnest, his hand steady.

"Why not?"

"I could not do such a thing—really—you insult me—you insult Karl—what you suggest is disgusting, impossible!"

"Not at all."

"You are abominable."

"Oh, I wouldn't say that."

She made as if to rise but he waved her back with a reassuring gesture, smiling. "Please," he whispered.

She calculated swiftly.

Abruptly she felt his hand on her knee, not heavy, but friendly, reassuring. His eyes were bold, but they twinkled.

"Send him to Budapest," Mia said. The weight of his hand relaxed, and he gave her a light pat on the knee.

"Okay. I'll give you a ring tomorrow."

4

James Newton Drew now led Mason into the next booth, saying, "Well, here we are, Jarrett, at last!" Patches shone under his bright, boyish eyes like smudges drawn by a finger dipped in soot. As he began to talk a messenger from Radio-Austria arrived with a telegram; Drew read it, then crumpled it in his fat, hairy fist and hurled it down.

He exclaimed, "I ask you!"

Some weeks ago, even more zealous for economy than usual, the I.P. had ordered him to drop the local news service of Telegrafen-Compagnie, the local agency which provided the best Balkan coverage. Tonight's telegram was a sharp rebuke from Drew's home office notifying him that he had been nine minutes late on a story early that day about a shake-up in the Rumanian cabinet. If he had not been compelled to drop Telegrafen-Compagnie he would automatically have had this item at the same time as his competitors, the A.P., U.P., and I.N.S., and would not have been scooped. "Jove, what they ask of a man!"

Controlling himself he said in a voice both peremptory and ingratiating, "Now, about this *Ehrengericht* business—let me explain from the beginning." He fished in his pocket and pulled out a clipping from the *Abend*. His eyes blinked, and for a second he looked embarrassed, but even in the midst of his indignation he gave out an air of attractive courtliness. What a mixed-up character, Mason thought. He remembered the day they first met; Drew had growled, "Well, hope you're not one of those Americans who have developed European habits and shake hands every time they meet!"

"Shoot," Mason said now.

The matter seemed to involve two Yugoslavs, a local journalist named Markovitch, hitherto thought to be respectable, and a Croat refugee and double traitor, by name Patchek. The latter, pretending to be an enemy of the Belgrade regime, had visited the Weissenhof table several times a month or so before, and then, returning to Yugoslavia, sold out to the Yugoslav police or perhaps had been a secret agent all along. Now the official Yugoslav newspapers were making a considerable play with the so-called revelations of this creature Patchek, and the *Abend*, published in Vienna, had that day printed a summary of his "disclosures." Patchek wrote among other things that he had steadily frequented the Café Weissenhof, which was infested with "low-type journalists vitriolically hostile to the Yugoslav regime," who condoned terrorism and encouraged seditious movements against King Alexander and the Belgrade government. The chief of these "heinous conspirators" were the man James N. Drew and his "foul henchman," David Bleschke, a well-known "agent-provocateur and crook." Moreover Drew was assisted in his "nefarious work" by his mistress, the woman Altmann, now known as the Gräfin von Zwehl, a former procuress, strumpet, and "hysterical old scorpion," who was further described as "an abortion in human form."

Mason put down the clipping. "Well, well!"

"Read the last sentence."

Mason read: "Among members of the Weissenhof circle are Dr. L. Sandor, Washington Sun; Dr. K. Tetzel, American news agency; and Mason Cherrett, Chicago Star." Mason pushed a spray of black hair off his forehead, compressing his lips.

Drew continued: "Maybe a few crooks and spies do hang around here at the Weissenhof, but they don't sit with us." With a gesture he indicated the booth holding Orlovsky, Zeissman and company. "And it is true that we welcome Croat and other anti-Serb refugees, because we believe in freedom of the press and it's part of our job to do so. But, clearly, this story goes too far, and it's our duty to ourselves to do something about it, quick!"

"How did the Abend happen to pick the story up?"

"That's just the point. I've been in touch with their editors, and they say that none other than Markovitch gave it to them, vouching for it. That's why the Ehrengericht will be concerned with him, since we can't reach Patchek."

Mason looked astonished. "Markovitch? Our Markovitch?"

"Yes. He peddled it to several papers, but nobody would touch it except the Abend."

"The plot thickens," Mason said.

"You're telling me."

Markovitch, the correspondent of a Belgrade newspaper, was also the secretary of the Vienna Union of Foreign Correspondents, to which Drew, Sandor, Mason, and most of the foreign journalists in town belonged. Mason had met him several times. A pleasant, self-effacing, old-young man he seemed to be, useful in ironing out red tape, arranging junkets, and lining up official interviews.

"Why should Markovitch stick his neck out by peddling stuff like this?" Mason tapped the clipping.

"Orders from his government, no doubt," Drew replied. "He's an official Yugoslav."

"Does Markovitch admit to having given the story to the *Abend*?"

"Not only that—it was he who translated the stuff from Serbo-Croat into German!"

Mason pondered. "Bleschke has a clear libel case here. So have you. Why don't you sue?"

"Sue? In *Vienna*? My dear sir!"

"Why not just sock Markovitch in the jaw?"

Drew, leaning back, looked aghast. "You haven't been here long enough, Jarrett. Sock a man in the *jaw*? Why, you could go to jail for that!"

"Have Bleschke sock him in the jaw."

"I don't control Bleschke, my dear sir."

"You might challenge Markovitch to a duel," Mason proffered.

Drew paid no attention to a remark so obviously facetious. "Now, here is the draft of a letter I'm sending to the president of the Union tomorrow, demanding the immediate summoning of an *Ehrengericht*, Court of Honor."

"Just what *is* an *Ehrengericht*?"

"What the word implies. Any member of a professional organization in Vienna can demand the calling of an *Ehrengericht* if a matter of personal honor is involved. A judge is appointed, witnesses are heard, and the case is investigated, all within the closed walls of the organization itself. A person found guilty of dishonorable conduct is expelled. That, in this town, can ruin a career. Well! I'll put it in the works, and I imagine charges will be brought against Markovitch next week."

"Where do I come in?" Mason asked.

Drew said, "Why, I thought I'd told you. I'm nominating you to be my representative, my second so to speak!"

Mason swallowed. He prepared to return to the *Stammtisch*, but Drew restrained him. "Something else on my mind, Jarrett." A pained, pointed expression came into his heavy gray face.

"Planning any trips soon, may I ask?"

"Not at the moment, no. I've just come back from Budapest and Bucharest, as you know."

Drew looked disappointed; his fist closed on an empty glass. "Well . . . well, that makes it difficult. I don't want to embarrass you, particularly since you're being so good as to be my representative on the *Ehrengericht*, but . . ."

Mason should have guessed, but did not know what was coming. "What's on your mind?"

"Well . . . I wondered. You pay me five dollars a day to cover for you when you're out of town, and I was wondering if . . . if you were thinking of taking a long trip in the near future, you could advance me what I'd get out of it—let me have it now—a loan, an advance, so to speak."

Mason froze slightly. "How much do you need?"

"Fifteen hundred Schillings—two hundred dollars." Mason was taken aback. For Drew, for Vienna, that was a lot of money. By unwritten law no newspaperman ever asked another what his salary was, but Mason was certain that Drew did not earn more than $150 per month. Sandor probably got $350 and Donald Bishopson $600.

Mason said carefully, "I don't like the idea of being an embarrassment to you later. Two hundred dollars means that I would have to be out of town forty days before you'd be clear, and it may be a long time before I'm out of town for forty days."

"Well . . ."

"I'd just lend you the money, no nonsense about calling it an advance, but it's near the end of the month and we're pretty short."

Drew's pride rose. "I wouldn't take it except as a strictly business proposition."

"In that case, I think I'll have to ask permission from Hilliard in Chicago."

"Sure. Well, I thought I'd ask. No harm in asking, is there? Maybe you could query Chicago, and let me know."

"How soon do you have to have the money?" Mason asked.

"Monday noon."

Mason made an inward whistle. "All right. I'll let you know."

Drew rose with the commanding words, "Time to get on the news," and Mason wondered what he would think if he knew about the story he and Sandor were sitting on. As they reached the *Stammtisch*, the eleven P.M. news bulletins arrived. Sandor ripped through the flimsy envelopes and exclaimed "Good! Good!" and "What? I mean!" as he scrutinized each paragraph rapidly. "Ha! Dr.

Benes will speak now again in the twenty-third! Time for Horthy to watch out!"

Sandor explained the background of each item. Erji looked proudly, lovingly, at her husband, but with downcast eyes—as if to indicate modesty before his huge and overflowing fund of erudition.

"Hallo, hallo—I mean!" Sandor called out. "What have we here? There has been a reorganization in the Ah-Oh-Gay. Old Neuwaldegg is out as General Director. He pronounced "General" with a hard G. "It says only because of routine. Neuwaldegg has seventy years, it is the correct retirement age. But I wonder. . . . Inter-est-ing! The successor of Neuwaldegg is Herr Generaldirektor Dostal. Let me think over. But, of course, do I remember aright, Dostal, Dostal . . . it was Dostal exoctly last year who had cawntact in the secret Heimwehr funds!"

"Is the A.O.G. a very important bank, say like our Continental and Commercial?" asked Mrs. Henderson.

"An important bank? Eggs-cuse me! It is the bank of banks. It is the colossus all with ears, it can see and smell, it has tentacles everywhere, it owns all of Owstria!"

Mason thought, Well! So my good friend Hilda was right about a reorganization there!

Sandor was saying, with strong emphasis, "A reorganization of the Ah-Oh-Gay can mean much. The end of this story is not yet!"

5

At just this moment, enraptured, their ears still reverberating with the thick beat of an impeccably performed *Rosenkavalier*, Paula Jarrett and Kitty Jameson made their way out of the Opera. Kitty had never been in Vienna before, and wondered if they could spare a moment to have a drink at Sacher's, which she had heard about all her life but never seen. They entered the hotel with its intricate series of small salons—crimson-brocaded walls, sparkling candelabra, gilt molding rising from marble pediments, lamps with fluted parchment shades—and found their way to the bar.

They ordered stingers, a drink which had lately become fashionable in Vienna. The Viennese did not pinch, but they certainly knew how to stare. Paula and Kitty surveyed the room as guests in the room surveyed them back, eyes lifted. *Herrgott!* There was absolutely nothing in the world to compare with young American women of this particular genre—so glossy, bright, with such ease and pride of posture, always with such unbelievable ankles and the wonderful teeth; girls born of good families but whose parents had probably made stringent sacrifices to send them to the best schools, who had had none but the healthiest of foods since childhood, so that their bones grew straight and true; sophisticated, but still fresh; chic, but not rich; no jewels. Moreover the Viennese connoisseur, and several of these lolled in Sacher's that night, would not fail to note the embracing quality that gave added point to all the rest; you could tell it at a glance, or by the simplest inflection of their voices—they had what was known as "class": they were ladies.

Paula and Kitty picked up their talk. "So there's nothing new about me, really," Kitty said. "He can't leave his wife. Or won't. I'm sick of it, but I always go back to him."

Kitty's lover had been one of their teachers; he was twenty-four years older than Kitty and had fallen madly in love with her when she was a graduate student and had never let her alone since.

She said glumly, brooding, "It's been going on for five years now. As a matter of fact it was he who got me this job in Athens. Maybe he really has decided to get rid of me, or maybe—you can't tell, he's a complex devil and even has a few good points—he wants to make it easier for me to leave him. But every time I do walk out he goes crazy. Matter of fact, after a whole tornado of anguished farewells, he cabled me in Paris day before yesterday to say that he might be able to meet me in Athens in the fall."

"What's his wife's hold on him?"

"Just marriage!"

They both laughed.

"I can understand why he doesn't give you up, you're such a delicious duck," said Paula, "but I really think you ought to break it off for good and leave him. If he won't marry you, he's just using you."

"It isn't quite as simple as that. He says he can't bear to live without me, but that we could never build up a good life together on the ruin of somebody else's—somebody innocent—namely that nice boring woman his wife."

"Oh, bosh. That's his excuse, not the reason."

"Possibly."

"Of course you're still mad about him."

"Well, he's marked me. He told me once, with that maddening complacent smile, 'Catch a girl when she's really young, then she'll never get over you.'"

Kitty was blonde, tall, almost as tall as Paula, and had light greenish eyes; behind rakish, heavily rimmed glasses her lashes stuck out like stiff little spikes in a crown. Her throat, where blue veins were faintly, provocatively visible just under the surface of the skin, was long and had a slight bulge. Her small mouth, Mason once said fancifully, looked like the ace of hearts. Any man, by the merest touch of her cheek, would know that she would be marvelous in bed. Altogether, she was not at all the type that one would ever dream was an archeologist.

The sallow, listless-looking pianist, who had a bald head the shape of a pear, observed them closely, and, saluting their nationality, plunged into the newest American songs to reach Vienna—"Liza" and "A Little Kiss Each Morning, A Little Kiss Each Night." Paula saw, without jealousy, that it was Kitty to whom he was playing, not herself. It never fails, she thought. There was honey on Kitty; men sipped and stuck.

"What about you, Paula?"

"No babies," Paula said. "Otherwise, bliss."

"Hmmm."

"We've just about gone through the book. I've been to a dozen doctors, they all say the same thing—there's no real reason for me to be sterile, none at all. Nothing's discernibly wrong. I'm regular as a clock, I do that temperature thing, count days like minutes, try to catch that darned egg dropping, but it never seems to work."

"Some day it will just happen-a."

"But I'm almost thirty, and I've practically given up hope. The last doctor I saw said that something in my system, that was the actual word he used, system, killed the, uh, juice. Can you imagine that—as if I were some damned emasculator!"

"Does Mason want children?"

"Oh, yes. He's been through tests too—so humiliating for him, but he never complained at all. He'd be a lovely father."

"Well," said Kitty, "I get pregnant if a man talks to me on the telephone. I suppose the trouble with you is that you're such an old puritan."

"Me?"

The pianist, watching them out of the edge of his eye, sprinkled his fingers on the keys to produce "Star Dust." Now the senior Ober was watching them with relish too, and the Piccolo kept hovering much closer to their table than was necessary. The Ober hissed to the Piccolo, "*Gehen Sie an!*"

"The way you were brought up, and all that guff," Kitty resumed. "Mother's talk."

"Well," said Paula cautiously, "I know that being taught to be strait-laced, if it goes far enough, can make a girl frigid, but it can't make them *sterile*, surely."

"Everything is sort of tied up together."

"You don't say, Frau Doktor."

"Mason is so worthy," Kitty said after a pause. "He's even wholesome."

"He is not!" Paula responded to this insult with spirit. "He's good, he's considerate, he has a heavenly disposition except sometimes, but at bottom," she concluded fiercely, "he's not worthy at all, he's a monster, *frightful!*" Kitty looked up at her. "Deep down, he never thinks about anything except himself."

A Viennese bursting with musical patriotism went up to the pear-headed piano player and demanded "*Zwei Herzen im Dreivierteltakt.*"

"What exactly do you mean?" Kitty asked after a moment.

"Just what I say. He's not in the least subjective or analytical, he's never introspective, he's never given a thought in his entire life to the why of things, but basically nothing at all interests him except his work and his career—himself."

"Well, isn't that a characteristic, more or less, of all healthy people?"

"Perhaps, but it's hard on a wife. Sometimes I look at him and he simply isn't *there*—no contact."

Kitty smiled. "I don't think you're too badly off. Doesn't he come back to earth quickly when you want him to?"

"Yes, but if you really love, you should think of the other person too every once in a while."

"I could gather from that remark a sense that you're feeling a bit neglected."

"Vielleicht."

"Have you ever been unfaithful, Paula?"

"Goodness, no."

"Has he?"

"He swears he hasn't, and I believe him. But he certainly has a wandering eye."

Kitty laughed. "Just eyes don't matter. As long as the impulse stays above the neck, it's all right."

6

A moment later Kitty, for some cryptic reason, as if the impending event might have significance, nudged Paula, and she saw a tall man with a straight soldierly bearing and a russet-colored hussar's mustache come through the door. The thought immediately came to her that he resembled the mythical type of officer who was supposed to have sat naked, except for a busby, in the private rooms at Sacher's in the old days, drinking, gambling and scattering rose leaves at pretty girls and otherwise misbehaving in a scandalous, dated manner. He seemed to be gracious, self-satisfied, and effete. The Herr Ober bowed like a blade pulled out of a knife, and led him to a table.

The tall man sat for a moment alone; he tap-tapped at a cigarette, glancing about with a bored expression. He saw Kitty and Paula, and his chin rose, not superciliously, but in a manner that seemed to say, in spite of its easy casualness, "I will deal with you in good time!" He continued to survey both girls appraisingly; he caught Paula's eye, although she did not intend this, smiled, and then did something surprising—he yawned. Paula, slightly taken aback, resumed talk with Kitty, and the man, turning away now, stifled with his hand another long, comfortable yawn. Then he seemed to fall sound asleep. The girls stared covertly at him, then, eyebrows raised, at each other. They were not used to being yawned at.

A moment or two later the man was standing by their table, well mannered, bowing.

"I have not even the excuse that you look lonely. You look nothing of the kind. You are absorbed in one another, as only young American women can be. I beg you to forgive my slight forwardness. May I not ask you to join me for a drink?"

Paula smiled brightly. "Thanks, I'm sorry, but we're just going." She called the waiter. "*Rechnung, bitte.*" She explained to the man, "We're late for something."

"A rendezvous, no doubt?"

"Not quite," Paula said. The waiter brought their bill.

"It is outrageous that two young women so attractive should be permitted to drink alone."

"No dice, pal," said Kitty. "Can't be helped."

The man sat down. Her slang was an invitation.

"One moment only, I implore you. You are new to Vienna? I go often to places around the town, but I have not seen you before."

"Well, as a matter of fact," Paula said pleasantly, "I live here, but my friend is just passing through."

"You would not sacrifice"—he underscored the word—"sacrifice five minutes of your time, just five minutes?"

How European, Paula thought—the use of such a silly, overstating word as "sacrifice." There was, however, something undeniably winning about this person. He turned now to Kitty, and Paula studied him. There was a certain vacuousness in his face, as if he might at any moment give way to childishness; but also a luster; also a puzzling element she had never noticed in anybody before, of immunity, of being exempt, removed from ordinary responsibilities and consequences.

"Let me at least say that, if you do feel that you must go now, I shall not forget either of you."

Kitty asked, "Why?"

"Because," the man proceeded calmly, "you, *gnädige Frau,*" addressing Paula, "remind me of a snow leopard." He smiled. "And you, *gnädigstes Fräulein,*" turning to Kitty, "of a cheetah out in the bush."

Both were startled.

Paula asked, "Are you a big-game hunter, by any chance?"

A dramatic change came over the tall man's face; coloring, it appeared to swell out; the russet mustaches twitched, and a wary, bitter light came into his eyes, sunk deep in lined pockets; but then he began to laugh; throwing his head back he laughed, laughed uproariously. Pulling a handkerchief out of his sleeve he wiped his eyes.

They stared.

"Not very long ago, perhaps a decade ago, when both of you were still children, I was employed . . . employed . . . in a novel—to me—occupation. This was in the worst period of our inflation. The cinema houses, importing a film, could afford to buy only one print even for a chain of theaters. I, I, I rode on a bicycle from one cinema to another, several in number, from one to the other, pedaling with mad fury across the town, breathless, transporting Reel One from Theater One to Theater Two and then on to Theater Three, then returning to Theater One for Reel Two and repeating the entire process until the night was done!"

They were too amazed to say anything.

The man's thoughts were precise: Both these young women are bien élevée—patrician. The one with that hair is virtuous, the other not.

He went on aloud, "The evening is still young . . . at its tenderest. I will not take advantage of your courtesy, my five minutes are up, but might I not be your host elsewhere for half an hour? We will proceed to a small night club known as the Koenigen. Singing there at about this time is an extraordinary young woman, who wears a monocle. She has a most remarkable voice and will go far."

They shook their heads. "Sorry, but we really have to go," Paula said.

Yes, the one who spoke was virtuous, hence boring. The invariable curse of virtuous women was that they were boring. But this particular young woman, the man reconsidered, might turn out not to be boring.

He rose. "I won't burden you with further expression of my disappointment. But in case we ever meet again I would like to assure you that you have nothing to fear from me." Now he would punish them a little, and his look became one of amused impudence. "Why not? Because all I care about, all I seek, is money, and it is clearly apparent that neither of you have any."

At the door he sweepingly kissed their hands, gave Paula his card, which she dropped into her bag without looking at it, and asked for their names. Kitty said, "My name is Jameson, but I'm going to be away in Athens for the next six months, so it won't do you any good. Her name is Paula Jarrett, and you can find her two or three nights a week at the Café Weissenhof."

Out in the street, wet with the soft rain, gusty with wind, Paula pressed the butt of her palm to her forehead, shaking her head, laughing. "Did you ever? The vanity of the human male! Well! Come on, cheetah."

Kitty said, while they waited for a taxi, "Something really peculiar happened to me on the Orient last night. I darned near got raped, I think. Man said he worked for a newspaper, I wonder if you could conceivably know him. He must have been in the Calais car, coming from London. I came from Paris, as you know, and I didn't see him until the two sections of the train hooked up, somewhere in Switzerland. I slept all afternoon and went into the Wagon-Restaurant for dinner, late. The regular service was over, but they made me some scrambled eggs. And here was this type holding a kind of court in the empty dining car, talking to the waiters as if they were all his devoted retainers who would be bound to hang on his every word. And, as a matter of fact, they did. I couldn't help listening. Actually what he said was quite interesting, about politics all over Europe, although it was obvious that he was a bit of a show-off. How lonely can a person get! Talking to a lot of waiters! Then he asked if he could sit down with me for a moment, and he talked some more, not badly. I went to bed, and half an hour later, there came a very light, scratchy knock on my compartment door. I was stark naked except for my slip and had taken my glasses off, couldn't see a thing. I thought that we had reached the Austrian frontier, and that the conductor was asking for passports or something. Of course I should have known better, but I didn't think. The conductor would have knocked harder, with that key he always has. Anyway I opened the door about an inch, and there was my

friend from the dining car! He got a little rough, I had to slam
the door right in his face, but he had grabbed the edge of my slip
or the slip got stuck in the door, I don't know which, and to get
it, I had to open the door again, and now I really was stark naked.
Well, I got my slip back, and slammed the door once more. That was
all—except that he *came back!*"

"What did you do then?"

"Told him through the door not to be a silly ass and to go to
bed."

"Did he?"

Kitty gave her a look, and Paula laughed.

7

Paula and Kitty, their hair glistening where the moist wind had
curled and polished it, sailed into the café. Mason jumped up to
greet them, kissing them both, and with his arm close around
Paula's waist led them to the *Stammtisch.* Erji Sandor murmured a
word to the Countess to the effect that it was always pleasant to see
husbands behave with such nice demonstrativeness to their wives in
public. But Mason felt tense, twisted, uneasy. How was he going to
handle this unexpected crazy situation with Sandor? What on earth
would he tell Strothness in the morning? Paula would have to
straighten him out, tell him what to do.

Paula introduced Kitty to the group, "Dr. Jameson . . . Dr. Jameson . . ." and the Hendersons were presented. At that moment, Mark
Thorne and Mia Tetzel walked in from the other bay. On Mia's
face was an expression of elevation, distress, and sacrifice: she might
have been Iphigenia. Then Paula became conscious of strong under-
currents at the table. How could it be possible? Was she hearing
right? Thorne was saying to Kitty in an undertone, "Why . . . hello!
We meet again!" She stared hard at Kitty; the spiked crown of lashes
hid her eyes; Thorne must have been the man on the train last
night!

Erji, with her sinuous intelligence, observed Mason. Not only did
she like him enormously: she really understood him, perhaps better
in some ways than Paula did, and she could detect that something

was bothering him painfully, harassing him. She thought: Mason has power—ambition too. My poor Laszlo—born without a trace of either!

Thorne asked Paula what she would like to drink. "Double stinger," she replied, and Thorne appraised her with mild surprise. She had met him once or twice before. There could be no doubt that he had a strong physical magnetism, and she felt curious about him now if only because of Kitty. He talked well, and his manner was bold and alert. He gave her a sensual admiring look, and moved closer. When she withdrew slightly his expression became slightly mocking, even insolent, and he deliberately kept himself close, an inch away. He did not touch her, but she could feel his warmth. Warmth leaped over the slight gap between them all the way from shoulder to knee. She flushed, and his look became one of amused, victorious satisfaction. It said, "I know you, and you know me and what I'm after. I've discovered that you have a vulnerability and this pleases, annoys, and frightens you!"

Furious with herself, Paula flushed again.

John Dixon asked what everybody would like to eat. "Würstels— thank you, Chawn," replied Sandor. The Weissenhof was renowned for its Würstels—delicate little pink sausages with crinkled skins, served with *Mohnsemmel,* poppyseed rolls, crisp out of the oven.

Mason saw Karl Tetzel approach Paula with his suave, graceful, adhesive Central European manner, and heard him ask her if she would like a game of chess. A few weeks ago he had started giving her chess lessons. She did not particularly want to play at this moment, but she liked Tetzel and was sorry for him. "Of course—delighted." Tetzel, his hand gently under her elbow, steered her by the forearm into the other bay. What a difference between his touch and Thorne's! What was Thorne *really* like, Paula asked herself. Did he always convey this note of challenge? Had Kitty ("She's incorrigible") told the whole truth about the encounter on the train? *Could* she have let him in the second time, if indeed the man had been Thorne?

Now Thorne addressed Kitty with a pleasant, commanding gesture. His voice combined earnestness and vivacity, and Mason, talking to Mia, could not help overhearing a word or two. They seemed to be mysteriously carrying on from a previous conversation and Kitty appeared to be talking about, of all people, her father. "So Samuel Y. Jameson, the creator of innumerable giant architectural master-pieces, went off on a day's notice to Brazil, leaving my mother rather dramatically in the lurch. Then he fell in love with that . . ." She grimaced. "They were married a couple of years later. . . ."

"Happily?"

"Oh, I guess so."

"Well, it sometimes takes two marriages to make a marriage."

"My score, zero."

"Marriage is an extremely serious matter," Thorne said.

"So is living alone."

Across the big table, Mia became as pale as a person stricken with illness: she appeared to be totally out of focus, so constrained and cloudy that she did not know what Mason, trying to be agreeable, was talking about. He could not reach her. "What . . . when? . . . Oh!" she muttered.

Thorne, after a quick, friendly, conspiratorial smile to Mia, as if to reassure her, turned to Mason. "Well, how's the old soldier?" he addressed him.

Mason detested being called an old soldier. He replied briefly, "Oh, all right—depends on the time of day."

"Paula looks marvelous. You must keep her in good shape."

Did he?

"I wish I knew her better," Thorne went on. "I have a feeling she must be an extremely *complete* young woman."

Complete is the one thing she isn't, Mason thought.

"She obviously has looks, brains, character. . . ." He continued to praise her fulsomely, and Mason became embarrassed. He re-membered Thorne's wife in London—wore her hair in a bang; played the flute; dressed in batik.

Sandor's voice, the voice of a man absolutely without guile, who had never harbored an atom of ill will toward anybody in his life, could be heard purring toward Mrs. Henderson, "You have heard the new joke about our charming, corrupt Vienna? It is that nothing can be expected of a city where the day has to begin with getting up in the morning!"

"Is that right?"

"I want to repeat this so I'm sure I've got it straight," said the

Congressman to Mason, "for my friends back on the Hill. The crux of your situation here is that you have two private armies, the Socialist, what's it called, Schutzbund, which seeks to defend its position in Vienna, and the reactionary, clerical Heimwehr, based in the countryside and allied to the government, trying to seize power."

"That's about it," Mason agreed.

"Now tell me about the other countries you deal with—give me a sentence, say, on each."

This was the sort of thing at which Mason excelled. "Hungary—a pool of wheat, one third of the total arable land owned by a handful of feudal aristocrats. Who—or what?—runs Hungary? Members of an antilegitimist secret society, the Double Cross. Chief issues? Habsburg restoration and revision of the frontiers."

The Congressman listened attentively.

"Poland? It has a crucifixion complex—always rising from the dead. Run by a clique of colonels, Pilsudski's men. Its viability doesn't depend on itself, but on Germany and Russia. Rumania? A royal circus in Bucharest on top of a huge half-starved peasantry. The government is being cut into by a reactionary gang called the Iron Guard. Fantastically corrupt—no party in power in Rumania has ever lost an election. Yugoslavia? Deep subnational fissures. Flirting with Germany a bit. The dictatorship isn't doing too badly, but remember, no Serbian head of state ever died a natural death. Bulgaria? Always picks the wrong side in wars. Albania? A lump of rock. The king was Yugoslavia's man, then sold out to Italy. Greece?" Mason paused; he put his hands forward, and his light clear laugh rang out. "When you shake hands with a Greek, count your fingers!"

He proceeded to tick off Czechoslovakia and Turkey.

Knows his stuff, Henderson said to himself, thus giving him the highest American accolade.

Paula returned with Tetzel. She murmured to Mason, "Of course he beat me, darling, even giving me a knight and a pawn, but he used a dirty new opening I had never played before." Mia, who now appeared to be squirming with restlessness, rose from the booth to take Karl home, and Thorne walked them cordially to the door, saying good night with his frank, hearty voice. Erji said to nobody in particular, yawning, "What for happiness! Tonight I sleep ze sleep of sleeps!"

Herr Julius, assisted by his underlings, arrived now with plate on plate of Würstels. "Ach, the true, the original, the incomparable Vienna Würstels!" Sandor muttered hungrily. He, Drew, and the others began to eat. The Countess, with her eyes flashing, but with a peculiar false demureness, looked about, and saw the Congressman, leaning back, push his plate away with a resigned, dyspeptic sigh; sausages, at this or any hour, were not for him. Suddenly came a swift, almost invisible movement; the Countess, faster than the eye could follow, plucked at her mouth and, with a gesture in which arrogance, malice, and a kind of hideous delight in her own perversity were compounded, deposited her false teeth, the result of the encounter with Graf Rudi, on the Congressman's plate. Demoniacally proud of the sensation she made, leering, prim too, even coy, she murmured to Mr. Henderson, "To help you eat!"

Erji was the first to grasp fully what had happened. She was agonized. This was an insult to all the decencies, an affront to human nature at large. She twisted her head back sharply, blindly, to shake off angry, humiliated tears, and cried out, "O weh, O weh!"

On the Countess' face descended a mask unutterably blank. Drew barked gruffly, apologetically, to the rest of the table, "She's off her nut!" The little tipsy White Russian, Orlovsky, came up swift as a flash to inspect the teeth, and John Dixon, ashamed of himself for the thought, wondered if he could ever work a scene like this into a play.

8

By running for it, Karl and Mia Tetzel caught the last bus to Hietzing.

"Now I will tell you what happened," Mia said when they reached home. She gave him the gist of the story.

"Thorne will telephone you quite early," Mia said, "and you will go to Budapest. Expenses will be paid, and it will be your first out-of-town assignment in several years. He will telephone me later and I presume I will meet him at the Majestic, and he may ask me to dinner afterward if he is sure he will not be seen. I am unhappy, but willing to do it for you."

"No, you will not do it!" Karl exclaimed. His eyes had become hard brown stones.

"It is a small and altogether temporary thing to do. He is a beast, but it will matter nothing provided he can be trusted to make the raise." She was shivering. "The raise is everything."

"Mia, I forbid you. It is impossible and out of the question!" he said fiercely. "This is an indignity—unspeakable!"

Her voice was taut. "Do not think I am happy about it."

"You do not love me, or you could not even conceive of such a thing."

"It is because I do love you that I do it."

"Thorne is handsome. He has made an offer, and you are attracted to him."

"No," she lied.

But she said to herself, How awful. This is the most awful thing. Wearily they went to bed.

9

At the Weissenhof, the waiters yawned, and the Piccolo yanked iron shutters down over the windows, as the cry of "I pay, please!" came from various tables. The Weissenhof was about to go to sleep. The Hendersons, whom no one in the circle would ever see again, said their farewells, and the Dixons led them off to their hotel. Nobody wanted to discuss the scene the Countess had made, or the way Drew had hustled her out of the café, his hand over her mouth. Thorne and Kitty, Sandor and Erji, Mason and Paula, walked out to the street, feeling the satisfaction that comes to a cohesive, intimate group when outsiders are at last cast off. The rain had stopped, and the *Föhn* was over. Thorne asked everybody to join him in a pubcrawl; Kitty said it was too late. "Just one drink at the Koenigen up the street," Thorne suggested. "No," Mason replied, somewhat sharply. "It's quite an attractive place," said Thorne. "I'd like to see it," Paula said. "Let's not," Mason repeated. Thorne then prepared to go off with the Sandors. Erji would stay up all night any night in the week. "Auf Wiedersehen," everybody said. Thorne would, Mason knew, continue to wander from bar to bar even if the Sandors left him, and, no matter what time he turned in, would be up early—such was his temperament as well as constitution—bold of eye, firm of cheek, and aggressively friendly with room service.

Mason said to Kitty, "I've scarcely had a chance to say a word to you. You look lovely." They were walking toward her hotel.

"Thank you. Why didn't you want to go to the Koenigen?" Kitty asked. "I thought you loved places like that."

Mason had never told Paula about Hilda, the girl with the monocle, or Trudi, the hat-check girl.

"It's no place to take a wife."

"Pooh!" said Paula.

"I'm not a wife," Kitty said.

Paula yearned to ask Kitty about Thorne, but she hadn't had a moment alone with her. "Kitty, was the man on the train Thorne?"

"Seems to me he was."

"What man? What train?" asked Mason.

"May I tell Mason about your adventure on the train?" Paula asked.

"Sure. Keep it clean, though."

They walked along.

"Wasn't it something called the Koenigen that the man in the bar wanted to take us to?" Paula asked.

"Yes," replied Kitty.

"The what in the what?" asked Mason. "I seem to be left out of everything tonight."

"I haven't had a chance to tell you," Paula said. "We were picked up in Sacher's by a rather odd type—attractive, though. Weren't we, cheetah?"

"Yes, snow leopard."

"What is all this?" Mason asked, cupping an ear.

"Oh!" Paula stood rooted for a second. "I forgot. He gave me his card." She fished in her bag under the yellowish glare of a streetlight. "Well, for goodness sake! He's an archduke!"

"No!" exclaimed Kitty. "Gracious!"

They huddled together, peering at the card, innocent, impressed, gawking. Archdukes were, technically speaking, forbidden to use their titles in Austria, but several continued to do so and, as a general rule, were still treated by most Viennese as royalty, which indeed they were. Mason passed his finger over the heavy engraving on the card. Archdukes did not come a dime a dozen by any means. This one had exceptional genealogical distinction.

"Imagine it—he was pretty glossy and superior, but I never guessed that he'd be anything as exalted as this!" Paula said. "Kitty could have done anything she liked with him."

"Why not you?" Mason smiled.

"Oh, he'd never want to see me again." Paula retreated into her special variety of self-deprecation.

"I remember a mailer I wrote a couple of months ago," Mason said. "Do you know, those Habsburgs ruled here for sixteen solid generations. Their holdings included parts of fourteen countries, and the Archduke Franz Ferdinand, whose assassination caused the war, had more than two thousand royal ancestors."

"What's this one's name?" Kitty looked at the card again, staring close.

"Well, he seems to have a lot of names—Renatus, Ferdinand, Joseph, Franz, Maximilian, Hugo, Felix, Wilhelm. I haven't the faintest idea which one he goes by."

They reached Kitty's hotel, and Paula made arrangements to meet her for lunch before seeing her off the next day; Mason promised to join them if he finished work in time.

What was Kitty really like, Mason wondered. She was bright, a good sport, a darling. Her flipness was no more than a kind of defense, and probably concealed a good deal. But could she be hollow, shallow, underneath? Did she lack the capacity to give genuine abiding love, as Paula could?

It was all tied up with that damned professor. He had, so to speak, fixed her, stamped her. But why couldn't she get rid of him? Was it a matter of inertia, lack of confidence, broken will, or what? Or was she merely, in a word, weak? Yes! But in that case why were she and Paula so extraordinarily close? Paula didn't like weak people as a rule. Well, they complemented each other in a paradoxical sort of way. Kitty appeared to be superficial, but she had a Ph.D. and had done brilliant academic work; Paula lived only for pleasure, or so she averred, she did no work at all, except to help him, had no job of her own, but she was a much more serious character.

Arriving home Mason and Paula had a Gösser. The sharing of an immediately preceding experience was almost the pleasantest part of any evening. Had *he* caught that flash when So-and-so said Such-and-such, had *she* noted the implications of that apparently casual grimace by X toward Y? Eagerly they filled each other in. She offered her back, which meant "Unbutton me"; as he fiddled with her dress she said, "Don't *pull!* Don't hurt the *cloth!*" and they rocked together in a light embrace. Sitting down to yank off his shoes while she placed herself before the dressing table he told her the hard news of the evening—Sandor's confirmation of the Customs Union story and Drew's business with the *Ehrengericht* and request for money.

Paula pondered. "Don't wire Chicago. Just possibly Hilliard might say no. Give Drew the money, and we'll manage somehow."

"I'd have to account for cashing a draft that big," Mason said.

"It's almost the first of the month. Take it out of our salary then."

"You're a darling girl. Do you suppose anybody else has a wife so nice? Now: what's Kitty up to?"

Paula told him the story of the episode on the train.

"You don't suppose she really could have *slept* with Thorne?" she asked in an outraged voice.

"Why not?" Mason said, preserving his masculine equanimity. "A girl who's bereft is terrifically vulnerable. You know how it is, there comes a time when a woman's judgment can go berserk. She's so delighted to get a positive reaction that she'll do anything, anything at all, and believe anything of anybody."

"I don't think I would," Paula mused. "Darling, when you pick up girls in bars, if you do, you don't do anything with them, do you?"

"Not a thing."

"Cross your heart and hope to die."

"I'll cross my heart, but I won't hope to die. What would you do if I *did* do anything with girls?"

Her voice was cheerful. "Slit your throat, and then take poison."

She disappeared into the bathroom and returned scowling, "I do think you might ask me if *I've* ever misbehaved."

"I know you haven't."

"You're far too sure of me." She sounded hurt. "Or maybe you don't care. If you came into a room and found me in bed with twenty blackamoors, all you'd say would be 'Good evening,' or 'I beg your pardon.' "

"Not tonight," Mason said.

"I must say you're very nice to me. Is it because you really do love me, or just want me to be happy?"

"Both."

A smile lit her face, and again two perfect eggs, or plums, made ovals under her cheeks.

He lay on his side in the warm darkness, brisk, bouyant, his knees partly bent, cupping her body with his. Her mood seemed to be dreamy and remote and he sensed that she was not quite ready, and he waited, content, perfectly sure of himself, as he had not been since that strange night after the quarrel about the *Star*. She turned, grasping him. His chin cut a groove into her shoulder softly, and he lowered his head so that he could kiss her delicate erect breasts. Dreamily, drowsily, she made a ladder of small kisses along his cheek. Soon she became utterly open for him, then locked herself closed. "There—ah!" "Oh, you're lovely, lovely." They became a single vibrant body and tonight she was not superior or removed and the divine, delicious bubble in her swiftly burst.

Later there came a postmortem about Jim Drew and the Countess.

"Why doesn't he simply leave her? How can he stand it?" Paula asked.

"She's doomed without him, and he's both stuck with her and sorry for her. That's her main hold on him, I imagine. Her weakness is her strength, which, as a matter of fact, is a characteristic of a lot of people of your—as they say—sex."

"There may be something else. He's a snob."

"What? You're being fanciful."

"No, he's a southern boy, poor white trash, and it flatters him to be living with a Countess. To show chivalry to her, no matter how horrible she is, gives a lift to his own ego."

He took up her question in reverse. "But why doesn't she leave *him?*"

"He's all she has, and as you've just said, she'd starve without him. But think of something else as well. She holds on to him like grim death because doing so proves her superiority. To accept him, with all his heavy vanity and naïveté, you know, all his defects, proves her capacity for sacrifice and that she's a great woman."

They fell asleep holding hands.

At about four in the morning the sharp, stinging ring of the telephone awoke Mason. Strothness was on the wire, and sleepily he tried to grasp his words.

"We're all set, Mason. I have full, authentic confirmation now, and I'll file tomorrow. You file too, cover the Vienna angle. We'll clean it up."

Mason was wide awake. "What happened?"

"Well, perhaps I forgot to tell you, but at about the time I telephoned London I shot off a quick wire to Hilliard in Chicago, tipping him off as to what might be coming. Apparently Hilliard, right on the ball, telegraphed that new fellow of ours in Moscow, Throckmorton, and he certainly must be on the ball too. It never occurred to me to try to get in touch with Moscow myself, although the Russians are bound to hate the idea of a Customs Union just as much as we are. Throckmorton must have good connections. He alerted the Soviet Foreign Office and got through on the telephone to a Czech Member of Parliament in Prague, a Commie of course, who in turn got in touch with a German official here, very high up—sorry I can't give you his name. And he telephoned me half an hour ago to say that the story is absolutely true and that Berlin and Vienna planned to announce it sometime next month. Well, we'll beat 'em to it, and maybe upset their little applecart!"

Paula uncoiled herself and murmured sleepily, "Who's calling? What's happened?"

Mason said to Strothness, "Sandor has the story too. In fact I got confirmation from him late tonight, but I didn't call you because"— he evaded—"I knew I'd be talking to you in the morning."

"The more the merrier, provided we get in first. Sandor can't file till tomorrow night."

Mason hung up, and said to himself, Berlin, the Soviet Foreign Office, a German tipster here, Warsaw, Labour M.P.s in England, trade unionists in the Rhineland, Sandor's friend, Paris, the A.O.G., a Czechoslovak Member of Parliament, a German official in Wilhelmstrasse, all play a role in this, but the very first hint of confirmation came from a Vienna night-club singer living with a hat-check girl. Tomorrow the world will shake. Austria, what a country! Austria, I love you!

He couldn't sleep. After a moment he crept from bed and tiptoed to his office. It was seventeen minutes after four. With luck, Sandor could just, just, file a brief bulletin to Washington in time to make this morning's paper. God damn it, Mason thought, this story is Sandor's just as much as it is ours, and even if I am killing a beat for my own newspaper and maybe risking my job it's not *right* that Sandor shouldn't have this confirmation now. What the hell is life for if not for the love of friends. Quickly he dialed Sandor's number.

No answer. He dialed again. Again no answer.

The Sandors must still be out with Thorne, chitchatting in some bar.

For a second Mason flirted with the idea of writing a paragraph and sending it to Washington himself under Sandor's signature. No. Quixoticism could go too far.

Wearily he plodded back to bed. Paula was sound asleep and a wave of infinite affection for her swept over him. Then he was struck painfully by a sense of guilt because he had not told her the whole story and indeed she knew nothing whatever of his life, such as it was, in the Koenigen. He touched her on the shoulder, shaking her. "Wake up. Let's make some coffee. I have a long story I want to tell you, about something in that night club called the Koenigen."

IV. COURT OF HONOR

Mason roused himself early. He had a lot to do. He was very sleepy. Paula, lying curled like a question mark, did not stir. Frau Gertrude made him breakfast, and he walked down the corridor. First, call Sandor; second, inform Dr. Wiskiewicz; third, arrange an appointment, if possible, with Dr. Wimpassing, the chief press officer of the government. The Chancellery shunted him off to Wimpassing's first assistant, Regierungsrat Dr. Hohnstedt, a career officer no longer young.

Mason saw Paula peek through the office door, a robe over her shoulders. The iron rule whereby he was supposed never to be disturbed while actually at work was broken not more than a dozen times a day, usually to his secret pleasure. She looked confused and extremely sleepy, with her pale torch of hair shining in separate fine threads of copper and gold. They had not gone to sleep again until almost six in the morning.

He was glad to see her but said, "Hey, go back to bed." His voice became solicitous. "You shouldn't be up so early."

"If you get up, I get up. I'm a good wife, aren't I?"

"Quite often." Mason smiled.

"Darling, darling, have breakfast with me now."

"I can't, I've had it. Hohnstedt is seeing me at ten, and it's nine-thirty now."

"I know, but I can't bear to have breakfast alone when you're here. You're away so often."

"That's an old complaint, Paula."

"Hold me, hold me," she implored. She bent her head sharply forward, almost at a right angle to her body, and stuck it against his chest, rubbing it, then put her arms around him hungrily, and let her whole weight sag against him. She could turn swiftly from being wand to willow, as he well knew. "Hold me, hold me," she repeated.

"Paula, dear, I've got to go!"

"Just one cup of coffee, please."

"Okay." He sighed, exasperated.

"Never mind, darling. I know you really are in a hurry. And you need me more than I need you."

His brows arched quizzically. Leaving the flat he called over his shoulder, "You'll have to do the papers alone, and please watch out for Bleschke's call."

Her German was substantially better than his, and usually after breakfast she helped him go through the newspapers before she did the shopping. At eleven every morning Bleschke, Drew's man, telephoned with the early news.

Mason hiked toward the Hauptstrasse. Now that the *Föhn* was over, the air, crisp and dry, held a sharp crackle; it smelt positively of ozone, of electricity, as it often did in Vienna after a storm. Like most boys born on a farm, Mason was exceptionally sensitive to weather. The first time he had experienced this smell of ozone, spreading his nostrils wide and tickling them like invisible bubbles of champagne, he thought that something had gone wrong with the power system of the town and that electricity was escaping somewhere. He could not believe that this fresh crackling spark could come merely from nature.

A taxi passed and when Mason hailed it the driver slammed on the brakes so hard that it rocked on its ancient haunches like a hobbyhorse. Near the Ring, where blinked one of the three veritable traffic lights in the whole of the city at this time, he said to himself, in tune with the universe, "In ten seconds the driver will say something about the price of coffee." The driver said, as they reached the Bundeskanzleramt, "Something ought to be done about the price of coffee."

Here was the stately cream-colored building, the seat of the Austrian government for generations, where the Congress of Vienna met in 1814. It had not changed much since. In the tall gilt-and-rose reception room with the magenta curtains Mason sat seeing himself in a dozen mirrors under a chandelier that must have weighed as much as a tree. Dr. Hohnstedt received him promptly. Mason, although exhilarated, felt somewhat embarrassed; his behavior was not at all that of the triumphant, cocky newspaperman confronting the powers that be with a successful coup and demanding information. Indeed, he fixed his gaze on the highlights on Dr. Hohnstedt's brightly polished shoes, and looked shy. It was a new experience for him to tell a government that he was about to print something that it would dislike extremely to have printed. Dr. Hohnstedt had for some time been an enigma to Mason, but they were friendly. Mason asked him about the Customs Union, whereupon he exclaimed, "But this is an extremely serious matter, Herr Jarrett. I assure you, on my word of honor, that I know nothing whatever about it. Excuse me, please." He returned in a quarter of an hour, red in the face. "The Minister is busy in the Parliament. Where can he reach you on the telephone at one-fifteen?" Clever Dr. Wimpassing, Mason thought. He was probably in the next room, and he knew perfectly well that one-fifteen was just on the edge of the time Mason had to file. Talk at that last minute would be useless.

"One-fifteen is a little late for me. My deadline is one-thirty, and I have to have a story written before that."

Dr. Hohnstedt said nothing, but his features seemed to betray the nerve-destroying dilemma of all civil servants—he had to be on the side of his government and defend it no matter what he himself might think.

"Might I ask you now—is the story true or not?" Mason inquired politely.

"I am not empowered to give such information."

"Even so," Mason went on, "I'd like to ask you if there is any official Austrian reaction to the story."

Again Dr. Hohnstedt, toothily courteous, left the room. This time he returned in less than a minute, with the words, "The Herr Minister will call you at one-fifteen."

Damned helpful, the Austrian press department! Mason took leave and reached the street. He took time out to send Hilda a large box of chocolates and Trudi a spray of flowers, with notes of thanks, and then hustled to the British Legation, to tell Yancey, the counselor, the gist of what had happened.

"You look as if you had been up all night. Have a nip?" Yancey brought a bottle out of a cabinet.

"I got to sleep at about a hundred and fifty in the morning. There's a hell of a story about to break."

Horace Yancey, like almost all British diplomats, was well informed, but he had heard nothing at all of what Mason now told him, and Mason was flattered when, after hearing him out, the Englishman said, "But I must inform Sir Eric about this at once!"

Yancey, who did not remotely resemble the conventional picture of the career diplomat, laid out for Mason some political developments to be expected, and briefed him on trade figures. He wore loud striped shirts, carried irreverence to the point of active indiscretion, had a shiny nose, could be arrogant as Lucifer, and behaved in general as no American diplomat would ever dare to behave, in that he was always himself and the devil take the others. He was the eldest son of a peer, but took a strong pro-Labour line in British politics.

Proceeding to the American Legation, Mason asked to see Mr. Rhoads. Mason's regard for him was low, but he knew that it might stand him in good stead later if the American Minister, no less, were to hear from him, personally, before he could possibly hear it from anybody else, the news that Germany and Austria planned to make a Customs Union. Mason was not one to neglect a chance to further his own interests if he could do so in a quite nice way. Mr. Rhoads was impressed by the news he brought and took notes on what he said.

Home, Mason checked with Strothness, called Sandor, banged out his story, and, a little after one, put in his Paris call. Everything from all the *Star* bureaus all over Europe, except London, went by telephone to Paris, the relay point for transmission to the United States. While waiting for his call he saw on his desk the letter Drew had written the president of the Union about the *Ehrengericht*. He had forgotten about it momentarily.

This is to request that you summon at an early date a Court of Honor (*Ehrengericht*), as provided for in our constitution, for the purpose of deciding whether or not our fellow member and secretary Dr. Vladko

Markovitch is to be considered longer fit to remain one of our colleagues.

It took Drew two and a half pages to say the rest, describing how Markovitch had translated and "caused to be disseminated" an article which denounced as criminals of the worst type

(a) an honorable Hungarian journalist, David Bleschke, who conducts the Danubia Press Service, and (b) myself and the honorable woman who has the honor to be my fiancée.

Drew concluded:

As my judges for the *Ehrengericht*, I name the following:

> Mr. Mason E. Jarrett
> Dr. Ricardo Stein

Christ! thought Mason.

A note from Paula waited on the desk as well:

Bleschke was nix. The papers are full of long sentences. Kitty and I are lunching at the Bristol, join us if you can.

Your eyes are always very, very brown when you are sleepy in the morning.

> X X X O X
> P.

The "O" meant something very special.

Punctually at one-fifteen the telephone rang, and Mason heard the purring voice of Regierungsrat Dr. Hohnstedt. "Alas . . . the Herr Gesandte Dr. Wimpassing . . . still engaged in urgent business on the floor of Parliament . . . unable to communicate with you himself . . . wishes me to state . . . certain preliminary negotiations to explore the possibility of a Customs Union between Germany and Austria have taken place . . . but as yet there can be no official declaration. Premature publication of important details might cause irreparable damage. The Austrian government cannot now make known its attitude toward negotiations only tentative and 'nonactual' and will neither confirm nor deny that any further discussion will occur."

It's a statement anyway, it admits that certain "preliminary negotiations" *have* taken place, Mason thought. He scribbled a new lead quickly. He might well have asked Hohnstedt for further elucidation but he did not do so because this might have led to bickering and argument without concrete result. There was no point in rubbing the government the wrong way, or putting its back up, now that he had what he needed. His business was not to quarrel with Austrian officials, but to write the news.

2

Another person who rose early that morning was Dr. Karl Tetzel. He and Mia, who were both somewhat lazy, often stayed in bed till noon. The bed was warm and what doctors sometimes said about making love in the morning was not correct, particularly if there was time for a bit of additional sleep afterward and there was nothing else to do beyond reading the papers, all seventeen of them. New York had five morning papers; Chicago two; London nine; Vienna seventeen. Mia as a rule got up before Karl did, to put the coffee on. Later, with the combination of tenacity and inertness that often characterized him, he would dress carefully, eat the meal that was both breakfast and lunch, and go down to the Journalistenzimmer, whence, if any news cropped up, he would put in his call to Thorne in London. Occasionally Mia joined him later in the afternoon, but more often she wandered off alone.

This morning, after a night during which he had slept little, Karl dressed with haste. Mia had taken two of the shiny little white bullets that are supposed to shoot sleep into you; she did not wake. He took a crumpled, greasy five-Schilling note from her purse, and explored the cupboard out in the hall. Here he found the revolver, made by Skoda, that his father, the former policeman and Schutzbund fighter, had given him, and which he scarcely knew how to use. Then this young man, who had been destined to be a teacher of political economy, glanced at Mia and, with a gesture in which love, guardianship, and defiance were commingled, kissed her on the forehead. His lips arched upward and, with his large, almost animal-like eyes glittering, he tiptoed to the front door, closed it behind him silently, and skipped down the worn stone stairs.

At the Majestic he asked for the number of Herr Thorne's suite, crossed the lobby while cautiously watching to see if anybody he knew was there, and took the elevator up. The gun clanked against the large bunch of keys in his side pocket; he smothered the noise with his hand, then stuffed a handkerchief into the pocket.

Burning in Karl's mind, brought back now from past to present, was every humiliation he had known in the past decade. He was acting not merely out of resentment at Thorne's insult to his wife's virtue, real as that was, or outrage at the vulgarity of the trade Thorne proposed. What kind of a life could he have with Mia hereafter, if she betrayed him to make his salary bigger? But beyond this were other factors that scarcely had to do with Mia at all. He recalled episodes in which he had been abused and degraded—the stinginess he had had to endure from various bosses, the insults based on indifference which were the worst of insults, the assumption that he was no more than a vessel to be kicked around at will. The nonrecognition of his own worth, his own merit, was what mortified him most. Karl's face shone with rage, hatred, and the taste of revenge to come.

He peered along the corridor, where the room numbers were ornately scrolled in thin gold against dark mahogany panels. His heart was pumping. He waited for two passers-by to disappear. When, at last, he reached Thorne's door, the corridor was empty. He rapped hard on the satiny wood of the door, but no answer came. He rapped again. Finally he heard steps, and then Thorne's voice muttering, "Come in—who is it?" The door swung open and there stood Thorne, who had obviously just come out of the shower; his bathrobe was unbuttoned, and his hair still wet.

"For God's sake!" Thorne greeted him. His manner could not have been friendlier, in spite of his surprise, as he led him into the suite, pushing a chair forward and saying, "Well—it's early in the morning for a visit." On a serving table were the remains of his breakfast. Two or three cigarettes had been ground out in the debris of a scrambled egg. "How are you, Karl? Sit down!"

"No!" exclaimed Karl. "You have suggested something to my wife . . . indecent! . . . dishonorable . . . I refuse!"

"Well—Jesus Christ!"

"Unheard of! She is not to do it!"

"I was tight last night. Everybody was a little tight. Can't you take a joke?"

"Not that kind of a joke!" Karl, his hand trembling violently, grabbed Thorne by the collar while he pulled at the gun in his pocket. Thorne stared at him, utterly incredulous, shook himself free, slapped him hard across the cheek, and with an expert gesture knocked the gun out of his hand. It plumped to the floor, and he kicked at it, propelling it over the carpet with the side of his bare foot.

"Pull yourself together," Thorne said sharply. He crossed the room, picking up the gun. "Of all the crazy nonsense I've ever heard of!" He examined the gun. "Quite a little toy—it could blow a hole through an iron door!"

Karl stood there leaning forward, wavering. He made an effort to regain both his equilibrium and his dignity, but now he had the additional humiliation that this brute of an American had disarmed him with a finger, and was not even frightened, although very angry. An inexpressible sadness released the taut nerves in Karl's body. He sat down, pulling a hand flat across his forehead as his head sank. "Very well. To kill you would be silly. But last night you made a dishonorable proposal to my wife, and I wish you to know that it is categorically refused."

Thorne stood there, coarse, vital. "Take your damned gun." He threw it at Karl. He did not even bother to unload it. "I don't want the damned thing around here!" He walked to the telephone, and commanded briskly, "Room service!" To Karl he said, "Now, behave yourself. I need a drink, and you need one too. Or a cup of the Majestic's finest?" He ordered coffee and some brandy.

Karl did not move.

"Control yourself, man!" ordered Thorne. "Of all lunatic ways to start a day—well! Now, let's get this business between us straight. Once for all—then we drop it. I hadn't the faintest idea of insulting you or Mia. The whole thing, hell, it was just a joke."

Karl carefully poured milk into his coffee, with his delicate, proud hands scarcely able to hold the cup.

Thorne watched warily as Karl burst into talk. "I wonder if you, Herr Thorne, in your position, can understand fully what it means always to have a sense of defeat. I win at chess, but that too is a defeat, because I should be expending my . . ." he groped for a word, "processes . . . on things more real, more productive. I love Mia, she loves me in return, but she despises me as a failure. She will do anything, almost anything, to have a little more of the comforts of life, not only for herself but for me, but everything to which I am connected, everything, seems always to end in failure. I am not talking in self-pity, Herr Thorne. I will not make any such excuse as that I am ill-starred. But I have intelligence, I have skill. Why, why, am I always left behind?"

Thorne became acutely uncomfortable.

Karl continued to talk, and Thorne took a quick decision. He did not feel contrite or guilty in the slightest about his proposal to Mia, and he was thoroughly repelled by Karl now, but he felt that he owed him a gesture. Karl was hysterical, and he could not afford to have another blowup. Besides, this stupid, silly episode would take the cream off any further adventures in Vienna. He reached for the telephone and asked for the porter's desk, saying meanwhile to Karl, "I was going to stay here a couple of days longer, but I've changed my mind and I think I'll leave today." When the concierge's voice came on the wire, Thorne spoke into the phone. "Klaus, get me a place on the Orient to Istanbul this afternoon." Thorne patted Karl on the shoulder. "You'd better go now. Don't worry. Give Mia my best. As to your raise, I'll put it through to New York right away, and if you don't believe me you can hang around the desk downstairs and watch me send the telegram. And I guess we can manage that extra hundred Schillings for expenses."

Karl did not take his eyes from his face, and Thorne sensed clearly that he would never cease hating him. "And be careful with that damned gun of yours." Karl left the room at last. Thorne thought, The poor son of a bitch, I'll give him a couple of months, then I'll have to fire him.

Karl tottered downstairs from the lobby to the men's room, and was violently sick.

3

Mason decided not to join Paula and Kitty for lunch after getting the Customs Union story off. Friday was mail day for catching the boat train to Cherbourg or Havre, and he had his weekly news notes to do. These only ran to a hundred fifty words each, but were troublesome to write. The *Star* printed them (very old-fashioned) in the form of single paragraphs, signed at the bottom, and they were popular with the sixty or seventy American papers that subscribed to the *Star's* foreign service. The subjects Mason chose this week were a report from Budapest that an avant-garde theater there was planning to produce an old play by Benito Mussolini, an item from Prague to the effect that the public hangman had had six hundred proposals of marriage in the last ten years, and the discovery in the Dodecanese of a fragment of sculpture possibly by Phidias.

Paula came into the office and described how, after lunch, she had taken Kitty to the train. "And," she recounted, "you could have knocked me *dead*—there was Mark Thorne climbing into the next car! You know how one section of the Orient splits up between Athens and Istanbul. Kitty was in the Athens car of course, and it seems that Thorne is on the way to Istanbul. Now, I know Kitty pretty well and I don't think Thorne is much of an actor—anyway, they couldn't possibly have planned it that way. They both looked absolutely *stunned!*"

Mason said, "The Orient splits at Nish, below Belgrade. It gets there tomorrow afternoon, so Thorne and Kitty ought to have about twenty-four hours together."

Paula sighed in the accent of an older generation, "Well, I never!"

The telephone rang—Jim Drew. His voice, usually so courtly, was sharp. "Say, Jarrett, about that two hundred dollars we talked about last night. Thanks, but I won't be needing it." He rang off.

Pulling his brows together Mason mimicked Paula with a "Well, I never!" of his own.

＊

Strothness's beat, together with Mason's parallel story and followed by Sandor's the next morning, made a sensation all over the world. At first both the German and Austrian governments sought to equivocate, to cover up, but it was no use; by Monday they were forced to issue a full-scale, official announcement of their detailed plans for the Customs Union project. This was, of course, a grave embarrassment, because they had counted on a period during which they could make elaborate diplomatic preparation, waiting for a propitious moment, before letting the news be known. Now Paris, Warsaw, Belgrade, Prague, Bucharest seethed. Sober leader writers in London called the event the most sensational since Versailles; correspondents everywhere on the Continent received queries from agitated editors. Does this mean war? Drew said to Mason at the café, "Well, Mister Jarrett, I see that you have been busy under the surface lately, huh!"

For four days running Mason held the front page with a story from Vienna, something that hadn't happened since King Carol flew back to Rumania to regain his throne. Not only did other capitals seethe; so did Vienna itself. Speeches, mass meetings, demonstrations made news as Austria divided on the issue, and it became clear that a serious cabinet crisis impended, with Monsignor Ignaz Seipel probably being called upon to form a new government.

Toward the end of the week Mason ran into Dr. Wimpassing in Parliament. The Herr Gesandte looked as if he wanted to cut him dead, but did not quite dare do so. Mason's reaction to this was ambivalent. He did not, any more than before, want to go out of his way to affront the government, but if it chose to be unfriendly it could go to hell. Mason was delighted with his success on the story, and felt that he was invulnerable. What could the government possibly do to him, since all he had done was write the truth?

But that was certainly a frigid look in Wimpassing's normally impassive eye.

4

Another week passed, and now spring was kicking its way down the rugged, sylvan Austrian hills; in Mason's imagination the days flashed by like a procession of ancient galleons with square sails whipped by fresh winds. Karl Tetzel rose from a chess game with Dr. Heinrich Ritter when Mason arrived one afternoon at the Weissenhof and approached him with a gingerly, somewhat faltering voice. "Could I perhaps talk with you a moment? Something personal—it would be welcoming to me if I could have the benefit of your advice."

"Sure, sure," Mason said.

He tried to make him less nervous. The deerlike eyes were flickering. But he's certainly good-looking, Mason thought. He had a broad upper lip, on which a single line of mustache was sharply traced.

Tetzel said, "Hypothetically, if a man has a quarrel on a personal matter with the head of his service, if he considers himself wantonly insulted and aggrieved, is it incumbent on him as a man of honor to quit his job?"

Mason thought rapidly. "That's a tough one, Karl. To answer with any sense I'd have to know more. How hypothetical is this, incidentally?"

He waited. Something must have happened between Thorne and Tetzel.

Karl said, "Perhaps in a day or two I will be able to tell you more."

"I don't think anybody should quit a job these days except under pressure of the most extreme circumstances." Tetzel's eyes dropped. "Jobs are damned hard to find, if you don't mind my saying something original."

Dr. Ritter buttonholed him, and, spluttering, demanded to know what step the Germans and Austrians could take to counteract French maneuvers against the Customs Union. The Herr Gesandte Dr. Wimpassing had assured him that the malign efforts of the French would be frustrated and circumvented no matter what the cost. They talked a moment, and Ritter, satisfied, whispered to him, "I have not forgotten the great, great favor you did me recently. Soon, soon, I will repay."

"Forget it, Heinrich."

Mason went on to the Journalistenzimmer, where he found Drew and asked him what was happening in regard to the *Ehrengericht*. Drew shrugged. Having initiated the procedure, which had apparently exhausted all his energies, he was content to wait; his heavy face showed no interest. Sandor, who had been watching the news ticker, choked with sardonic laughter and said to Mason, "You are ill stuck with that thing! But nothing will come on it, I mean!"

Mason returned to Drew, persistent.

"But, Jim, we ought to get started soon. I'm losing my grip on who is supposed to have insulted whom."

"My dear sir, an *Ehrengericht* is a serious matter. It's up to Gatterburg, the president of the Union. He'll probably call a meeting next week. "Oh—I hear that Donald Bishopson has agreed to represent Markovitch."

Bishopson! Mason quailed.

He had several errands to do. Near a shop on Kärntnerstrasse with enticing expensive confections in embroidery and crystal he almost stumbled over a beggar who, arms upstretched, was actually kneeling on the curb, praying. Three boys in rags, one of them playing a violin, leaped after him with a whimpering call for alms. Not a mile away, he knew, stood regally the opulent palaces in the Belvedere quarter; one was the principal town house of the head of the House of Rothschild, and the word was that it still employed enough British servants to man two football teams. Well, don't blame Vienna; plenty of other cities were mixed up between rich and poor.

Climbing the low belly of hill at Haydnplatz Mason passed again, this time by daylight, the monolithic building which housed the A.O.G.; here too stood its formidable rivals, the Credit Anstalt and Wiener Bank-Verein. The violet windows of the A.O.G. flashed obliquely in the sun. Mason glanced at the upward slanting street and had the vagrant thought that the A.O.G. itself, not the street, was on uneven keel; he said to himself, Hello, that bank isn't on the level. There had been no financial news at all lately. He wondered how the new A.O.G. directorate was getting on. He must ask Sandor if the collapse of the Customs Union project had made any difference in the commitments of the Austrian banks to their creditors abroad.

Near Fleischmarkt he could not resist poking into a narrow passage reached through a cobwebby net of old streets. Here, half hidden in a shadowy arcade, was a shop to which young John Dixon had introduced him several months before. In discreetly recessed vitrines were hung photographs of young women, blown up to large dimensions; the displays changed week by week, but their nature remained the same. Here were the most luxurious, the most provocative, the most sensuous nudes he had ever seen. They carried a characteristic Viennese note of pure seductive wantonness. Heads of the models were, as a rule, clouded over—still, you could see some of the features. Suddenly Mason's attention became fixed; the new girl this week reminded him of somebody—could she be somebody he knew? Who? He looked more closely, abashed. Mia Tetzel!

Dumbfounded he looked hard again. The likeness, even if blurred, was unmistakable; two such Venuses could not exist even in Vienna. So this was what Mia did when she disappeared from the café on long, lonely afternoons. Posed for erotic photographs! Did Karl know?

Mason entered the shop. The photographs outside were, he knew, the merest foretaste of the spectacular treasures, if you could call them such, to be found within. Here were drawers, cabinets, cupboards, stuffed to bursting with pornography. Mason, when he had first penetrated into this cave of wonders, or horrors, with Dixon, had never conceived that such etchings, implements, objets d'art, contraptions, of such extravagant evil refinement and variety, could so much as even exist. Today the proprietor, Herr Abt, showed him some nineteenth-century Von Bayros prints. Imagine anybody doing *that* to *that* with a violin bow! Literally, Mason could not keep from blushing.

"Who's the new girl outside?" he asked Herr Abt, striving to sound casual. Herr Abt had tiny hands, glossy nails, and dark hair in single strands slicked over a bald pate.

"Ah! If you only knew. Respectable!"

When he reached home Mason found a message to the effect that he had been granted a long-sought interview with Thomas Garrigue Masaryk, the venerable philosopher-statesman who was President of Czechoslovakia. Interviews with Masaryk were rare, and he was pleased. The *Star* liked interviews. Mason's ambition was to get eventually an interview with every head of state in his area, but so far he had succeeded only in Greece, Poland, and Rumania. Now Masaryk fell into his lap. He could only presume that the Czechs were granting him this favor as an indirect gesture of thanks for helping to break the Customs Union story. The Czechs had a highly developed sense of quid pro quo.

He caught the night train to Prague, had a satisfactory talk with Masaryk the next day, and flew back to Vienna at once. The plane, a tri-motor Junkers with corrugated wings, held no fewer than sixteen passengers—sensational, the last word! He was mildly surprised, arriving back at the villa, to see Mia Tetzel there, having tea with Paula. Paula had not expected him to arrive so early and, embracing him, protested vigorously when he told her that he had flown. She hated airplanes and did not like him to fly.

Both Paula and Mia seemed secretive, as well as unnaturally intent on the words of the other. Mia looked as if she had been weeping, and Mason noticed two tiny specks of mucus at the points of her eyes. He kissed her on the cheek, and could not keep from thinking of the photographs in Herr Abt's window.

She left after a few moments.

Paula said, "Something perfectly awful has happened to Mia, really awful, and Karl is threatening to quit his job. It's all mixed up with Thorne—your friend, that snake!"

"What happened?"

"She's in an absolute torment about Karl, which is one reason she came to me. She wants you to do your best to influence Karl not to quit if he asks you for advice."

"He already has. But what's the story?"

"Thorne made her a proposition, to sleep with him *in exchange for a raise for Karl!*"

"Phew," Mason said.

"She refused, of course."

5

Mason learned the next morning that the procedure for the *Ehrengericht* had at last been established. He and Dr. Ricardo Stein, Drew's advocates, would meet Tuesday with the two men representing Markovitch—Dr. Lothar Unzicker, the well-known foreign editor of the *Wiener Sternblatt*, and the pale-eyed Donald Bishopson, the Scotsman with the brief tongue and flinty manner who was chief correspondent in Central Europe for the New York *Register*. These four would then appoint a fifth person as a neutral arbiter, hold sessions at some convenient coffeehouse, call witnesses, come to a recommendation, and put the matter up to the Union as a whole— whether or not Markovitch should be expelled.

Mason didn't know Bishopson at all well. Now that things were coming to a head he thought that he might call him and talk the matter over, although this was probably against the rules. The devil with the rules. "It's irregular," Bishopson said over the telephone, "but never mind, I'll meet you in the Bristol at two-thirty."

Bishopson had a tight, stiff voice, as if whiskey-bitten, although he drank little. He never came to the Weissenhof; to have encountered him there would have been like running into Ramsay MacDonald in a house of ill fame. He was the only American or British correspondent in town who worked in an actual office of his own instead of the Journalistenzimmer, had his own car, and played golf on the single course (nine holes) Vienna had. Bishopson's flinty, commonsensical aloofness had always repelled Mason slightly. As a matter of fact, they lived in altogether different worlds. The Jarretts cultivated the youthful artists, the musicians, cartoonists, young lawyers, actors studying with Reinhardt, and visiting novelists sampling the local Gemütlichkeit. Around the Bishopsons were the diplomatic secretaries, the businessmen, rich people with Schlosses, those interested in amateur theatricals, and ladies of the American Women's Club. Bishopson even belonged to something called the Beefsteak Club, which met for formal stag dinners once a month and at which the members and guests wore, believe it or not, dinner jackets.

The Bishopsons entertained widely, but the Jarretts had never been invited to their apartment. They discovered that this was because, when he and Paula arrived in Vienna, they had neglected to "call," to leave cards. Mason had never left a card on anybody in his life and thought that any such procedure between fellow newspapermen was the weirdest nonsense. Later he felt that Paula, who seemed to be rather lonely, might like Helen Bishopson and suggested that they should take some step toward becoming better acquainted with the Bishopsons.

But Paula said, "Oh Mason, you don't want to play around with that snobby crowd."

As a matter of fact Mason would have liked to have known the Bishopson circle better himself because he had a voracious curiosity about people and yearned to be on good terms with everybody. The truth was that Paula was much more bohemian than he. Mason had an instinctive, ineradicable feeling that radicals, people who were unconventional or off the beaten track, were somehow disreputable; he would never conceivably have chosen to live in Greenwich Village. But Paula, born of the most conservative stock, was much less bourgeois. Mason was a vagabond, but secretly craved respectability; she the opposite.

Mason found Bishopson waiting. He wore a blue shirt with a tight, white stiff collar. His forehead, nose, and chin all had an identical slant—three short lines. Mason knew one thing about him that he liked extremely—he let his two assistants, the chief of whom was a stout, energetic Hungarian named Hestery, sign their own dispatches. In the journalism of that day it was an accepted rule that only the chief of a bureau had the right to sign dispatches, no matter who wrote them. Subordinates did not get bylines. This was a rank injustice. One well-known case concerned the chief of a big agency in London who won a Pulitzer Prize for a series of stories written in their entirety by his anonymous assistant. Bishopson held strictly to the principle that every man should get individual credit for what he did.

"Now, see here," Bishopson began at once in his harsh, throaty voice as they ordered coffee. "This Markovitch fellow is no particular friend of mine, and he's certainly not a Galahad, but I think he has a case."

"*He* has a case?" Mason found himself flung on the defensive.

Bishopson cleared his throat with a dry rustle. "Aye. What's Drew's point in this business, anyway?"

"The obvious point. Drew takes the line that it was completely unjustified—wildly libelous, in fact—for anybody to stigmatize the crowd that hangs around the Weissenhof as a gang of spies, thieves, and liars. What right did Markovitch have to hawk around an article saying things like that?"

"No right whatever, but he had orders from above, no doubt. You know what Balkan journalism is."

"Fact, Bishopson, I'm not so keen on this silly business myself, but—you see, a lot of us go to the Weissenhof three or four times a week, and it's awkward to have it printed that we're a gang of crooks."

"Oh, quite. But Markovitch didn't say that you were *all* crooks and spies. This fellow Bleschke, the man mainly aggrieved, next to Drew himself—do you know anything about him? I've made a little investigation. It's entirely possible that he *is* a spy."

"I doubt if you could prove that." Mason stiffened. He felt that he was being weak and ineffectual. He must pull himself together. Did he feel inferior to Bishopson because of Bishopson's better job and social prestige?

"I buy Bleschke's news service," Bishopson continued relentlessly, "I more or less have to, but from what I hear his antecedents aren't the best. I don't know if he's a terrorist or a murderer; I do think he's probably a shady character." Again came a harsh rustle at the base of the throat. "Now, as to Drew—"

"Perhaps you don't know Drew well," Mason interrupted him. "He's a queer fish, obviously. A bit of a megalomaniac, perhaps, even though he has nothing but the I.P. job and the coverage he does for the rest of us when we're away. It's very important to him to keep up the queer . . . I don't know quite how to describe it . . . queer emotional leadership he has over the Weissenhof table. The Weissenhof is his home, his refuge, his citadel." Mason took a new tack. "Besides, he's altogether mixed up—not at all stable, but he's quixotic and generous, and maybe he's simply backing Bleschke up because they're friends. Finally, to describe the Countess, his fiancée, as Markovitch did was certainly outrageous."

Bishopson gave a curt laugh. "Fiancée?"

"Well, that's what Drew likes to call her."

"Aye. But what else is she? You know," he went on, his manner becoming more friendly, "Drew isn't so awfully damn popular with some of the people in the Union. There's some talk that Markovitch may institute a counter-*Ehrengericht* against Drew, on the ground that Drew's letter to the Union insults *him*. He may ask for *Drew's* expulsion from the Union."

"My God!"

Bishopson laughed his short, dry laugh. "Aye, it's a dilemma. But we're in it, you and me, and we're both honest men in this den of thieves. Suppose we try to work out a solution together."

"Sure—that's why I called you," Mason said.

But, stiffening again, he wondered if Bishopson had not been cleverly bargaining all along. After all, as the case now stood, there could be no doubt but that Drew was certainly in the right and Markovitch in the wrong; he mustn't permit himself to be pushed off base this way.

"I can say for Drew that we would welcome a counter-*Ehren-gericht!*" he declared.

"Well," Bishopson receded, "I'm pretty sure we can avoid going as far as that. As to a solution, what exactly does Drew want?"

"He wants Markovitch discharged from the Union for unprofessional conduct, together with an apology."

"He'll never get it." Bishopson leaned back. "Anyway, it's all going to be a damned nuisance—and just as the tennis season starts. Do you play tennis, Jarrett? Look you here, I remember a good short story of yours several years ago—it was in one of those Paris magazines. Writing any more?"

Startled, Mason could not conceal his pleasure. This was the first time anybody in Vienna had ever mentioned fiction he had written. He knew the story Bishopson was referring to, and recollected the struggle it had cost him.

"No, I haven't touched fiction since we arrived here."

"Well, you ought to give it a try again some day."

He called for the bill, and each paid for his own coffee: this was a Vienna rule. Bishopson said, "Let's get going—it's almost three, time for this celebrated Court of Honor to begin."

"I'm afraid we're not in agreement," Mason put in.

"Well," coughed Bishopson throatily, "if we're not, there's not much chance that anybody else will be. But I know how these things go—it will be a week at least before we begin to talk hard facts."

They walked down the Ring to the Imperial, where the meeting was to take place, and Mason said to himself, This Bishopson isn't a bad sort of fellow after all.

6

Mason and Bishopson arrived on time, which meant that they were about fifteen minutes early. Then young Dr. Ricardo Stein entered the café. For several reasons Mason was curious about Stein, his associate in the *Ehrengericht,* and eager to know him better. They had met half a dozen times, but only casually. Stein, who was about twenty-six, derived from a distinguished rich Viennese family; his father, a well-known jurist, had one of the most successful legal practices in town. But the family had an ardent socialist tradition; young Stein had been named for Ricardo and brought up on the Fabians from the cradle. He had a degree in law and worked in his father's office, but, for fun and to gain experience, he was doubling in journalism and was now second man in the local bureau of the A.P. Another thing that interested Mason about Dr. Ricardo Stein was that he had his own small airplane, a baby Heinkel II Z-Kub, and flew it everywhere.

"When are you going to let me take you for a bit of a flip in it?" Stein had asked a few weeks before.

"Any time," Mason said, "but Paula doesn't like me to fly and I'll have to ask her and think about it."

Mason Jarrett, so thoughtful a man! reflected Stein. Most of his American colleagues were so fantastically hidebound by their wives, so unmercifully under the conjugal thumb. Thank goodness he himself would never be that way, Stein thought. He was still a bachelor.

Mason greeted him as they sat down with Bishopson at a special table in the café. He was a small man, delicately built, with blond curly hair and a sunny appearance, but his mind was hard and he affected an exceptionally precise, almost pedantic manner of speech. He was also capable of becoming excessively legalistic on occasion. Mason dreaded this. Nothing was simple in Vienna, but of all matters inordinately complex Viennese legal procedure was the most complex.

The last of the judges to arrive was Dr. Unzicker. A heavily built, iron-gray man of sixty, he was both formidable and benign.

"Well, let's get started," Mason said briskly. He didn't usually take the initiative like this, but something made him want to be decisive at once, possibly to compensate for the weakness he had felt with Bishopson. "First of all, as established by the rules, we ought to choose a fifth man as chairman. . . ." So he laid it down. Unzicker looked at him quizzically; Bishopson said nothing. Apparently Bishopson was shy in company, which was why people thought him stiff. But he was stiff. Look at him now, straight as a gun, checking over some of the documents; he had put on small, rimless pince-nez, much too small for his face. When he did talk, Mason discovered, his German was slow but admirably correct.

"Well, how about it?" Mason was still aggressive. "We have to select a president, a neutral arbiter. Who shall it be?"

Dr. Unzicker, who had a couple of papers in his hand, gazed at him evenly. These youngsters, with all their lives before them, with their good intentions, their ideals . . . ignorant still, rash, babes in the wood . . . no barnacles on them yet, no blots or burrs . . . not unattractive. These youngsters, who know so little of life, who might in time have to learn a good deal more, so ignorant, so rash. . . .

"I haf wid me here a documENT," intoned Unzicker in English. "If it pleases you now to listen a liddle, I vill read dis documENT."

"I have all the documents too," Dr. Stein interrupted. "First, I appeal to you, gentlemen, I beg to appeal to you, we must follow the law in this serious matter, we must choose our president."

Dr. Unzicker turned his fixed, bland gaze on Stein. "Perhaps you vill bear wid me a liddle. I haf dis documENT, it vill interest you a liddle, I think."

"My idea is this," Mason cut in. "We obviously ought to have a president who is neutral from the point of view of nationality— that is, someone who is neither American or Yugoslav. An Austrian would do. Or British. Not a Hungarian, since Bleschke is Hungarian. The president should speak English if possible. Of course he has to be chosen out of our own membership, the membership of the Union. Now . . ."

Dr. Unzicker held his paper under his chin, flapping it, patient, waiting.

It wasn't going to be easy to find a truly neutral president satisfactory to all. Bishopson suggested the New York *Times* man, Dr. Seitz, venerable and aristocratic, but apparently he was out of town—on a bustard hunt in the Burgenland. Stein suggested Sandor, but Mason knew that he would not under any circumstances take it on. Bishopson suggested Ernst Boericke, the correspondent of a Swiss agency, a friendly and popular little man, but Stein recalled that his service went to Markovitch's newspaper too, and that he therefore might be considered to be prejudiced. Wheels within wheels, Mason saw.

"Chentlemen." Dr. Unzicker finally gained attention. "I haf now to tell you, I do not think you vill haf the necessity to elect a bresident."

With a flourish he put a letter on the table signed by Markovitch, in which the Yugoslav apologized for the Patchek stories and promised to make a retraction available to any newspaper in Vienna which would print it.

Mason gulped.

Bishopson said nothing, but coughed, and through his small pince-nez read out slowly an English version of the German text. Markovitch's apology was complete. He said that Patchek had been mistaken in assuming that the Weissenhof was "a nest of spies"; he said that there had been no intention of insulting any person or persons who were accustomed to assemble there; he said indeed that the Weissenhof was a distinguished place of rendezvous, celebrated for the patronage of such well-known correspondents as "Drew, James N., International Press; Dr. Sandor, Washington *Sun;* Dixon, John P., Chicago *Daily* [sic]; and Charrett, Mason, of the Chicago *Star* foreign office." He extolled Drew's virtues, and apologized for the language that had been used about Bleschke and the Countess. Then Unzicker produced another letter, which Markovitch was prepared to send to Drew, confirming all of this to him personally. My God, what an anticlimax—how Viennese! Mason thought.

"I think we can take it for granted that there will now be no necessity for an *Ehrengericht,*" said Dr. Stein, after a bewildered pause.

"I don't think anything more needs to be done," Mason said. "If Dr. Stein agrees, we as Drew's seconds will vouch for it that he will accept this apology, and the whole matter is closed. Okay, Ricardo?" Stein nodded. "Then we're satisfied."

All that remained was to work out procedures. "Nothing in Austria is ever simply dropped," said Stein. They argued for half an hour, and then decided that everything could be considered satisfactorily liquidated if, first, the *Abend* agreed to print Markovitch's retraction, and, second, if Drew wrote a formal letter to the Union withdrawing his request for an *Ehrengericht* and offering "satisfaction" to Markovitch.

With everything thus settled, Mason and Bishopson left the Imperial together.

"What's your explanation?" Mason asked.

"Easy." Bishopson gave his clipped half laugh. "The Yugoslavs got scared. They thought that Markovitch might lose his job as secretary of the Union, which is a key post they like to have."

Of course! More wheels within wheels. Mason reflected that what all this amounted to was that Drew had won his case, that is, Markovitch apologized, but it also meant that Drew had not got what he wanted, that is, Markovitch's expulsion from the Union. He wondered if Drew would be clever enough to deduce both conclusions.

Near the Opera, Mason and Bishopson shook hands. "Let's meet again," Bishopson offered. "My wife and I have been envious of you, Jarrett. You seem to know a lot of Viennese and to get along with them well. We scarcely meet anybody except the British and Americans."

❋

"Sure thing," Drew said. "I'll agree to liquidate the matter. What's the odds? The man has retracted and I'm not vindictive." Mason waited in the Journalistenzimmer while he wrote the necessary letter. He waited for more than two hours. The letter turned out to be three pages long, and was stuffed to the edges with silly pomposity.

Mason sniffed. "Can't you make it shorter?"

7

Paula, the young realist, like practically everybody else in Vienna, was doing her accounts. She hated to work at a desk, and sat cross-legged on the big sofa, with her face concentrated, mouth grim, and papers strewn about her. She was wearing slacks—new to Vienna then. Mason had admired the slacks from the moment she had been bold enough to get them: they showed off nicely her slender long legs and boy's behind.

The April sun poured into the room, and the gramophone was playing a Vivaldi concerto, with its piercing and unearthly sweetness, very loud. Mason reflected, not a very original reflection, that the most modern people always seemed to prefer antique works of art; Paula was fascinated by Alban Berg, but Bach and Vivaldi were what she played for pleasure; Picasso absorbed her, but her favorite painter was Piero della Francesca. As to music she played it loud, because otherwise, she liked to say, you couldn't hear it when it was soft. He did not altogether follow the logic of this, but accepted it.

Paula groaned. To pay bills in Vienna was a laborious and complicated process, since personal checks were never used for household payments or purchases for the simple reason that nobody in Vienna trusted a personal check. Citizens paid the butcher and baker and candlestick maker by taking the necessary cash, in person, to the nearest post office, together with a form known as an *Erlagschein* made out to the recipient. The post office then proceeded in an altogether mysterious and fantastically complex manner to track people down and pass on the required amounts to those who had postal accounts. The first German word Mason ever learned was *Erlagschein*.

With a pen between her teeth, Paula muttered with fierce abstraction, "I'm almost finished. What's nine times seven?" Being a product of an education just about as good as the America of that day could provide, she had never mastered the multiplication tables, loved to split infinitives, and was shaky on geography.

"Sixty-three, unless Einstein changed the rules last night," Mason said.

"You'll be pleased, I've struck a balance, and we have exactly 147.20 Schillings in the world." She compressed her lips. "Damn!"

A month or two before they had sought to work out their financial situation squarely, but with little result. Frau Gertrude had come in while they were talking. "*Gnädige Frau.*" Her face had looked apologetic, as it always did when she asked for household money. "*Darf ich schon wieder Geld haben?*" Paula had looked helplessly at Mason and he fished one hundred Schillings from his wallet. Later that afternoon she had said, "Mason, I'm sorry, darling, but I have to have one hundred Schillings too. I *have* to pay something down to the dressmaker, and we're being dunned for several bills."

He couldn't stand it if any bill wasn't paid by the tenth of the month.

"A certain mathematical problem arises. I haven't got another hundred Schillings. Lord, Paula, is every Groschen gone already?"

He had paused, looking unhappy. "Didn't I give you a hundred Thursday? I'm damned if I know where all the money goes."

"I've told you what prices are. And if you didn't always insist on having wine at dinner—"

"If we can't have a little *wine* once in a while, why—! Darn it, I never have a cent myself."

This was true enough. But she had gone on. "You know my mad passion for shoes, and I haven't had a new pair this year. And it *would* be nice to have an occasional glass of fresh o.j. for breakfast!"

Like many married people they had their own private code. "O.j." was orange juice, "h.o." hangover, and so on.

"Come, come, we're much better off than most people here," he said. "We don't lack anything, and we live very well. Don't worry so much about money—we'll scramble along somehow. Money isn't everything, after all!"

"It is too," Paula said. "Money is the most important thing there is."

Today, this luminous April afternoon, having discovered that they had one hundred forty-seven Schillings, or about twenty dollars, in the bank, she rose and patted him on the cheek. He had just finished two mailers on Transylvania, and had fallen into a doze. He didn't stir. "Well, I've done my work, now I'll do yours," she said cheerfully. Scuttling toward the office she paused for a second to look at herself intently in the hall mirror, and exclaimed, "My Negro lips!" She continued to inspect herself in mock despair. "And if my hair turns any darker I'll look like a tomato within a year!"

He woke up. "Tell me someday why you like to depreciate yourself so much," he said mildly.

"I'll tell you now, you goose. It's because I haven't got a bay-*bee!*" she chanted.

Mason had a different idea. He thought that her trait of self-derogation must derive from her mother, who had brought her up to be perfect in all things. This obviously had not been possible, and the result had been to destroy her confidence.

"A bay-bee!" Paula repeated.

Mason half rose, then subsided. This wasn't a moment for going into all *that* again. Besides her voice had been quite casual, not serious. God, if only they *could* have a baby. Nothing on earth or heaven would please him more. He remembered years back—the agony, frustration, blackness, the long periods when it seemed that nothing could restore her faith in herself, nothing could alleviate this all-embracing, month-by-month, irremediably mounting shock of discovery that she did not conceive. *That* was when they had really come to grips with one another, learned to know the heart within the heart.

But now . . . Mason thought that never in their marriage had he and Paula been so happy as in the past few weeks; never had they been closer. Day had followed radiant day.

In his shambles of an office, such a contrast to the neatness of the rest of the flat, Paula worked an hour. One of her chores was to type out in quadruplicate the dispatches he sent by telephone—often indecipherable longhand notes—which had to be mailed every day to the *Star* bureaus in London, Berlin, Rome, so that each man in the organization knew what the others were filing day by day. There was also Mason's scrapbook to maintain, his accounts with the telegraph and radio office to keep in order, notes to classify, mail stories to check, and clippings to file for his rapidly expanding morgue.

She looked tired, worn out, when she returned to the living room, and they strolled in to dinner. Frau Gertrude produced a *gefüllte Kalbsbrust* and, for dessert, snow cookies with a ginger ice. Mason ate as if he had not had a meal in a month, and then, after coffee, began to go through the evening papers. They had decided not to go down to the Weissenhof that night. With the unexpectedness that was one of the qualities she enjoyed most in him, he said casually, "Paula, you spend far too much time on the accounts and over my files and all that. Let's get a secretary."

"A what?"

"They don't cost much."

Just like the crazy man, not a cent in the world, and now he wants a secretary.

"But what do we need a secretary for?"

"Help with the papers. Free both of us from a lot of nuisance and routine."

She asked herself, When did this bizarre idea get into his head?

"I've been thinking. We could get somebody part-time for two hundred Schillings a month, say thirty dollars, maybe less."

"All right, sweet. What gave you this idea, incidentally?"

"Don't quite know. Maybe one thing was meeting Bishopson. He seemed so, oh, I don't know quite what to say, responsible and efficient, and we're always bogged down in a mess."

"We are not!"

Next day they put an advertisement in the Tagblatt, and what happened then appalled them. Everybody unemployed in Vienna read the Tagblatt, and it seemed that all the cultivated jobless in the city gathered for a collective assault on the Jarrett household.

There was the small man with the shiny celluloid collar, who had once been a clerk in a great embassy, and who told Mason that he had such a desperate hope to get a job at last as a wedding present, on his fiftieth birthday, which was next week.

There was the lank infantry major, A.D., retired, who sat as straight as a baton, who had a tic, and who, after Mason said he couldn't possibly use him, simply sat there, and refused to go.

There was Dr. Emmeline von Waldenau, who had lived quite comfortably on her husband's pension—until the inflation. She knew five languages, and might now have to sell matches in the street. She carried the recommendation of a bank for which she had done some translations after the war; it was so tattered that strips of pale pink adhesive tape held the folds together, like a worn map. "I would have so much liked to enter the mysterious gates of the world of journalism," she sighed, carefully refolding the letter along the taped edges and bowing her way out of the office.

There were young men and women struggling through the university, to whom two hundred Schillings would have meant precious books, or fees without payment of which they could not take their examinations. The young men were the most heartbreaking. Hundreds of them lived in Vienna, many from good professional and civil service families, who were struggling for their degrees in philosophy or law or what-not but who might never, never find a job in the fields they had so hopefully, hopelessly chosen.

Mason was so outraged by the pain of dealing with these job seekers that he decided to hire no one at all, for fear of being haunted by those he would have to disappoint.

❈

The Wallensteins asked the Jarretts to tea to meet their son, Otto, who had just returned from England. The Frau Dozent greeted them. To Mason and Paula she was not only a t.b., true blue, but a t.t.b., true true blue, their highest compliment. She had the habit, when at rest, of holding her head slightly sideways, on a longish neck, with the tendons taut, so that she looked like an inquisitive pert bird. She was youthful-looking, talkative, and chic.

Frau Ingenieur Blohr, her mother, very old now, almost blind, sat in a Regency armchair with a thin, silvery spotlight of sun— from an aperture in the dark crimson curtains—faintly tinting her face, like an old woman in a Rembrandt. The Herr Dozent prowled electrically from guest to guest, restless, energetic. Mason thought that he was the healthiest-looking man he had ever met. Compared to him—Mason fished for a name at random—Mark Thorne, even though robust, looked like a slug.

The Dozent patted Mason on the stomach, as if to suggest tactfully that if he didn't look out he might have to think seriously about taking off a pound or two.

It would be difficult to conceive any two establishments in the same building so different in decor and atmosphere, Mason thought as he observed the Wallenstein salon. He and Paula had converted their floor into something scintillating, open, fresh, but these rooms were closely stuffed, elegant, and closed. A glow came from the silver service on a marquetry table, and the rugs, particularly an old Sennah, had a thick, glossy pile. Paula too was looking about with delight at the Meissen in a cupboard, the heavily interwoven design on the tapestry of the broad bellrope, the sheen on the gray-dappled marble of a Louis XIV console. It wasn't her taste, except the china, but to appreciate it gave her joy.

Nella Blohr scrambled in, fresh, freckled, gave them a school-girlish frown, and, as the Frau Dozent poured tea into exquisite dark rose cups, picked up a book and, her nose in it, paid no further attention to anybody. She sat bent over, her sand-colored hair spilling forward: her knees and toes were squeezed tightly together, her heels outspread. Presently Mason felt that, without giving him a look, she was trying to project herself forward intently so that he would break through and say something to her, or make some gesture

to penetrate her own assumed lack of interest. It occurred to him
to play the same game. He looked at her steadily, amusedly, to see
if he could entice her into looking up even if he said nothing. She
did, at last, and gave him a flashing smile.

Otto was presented. He gave an impression of physical awkward-
ness—a colt. But he was a nice-looking boy, with an open round face
under a pompadour of golden-brownish hair. He must be about
twenty.

There came talk about London, his studies there, and the British
political situation. Paula asked him what he intended to do during
the forthcoming summer, and he said that he was at loose ends,
since plans for a boating trip in the Adriatic, made with a group of
friends, had fallen through because he couldn't afford his share of
the expenses. Mason listened—he talked well, and except for the fact
that he hardened some of his "d's," saying "respectet" for "respected,"
his English was very good. His principal feeling about Mason and
Paula was, Mason sensed, curiosity; after all, nobody else had ever
invaded these cultivated and exclusive premises. What would the
American barbarians be like? Now he talked with animation about
the local theater. He got into an argument with Paula about the new
Lehar operetta, and quickly, suavely, withdrew from his own position
when she reiterated hers. Was he too polite? Or unsure of himself?

Again Otto mentioned that he didn't know what to do for the
next few months. Mason, with astonishment, heard Paula say,
"We're shorthanded and need some help—typing, filing, helping
with the papers. You wouldn't possibly be interested?"

Otto too looked much surprised. "Perhaps I would."

Mason and Paula said their thanks after an interval. Mason
grimaced as soon as they left. "That was certainly unexpected! Whatever put it into your head to suggest hiring *him?*"

"Well, if we are going to hire a secretary we might as well have
an attractive one."

Bleschke was on the phone with a big story when they returned
upstairs. The cabinet crisis had come to a head and Dr. Schober,
the Vice Chancellor and Foreign Minister, who had been largely
responsible for the Customs Union scheme, had been forced to
resign office. The French demanded his head as a price for continued

help to Austria. This would mean violent political turmoil, a new
Austrian government, and unpredictable disequilibrium in the future. Mason blinked. He picked up the phone to call Strothness in
Berlin. Strothness had certainly opened the gates wide with that
call of his a month or so before. What froth, what flood, might
continue to pour out as a result?

8

He caught the train by running hard down the platform; Sandor, on
the lookout, gave him a hand up, and they joined John Dixon and
Vilmos Hestery, the gigantic Hungarian who was Bishopson's assistant. Panting, he unfolded the *Extra-Ausgabe* he had grabbed at the
last moment on the way to the station—a single page of the *Neue
Freie Presse*, a flyer with enormous headlines, which was the way
Viennese newspapers produced extras. The train click-clicked slowly
over the long slanting rails and curving switches, then gathered
speed. The four journalists put their heads together, excitedly reading the paper. The Heimwehr had made a Putsch in Styria.

Quick work, thought Mason. Obviously the Putschists were trying
to take advantage of the disintegration and confusion caused by the
Schober resignation. Strothness certainly *had* set a ball rolling!

"Have I not told you it would happen? Have I not warned you?"
Sandor wiped perspiration from his forehead. "Now is the time of
warfare and destruction. Now comes the time of great catastrophe."

"Oh shucks, Laszlo, it may be over by the time we get there. Incidentally, has it occurred to you that you and I, after Strothness,
probably have a bit of responsibility for what's happening?"

Sandor looked surprised.

"No. You are too American and logical. Events in chain do not
have such a positive, neat relationship."

"What's your theory of cause and effect? What makes things
happen?"

Sandor's smile gleamed. "The cause of everything is everything.
Or, rather, since Einstein and the modern philosophers, the cause of
everything is nothing. Console yourself, Mason. If the Customs
Union story had not been broken by us, the results could now have
much worse been!"

A man named Kohler, one of the dissident Heimwehr leaders, had gathered together a band of peasant ruffians, which had swooped down the night before upon the towns of Bruck and Leoben, and then issued a flamboyant manifesto proclaiming himself dictator of Austria and pledged to renew negotiations on the Customs Union. His revolt was part of a nationwide plot, but it misfired except in Styria; the remainder of the country remained quiet, and Kohler was left holding the bag. His proclamation said that he was marching on Vienna, but the government acted promptly against him. Though the Heimwehr was its unofficial armed force, it could not possibly countenance illegal measures, not to say violence, on such a scale.

All this had become known in Vienna early in the morning, and Mason and his colleagues were hustling down to the scene hoping, in their journalistic way, that the fighting would not be over before they got there. "Dear me, dear me, we shall be late, the train is already late," Sandor groaned. He sat watching and mumbling, measuring the progress of the heavy train, when, reaching the hills, it slowed up puffing and waited at Gloggnitz for the second locomotive it must have to help push it through the Semmering Pass. Sandor had a timetable and map in his pocket. These he inspected carefully as station followed station; he would look at his watch, fumble nervously putting the watch back in his pocket, search the timetable again, and mutter, "Thirty-two minutes late . . . Now thirty-one minutes late . . . We are gaining . . . no. Dear me. Thirty-two minutes late . . . Ach! thirty-five minutes!"

He relaxed and began to chuckle when they started to coast downhill after the pass. "Ha! We will gain time on them now!"

They reached the river Mur. "I ask you, Mason, watch it, the watershed of the river Mur. It will be the chief combat of the war."

"If we don't get there pretty soon, the war will be over."

"I do not mean this war, I mean! I mean the great Italian war to come, when Mussolini, our Lord High Protector, clashes with Germany over the ruins of our poor little Owstria!"

They walked up to the restaurant car, bounced from side to side in the aisle by the rocking of the train. You could buy third-class tickets on any Austrian train, and then, by no more expensive a gesture than winking at the conductor, stay luxuriously rooted in the dining car for the whole journey. It was around eleven in the morning now, time for goulash. Almost all the big expresses had goulash simmering in the pot in the dining car at almost any hour.

"IIa!" Sandor chortled. "Could not something outside explain our slowness? Perhaps the Kohler lads have mined the track! Would it not be wonderful, Mason? I ask you, we are on a Putsch train, and perhaps we will be blown up while I am exoctly with my goulash on the train!"

*

Dismounting at Bruck in the railway yards they found no transport available and walked warily toward the town. Barbed wire was loosely piled up in shimmering billows where the road forked, and a cry came: "Halt! *Nicht weiter!*" A government soldier stuck Mason in the belly with his gun, which had a bayonet on it. Sandor explained that they were newspapermen and asked him to call an officer. Mason felt extremely uncomfortable. The point of the bayonet made an actual small V in the cloth of his shirt. The soldier was a sallow youth who had not shaved that morning and whose Adam's apple, as big as a toad, worked up and down. His hands, with a finger on the trigger, were quivering. But Mason, although nervous, did not feel much outright fear because of a sense that he was an observer to this action, not a participant. He had the foolhardy conviction that this was not his war and he had nothing to do with it and that therefore nothing could happen to him.

An officer, swollen with self-importance, looked at the credentials Mason and Sandor carried and told them to proceed at their own risk. The soldier spat, lowering his gun. Mason breathed. Hestery and Dixon, together with a small group of other correspondents, advanced, and then Mason heard rifle fire—the sound was that of a long whip being struck smartly across a pavement. Shorter crack-cracks echoed, and the officer pointed toward the hills. "There's a little sniping still. Look out."

Sandor, though he took the lead in walking forward, became agitated. Always he had exaggerated respect for authority; his tendency was to obey orders prudently, revere superiors, and overvalue underlings. His father's influence, Mason thought. Controlling himself, Sandor suggested that they make their way to the mayor's office, which would be a natural focus for what news might become available.

John Dixon, wearing plus fours, bareheaded, smoked a pipe nonchalantly, but was pale. Nobody paid the slightest attention to the group of journalists finding their way through the confused crowd of soldiers and townsmen. A squad of infantry clumped down the street with a rough, metallic tramp, and from the woods, more rifle fire came with a *wheee-ish* noise. Then came the sound of a heavy, old-fashioned, rust-encrusted iron pump handle being laboriously crunched up and down—artillery. The government's artillery was firing back. Hestery grabbed Mason by the arm and pushed him aside. Mason looked down. He was astounded. Obviously the man was dead, and must have been killed only a few minutes before. His impulse was not to look again. But he could not resist looking. This was the first time he had ever seen a man killed in military action. The dead man wore blue overalls—a worker. Leaking out on the road was a puddle of brains, like a tomato omelette.

The crack of rifle and machine-gun fire became a spreading, continuous crepitation. Dixon broke for cover, and the others dove after him to the lee of a white plaster Gasthaus. The group, breathless, squeezed through a lattice fence, penetrated into a garden, and, entering the Gasthaus from the rear, emerged into the taproom which faced the central square. Here the scene was astonishing. Young men wearing tall hats with stiff chamois bristles were entrenched across the square and shot wildly toward the Gasthaus, while the government troops, lying on their bellies behind pots of flowers, fired back. But meantime on the terrace of the Gasthaus itself waiters in white aprons hustled in and out bearing platters of beer. Youngsters, to show their courage, dashed out on the square between volleys, circling like skaters, sickle-shaped, their bodies almost parallel to the ground. Stout women in bright green leggings and a miscellany of other townsfolk and sightseers drank thirstily, and, almost as if they were taking sides at a football game, yelled, moaned, or cheered as the rifle fire continued. A man fell, and the nearest waiter tripped, spilling a seidel of beer.

"Owstria, Owstria!" murmured Sandor incredulously.

When the shooting stopped the journalists progressed forward.

They found the mayor's office. The mayor shrieked. He was raving, almost out of his mind, shrieking. Bruck was a peaceful city. There had never been any trouble in Bruck. The administration was solid, clean, respectable. Then this miserable Kohler, this adventurer-thug, this miscreant-criminal, this murderer-lunatic, got it into his head to make this criminal, silly Putsch, to invade Bruck, to gather his ignorant peasant boys for the murderous fantasy of a "march" on Vienna, to issue his fabulously stupid, evil "proclamation," to send his men *shooting* through the peaceful streets of Bruck and Leoben, to start *killing* people, to shoot and maim and *murder* workers defending their homes and women and children on the streets. That was all that Kohler had done. Then when he saw that the Putsch was failing, he fled ignominiously. He had been caught half an hour before in Kapfenberg. He ought to be hanged. But what would happen? He would get a sentence of three or four years from a Christian Social judge and in two or three months would be pardoned and out on the streets again. Treason! Murder! Lunacy!

The mayor shook his head so violently that tears of rage and anguish flew off his face.

The buzz of a small airplane came from overhead and it swooped low as Mason strode out into the square. A soldier aimed at it, moving the rifle with slow precision, but Mason had a sudden sharp intuition and banged him on the arm before he could fire. "Ours!" Mason exclaimed. The plane rose like a gull, circling, dipping, and then disappeared behind a green shaggy bluff. About twenty minutes later Dr. Ricardo Stein and Dr. Karl Tetzel appeared, hanging on the edge of a truck, and pretending to be possessed of perfect equanimity. Stein had flown Tetzel down with him from Vienna. They had not seen much, and Mason quickly filled them in.

Those who, like Mason, worked for afternoon newspapers tried to get through to Drew, who was waiting at the Journalistenzimmer to relay their dispatches, but the telephone lines were down. After lunch one of the mayor's assistants took them to the morgue. One woman had been shot through the shoulder with a dumdum bullet and her lungs had been blown right through her chest. A youthful attendant, his eyes slaty, pulled the blanket off the body. Mason would not have believed that there could be such a wound. Dixon dove for a door, and managed to get outside before being sick.

Mason suggested, "Let's have a look at the hospital." One lad of seventeen was lying there unconscious; he had never been mixed up in politics in any way, but was catching a train for a holiday in the mountains when a mortar shell hit him in the shoulder. He would almost certainly die, the doctor said. A woman moaned steadily. She had been shot in the stomach.

"Oooh! Oooh!" she kept crying. "Take me away! It hurts!"

Sandor and Mason stood over her bed.

"Oooh! Ugh—oooh!"

At that moment, a girl on a cot a few feet away died. Her left arm had been torn off. She was seven.

Mason and Sandor, Hestery and Tetzel, caught the night express back to Vienna. Dixon changed places with Tetzel and flew with Stein. The story was over. Now all they had to do was write it. "Ach, dear me," Sandor said. "I mean, what shall one be able to do?" Never before had Mason seen his forehead white and not red. What would they write? What did the story mean?

Mason, gulping, tried to think clearly. Could this be real? Children with arms blown off? He recollected the refreshment he had felt after the talk with Masaryk in Prague. These events today were a long way off from the life of the mind, belief in progress, in the triumph of right, the conquest of chicanery by principle. This was gangsterism, politics by brute force, smash-and-grabism, infamy. This kind of thing made a mockery of rationalism. What was the point of educating people to be artists or philosophers who believed in the human spirit and the life of the mind when some irresponsible villainy could cause a woman's lungs to be blown out through her ribs and chest?

❋

Mason did not know anybody in Vienna he liked better than Bishopson's man, Vilmos Hestery. Nobody could be with him for ten minutes without recognizing that he had largeness of soul as well as body. He had had a fine career in the Hungarian army, and a quarter of his big neck was shot away; under his jowls shone a patchwork of large glazed scars, which looked like transparent paper pasted on the flesh.

He patted Mason on the knee: it was like being hit by the trunk of an elephant. "You are agitated by what you have seen today. I will tell you a story now." The train was puffing, panting, creaking. "Once a year, every year on June fifteenth, I pray. Carefully I crouch down on the floor, and on these fat knees of mine I pray. On June fifteenth, 1917, I, who had risen to be a captain, led four hundred Austrian troops into action on the Italian front, on the Piave. What did I come out with? Sixty. We were trapped on an island during the advance. The island consisted of sand. No cover. We could not dig into the sand because at twenty centimeters water seeped in. Like so." He held his hands one above the other. "Men dying, blown to bits, fired on even by field artillery at point-blank range, and all we could do was wait till the broiling sun should set. And do you know why? Because Austrians have among other bad habits the very bad habit, particularly bad in wartime, of being unable ever to keep their loud, filthy mouths shut. Every precaution was taken for our offensive that day, every precaution except to keep our God-damned stinking mouths shut. There was not a soldier in our army, or for that matter in theirs, who did not know that June fifteenth was the day for our offensive. Our staff had gone so far as to requisition headquarters in inns across the Piave for our victorious Commander-in-Chief, may his name stink forevermore in hell. The staffwork was so efficient and secret that, it was glorious, even in the Vienna coffeehouses, on the Opernring itself, everybody— and I mean everybody—knew that the advance was to begin at seven-thirty A.M. on June fifteenth. Blab, blab, blab! I saw, in villages where my own men were billeted, *Italian* peasants praying devoutly for the defeat of our offensive—several days before it started. Austrians!" Hestery cocked a snook at the dining car waiter, who drew back startled. "*Dreck!*" Hestery shouted. "*Scheissdreck!*"

Tetzel drew Mason aside when the train started to slide downhill, after the Semmering Pass, making a sound on the smooth rails like *lollipop-pop-pop*. Obviously he wanted to tell a story that might be long. Mason said, "Karl, not now. I want to think out what I'm going to file."

Still teasing Mason, puzzling him, worrying him, no matter what Sandor had said, was the relationship he and Strothness had with all of this.

BOOK TWO

The Bank

V. THE SCANDAL

"Haven't seen the papers yet," Mason said to young Bleschke. "Any news?" The lilacs were blooming now, and the Wallenstein garden bore soft plumes of lavender and white. Mason felt cheerful, large, exuberant.

"Nothing fery much, Mr. Yarrett. The government he is going to push the disarmament bill against both private armies. It's maybe not true but the Presse she says it. Let me see . . . anything else . . . Oh! A small news note maybe—there is a case about graft over caviar in Rumania, and in the Moslem regions of Yugoslavia it is considered to make abolition of the fez and veil."

"That all?"

"Yes, Mr. Yarrett. It's all I haf to the moment."

"We don't have much to write about these days, do we?"

"Not since the Kohler Putsch, Mr. Yarrett."

"All right, ring up again if anything shows."

Mason went through the papers, picking his way carefully to find the verbs. Usually he read the *Arbeiter Zeitung*, the Social Democratic organ, first, because it was a cleanly made sheet, had a concise news coverage, and was written in simpler German than the others; sentences in the leading articles were not, like those in the *Tagblatt* or *Presse*, ten or fifteen lines long. Tucked in an inconspicuous corner he saw something that interested him:

SCANDAL IN FOREIGN PRESS

We have received lately the information that certain journalists, including the representative of one well-known foreign news agency, have been the recipients of certain sums, not small, from an important Vienna bank.

It has been known for some time in our circles that the bank in question, for reasons best known to itself, has begun to make "gifts" to persons in a position to control or influence various channels of information to the world abroad.

Mason picked up the telephone. "Say, Bleschke, what the hell, look at the *Arbeiter Zeitung* on page five and tell me what it's about, will you?"

Everybody used the word "young" for Bleschke and his face was unlined and expectant, but he had to be around forty if the story Sandor told about him was correct. A student in Budapest, he was sitting with antigovernment journalists in a café in 1918; they discussed politics hotly and Bleschke said, "Tisza! That scoundrel! I wish he were dead. Maybe he is dead." And by the oddest of coincidences Count Istvan Tisza, the Hungarian Prime Minister, was in fact dead; he had been shot an hour before. A police spy disguised as a waiter overheard the conversation, and Bleschke was arrested for suspected knowledge of the murder plot. He was quite innocent, but he got seven years in jail.

Bleschke was all but starving when Jim Drew picked him up in Vienna years later. Drew conceived the idea of organizing his own local news service, with the aim of breaking the monopoly on Balkan news held by the various governments; he hired Bleschke to organize and run it, and then withdrew into the background, disclaiming any responsibility. This was the origin of the Danubia Press Service, which had twenty or thirty subscribers now. No one knew whether Bleschke had already repaid Drew's original investment, or if the American still got a share of his earnings, which, at the best, were meager.

Bleschke, with his mellow voice, returned Mason's call in a few moments. "The bank article I had not seen. I think it is nothing much, Mr. Yarrett."

Sandor called Mason a little later. "You have seen a story in the *Arbeiter Zeitung*, page five? Please look at."

"I've seen it, Laszlo."

"Now I ask you, what do you think?"

"Which bank is it?" Mason asked.

"Which bank? You ask, which bank? *Eggs*-cuse me!"

"Not the A.O.G.?"

"Of course the A.O.G. What other bank would it be?" Sandor stuttered. "It is what I always told you, do not trust any bank in Owstria. Ach, dear me, it will be the fireworks soon!"

"Well, if the A.O.G. passed out money to journalists to influence opinion abroad, the next question is—who got it?"

"Exoctly! It is not a pleasant business at all. Of course the story will get no further. No one will dare to print more. It is too libelous, even for Owstria."

"Won't the A.O.G. be mentioned by name?"

"The A.O.G.—by name? EGGS-cuse me!"

"Well," Mason laughed, "if you hear of anybody slipping out a little dough to any hungry foreign correspondents, we haven't paid the rent yet and please give them my address."

2

Little other news was running today, and Mason sent a brief dispatch to Chicago about the *Arbeiter Zeitung* story. It continued to arouse his curiosity. Why should an "important bank" pass out bribes? How had the alleged facts become known? He found it difficult for the moment to concentrate on his backlog of mailers. Mason had a habit, bad by orthodox standards, of hoarding news. He would collect stray inconspicuous items about, say, the westernization of Turkey or political fermentation in Greece, sit on them, wait till some new event made the whole subject live, and then let loose with a full interpretative dispatch. He liked to think that if a reader in Chicago followed him closely, day by day, he would miss nothing really important anywhere in Central Europe or the Balkans, month in, month out. Alert, although the bank story still tickled the back of his mind, he finally got to work on a Polish situationer that needed doing. If he missed a story by cable he tried as a rule to deal with it later by mail, dressing it up with a new approach.

Paula, just out of bed, was leafing through dresses in her closet. There were not many dresses, but the choice was difficult. One of her most beguiling and sometimes maddening traits was her conviction— or simple assumption—that her voice, no matter how muted, even if she were talking from a half-closed closet, would follow Mason around corners and inevitably reach him even through closed doors.

"Mason!" she called, and began to talk.

His office door was open, but he could hear nothing of what she said.

"What was that? Didn't quite hear!"

Silence, then another call.

"Cumshone." This was his way of pronouncing "*Ich komme schon*" —"I'm coming right away." He put down his story.

"I'm lunching with the British and it's going to be very, very dressed up. I've worn the beige to death and I can't stand this black any more. What shall I wear?"

"For God's sake, Paula, did you interrupt my work just to ask that?"

"What could possibly be more important or interesting than how your wife is dressed at a big diplomatic lunch?"

"Wear anything you like. Go jump in the lake. But don't interrupt me at deadline time, you louse."

She made a face.

Mason was having lunch with Donald Bishopson. The affair of the Yugoslav *Ehrengericht* was not yet finally liquidated, as Dr. Stein had said that it ought to be. Mason still had in his pocket the preposterous lengthy letter Drew had written. Mason showed Bishopson the letter and he coughed flatly. The very fervor with which Drew was magnanimous to Markovitch for his retraction vitiated his generosity. "Well, for myself," the lean Scotsman said, "I find this entirely unacceptable."

The more Mason saw of Bishopson the more he respected him. Obviously Bishopson had no special regard for Markovitch, but he held strictly to an attitude like that of an attorney appointed to defend an unpopular cause; he would do it justice, he would see it through. Not by a word did he feel it necessary to give expression to this.

"What should we do?" Mason asked.

"Let's write a different letter, and make Drew sign it."

Together they concocted one.

Gentlemen:

Having read the complete retraction by Dr. Markovitch of articles in the Vienna press translated by him which reflected on the honor of certain journalists, also of their friends and associates, who frequent the Café Weissenhof, and accepting also Dr. Markovitch's complete, unequivocal

apology, I hereby express myself as amply content with this action, and
withdraw my application for a Court of Honor.

Sincerely,

James N. Drew

"I think that ought to do it," said Bishopson.

"I hereby appoint you my trouble-master," Mason said. "*Herr
Schwierigkeitenbeseitiger,* I thank you."

"Your German is getting hot."

Mason took the letter to the Weissenhof, where he found Drew.

"Sure, sure," Jim said, reading it, blinking. "*Macht nichts.* I'll sign
this one if you think it's better."

"Good. What did you think of that bribery story in the paper this
morning?"

"Just a Socialist squawk. Nothing in it. Wouldn't give it a
thought."

Paula said that evening, "Do you love me, sweet?"

"Yes."

"Say it."

"I love you."

"How much?"

He was perfectly serious. "As much as I am capable of loving."

"Tell me again, how much."

"As much as a man can."

"Goodie." She sighed with contentment. "*Too* much?"

"Of course."

She laughed. "What's my name?"

He kissed her, but felt mildly irritated.

3

Now, as a direct result of the Yugoslav *Ehrengericht,* an important
development occurred in the life of Mason Jarrett. He became a Herr
Präsident. Here in this city of titles, this city where every minor
official was a Hofrat or a Sektionschef, he finally received a title himself. No longer was he merely Herr "Colleague," or, inaccurately, Herr
"Editor." Had shopkeepers known it, he now deserved better than the
mythical Herr Doktor they still sometimes bestowed. Mason Jarrett

became president of the newly formed Anglo-American Press Association.

At the Weissenhof one evening Sandor had spoken: "I have now an idea with me. Let us take a lesson from the Yugoslav *Ehrengericht* and organize ourselves. The Union is too slipshod, too feeble, too full of *Schlamperei*, to be of use. Not two-fifths of the membership is honest jo-arnalist. This is also true of the other jo-arnalist organizations. All are full of press agents, Balkan spies, and people who perhaps write one article a year. Let us set up our own organization and include only the legit-imate correspondents of British and American newspapers and agencies, of the most genuine, I mean!"

Mason agreed enthusiastically that this might be a good idea, and sounded out Bishopson. He was dubious at first, and then said, "Well, it will help pass the time, and I daresay will be worthwhile if only because it will annoy the government so much."

Sandor, Mason, and Bishopson set themselves up as an organizing committee, and found that twenty-four correspondents were eligible for membership. Before the week was out, twenty-three joined; the twenty-fourth, Morton Brewster of the Chicago *Tribune*, was absent in India. Opinion was general that Bishopson should be the first president, but he flatly refused the nomination, as did Sandor, and it fell to Mason instead. He was aghast. He was totally devoid of group spirit, and had scarcely ever in his life even belonged to any organization of any sort before. But Paula said, "Oh, let's take it on!" What moved Mason most was his sense of comradeship with his colleagues. They were all members of a community, a colony, and should hold together.

They ticked off the names of the charter members. There were Drew, of course (somewhat lukewarm), Tetzel and little old Dr. Ritter (puzzled), Dixon, Stein, and the three agency greyhounds, the tough, rangy killers. Then Mason counted Hotchkiss of the New York *Herald Tribune*, who had recently had a severe hip injury in a skiing accident (his wife a youthful Viennese, pretty, taffy-colored curls); Allbright, Boston *Times*, whose whole soul was wrapped up in an avant-garde story magazine he and his wife had just founded; Wheatley of the *Daily Telegraph*, the son of an illustrious Oxford mathematician and one of the shyest men Mason had ever met; and

Hanley of Reuters, the red-cheeked Irishman, who was a passionate fisherman, knew every trout stream in Austria and had written a standard guidebook to the country.

As Bishopson predicted, the new group came under official suspicion at once. The Press Bureau of the Bundeskanzleramt, Chancellery, took a distinctly cool view. The word promptly went around that the British and Americans, led by this newcomer Jarrett, were operating against the rules, changing hallowed procedures, stirring up ferment, and improvising something totally unnecessary. Something must be *behind* this movement of the Anglo-Americans, somebody must be launching it with ulterior motives, it could not possibly be just what it claimed to be, there must be something underhanded involved. The presumption that it could be a perfectly innocent organization, devoted solely to the mutual professional interest of its members, was, on the face of it, absurd.

Mason called the first meeting to order in the Journalistenzimmer, and became concerned when he saw Drew's face—dark, troubled, and, above all, hurt; he kept moistening his lips and gulping silently. Clearly, Drew thought that the presidency should have gone to him, and was seeking to conceal his mortified chagrin. The vice presidency, they had decided, must go to somebody British, since Mason was American. The choice narrowed down to Wheatley and the representative of the London *Times*, and Wheatley won after a stiff little tussle. The British took things like this very seriously. Dr. Ricardo Stein became secretary, and the giant Hestery treasurer, so that a Viennese and a Hungarian both had posts.

Mason and Wheatley talked together for a minute. Mason knew that they were bound hereafter to have a good deal to do with one another, and he wanted to know him better. How, he wondered, would he be able to penetrate Wheatley's shyness, his predisposition to uneasy silence? But was it merely shyness? Was he striving to isolate himself because he had something to conceal? Mason observed him carefully: tall, tweedy, stooped and bespectacled as only an Englishman can be, with teeth that had lacked dentistry in childhood and loose, ashen hair. Mason said that they would have plenty of problems. After a painful delay Wheatley emitted the single word "Quite!"

The meeting broke up. As Mason walked out Drew pushed past him and snapped gruffly, "Well, so long, fixer!"

4

Before the week was out the name of the A.O.G., Allgemeine Österreichische Gesellschaft, did appear prominently in print in connection with the bribery story, in spite of Sandor's prediction. What was more, it was mentioned in the most respectable and bourgeois of all the great Vienna dailies, the esteemed *Sternblatt*—and one of the few that didn't owe the A.O.G. money. The *Sternblatt* repeated the *Arbeiter Zeitung* story, called the A.O.G. the A.O.G. by name, asked what its motives could be in passing out money to journalists, and demanded an explanation and investigation.

Sandor and Mason met at the Weissenhof. "They wouldn't dare mention the thing so strongly if it wasn't true," Mason said. "To come out so flat they must know something. How do you suppose the *Sternblatt* came to take it up?"

Sandor said, with a gleaming, ironic smile, "Because maybe somebody was stupid. Because maybe somebody on the *Sternblatt* did not get *his!*"

Mason would not have been surprised had the A.O.G. issued a lofty denial of the *Sternblatt* story, or refused to dignify it with any rebuttal at all; but he was amazed when, two days later, every newspaper in town carried the following item:

The Direction of the A.O.G. informs us: Reports in the press about "bribery" by the A.O.G. of certain journalists are incorrect. The facts in the case are these. Because of the considerable amount of foreign capital invested in the A.O.G., it was deemed proper and necessary that public opinion abroad should be correctly informed about the bank's affairs, particularly since the affair of the Customs Union. To cover expenditure in this direction, the sum of 300,000 Schillings was authorized. It concerned only the formation and functioning of an efficient foreign information service. The public of Austria was not influenced in any way.

Mason whistled. "Three hundred thousand Schillings is forty-three thousand dollars, and you could practically buy the Ringstrasse for that and decorate it with cupids!"

People began to ask questions. How had a Socialist newspaper got the news first? Who was the representative of the "well-known foreign news agency"? Did the A.O.G. spend the money on correspondents who lived in Austria, or abroad, in setting up "an efficient foreign information service"? Three hundred thousand Schillings might, if it were divided up into small sums, have gone a long way. Who got what?

"Three hundred thousand Schillings!" Sandor echoed. "Enough to corrupt the body politic of Owstria, let alone a few miserable of scripters!"

Mason scuttled home and filed another story.

5

The Weissenhof had, as was inevitable, a lively evening celebrating the formation of the Anglo-American Press Association. Mason brought with him two visitors who had descended on him, a professor of economics at Columbia and the editor of a newspaper in Omaha, and Paula had in tow an artist, Hofmeyer by name, who was doing the sets for a new production of a Schiller play at the Burg Theater. The journalists were jubilant. Somehow Mason, the nongroup man, had fired them all with a collective spirit.

Tetzel took him aside. "It is not a public matter yet, but you will recall our preliminary talk recently and I had no chance for further conversation on the train. I must tell you—I have decided now that it is absolutely necessary to quit my job."

"Take it easy. Wait a while. Maybe whatever it is that's troubling you"—Mason hesitated—"won't seem so important after a while." He must not give Mia away, or Paula either. Obviously Karl did not know that Mia had talked to Paula.

"You know of no openings at all?"

"I'm afraid not."

Of course what Tetzel hoped was that Mason himself might offer to take him on as second man. But Mason had no budget for that, and besides he had just hired Otto, who, Paula thought, had better be disguised for a while as "entertainment" on the expense account.

He went on: "I don't know a darned thing, but I'll keep my eyes open." He hesitated again. He could say just so much, but not a word more. "From what you said last week I gather you've had some sort of row with Thorne. But, listen, even if Thorne acts like a crazy bull in a china shop sometimes, he isn't too bad a guy at bottom. Be patient. Maybe he's rough and obtuse, but for God's sake don't do anything rash. Think of Mia!"

"Actually he has given me a small raise, but that is part of the trouble. I would like to tell—"

Mia approached them from where she had been sitting at a different table. Clearly she suspected what Karl was talking about and did not want him to go on. Obedient to her command he drifted toward the chess games. She ground her knuckles into her eyes and an outer disk of her metallic marigold hair shook loose. She acted as if she cared nothing of what anybody might think of her.

Mason described the bribery scandal to the editor from Omaha, who laughed. "Sounds like small potatoes to me. We have politicians back home who steal the city hall!"

Mason said, "This is a town where they take the concept of honor very seriously." He expounded this theme.

"Honor among thieves, no doubt!" the Omaha editor exclaimed. "You're getting Europeanized, Mr. Jarrett!"

Mason protested, hunching his shoulders, hiding his chin, and making the gesture of shadowboxing with him.

Drew came in with the news that the French had at last succeeded in bottling up the Customs Union project by having it referred to the Hague Court, which would kill it. Erji inquired of him, "Where tonight is Cawntess?"

"Stumbled into a coat hanger, has a black eye."

Nobody had seen her since the evening with the Hendersons.

Mason and Drew saluted one another; Drew had, it seemed, recovered from his spurt of jealousy and Mason, who had never harbored a grudge for longer than ten minutes in his life, gave him every opportunity to lead the talk. Drew, rolling his heavy head around, clucking with his tongue, set out to impress the visitors. Jarrett might be president of the Anglo-American, but he, James N. Drew, still bossed the Weissenhof. Pontificating, sipping his *Einspänner,* he talked with vivid authority.

"My dear sir," he turned to the professor from Columbia, "the present situation has headaches for everybody. But wasn't it smart politics by Buresch to relax tension by lightening up on the new tax bill. That Buresch! No one else in the government has any sense." (In a few weeks Drew might be calling Buresch, the new Chancellor, all kinds of fool and idiot, Mason knew.) "Jove, the Socialists are on the run, I tell you!" (But his tone showed no special enmity to the Socialists; he was simply delighted to make a prophecy and gloat in the anticipation of having it come true.)

Mason had a sudden memory of seeing Drew in the Journalisten-zimmer soon after meeting him for the first time. On his desk was a great slippery pyramid of unopened mail and a heap of newly arrived copies of the New York *Times*. No man could be poorer than Drew, but he paid thirty-two dollars a year out of his own money to get the *Times*. Neglecting the mail, he busily clipped from the pile of *Timeses* all the Central European and Balkan news they contained, which he then did not read. By the physical effort of clipping them, he had justified his subscription. Mason had wondered then why Drew kept on staying in Vienna, year after interminable year; he was an excellent newspaperman and could have easily found a much better job in London or New York. But Vienna gave him the frame he needed. The key to Drew, as Mason gradually became aware, was ego, moreover ego expressed in the public sphere. He wanted to be famous, he wanted to be a great man. And this was why he stayed on in Vienna, because he had established his position, his platform, here; there were no other claimants to his throne.

"Going back to America when I'm fifty," he had boasted. "I'll have finished with Europe then, and my intention is to run for Senator from Tennessee!"

Now, Drew busied himself with the *Abend-Nachrichten* bulletins, while Hofmeyer, Paula's friend, told stories about the antiquated procedures of the Burg. Paula had met him at a dance. He could not stop looking at her. He tried to catch her eye invitingly and to reach for her hand under the table.

Mason, hearing a slight commotion at the door, looked up and saw a tall, soldier-straight man with a russet hussar's mustache enter. He recognized him at once—this was the person he had seen that night in the Koenigen. But what was he doing here? Pink of face, glossy in approach, the man advanced straight to Paula, bent low, and stood next to her, poised, urbane, but looking a little foolish. Paula was startled, then pleased. With a swift private glance at Mason, and while still politely giving her attention to the man, she said, "Hope I've got your name right—what name do you go by? Willi? Ah, the Archduke Willi," and introduced him around the table.

Chairs scraped.

"This then is your husband?" the Archduke proffered, bowing gravely to Hofmeyer.

"Oh, no!" Paula's laugh was clear. "*That* one!" She pointed Mason out. Hofmeyer was disconcerted.

"Ah, I think I have seen him somewhere before," said the Archduke, surveying Mason.

Never before had an authentic Archduke visited the Weissenhof. Herr Julius, the Oberkellner, took this honor in his stride, merely muttering as usual, "*Bitte, meine Herrschaften, was ist gefällig?*" and was the only person to address the Archduke with the term *Durchlaucht*; the other waiters stared. Willi sat himself down next to Paula, and described pleasantly a shooting trip from which he had just returned; then, in a tone that lay just outside the province of impertinence, he talked to her with an air of intimate confidence, and wanted to know where she bought dresses, who her coiffeur was, what her favorite perfume was and exactly what she had been doing all that afternoon.

Sandor drifted in from the Journalistenzimmer and, stunned, recognized the new figure at the table. In a loud whisper, which everybody could hear, he questioned Erji, "What is happening here around!"

The Omaha editor addressed a series of questions to the *Stammtisch* about the succession states. Drew yielded to Mason, saying, "Of course Jarrett has just come back from Prague, and saw Masaryk there," but he said this in such a proprietary manner that it seemed that he was appropriating Mason's own story, with pride in the accomplishment of a protégé.

Interested, the Archduke looked up. What did these gauche, untutored Americans know about the realities of Central Europe? He himself was entirely nonpolitical; he had to be; nevertheless he and his family had been dispossessed by the new countries and he knew a good deal about them. Mason spoke up in answer to the Columbia man, "The common denominator in all the succession states is how to make freedom viable. Nationalism has won, but will it work?" The Archduke was impressed by the crispness and accuracy of this, and glanced at him with an approving eye.

Promptly the question was posed: What did His Imperial Highness himself think would be the future of Czechoslovakia, Poland, Rumania, and the other countries which had sprung up out of the broken body of the old regime? On the Archduke's proud and exempt face came an expression of slyness, good humor, and intelligent aplomb.

He replied with a single word, "Humpty-Dumpty!"

6

Not another word was printed in Vienna about the A.O.G. scandal after the bank issued its *dementi*. Probably it had taken the unusual step of making a public denial partly in order to shut the newspapers up, since nobody could print a word now except at the grave risk of a libel suit. What a person had to have now was detailed proof, evidence, the goods. Mason wanted even more than before to stay abreast of the story. He was impatient to do something about it, but first, following his instinctive temper, he thought he should dig up background on the bank itself. The best available source would be Sandor, and he arranged to meet him at the Imperial the next morning.

Crossing the Ring he dodged between the trams, colored red and cream, which seemed drowsy and aimless; sometimes they ran in pairs, or even triplets. At the Imperial the revolving door, scraping against a rough mat, squeaked. Erji, drinking her first *Weisse Ohne* of the day, exclaimed, "Oh, why, why did you and Paula go home so early last night? Sandor and I, we went to Koenigen with Archduke and the Tetzels, girl with monocle, she sang, and Archduke he volz with Mia one solid half hour. Then with me," her voice was invincibly good-humored, "five minutes!"

Sandor said, "Now, to begin . . ."

The *Stammtisch* here at the Imperial was quite different from that at the Weissenhof. Its members were senior correspondents, men of

long-standing reputation and international renown. People like James
N. Drew or Dr. Heinrich Ritter almost never came to the Imperial.
Along with the journalists, important bankers, diplomats, and politicians were to be found here; news sources came to the Imperial
as well as newsmen. Sandor and Jarrett were the only correspondents
of American papers who belonged to both the Weissenhof and Imperial circles. Several German correspondents, who had been accustomed to high-hat Mason, surveyed him this morning with
considerable interest, and even appeared to have mastered his name
at last; this was of course because he had been an important actor in
breaking the Customs Union story.

Two or three of the men who gathered here, like Van Der Martens
of the Brussels *Monde*, Paul-Henri Milleforte of the *Grand Parisien*,
were political reporters of the highest rank. They would no more
touch a feature story than eat garbage. They filed column after
column every day on politics, just politics, the more abstruse the
better. They were politicos themselves. They were as expertly erudite
in their fields as an American sports writer covering a World Series
in his. Several—this had been a surprise to Mason—were paid substantially bigger salaries than any American or British correspondent
in Vienna, and were known all over Europe for their authority. Mason
had also been fascinated to find out that the Germans among them
did not sign their dispatches but used cabalistic symbols—an asterisk,
a dot in a circle, a cross in a square. Devoted readers of their newspapers knew their work so well that they recognized these symbols
and could identify the men behind them.

Here at the Imperial a *Nussbraun* cost one Schilling ten, twice
what it was at the Weissenhof. The journalists met in a low-ceilinged
room where a mirror covered an entire wall. "The better to see with
who is coming in!" Sandor had explained.

Mason ordered his *Gabelfrühstück*, second breakfast; invariably he
had a *Schinkenbrot*. A *Schinkenbrot* was, at the Imperial, an exquisite
object; to have called it merely a ham sandwich, which it was, would
have been an impertinence. On a slice of extremely soft rye bread,
with a flaky crust, heavily daubed with butter, were superimposed
three or four slices of delicate Prague ham, to equal the thickness of
the bread; atop this lay a scroll of gherkins. This structure was sliced

crosswise into half-inch strips, but one edge of the bread was not cut, so that the strips remained attached to it. Gently, expertly, the connoisseur of *Schinkenbrot* pulled off slices of the sandwich strip by strip, leaving the far edge of crust to the last. Mustard, far too crude a substance, was not served.

Sandor leaned forward. "We will begin in the early years of the last century." He described how the A.O.G. was founded as a rival to the great Rothschild banks, like the Credit Anstalt; how large British interests and the distinguished French banking family, the Descazes, invested in it; how it had set up an interlocked system of private banks in cities like Frankfort, Brünn, Rotterdam, and Cracow; how it financed kings, archbishops, and counter-revolutionary leaders (though not on the scale of the Rothschilds); above all how it made a specialty of buying into industry—cloth, foodstuffs, armaments, railroads, wine, tobacco, asphalt, indigo.

"People they say the Louvre it is in Paris," Sandor said. "There is another Louvre here in Vienna. It is the town palace of Count Alfred Diederbach-Aflenz, the head of the family which still controls the A.O.G. Inside is one of the most wonderful private art collections in the world. Of the art treasures the most beautiful is Count Alfred's iron safe; in it are placidly reposing twelve million of gold crowns!"

Concurrently came dealings in foreign exchange for various governments. "I tell you the truth on it. The A.O.G. simply could not handle all the business itself. There was too much business." So a man named Schiller, who was close to the old Emperor, founded another bank, the Donau (Danube) Finanz-Verein. Competition between the two became bitter, particularly when the imperial family threw most of its enormous business to the Donau. "Then, I ask you, what comes next," said Sandor, his palms up, "war in 1914!" Both the A.O.G. and the Donau helped finance the military operations of the Austro-Hungarian government, sold munitions, and built factories that made cheap uniforms and shoddy boots for huge profits. But after the war came sharp, painful readjustment. All the big bankers, like the Rothschilds with their Credit Anstalt, found themselves serving, not an empire of fifty million people, but a shriveled little rump of a country cut down to six million. Did they take heed, reduce operations, cut salaries, retrench? "They did not!" Sandor exclaimed. Vienna, the A.O.G., and the Donau all had one thing left, if nothing else, and this they intended to maintain at all costs—pride.

Sandor sipped his *Nussbraun*. Mason said, "What next?" Erji put down the French novel she was reading.

"Came next the inflation. The A.O.G. and its rivals rode it out largely by buying further into industry. It was the easiest thing in the world to make money. All they had to do was borrow millions at a fairly low rate of interest and lend it at a very high rate to the new mushroom industries struggling in the succession states." Sandor paused. "What is a bank? It is a ben-EV-olent institution that borrows money at three per cent and lends it to someone else at eight, twelve, or fifteen per cent."

"Where did they get the money?" Mason asked.

"From England and America, of course!"

Those were the days when youthful British and American bankers, with such nicely modulated voices and such pretty polka dots on their neckties, with such a razor edge to their white collars and such a glabrous pink to their smoothly shaven cheeks, and with such a profound knowledge of elementary high school economics, stood row by row on the street corners of Central Europe, where interest rates were higher than anywhere except the more sensational South American countries, and pleaded with the local banks to take their money away.

"And then," Sandor went on calmly, "the Donau Finanz-Verein did something it ought not to. It failed!"

That was a little over a year ago, just before the Jarretts came to Austria. Bankers in America and in England, tightening up after the Wall Street crash, called some of their Central European loans. So the Donau had to call its loans. But industry along the Danube was going to pot. Mines were drowned, textile mills were strangled, and a cemetery of dead factories marked the region between Prague and Bucharest. Hotels, timber companies, cement works, failed. The industries could not collect their own debts, and could not repay the banks.

"Well," Sandor said, "I can tell you there was such a crisis as you cannot listen to. Old Rohrbach, he was the Chancellor, he had to do something. He knew nothing about finance. He thought a bank was something you put money into."

He was, however, a shrewd old man. Clustered around him were the doomed Donau directors, fatigued by gesticulation, and his own advisers from the Austrian National Bank. Something had to be done at once. If the Donau simply went under, without warning, panic would be so great that the currency might slip, other banks would fail, and the whole country might collapse. "I wish," said Dr. Rohrbach to his associates, "that you would find and bring to me Count Alfred Diederbach-Aflenz."

Sandor wiped blisters of sweat from his forehead.

Count Alfred, even though his family had controlled the A.O.G. for generations, was not much interested in banking. He was a small, frail-seeming man, with thick glasses and a waspish voice, whose abiding passion was postage stamps; his collection was the largest in the world next to that of King George V. As avocation, he went shooting; he shot quail, partridge, duck, pheasant, chamois, stags, and bustards. It took most of the day to find him in Carinthia. Dr. Rohrbach's men took him to Vienna without giving him time to change from his hunting clothes, and he arrived at the Chancellery at midnight, blinking.

"Count Alfred," said Dr. Rohrbach—they had been friends for years—"you are going to save me, the Donau, and our beloved Austria." It was, as a matter of fact, not a bad bit of business, strictly in the A.O.G. tradition. Count Alfred was no fool, and he knew quite well that the crash of a fellow giant like the Donau could damage his own bank severely. Besides it was rather a neat thing for him to buy up the old Donau on such advantageous terms. He knew all about the snubs administered to his father by the court, and his humiliating quarrels with the upstart Schiller; he remembered, from his youth, unpleasant episodes in the long struggle between the A.O.G. and the piratical Schiller interlopers. And now! He strode across the Donau ruins! It seemed, as Count Alfred thought it over, that this was a nice new bit of A.O.G. history he was writing. "Very well." He blinked. "Give me the papers, and I will sign them."

So to the people of Austria the first news of the Donau crash was that there was no crash. But now the A.O.G. had two hundred million dollars more to supervise in Austrian industry.

Mason thanked Sandor and kissed Erji on the cheek, then sauntered up the Ring. His thoughts went back to the bribery scandal. Why, why, would a colossus like the A.O.G. bother to bribe a handful of journalists at this particular time—why, why? Of course three hundred thousand Schillings meant no more to the A.O.G. than thirty cents meant to him, but even so, why? Suddenly he had a small, pointed intuition. It seemed too fanciful, too grotesque, to accept rationally; however, there were times when an element in a situation could be smelled. Mason, pacing along, caught himself in the physical act of sniffing; and he had a very good nose for news.

Passing the Majestic he thought of something he had neglected— to pay Klaus, the concierge, his retainer for the month. Klaus was one of his tipsters and news sources. He telephoned him once or twice a week, reporting on what prominent Americans were passing through Vienna and communicating nuggets of local gossip. As Mason approached him he was simultaneously, effortlessly, reassuring an American woman about her tickets for the Opera that night, listening to an angry complaint on the telephone from somebody on the seventh floor who couldn't get a window open, steering one impatient client toward the cashier's desk, and telling another that the best small night club in town was the Koenigen ("Be careful of those pretty *Animierdamen*, and be sure to hear the songs of a girl who wears a monocle"). He accepted unobtrusively one hundred Schillings from Mason Jarrett and slipped the bill into his hip pocket not only with the utmost fluidity and grace but with a gay, secret flourish, while fixing up somebody's tickets to Budapest.

What an operator, Mason thought. His confidence and euphoria were as conspicuous as his efficiency; he positively radiated skulduggery and cheer. Mason liked and admired him very much.

"Klaus, you slipped up on a man named Henderson two or three weeks ago, a Congressman from Illinois. Not important, but you shouldn't have missed him."

"He wasn't in the house."

"Yes, but I'm assuming you're keeping an eye on the other big hotels too."

"Of course, Mr. Jarrett. Sorry about the Congressman. I hope the gnädige Frau is well."

"She's fine."

"Too bad about that pup," Klaus said.

"Yes. What happened to it?"

A month ago a rich, hysterical German woman living in the hotel had given one of her dachshunds to Klaus and he in turn had offered it to Mason for a modest price, but he had had to say no because of Paula's tendency to hives. It was one of the prettiest Dackels he had ever seen.

"You'd never guess," boomed Klaus, escorting Mason to the door. "I give it to Johann, our night porter, and, guess what, Johann is making a pile of money out of him—putting him out to stud, one hundred Schillings each and every time!"

Mason looked impressed.

"Johann offered me a twenty per cent kickback, but I didn't want to take it. Poor little dog is all wore out."

7

"Mason," exclaimed Sandor over the telephone, "it has now reached a step. You will have to make action, I mean!"

"I don't want to hold the bag for all the crooks in town. Let's be careful."

"Names are being bandied about. I do not know what to say about. In our own defense, you must make action!"

"All right, we'll call a meeting of the Anglo-American. Let's fix it for Friday at three o'clock."

Mason's impulse, in spite of the commotion now rising about the bank scandal, was still to proceed cautiously. He didn't want to lead a crusade. It would be more prudent to wait till the other journalists' associations took some decisive step. After all the Anglo-American Press Association was not directly involved in the affair, and if he made an official protest the other organizations might smugly retire, leaving him to fight alone.

But the telephone rang again, and Mason heard Bishopson's hard voice. He coughed at the top of his throat.

"Jarrett, my man Hestery is just back from the Parliament, where all the deputies are talking about who got the A.O.G. money."

"It's embarrassing," Mason said.

"It's damned embarrassing. Old Unzicker said that if the A.O.G. was setting out to bribe journalists he hoped they'd have the good sense to bribe the important ones. For instance the heads of the big international agencies or big American bureaus, for instance the New York *Register*, that is, me."

Mason whistled.

"I want it stopped," Bishopson said.

"Well, let's stop it. I suppose we ought to try to get some assurance from the A.O.G. that none of us is involved. I'm calling a meeting Friday, and we'll talk it over then."

"It may not be so easy," Bishopson concluded, "to get the assurance we ought to have."

The meeting Friday caught the American and British correspondents unprepared. The Anglo-American had, as a matter of fact, scarcely begun to function as an organization. But Mason had gone so far as to set up headquarters in the Majestic, and had worked out plans for a fortnightly lunch like those given so successfully in London and Paris by the analogous press associations there. To each he hoped to invite some local dignitary or political personage passing through town for an off-the-record talk. This would be unprecedented in Vienna. Even his own members had difficulty in grasping the idea. But although he had no confidence at all that the project would work out (who in Vienna had ever even heard of the concept "off the record"?) he was determined in a vague sort of way to give it a try.

He rapped with a spoon on a coffeecup and called the meeting to order, only twenty minutes late.

"I understand the A.O.G. has undertaken some adventures in the world of journalism," he began lightly.

His attempt at humor was not appreciated, and an agitated discussion began at once.

There were several distinct groups within the Anglo-American, he soon perceived. Most of the British stood for moderation; they conceded that the scandal might have serious repercussions, but saw no reason to lose their heads. The Austrians and Hungarians were those most disturbed. It was they, after all, who had the worst jobs and got the least pay; if any correspondents had been corrupted, they were the ones who might most easily have been expected to give way to temptation. The native Viennese who worked for British and American newspapers, like Dr. Seitz of the New York Times, Dr. Karl Tetzel, and little old Dr. Heinrich Ritter, churned with indignation. What they wanted was to bring a lawsuit. They would sue the A.O.G. and force it to publish the names of journalists who had been bribed, thus clearing all the rest.

Mason said from the chair, "Dr. Stein, give us your opinion; is a suit technically possible?"

Stein said that no suit could easily be brought at the present stage. The A.O.G. had mentioned no names but had merely stated that it had spent three hundred thousand Schillings for the purpose of "influencing" sections of the foreign press. The expenditure might have been perfectly legitimate. The bank could, for instance, have set up a public relations bureau—in Paris, say—that nobody in Vienna knew about, or it could be operating from London or New York. Stein was shouted down. No, no, everybody protested, no, no; specific individual bribes must have been given to specific individual correspondents right here in Vienna! "But how can we prove this?" Stein demanded. Talk raged.

Bishopson had an idea. Get in touch privately with Sir Reginald Whitt, who was a British director of the A.O.G.

Jim Drew had an idea. Form a deputation to call on Count Alfred Diederbach-Aflenz, and demand an explanation.

Hotchkiss had an idea. Go to the Arbeiter Zeitung, which had first published the story, and ask the editor what other material, if any, might be available.

Dr. Ritter had an idea. The voluble Ritter was spluttering with defiance, anger, and outraged innocence. Let the Anglo-American join forces with the other journalists' associations.

The correspondent of the Daily Express of London had an idea. Let them get some Socialist member of Parliament to bring the matter to the official attention of the government.

Mason let the talk bubble, and then put forward an idea of his own: why not try an unexpectedly simple approach, namely to write a letter to the A.O.G. asking for nothing but a clean bill of health for all members of the Anglo-American Press Association? If they got this, and there was no reason to assume that they wouldn't get it, the affair would be automatically closed so far as they were concerned. Mason's suggestion was adopted, and Bishopson and Stein proceeded to draft the letter.

It read:

Gentlemen:

We have seen in the press reports to the effect that the A.O.G. has distributed sums of money to various journalists, together with your explanation and your admission that the sum of 300,000 Schillings is involved.

We must say that we are not entirely satisfied that unpleasant rumors naming various correspondents may not continue, and we wish therefore respectfully to ask your cooperation in regard to our organization. As you may see from the subjoined list of our 23 members, we include all the principal correspondents of British and American newspapers in Austria, and our services cover the entire English-speaking world and much else. None of us has ever had any connection with your bank or its designs for publicity. In order that the highly disagreeable rumors may not spread further, will you not kindly give us your assurance that no one of our members is in any way involved in your distribution of funds.

Yours faithfully,

Mason E. Jarrett

Mason was disconcerted by the reply he received a few days later:

A.O.G., Direktion, Wien.

Highly Well-born Sir:

In reply to your esteemed letter addressed to our Generaldirektion, we permit ourselves to answer you. In the communiqué of the A.O.G. published recently in the Press it is pointed out specifically that as a result of aforementioned circumstances, no influence to the Public resulted. We believe that with a repetition of this declaration all legitimate interests, including those of your organization, are satisfactorily served. With this statement we wish to close the matter.

Accept, honored and highly well-born Sir, assurances of our deepest consideration.

To Herr Doktor Präsident Jarat
Wien.

The signature was illegible, and, as was usual in Austrian business letters, had been scribbled between the lines of a rubber stamp.

Sandor spent an hour or two browsing in the *Arbeiter Zeitung* building, hoping to find out how the story had originally become known. A man in the auditing department of the bank, by name Gstottner, a vehement Social Democrat, had worked for nineteen years in the Donaubank before it was taken over by the A.O.G., and after the fusion the A.O.G., in its noble beneficence, paid him exactly one half of what he had received before. Gstottner had three children to support, and his wife was ill. Every day, with calm and deliberate scrutiny, he explored every iota of A.O.G. business that came before his eyes; he checked, and then remembered, certain figures. When these, taken together, became suggestive, he got in touch with a close friend and party comrade who was a sub-editor on the *Arbeiter Zeitung*, and told him what he knew.

Mason, wandering into the café, decided to give voice to the small idea he had had a few days before, and approached Jim Drew.

"I've been taught to think of the A.O.G. as if it were the House of Morgan, but you don't suppose it could be in any kind of trouble, do you?"

Drew blew through his closed lips, making a rough purring sound. "My dear sir, the A.O.G.'s paper is accepted in every city in the world on the same terms as government treasury bills."

Mason went to Sandor, who said in turn, "Don't be fanciful, I mean! The current A.O.G. dividend is fourteen per cent."

Inveterately and shamelessly American, Mason thought that he might try another direct approach. He walked over to the A.O.G. building, sitting on its hill with proud impregnability, and sent up his card to the Generaldirektor. He had a shock. Above all, the Viennese were polite. All else might leave them—glamour, riches, power; but politeness, never. Yet Mason was shown out of the office of the secretary of the Generaldirektor after exactly two minutes as coldly as if he had been a beggar intruding into the Hofburg to ask for an audience with the President of the Republic.

"The matter of the press fund is closed," the secretary said icily. "Kindly contain your remarks to the news department of the government."

Mason trod down the marble steps, with their shiny brass railings, and reached the street. A passer-by bumped into him, and he was surprised to discover that his fists were clenched. So the matter of bribing journalists was closed, was it! So the A.O.G. was going to lord it over them, was it! Once more he surveyed the baroque mountain of the building, and saw again its windows, with their strange violet glare, flash and glisten in the sun; they were oblong eyes, which said, "You are watching us, but do not forget that we are watching you as well." He came closer, and standing there for another moment, as he had stood before, he weighed the great inanimate structure, measuring it, as he sought to look through the warped violet windows, observing the heavy cornices and ornate moldings and the confident arch of the porte-cochere. He looked down, and saw his own slanting shadow on the pavement. People trod on it.

Once or twice as he waited, heavy automobiles drew up to the bank, and quick-stepping men gave astringent orders to their chauffeurs. Mason was not a fighter by instinct or desire. But he said to himself, Guess I'll have to call another meeting of the Anglo-American pretty soon!

8

At a reception at the Rumanians, the Jarretts ran into Von Traum, the German whom Mason had telephoned the night the Customs Union story broke. He invited them to tea the next day. He had a job with a Pan-German publicity organization as well as a minor newspaper, but he gave forth the air of a man expecting something much bigger to turn up. There was a curious tang to him, which seemed to be associated with a white scar cutting into the side of his upper cheek, as if the wound had recently been disinfected although it must be years old; above the scar, just over the shaft of his spectacles and below a thatch of thinning ocher hair, the veins stood out like the delta of a river. When he talked and became excited the scar showed whiter and the delta became red.

Von Traum welcomed Mason and Paula with his quick, forced

flat smile. His establishment was small and pared to the bone of any ornament—almost icily clean and orderly. There were no servants. Von Traum summoned his wife; his voice was that of someone used to command, not without asperity. Frau von Traum replied from the kitchen that she would bring tea in a moment. Served plainly in thick white cups, it came accompanied by the most inexpensive cakes. Von Traum, darting forward, shoulders quivering, reached for a brittle small cookie and ate it as if he were hungry. The tea was the color of molasses.

Paula chatted with Frau von Traum, a shy woman, tense with nerves. Von Traum's conversation was angry, eager, and defiant. Mason thought that this man must have been an officer, and asked him, "How long were you in the war?"

"Four years, four months, four days! In other words, I saw it all. I commanded a machine-gun company in France. I was wounded four times, gassed once. It was a long war. But, *Herrgott,* I would like to have another!"

"Why?" Paula asked, shocked.

"To bring order."

"Well, we're all pacifists in our family."

"To be a pacifist is to be an ignoramus!"

Mason rose. "Come now—"

"Excuse me," said Von Traum. "I beg your pardon. I meant nothing personal."

Must be careful not to lose my temper, Von Traum thought. This Jarrett is the man who knew all about the Customs Union well in advance, he must be handled carefully.

This man is a true fanatic, Mason thought. Not like those Heimwehr lads in their sleek uniforms, slippery, lax, bulging around the belt.

"As a matter of fact," Von Traum resumed, "you Americans have had rather little experience of war, and hence do not understand its realities."

"We didn't put up such a bad show once we got to Europe in 1917," Mason said mildly. "In fact we licked the pants off you."

Von Traum attempted with spirit to rebut this, but Mason changed the subject by asking him about his career in journalism.

The German sketched his history. His wounds disqualified him from the Reichswehr after the war, he had no other profession but that of arms, he could find no work in Germany. Here in Austria he had found a minor job in journalism, but his paper could pay him little. He was making a study of German economic penetration along the Danube, from documents, and he desperately wanted a brief trip to the Balkan capitals to give it firsthand color. For fifteen hundred Schillings he could do the whole job. His paper didn't have fifteen hundred Schillings. There wasn't fifteen hundred Schillings in all the world! He talked of other work he might be doing, for instance a survey of secret rearmament in Hungary. He was living only half a life. All his potentialities were being wasted, chafed away, on his miserable little job, which he had to keep—and be thankful for—to live.

Frau von Traum said, "Gustav, not so loud, I beg you, please!" Indeed his voice had risen.

Carefully Von Traum did not mention his secret connection with other institutions in the Reich.

Mason asked, "What do you think of the political situation, Herr von Traum?"

"In Germany? As to politics, the Nazis have a hundred and seven seats in the new Reichstag, six million votes. And ten years ago they were nothing, five years ago a handful. Watch them, like the little trees, grow and grow. In two, three years, Hitler will rule Germany. It is as certain as that the sun will rise tomorrow."

"How about Austria?"

"Austria!" Von Traum's face became sardonically beatific. "Austria!" His eyes rolled under their lids, his hands flapped downward from the wrists, he tilted his head back, his scar shone purple, he laughed and laughed—to indicate the absurdity of Austria, the hopelessness of Austria. Then he clicked his teeth. "The Austria of today is a historic monstrosity, as you well know. It is an impossibility. It has no future, not even a present, because of the economic load crushing it to the ground. It is a joke, a nuisance, a bad dream. The Customs Union might have saved it, but now all hope in that direction has been cut off. Signs grow of economic discontent. Credit is very, very tight."

"Can the Italians help?"

"The *Italians?* Mussolini will be swallowed up by the Führer!"

Frau von Traum poured more tea, and Von Traum, reaching into a cabinet, brought out a bottle. "A glass of Tokay? The Hungarians are a light-minded people, totally inferior in most respects, but they produce a pleasant wine."

His voice became less crackling. "Now enough of politics. Let us discuss the things our so-beautiful Vienna really cares about. Have you seen the Schiller revival at the Burg? It is good, perhaps a shade dull, but soundly German. I am told that the Josefstädter has a new comedy, decadent but not unamusing, but I have not seen it—the author is, I believe, Jewish, and so is the director. The cast, however, is said to contain good Aryan actors." He turned to Paula. "And are you fond of music, *gnädige Frau?* Yes? I go to the Opera incessantly—in the cheapest seats of course!" He rubbed his hands. His expression held a combination of envy and voluptuousness.

"Of course I have little patience with much of the modern repertoire, but give me *Meistersinger!* Give me anything of Wagner —ah!" His eyes glittered. "Do you ever, incidentally, go to the Rheingold Bar on Silbergasse? The Austrians, they are foolish and drink too much beer, but the piano player there is excellent—and not Jewish, incidentally. It is rare to find someone non-Jewish in the entertainment world of Vienna. Now I am curious to ask about your friends—what people do you, such representative Americans, see here? Who are you fond of among your colleagues? Dr. Sandor? Ah! Of course he is one-quarter Jewish on his mother's side, and I believe that his wife has gypsy blood—impure."

Mason bridled.

So did Paula, who said warmly, "Let's not get into talk about the Jews. My husband and I both like Jews, admire them, and see a lot of them constantly." There came a second's uneasy pause. Frau von Traum looked frightened. But Von Traum decided not to lose his temper. He said merely, "Ach, *gnädige Frau*, if you bear with the course of history a little, you will see. But as I have said, you Americans have so little experience of the realities of life. In particular you know nothing about the occasional necessity for violence!"

Mason had a sudden thought. "Ever seen an electrocution, Herr von Traum?"

"A what?"

"An electrocution—I saw one in Chicago once."

"Don't tell that horrible story, please!"

Mason proceeded: "They led the convicted man to the chair with his legs shackled, but his arms were free. He flipped a cigarette contemptuously at the warden. Then they strapped him into the chair, tight, very tight. A kind of helmet concealed the prisoner's eyes, but his teeth separated into a tight, leering grin. The executioner turned a wheel, not a switch, click-click, softly. Slowly a flush rose from the exposed chest of the prisoner to his throat and face, and then the body began to swell—perceptibly swell—around the shoulders and chest as the face turned bright red. There came a whiff of smoke from behind the neck and then we could smell it, like a steak on a grill. The doctors took a look, and the warden said, 'I pronounce this man dead.' The straps were released. They had been pulled so tight that the body didn't quiver at all when the current went on, but as they were released the entire swollen body deflated at once, and out of the man's dead mouth came a loud Whooooosh!"

Von Traum's face took a taut, nettled look. He said contemptuously, "I talk of nations, wars, great national movements. You discuss an episode in gangsterism."

Paula intervened: "That's just the point. Gangsters sometimes take over nations. You're a Nazi, aren't you?"

❋

The Jarretts had to hurry home because they were expecting Dr. Ricardo Stein to dinner. They had asked him to bring anybody he chose to make a fourth, but he preferred to come alone. Mason had never seen him with a girl. He thought that he was probably a typical European in thinking of marriage as something inextricably bound up with his career and who hadn't found a girl yet whom he considered to be the proper wife for a rising young lawyer-politician-journalist.

Paula just had time to change her clothes ("I look a wreck—will

that green thing be all right?"), peek in the kitchen and say hello
to Frau Gertrude, notice that they would be having a chestnut flan,
mit Schlag, for dessert, pat the table linen approvingly, and light
the candles, when Stein arrived.

Mason liked Stein more and more, if only because they had
similar tastes. The Jarretts had visited his flat recently and found
there many of the same books they had, identical music on the
piano, and the same death mask of Beethoven on a wall near the
same Van Gogh print of a wheatfield under boiling clouds. Besides
he was such a sunny person, even if his manner was sometimes
doctrinaire.

Stein had flown back that afternoon from Linz, where a prolonged
strike was tying up a big chemical factory. The owner, financed mostly
by the A.O.G., had about as much understanding of labor as a mill
operator in England in the early eighteen-hundreds, Stein said. The
situation seemed insoluble. Rather grittily, he put out his hands
helplessly and half laughed. "Of course the propertied classes, even
now, actively want unemployment," he proceeded. "Owners of
enterprises, capitalists, deliberately stimulate unemployment, and
indeed unemployment is to some degree a convenience to them,
even a necessity, because it ensures a cheap labor market, labor reserves. Capitalists deliberately make unemployment in order to be
able to get labor cheap."

Like a bullet, these sentences shot into Mason's impressionable
head. Was that true? Really? How disgraceful! He demanded enlarge-
ment of the idea. Stein talked easily and fluently, and Mason became
excited. Stein's curly blond hair shone in the candlelight, his smile
was vivid and responsive, and he listened well. What a nice guy,
Mason thought. He's attractive, Paula thought.

The telephone rang with its shrill long-distance bleat.

"Hello? Phil! Yes—how are you?" Mason made a gesture to
Paula, indicating that this might be something important, because
Hazelwood seldom called them. "No, I haven't heard of it. Sounds
rather fishy to me, but I'll check up. Yes? . . . . All right, if there's a
story in it, I'll call you back. . . . Yes, we're fine. Paula, top of the
world. . . . Thanks. . . . So long!" Hazelwood wanted to know if
there could be any truth in a report reaching the Quai d'Orsay to

the effect that Hitler was making a secret trip to Austria. Would the Austrian government let him in?

"Hitler is very dangerous," Dr. Stein commented. "He is by no means a joke, as our complacent government seems to think. That is partly because he too is a socialist. Oh yes, Nazis are socialists too. That is one of the things that make them so dangerous. They preach a fraudulent and poisonous kind of socialism that makes false promises to the little man. The idea that a gang of big Rhineland industrialists produced Hitler by giving him some banknotes in a back room is a serious misreading of history."

Mason asked Stein if the Social Democrats in Austria would try to form a government now that they were in a technical position to do so.

"Hardly! We don't believe in suicide. If we formed a government, the Clericals, the Heimwehr, and the pan-Germans would unite against us. We wouldn't last ten minutes."

"If you don't believe in suicide, why do you let the government take your arms, the Schutzbund arms, away from you?" Paula asked.

"We don't believe in arms," replied Stein with his sunny smile. "We believe in reason."

"But you have to defend your own right to exist, don't you, if your opponents deny that right by force?"

Paula had put her finger on a touchy spot. "Ye-es," Stein said, taking off his glasses and polishing them. "Ye-es, but we are democrats, we base our entire structure of policy on the good sense of the common people. Our whole belief can be summarized in one word—education. We believe in gradualness, in evolutionary growth, and we continue to grow steadily and satisfactorily. Give us time, give us education, and in a brief interval—what are five or ten years in the whole historical process?—we will command an absolute majority. Probably we shall come into power two or three general elections from now. In the meantime, we are content to wait and do our work, to hold fast to our position. We let the country more or less take care of itself, while holding on like tigers in Vienna, where our position is secure."

"But I thought you were supposed to be a revolutionary party," Paula said.

He looked up at her brightly, appreciating the pertinence of this remark. "That's more or less a thing of the past, because nowadays, barring occasional strikes and the like, we represent workers in work."

"But suppose there aren't any more general elections," Mason cut in. "Hasn't the Heimwehr gone on record for a totalitarian state like Italy? Doesn't it want to make a dictatorship?"

"The Heimwehr got a hundred and fifty thousand votes in the last election. We got two million."

"But that's just it!" exclaimed Mason. "They know they haven't enough votes, therefore they will be tempted to use force."

"We will repel them by the power of public opinion. Moreover, the government isn't quite as bad as we sometimes think. For instance, it put down the Kohler Putsch."

"There may be more Putsches coming. Why don't you forbid these Heimwehr mass meetings in Vienna? There's one tonight right here in our neighborhood. You have the authority within the municipality, haven't you?"

"My dear Mason, what ethical ground would we have to stand on, democrats ourselves, if we used the weapons of the Heimwehr or the Nazis and forbade them free speech? We believe in free speech for everybody."

"Even for your enemies, even for those who wouldn't give you free speech if they were in power?" Paula asked.

"Certainly."

Paula, her little finger arched against her lips, shook her head. What he was saying was magnificent, but in the modern world it seemed extraordinarily quixotic and unreal.

Mason thought, How refreshing! He compared Stein with Von Traum. Here's a man who believes in reason.

9

Mason checked the Hitler rumor with Regierungsrat Dr. Hohnstedt at the Chancellery the next morning. There was nothing in it. Hohnstedt was, to his surprise, quite friendly, and even gave him enough details about the official Austrian attitude toward Hitler to make a small story. Mason called Hazelwood, wrote a dispatch, and gave it to Otto, who was working out very nicely, to copy and transmit. But most of his mind was still concentrated on the A.O.G. affair. What could he do to hurry up procedures? *How* could he break through the burcaucratic deadlock?

Paula sailed in after lunch ardent, fervent, even if a realist; he kissed her and she slid away, head atilt, saying, "You'll never guess what I've been doing."

"You've been having a drink with a man."

"How'd you guess? Y-E-S." Amusement, a touch of impudence, frank confession were mingled in her voice; the whites of her eyes flashed, matching her teeth; she was pleased—proud, too, of Mason for catching her out.

"Who was it?"

"The Archduke—Willi."

He waited. It was the atmosphere of Vienna, the city itself, that made the A.O.G. business—and much else—so hard to grasp.

"Don't look so alarmed, you funny." Her laugh tinkled. "I was having lunch at Erji's—their little boy has whooping cough by the way—and whom should I run into in front of Sacher's—obviously he had been having a fine lunch too—but our friend Willi, the Archduke, himself. He walked with me as far as the Imperial, and suggested a cup of coffee. So we had one."

"I take a somewhat dim view of this. He was probably lying in wait for you."

"Oh, I'm sure of it."

"What did you talk about?"

"My glove size."

Mason made a face.

"Seriously, he's very nice. He likes to flirt and he makes slightly outrageous remarks, but he's interesting and well informed. He was extremely polite about you, and said that he always has bad luck—whenever he has designs on a pretty girl he meets the husband too and then likes the husband better. I've asked him to cocktails Tuesday."

"I see through him as clearly as through a glass wall. He's after you."

"Well, he goes about it with a certain courtliness."

Mason was slightly nettled. "I don't think you'd have the faintest interest in him if he weren't an archduke."

"I'm not sure of that."

An ironic gleam came into Mason's eyes "Snow leopard, he's just trash."

For the next day or two Mason was totally preoccupied by the A.O.G. affair. Paula found herself alternating between oversolicitude ("Darling, you look troubled—what's the matter?"), which bored him, and being at him all the time. Invariably, when it was she who was cross, she began the conversation by saying, "Are you cross? Why are you so cross?" He became restless and out of reach, wondering why he had not learned earlier a maxim that should be learned soon in all marriages, namely that women are insatiable; give them the Kingdom of Heaven, and they still want more.

One afternoon Mason mixed a drink and eased himself down on the sofa beside her. Obviously something bothered her. He had seldom seen her so on edge.

"What do you want to be?"

"Baudelaire."

He laughed. "What do you want to do?"

"Live with a musician for a year."

"If you weren't married to me, whom would you like to be married to?"

"Keats."

"Didn't he need a maternal type?"

It was Frau Gertrude's day off, when, as a rule, they had a bite in some café nearby, but tonight Paula wanted to cook. He groaned. She disappeared into the kitchen and there followed a series of small catastrophes. She used nine eggs unsuccessfully in an effort to make Hollandaise, and even managed to scorch the artichokes; then the steak caught fire, and burst into flames. Mason tramped into the kitchen through jets of smoke, pulled the grill out, and put out the fire.

He shouted: "At least you might learn to cook! You've almost set the house on fire! And what are those egg shells—what were you trying to make? Why don't you start on something simple? Eggs cost a quarter each! You can't even toast a slice of bread!"

"Oh glory, everything happened all at once and I just got confused."

"You love good food and you're one of the few women I've ever met with a genuine palate—why can't you cook?"

"You don't have to be able to paint like Velásquez to enjoy Velásquez!"

A stopper. He looked black.

Before bed she rocked in anguish at her dressing table, head hidden in crossed arms, groaning.

"I was six days late, and it's the first time *that's* ever happened! I've been hoping against hope all this week. Now I suppose it's just impossible, it won't ever happen, I give up! Hopeless, hopeless!" She looked at him with fierce indignation. "But you don't care! You don't care a bit!"

"I do care."

He moved toward her.

"Don't be so darned considerate! It's not sympathy I'm looking for!"

He waited.

"If you *did* care you'd be denouncing me, not trying to give me comfort. You'd say, 'You are not a whole woman, because you cannot conceive. You are defective, useless, a monster, not a woman at all, because you cannot conceive!' "

Not for an hour did she become quiet.

But the Jarretts were not among those unfortunates who had to destroy each other to prove their love; they did not hoard trophies, spiritual trophies, in the form of crushed souls, to assert domination; their marriage was not a process in which continuing affinity could only be proved by incessant quarrels; they did not, out of weakness, take pleasure in the wounding of the strong.

The next morning Paula smiled at him, "Your eyes are the brownest brown. But your mouth is terrible. It smiles three different ways."

It was her way of making up and saying that she was sorry for the scene the night before.

❈

Sandor said, at the café, "You have heard the news about your friend Von Traum? He has been appointed correspondent here of the *Völkischer Beobachter*, one of the key Nazi posts in Owstria!"

10

Now, to Mason's satisfaction, the A.O.G. scandal left mere journalism, and entered politics. The Social Democrats brought the affair to the floor of the Chamber, and after an astringent debate the Finance Minister of the Austrian government was compelled to promise a complete investigation.

In the town, on the streets, in the coffeehouses, the scandal became personified, crystallized, in the form of a list. Individuals had been bribed; the A.O.G. must at least know to whom it had given money; therefore some kind of list must exist. Many citizens, full of *Schadenfreude*, were torn between embarrassment and gleeful satisfaction at the obvious discomfiture of the A.O.G.; many did not know whether to rejoice—or not—at the bad luck of the journalists said to be involved. Dozens of names were being mentioned by this time. Nobody's reputation was safe. Ah yes, old Nierstein, that shady, decrepit correspondent of the *Orakel*; he must have got his, all right! No wonder the dignified foreign editor of the *Eklipse* had bought a new Steyr automobile the month before! A long way three hundred thousand Schillings might go. Friends in coffeehouses tittered and winked, and certain old acquaintances began to avoid each other. Almost the only men who were never mentioned at all, Mason gathered, were the three outright, acknowledged crooks who sat on the fringes at the Weissenhof every evening, Zeissman, Orlovsky, and Tinkham, whom nobody in his right mind would ever bother to bribe because they had been bribed by everybody already. One story even said that Zeissman had approached Sandor asking him to use his influence to have him put on the list! Mason grunted.

After another acrid scene in Parliament came a formal statement from the Finance Minister, the esteemed Dr. Bach-Dengler. He admitted that a list existed, but refused to publish it. Instead, according to a decision of the cabinet, the list would be submitted to

the Central Institute of the Vienna Press, for further investigation
and report. How characteristically Viennese, Mason thought. Such a
clumsy and obvious way to try to bury the whole matter! The list,
the Finance Minister proceeded, would continue to be secret to
the public at large, but the A.O.G., moved by its customary public
spirit (a touch of irony in the Minister's tone?), had agreed to
submit it in confidence to this professional organization, in the
province of which the whole matter was now put; action would
follow when a report was made. The Central Institute of the
Vienna Press would, if any of its members were found guilty, dismiss them and they would presumably lose their jobs. The other
journalists' associations (there were, incredibly, eight in all in
Vienna) could then do likewise, if any of their members were involved. Until the Central Institute of the Vienna Press concluded
its investigation the government and the A.O.G. washed their hands
of the whole business.

"Lord, we ought to see that list," Mason said to Bishopson. "Anybody's name might be on that damned list."

"Aye, and whether they're guilty or not. Ever heard of an easier
way to frame a man?"

But this was not what was worrying them. Neither were fools,
and the thought had come to both by this time that perhaps some
member of the Anglo-American had been bribed.

✳

The President of the Central Institute of the Vienna Press was
a certain Herr Hofrat August Zoltan, a slippery, compact little man.
Most members of Herr Zoltan's organization were not foreign
correspondents, but editors, reporters, and copy readers on the
local newspapers. Why, then, had this particular organization been
charged to report on the A.O.G. affair, since the affair was supposed
to involve foreign correspondents? Well, Sandor explained, the
Zoltan group had a semiofficial status, under the thumb of the
government, and representing the press as a whole, could the more
easily deal with—or hush up—the entire affair. What would the
technique of investigation be? Through an Ehrengericht, of course,

Sandor said. Another *Ehrengericht!* Mason held his head.

The majority of Zoltan's members were *local* journalists, yes; but some of these, it happened, represented foreign newspapers as well. Thus they might, in their capacity as local reporters, be attached to the Zoltan group, while, as foreign correspondents, they could at the same time belong to one of the foreign correspondents' organizations. Of these latter, the biggest and most important was the Union, to which Drew had appealed in the matter of the Yugoslav *Ehrengericht;* next came the Gesellschaft, which was venomously jealous of the Union; then the Reichsdeutsche Presseverein, composed exclusively of correspondents of German newspapers; finally the newly born Anglo-American; the others didn't matter.

Mason had an idea, and called a meeting of the Anglo-American. He proposed that he, as president of the Anglo-American, should get in touch with the three other chief presidents, whereupon they would jointly call upon Zoltan to demand details of the list from him. This proposal was adopted, and Mason, after much frustration and delay, got the grudging consent of the other presidents to meet with him. Duly the four presented themselves to Zoltan.

Gatterburg of the Union: an oily fellow with thick-lensed glasses, slightly greasy, and alert hands which he rubbed together continually; he worked on space for a French agency, and had not had a regular journalist's job for years. The presumption was that he made his living mostly by being president of the Union; he was quite possibly a blackmailer, and was the fond head of a large, indigent family.

Old Pflug, the president of the Gesellschaft: a gray man, whose mustaches curved down so that he seemed to be chewing them perpetually; once, many years ago, he had been deeply involved in Serbian politics and even today he could recall the names of successive Serbian Prime Ministers long before the war; he sat for hours on end at the *Stammtisch* of the Imperial, hunched over a charred cheroot and telling of the time when—when he had not been president of the Gesellschaft.

Dolliner, of the Germans, an altogether different type: softspoken, intensely cultivated, intensely disillusioned. He had been a poet once. He was no longer a poet. He had represented his Frankfort newspaper for years in Moscow after the war, and his wife was Russian; he played the violin well. He seldom had time to play.

Zoltan, with his button-shining eyes, his hair like patent leather, passing one palm smoothly crosswise over the other, welcomed the four presidents in his office in the Telegrafenamt, above the Journalistenzimmer.

My goodness, I've never seen anything like this, Mason thought. This is really too Viennese and childish. The conversation was indescribably unreal. An old man whose pen scratched in conflict with wiry hairs from his own beard leaned close to a block of paper and laboriously, with extreme deliberation, wrote down a longhand record of what everybody said, while muttering, "Ah . . . um . . . ach . . . brr . . ." Gatterburg, Pflug, and Dolliner all made speeches twenty minutes long, in which they artfully maneuvered for position; when, with infinite deviousness, they at last reached the point at issue and actually dared to mention the list, they did so with exquisite circumlocution, giving the impression that they were describing an altogether abstract problem in quite a different century and world.

Each president was accompanied by an attorney. Mason's was Stein. It was Mason's turn at last.

"Look here, gentlemen, I'm not sure I've understood everything you've said, but I've caught the drift, and Dr. Stein will fill me in later if I've missed anything. I want to make my own point very simply and briefly." He waited for the longhand stenographer to catch up. "I've come here today for just one thing, and I imagine that all of you want the same thing. My organization, which consists of all the correspondents of British and American newspapers in Vienna, wants nothing more than a simple assurance that none of us is involved. We can get nothing out of the A.O.G. or the government, our honor is impugned, and we want to be cleared. That's all."

The others, except perhaps Dolliner, were shocked by such directness. Old Pflug had talked twenty minutes, saying nothing, because he had expected to bring up Mason's point, which indeed was also his point, in another speech at the end of another twenty minutes—

if it became necessary. Gatterburg too gave Mason a hostile glance, and began to grumble. Only Dolliner looked friendly.

A fantastic thought flashed through Mason's mind. It was entirely possible that Pflug and Gatterburg, also Zoltan himself, were themselves guilty of the misdemeanor they were investigating. Pflug, Gatterburg, and perhaps Zoltan might very well be among the journalists whom the A.O.G. had bribed. They themselves were probably on the list! Here they were, adjudicating on an affair of honor, the end of which might lie no one knew where, and the judges themselves could easily be among those who had been corrupted! Such hypocrisy is beyond belief, Mason thought.

He controlled himself, saying again to Zoltan, "I repeat—that's all I want, formal assurance that nobody in the Anglo-American is involved."

"I cannot give it to you, Herr Präsident."

"Why not?"

"Because," Zoltan said, "we are embarking on this *Ehrengericht* in circumstances of the strictest confidence, at the request not merely of the A.O.G. but of the government itself. The list is private, secret, and confidential."

"Does that mean," Mason asked, glad to get the thought out at last, "that some of my men are on the list, and that you refuse to let me know about them?"

Silence came to the room as Zoltan stared at Mason coldly and the stenographer's pen busily scratched. At last Pflug said, "No personalities, I beg of you, Herr Präsident."

"Mr. Jarrett," stated Zoltan, "kindly restrain yourself." Gatterburg nodded. Dolliner maintained silence.

"Well, my God!" Mason, the edges of whose eyes had become bloodshot, exploded in a loud voice. "What on earth *is* going on here?" He turned savagely on Zoltan. "What, may I ask, is the point of this meeting? Didn't we arrange to meet here in order to ask you, Hofrat Zoltan, you, precisely the question I've just asked?" He turned to Pflug, Gatterburg, and Dolliner. "Why aren't you backing me up? What we came here for was to see the list. You, and you, and you! If not, at least to find out if any of our members are on the list. Isn't that correct? We want that damned list! We cannot permit

you, Hofrat Zoltan, to make an investigation in secrecy on matters
of this sort that may concern us intimately. We cannot permit you
to play with the names of our men in your bloody confounded
Ehrengericht. What about us? We're in the dark! Black dark!" He
was becoming inarticulate with rage. The pen scratched. "By God,
you'll never put this kind of thing over on me!"

Gatterburg and Pflug made new speeches twenty minutes long,
in which they sought once more to evade the point brought up so
indecorously by the uncouth American, while having to agree that
his point was justly taken. Then Dolliner spoke up and supported
Mason firmly.

To all four presidents, Zoltan made the same reply. It was impossible for him to divulge to any human being any names on the
list. The rules of the *Ehrengericht* as operated by his organization,
the Central Institute of the Vienna Press, forbade it. It would be
contrary to the desire of his eminent friend, he might even say colleague, the Minister of Finance. It was contrary to the desire of
the Press Bureau of the Chancellery of the Austrian Republic, as
represented by Herr Minister Dr. Wimpassing. It was, finally, contrary to the desire—he lowered his voice slightly, as if in reverence—
of the Generaldirektion of the A.O.G.

"Now, listen," Mason snapped when Zoltan had concluded. "You
have the list in your pocket, haven't you? Let's cut through all this
nonsense. I'm going to ask you one plain, simple, direct question.
Are you going to let me see that list, or not?"

"It is impossible. I cannot."

"Then," Mason said rudely, "I think you're a scoundrel, and I'll
fight you to a finish."

11

The next day Zoltan sent Mason a letter deploring what he called
the slight misunderstanding of the afternoon before. The letter expressed to Herr Jarrett, as a fellow president, the most profound
apologies for the unfortunate course the conversation had chanced
to take. Now Herr Präsident Zoltan, calling to mind the great esteem
he felt for Herr Präsident Jarrett, had decided to make a slight
amendment to his position. True, he could not give Herr Jarrett
a copy of the entire list. That, for reasons already gone into, was

out of the question. But he could, since Präsident Jarrett seemed to have become so unnaturally exercised about the whole matter, formally assure him that no members of the Anglo American Press Association were involved in the corruption affair of the A.O.G. *who were not also members of Herr President Zoltan's Central Institute of the Vienna Press.* Nobody was accused of corruption who did not belong to Zoltan's group. That was why he, Zoltan, had been given the list. Nobody *exclusively* a member of Anglo-American or any other organization was involved at all.

Mason snorted. Now he had something concrete to go on at last. He got in touch with Bishopson and Stein, and they checked through the membership list of the Central Institute of the Vienna Press. Only one man in the Anglo-American was also a member of the Zoltan organization. The man—Mason became agitated—was Dr. Heinrich Ritter, the little sparrow of a man who spat when he talked and to whom he had given twenty Schillings the night the Customs Union story broke.

※

Tired, Mason took a stroll in the garden. The great tree with its double-twisted trunk had burst into a foam of white blossoms. He chatted for a moment with the old gardener, a man who could make roses grow, so it seemed, by whispering to them. In the bower behind the forsythia Mason encountered Nella Blohr. Her hair was pretty and her cheeks freckled and she had a heavy mineralogy textbook under her arm. In the calm light he saw the color of her eyes.

"Been studying? It's nice to study in a garden."

"I overheard you talking to the gardener. Your German really is awful, isn't it?"

"It's a language I don't like. I get bored trying to chase down the verbs."

"Why don't you take lessons from Otto, instead of having him clip and file all those old papers for you?"

"What I do with Otto is my own business. You're a sassy little puss, aren't you?"

Her eyes were level, appraising. Was she daring him to make some gesture?

"I think I've learned something else about you. You're a rebel, and you're full of tricks."

"Everybody in my family likes you," said Nella, "but I'm not sure I do. You're far too controlled."

He leaned forward, grasped her shoulders, and kissed her straight on the mouth, hard.

She twisted, squirmed, and scampered away.

✳

Mason had his weekly batch of news notes to do today. He wrote two quickly—one about hordes of grasshoppers in Central Hungary so large that they had stopped railway traffic, the other about a record price, $35,000, paid for Chaplin's *City Lights* in Prague. Now he must decide finally what to do about old Ritter. He called him, and a hollowish voice on the telephone replied, "Dr. Ritter has been called suddenly, urgently, to Budapest. I do not know when he will return."

Irritated, frustrated, Mason tried to think out what new step to take. He felt beaten down. The labyrinthine quality of Vienna had vanquished him. He drifted disconsolately into the living room, where Paula, who had been thumbing through the last *Vanity Fair*, looked at the clock; it was ten minutes after five. "Where's Tetzel?"

Regularly, on Thursdays at five, Karl came to give her a chess lesson. Unlike most Viennese he was always punctual, and after another quarter of an hour, she felt a jab of worry. Mason called Tetzel for her; no answer at home, nor could he be found at either the Journalistenzimmer or the café.

"Don't worry about it, he's busy chasing some story, or is up to something else and didn't have a chance to phone," Mason said. But neither he nor Paula could keep from being concerned. For the past week both Karl and Mia had seemed to be aching with strain, as if they had become unendurable to each other.

"Mason!" said Sandor on the telephone after dinner. "I beg you, come, come to the café at once. There is news so terrible . . . shocking . . . I cannot deal with alone!"

Mia Tetzel had killed herself that morning. She had taken thirty of the little white bullets that shoot sleep into a person, not just one or two.

VI.   THE BANK

Breakfasting with Herr Kommerzialrat Dostal, the new Director-General of the A.O.G., were two of his closest associates, Dr. Hermann Treuwalt, the bank's principal finance man, and a certain Hofrat Paultraxl, who was responsible for what were called "external" contacts. Dostal, thoroughly civilized, a man of penetrating intellect, but who made the mistake of being contemptuous of persons less rich ("Eh, I could buy *him* ten times over!" was one of his favorite phrases), knew both Treuwalt and Paultraxl well, and trusted neither fully. In particular he was well aware that the Hofrat was a slippery fish. They had risen together over years in the bank's hierarchy and had been the principal operators in the recent reorganization and the decision to go all out for new industrial commitments in Germany, if possible under the protection of a Customs Union; but Dostal was certain that Paultraxl would seize any opportunity to knife him if it could be done without serious risk.

"Very well," Dostal said, summing up the discussion. "Agreed on the pensions matter. Agreed on the new investments in Brünn and Bratislava."

"I have certain reservations in regard to Brünn," said Paultraxl.

"That I know. But since we face today the first full meeting of the new board, it will be prudent if we three at least present a picture of close harmony. Now, Treuwalt, I would like your estimate of our general picture in relation to the Austrian National Bank."

Leaning forward to listen with care, Dostal pushed back a strand of his rich, chocolate-colored hair.

While Paultraxl buttered another crisp *Semmel*, Dostal, passing him the honey, observed him unobtrusively. A man skillful in diplomatic maneuver, Paultraxl maintained well the complex relationship of the A.O.G. to the government, the Ministry of Finance, and the National Bank. He thoroughly earned the $105,000 a year the A.O.G. paid him. But, even though his position demands it, Dostal said to himself, he plays too ostentatiously the role of an itinerant Talleyrand. Paultraxl, plausible and alert, was always seen at the important legation parties and the receptions at the Hofburg and Ballhausplatz; he shook hands with a person carefully, greeted the person with the precisely correct degree of warmth, and never forgot a face or name. I can easily get rid of him if he becomes unmanageable through too much ambition, Dostal thought. I can make him Austria's delegate to the finance committee of the League of Nations.

Treuwalt concluded his remarks about the National Bank. Dostal said, "Would you now kindly bring us up to date on our commitments in dollars and sterling," while thinking, as he surveyed him, Once a parvenu, always a parvenu. Look at that nose of his, virtually scraped off by the grindstone. Whereas Dostal had come of a rich family, Treuwalt was a poor boy who went into the Civil Service (he was at the top of the lists in the 1913 examinations), and became indispensable as a technician in the Finanzministerium. Treuwalt was a bachelor who lived for nothing but the A.O.G.—and the $95,000 a year it paid him.

He concluded his remarks, and lit a pale, velvet-skinned cigar.

Dostal rose. "No more business, eh? Come, gentlemen, come."

Dostal's villa stood on Peter Jordanstrasse, about half a mile from where Paula and Mason Jarrett lived. The three bankers took their places in the Generaldirektor's gaunt limousine. It was now 9:15. The car reached the A.O.G. at 9:32. The Herr Direktor admired promptness. Outside the bank the old porter, who had served the A.O.G. for many years, and who had white whiskers like those of the Emperor Franz Josef, stood poised and alert. The car rolled up the hill, a traffic policeman whistled shrilly to clear the way, pedestrians hopped, and the porter leaped forward from the curb. Generaldirektor Dostal and his two associates were inside the bank in half a minute and walked with a hard rapid pace to their offices. Dostal's staff rose and stood at attention as he entered. Herr Direktor Dostal was something of a martinet.

"Dostal is a machine," Paultraxl muttered to himself on reaching his own office. "Nothing more than a machine, and hence susceptible to breakdown."

Dostal has too many interests, he is wearing himself thin, Treuwalt thought with satisfaction, as he too reached his desk.

Sylvanus Dostal was, in truth, the hardest-working man in Austria. He believed in industry. He believed, in fact, in two kinds of industry, his own and those in Central Europe he had purchased. He owned the cement works in Wiener Neustadt, a small arms factory near Linz, and the briskly rising new automobile company in Brünn. Ringing for his principal secretary he prepared for the day's duties and tallied up his score on yesterday's stock exchange: this was always his first act every morning. Business in general was not good, but he was a cool, careful speculator and continually made money; in fact, next to the head of the House of Rothschild and Count Alfred Diederbach-Aflenz, he was probably the richest man in the country.

The Generaldirektor proceeded to conclude his preparations for the board meeting at ten-thirty, and took a minute off to put in a call for a horticulturist; his hobby was growing roses. Meantime he went over the list of directors scheduled to be on hand. There was Fischer, the A.O.G.'s specialist in industrial loans. Few liked him; none questioned his ability. There was Eckmuhl, cold as a glacier, who had come to the A.O.G. from the Donau. They earned $80,000 a year each. (Too much, Dostal said to himself, with his big slug of a nose quivering.) Then several of the foreign directors, whom Dostal had entertained luxuriously at dinner the night before, had arrived for this special meeting, including the senior representative of the Descaze dynasty (corpulent, aggressive) from Paris, Dr. Pepperkorn from Leipzig (foxy, a big plunger), the Czech munitions man Probaska, two Hungarian aristocrats (ancient, exquisite, brittle), and of course Sir Reginald Whitt of Simms and Sons, Ltd., and the Bank of England.

Dostal's nerves were ragged from overwork, and deep furrows, like slanting grooves, ran from the sides of his nostrils to his thin lips. But ragged nerves had never interfered with his efficiency. Today the agenda included several widely different items. One was the disposal of a large number of bank shares belonging to Count Alfred, who, it appeared, unaccountably wanted to get rid of them. Of course Count Alfred would not attend the board meeting himself. He never did. Treuwalt represented him. Another was the reconstruction, if possible, of the Behemoth Corporation, a steel company controlled by the A.O.G. which (a dead secret to the public) was on the point of disintegration—perhaps complete collapse. Still another was the unutterably trivial and absurd corruption affair of certain journalists, which, it seemed, had provoked a scandal.

✵

That evening Mason called Dr. Ritter for the fourth or fifth time. He said to Ritter's daughter, "Yes, I know that Dr. Ritter went away to Budapest. Yes, I know, but when is he coming *back?*"

"We have no information."

The fact that Ritter was the only man in the Anglo-American who also belonged to Zoltan did not, of course, prove that he was guilty.

Not necessarily.

Mason banged down the phone impatiently.

2

Mia Tetzel's death cast a cloud over the café that had not yet lifted. The shock arose not merely out of regard for Mia herself and pity for Karl but because the event seemed to be so mysteriously unreasonable. Even if she was often moody, Mia had always appeared to embody the strong, primitive, outflowing forces of life. Paula could not get out of her mind some visual memories of Mia, and remembered a swimming party at Baden the summer before when the Jarretts and Tetzels first came to know one another—Mia standing by the pool, poised to dive with her columnar but perfect legs held straight together, body creased at the waist, arms flexibly forward, and bright, fine metallic shavings of golden hair curling from her bathing cap.

What, what, could have been the distress dire enough, the torture severe enough, to make her kill herself? Or could she, as some people do who take tragic and irreversible steps, simply have lost control

through a momentary outburst of spite, crossness, testiness? Or could
it have been an accident? The psychiatrists said that suicide was
often a displacement for a hidden, stifled desire to murder. Whom
did Mia want to punish? Karl? Thorne? Whom did she want to kill?

Tetzel, who looked as if he were being eaten alive, drew Mason
aside at the Weissenhof. With precision, not hurrying it, he told him
of the meeting with Mark Thorne a month or so before, Thorne's
proposal to Mia, her response, and the incident that followed.

"So now you understand why I wished to quit my job. Any association with Thorne made me feel tainted. My reckoning with him
will come later. But now . . . I must ask an opinion about Mia herself.
Why I seek your advice is because I know I can trust your discretion,
also you have of most things an objective, highly balanced view. In
any case I must unburden myself to somebody, or I shall go mad.
The question I cannot answer is—did Mia agree to go to Thorne
because she was secretly attracted to him and wanted him, or did
she in truth arrange to send me away, make the rendezvous with him,
purely for my sake? Which?" He put up a warning finger. "No, no,
do not give the easy, the expected answer. I do not seek consolation.
I seek the truth."

"How can I answer that, Karl? I didn't know Mia well enough."
What Mason could not ask was the blunt, obvious question that
would be most relevant—did she have many love affairs? He evaded:
"You must have loved her very much."

"Yes, but I killed her."

Mason was startled, but thought that he must be using a figure of
speech. "Did you talk to Mia about all this?"

"Yes, interminably, I hounded her with it, day after day, night
after night, hour after hour. That is what killed her."

"What did she say?"

"Her answer was always that she did it for me, for us both. But of
course she always took a certain morbid pleasure in torturing me.
That is probably why she told me of Thorne's offer in the first place."

"In any case, why not take her word for it?"

"I cannot."

"Surely if she had simply wanted to have an affair with Thorne
she wouldn't have told you about the rendezvous?"

"How, then, would the raise have been explained?"

"Oh, any number of ways."

"You perhaps think that she wanted Thorne for his own sake but found it convenient to use the occasion of the rendezvous to get a raise for me as well."

How remarkable can be the convolutions of the Vienna mind, Mason thought.

Tetzel gave him a long, hard look. "But in any case it was a horrible thing to agree to do, was it not?" Now his face held not merely a look of pain and remorse, but a note curiously perverse—almost of satisfaction, of vindication. A thin smile separated his arching lips.

"I have more to say. There is worse to tell. Not only was I responsible for her death by driving her to desperation, by hounding her, but directly as well, out of wounded pride and jealous rage. We had a bitter quarrel that night, and I told her that I had finally determined to quit my job with Thorne. She was terrified. She thought that she had cost me our livelihood. Her misery, her desperation were extreme. At about three o'clock in the morning she awoke. She did not know that I had wakened too. I lay absolutely quiet. She went to the bathroom and I heard her open the medicine cabinet, then turn on the water tap. It must have been then that she took the bottle of pills. My body stiffened with horror. I started to rise, then sank back. Both of us were totally exhausted, and, incredible as it may seem, just as I was about to jump up, shout, slap her on the back, call a doctor, summon an ambulance, make black coffee, march her around the room, I lost all power to do anything. I became dazed. But, you say, how did I know that it was poison she took, not simply aspirin or some harmless other drug? My reply is that she had been taking too many sleeping pills lately and I had hidden the bottle on a top shelf behind innocent bottles. I could hear her search. She climbed back into bed, giving a terrible choked sigh, and, while struggling to rouse myself, I fell asleep. Of course this could not have occurred if I had not subconsciously wished not to interfere with the course of action she had undertaken. I wished her to be punished, to be dead. I could not conceivably have fallen sound asleep at that moment of all moments in my life unless my concealed self, my submerged self, had not wished for her death, her punishment. I sought revenge. I could have saved her. But when I woke up, she was dead."

Mason could think of nothing to say.

"Now what is my life to be? Where do I go? What shall I hold on to? What exists?"

Tetzel added sententiously, "To some extent I blame the *Zeitgeist*. How can anybody be happy in this diseased society of ours, with all values confused? How can anybody achieve a decent personal life, since we no longer have the capacity to control or manipulate the main impulses that go into making a life? Perhaps the personal life should be discarded and forgotten." He seemed to become confused. "Perhaps it is impossible to atone except through abstract faith . . . but faith . . . faith in what?"

They walked back to the *Stammtisch*.

Tetzel said, "Of course if I did not have unfinished business, I would follow Mia to the grave . . . kill myself at once."

"What unfinished business?"

"You will see."

3

Mail from the United States, which came in a large batch once a week, arrived the next morning. Even before opening his letters Mason, as always, pounced on copies of the *Star* in their sleek brown tubular wrappers. He wanted avidly to see how his stories had been played—how well the cable dispatches had been handled, what mailers and news notes had come up. The *Star* had a unique system whereby foreign news from its own staff appeared always on a single page, page two, except of course for really big stories which made page one. On page two, day by day, appeared Hazelwood, Preble, Strothness, Throckmorton, the *Star* men in the Far East, and those in subsidiary bureaus like Geneva, Stockholm, Rio de Janeiro, Madrid. Competition to make page two was hot. Mason was often bored with his local routine, off in a trance, or dissolved into simple incapacity by the prevailing Viennese atmosphere of put-it-offism, but he seldom forgot page two. If a few days passed and he had no story he became frantic. Today, wrenching the papers open, he saw that his Hungarian series had been presented nicely and that several routine cables stood at the top of the page, but to his amazed consternation he could find no trace of the two brief stories he had sent about the A.O.G. Mason was furious. He was outraged. Not for months had any cable of his not been printed. To have had something he had written thrown in the wastebasket without explanation by some dolt of an assistant foreign editor was too much to bear; he felt as if part of his very flesh had been brutally sliced off. It was scandalous—revolting! He could not believe it. He continued to tear the papers apart. Back in the financial pages, all the way back, hidden, surrounded by stock exchange reports, he found at last a much-cut version of his first bank story, the announcement of the scandal. Well! At least they had printed something! But of the second story dealing with the reaction of the A.O.G. there was no trace at all.

George Hilliard must be out of town. Some insufferable dumb crumb must be filling in for him and had made this outrageous blunder. This was Mason's first thought.

The second was more serious. All big banks had multiple interlockings and the *Star*, since its recent change in ownership, must be heavily in debt to Chicago—and no doubt other—financial interests.

Had anybody in Chicago thought that it would be unwise to spread scandal news about such a splendid, respected colossus as the A.O.G.?

No, no!

That was not the kind of paper the *Star* was.

Mason found Paula, the realist, in the living room.

"There could be another explanation," she said after listening carefully. "Perhaps you're exaggerating the importance of all this. Is it really as big a story as you think?"

"I didn't overwrite it."

"The fact that a couple of newspapermen get bribed by a corrupt bank in Vienna isn't necessarily worth an eight-column headline in Chicago."

"Yes, but there's a principle involved, a universal principle."

"Of course, but even so . . ."

They became plunged into an argument about the nature of honesty. Mason, somewhat hesitantly, tried to make his position clear. Could he himself say that he had never told a lie in his life? Certainly not. He had never been guilty of embezzlement or forgery, but when he crossed frontiers didn't he fib to the customs inspectors? Didn't he tell minor social lies? Would he not lie, if necessary, to save the honor of a friend? What about helping a man who needed a job by giving him a better reference than he deserved? But to write things you knew were not true, to accept a bribe in order to disguise or conceal the truth or to disseminate lies—that was something in a totally different vein. That undermined everything. It violated the basic code.

"But think it through, darling," Paula said. "Lying is hateful, but for a man to tell a lie doesn't necessarily mean that he's dishonest. Bribery is hateful, but there are bribes and bribes. Suppose, just for the sake of argument, that every time you went to the Czechs you got the worst seat at the table, and at the Hungarians the best. Wouldn't that influence you just a little against the Czechs, and tend to make you a bit pro-Hungarian in time?"

"You're being ridiculous. That's on an altogether different level."

"Yes, but how exactly do you differentiate between a bribe, a tip, and a gift? I know you're the most honest man alive, but didn't you accept that smoked turkey from the Poles last Christmas?"

*

It seemed to be definitely established now that Zoltan's list contained between forty and fifty names: forty-two, the best reports agreed. Forty-two Viennese journalists guilty of taking bribes! What made the situation worse, as most of Mason's colleagues saw it, was that the sums given to individual correspondents were so absurdly, ignominiously small. The largest single payment was said to have been 5,000 Schillings, and many were only five hundred. Selling one's soul for seventy dollars! The factor in the case most trying to everybody was the pall it cast on personal relationships. Mason had drinks that afternoon with the well-known correspondent of a Swiss newspaper, Ernst Boericke. He was a small man, whose lips always seemed to be slightly, gently parted, as if he were about to speak but would not do so until speech should be permitted, and who stood on tiptoe. He was a great one for the formal Viennese manner of address, and used phrases of greeting like "Meine Hochachtung!" or "Meine Verehrung!" Mason would have been perfectly prepared to accept the fact that Ernst Boericke might beat his wife, terrorize his children, spread scandal about his neighbors, or occasionally give the Bulgars, or the Albanians, or Whom-you-will, the benefit of the doubt in a news story; but could he have taken seventy dollars across, or under, a café table from some slippery-handed agent of the A.O.G.? No—preposterous!

Mason arrived at the Boerickes' alone because they had several dogs and a large Persian cat. He remembered what had happened the last time. The cat made a beeline for Paula, who cried out when the animal leaped into her lap. In a moment, her arms had turned bright red and welts began to appear on her face. The Boerickes were alarmed. They locked up the dogs, which had begun to bark around her chair, and put the cat away; clearly they thought that Paula must think that they were unclean. "It's just my idiotic hives—a rash," she sought to explain, furious with embarrassment. Today the Boerickes, although much too polite to say so, were obviously relieved that Mason had come without her.

Mason and Boericke had a long discussion about the dilemmas involved in the A.O.G. affair, philosophical and otherwise. Boericke said, "My idea would be not to think in terms of principles. I suggest that we take a simple ad hoc attitude on each case—let each individual case be judged on its own merits." This bit of conversation made a strong impression on Mason. Paula had discouraged him this morning, but this little man, if only because of his simplicity, helped to put him straight. It was a surprise to him that Boericke should advise him not to think in terms of principles. As a rule all Europeans did. The way to get along with Europeans was to agree on principles first. This was because even the worst of them had standards of some sort.

Boericke had a pingpong table and they played a few games. Mason put down his racket chastened. It was still a law that any European in Vienna could beat any American at pingpong.

"Keep after the whole business," said Boericke as Mason set off down the street. He added in a moment of illumination, "Keep after it, not for the sake of others but for yourself."

4

Apparently confident but not at all sure of himself, groping inwardly, Mason called the meeting to order. The Anglo-American had not met since his conversation with Zoltan, but this delay did not displease Mason because he wanted to talk alone to old Ritter first. Now, however, the pressure had become such that he could not put things off any longer. Besides, it was now clear that he had become engaged in a fight, a struggle. It was not the ethical principle at stake that challenged him most, or even the nature of the story. Something mysterious and disagreeable was going on which deeply involved him and his friends, and he was going to get to the bottom of it, no matter what.

He said first that Ritter's membership in Zoltan's group could not be considered actual evidence against him. But Ritter was still absent in Budapest, and there the matter lay. The *Daily Herald* man pointed out that Budapest was only five hours away and to make a special trip there should not be too onerous. Mason shrugged, saying that if the opinion of the meeting was that he should go to Budapest he was perfectly prepared to do so. He added, "But I would like instructions. What shall our procedure be? Ask Ritter straight off if he's a crook?"

A swirling babble of talk followed. Mason banged on the table to restore order.

"Mr. President," said John Dixon, "there must be a way out of this. We must go to the Finanzministerium, or the A.O.G. itself, and get those lists!"

"How? By pulling a gun on the Finance Minister or Herr Direktor Dostal?" Mason cried impatiently.

The *News Chronicle* correspondent said, "I dislike Austrian solutions, but perhaps the best thing would be to bring a suit."

Mason became so overwrought that he exploded, "What the devil is going on here, anyway? What *is* all this *Kitsch*? We're running around like chickens with our heads cut off! Now, listen. I did my damnedest to get that list. I didn't get it. I don't think anybody else will get it. But we're getting confused by a lot of hocus-pocus. For God's sake, let's not lose all sense of reality! Listen," he shouted, banging the table again. "*I* didn't take any money! *I* wasn't bribed by the A.O.G.!" He flung his hand around the table, pointing. "Did *you* take any money, Bishopson? No! Did *you*, Drew? No! Did *you*, Sandor? No! Did *you*, Wheatley? No!

You, Stein? Did *you,* Hestery . . . Tetzel . . . Dixon . . . Wolfe . . . Bass . . . Clippert . . . Hotchkiss . . . Hanley . . . Simms . . . Allbright? NO! Did any of *us* get anything? NO! Not a damned Schilling. Well, then, what's all the fuss about—let's just repeat that we're in the clear, and let it go at that. *Schluss!*"

Dr. Stein said precisely, "Perhaps we could settle the matter for good and all by each of us signing a statement of innocence and publishing an announcement that we are all quite innocent."

Bishopson interrupted with a dry cough. "We can't very well publish it that we're all innocent, if one of us is not."

❋

At last Dr. Ritter returned. He telephoned Mason and they met at a café off their usual track. Ritter began by explaining elaborately the reason for his absence and his failure to attend the meeting of the Anglo-American. The old man, soaking a biscuit in his creamy, soft-brown coffee, was aggressive. He spluttered, and a smear dripped down one coat lapel.

"Mr. Charrett, I do not wish you to assume anything incorrect. . . . Do not think that I tried to evade . . . It was sudden business, urgent business, that kept me in Budapest."

Mason, knowing that he was lying, nodded, and then sketched out the situation carefully. "Would you join us all in a pledge," he proffered, "some sort of joint statement we might prepare declaring our innocence?"

"As I understand it, the Zoltan organization is empowered with the investigation. All is in order." Ritter looked cunning. "Why should we interfere?"

"Because we're not satisfied that the Zoltan investigation will be honest, and the whole business concerns us too. Zoltan refused to give me any details at all and is blocking us all from information."

"I am told that the *Ehrengericht* of the Zoltan organization begins actually today. After all, what business is it of ours, Mr. Charrett? Ah"—he swirled another biscuit in the coffee—"you are not a Viennese, you do not understand the special circumstances that apply. Ah, this whole business, what is it but a series of misunderstandings . . . of clumsy errors . . . and this is not New York, Mr. Charrett, it is not

London or New York or Tchicago." Plop, plop, exuded vigorously
the tiny bursts of spittle.

"Well, I'm given to understand by my betters in our organization
that it's up to us to defend what's called our honor." Mason tried
to make his tone light.

Old Ritter shrieked with harsh laughter. "Honor? In Owstria?"

Mason could not bring himself to ask the direct question necessary. Seldom had he felt more uncomfortable. It was too utterly embarrassing to ask a man old enough to be his father if he had taken
a bribe or not. Besides, Mason thought, there was no need. It was
all too distressingly obvious.

He took another tack. "I understand that one member of the
Gesellschaft is said to be involved, and he's taken the more or less
graceful way out—in order to protect his organization as a whole he's
resigning from it. And I hear that three men in the Union are doing
the same thing."

Ritter did not accept this hint, except to look up at Mason. Then,
sibilantly, with gestures indicating delicate gradations in meaning, he
brought forward a suggestion. "Take a hypothetical case," the old man
said. "Purely hypothetical." Plop, plop. "Assume, for the sake of
hypothetical discussion, that someone in the Anglo-American *did*
take money. Unthinkable, of course! But assume it. For the sake of
hypothetical discussion, assume it. Suppose that someone in our organization *has* been bribed by the A.O.G. But if in this hypothetical con-
tingency the hypothetical person involved sent the money *back*,
returned it to the A.O.G. intact—what then?"

"That's an idea with interesting possibilities."

Before he could comment further Ritter burst out, "So sorry I
could not come to the meeting! A misfortune, I see now. But it was
business, urgent business, in Budapest. . . ."

Mason tried to pursue the opening Ritter had given him. "Suppose
we make the hypothetical case about returning the money non-
hypothetical. . . ."

It seemed that the old man must have changed his mind, because
he lost control of himself. Hissing with fury he said, "And you, you,
Herr Charrett! Might I ask what business any of this is of yours?
Who are you, an American, an outsider, to invade our peaceful

Vienna, to stroll through the streets like an overlord, a conqueror, in the name of being merely an observer, and to destroy people's reputations, ruin their lives—and for what? To prove what? To demonstrate how correct and upright your standards are, you who come from a criminal city like Tchicago, where even the police, the high authorities, are bribed! Tchicago, the citadel of all gangsters, all crooks, where every newspaperman is on some bootlegger's payroll! You are a foreigner, an outsider, a stranger from a world where only hoodlums rule, and you dare to tell us how to behave! No, no, Mr. Charrett! Come off your high horse! How dare you confront me with this unspoken accusation, you who are not in any way part of me, and yet it can destroy my life!"

"Come now, Heinrich—what I'm trying to do is protect you. Wait a minute! I'm trying to *help*—"

Tottering, old Dr. Ritter left the café and sailed off down the street. The poor devil, Mason thought. He took some, all right.

※

Mason walked across the Ring to Bishopson's office.

"He didn't admit to a thing," Mason said, "but he's guilty, that's certain. Otherwise he would join us in a pledge, or resign from the Zoltan outfit." He found himself under an inexplicable compulsion to defend Ritter. Although he wanted above everything to break the case open as a whole, he did not want any friend to suffer. "Now, one thing seems reasonably clear, that it's not really Ritter's own fault. It's the fault of the system. You pay a man fifty dollars a month here in Vienna, a darned expensive town! . . . It's the fault of lousy newspapers and lousy newspaper agencies that know they can always underpay men, underpay them disgracefully, because there are so many idiots in the world wanting newspaper jobs, and so many drifters all over Europe who think that because they know how to write a letter they can become newspapermen."

Bishopson cleared his throat grittily. "Just the same, I hear the old boy has a good deal of money stowed away. He's probably better off than we are."

"He wouldn't have to be very well off," Mason said, "to be better off than me."

"What exactly is Zoltan's procedure?" the Scotsman asked. "We'd better find out, in case we have to have an *Ehrengericht* of our own."

"Apparently Zoltan sits with a committee of three and takes evidence from those involved. It's like a court, witnesses are on oath, attorneys are permitted, but it's certainly not a very scientific method. Those members found guilty are publicly named and expelled from the Zoltan organization—then presumably they'll lose their jobs. After that the public prosecutor takes action in the interest of the Austrian state. Oh yes, bribery is a felony under Austrian law, and anybody guilty may face a criminal trial and go to jail." Mason paused. "Meantime, the A.O.G. men who passed out the money aren't touched at all!"

"I have a feeling they may be touched sooner or later," Bishopson said decisively in his dry, clipped voice.

"Since Ritter is a member of the Zoltan organization and Zoltan has all this paraphernalia in the works, isn't the old man's point well taken? What business is it of ours, after all?"

"Mon, Vienna is beating you down—you're getting soft. You've succumbed."

"No, not at all. After all our first duty is to protect ourselves. Why take the lead in confessing that we, the Anglo-Americans, harbor a guilty party? Let's delay a little—stall. If Zoltan finds Ritter innocent, we're clear. If he's guilty, *then* we can take steps on our own."

"Perhaps. But, after all, we founded this organization of ours with one specific purpose, to keep all the *Schlamperei* out, to keep us clear of just this sort of entanglement. We were to be the one honest organization in town, the one group of journalists with correct professional standards. And now straightaway we're evading a critical issue in regard to the possible bribery of one of our own members. Should we not," Bishopson continued in his implacable tone, "demand of ourselves what by implication we demanded of the other organizations, no matter who suffers?"

"In other words, expel Ritter."

"Aye."

"But, my God, you can't take the responsibility of publicly disgracing a man over seventy!"

"Maybe he ought to know better at that age."

"But, my dear fellow, if we throw him out, he'll starve!"

"Oh," said Bishopson, "sentimentally I quite agree with you—quite. I'm simply trying to explore the matter from both sides."

Mason persisted, and finally Bishopson came over to his point of view. They decided not to investigate Ritter for the moment; instead they would delay—go no further until Zoltan's report appeared. If Zoltan found Ritter innocent, then the business was closed so far as the Anglo-American was concerned. If he was found guilty, well, there was still plenty of time to act. They were passing responsibility over to Zoltan, but never mind.

5

Mason and Paula dined one evening that week at the Wallensteins'. The only other guest there whom they knew was Dr. Ricardo Stein. Mason caught himself looking out for Nella, but she did not appear, and he felt a twinge of disappointment; thinking of her, his mind formed the image of somebody biting into a fresh apple, light, tart. Nor did Otto appear. After dinner, Mason slipped into a tête-à-tête with Stein, while Paula, across the room, stood with a man who had been introduced as Herr Oberbaurat Dichter, a cousin of the Wallensteins. As he talked, becoming attentive to Paula, he cackled. He had a wide upper lip covered with a violin-brown mustache; violin-brown hairs showed from his nostrils. An American lady? So! And a resident in Vienna for almost a year? So! The Americans were so rich, they had such nice theories, theories were always nice when you were rich! (*Cackle!*) There was Vilson, Voodrow Vilson. He had nice theories about the independence of small nations, what a blundering ignoramus-miscreant-malefactor-fool was that Voodrow Vilson! And the debts, the war debts, the Americans with their nice, democratic theories they turned Europe upside down and gutted it and then ran away and charged the world for it. Americans! Voodrow Vilson!

Paula, zealous, was not one to take this lying down. "Among other things Wilson fed your country here after the war and kept it from starving," she said warmly. "And you've resented it ever since."

He spread his palms out. "*Gnädige Frau*, the war made universal cataclysms. Broken apart by the Vilson theories, we could not take proper care of ourselves."

"I think you're too superior. We didn't start the war, did we?"

"The Russians started the war, gnädige Frau."

"What? It wasn't the Russians who invaded Belgium!"

He looked astounded, saying, "You talk of things you can know nothing of. You are a woman, a lady—"

"Oh, please don't tell me that I have no business talking politics. So many people here seem to believe that it's something perverse and monstrous if women try to think for themselves."

"Our women are not so educated, it is true. It is unusual among us to find a woman who thinks. Wives in our country travel a straight line between bed and kitchen sink."

Herr Dichter had been very rich, the owner of coal and iron deposits in Silesia, he told Paula; but he had been dispossessed when part of Silesia went to Poland after the war. He had been educated to be an architect, but not since 1919 had he done any work. Living on capital, he managed to get along, but only just; he lived in his mother's house, in two small rooms on the top floor; in the hall cabinet stood his boots and shoes, twenty-three pairs of them. He had not bought a pair of boots or shoes since the war, nor a suit of clothes. He had twenty-nine suits of clothes. Luckily he did not grow fat (cackle!), and his clothes would last him all his life. He got up early every morning and then there was all day, every day, day after day, to fill up, and for twelve years he had had nothing whatever to do. He kept himself fit. He had brains. He had experience and ability. (Cackle!) And day after day, for twelve mortal years, there had been nothing in the world for him to do.

"But you haven't really looked for work, have you? Surely you could have found something to do if you really wanted to, couldn't you?"

Across the room she saw Mason chatting amiably with Nella, who had just sauntered in. Herr Dichter moved closer. He said, "Gnädige Frau, you have rebuked me. Gently, but a rebuke just the same . . . I would like extremely to talk to you at some length. Could we meet again?" She became aware as he spoke that this ridiculous, useless, anachronistic old drone had become violently stirred by her; his eyes did not leave her face, and he moved sideways slightly so that their hips touched. Acutely uncomfortable, she wheeled away sharply, but he put his arm out, attempting to imprison her in a corner. This man wanted her. Look at him. "Frau Jarrett, I would beg . . ." She shook her head, evading him. What idiocy, Paula thought. Slipping from the cage he made with his outstretched arm she muttered a polite word of dismissal and started to cross the room to join the Wallensteins. Herr Dichter clutched her shoulder; she made herself free. Then, astounded, she heard him say, with an expression almost menacing, "You have aroused me physically. Now I will not sleep all night!"

She saw that Mason and Nella, on a sofa, were laughing together, and she stood with her arms limp in the middle of the floor, stranded. Dr. Ricardo Stein rescued her, and she gave him a grateful look. What an attractive girl Paula was, Stein thought. But one of the first laws of life among journalists in Europe was never to covet your friends' wives.

❈

Paula told Mason about Herr Dichter, and Mason was reminded of another relic of the ancien régime who had made a vivid impression on him. Count Dolhazy, a venerable Hungarian aristocrat, similarly represented a world now obliterated. Mason and Paula had met him and his family in a pension in Schönbrunn, where they had lived briefly before moving into the Wallenstein villa. In his youth Count Dolhazy was so rich that he had a special car on the trains taking him to fashionable spas; in his mature years he served the Emperor as an ambassador to several minor capitals; then he lost most of his fortune gambling; after World War I the inflation wiped him out. Lately he had become involved in a scandal over "borrowed" jewelry; only his name kept him from jail. He took a diamond necklace from one shop on the Kohlmarkt, "on trial," and then sold it to another.

Living with the Count were the Countess, their nine-year-old daughter, and the governess. The Jarretts were never introduced to the governess, but it did not take them long to discover that it was she who was the child's mother. The Countess had a superb manner. Two of their servants, who had not been paid for almost a year, made a squalid scene one day. "Their impudence!" the Countess exclaimed to Paula. "Of course I thought of a way presently to calm them down. I threatened to discharge them—without notice! They would have had to leave. I can tell you that brought them to heel, and they slunk off quietly!" The Dolhazys hadn't paid their bill at the pension for months. Since they had no money, payment was obviously impossible. Once Mason came home in midafternoon to find Frau Schultheis, the wife of the proprietor of the pension, weeping because the dining room furniture was being moved out. She and her husband had bought it on the installment plan, and for want of a few thousand Schillings it was now lost. Frau Schultheis sobbed, "If only Their Excellencies could manage to pay their bill!" But it would have been unthinkable for her to ask them to pay it. That evening Count Dolhazy kicked his chief retainer, Franz, who had been with him for more than thirty years and whom he loved like a son, downstairs, and then rushed into the street bawling aloud. . . .

Mason had little patience now with people like Dichter and the Dolhazys. All that kind of antediluvian nonsense was done with, finished forever. Then he remembered that single word of the Archduke's at the Weissenhof: "Humpty-Dumpty!" Perhaps the old Empire, evil as it was, had served an indispensable purpose after all. Could any structure fabricated out of the new nations replace it to make Central Europe a cohesive body again? Was the basic concept of imperial unity necessarily wrong? Was nationalism necessarily always right?

He would have to talk it over with Paula in the morning.

6

After dropping his chess lessons with Paula for a time Tetzel resumed them. He appeared to be worn out, and his talk still carried a note of angry suffering. At last he had quit the job with Thorne.

He approached Mason after the chess lesson the next afternoon. "To succeed me with Thorne I have suggested Ritter, but perhaps the A.O.G. scandal makes that impossible. So something only rarely available in Vienna is to hand for somebody—a job. As to myself, I need much less now that Mia is gone." His face became contorted. "It matters little if I starve. I could find work as a clerk . . . a salesman . . . even a laborer. But I admit clearly that it would be more pleasant to continue to be a journalist."

He looked appealingly at Mason, who replied, "I have an idea. The

Anglo-American has this damned A.O.G. thing hanging over our heads."

"Yes?"

Mason himself had continued to be so obsessed by the bribery case that he could think of little else. *How* could he take more effective action?

"If we knew more about what's really going on at the A.O.G. it would help. Why can't you do a little quiet snooping for us? There must be quite a few Social Democrats, decent citizens, working there. Try to ferret them out, and let's get a line on what's happening."

Karl showed interest.

"I'll work out later how to pay you. I think Bishopson, maybe Wheatley too, would share the expense with me. Or perhaps we could use dues from the Anglo-American. It wouldn't be much, but it might tide you over."

A remarkable change came over Tetzel after this conversation. From having been crushed by Mia's death, he appeared to find some measure of release, at the same time that freedom from Thorne gave him satisfaction. He developed more confidence, more push. He had always been adhesive, but in a soft way; now, even in continuing moments of anguish and chagrin, a new element in that tenacity could be seen together with a hard, stubborn bitterness.

A call came one afternoon from a certain Herr Albert Sachs, who told Mason that he had a letter that he must deliver personally. When they met Herr Sachs gave him a written communication from old Dr. Ritter, who, it seemed, was out of town again. Everything in Austria always had to be so fantastically indirect. The letter read:

Dear Colleague:

I request you to make clear the following facts during my absence which is professionally unavoidable. You will remember our recent conversation. I have returned the money in question to the person who gave it to me, Herr Gmunden, and I enclose herewith Herr Gmunden's receipt. Thus all possible combinations concerning my person in the A.O.G. affair are null and void.

Heinrich Ritter

Mason glanced at the receipt. Little old Dr. Ritter had sold his soul to the A.O.G. for five hundred Schillings, seventy dollars.

Herr Sachs bowed and departed, coldly. Obviously he thought that Mason was a cold-blooded miscreant bent vindictively on the ruin of his old friend Dr. Heinrich Ritter, the A.O.G., the Austrian government, and the fair name of Austria itself.

Now Mason had the name of the A.O.G. payoff man, or one of them—Gmunden. The receipt, however, gave no indication of Gmunden's first name, address, or business. He called Tetzel and gave him the job of trying to track Gmunden down. The next day Karl telephoned to say that he had found out who Gmunden was— a former civil servant who had been dismissed from his post in the Finanzministerium following a scandal, and who now did odd jobs for the Chancellery, A.O.G., and other institutions—but could not locate him or get any hint as to his address.

"Well, go after it, *Herr Sonder-Gesandter für Verderbnis im Bankgewerbe.*"

It amused Mason to call Karl his Special Emissary for Corruption in Bank Affairs.

Mason felt feverish that night, went to bed with a chill, and woke up with an illness that defied diagnosis for several days. Then it was found that he had an absurd child's disease—whooping cough. The villa shook with his coughing for a week. Paula, not a particularly good nurse, because she hated and feared illness, was moved by his distress. "Oh, ducky, you look so awful. Your eyes are practically sunk through your head! Otto, try to cheer him up. And we'll play *J'attaque* after dinner." This was a French game he liked.

Later in the week Tetzel made his first full report. The list had been prepared in the department of an officer of the bank named Paultraxl, and had been assembled on the basis of the most fragmentary information. The bank scarcely seemed to know one newspaper from another, or what correspondents worked for what paper; a man who did occasional feuilletons for some provincial rag in Ruschuk, Bulgaria, had equal status with the correspondent of the *Echo de Paris.* Men were listed in connection with publications they had never represented, and some names had apparently been put down at random. The payoff men, besides getting their own cut, tossed in the names of friends who would be delighted to pick up a spot of cash. Names were even put down of men who never got any money at all. Mason remembered that Bishopson had pointed out that this would be an ideal way to frame a man. Paula looked shocked and alarmed when he mentioned this, but then recovered. "They wouldn't dare!" she declared.

Mason said to Tetzel, "But you couldn't get your hands on an actual copy of the list?"

"No."

7

By this time young Otto Wallenstein had virtually become a member of the Jarrett household. He worked at all hours if Mason needed him. He took Bleschke's daily call, dictated the noon dispatch to Paris, handled the mail, and often had lunch at the Jarrett table. Often Paula asked him to sit down for a slivovitz or vermouth late in the afternoon. Mason had begun to play tennis once or twice a week with Bishopson, and practiced with Otto at the nearby Tennisplatz. He was quite good and sometimes beat him, but Mason was not competitive at all on this level and did not mind.

Mason had cabled nothing to the *Star* about the A.O.G. for some time. Actually there had been little hard news to report. If Chicago had not thought that his first two stories were worth much he could hardly expect a better fate for the minutiae of negotiations with Zoltan. Besides almost everything was still under the surface or off the record. But Mason felt that Chicago should, at the very least, know the outline of what was going on. He decided to summarize the whole story and describe recent developments in private letters. Otto did not know shorthand, but was nimble. Slowly Mason dictated a long letter to Hilliard, a shorter one to McFarland, and still another— a formal note enclosing carbons of the other two—to Mr. Plover. It was always wise to keep delicacies of protocol in mind.

Otto said, "Mr. Jarrett—"

"Call me Mason for God's sake."

Otto flushed. His face filled with blood easily, like his father's. "Mason, you would not mind, I would beg so much to ask, I do not understand the hierarchical position of your executives—would you explicate?"

"Explain, not explicate. I have four bosses in Chicago. Sure. We'll take them in ascending order."

"Hilliard's the foreign editor. He's conscientious to the bone, uncomplicated, totally nonintellectual. He's a former agency man, fast and fair and an absolute stickler for accuracy and good content. What else? Well, he's crazy about golf, and has two sons."

"What age is Mr. Hilliard?"

"Thirty-five—no, thirty-six."

"What does he look like?"

"You are full of curiosities, aren't you, Otto!" Mason grinned. "Tall, lean, sloping shoulders, bright suave face, sharp parentheses at the sides of his mouth, like big caraway seeds."

Otto was pleased by this.

"Next, the managing editor is Hiram J. McFarland. He's around fifty, sensitive, subtle, introverted. He's frail—looks waxen, with a drooping black mustache. All he really cares about is good writing, and he's fostered a whole school of Chicago writers on the Star. His notion of small talk, if you run into him in the elevator, is 'Well, how's life?' and he'll hold up an edition to delete a comma."

Mason went on: "Richard Maxwell Plover, editor. Seventy, I imagine, and he's been editor of the Star for thirty years or more. He never calls anybody anything except 'mister' even if they've worked close to him for a quarter of a century. 'Mr. Hilliard, Mr. Edmondson, et cetera.' He has a shock of heavy white hair so white that it looks powdered, and he asks you out to lunch Sundays in a big place in Winnetka and says grace at meals.

"No, he's not particularly old-fashioned: just seems to represent a different age. He's the most fair-minded man I ever met, with integrity, decency, courage, and he has a ferocious temper too."

Mason rose, walked to the window, and sucked in some fresh air. His fourth man was Rufus Knowles, publisher.

"A New Englander, bought the Star not long ago. Heavy-set, red-in-the-neck, fiftyish. He owns textile mills and a steel company too, I believe. He pronounces the word 'foreign' 'farn.' He's very

proud of the *Star's* 'farn' service, and leaves it pretty much alone—
he knows it's what keeps us from being just a provincial newspaper.
When he whistles, we hop. Handsome wife, six children, civic leader,
strong Republican. I've only met him twice."

Otto asked, "These editors, these owners and executives—are they
all very rich men?"

"No, not at all. Mr. Knowles has plenty of money, sure, but he's
not rich in the European sense—he's self-made, he doesn't derive
from inherited wealth or a great private fortune. The rest are men on
salaries—not very big salaries at that."

"What kind of stock do they come from?" Otto continued.

Mason had been watching Otto with some attention. His
hands were still roundish, almost like dumplings, with the knuckles
scarcely visible, and his large inquiring eyes were those of a child.
The golden-brown brows were soft with a faint herringbone pattern.

"Stock?" Mason coughed. "Basically middle class, I suppose. Oh, I
see what you're getting at. We don't think much about 'stock' in that
sense in America. We're a very mixed society."

As a result of this conversation, Mason found himself free of a
discomforting thought which had come to him several times since
the day he found that his A.O.G. stories were being neglected by
Chicago. None of these men could possibly have been party to any
attempt to kill a story because an influential bank was involved.

"What are your own origins, Mr.—I mean, Mason—if that question is not impertinent?"

"My father ran a big wheat ranch in Montana, but he died when I
was twelve. Later my mother worked in a shop."

"But what was your *blood*, what was Mrs. Jarrett's *blood*?"

"What do you mean, 'blood'?"

Otto looked embarrassed. Certainly he had discernment to a
marked degree for somebody his age, but—Mason fished for a
word—he was a little covert. He helped him. "Paula's family goes back
a long way. She's of straight Anglo-Saxon origin, never watered down,
but pretty much played out now, full of ancestors who came over
on the Mayflower and signed the Declaration of Independence, all
that sort of thing. I'm much more plebeian. I have Scotch, Irish,

Huguenot, maybe a touch of Spanish blood—also Indian. Jarrett was a French name. My mother's maiden name was Smith."

"Did anyone in your family, or Mrs. Jarrett's, ever marry anybody Jewish—have you any Jewish connections at all, even if remote?"

"I don't think so."

"Are there many Jews on the Chicago Star?"

"A few. Jews don't go in for journalism much in the Middle West. Our best rewrite man, Meyer Silver, is Jewish, and so is Doc Eckstein, our Shanghai correspondent. Lester Moses in New York may be a Jew, but I'm not sure. Moses is an old New England name, but it could be Jewish too. I've never thought to ask."

"You have never even asket?" Otto looked incredulous. "Do the Jews on your staff face prejudice?"

"A little, perhaps."

"Here in Vienna is a positive inferno of prejudice!" Otto rose gawkily.

"I know that, Otto."

"You must never breathe a word of this to my family. It would kill them." Otto lowered his voice. "I would like to confess something, Mr. Jarrett. I often wish that I were not Jewish. I cannot stand sometimes that I am Jewish. My father in particular would be extremely hurt to hear me say this, but I am sorry that I am a Jew!"

"Maybe you take the subject a bit too seriously."

"Seriously? You do not appreciate the extent of our plight. Do you not realize that, if the Nazis take Austria, my life will be destroyt even though nobody would take me for a Jew by my looks and besides, I repeat, I do not wish to be Jewish."

❊

Mason that evening asked Paula what she thought of Otto. Paula replied, "I like him a lot, but I don't think he has much s. of h."

The phone rang.

"Yes, Bleschke?"

"It is not a story maybe, but I thought you would be interested. There has been a shake-up in the Reichsdeutsche Presseverein. Dolliner has been ousted as president, and his successor is the new

Hitler correspondent, Herr von Traum."

Mason turned to Paula grimly. "I don't know how much sense of humor Otto has, but before long he may need all he's got."

8

Once a year the Sandors gave an evening party to celebrate their wedding anniversary. They were discriminating about their guests, and Mason had noticed at other gatherings of theirs that you could pretty well categorize the Central European colony in Vienna by those whom the Sandors had to their apartment. The criterion was not one of money, rank, or power. It was an infallible sense of soundness in regard to people from the Danube regions. You would never, for instance, see Bleschke at a Sandor party, or Markovitch, or Von Traum. You might well see Dolliner or the Boerickes, but Zoltan, Gatterburg, and Pflug (whom Sandor was quite willing to greet cordially at the Imperial), never. Erji was a charming hostess. After midnight she was apt to become giddy, out of excitement and happiness. The Sandors did not provide an excessive amount to eat or drink, but the *Lachsschinken* was always of the finest, and the Austrian wine heady and tart. Then too there was always a keg of beer—a whole small keg, the installation and proper handling of which was an art not to be surrendered to beginners. Mason knew well and loved their flat hidden on top of the office building in the Innere Stadt. You had to put twenty Groschen in the elevator to make it work, whereupon it wheezed stertorously upward, a cage in a shaft uncomfortably isolated by ten feet of open space from the circular staircase surrounding it. The last flight had to be done on foot. The contrast was striking between the bare, echoing staircase of the building altogether deserted at night and the Sandor apartment, with its pleasant glow and warm sense of being lived in well, its furniture with a high gloss, and glazed old paintings. In the principal room an elaborate crystal chandelier, which Erji loved more passionately than anything in the world except Laszlo and their son, cast sparkles of light on marble-topped tables and stout Biedermeyer chairs.

Sandor greeted Paula and Mason from a console where a silver tureen gleamed over a blue flame wavering like a butterfly. "Ah, we have now the family of Jarretts!" His friendly eyes gleamed through his heavy spectacles, beneath the sloping, rosy brow. "Welcome to our *Paprikahuhn!* Welcome to our *Nockerln!*"

The American military attaché, Colonel Baggs, was there; Yancey, the British counselor, and his Greek wife; the French expert from the National Bank; a pair of psychoanalysts; Dr. Hohnstedt (twin highlights on his polished shoes) of the Austrain Press Bureau; an oboist from the Philharmonic; and of the foreign correspondents a fair selection, including Drew, Dixon, Wheatley, and the Chicago *Tribune* man, Brewster (born in an Iowa hamlet, wrote beautiful lucid leads), who had just returned from India.

Then, somewhat to Mason's surprise, he saw Willi, the Archduke, whom Erji had prevailed upon Sandor to invite. At first Sandor was too shy to comply. "He come, do not doubt, if he know Paula Jarrett coming too!" The Archduke, suave, glossy, but with a look of mild hauteur, gazed with sleepy eyes on the assembled company. Mason advanced to greet him as he bent to kiss Paula's hand. No longer did Mason think that he was a worthless gigolo. They had had an illuminating talk the day he had come to cocktails at the villa. Tonight Willi was almost repellently immaculate, as well as immaculately polite. Every hair in that russet mustache had been brushed to stand at attention, and Mason thought that his small reddish-brown eyes, even though half closed, looked like dark raisins in carefully tended flesh.

"Later will come Tom Cairn," Erji declared, surveying the room. At once, both Mason and Paula (in a dusky golden dress with a high collar) felt a tinge of excitement. Cairn, the radio reporter, whom they had never met, was one of the best-known American journalists in Europe, a star.

A circle formed around Mason, which Paula observed with pleasure. No man could possibly want less to be a leader, but a leader he had turned out to be. Guests who did not know him were curious about this amiable but determined-seeming young person, with all that freshness and power, but an air of constraint as well, who was the head of the Anglo-Americans.

Around the room sat chattering guests with plates of the steaming chicken and dumplings on their laps, sipping wine or gulping beer. From door to door a diaphanous scarf of tobacco smoke floated over their heads, catching on at times to Erji's pride, the large and glittering chandelier.

Yancey, with his sloping heavy shoulders, swarthy skin, and blunt oily nose, was talking about the bribery affair. He was wearing a purple shirt even louder than usual, and his face had a nice untidy look. "Any of you lads here taken any money?" he asked with rude jocosity.

"Sure, we're rolling in it," Mason said.

"Good. Seen that list yet?"

"No."

"Better get hopping."

Mason thought, Only a man perfectly sure of himself can be as rude as Yancey is. But they had a good relationship.

"I'm told that the new directorate is having a lot of trouble over personnel," Yancey said. "Things aren't the same since Neuwaldegg retired. He was the brains of that bank. Dostal and Treuwalt aren't up to him, simply aren't in his class, although Dostal is an able man. And, of course, old Count Alfred isn't interested any more. Odd fellow, the old Count, I knew him well years ago. But he's an anachronism, his day is done."

Mason salted some of this away for future use.

Drew, in his best boyish manner, asked Yancey to explain why, in his opinion, the A.O.G. had started to throw its money around. Mason noticed that Drew's cuffs, flapping around his fat wrists, were frayed. And, although this was a gala party, he had not shaved.

"I imagine it could conceivably have something to do with the Customs Union," said the Englishman. "In case anything like that ever starts up again, they want to be able to control the publicity better."

"What's the situation on foreign exchange? Are the reserves holding up?" John Dixon inquired.

"Here's the man to ask." Yancey pointed to the French adviser to the National Bank, then turned to the Frenchman himself. "I'm delighted that you people seem to have stopped your currency withdrawals."

"What do you mean by 'my people'?"

"The Banque de France."

The Frenchman said somewhat stiffly, "I do not represent the Banque de France. I am the French technical representative at the Austrian Ministry of Finance."

Mason laughed. "I thought *all* Frenchmen represented the Banque de France!"

The Frenchman gave him a glacial smile, then inspected his narrow fingertips.

"Of course," said Yancey, "now that you've got the Customs Union safely throttled at The Hague, you can afford to relax on currency manipulations."

The Frenchman resumed a study of his fingernails.

"Do you think there's any chance the Zoltan organization, what the devil is it called, will make an honest report?" asked Colonel Baggs.

"Eggs-cuse me!" Sandor laughed ironically.

"It's possible," Drew disagreed with Sandor. "Quite possible. Remember, the Socialists are hot on the whole thing, and probably a majority of Zoltan's men are Socialists."

"Zoltan *must* whitewash," Sandor insisted. "He has one hundred fifty members in all. Suppose the forty on the list are all guilty. It will break his organization."

"Watch the Socialists," Drew said with emphasis. "Parliament will be the center of this story soon. Watch two things—the line the Germans take, under this new fellow Von Traum, and the Socialists in Parliament."

Mason left the group, and approached the Archduke in the other room. "We were talking about the A.O.G. back there." He pointed behind him vaguely. "Do you know Count Alfred Diederbach?"

This might be a way to break through the A.O.G. wall of secrecy.

"He is very well known to me indeed. I have known him since I was a boy of six. . . . His relations with my family—very interesting!" The Archduke's eyes flickered. Then, to Mason's surprise, he burst out laughing. He laughed so hard that tears came to his eyes; he took a handkerchief from a sleeve, and wiped his eyes, still laughing, then blew his nose vigorously. "Ach . . . ach . . . the younger generation of commercial people—all guilty of what I can only call snobbery in reverse. They think that because we of our family were imperial, we are fools!"

Mason tried to pursue his question further, but was interrupted. Paula introduced several of the newspaper wives, dying to meet an authentic Habsburg prince, to the Archduke. A minor flurry attended the arrival of the Polish minister, attended by Mason's old friend Dr. Wiskiewicz, with his curious ginger-colored head. The Welshman Simms, the only Nazi among the Anglo-American correspondents, who had not been invited but who came with somebody else, got into a furious argument about the Sudetenland with the Czechoslovak press attaché. Somewhat officiously, young Dixon superintended the beer keg, while Sandor gave confused instructions about the food. When excited Sandor talked to the servants in Hungarian, a language they did not understand. Erji snatched up a Slovak stringed instrument, something like a guitar, and in a throbbing voice, high and piercing, she sang gypsy songs, songs of the puszta, songs of her childhood, piercingly dissonant and yet melodious. Then some of the Hungarians began to dance the czardas. With their arms rigid, holding one another's shoulders, they danced with knees stiff, shoulders high. "Hi! Hi!" everybody shouted. "Hi, hi!" Erji sang back, wildly. Her thin throat bulged out, her eyes flashed, her big white teeth, with the little slit of window, glittered. "Hi! Hi!" The czardas went on, with its wild, weird dissonances, and the floor quivered almost as a pier might creak and quiver when pushed by a heavy ship. Stamp, stamp! "Hi! Ho!"

Somebody turned on the gramophone—a waltz. Willi rose, approached Paula, beside Mason, bowed, and circled with her over the floor. He was extraordinarily expert; she was pretty good; others joined them waltzing, and in the soft silverish light, the room became a cage of gracefully interlocked and circling couples, under a haze of smoke, which was now coiled under the chandelier like a ring around the moon.

A stir came at the door, and Sandor, his nose more than ever like a mound of bright red strawberry marzipan, greeted a new arrival— Tom Cairn, the star radio reporter for N.B.S.

Erji led Cairn around the room, and he shook hands slowly with everybody, looking each person levelly in the eye. He greeted Mason

with particular attention, saying, "I've heard such a lot about you—
I'm glad we're meeting at last. And which is your wife? Oh, of course,
I should have known from the descriptions I've had of her." He was
earnest, direct, and graceful. But Mason felt at once that there was
something strange about Tom Cairn's manner. His hands trembled—
he must indeed be a bundle of nerves, as everybody said—and his
eyes, even when they searched you, had a queer enigmatic stare,
as if he were slightly dazed, a man in a trance. He asked for a Scotch
and, withdrawing to a darkish corner, sipped it slowly as a circle
formed around him. Close by stood the Archduke, arms akimbo.
But it was Tom Cairn who was holding court.

Mason felt a small twinge of jealousy. An hour before it had been
he who was holding court. Cairn could be a deadly rival, Mason
thought. Watch him.

Cairn's voice, the celebrated silken voice with the chuckle running
in it, was calm.

"What brings you to our Vienna backwater, Mr. Cairn?" one of
the women asked.

"I have an appointment with Monsignor Dr. Ignaz Seipel for a
radio interview. I'm told that he's a sinuous character, as well as a
genuine man of God. The paraphernalia of broadcasting is completely
novel to him. We had a preliminary conversation today and it seemed
to stagger him that we will have a talk which will be transmitted
instantaneously across the Atlantic, even as we speak. The first
question I shall ask him is what he thinks God thinks of a mechanism
that can carry a voice, live, from the imperial corridors of the Hofburg
into the parlors and sweatshops of New York!"

Too fancy, Mason thought—a shade pretentious too. But maybe
he's just trying to catch his audience. He certainly shows ease, command. But what's wrong with him?

"What do you think of Hitler, Mr. Cairn?" a woman inquired.

"You remind me of the good lady who asked Henri Matisse what
he thought of modern art. The master replied, 'N'avez-vous pas de
petites questions, madame?' Have I met Hitler? Yes, several times,
but only once for an extended talk. It lasted four hours, and it took
me a week to get over it. You know the curious ceremonial they put
on at the Brown House when you're first received? It's quite revealing

—something out of Wagner, but with all the voluptuousness and stress translated into a kind of peculiar, refined asceticism. The day I had lunch there Hitler ate nothing whatever except a few raw carrots. But what beautifully special carrots they were, the most exquisite of carrots, carved and cut in curls. Incidentally, Hitler is a virgin."

Somebody giggled, and attention in the room became fixed. Dauphine Dixon, smiling, reached swiftly for her notebook.

With the easiest gesture in the world, but still with his eyes oddly glazed, Cairn turned to Mason as if he had known him all his life and asked in the tone of a man discussing the price of soap, "Mason, would you, if British, give up sexual intercourse for a year to be Prime Minister? Would you, as an American, give it up for two years to be President?"

Erji choked with horrified laughter.

Mason said, "No!"

Paula tried hard to avoid any eyes.

"To be Shakespeare?"

In spite of himself Mason hesitated.

"Ah, that's more difficult, isn't it!"

"No, not really." Mason smiled. Why, the son of a bitch, he's pretty good, he thought, chuckling.

Sandor looked embarrassed, while others laughed in outer corners of the room. Dauphine scribbled in her notebook fast.

"To return to Hitler," Cairn proceeded with the utmost smoothness, and as if there had been no interruption whatever, "the main thing to say is that he's bound to make a war. He's by far the most dangerous personality to have arisen on the Eurasian continent since Genghis Khan. That is because of the mystical union he has established between himself and the German people, a nation of sheep until they are put into uniform, and because he combines in his own person the two most powerful forces in the modern world, nationalism and socialism. The N.S.D.A.P. is rightly named. Mussolini? A jackanapes. Dress him in a clown's shirt and let him sing Pagliacci. Stalin? A lump of granite. If he has nerves, they are veins in rock. His contribution is, however, perfectly enormous—he's made the Russian Revolution work. Nobody seems to appreciate that the most important event in Europe since Versailles is, next to the rise of Hitler, the success of the Five-Year Plan."

Argument was vivid. Cairn turned to other fields, more lightly, and told stories with measured, confident charm—anecdotes about King Alfonso, who had recently been deposed in Spain, and the subtle wiles of Venizelos in Greece. Apparently Cairn knew him well; at any rate he called him by his first name, Eleutherios.

"By the by, I don't know if you're following politics at home closely, but Herbert is not going to have an easy time at all next year."

"Herbert who?" Paula asked.

"Hoover."

Now the czardas sounded again from the next room, and the circle around Cairn began to break up, which left him stranded and, it seemed, a trifle nettled. His voice rose, and he talked harder. He loved gossip, and for a moment he chatted with the Archduke about one of his half sisters, whom he knew, and whose second husband was a paper manufacturer in Binghamton, New York. Cairn turned to London as a field, and made passing references to Lytton Strachey, the price brought by some Georgian silver recently at Sotheby's, the origin of the use of the color red for buses, the romantic history of a pastry chef at Boulestin's, the American at Cambridge who did not know that the Duchess of X had been an actress, and the cabinet minister who had to be carried away from lunch at the Carlton feet first.

Few were listening to Cairn now but Mason. The other guests were not being rude, but were moving back and forth at the buffet or dancing. But Cairn's monologue continued. Then in a flash Mason guessed. Cairn's voice, even if a shade strident, was perfectly controlled; his gestures, even if nervous, were no more than what was appropriate to the occasion; but Mason guessed; he understood; Cairn gave no clear sign of having had too much to drink, but he was drunk, dead drunk. Probably he had been drunk from the moment he arrived. His performance was that of a robot, an automaton.

Presently the Archduke said good night, urging various guests to join him in a visit to a night club called the Koenigen. A group followed him, including the Dixons. John said to Mason, "So long, Mace. The script ought to get to New York today. Gee, if only that agent, Howland Snyder, likes it, but agents are such God-damned fools!"

Cairn led Paula toward the bar; now the pace of his words was slower, and his hands were twitching. From the next room the "Hi! Hi!" and crashing beat of the czardas dancers continued, and Erji, her hair loosened into a flying brown coil down her back, flung the windows open. Fresh air gushed in. Mason sat with Vera Yancey while Cairn and Paula talked, mostly (Mason could casually overhear) about music. Cairn was apparently very musical. He told a story about Boito and an error in the first draft of the libretto for *Otello*. It was two o'clock in the morning; three minutes later it was four o'clock. The party had thinned out now. One Balkan guest, sodden, fell asleep on the sofa, and the animation even of Dr. Wiskiewicz was receding. Then an astonishing thing happened. Cedric Wheatley of the *Daily Telegraph*, who had scarcely ever been heard to say a word at a social gathering, rose, and, formally addressing what remained of the party, told in a loud voice a prodigiously long anecdote about the China coast, where he had lived for some years. One detail had to do with a snake, supposedly dead, which woke up and started to sip the soup it was being served in, to the horror of the guests at a dinner party. When Wheatley concluded there came a round of hand-clapping; abruptly he sat down and, missing his chair, crashed to the floor. At the same moment a small bird—brown, squat, with a square tail—fluttered stolidly along the windowsill, perked its tiny head, with eyes sharp, toward Erji, and flew confidently into the room. It approached Cairn, whipped around him madly with a whirring sound, the sound of a pack of cards being shuffled rapidly, and almost—but not quite—settled on his outstretched hand.

Cairn stared at it bewildered. "An omen," he intoned.

The bird pirouetted, still whirring, and flew out after bumping its head against a billow of curtain.

"An omen of what?" asked Mason.

"I'm not sure. But an omen, certainly."

In a chorus of farewells the party broke up. Mason, Paula, and Cairn clomped together down the long twisting tube of stairs. At

the bottom Mason remembered that he had forgotten to leave
Tiinkgeld for the cook. Power for the elevator had long since been
turned off and eight flights up was a long, long climb. Taking breath,
he set out.

"Your husband is a very conscientious man," Cairn said.

"He's a mixture of a lot of things, but he *is* conscientious, yes,
very."

"Unlike me. Does he *care*?"

"About what?"

"It."

"What do you mean, 'it'?"

He turned to her with an indignant roar. He had broken out of his
shell at last.

"It—life—the forces of the universe—politics—*it!*—IT!"

"I honestly don't know," Paula said. "He's an artist at heart, who
got sidetracked into news. He doesn't care about politics in the least,
not really. But people, *stories*, fascinate him."

"So. Are you domesticated?" Tom Cairn asked.

"If you mean by that am I faithful to my husband, yes."

"Do you sew buttons, apply witch hazel, mend hangovers?"

"Come to lunch tomorrow, and we'll give you a glimpse of our
domestic procedures," Paula said.

They heard Mason's footsteps banging down the stairs.

"Mason, darling. I've asked Tom to lunch tomorrow," she called
toward him.

"Good."

"I'd love to come," Cairn said.

9

Tom Cairn was a smallish, neat, graceful man, delicately built.
Beside him Mason looked like a tall sack filled with boulders. He
had close-cropped graying hair, which made his eyebrows, still jet
black, conspicuous. Had not his chin been both broad and sharp,
jutting out under a wide mouth, the brows would have made him
seem top-heavy. Cairn was three flat horizontal lines—gray skull,
black brows, big mouth. He did not, Paula soon found out, behave at
all in the conventional manner of a star—no swagger, no walking

stick, no hired limousine to hand. But he did wear dandyish waist-coats, brightly colored. Of course Tom Cairn had been everywhere, done everything, long before getting this new tremendous job on N.B.S. The rumor was that he got $25,000 a year—plus expenses! Since he was traveling practically the whole time, he could save almost all his salary, Mason and Paula calculated. Around Tom Cairn all manner of legends had already accumulated. Even the facts were interesting enough. He had played an intimate role in the Rhine-land separatist movement, participated in the Rif rebellion, fasted with Gandhi, dodged bullets in Ireland, and interviewed everybody from Clemenceau to Hindenburg.

One o'clock came the next day, one-fifteen, one-thirty. No Cairn. Mason telephoned the Majestic. His room didn't answer.

"Well, he just forgot," Paula said, disappointed. "Or maybe he's browsing in some bar."

"No, my guess is different."

He asked for another extension at the Majestic.

"Klaus, Jarrett here. You have in room number seven-one-two a certain Mr. Thomas Cairn."

"I know, Mr. Jarrett! Tom Cairn, the Voice of Four Conti-nents!"

"No less. Klaus, would you do me a favor? Send one of your boys up to seven-one-two, or, better, go yourself. Bang on the door or break it down. Then call me, or have Mr. Cairn call me, will you, right away."

Back on the telephone within a quarter of an hour, Klaus reported, "Our locksmith succeeded with the door. Mr. Cairn had cut off his telephone, but now here he is."

"*Hello!*" said Mason cheerfully. "You're late—what's happened? We're expecting you for lunch."

"Who's this?"

"Mason Jarrett."

After a pause, a dead, flat voice asked, "Where am I?"

"Dreamland, obviously."

"Who did you say you were? Mason Jarrett? Of the Chicago Star? What city am I in? What hotel is this?"

Mason did not know how much of an act Cairn was putting on. He heard Klaus offer hurried explanations.

"Well. And you say we've met? Where?"

"Last night at Laszlo Sandor's."

"The Sandors. Oh." There came another long pause. "I seem to remember something about a bird."

"Well, come on to lunch—we've got a bird on the fire. You have the address in your wallet, or Klaus will give it to you. Hurry up."

Cairn said, "Give me half an hour."

At the Jarrett door he looked sheepish, as if he wanted to say, "Please like me, no matter what." He surveyed them with some care. "Of course . . . it all begins to come back to me." A smile stretched his lips. "Rather embarrassing, isn't it? Happens to me about once a year. . . . I black out."

Mason nodded. He had met alcoholic somnambulists before. And he had noticed how slowly Cairn had sipped drinks—a sure sign of a person who takes alcohol seriously and respects its power.

"It's scary. It's not *just* caused by alcohol, incidentally. I suppose I talked from Christmas to the moon and back. You'd better both know at once, I am one of those unfortunate types who talks even about Bulgaria before breakfast. But did I disgrace myself? Did I do anything untoward?" They reassured him. "That bird! First I thought it was my mother, but now I believe it was my first ex-wife."

"How many ex-wives do you have?" Paula asked after a moment.

"Only two."

"Do a lot of women you know take the form of birds?" Mason put in. "What kind? Ostriches? Harpies?"

They sat down to lunch.

"Titmice?"

"Mason, stand in a corner and shut up."

"I can see that you have succeeded at the hardest job in the world," Cairn said, "marriage. A man is hard on a wife." He turned to Paula. "Haven't you found that to be so? Particularly if a man is a writer. The life of an artist is impossible because, except in the rarest of instances, the demands made by the artist on himself are greater than the rewards of any accomplishment he can reasonably hope to achieve.

Hence: misery for the partner. Now please tell me everything you know about Monsignor Ignaz Seipel."

In the next hours the Jarretts and Tom Cairn achieved without effort a mood of complete ease, comradeship, and unity. The spell of their communication was absolute. Mason felt at his very best. There was something in Cairn that drew him out. He lost altogether the jealousy, the intimation of rivalry, that he had felt at Sandor's. He liked Cairn so much that he felt it was too good to be true: he was fearful now that he would not live up to his expectations, and might do something to break the spell. At twilight Cairn asked if he might put in a call to London. Mason walked him into the office. Assuming that he might have something private to say, he made as if to leave him, but Cairn pat-patted the air at him with a gesture that meant, "Don't leave me. Sit down." Cairn said into the telephone, his voice somewhat defensive, "No, I haven't started on the research yet. Haven't opened your envelope, in fact, but I will tomorrow." He put down the phone after a few minutes. He said, as if to himself, but answering an unexpressed question in Mason's face, "No, no, not my wife, not my secretary. A girl who's helping me. I'm very close to her." He sighed. His face became sober and deliberative. "My luck with women isn't very good, I'm afraid. I don't want to get involved again, but I always seem to be stumbling into things. I meet a girl and she attracts me and perhaps I even attract her; we become committed, and then later I find that she's altogether empty under the attractiveness—nothing there. I'm bored to death, and then it becomes such a problem—how to become extricated, how to achieve graceful extrication, if that's a way to put it."

"Not a very novel problem," Mason said. They walked back along the corridor. "Why don't you try falling in love?"

"Can't be done by volition, which you know as well as I. Besides, that's *bondage!* I had that once. Thought a girl was just a pleasant bedfellow, and then found that I really *was* in love with her, loved her madly. A terrible experience—shattering."

Mason gave him a look. Rejoining Paula they had another drink. The tremor in Cairn's hands became worse.

"What would you do if I asked if I could take a nap for half an hour? Give me a bed. Then I'll take you out to dinner."

It was six o'clock, and he slept till ten.

They went out and stayed up all night again.

Outside the Majestic, at dawn, Mason said, "Let's hire a car and go out to Edlach for the weekend."

"Oh goodie, let's!"

They were tottering, but went.

Edlach was a sylvan pretty village near the Semmering Pass, underneath the Rax, the great sheer pedestal of mountain rising out of the lacy green mist in the pass. The hotel had a small *Strandbad* set in golden sand and resembling an utterly transparent flat thin oblong slice of blue stone, behind shrubbery and neat banks of buttercups, pinks, and alyssum. Peasants, wearing green vests with silver buttons and dinky felt hats, led dogteams carrying milk down from the upper pastures, and along the roads Christmas-tree ornaments—used as scarecrows—flashed in the tall rye, the color of smoked salmon, near white cottages painted with bright, rude frescoes. Late wild violets grew in shady corners. A thin moon, the shape of a dog's tooth, appeared that night. It was all too impossibly romantic.

They took a mild walk the next day, rode up the Rax on the *Scilbahn*, got lost on top in purplish clouds, avoided the gray-greenish rain that came in midafternoon and made tiny yellow puddles in the dust, and had *Gugelhupf* for tea. They even played a little tennis, and Mason was surprised by the prowess that Tom Cairn, with all his delicate, faintly epicene quality, commanded.

Soon it was time for dinner. Under a jacket of Greek silk Cairn wore a scarlet waistcoat with gold buttons.

Paula decided, as many had decided before her, that Tom Cairn was one of the most charming persons she had ever met. One major constituent of charm is candor, and, gracious, she thought, he certainly has enough of that. He told appallingly frank stories about some people he had known, and stories even franker about himself. Before long she found herself comparing him to Mason. He was as loquacious as Mason was laconic, as fancy as Mason was, for the most part, simple. Cairn was five or six years older. He was much better educated; he knew four or five Western languages well, could get along in Russian, and was now studying Arabic. Following a recent trip to the Middle East he had become devoted to the Arabs, and, he told them seriously, he was thinking of becoming converted to Islam and retiring from European society to live, pray, and meditate in a Moslem sanctuary.

Mason was solider and had more sense. Yet Cairn—behind his frivolity, his somewhat artificial gaiety—had content too. He was phenomenally erudite. This did not keep him from making a continual crossfire of little jokes ("Oh, well, the Tyrolese, they're the missing link between the Swiss and the human race") and talking gossip incessantly. Mason had better judgment, but less vivacity. To Cairn there was often attached a positive iridescence. Mason had a good deal more contemporaneity. Fascinated by the present and keeping himself well posted he always knew what actors were playing in what new Broadway play, what new books were coming out in London or New York. Cairn, on the contrary, seemed to be remote from the present except in connection with politics. Out of his pocket protruded Dante or Aristophanes, not the New Yorker.

There arose among the three a warmth, a closeness of understanding and association, unparalleled in their experience; the rapport they felt, the community, the devotion to one another, arose spontaneously, without a trace of constraint, and with the full rapture of unashamed youthful give and take. Mason, thinking back to that weekend, wondered above all how they could have been so extremely young in their attitudes and preoccupations—so desperately earnest, so serious as well. How splendid it had been, but also how faintly ridiculous, to have felt so secure, to have had such unquestioning delight in life, when none of them had yet crossed the jagged divide which separates the years of taking in from those of giving out. How naïve, how youthful they had been not to have recognized that infamies and mortifications to come were the price that innocence, sooner or later, had to pay in order to become experience!

That night, very late, there came a rap on the Jarretts' door. Mason sleepily rose, grumbling, and let Cairn in. Paula lay flat with her face deep in the pillow and her hair a splash of pale fire in the moonlight penetrating the half-drawn curtains. She wriggled up and slid into a bed jacket. Cairn said, "I'm lonely—couldn't sleep." For half an hour he scarcely spoke. He muttered to Mason, almost roughly, in a voice that contained a slim element of veiled contempt, as well as envy,

"You . . . you . . . who never have to stare night after night into the *abyss!* Even alone, you'd be good company for yourself. . . . I have wings, you haven't, but you'll outfly me by miles in the end."

"The hare and the tortoise, what?" Paula said.

"I hate anything that has to do with rabbits, and Mason resembles a tortoise in no way whatsoever. But he has *character*, which I haven't."

Mason said nothing.

Tom shook him by the shoulder. "And I can't bear it, literally can't bear it, that you're so much younger!"

"You think too much in terms of competition, Tom," said Paula. She thought also that he had a slight tendency to self-pity, of which Mason, thank God, had no trace whatever.

"No, you're being unjust. In my own field, I have no competitors. What I am trying to express is my sense of oneness with Mason, and it *hurts* me, that's all, that we're not all the same age. I wish we were all twenty-seven!"

"I don't mind being your junior," Mason said.

"Matter of fact, you sometimes seem older than Tom," Paula said.

"Do I?" He bristled slightly.

"I meant it as a compliment."

Cairn spoke violently, "Our relations have already become intricate. You, Mason, although there is no single drop of homosexual blood in your veins, have fallen in love with me—and I perhaps with you. Oh, don't be crazy, I don't mean physically. Paula loves you, and you love Paula, but I, just to mix things up a bit, might very well fall in love with Paula too—Paula, however, not with me, because she feels she cannot quite reach me. She's madly attracted to me, but with no physical feeling. Right?"

Such divination was uncanny. Paula tingled, and then felt vaguely frightened.

He rose into a babbling swirl of complex self-analysis. "You know nothing about me, really! Do you know I have five children scattered about—five! And yet . . . yet . . . I have more basic harmony with men, some men, than with women, adoring women as I do. That bird the other night—it was sent to me as a warning, of course. Not to become too embroiled, too entangled, with you two? No, that can't be it. Let me tell you about the time a beetle rose out of a rug and flew toward me when I was staying at the British Embassy with Connie. . . . Connie *who?* You don't know *Connie!* But he was the ambassador! Well, Connie reminds me in turn of Cyril Baxter and the day in Teheran I fell asleep in that rose garden. Baxter, the architecture of whose life was completely undermined when his wife ran off with the King's mistress, but who recovered partly through my influence . . ."

Paula adored every word.

They got to sleep at five.

The next day, after a late lunch and a nap and laughter out in the soft rain and a good deal of beer at dinner, they drove back to Vienna. A mist rose; the car moved along behind the twin furrows made by its own headlights as the windshield wiper spoke like a locust: *Duzz-hunt, Duzz-hunt!* They reached the Ring. "Well, here we are," said Cairn, "time to scamper." Mason and Paula took leave of him at his hotel. Paula kissed him on the cheek; he took her face in his hands, slowly, and returned her kiss full on the mouth. "You kids stick together," he said firmly. "Don't smoke in bed, and you, Paula, you can be a pretty hard bit of goods at times, let Mason alone to fiddle with his fantasies all he wants. When you solve the problem of why people can't be happy being happy, in terms of me, call me up. I love you both." It seemed silly, but all three were close to tears.

VII. AT BAY

Tom Cairn took them to his Seipel broadcast and then had a long talk with Mason about the A.O.G. affair, urging him to write the story. Wait till some new development came which he could use as a peg, and then let fly with something so big that Chicago could not possibly ignore it, Cairn suggested. "It's crying to be published," he went on. "You won't be able to sit on it much longer." That afternoon Mason was stunned by a cable from Hilliard which said that his letters on the case had just arrived in Chicago and unless he cabled promptly to the contrary Hilliard and McFarland themselves would concoct a story out of his memoranda and run it as a dispatch—something unprecedented. "You are scooping yourself," Hilliard said.

Elated, Mason rushed in to Paula. So she had been right—of course. The story had not been big enough to get big treatment from Chicago when he first filed it; now it was.

He met Bishopson and Sandor at the Imperial, telling them that the *Star* was printing the story and, somewhat embarrassed, explaining the peculiar circumstances. It was very important that he should not appear to be deliberately beating any of his colleagues on this. If he filed, they should all be informed so that they could file as well; he must never use any special knowledge coming to him as President of the Anglo-American as a source of news. In particular he must let his Chicago opposition, Dixon and Brewster, know exactly what he was doing, so that they could send stories too.

Von Traum marched into the café; the German stank faintly of eau de cologne. He greeted Mason with the words "Now I too am a

Herr President, truly your colleague, and it is clear that we may have much future business in common. Parallel lines *do* meet sometimes—ha!" As always there was a glare in his eye, a rasp to his laugh, and cold desperate bitterness in his conversation. Mason, hating him, nodded. "You too are preparing also for a showdown with the A.O.G.? We must not let ourselves be put upon further by these Austrian *Schweine*, with their filthy standards and impure blood. I shall soon take the step of recommending to my group that the leading German newspapers should terminate their services to Austria, in other words declare a boycott of all German news to Austria, until satisfaction is reached."

That would certainly be something! It could put the entire Vienna press out of business, since German news was so vital. But could not Von Traum be bluffing? Had he any power except in connection with a few Nazi sheets? He asked, "Why are you so keen on this, Von Traum?"

"Honor!" he screeched.

Quatsch, Mason thought. The Nazi game is to do anything possible to weaken the Austrians, subdivide them, upset public confidence. If the A.O.G. suffers, that's nothing to the Nazis. They're against the big banks and they don't give a damn for the A.O.G. even if it has big pan-German connections.

Tetzel called Mason that evening.

"I have made contact with a young woman who is one of us, a secretary attached to the bureau of Hofrat Paultraxl. The bank is holding secret to itself the fact that the list supplied to the Finanzministerium and handed over to Zoltan is *only one of several lists.* There are *other* lists!"

On hearing this Mason at once called an emergency meeting of the Anglo-American, which empowered him to write to the A.O.G. again, citing this information, saying that the existence of new lists, if true, changed the entire situation, and demanding an immediate explanation without regard to Zoltan. Now it was a showdown.

Two days later came the bank's reply. In icy language it rejected the Anglo-American demands and threatened ominously to take legal action against anybody who pursued the matter further.

This was all the peg that Mason or anybody else needed. He wrote a long, meaty dispatch. Response from the *Star* was quick. Hilliard wired: FRONTPAGING YOUR BRIBERY KEEP AFTER IT, and then, something most unusual, came a message from Mr. Plover. YOUR BANK STORY AROUSING KEEN INTEREST ALSO SOME DISAPPROBATION FINANCIAL CIRCLES HERE STOP KINDLY DOUBLE CHECK ALL FIGURES THIS MATERIAL MUST NEEDS BE FOOLPROOF AND IRONCLAD.

No editor in the world but Mr. Plover would use such a locution as "must needs be" at thirty cents a word.

2

"The man chiefly responsible for publication, also the man most active in pushing the matter in general, is a certain Jarrett," said Herr Generaldirektor Dostal angrily. He, Treuwalt, and Paultraxl sat in conference. He picked up a dossier resting on his rosewood desk, and rattled a handful of cables and dispatches.

"Jarrett, Mason E.," Dostal proceeded. "An American, correspondent of the Chicago *Star*." His voice was irritated. "Jarrett's article has appeared not only in Chicago but in several other cities, financial centers, including New York, where publications take the syndicated service of Jarrett's newspaper. There are other articles as well by other American correspondents." He flung the batch of cables down.

"We should never have conceded that any money was disbursed or turned that list over to the Finanzministerium," averred Treuwalt, glancing with hostility at Paultraxl. "That was your recommendation, and it has been the root of the trouble ever since."

"Yes, I admit that it was my recommendation," said Paultraxl. "But also I must point out that the matter was thoroughly discussed by all of us, and a unanimous decision reached."

"Humpff." The grooves bearing down from Dostal's nostrils deepened. "In any case there was little else that could have been done. We had to silence the opposition in Parliament and satisfy certain personages in the government as well."

"What do we know about this person Jarrett?" asked Paultraxl. Dostal, putting on his glasses, read from the dossier. "He lives in Döbling. In his early thirties. Married, no children. He is not a member of any party. He has apparently never taken any political line at all. Good relations with the American Legation and all the American groups in town, also the British. Plays closely with the Czechs, Poles, et cetera. Apparently very active in forcing premature publication of the negotiations for our Customs Union—ah!"

"An enemy," said Paultraxl.

Dostal proceeded, "In Vienna about a year, his German faulty, frequents the Imperial and Weissenhof, has no suspicious connections of any kind, but goes occasionally to night clubs."

"Hmmm." Paultraxl looked interested.

Dostal proceeded: "His income is five hundred dollars per month and his newspaper pays generous expenses. His account with us has always been in perfect order. Somewhat extravagant, he lives well. When he travels he does not accept free railway tickets or other favors. Humpff, the fool. He has consistently sent altogether neutral dispatches. Careful check on all his recent telegrams; they are closely factual. He is not vulnerable from that point of view. We cannot have him expelled from Austria without serious complications."

"The entire development is absurd," said Paultraxl. "An American *Dummkopf.*"

"You assure me," Dostal turned to him, "the list was the same as in other years? The procedure was the same, little gifts and tips, scattered among minor officials, journalists, agents and hangers-on in the cafés? It has always been done. Nothing exceptional was done this year, except that, for certain reasons, we decided to make the sums more considerable. Eh?"

"Even so, not much," Treuwalt said. "Think what we pay the Heimwehr."

"And now the Nazis too!" Dostal's voice became more irritated. "They are rising somewhat in strength, and it is necessary to keep some goodwill on all sides. They might even form a government some day. It is totally offensive to have to pay Nazis—scandalous! They are animals. But we must continue to subscribe to the old policy, have our bread buttered in every quarter."

"Something should be done to stop the Americans," Paultraxl said decisively. "Zoltan and his group do not matter much, though it will be embarrassing if they publish full details of the list or discover about the supplementary lists, which are more important. The Germans I do not take seriously as yet, because Von Traum has little influence except among the pan-Germans. The Americans I do not like. Their last general meeting—they have decided to push the matter through. They are willing to Whitt and the English. Now come the stories in New York and elsewhere. The Americans keep the scandal alive. Somehow they must be stopped."

"I have suddenly an idea." Herr Generaldirektor Dostal picked up the telephone. "It is not a big idea, but it may be something." He spoke to his secretary. "Get me at once the Chief of the Austrian Press Bureau." While waiting he turned to his fellow directors. "This Jarrett, like all Americans, may be vain."

3

The Austrian Press Bureau, as Mason and his colleagues knew well, was an intricate and curious organism, an inheritance from the days of Metternich. Most of the new Central European countries paid close attention to the fine art of propaganda. They maintained efficient staffs to receive newspapermen, make their passage easy, and assist their work; they assembled information, arranged interviews, and volunteered to provide research on any special problem. Not so the Austrians. The Press Bureau of the Bundeskanzleramt came close to being invisible. It considered the press, with which it had to deal, as something beneath its dignity. Dr. Wimpassing, the Director, had little interest in his nominal job. What interested him was politics. He was the Chancellor's principal contact man and private manipulator in Parliament. When Mason arrived in Vienna he had applied for an appointment with Dr. Wimpassing as a matter of course. In any other country in the world the head of the Press Bureau would have greeted the new resident correspondent of an important American newspaper with cordial alacrity, not merely out of courtesy but for obvious reasons of expedience; but Mason waited five solid months to be received by Dr. Wimpassing. This was not because of any hostility to Mason Jarrett or the Chicago Star. It was because Dr. Wimpassing was too busy. So, now, Mason felt a spasm of curiosity when he received an urgent message to the effect that Herr Gesandter Dr. Wimpassing, the Chief of the Bundespressedienst, would like to see him the next morning at eleven.

"Ah! *Lieber Herr Kollege!*" Mason was astounded. Not only was he received punctually, but Dr. Wimpassing positively oozed with friendliness. The Gesandte, tall and lean, had glabrous cheeks, shaved so closely that they looked raw, and silver-shining hair. He wore octagonal-shaped smoked glasses, and had long spindly legs.

"But no, I cannot call you longer my *lieber Herr Kollege*, I must call you now my *lieber Herr Präsident!*"

Mason did not have to exert himself to recall how frostily indifferent the Press Bureau had been to the organization of the Anglo-American Press Association. "My *lieber Herr Präsident!*" Dr. Wimpassing repeated, almost cooing. He clasped Mason's hand with both of his, led him to an Empire sofa upholstered in turquoise silk, and poured forth a monologue.

Dr. Wimpassing congratulated his dear colleague on the formation of the Anglo-American Press Association. He congratulated him on being the first president of the Anglo-American Press Association. He trusted that his dear colleague, fellow worker, and *lieber Herr Präsident*, was enjoying thoroughly his sojourn in Vienna. He prayed that the same was true of the wife of the *lieber Herr Präsident*, and that she was in good health. He wished his friend and *lieber* colleague, the Herr Präsident, to know categorically that the Austrian government approved most heartily of the formation of the Anglo-American Press Association. It was so valuable to have these little, ah, journalistic groups active on the scene. They promoted friendship. They promoted, ah, solidarity. They promoted, ah, a good spirit between Austria and the world abroad. The Austrian government was, at this particular moment, it just so happened, in particular need of sympathetic understanding by important circles in the world abroad. It would much appreciate the handling of certain types of, ah, news, in Vienna by resident correspondents in a friendly, sympathetic way. Hence it wished to give concrete expression of its approval of the formation of the Anglo-American Press Association and the election of Herr Jarrett as its first president. So, would not Herr Präsident Jarrett accept a token of appreciation from the Austrian government? The Austrian government would be overwhelmed with pride, joy, and honor if the Herr Präsident would find it possible in these rather, ah, difficult and troubled times, with so much about Austria unappreciated and in fact all but unknown in the world outside, while difficulties of incalculable force might soon be facing the Austrian Republic, to accept the small—ah, but honored!—demonstration of esteem which the Austrian government wished to proffer. The Austrian government, of which he, Herr Gesandter Dr. Wimpassing, was the representative, in a word offered to Herr Präsident Jarrett, president of the Anglo-American Press Association, the Order of the Phoenix, Second Class.

"A decoration?" Mason exclaimed, astonished.

"A decoration!"

Dr. Wimpassing beamed. There came an awkward pause.

Mason said, "Thanks very much, Dr. Wimpassing—"

"Ah—"

"Thanks a lot, but I'm afraid I can't accept your decoration."

He got out of the office as quickly as he could. "By God," he muttered to himself, half-grinning. "Now they're trying to bribe me!"

❋

Herr Generaldirektor Dostal turned to Paultraxl testily. "Let us try something else. I leave it to you—take special action. There must be *something* on this Jarrett." He summoned two other directors, and, grunting, muttered, "Now we proceed to something serious. Gentlemen, I wish to discuss certain factors that are bound to show in our next balance sheet. First, as to outstanding debts to foreign creditors . . ."

4

Mason had a cable from McFarland suggesting a mail series on the Vienna housing program, something unique in Europe. Apparently he had heard enthusiastic comments about it from a Chicago friend who had recently visited Vienna. Mason was sick of writing mailers, but a service message from McFarland was a command. Besides, the *Star* was one of the few American newspapers that did not discriminate against mail stories, which, if they were interesting enough, got exactly the same treatment from the foreign desk as did cables, and had equal chance to make page two, or even page one.

Mason got in touch with Dr. Ricardo Stein, who offered to help him, and they set out together. He and Paula had become very fond of Stein. It was a brilliant, warm May day. The sun shone fully and calmly. Stein took him to the Schiller-Hof near the Danube canal, and pointed to the courtyard. "It's the largest residential building in the world, three-fifths of a mile long, and it holds four thousand families." There was a good deal of emotion in Stein's voice, in spite of his precise, somewhat pedantic manner. He led Mason along a series of blue-buff terraces, sharply divided into sectors, where whole streets penetrated boldly under stucco arches to cross the gigantic courtyard. The roof, like that of a medieval castle, was crenelated, and at the corners stood parapets and towers.

They climbed a broad staircase, and Stein rapped on a door that he picked at random.

"Of course," Stein was saying, "if a worker loses his job, he's relieved of the obligation to pay rent until he finds work again."

"What?"

A woman in an apron opened the door, apologetically wiping her hands. "From the Gemeinde? To visit us? But come right in!" She was the wife of a railway worker and spoke in a broad argot, saying "Jaw" for "Ja." Peering through the small, square nest of rooms, clean as soap, Mason remembered stories he had heard about the colossal "extravagance" of these municipal flats. Now he saw that they were not extravagant at all, but sensibly built, modest, and inexpensive to maintain.

"What rent do you pay?" Mason asked.

"Sixty-seven Schillings a month."

Mason whistled—nine dollars and a half! Stein led him to another Stiege, and they dropped in without warning at two more flats. In the first the man of the house, a metalworker in a branch of the Behemoth Steel Works, where business was slack, had been out of work for six months. His wife was recuperating from tuberculosis, and if they hadn't been lucky enough to be longtime residents of a Gemeinde-haus, they might have starved, she said. Now she had a job in the tenement's laundry. In the other the wife was an intellectual, a Ph.D. who worked at the party's research center; her husband was a dentist. Mason hadn't known that people other than manual workers were permitted to live in the Gemeinde houses. Stein explained that in the past year or two a number of professional men and women had been taken in—doctors with jobs in the municipality, traffic engineers, civil servants in the Ministry of Health, even a few writers, musicians, artists.

"You've got all this now," Mason said to the dentist's wife. "You know what it means and what it represents. Would you fight to defend it?"

"*Jawohl!*" She pointed to the Danube canal near Heiligenstadt, half a mile away. "There the barricades begin." She crossed her arms, which, for an intellectual, showed substantial muscle. "We are ready."

"But don't a lot of workers get soft, living in apartments as comfortable as these? Doesn't it turn them into bourgeoisie, so that they'll be less good party members in the future?"

Stein realized that this question had point, but the dentist's wife argued with fierce dogmatism that what he said could not be true.

They visited the clinic, the library, and in particular the kindergarten, which had shiny cork floors, washbowls set conveniently low, modern functional toys, and small-size deck chairs and other special accouterments—the sort of equipment that, in other cities, would be available only to children of the rich. Attendance cost thirty cents a week. At a lunch given for them by the staff Mason felt something expand within him. These teachers, doctors, administrators, were all good people. They looked at him with proud, grave, guarded eyes. They were idealists, but they worked hard for an immediately realizable objective. Perhaps they had personal problems and conflicts, just as he had, but their lives seemed to have become solidly integrated into that of the community. They were molding and shaping the life of a whole city, giving it a fruitful design, and it was no wonder the Gemeinde homes ranked incontestably as Vienna's finest contemporary monument.

Look at Stein now. Mason suddenly realized that he envied Stein. Stein was a sunny person, but he knew exactly what constituted his relationship to the external world, what he believed in, and what disciplines he had to submit to in order to achieve enjoyment of his beliefs. In contrast, Mason felt lost, empty, aimless. They picked up their car and visited several other of the great houses scattered around the city, the La Salle-Hof, the Goethe-Hof, the Karl Marx-Hof, and, one of the newest, the George Washington-Hof, painted a slick, clean combination of cream and green. "As you observe," said Stein, "we name the houses for eminent revolutionaries!"

"But you won't let anybody in your houses who isn't a member of the party—is that fair?"

"You are quite misinformed. The new houses are primarily for workers, and it so happens that most of the workers belong to us."

"But suppose, say, a man with a small business, a teller in a bank or a clerk in a department store, applied for residence?"

"Anybody is entitled to apply," Stein explained. "A committee sits, and each case is judged with care. We take first those who live in unsanitary or condemned buildings, those who are ill or those who cannot afford decent quarters or a satisfactory diet for their children."

"But in practice you take mostly Social Democrats?"

Stein shrugged. "We have built dwellings for one hundred and sixty thousand families. To house all of Vienna properly we will need to build twice or three times that. And why should we give the first fruits of our program, for which we have fought so hard, to our enemies?"

"How is all this paid for—out of the taxes of the rich, of course!"

"Not quite." Stein laughed. "The funds do not come out of taxes at large, but only from a special levy on landlords and landowners, which is not exorbitant. No capital investment is involved at all. That's why we can afford such low rentals."

"In other words part of the rent I pay the Wallensteins contributes to the rent of the Gemeinde tenants."

"In a sense, yes. Incidentally, why don't you and Paula apply for a Gemeinde flat?" He added dryly, "It would save you a considerable amount of money. I should imagine that you would find adequate quarters for about fifteen dollars a month."

5

Mason thought that he had gotten rid of his cough, but it returned; he whooped, hacked, and began to run a temperature. Paula refused to take this seriously. "It's all in your imagination, darling," she bantered. "You're trying to get rid of something, to spit something out, to get it off your *chest!*" This did not make Mason feel any better, but of course everybody in Vienna became an amateur psychoanalyst sooner or later.

Mason went to see Antioch, their doctor, a stocky, warm little man with eyes overhung by bristling untidy brows.

He looked him over.

"You are young, therefore it is nothing," Dr. Antioch said. "Nevertheless I do not like all that I find. Could you take time off for a week or two in the Alps—not necessarily in a sanitarium, but anywhere high in the sunshine, where you could rest?"

"Too much going on," Mason said. "Impossible."

The doctor nodded. "Do you know by chance anybody who has an airplane?"

"No," replied Mason automatically, and then reconsidered, thinking of Stein. "Why, as a matter of fact, yes, I do."

"It is a new experiment in therapy for the aftermath of whooping cough and certain other respiratory ailments. Fly half a dozen times, an hour or so each time, at seven or eight thousand feet—quite possibly the irritation will clear up."

This sounded far-fetched to Mason, but Antioch had imagination as well as skill and he trusted him.

The doctor spoke as if he were talking to himself. "Myself I am not a psychoanalyst, not even a psychiatrist except insofar as any physician has to be a psychiatrist to be able to endure most of his patients. I shall be pleased if a series of flights clears up your cough. If not, come back to me at once. There may be other elements involved—factors of stress, emotional or otherwise. Are you under any particular strain right now? You need oxygenization, that is to say, refreshment, that is, air, that is, freedom from obsessive thought. Anyway, get rid of the whooping cough. You are a large man, but your lungs are, it happens, small. They are your weakest point, and it is my experience that disease always likes weak points." Dr. Antioch lit a cheroot, which had an evil smell. "I believe firmly that most illnesses have a double origin. A physical irritation, invasion by a microbe, a traumatic disturbance, call it what you will, forms one element. The mental or neurotic component is perhaps more important. Few people, except tuberculars, become seriously ill if they are in the midst of important work. Few honeymooners develop serious complaints. . . . I would add something you may think fanciful—that disease often attacks that part of the body most precious to the sufferer. I have known singers to develop cancer of the vocal chords. Well! To be serious: you must get rid of your cough at once, and let us experiment with the airplane. I do not want to be involved with you if you acquire tuberculosis. You would cost far too much in nuisance and would be very difficult to handle."

Mason rose.

"You have not mentioned the *gnädige Frau*. She is well, I hope."

"Very."

"No eczema, no hives, no rash?"

"Hardly any trouble for months, I'm glad to say. Of course we avoid animals, and keep away from people with pets."

"It should not be necessary. I am more than ever convinced that factors of sensitiveness, of suppression, are involved."

He walked Mason to the door.

＊

Dr. Ricardo Stein agreed at once, with his perpetual sunny smile, to take Mason up for a series of flights, and Paula, for all her fear of airplanes, accepted the proposal after argument. The concept of therapy by aviation challenged Stein's rationalist mind. They drove out to Aspern across the Danube. The aircraft seemed appallingly small and frail. Mason felt that he was mounting a wasp's back when his friend tucked him in and they took off. The earth wheeled sideways; tilted alarmingly; receded swiftly; Mason could feel the strong bite of the engine, pushing them steadily forward—up—up— up. Wind whistled in the open cockpit; spars and braces shook. They followed the yellow trough of the Danube and then swung into a broad crescent, bumping violently, over the Wienerwald hills. The wings of the small plane rustled as if they were canvas sails, and, edging along a cloud bank, it seemed that they flew through a storm of chrysanthemums.

Stein made a sharp turn which brought Mason's stomach into his throat, whereupon they straightened out and coasted down over the center of the city. Gesticulating, he pointed out various sights, like the Karlskirche, a squatting bullfrog, and St. Stephen's. Mason even identified the A.O.G. building. It came time to return, and he felt that he was sliding, sliding, down the sloping side of an isosceles triangle. Stein manipulated the stick, making a neat, airy gesture, and before Mason realized what was happening they bumped with a soft squash at the far end of the billowy green field.

They repeated this adventure every day for a week, and Mason learned to love to fly. Stein let him play with the controls and they continually slipped back and forth over metropolitan Vienna at fairly low altitudes, so that he had unparalleled opportunities to see the city from the air. Firmly fixed in his mind were the shafts of long streets intersecting the Ring and the massive blocks of Gemeinde tenements along the river. On the last flight, Mason almost—but not quite—landed the plane himself; it made long swooping bounds over the turf like a kangaroo, until Stein grabbed the controls. Stepping out, he patted the little ship on its nose affectionately, as if it were something alive, as one might pat a horse, its nostrils steaming, which had just won a good close race.

The phone rang as usual the next morning—Bleschke. There were days when Mason could scarcely bear to listen to the bland monotonous voice ticking off possible human-interest stories. Exiled Archduke Otto declared to be an honorary citizen of a village in the Tyrol. Dedication in the Votivkirche of the largest candle in the world, which would burn for 150 years. Failure of the grain crop in the Sanjak of Novibazar. That was a nice name, Mason ruminated. It belonged to a region of Yugoslavia he had not yet visited. Much else in his enormous territory was still unknown to him. He had never been to Ljubljana or the Black Sea ports of Bulgaria; mountain resorts in the High Tatra were still unprobed. He started to scribble on a pad. Scarcely a day passed without his making lists of stories he would like to tackle. He loved to plan. Now he drew up a calendar, month by month, for the year to come, together with an agenda sheet, estimating the time necessary for self-imposed assignments. June: a mail series on the Vienna theater; July, a trip with Paula to the Vorarlberg and Carinthia, for stories which would appeal to tourists; August, the spas in Bohemia and Moravia; September and October, Yugoslavia, Macedonia, and Albania. But this was silly. Whether he would do any or all of it would depend on the way spot news was running. He tossed the calendar and agenda sheet into the wastebasket. Directly then he retrieved them from the wastebasket.

He looked out to the Wallenstein garden through the double sheet of his office window. A fly, rubbing its mandibles like a Chinese using miniature chopsticks, was caught between the two panes. In the garden each individual flower looked individually, personally, polished, particularly the tulips. Mason had to get to work, but he still dawdled, dreaming. He shuffled into the dining room to have another cup of coffee. Overwhelmed, almost suffocated as she was by the colossal weight of her love for him, Paula nevertheless still found it insufferable, intolerable—the way he sometimes moped around the house for hour after hour in the mornings, sloppy in a bathrobe. How he threw his clothes around! That morning she had found one of his socks on her dressing table—how was it possible?

Around five that afternoon came an unexpected call. Paula was out looking at some Lowestoft in the Dorotheergasse auction rooms. He recognized the husky, vibrating voice at once. Hilda apologized for telephoning him, said that she did not want to discommode him in any way, but, in his own interest, felt that she had to see him as soon as possible. A personal business—urgent. Could he make himself free to drop in at the Koenigen at nine?

When Paula asked him after dinner (jellied bortsch, stuffed peppers, *Salzburgernockerl*) where he was going he replied easily, "To see a girl in a night club, of course." She laughed, not dreaming that he told the truth. "Good luck, darling." At the Koenigen, Trudi greeted him with her gentle "*Servus.*" What a sweet, decent little girl, Mason thought. She pointed to a table in the rear of the establishment, where, to his considerable astonishment, he saw Hilda sitting with Willi, the Archduke. Hilda looked lovely. Her hair was like Montana wheat planted in contours on a slope of hill, he thought fancifully. At once, joining them, he detected an atmosphere, not of coldness, but of stern, questioning appraisal. The Archduke and Hilda were both measuring him like judges at a court-martial.

"What's up?" Mason asked, startled.

Hilda said, "You seem to be mixing up in very dubious affairs, my good friend. For one thing you have just cost me a thousand Schillings."

Mason ordered drinks. "How? What's going on?"

The Archduke fidgeted.

"An attempt was to be made to blackmail you. I was to receive a thousand Schillings for my participation."

Mason smelled A.O.G. at once.

"We are doing you a large, large favor, and undergo a certain amount of risk to do so. I will explain, and then you must tell us your side of the story."

He tightened.

"Do you remember the evening, I think it was the last time we have seen you, perhaps two months ago, you asked Trudi and me to find out for you what a group from the A.O.G. was talking about."

"Yes, of course."

"Now it is the A.O.G. which wishes to find out things about you." She paused significantly. "What were you looking for that evening? Why should the A.O.G. wish to disgrace you now? What is the connection?"

Her manner was calm, but still appraising. The Archduke, red in the face, seethed with what seemed to be indignation, suppressed hatred and excitement.

Mason said, "Nothing that night had anything to do with the A.O.G. itself. I was running down a story about the plan to make a Customs Union between Germany and Austria. I had a sudden hunch that the A.O.G. men might confirm that negotiations were going on, which, thanks to you, they did."

"Still I do not understand."

The Archduke grunted.

"It's a complicated story. The gist of it is this." Mason told them about the bribery affair.

Hilda said, "Ah, now it becomes clear. You are the spearhead of the investigation, and they wish to silence you." She paused, murmuring, "Money . . . money! The source of good and evil both."

"Do not talk in such clichés," said the Archduke.

"It is my mentality. Do you know"—she turned to Mason—"I have earned a living since I was eight. That is not an exaggeration. I was made by my parents to be a model for the advertisements showing

happy, pretty children. There was one series for a toothpaste. I opened
my mouth wide and smiled, radiant, showing all my teeth, like this"
—she grimaced with the parody of a grin—"and then later the photographer, who was a hunchback, made me always a proposal of extreme
indecency. And I was eight! Back to the camera, the toothbrush in
one hand, and then opening my whole face with the smile, then touching the teeth with the toothbrush now covered with pink paste—
uhh! Money, money! To you perhaps it is nothing, but to me, even
today, a thousand Schillings is a major sum. Moreover it was to have
been an advance payment on a larger fee."

Mason did not know what to say except a lame "Well, thanks,
thanks a lot. Really, I can't tell you . . ." He was quivering with anger
at the A.O.G.

"Never mind."

He knew that it would be tactless to say now that he would make
the thousand Schillings up to her. He said, "Now, please, tell me
more. What were you supposed to do with me in this blackmail
business?"

Hilda shrugged her shoulders; the monocle slipped off. "The idea
was to get you into a compromising position, make a scandal, dis-
credit you, make you disreputable so that you would not be believed,
even force you out of your job or to leave the country. Any number
of combinations would be a possibility. Traps could be set. You and
Trudi might be found in bed together."

Mason laughed, but his blood was boiling. "That would be very
pleasant."

"Not after the photographers entered."

He proceeded: "But how did all this get to you? How was it
arranged? Who was the emissary?"

"I . . . I!" said the Archduke. "Often I do small jobs for certain
institutions. Occasionally the A.O.G. calls for me. A director there,
Paultraxl, told me of the wish to make you an object of scandal. And
now, I take rare pleasure in it, I am double-crossing Paultraxl!"
His eyes danced. "I shall report that you cannot be reached, as
indeed I know you could not be. The clumsiness of it, the effrontery,

the stupidity! As if successful blackmail could be performed in such a manner! A plot so childish—they must be losing their minds. But, my friend, I think perhaps you are getting into deeper waters than you know. I would advise caution."

"Why are you doing this for me, Willi?" Mason asked.

The Archduke began to laugh, as he had laughed that night at the Sandors', and could not stop. He became hysterical, rapped the table, and then, seeking to control himself, said between gasps of laughter, "Because . . . because . . . I like . . . your wife!" He gulped a drink and began to bang on the table with a knife and fork.

"I . . . I . . . who should be sitting this moment in the Hofburg, am forced to crawl secretly on missions so disgusting, so degrading. . . . For me, me, to have to become a blackmailer! I, who have rights as a human being, let alone a royal prince, to have to prowl night by night in the bars and cafés, doing shadiness! It is not to be borne, and I have had enough of it!"

He flung himself out of the establishment.

It was time for Hilda's first number, and sitting with Trudi, Mason listened once more to the sheer animal bellow rise out of her slim throat. The force of her voice seemed to be greater than what the body could contain. Then in the next song she became muted, husky, whispering. "Kleines, she's certainly at her best tonight," he said to Trudi, who nodded with rapt pleasure. He noticed the peculiar slight ripple in Trudi's teeth, and thought of how much he liked her. How keenly he would like to see both these girls more often. Impossible! No matter how innocent, impossible! It was the sort of thing that Paula, the puritan, could never possibly understand, much less accept, and, what the hell, Paula was his wife, wasn't she? And indispensable. But he could not help feeling convinced that an inch of freedom never hurt a man.

Hilda came up to his table after her songs.

"Have you known Willi long?" Mason asked.

"Oh yes. One of my truest friends. Besides," she added negligently, as if it must be something that Mason knew, "besides, he works here, more or less."

"Works here?"

"He is paid a small retainer, and gets free drinks as well, for hanging around the fashionable hotels, making friends, cultivating people, and persuading them to come here for the evening."

Christ, Mason thought.

"He is also very well known in the underworld. *Ja!* He has contact with swindlers, big thieves, even assassins. But he is a very good man, in spite of spoiling."

They talked, smiling at reminiscences of the summer before. Mason had to go, and her face became pensive.

"A penny for your thoughts, Hilda."

"Tomorrow is my day off and I think of the *Bauernschmaus* I will cook for Trudi."

∗

While talking to the girls Mason had tried to keep his rage and resentment at the A.O.G. to a decent minimum. Now walking home he boiled over. Get those bastards! he said to himself. Get them!

6

The Jarretts had had no word from Kitty Jameson since a postcard reporting her safe arrival in Athens two months before; now a letter came. Reading it, Paula gave several appreciative bursts of laughter, and then frowned heavily, murmuring, "Oh! . . . Ah! . . . No!" She thrust the letter at Mason with a fierce gesture of refusal. "No, no," she repeated, and commanded, "Mason, stop dreaming—read this. Kitty's in trouble. She must be stark, staring mad!"

After describing details of her job, the status of the Agora excavations, the social life of Athens, and her opinion, not high, of contemporary Greeks, Kitty concluded:

Incidentally, I don't know if you remember all the nuances of that departure from Vienna, but your mad, compelling, persistent friend Mr. Thorne changed his ticket, once he was on the train, came down with me to Athens, and stayed a day or two. Now he's come back. Says he needed a holiday in the sun, and was able to contrive some office business as an excuse. I don't know where he gets the money, but he's hired a boat, and next week we're going to do some island hopping.

Mason put the letter down. "What do you mean, she's in trouble? She's just having an affair with Thorne."

"Isn't that trouble?" Paula became more agitated. "I'm going down to Athens right this minute, and rescue her!"

"You'll do no such thing."

"But that man is a monster! You've said so yourself. Look what he did to Tetzel—he caused Mia's suicide!"

"Well, now, I don't know that that could actually be proved. Nobody ever knows exactly what makes things happen. Character is destiny, isn't it?"

"Don't be so darned calm and reasonable, please! You know how vulnerable Kitty is, and that man will ruin her. I've got to save her somehow, anyway protect her."

Mason held no particular brief for Thorne and, as always, he admired Paula's ardent and impulsive generosity of spirit, but he couldn't see her trucking all the way down to Athens, more than two whole days on a train, on such an errand. He protested, "But Thorne, after all, may be preferable to that damned professor—"

"Thorne's impossible!"

"Perhaps. But it's Kitty's life, not yours. What business is it of yours, ours, anyway?"

"*Business?*" Paula became angry. "She's my best friend, isn't she? What are friends for, anyway? I can't let her get into another unending, hideous mess with a brute like Thorne, after all the trouble she *has* had with the professor. Relationships count. I have a responsibility!"

"No, you haven't. All you'd do would be to barge in where you're not wanted, and spoil what's probably a quite nice love affair."

❋

That afternoon Cairn called from Warsaw, where he had arrived hoping to interview Pilsudski. One of Tom's most engaging qualities was the concentrated delight with which he threw himself into the life of his friends. The A.O.G. story gripped him. He wanted not merely to be helpful to Mason, but to be part of the adventure himself. Today he told Mason to try to get a complete list of the A.O.G.'s industrial investments and work out, if possible, a list of interlocking directorates—also indicate how sound the investments were (or were not) and what interest rates were being paid. Mason listened carefully and summoned Tetzel and put him to work.

In his adhesive way Karl dutifully dug up most of the details Cairn wanted a day or two later, and Mason pored over the figures. Formidable, amazing! The A.O.G. owned or controlled the three leading Vienna hotels, nine construction companies, and two machine-tool plants. It had twelve million dollars in breweries, thirty million in electrical appliances, seventeen in sugar, thirty-five in textiles, fourteen in paper mills. Forty million dollars in four different railroads; thirty-three million in insurance! Then there were very large sums in glass, shipping, mining, timber, and cement.

One A.O.G. director, Treuwalt, had, it seemed, borrowed more than $5,000,000 from the A.O.G. at four and a half per cent and lent it to a company of which he was the principal shareholder at seven per cent, pocketing the difference. This of course was too libelous to use in a news dispatch. But Mason could send a story on the full list of A.O.G. holdings, together with all the material he had on interlocking directorates, without risk. He did so and his story was almost immediately cabled back to Vienna, where it appeared under large headlines in the *Stunde*. Incredibly enough a full description of the A.O.G.'s industrial holdings had never been printed in Austria before, and it made a legitimate sensation.

*

Mason was surprised the next day that Paula still felt that it was her duty to do something to save Kitty from Thorne. She did really want to go to Athens, but he held firmly to his view that this would be a foolish mistake. Thorne and Kitty might have a hell of a difficult time, if their affair was serious, but it was also entirely possible that they might be happy together. Mason's belief in imponderables was, as always, strong. Life was a matter of probabilities. Paula, on the other hand, could not be shaken from her belief that if life was worthwhile, as she most definitely thought it was, it must logically follow that it has structure; therefore cause and effect must operate. At the age of nine she had learned that if she ate licorice she would be sick; ever since she had taken it as a matter of simple, automatic faith, like the multiplication tables, that consequences follow actions, and that unwise actions can produce dire consequences.

Mason had a cable to write about reports of trouble along the Bessarabian frontier, and was awaiting Bleschke's call.

Paula came in.

"What about Athens, Mason? I really think I ought to go."

"Honestly I don't think it's a good idea."

"Virgin Mary!" she exploded. "Am I a slave?"

"You know darned well you're not a slave."

"It's all a question of money," she said bitterly.

"Money?"

"If I had a penny of my own, you'd not be able to stop me. If only I had money, money! The basis of all masculine superiority is financial, and I think it's sickening. Why should men have all the independence? I'm going out and get a *job!*"

"Now, really, Paula. And I'm not stopping you. All I'm saying is that I think it would be foolish to go."

"You are stopping me, because you know I'd never do anything without your consent. Also you're being frightfully hypocritical when you pretend that you're *not* stopping me."

"You put me in a difficult position. I'm not giving you an order. I'm telling you what I think."

"You are too giving me an order, but you won't admit it. Well, never mind." She gave him a somewhat wan smile, accepting defeat.

The American mail came in. Mason opened with interest a letter from Mr. Plover. He did not have letters from Mr. Plover often. "Look at this," Mason said to Paula.

Dear Mr. Jarrett:
We have been printing with interest your dispatches about the corruption matter concerning the Allgemeine Österreichische Gesellschaft. I am relying on it that you are firmly correct, not merely on all your facts, but prudent and of good judgment of the circumstances you deduce therefrom.

Meantime I have to report something in the same realm that will be of interest to you. Yesterday an Austrian gentleman called upon me, having arrived from Washington for this specific purpose. His assertion was that his capacity was purely unofficial. But it seemed to me obvious that he must have some connection at least with the Austrian authorities. The purport of his conversation was that he understood that the *Star* was thinking of withdrawing you from Vienna, and assigning you to another post. I told him that we contemplated nothing of the kind, and that so far as I knew you were perfectly happy in Vienna and hoped indefinitely to remain there. He then suggested that "certain institutions" in Austria would appreciate it very much if, in fact, we did transfer you from Vienna, and filled the Vienna post with another man.

Perceiving that this was the object of his visit, I at once showed him the door.

Yours sincerely,
Richard Maxwell Plover

Paula muttered, appalled, "Well! Of all the *nerve!*" The thought of going to Athens vanished from her mind.

7

Mason had some letters to write that night, and found that he had run out of carbon paper. He walked into Otto's room, where he rummaged through the cupboard without result, and then yanked open his desk drawer. There, carelessly flung on a pile of envelopes, he saw a black leather notebook—obviously a diary. Mason did something totally odious and reprehensible. Idly he opened it, and then began to read.

Most entries, written in careful English (clearly Otto was exercising himself), had little interest. Notes on philosophic studies; remarks about girls he was taking out; some bits of self-analysis. He had been profoundly moved by *Of Human Bondage*, and was worried to the point of desperation because he could not identify all four of the encores that Mischa Elman had played at a concert the night before. Then a notation caught Mason's eye:

Observations on the Amerikaner.

The *gnädige Frau's* German is quite good, but his! Every other word is *doch* or *schön*, and he has no knowledge whatever of the subjunctive. The way he mixes genders!

One afternoon he talked about the editors of his newspaper—this taught me much. But how can such a newspaper send to Vienna here a correspondent who does not know perfect German? Unthinkable! Americans are super-confident! !

I have at last determined the color of the gnädige Frau's eyes. They are both brown and green, the color of oak leaves.

Mason could not keep from reading on.

The Herr continues to baffle me. He has not read Kant, not even Spinoza. Fie, fie!

Both the Herr and the g. F. treat me with the utmost consideration. Compared to us they are somewhat barbaric (? barbarous?). It is extremely necessary that my English shall be perfected soon. The Herr reads constantly, but he has no interest in ideas at all. I asked him today if he believed in free will or determinism, and he gave me an answer so astounding that it is almost impossible to write it down. Laughing, he replied, "Both!"

Such irresponsibility!

To the cinema with my cousin Nella. We discussed the Americans again. She is baffled too. Nella says that his secret is that he does not wish to dominate. This is a characteristic most unusual in the male. Is it caused by a certain quality of superiority, or by indifference?

Well, well! Mason thought.

For all the Herr's vagueness, he has a great deal of drive, more than she. On the other hand her vitality is superior. There is clearly a distinction to be made between "drive" and "vitality." When he finishes anything, he relapses into lethargy. She continually keeps on going. Of course she is by far the more cultivated. She has style, of which he has little. But here again Nella and I entered into serious argument. She says I am mistaken in thinking that the g. F. is more sensitive than the Herr. He, she says, is much more perceptive, in tune with more nuances, than is she. But resolutely I refuse to believe this.

Journalism, as practiced by the Americans, is held to be "objektiv." The Herr says that his whole duty is to write the truth. But I asked him today if he would be willing to define for me the concept of truth. Did he mean truth in the pragmatic sense, in that it was something verifiable, or were his standards larger? He gave me a most peculiar look and said nothing. Has he true principles? Astonishing!

He would have to give this brat a good talking-to.

The *gnädige Frau* looks into mirrors much of the time, primping. She asks him three or four times a day what to wear. *But this does not derive so much from vanity as from underconfidence.*

The Herr does not understand this. He thinks even that she is arrogant and conceited, but in reality she is timid, not knowing her own value.

There was a scene last night of such a wildness. A craziness, no less! They had bought a quantity of raw silk and a dressmaker had out of this made them pajamas. These they were *dyeing!* Frau Gertrude had gone home and they did not know that I still labored. I must *master* Hegel. In the kitchen, incredible, fantastic, they had made pots and pails of different colors—peacock blue, a glaring pink, orange. Pools of the dye spilled and began to run on the floor and mix—frightening! I passed by the door and the g. F. said, "Come in, Otto, help us." The Herr took one pair of pants, bright green, and started to wring it out over the sink at the same time that she spilled a pot of purple. Screaming with laughter she put her finger in the pot and touched it on his nose, making a spot. He howled with laughter too and daubed her with green on the cheek. *Phänomenal!* Then they hurled the wet newly dyed pajamas over the whole of the kitchen, splashing themselves with color and ruining their clothes! They sank back exhausted, rocking with laughter. Then she caught my eye again and said, *"Now let's paint OTTO!"*

I fled. I think that perhaps both were drunk.

Mason slipped the diary back into the desk drawer carefully and tiptoed out.

Karl Tetzel dropped in the next afternoon, and Mason took him for a stroll in the garden to work out their next course of action. Behind a flowering border they encountered Dozent Dr. Wallenstein sauntering with Nella, and Mason introduced Tetzel. This was the last week of Dr. Wallenstein's tenure at the university, after a quarter of a century, and he looked tired—suddenly years older. He took Mason by the arm, while Tetzel and Nella walked ahead. In this light Nella's hair looked the color of oatmeal. Her small, youthful breasts pressed upright against her cotton dress.

"My son . . ." Dr. Wallenstein began. "He is doing well, I hope? You are not dissatisfied? He is dutiful?"

"I don't know whether he's exactly dutiful," Mason replied, "but he does his work well." He thought of the diary. "In fact I have no hesitation in saying that I think that he is a most remarkable young man."

"Ah!" the Dozent beamed. "He lacks humor, but my wife is furious if I tell her that. I have hopes. . . ."

"Your son will go far," said Mason firmly.

Tetzel's eyes were proud, flashing, as the Dozent led Nella away. He looked positively jaunty, a word Mason certainly would never have associated with him before. "That is a very attractive girl," he was saying, "I have asked her to have tea with me tomorrow."

Mason felt a twisting stab of totally unreasonable jealousy. Nella meant nothing to him except as an object of curiosity, but that Tetzel could ask her to tea freely, flirt with her, make advances, perhaps make love to her, made him feel unconscionably fettered, old, committed. Tetzel was a free agent; he was not.

He climbed upstairs and Paula, talking on the phone, waved to greet him. Cairn was on the wire again, and his voice, positively iridescent, became more intimate as he rang off with the words "Don't ever forget—I'm madly involved with you!" Mason advanced into the room and she had an uneasy thought. Was that "you" of Tom Cairn's plural? But of course—it had to be!

Paula said, "That was Tom once more, he got the Pilsudski interview. I told him about Plover's letter, and he's very concerned. He says you can't take these A.O.G. threats lying down. Europeans aren't Americans. Here in this wilderness if you're slapped you have to slap back."

"Of course."

"Tom says that there's no telling what they may try next, and that you ought to work through the British if you can, not the Americans."

"I'm ahead of him."

8

Mason dropped in to see Horace Yancey at the British Legation the next day, having decided that Yancey would be a better instrument than the Archduke for what he wanted. He had come to know him much better since that morning he had told him about the Customs Union. He brought him up to date on the A.O.G. affair and asked him a favor: could he arrange a meeting with Count Alfred Diederbach?

Yancey agreed with alacrity, and called him later.

"I've built you up into quite a bill of goods, and Diederbach says that he'll be delighted to have us to lunch—he suggested Thursday. Right with you? Good. I'll slip out to look at the Rembrandts after the coffee, and you can have all the time you need with him alone. Won't need much, I'd risk predicting. The old man's a bit dotty, as I hope you know. Pick me up at half past twelve."

What the devil would life be like without friends, Mason asked himself. The obligations of friendship can be onerous, even if unstated; now he was in direct debt to Trudi, Hilda, the Archduke, Yancey—who else? Well, a lot of people were in debt to him. Some mysterious celestial bookkeeping would make the accounts even in time.

He returned from lunch Thursday more exhilarated than he had been in a long time. He sat Paula down next to him and began to talk.

"Well—bless me! I've never had a more interesting hour. The house is fabulous. I've been in some rather grand British houses, and you remember that weekend in the Loire with Molly Casenaves, but this place beats anything I ever saw. Not so much for its luxuriousness but as an example of perfect taste. It was all of a piece. The footman's uniform, scarlet, white ruffles, matched the Delacroix perfectly. Every bit of furniture is a museum piece, of course, and calm in spite of all the gilt. What did we have to eat? *Truite à bleu,* frog's legs, and a *mille-feuille*—I swear it had twenty layers. Everything altogether French, therefore light, except the wine. Only one wine— a Berncasteler *Doktor Spaetlese Fuder,* worth its weight in the teardrops of an angel. Well, the Count greeted us with a peculiar, wary grace, polite, curious, as we came in. I've never heard him described accurately. He gave out the aroma of dried rose leaves in a jar. I don't mean he *smelled* of roses; just evoked that impression. His eyelids flutter. He has purplish spots, as big as coins, over his hands and cheeks. He must be *quite* old. He has a lot of charm. That old man made me feel that I was the most important human being in the world, but he drummed with his fingertips most of the time, showed

mild restlessness, and went off on tangents. I tried not to be trite, I
didn't tackle him on either of his hobbies—stamps or shooting. It
would have been silly, and he would have caught on at once to the
fact that I don't know a damn thing about either. I did ask an informal question or two about the silver and china, just to show him
that I wasn't an oaf. But what caught his interest was when I said
something about aristocracy in Chicago. He repeated, incredulous,
'An aristocracy in *Chicago*?' I described Lake Forest and told him
that the North Shore had one of the most closely knit, tightly inter-
bred, and truly distinguished aristocracies in the world. He couldn't
stop laughing when, pulling his leg a bit, I said gravely that his
palace almost matched the great Chicago houses for splendor and
sophistication. Yancey left us saying he had not seen the Fragonards
for a year and wanted to have another look at the Titian. Diederbach's
manner changed slightly. His voice was almost severe as he turned to
me, saying, 'Now, young man, tell me why you have been brought
to see me.' I explained that, in the past few weeks, his bank had tried
(a) to bribe me with a decoration, (b) to blackmail me, and (c) to
get my job by exerting influence in Chicago. A look of the most extreme cunning came over his face. His eyelids went up and down
furiously, his silver whiskers quivered. He said, 'But why are you so
dangerous, Mr. Jarrett?' I told him that nobody had ever found me
dangerous before. 'Why, then, if I may put it so, are you such a
nuisance, why is it necessary for us to go through all these complex
procedures, if indeed we do go through them, in order to frighten
or silence you?' So I told him the whole background of the bribery
affair, from first to last, trying to make it as lively as possible—just
telling it as a story. I don't think he had ever heard a word about the
case before. 'Ah, I see, I see, you consider it improper that certain
journalists should have received certain gifts. You did not receive
cooperation from the, ah, authorities, and after an interval you caused
to be printed your version of the case?' 'No, Count Diederbach, not
our version, just the facts,' I replied. 'And now my bank retaliates?'
'That's it.' After a pause Diederbach asked, 'And what are you going
to do next?' 'Continue with what I'm doing now, unless the A.O.G.
agrees to cooperate with us.' "

"What did he say?" Paula interrupted.

"He didn't say anything at all for a moment. His face looked rather sad. Then he spoke. 'What do you want of me, Mr. Jarrett?'

" 'First, call off your bloodhounds. Second, give us whatever assurance you can about the innocence of the American and British correspondents.'

"He rose, with a sigh, put his hand on my knee, and said, 'Well, you pose interesting problems.' Then he left the room, obviously going to the telephone. He returned, pink in the cheek, after what seemed to be an interminable time. And now his manner had altogether changed.

" 'I have consulted my people, and they contest vigorously the accuracy of your interpretation of these events. They advise me strongly to take no action whatever in your behalf, and they refuse to consider any act of conciliation toward your organization.'

" 'I wonder why,' I said. 'Don't people ever learn anything? I think they're making a great mistake, Count Diederbach. Now all of us have no recourse but to keep on writing the story.'

" 'I daresay.'

"I made a last effort. 'You could overrule your own people down at the A.O.G., couldn't you? After all, you're the boss.'

" 'I have no choice except to take the advice of my advisers. That is what advisers are for, Mr. Jarrett.'

"Yancey rejoined us, and we moved toward the door. 'I'm sorry,' was all I could think of to say.

" 'I'm sorry too.' But he didn't look sorry. We shook hands.

" 'What do you suppose will happen next, Count Diederbach?' I asked as we said good-bye.

" 'I do not know. In another age you would quite possibly be assassinated.'

"And do you know what? I think he really meant it."

9

While Mason was dictating a story to Otto about a Serbo-Croat crisis in Zagreb the telephone rang.

"Mr. Charrett."

"Yes?"

The voice was quiet, but imperative.

"Mr. Charrett, I would wish, is it to be bossible that you would come and see me this afternoon?"

"Who is it?"

"You do not know my voice, Mr. Charrett?" She said this neither as a question nor a rebuke, but calmly. "This is the Countess von Zwehl speaking, Mr. Charrett."

"Oh! Look, say, I'm awfully busy; I've got a deadline to meet this afternoon—"

"Do not tell Drew that I have telephoned, Mr. Charrett."

"What? Why not?" Mason had a flash. "But you'll tell him, won't you?"

"You are not stupid, Mr. Charrett." She paused. "I appeal to you. I am in need of you. For an hour, come to see me, advise me. There is a service you could render."

He agreed to drop in to her place around four.

"I thank you. I thank you from the bottom of my heart. Except that you know from Drew that I have no heart."

Mason arrived at the address she gave him. She rose graciously as he entered, gave him her hand to kiss, and prepared to serve tea. The cups and plates, once delicate, were chipped and worn. Mason had never seen a *Wohnung* of Drew's before, and he looked around with curiosity; it was not so shabby as he had expected. A bookshelf held a line of religious tracts.

"You and your wife, Mr. Charrett, continue to make an exciting element in the life of our old Vienna. One of my friends is a doctor, a neurologist. He says that it is extremely unusual for two people equally good-looking to establish an acceptable relationship."

What did all this presage? "Why not?" Mason asked.

She raised a bony forefinger coyly, and proceeded without answering him, "I have hurt"—she hardened the "d's" on words, so that "heard" came out "hurt"—"so much of your accomplishments and exploits in several fields!"

Mason sought to look modest. Praise from anybody always embarrassed him. He made a quick shuffling movement with his hands parted as if to minimize or ward off further flattery, with the words "No, no."

"Do not deny your accomplishments, Mr. Charrett," she continued. "What you have done, as the organizer of your press association, with your work on the case of the bank and its contacts with the world of journalism, ah, ah! I know about it all!"

She poured tea expertly, but her hands trembled; her physical gestures were like the voice of a man stuttering. "But I sometimes wonder if you know very much as yet of certain *realities*, Mr. Charrett." She gave an unusual stress to the word "realities." "I am worried about Drew and what to do about a certain matter. Something has happened. I need your help."

Mason thought: She's put Drew up to something and it's gone wrong; now she's trying to wriggle out, but she doesn't quite dare tell me what it is.

"Drew is a complex character, Mr. Charrett. I have liffed with him some years, and I do not altogether understand him. I save for him, every cent. Berhaps you do not know about my effort for him when I bersuaded him to invest in the Slovak iron shares." She hesitated significantly. "Now I need money for a very special burbose. Shall I confide in you what it is, Mr. Charrett?"

"Go ahead, please."

"The sum involved is a mere bittance, fifteen hundred Schillings. You would lend it to me, blease?"

What was going on? That was the same sum Drew had wanted to borrow several months before.

Mason leaned back, carefully balancing the under part of one knee on the other. "I'm awfully sorry, Countess, but you know how things are—fifteen hundred Schillings is a lot of money at the moment and I just haven't got it."

She was about to go into the matter more fully when Mason heard a key sink into a lock and saw the doorknob turn. Drew entered. Clearly the Countess had not expected him at this hour and it was also clear that Drew was astonished to see Mason there. The Countess sprang to her feet, put her hand dramatically on Drew's elbow, and whispered to him swiftly. He patted her shoulder with affection mingled with irritation, as one might console a child who has fallen into mischief. Turning to Mason he said, "Well, Jarrett, never knew we'd be honored by a visit from you here! Sit down! Say, what did you file on that Croat report this morning? The Belgrade government can't be in trouble, but even so . . ."

Drew munched a cake noisily, and the Countess stroked his hand; they seemed to be deriving active, overt pleasure from each other's company. They agreed about things quickly, laughed together, and included Mason tolerantly in their conversation as a casual outsider who could not be expected to penetrate or understand the comfortable community they made.

Obviously the Countess would never get a chance to broach to Mason what she wanted to talk about. He left after half an hour. Well, he said to himself, I know now why Drew stays with her. He likes the old girl!

❋

"Does it not sound as madness!" Sandor ejaculated on the phone to Mason the next morning. Drew, he reported, had had a violent quarrel with the Countess the night before. He had thrown a chair at her, mauled her, slugged her, and given her severe bruises on the face and throat. Now, as a result, she had brought suit against him. She had gone directly to a lawyer, shown him her injuries, and instituted an action against Drew in the civil courts. If he were found guilty of assault, as charged, he might very well be sent to jail.

Mason had a thought. Drew might have wormed out of her the fact that she had asked him for fifteen hundred Schillings, and this could well be the reason he had assaulted her.

10

Sometimes it was a luxury to have a drink by himself. Mason finished his chores for the afternoon and drifted down to the Grand Bar. This was crowded as a rule, but he went there when he wanted to be alone. He liked the sensation of watching well-dressed men and women whom he didn't know or have to know, the impersonal buzz and chatter from other tables, the sense of a world in movement—people searching, seeking, sometimes finding. The Grand Bar was utterly different from the Weissenhof or even the Imperial. Nobody had ever ordered a coffee there. The Grand Bar was the haunt of the rich, the celebrated, the successful. It was the haunt of ski champions, opera stars, big playwrights, wealthy young Heimwehr officers, and of course the coveys of little whorelets, poules de luxe. Mason loved to watch them. You could identify them instantly by their tightly drawn tawny stockings and silver foxes. They would watch you, but only with difficulty could you catch their eyes.

What a nice bar the Grand was, Mason thought, with its chic, come-easy-go-easy atmosphere. He ordered a Scotch and soda in a long glass. Scotch was always served in ridiculously small glasses in Vienna unless you ordered it otherwise. The room gave out a glow of warm browns. The satiny wooden walls were brown; the grain was fine, the polish high. Mason put his hands down and patted the wood of the walls so smoothly brown.

Mason felt a touch on his arm, and there was Bishopson. "Join us, won't you?" Mason groaned inwardly, but his friend pressed him, and, carrying his drink, he followed him across the room, picking his way over the high-heeled shoes and silken ankles of the poules. "You haven't met my wife, I think," Bishopson said, his voice tight, throaty. "And this is Miss Falk, one of our Viennese friends."

Mason shook hands with the two young women. Helen Bishopson was handsome and well dressed with a crisp, clinging hat. Because he had come to like and respect Bishopson so much, he wanted to be on his best behavior with his wife, who was saying easily, "I'm so glad to meet you at last, Mr. Jarrett. My husband talks about you often. And we're more than eager to meet your wife; everybody tells me how attractive she is. I'm sorry I've never called." Mason chuckled to himself. Mrs. Bishopson offering to call! He and Paula must be getting up in the world. But he appreciated her freedom of gesture, and told himself that he and Paula must have the Bishopsons to lunch on the first day possible.

Bishopson asked Mason if there was any news from Zoltan. None. But Tetzel had told him that morning that he had at last located Gmunden, the payoff man. Gmunden had been in Franzensbad on a cure, but was returning to Vienna the next day.

"We'll go to see him."

"Aye."

"They haven't tried to get your job yet?"

Bishopson's laugh was grim. "Not so far as I know."

They had another drink, and Mason recounted with relish the story of his lunch with Count Alfred Diederbach. The Bishopsons were listening attentively when, for the first time, Mason realized that the dark girl with them, Miss Falk, had an unusual quality. He had been so busy being friendly with Helen Bishopson that he had scarcely noticed her. Hello, he thought, she's lovely. She had what the Austrians called a *vollschlank* (fully thin) figure—a small waist, and then the firm round bosom of the Viennese. Her hands were nicely shaped, with long slim fingers, and her smile—she smiled a good deal—was warm. She seemed open, intimate, and warm, but with a demure quality as well.

Mason gathered that she was some kind of artist, but he didn't understand what kind. While he had been talking she was attentive and polite, as a well-bred person will be who is part of a group but who is not included in its conversation because of lack of knowledge of the background, but she said little, since she apparently was modest and did not like to put herself forward. But Mason had the feeling that she had not been bored, and had missed nothing.

He looked at her more closely. Her hair was dark, combed softly in curls and fluffed out in back. Lips bright, teeth good. She had a short, funny little nose ever so slightly crooked. Her eyes were a fascinating color—sepia? sable? charcoal?—he sought for the right word. They were intensely black, but at the same time, an impossible paradox, *pale*—the image rose of a child's box of watercolors, and of a blob of jet black paint just touched with water.

Mason overtalked. Her impact, although she said scarcely a word, excited him. He told anecdotes, directing them at Miss Falk, about events and personalities all over Europe, and tried to describe what the skyline near Central Park looked like at dusk on an autumn day. In the middle of this, the girl, obeying some urgent impulse, turned without explanation to Mrs. Bishopson and made a quick interruption. Mason was thrown off balance. Miss Falk saw this, thought that she had perhaps been rude, and, cheeks pinkening, turned to him with a smile at once genuine, sweet, and appealingly apologetic.

The Bishopsons rose to go. "I'll call and drop in at the studio again some time next week," Helen Bishopson said to Miss Falk.

Miss Falk waited. Mason, although unsure of himself, felt cer-

tain that if he asked her to stay she would. He looked her fully in the
eye, with an appraising, tentative air of invitation; decorously she
dropped her eyes, but with no hint of flirtatiousness.

"What's your first name?" Mason asked.

"Erika," she said.

11

Mason, late, scuttled across the Innere Stadt to the Weissenhof. He,
Sandor, and Erji had planned to meet the Countess and prevail upon
her to withdraw her suit against Drew, if possible. But she did not
appear, nor did Drew. There was no message, no explanation. Tetzel
entered with a bit of news. The Behemoth Steel Works, controlled
by the A.O.G., was on the point of shutting down; already one shift
of workers had been dismissed. "How do you know they're really
going to shut down?" Mason asked. Karl was a careful reporter, but
nobody Viennese ever seemed to be able to draw the line firmly
between rumor and hard news; time and again he had known local
tipsters to give false information innocently. He, Mason, could not
possibly afford to go wrong on any detail having to do with the
A.O.G. If Behemoth were indeed on the point of failure that would
indeed be a story, particularly since he could tie it in with the
scandal, but a mere rumor to this effect was not enough. Tetzel
promised to investigate further.

After a moment Mason prepared to go. Tetzel, smiling, confidential, told him that he had seen Nella Blohr several times.

"How did you make out?"

Karl's language was becoming more and more Americanized, and
he replied, "I did not even get to first base." He added with a touch
of bravado, "But I will try again. Who can tell, a home run may
some day come!"

At dinner this bit of conversation, a burr, stuck in Mason's mind.
As if out of the blue, he asked Paula what she thought of Nella. Paula
had an unerring eye for the weak point in a person, and she answered
in a single phrase: "There's a streak of commonness in her." Surprise
crinkled Mason's forehead. She added, "And she's the only one in
the family who has it. I think she's tricky too."

After dinner Paula played Mozart very loud, and Mason, yawning, flipped through some books from London. At about ten the telephone rang and he heard Jim Drew's voice, indignant and alive.

"Do you know whose name is on the A.O.G. list?"

"Whose?"

The voice barked: "The name of James N. Drew!"

VIII. PROBITY

The next day was busy, because the case was beginning to break open at last. As far as Drew was concerned Mason had mixed feelings. He was not so naïve as not to have thought for some time that he might possibly be guilty, and his talk with the Countess had intensified this suspicion; even so he could not believe that he could have been so careless and stupid as to have taken an outright bribe. There must be a catch in this somewhere. At least until the facts were known Drew must be protected.

Early in the morning Mason got Zoltan on the phone—that slippery little scoundrel, who was still the key to much. Mason said, "Herr Präsident, you gave me your word of honor some weeks ago that no member of the Anglo-American was on the list except Ritter. Now I hear that Drew is named. What is your explanation?"

Zoltan said, "Ah, so you have already been informed. I was at this moment about to call you. Something extraordinary has occurred. I have been instructed to report to you that the Chef du Cabinet of the Ministry of Finance will receive us at eleven A.M. tomorrow, to allow us access to certain . . . communications."

"I'll be there. But what about Drew?"

"We will discuss it in the morning. Perhaps you would be good enough to call on me at ten-thirty, and then we will proceed to the Finance Ministry together."

Mason picked up Bishopson and Stein, and they descended on Zoltan together; he was deferential, but his eyes flickered uneasily. Self-conscious, Mason was not at all sure of his own ground, but he opened the conversation by repeating the question about Drew he had asked the day before.

"Ah, Herr Präsident, I beg to assure you, I did not mislead you. Drew's name did not appear on the old list. I knew nothing about his involvement till yesterday, when I called him at once. Now have been found new lists which, unfortunately, contain many new names, several of men well known."

"In my country people are presumed to be innocent until they're proved guilty. It's a quaint custom, you may think. But I will not listen to one word against Drew unless I see some proof."

"I regret to say, proof exists."

"What kind of proof?"

"Drew is number six on the second list, and it is written that he received fifteen hundred Schillings."

Mason felt alarm at the mention of this particular, specific sum.

"Drew, in any case, is not my member, and I have nothing to do with him," Zoltan proceeded smoothly. "He belongs to you. You and your Anglo-American will have to have your own *Ehrengericht* to deal with him."

"We'll do nothing of the kind," Mason said. "I've had enough of these damned fool *Ehrengerichts*."

Zoltan looked sly. "Suppose the lists are published, as the opposition in Parliament demands. What then?"

"Let them publish and be damned."

Bishopson quieted Mason. "Well, it wouldn't be good for Drew's job, would it, if it suddenly appeared in cold type that the A.O.G. had bribed him for fifteen hundred Schillings."

"You will have to do what in my organization we have been doing," Zoltan said smugly. "Investigate, clear Drew, and get his name off the list if possible."

Mason grunted. What an irony! He and Zoltan would become as one. He too, for the sake of his organization, would have to put on an act full of humbug.

"Suppose we find it impossible to clear Drew—what then?" Stein spoke up. "Suppose he *has* taken money? Do we temporize, as we did with Ritter?"

Bishopson said, "Let's face that hurdle when we come to it." He turned to Zoltan. "You said a minute ago that the new list contains several new names. Are any of them ours aside from Drew?"

Zoltan looked puzzled, scratching at his shell of hair. "I think . . . yes! I do not carry all the names in my head but, yes, I think one other of your members is involved."

Mason, Bishopson, and Stein froze in silence.

"Who?" asked Stein.

Mason felt gooseflesh crawl down his back.

"I forget. But the name is on file at the Ministry."

❊

They picked up a photographer, Mason's idea, and drove over to the Ministry. Such a scene had scarcely been witnessed before. The Ministry of Finance was an exceedingly dignified institution, unaccustomed to obstreperous incursions from the world outside. An immense double wooden door, with huge iron knockers, guarded the entrance; then came a courtyard, steps, more doors, and an impressive coiled staircase, bare for yards on either side of the somewhat tattered crimson rug climbing in the center. The second floor unfolded into a series of dimly lit, suave chambers, with damask on the walls. Portraits of Maria Theresa, Franz Josef, and the last Karl gloomily looked down.

The Chef du Cabinet of the Finance Minister, Dr. Einfunder, received them. The Minister himself would not, unfortunately, be able to be present. Long ladders of paper, marked with names arranged like rungs, each with a check in red ink, a figure, or an indecipherable scrawl attached, lay on the Chef du Cabinet's desk. Dr. Einfunder wished to inform Herr Präsident Jarrett officially that the Anglo-American Press Association was now directly involved in the A.O.G. bribery case, by reason of the recent discovery that Herr Redakteur Drew's name was included on a new list.

Dr. Einfunder looked displeased when Mason's photographer set up his apparatus. Mason explained, "We've been in the dark a long time, and if any evidence involving us comes up I'd like to have a record of it. Do you mind?"

The Chef du Cabinet bowed. He had a manner common to upper civil servants everywhere which said, "Only I have fingers on every latch. Only I know all the bits and pieces that must be fitted carefully into the whole situation before it can be made to make sense. The Minister himself would be helpless without me." His instructions from above were to be polite and cooperative but as uncommunicative as possible. Anyway, this was a minor, tedious business. . . . Journalists were a low class, especially if American.

Now Zoltan became friendly with Mason and Bishopson. "We're all in this mess together now, boys," his expression said. He bubbled with satisfaction to be in the company of the Anglo-Americans, who, he must have felt, gave him support. He buzzed from desk to desk, and came back to Mason with odd bits of information. He whispered cheerfully—of course confidential to Herr Präsident Jarrett—that whereas thirty-eight of his men were now known to be involved, there were seventeen on the list who were members of the Gesellschaft, and fourteen in the Union. The Germans had five, and Herr Präsident Jarrett was lucky to get off with only two.

Trying politely to conceal his restlessness, Dr. Einfunder produced the correct documents. Mason, flanked by Bishopson and Stein, looked at them with curiosity.

The first was a note on a roughly torn square of quadrille paper. It read:

A File 4, No. 7
Five hundred Schillings (*Fünfhundert Schilling*) . . . given to . . . Herrn Doktor Heinrich Ritter, New York *Register wird hiemit bestätigt*.
Gmunden

"Hee! Haw! Hee!" laughed Zoltan.

Then for the first time Mason saw Donald Bishopson angry, and he was just about as angry as anybody he had ever seen in his life.

"What's this? New York *Register*? The *REGISTER*? MY newspaper! What hell's nonsense is this?"

Bishopson did not raise his voice, in fact it became ice-cold, but its impact made the Chef du Cabinet's self-satisfaction disappear and he looked as if he thought the ceiling might fall.

Bishopson turned white. "Hell's bells!" he exclaimed. He advanced with his fists tight, shoulders bulging, to the Chef du Cabinet, and said through clenched teeth, "The New York *Register*? My newspaper? This is deviltry! Grossness!" He had the Chef du Cabinet by the collar. "I have a libel suit in this worth a million pounds!" He started to shake him by the collar.

Zoltan interposed himself between them.

Bishopson said to Dr. Einfunder, "God damn you, retract!" The Chef du Cabinet tottered, and Mason thought that he was going to faint.

Zoltan hastily explained, "Carelessness, carelessness. The A.O.G. agents do not know one American or British newspaper from another. They think they are all the same. Probably someone told Gmunden that Ritter once worked for the *Register* years ago, and he thought that it was a good name to put down."

"No . . . calumniation . . . of you . . . much less of the New York *Register* . . . intended!" the Chief du Cabinet managed to breathe out, between gasps. "Ap-apologies!"

Bishopson said, controlling himself, "Gmunden may learn one of these days to find out the difference between one newspaper and another. So may you."

Mason, violently agitated, handed the square of paper to the photographer, who tacked it against the wall and aimed his box of a camera at it.

The second document came from Drew's man, Bleschke, and was longer:

DANUBIA PRESS SERVICE
David L. Bleschke, Chefredakteur
   Radio, Cable, and Telegraph Address: Danubia Wien
   European Headquarters: I, Kantplatz, 7. Vienna, Austria
In reply please refer to File Number: Z 31 F
LOCAL
Herr Gmunden, care the A.O.G., Wien
Dear Sir:

This is to acknowledge the receipt from you of the sum of 3,000 Austrian Schillings (Sch. 3,000.00)—twice 1,500 Schillings—for the complete services of the Danubia Press Service (a double subscription) for the full year (12 months) beginning of date today.

As a token of appreciation of your subscription (double) to our service we wish to state that we will not only (a) furnish you with our complete news service, but (b) volunteer to accept from you any news items which you may wish to furnish us. These we will pass on to our clients, as part of our regular service (source unrevealed), with the recommendation that they be given special consideration.

Among the British and American newspaper and news agencies to which any items you choose to deliver to me will be duly transmitted arc the New York *Times*, New York *Register*, International News Service, Chicago *Star*, Chicago *Daily News*, London *Daily Telegraph*, A.P., U.P., London *Times*, Boston *Times*, Manchester *Guardian*, Washington *Sun*, St. Louis *Hawk*, Reuter's, etc.

Thanking you for this payment and trusting that our service continues to be satisfactory, we remain, dear sir, yours faithfully, and with great esteem,

D. L. Bleschke, European Manager

Bishopson whispered, "Never saw such a letter in my life!" and Mason looked at it in consternation. The photographer, adjusting a heavy wooden tripod, attached the letter to the wall, while Mason, Bishopson, and Stein withdrew to a corner together.

"Look what Bleschke does," Stein pointed out, aghast. His face had lost its sunniness. "He not only takes three thousand Schillings from the A.O.G. on the pretext that the A.O.G. is taking out a double subscription to his service, understand that, a double subscription, but he writes down the names of all our papers as grateful recipients of what news the A.O.G. gives to him, with the promise that it will be given special attention, source unrevealed!"

They walked up to the desk. Dr. Einfunder looked embarrassed, and Zoltan giggled: "Hee! Hee!"

Mason, feeling his way, said smoothly to Zoltan and the Chef du Cabinet, "Of course, as both of you must clearly see, this letter doesn't compromise Drew at all. He isn't even mentioned."

But Drew's style stood out all over it, as he knew perfectly well. Bleschke had no command of written English, and the letter was full of Drew's unmistakably stuffy, businesslike grandiloquence. The dodge of the "double" subscription was typical. By openly, as it were, describing the A.O.G. contribution as such, Drew excused himself for having split the three thousand Schillings with Bleschke, if he had indeed split it. By inventing the pretext of two subscriptions he justified his receipt of part of the money, if he had taken any. It was all too outrageously transparent.

Nevertheless Mason proceeded coldly, as if preparing to dismiss the matter: "As evidence against Drew this letter carries no weight whatever. What else have you?"

The Chef du Cabinet said nothing.

Mason went to the desk where the papers were laid out. "Now if you don't mind I want to look at the lists themselves." At last!

He saw several names on the old list that startled him, but they were not British or American. On the new list the first few names were unfamiliar. Then came another series:

> No. 5. David L. Bleschke. 1500 Sch.
> No. 6. James N. Drew. 1500 Sch.

Bishopson said, "The fact that somebody has put Drew's name down on a list isn't proof of any kind. Anybody's name could be written down. Show us something with Drew's signature."

The Chef du Cabinet shrugged. Of course the Americans knew that Drew was guilty, but, for the sake of their organization, were seeking to protect him.

"How exactly are these lists made up?" Stein asked with his precise, pointed voice. "How is it that a new list is revealed only now?"

The Chef du Cabinet responded, "I do not know how the A.O.G. operates in these special fields. It is not my province." His stomach had begun to rumble. It was after twelve, and soon at the Jockey he would be having the *Tafelspitz*.

Zoltan said to Bishopson, presenting his pink, softly wrinkled palms, "Drew and Bleschke are close business associates. It is common knowledge that Drew helped to finance the Danubia Service. He is behind Bleschke in everything."

"But that isn't proof that Drew took half of what Bleschke got."

Mason asked Zoltan, "Who is our second member you were talking about? Drew and one other, you said." He put a sheaf of lists down. "No other names of ours are here."

"Bleschke," said Zoltan. "Is not Bleschke your member?"

"No."

Zoltan had been in error, and so had the Finanzministerium. Pens scratched, and the Chef du Cabinet came to attention. Bleschke, it just happened, wasn't a member of any of the newspaper organizations in town—probably because he couldn't afford the dues. He belonged to nobody. What an anticlimax, Mason thought. Bleschke, the first person to have admitted in writing that he took A.O.C. money, was the only person—so far—who could not be investigated and who was free of any possibility of inquiry into the charges. How Viennese!

Zoltan, who had darted out of the room for a moment, buzzed up again, glib, gleaming. Confidentially he could now give his friend and colleague Herr Präsident Jarrett some new informations. He had just discovered that Gmunden, the payoff man, had been given 57,000 of the original 300,000 Schillings to distribute. He had turned in notations of outpayments, not always accompanied by actual receipts, for only 46,000 Schillings. So the sum of 11,000 Schillings was outstanding—missing. Where was it? Heaven only knew. But probably in Gmunden's pocket. On account of the scandal, the A.O.G. would be afraid to sue.

Bishopson continued to address Dr. Einfunder imperturbably: "Of course, technically speaking, Bleschke has done nothing whatever improper. I trust you understand this. Bleschke runs a news service. Anybody on earth can pay him fifteen hundred Schillings a year for it; it's the regular rate for nonjournalist subscribers."

"You would make the greatest defense attorney in the world," Mason said to Bishopson. "I salute you, Herr Doktor, Rechtsanwalt und Sorgemeister."

Mason, Bishopson, and Stein had a hurried lunch. Bleschke did not matter; the man who mattered was James N. Drew. They hiked over to the Weissenhof, where both Drew and Bleschke awaited them. As Drew rose, his heavy shoulders sagged. Mason intercepted a look from his bright, boyish blue eyes, which blinked; it said, "Help! Save me!"

Outwardly, he was gruff and uncommunicative. Mason gave him a brief survey of what had happened, and then turned to Bleschke. "We've put in a hard morning. I think maybe you owe us a word of explanation."

The gist of Bleschke's reply was that he needed all the subscriptions

he could get. He had pretty well gathered in all the correspondents in
town, and now he was tackling the foreign legations, the banks,
institutions like the Chamber of Commerce, and so on—anybody who
might want to subscribe to a tipster sheet. The A.O.G. had volunteered to take two subscriptions, one for its foreign department, one
for the executive staff. Yes, it was true that Drew had written the
letter for him, but this was merely because he needed technical help
in English. Why write in English? Since when was the A.O.G. an
English bank? Bleschke looked embarrassed, and said apologetically,
"Well, it was easier to do it that way."

Drew said not a word.

"Well, now," Mason proceeded with Bleschke, "tell us a little
more. Somebody from the A.O.G. happened to pop into the Journalistenzimmer one afternoon, and, simple as could be, said that he
wanted a double subscription to your news service, and thereupon
handed you three thousand Schillings. Was that the way it went?"

"Well, not exactly—"

Bishopson cut in as if he had sand in his throat. "You mean that
the A.O.G. offered you some money, and then somebody had the
bright idea of covering this by the device of having them subscribe
to your service?"

Drew said, "You're making an unwarrantable insinuation, Bishopson."

"Shut up, Jim," said Mason. "We're trying to help, but we can't be
effective unless we know some facts. You're on that list, a fact embarrassing not only to you, but to all of us. What we're doing now is
trying to work out some way to get you off."

Drew grunted.

Bishopson asked Drew, "Have you got your original investment
out of Danubia? If so, when did you get it out?"

"My dear sir, I will not be questioned in this manner!"

"Sorry," Bishopson said. "I had an idea for a solution, that's all.
Never mind."

Too late, Drew realized that Bishopson had shrewdly offered him a
way out. He could have said plausibly that Bleschke owed him fifteen
hundred Schillings and had used half the A.O.G. money to repay him.

Mason asked Bleschke why he had specifically named all the papers to which he offered to transmit news from the A.O.G. His reply was evasive.

"Well," Mason sighed, "if anybody else ever comes along and donates you a couple of thousand Schillings, please don't give him Niagara Falls in return, and kindly keep the name of my paper out of it."

They wrangled a long, painful hour.

Nobody—neither Stein, nor Bishopson, nor Mason Jarrett—could bear to put the direct question necessary. Had Drew actually slipped in his pocket fifteen hundred Schillings from the A.O.G.? The nearest approach came from Stein: "One thing is still unclear to me. How do you explain that *both* you and Bleschke are named on the list we saw —and photographed—this morning, since Bleschke"—Stein's voice made a delicate, hesitant purr—"indicates that only he received the money?"

Drew grimaced. "Have no idea."

2

Drew and Bleschke left the café, and Mason wondered what to do next. He had no authority to decide by himself, since the case must be put up to the Anglo-American as a whole, but what should he, as president, recommend? Accept from Drew a formal letter of denial that he had taken any money, and declare the matter closed? Try him by an *Ehrengericht?* Or expel him—toss him to the wolves?

Stumped, pondering, Mason walked alone toward the Graben till he reached a bar he liked on Bognergasse. The barman, Max, was a friend, like Hugo at the Koenigen, but not as sophisticated.

"Good afternoon, Chentleman Charrett, vat a nice type of afternoon it is."

Max had had hard luck. For a time he was head barman in nothing less than the splendid glittering bar of the Imperial. Too ambitious, he decided to break away and found a rival bar across the street. It ruined him. Now he worked in this little *boîte.*

"How's business?" Mason asked.

"Filthy."

"Too bad you couldn't squeeze back to the Imperial."

Max shrugged. "I vill show the Imperial some day."

"How's your wife?" This was a recurrent topic.

"In the sanitarium at Breitenstein. It's the cross one bears."

Mason went to the phone, called Paula and asked her to join him. She was surprised. Nothing is more likely to delight a wife, Mason reflected, than a totally unexpected summons from a husband who tells her to drop everything and meet him for a totally unexpected drink in a totally unexpected place at a totally unexpected hour.

She looked luminous, if only because his call had pleased her. Everybody in the little bar watched her. Mason told her the events of the day.

"What did you decide?"

"Nothing, yet. In any case it'll have to go before the association as a whole."

"I'd try to avoid that, if you can."

"Why? I can't settle it on my own, or just with the officers."

"You could wangle it in some way, I think. Anyway, I'd try. Play the whole thing down." Her voice was earnest.

Again he asked, "Why?"

"For one thing, if you push on with it you'll damage the prestige of the Anglo-American. Second, you'll split it. More important, I don't think you'll ever be able to prove that Bleschke did divide the money with Drew. They'll both deny it till kingdom come, and then where are you?"

"Yes, but where does that leave us as an organization?"

"A dilemma," Paula conceded.

"A dilemma indeed. If we whitewash Drew we're not only condoning fraud, bribery, and God knows what else but we're doing exactly what Zoltan and the rest are doing—whitewashing the A.O.G. as well!"

"What line do you think the association will take as a whole if it gets the case?"

"Tuck and nip. Go and touch."

"You covered up for Ritter."

"The cases are quite different. Ritter is one of Zoltan's men, really Zoltan's affair, and Ritter has paid the money back."

"Couldn't Drew do that?"

"Where would he get the money?" Mason sighed. "The Countess tried to get it out of me!"

"And if Drew's found guilty, he'd be expelled?"

"We haven't got that far yet. I suppose so."

"Then he'd lose his job. You simply can't do it, darling."

"Why not?"

"Because of the nature of human relationships. Have some compassion! You can't ruin the life of a friend because of a minor peccadillo."

"Is it a minor peccadillo? After all, our whole code is at stake. If Drew's guilty he *ought* to be thrown out. There's a sort of unwritten law."

"No, no!" Paula cried. "You can't be party to anything so smug, so cruel!"

They had another drink without reaching a solution.

"Let's not go home," Mason said. "I have a sudden irresistible impulse, Miss Whipple, to get to know you better, and I think I might treat you to a dinner at Schöner's and then sit with you cozily in some movie for an hour or two."

Dinner was delicious, and the movie not too bad. They held hands in a back row, and kissed when they got home.

✳

The next day Mason, Bishopson, and Stein set out to track down Gmunden, the payoff man, in his lair. Taking Drew with them they drove to the address Tetzel had provided. Drew said nothing, but, rigid, held his head slightly bowed, while grinding the knuckles of one fist round and round in the other palm.

Mason sent in their names. The maid returned and said that Herr Gmunden was indisposed and could not see the visitors. Mason pulled out of his pocket the photostat with Gmunden's signature and sent this in with the maid. After a few moments Herr Gmunden appeared.

He limped, and walked heavily with a stick. There was a dust of dandruff on his collar, and he had heavy, hairy, dark brown hands.

Mason concluded his explanation. Gmunden made his fingers into a tent. "What is it you wish of me?"

Bishopson replied, "Well, Herr Gmunden, it happens that Mr.

Drew here happens by some accident to be named on the A.O.G. list, whereas in actuality, of course, as you must well know," Bishopson coughed, "he took no money at all. He should not have been put on any list in the first place, and we wish you to help us remedy this obvious injustice."

Gmunden stretched his fingers apart, then put them together again. "What could I do?"

Drew shouted, "You dirty scoundrel, you Gauner, you know perfectly well that I had nothing to do with that Bleschke business. You put my name on the list out of spite because we wouldn't give you a kickback on the subscriptions!"

Bishopson and Stein stared at him appalled.

"Shut up, Drew," said Mason harshly.

Gmunden said in a guarded voice, "That is not quite the case. But . . ."

He spoke at length, but it was difficult to follow what he said. Stein interrupted him. "Herr Gmunden, we can't wait here all day. Would you be prepared to write and sign a letter to the effect that you never actually passed over any funds to Drew?"

"What if I do not?"

Mason said pleasantly, "Our organization will soon hold a meeting to discuss the whole situation, of course." Drew looked startled. "Normally we meet in private. On this occasion we might decide to make it public. Testimony will be given, and evidence, such as these photographs, produced. The Vienna press . . ."

Gmunden went into another room and returned after a quarter of an hour, having composed a communication:

Herrn Präsident Jarrett
Anglo-American Press Association
Vienna
Dear Sir:

In connection with the list, which is in the hands of the Ministry of Finance and which is now being investigated by various groups, concerning payments by the A.O.G. to certain journalists, I wish to state that this list contains both "actual" and "nonactual" names.

That was certainly a way to put it, Mason thought.

Therefore it is explicable that the items such as those concerning Mr. Drew and Mr. Bleschke appeared on this list although they should have not appeared. I think therefore that it is my loyal duty to confirm that the money ensured exclusively for the subscription to the Danubia Press Service, and that neither of the named gentlemen received any "personal" payments.

Cagey son of a bitch.

You would make me very much obliged if you would accept this statement as a safeguard of the honor of the unjustly suspected gentlemen Drew and Bleschke.

Yours very truly,
[Signed] Gmunden

Mason, Stein, and Bishopson looked at one another and there was no need for them to give voice to their thoughts.

✳

The cablegram came after breakfast the next morning. Mason stuck a forefinger in the soft envelope and ripped it open. Paula saw that he went pale—so conspicuously that she asked in a shocked voice, "What's happened?" Quickly he rose and moved next to her as if to protect her, and then, with a hand on her shoulder, saying, "Bad news, darling," showed her the message. It came from her stepfather, and said that her mother had had a cerebral hemorrhage, altogether unexpected, and had died suddenly the night before.

Paula gasped. She put her fingers on her forehead, clutching the temples. She exclaimed, "Oh! . . . Oh, dear," and a puzzled, angry flash came into her eyes. "But why—why?" This was some monstrous, incredible irrelevance in the orderly procession of events: something must be incoherent in the pattern of the universe. Her cheeks tightened with indignation, her lips trembled, and she burst into a cry, not so much of grief, which would come later, but of shocked bewilderment and protest.

They decided that she ought to go home at once, if only to see her father, who would be heavily struck by this although he and her mother had been divorced for so many years; her father had never loved anybody else. Besides there was bound to be a tangle over the estate. Mason found out that if Paula left by train that night she could catch the *Aquitania* in Cherbourg twenty-four hours later, and he telephoned to Paris to arrange the transportation. To pay for this trip would mean a lot of scraping. They were short in the extreme. It was a bad moment. Mason had sent Stein a case of Scotch, which was still unpaid for, as a token of appreciation for their flights together, and still outstanding were some appalling bookstore bills.

They stood together at the Westbahnhof. Steam gushed from pipes under the cars; the clatter of hammers on wheels was sharp. "Buck up, old bean," Paula said.

"Bring back a decent American corkscrew, one of those that go both ways, and maybe a new pair of sneakers." He kissed her. "Be a good girl, darling."

"I don't want to be good, but I am," Paula said.

3

Mason found himself altogether lost without her. He discovered now how all-embracing his dependence on her had become. The elder Steins asked him to dinner, and, after crossing half the city, he realized that he had no idea of their address, although he had been to their house several times. Paula, of course, knew every address they used in Vienna, every telephone number, by heart. Mason had to make contact the next morning with Sandor's sister in Budapest, and could not remember her husband's name. He didn't know what to tell Frau Gertrude to order for dinner. He had not the faintest idea how to handle what seemed to be an unending procession of domestic problems, such as what to tell that damned upholsterer about the slipcovers and where, for God's sake, was the key to the trunk with all the summer clothes.

Day by day, his loneliness increased. He could not endure having dinner alone at home, and breakfast was a misery. The bedroom was cryingly empty without Paula, and he slept badly. Yet, during his frequent trips outside Vienna, he had seldom missed her. Working in a new city, exploring new problems, meeting and liking new people, gave him too much else to think about. That Paula was not home was what made the difference.

Came the day (how interested she would have been!) of the Anglo-

American meeting to decide Drew's fate. The rank and file of membership clamored for action, and the mood was savage. Mason, feeling his way carefully, laid down all the facts in as neutral a manner as possible. Drew sat silent, glowering, as Mason read out Gmunden's letter. Several correspondents were quick to perceive that this did not necessarily clear Drew at all, and Mason thought that he would perish of a humiliation he could not admit.

What had to be worked out was procedure. Only after confused and turbulent talk did a formula emerge. First Drew would be invited to make an explanation. Second, if this were not considered to be satisfactory, a vote would be taken as to whether or not he should be asked to submit his resignation. If a majority voted to ask him to resign, it meant, of course, that he was presumed to be guilty. The Anglo-American would be freed of any association with him and there would be no necessity for a long, painful *Ehrengericht*. As to Drew himself he would have to face alone whatever music might come later from other quarters.

Mason turned to Drew. "Jim, you've heard the sense of the meeting. I know it's awkward for you, but will you make a statement, give us some kind of general explanation?"

"No."

"Why not?"

"Never mind why not."

"It's the sense of the meeting that you should be given the opportunity to make a statement—"

"No. Won't say a word to you or anybody else."

"—given a chance to rebut Gmunden's letter—"

"If you want to fire me, fire me now, and don't prolong the agony."

Mason persisted, trying to help him: "If you don't make a statement, we'll have to vote—"

Drew gave up his inhibition about swearing. "Fuck you all," he said.

Pandemonium. Mason banged with his gavel. "Ten-minute recess," he shouted.

Now preparations had to be made to take the vote; slips of paper were passed out, and Wheatley and Tetzel were appointed tellers. Should Drew be asked to submit his resignation from the Anglo-American—yes or no? The correspondent of the *Christian Science*

Monitor (watery eyes, a Quaker, flaming liberal) rose and said he would have no part in this process, which he compared to a drum-head court-martial, and refused to vote. The *Daily Mail* man, passionate with anger and outrage at Drew, took the opposite line vehemently.

The vote was taken. Ten negatives, eight affirmatives, five abstentions. Drew was saved.

Mason caught his arm as they passed through the door. "I did what I could," Mason said.

Drew's voice was a snarl. "Thanks."

Sandor inquired of Mason when they were out on the street, "And how did you vote, if I may ask?"

He thought of Paula. He remembered how she often criticized him for equivocating, for sitting on the fence. "Abstained," Mason said, ashamed.

4

Strolling down Herrengasse, at the point where this proud gray street suddenly becomes narrow, as if throttled, and is darkened by shadows from overhanging rococo cornices, Mason ran into the girl he had met in the Grand Bar with the Bishopsons. He had just had a sandwich for lunch.

He said to Erika, "Why, Miss Falk!"

She looked startled. So that there would be room he stepped down to the street from the sidewalk, but even so he was taller than she.

The oddest of odd sentences came out of his mouth: "It's time for *Mehlspeise*."

A celebrated confectionary shop named Demel's was nearby, and seizing her by the elbow, giving her no chance to protest, Mason led her there. Along the counter stood such an array of delicacies as could scarcely be thought real—miniature chocolate cakes in crinkled gold wrappers; strawberry and pistachio ices carefully nurtured in individual bowls; silver candies, gold candies, and chocolates flecked with green and scarlet dots. On shelves behind could be seen homely jars of marmalade and poor pickled plums, looking down in envy at the brilliantly displayed, flashing trays of cream and chocolate. At the side, sandwiches so delicately complex that each might have taken half an hour to make were spread with intricate scrolled designs in salmon, yellow cheese, and gray foie gras.

A lady in a lavender dress and stiff, starched white apron took their order, in the room where the spiked gilt mirrors were arranged so that everybody could see, without craning, how charming everybody else was. Mason, for the fun of it, as if this were a celebration, chose gaily the most elaborate confection he could find—twin chocolate towers festooned with ornaments of stiff whipped cream, capped with cherries like hats on a doll, and hung with tiny skirts of pink spun sugar. Erika's eyes widened.

She had never had a tête-à-tête with an American before. Were all youthful Americans like this? He was like a big boy, but not gauche. He seemed to be fresh, healthy, alert—and how inquisitive! Yet also he gave forth a certain note of self-consciousness and guarded readiness for quick withdrawal.

"Tell me about your work," he was asking.

She gave a small, almost fragile shrug of disclaimer. Her work wasn't very interesting, she insisted modestly. Her manner was diffident, but without a trace of coyness. She was brushing a curl of soft dark hair up from her forehead. Shy, Mason thought.

No European would ask about a girl's work, Erika thought. It was the last thing a Viennese would talk about. A Viennese would ask her about what music she liked, or what she thought of the new night club in the Prater. Then Mason surprised her with a blunt question: "Do you work because you need the money, or aren't you fulfilled?"

Her lids dropped. "What shall I say? . . . I suppose . . . both reasons are involved a little, but it is mostly that I enjoy very much what I do." She looked up, flushed.

He grinned. "You're sweet. No woman is any good as a woman if just work fulfills her. But I have a feeling you're too modest; maybe what you do is more important than you think it is."

She turned the subject around. "Mr. Bishopson says that you write stories, as well as work for your newspaper. What are the stories about?"

"I haven't written a story for a long, long time—too busy."

Her question both pleased and disconcerted him. What were his stories about? If he did not know it was certainly proof that something was radically wrong with them. Becoming embarrassed, he stretched his legs out taut under the chair, twisted his shoulders, squirmed, and then, head sharply back, so that his neck cracked, looked straight up at the ceiling. He seemed to become younger than he was. He said, eyes half closed, musing, "Well, that's not the whole truth, I'm afraid. . . . It's true that I haven't had much spare time, but I could make time if I wanted to. . . . It's not what you say that counts, but what you *do*. I've lost confidence, I guess!"

But he said this as if he had all the confidence in the world. She looked sympathetic. She said, "To lose faith is the worst of all things, isn't it? How is a lost faith to be regained?"

Her pretty face became almost childishly serious. She's sweet, he thought. Almost too sweet, sticky-sweet.

He said, "First, avoid self-deception. Self-deception is the root of all evil, I sometimes think. And it's certainly a characteristic of practically everything in this whole darned town!"

"Yet . . . there must be room for some quality of illusion in life . . . some escape—oh, I don't know what I'm saying." She broke off in confusion.

"You mean that too much reality is too hard to take, and becomes unendurable in time?"

"If the reality is unpleasant, yes. But some realities are delicious, are they not?"

She gave him an apprehensive look, as if to indicate that she knew that the sentence she had just uttered could be misinterpreted as being an invitation: yet, issuing it, she had been modest, decorous, even sedate. He wondered how old she was—about twenty-four, he guessed.

He called for the check and pulled out his wallet, slipping some money down on the plate. Then he saw her reach for her purse. Good Lord! She wanted to pay half! He made the gesture of warding her off with stiff, upright, waving palms. "No, no!" he protested, laughing. "In my country it's the man who pays." He checked himself. "Or do we? In the long run, I suppose it evens out."

Out in the street he guided her toward a taxi, putting his big hand around her arm above the elbow firmly, warmly. He tightened his grip and slid the hand up an inch and she felt its warmth. She could feel that he didn't want to leave her. Erika said, "Perhaps you have a small moment. Would you like to see my studio?"

Had he been wrong about her eyes? He was not sure now that they were black-and-water. In the dappled sunlight he saw a touch of brightest, darkest blue.

Erika's studio, twenty minutes away, near the Belvedere, was a kind of workshop—an establishment specializing in what were called the "applied" arts. She designed glassware, leather bags, ashtrays, prints, scarves, novelties. The studio, part of a disorderly ancient barn, gave an impression of impetuosity, of being improvised from moment to moment, and was packed with drawing boards, cans of paint, piles of plywood and rolls of colored paper, fragments of pottery, a huge old-style studio portrait camera, and a loose pile of shiny dog-eared glossy prints, curving at the edges.

"This is Stefan," Erika said. She introduced a young sculptor in his early twenties, vigorous, unshaven, with peering eyes under shaggy, uninterrupted brows. Work was almost over for the afternoon; he prowled around with a frown, tidying up, putting wet cloth on plaster and paying no attention at all to Mason.

"Stefan is my son," Erika said.

For "son" Mason read "lover." Later he was not so sure. Erika put on a white smock over her dress, and Mason watched her; every time he looked at her she flushed. He had never known a girl who flushed so often or so readily. But she was more at ease with him now. She showed him some of her drawings and he felt a warm ripple of excitement when, standing together, the sides of their bodies touched. With delicate poise she moved away. She had a distinct talent, he saw, but not a very imaginative one. Her things were accurate, not brilliant, but sweet. That was certainly the word for her—sweet. And there was something romantic about her—elusive. She continued to talk in what he could only describe as an extraordinarily demure way, without a trace of forwardness or guile, but he felt that she was the kind of girl who half an hour before could have done almost anything and that it would leave no trace.

Stefan's face, watching him, took on an expression of disinterested contempt—even disgust. Obviously, to his eye, Mason was a bourgeois not worth consideration. Erika slipped behind a screen to tidy herself, and, emerging, sat on a stool with her hands crossed on her lap, rocking, smiling, like a schoolgirl with a note of mystery, demure, yes, but inviting too. Mason saw the shine in the curving hollows of her dark hair. Stefan scowled, opened a drawer, reached for something, and dashed it back and forth in his hand. He returned to Erika; she shook her head. He said nothing, but obediently she opened her mouth and he put the thermometer in. After a moment he took it out, and, walking to the window, screwed up his eyes under their shaggy, continuous brows, squinted, and shook his head, grumbling.

Mason asked, "Are you ill?"

Erika said, "No."

Stefan said, "Yes."

Erika said, "Just a little."

Mason telephoned her the next morning and asked her to lunch. She was tied up and suggested instead that he drop in at the studio again late in the afternoon. At once he discarded his plan to do some mailers, and said that he would be there.

He asked a hundred questions, or so it seemed. She derived from a middle-class suburban family, she told him; her father was a *Kommerzialrat*. She had had a governess when she was a child, and knew English and French quite well. "My mother told me in the middle of the war, when I was nine, 'Soon the war will be over, and we will drink champagne and there will be dancing on the streets.' Then at last the war did become over, but there was no champagne to drink and certainly no dancing on the streets."

She grew up greedy for life and restless and did not want to finish her courses at the university and became bored with her family. "Besides, they did not like at all my husband."

"Your what?"

"I am now virtually separated from him."

"What do you mean, 'virtually'?"

She blushed. This is really the most delectable girl, Mason thought. And he was struck by her frankness and detachment.

"But why do you call yourself *Miss Falk*?"

"I prefer now my own name."

"What's your husband like?"

"He is altogether . . . do I use the right word? . . . philistine, but I did not know that when I met him. He is very handsome and an athlete. He is the head of an import company, but business is now very bad. He has changed much. He is somewhat unpleasant in character, and has little honor."

But the unseen husband was not a problem; Stefan was. Mason couldn't find out what Stefan meant to her. Continually he stood at her side, a protector. At the studio, it was almost impossible to get in a word alone with her. But she wasn't in the least in love with Stefan, she insisted, nor he with her. He had tremendous talent, said Erika. Some day he would be well known everywhere. She was supporting him—that is, her husband was. Oh yes, her husband knew all about him. Wasn't the husband jealous?

"Why should he be?" Erika asked calmly. Her husband had a mistress, and Stefan had another girl. Mason held his head.

About a year before Stefan had seduced the very young daughter, she was only sixteen, of a prosperous doctor out in Vöslau. He was altogether finished with the girl by this time, he couldn't stand her any more, but she was madly in love with him and would not let him alone or let him go. Her parents now threatened to shut the girl up in an insane asylum if she ever saw Stefan again.

"A what?" Mason asked.

"Insane asylum. The girl's parents take it very seriously. I have to give the girl money too, because her parents won't, and Stefan has utterly none."

Erika had started the studio two years before, when she determined to strike out on her own; Stefan, whom she had met at the Kunstakademie, did most of the heavy work, and they had become quite successful—almost overnight. She had met Mrs. Bishopson and some of the other American ladies when, last autumn, the studio had had its first little exhibition.

Mason contrived to get her out of the studio and away from Stefan. They sauntered near the Belvedere, and she asked him if he liked pictures. Yes, he said, but he didn't know much about them— Paula was in charge of the art-music division. This was the first time he had mentioned Paula to her. "Perhaps you would like to see with me an *Ausstellung*," Erika suggested. They drove to a gallery on one of the small crooked streets off the Kohlmarkt and Mason saw the name of the artist on a poster in the window—Egon Schiele. The name meant nothing to him. They walked in.

Here, against a background of dead, pebbly oyster-white, the crippled and diseased limb of a tree: the flesh of the tree composed exactly as if it were human flesh, the muscles twisted and alive, and the branches bearing green, poisonous fruit. Across it, in metallic orange, the body of a woman—or was it a woman?

Here a group of naked men and women with eyes red as coals, taut arms and legs stretched so that the sinews gave a note of excruciating tension; but the arms and legs had no hands or feet, and were broken off into round grayish knuckles, like the thighbones of a chicken.

Here, a portrait of a woman. A girl's triangular face, foreshortened, under a vermilion scarf. The other spots of color were vermilion circles under the eyelids, on the stiff nipples, and at the point of each elbow. On the tense grayish white body were shadows of the palest blue-green; the belly was a delicate hill triangularly sloping; one arm held a horizontally extended bulging thigh, and the other broke off cruelly in a bare, knoblike knuckle.

Out in the street Mason was silent.

"What did you think?" Erika asked.

"Well, they're corrupt, almost diseased—beautiful too, like Vienna itself."

"Did you like them?"

"In some way they made me uncomfortable, but they excited me."

"I felt the same thing. But why should anything that gives pleasure and causes excitement make for discomfort too?"

"Ah!" He laughed. "I can detect from that remark that you're not a puritan. You don't understand people afflicted with a sense of sin. Erika, I'd like to ask you a question. When we met in the Grand Bar the other day what did you think of me?"

What a curious thing to ask, she thought. Perhaps it was true that he really did lack confidence. She chose carefully one of several possible answers, all quite honest.

"I thought you were an important person."

He was pleased. "Why?"

"You gave . . . you gave an impression of having both control and power."

They had *Jause*, sweets again, this time at Gerstner's on Kärntner-strasse, an establishment almost as renowned as Demel's, and then Mason drove her back to the studio. The taxi jolted over a bump, their shoulders brushed, and in the dark cave made by the cracked leather canopy of the taxi, his hand touched her knee. He felt his hand become warm through the cloth of the skirt on her knee. He leaned over to kiss her and they played with their lips for a moment. She seemed gentle, warm, and timid. They discovered small unusual deliciousnesses in putting their lips together, and then the contact between them became different and serious. He could not have imagined how trembling, supple, and very soft her lips would be. He drew her closer and her head rested sideways on his arm; he looked at her eyes, which became fixed, but floating, petals. He kissed her again deeply and she responded and began to shudder, squeezing herself against him; she closed her lips with his in a rhythmic, throbbing motion and her breasts, which had been taut and solid, turned suddenly soft; her mouth became cool, and she withdrew with a profound sigh, released. He was astonished. This from nothing more than a kiss! He cupped her head with the inside of his elbow, and kissed her eyelids as she hid her face. There could be no mistake, and his delight and wonder grew.

They reached the studio.

She straightened up, lifting her chin, twisting her head, shaking it lightly, with a transfiguring look of joy. "*Du!*" she exclaimed, triumphant. Never before had a girl in Vienna addressed him in the second person. "*Du!* I love you!"

He followed her to the door. She shook her head, putting a finger across her lips. "Stefan. Probably I can send him to Prague for several weeks, if you wish."

5

At long last Zoltan made his report. Mason, thumbing through the sheets swiftly, saw that it was a subtle combination of moral earnestness and eyewash. Four members of Zoltan's group were found "flagrantly" guilty of having accepted bribes from the A.O.G. and were expelled. Seven were "severely reprimanded," and nine others "reprimanded." The four whom Zoltan expelled were probably men whom he disliked for other reasons, Mason suspected, Zoltan used the A.O.G. scandal as a pretext to get rid of them. Life in Vienna made you cynical, all right. Verdicts from the Gesellschaft and Union, which were also minor masterpieces of the Vienna style, pompous, slippery, and evasive, soon followed. Two men in each were found guilty and dismissed.

Ritter was named in the Zoltan report; Drew was not. Ritter, it was announced, had paid the money back; this restored him to good standing. As for Drew it must have been Gmunden's letter, no matter how disingenuous it was, that kept him from mention. Mason had sent a copy of it to the Finanzministerium, with a strong covering letter emphasizing that it did not implicate Drew directly in any way.

Some further details of the report interested Mason. The 300,000-Schilling fund had been distributed in two different procedures, the "Oktober-Aktion" and the "Dezember-Aktion." Mason reached for a pencil. In the first Aktion 160,000 Schillings had gone from the A.O.G. to none other than Dr. Wimpassing of the Press Bureau— himself. So? Dr. Wimpassing, according to Zoltan, had spent this money exclusively "abroad" on behalf of the bank; that is, he had used it in foreign capitals for advertisements, publicity service, and the like. The A.O.G. had deemed such expenditure wise and Dr. Wimpassing was the logical man to take care of it. Therefore, concluded Zoltan, no journalist who actually lived in Vienna was concerned with the Oktober-Aktion in any way.

The sum involved in the Dezember-Aktion was less. Most of it went for "advertising," but certain amounts had been given to Herr Gmunden and two other agents to distribute as they saw fit, in order "to improve the local prestige of the A.O.G." Therefore only a minor portion of the original 300,000 Schillings could have found its way into the pockets of individual journalists. Therefore, Zoltan concluded, the whole affair had only touched his organization lightly, and his Ehrengericht had had little necessity for being. Therefore, now that his report was made, the matter could be considered closed.

Only three Viennese papers printed a word about any of this. In other words, Mason thought, the A.O.G.'s threats had, in a manner of speaking, paid off. The story was—so far—pretty well hushed up locally. But the *Arbeiter Zeitung* gave the full text of Zoltan's report and printed the name of every man on each list. Most of those who had taken bribes were Viennese—financial editors and the like—whom Mason had never heard of. He saw that five thousand Schillings had gone to Dr. Haber of the chief pan-German newspaper, an outright Nazi. Von Traum wouldn't like that to be known publicly! Thirty-five hundred Schillings to that ghastly old wreck, Herr von Schachtl, who had half a dozen Balkan papers on his string. *Und so weiter.*

Next day the affair reached Parliament, because the Social Democrats could not be refused their demand for a full-dress debate on the implications of the report. Mason hurried over to the Ringstrasse, and, dodging through the lobbies and corridors, climbed up into the press gallery. He leaned over, chin on knuckles, watching. Sandor joined him, and so did Bishopson, his redoubtable *Schwierigkeitenbeseitiger und Sorgemeister*, as well as Tetzel, his *Besonderer Kundschafter für Verderbtheit im Bankwesen*. Now the A.O.G. could no longer hush the matter up: every detail of the story became everybody's property.

Otto Bauer, the Socialist leader, compact and gracious, rose; he was a man of immense intellectual distinction, but too cloudy, Mason thought, too doctrinaire. Yet he made an effective speech. What right, he demanded, had the A.O.G., a private institution, to turn over 160,000 Schillings to the Austrian Press Bureau, an official division of the government, without public knowledge? What right had the Austrian Press Bureau to touch, much less to expend, the A.O.G.'s hush money, blackmail money, for any purpose whatsoever? Was the A.O.G. the servant of the Austrian government, or its master? By what incredible stretch of privilege was the A.O.G. empowered to use the official mechanisms of the Austrian government for the dissemination abroad of its odious and malignant propaganda? What right had the A.O.G. to bribe journalists, blaze open new paths of corruption, and conduct its shadowy affairs in this fashion at once shameful, scandalous, and even criminal?

Uproar. "Withdraw, withdraw!" shouted deputies on the government benches. Bauer refused to sit down.

"Order!" The speaker smashed his mallet down. Uproar again. "Order, order!"

"I ask that the whole matter be put in the hands of the Public Prosecutor," Bauer concluded calmly. "Let criminal action be brought against the directors of the A.O.G.!"

Criminal action! Mason tingled. And, in a way, he had started all of this!

The Finance Minister, smartly brisk, made a brief statement, and then the Chancellor himself—bearded, gray, immaculate—rose to answer Bauer. He made a long and complicated speech, deploring the affair, defending himself and the government, and asking that the debate be terminated. The A.O.G., he admitted, had behaved carelessly. He would even go so far as to say that it had behaved irregularly. He was not, however, prepared to say that it had behaved criminally. He regretted the emotional outburst of his eminent colleague Dr. Bauer. (Pfui!) He regretted unbridled emotion of any sort in circumstances so trying. He was sure that Dr. Bauer, like himself, was moved by the desire to uphold the clean name and reputation of their beloved motherland, Austria. The A.O.G. insisted that its activities were legitimate. All monies were dispensed for the orthodox purposes of publicity. The funds were given, in part, to Dr. Wimpassing, against whom no stigma could possibly be attached, so that the expenditure might be . . . er . . . regularized. (Boos and cheers.) As to the local funds, the A.O.G. insisted that it had few records or receipts. The gentleman who acted as the agents for the A.O.G. were unable to account precisely for their expenditures. Apparently 5,000 Schillings had been contributed to charities like Winterhilfe. (Laughter from the opposition benches.) The honorable and esteemed deputies of the Austrian Parliament would appreciate this act of . . . benevolence. (Renewed ironic laughter, then shouts of "Shame!") Another sum, 30,000 Schillings, had apparently gone to a foundation for the export of unemployed Austrian workers to the Dutch East Indies. (Laughter.) The rest—the old Chancellor put out his hands pleadingly—had been . . . er . . . distributed to journalists. The total sum in the public mind was 300,000 Schillings. A balance of 26,110 Schillings was, he believed, still in the coffers of the A.O.G. (Laughters, boos, and cheers.) So, in part, they were investigating the allegedly illegitimate expenditure of monies that had never actually been spent. (Counter cheers.) As to the personal payments to journalists, he could only regret them. The journalists involved had perhaps been ill advised to accept these . . . fees. The whole unfortunate matter might not have come into the open but for the imprudent, he might even say mistaken, zeal of a certain body of correspondents, who seemed particularly sensitive about their virtue. But now honor had been satisfied. Let bygones be bygones. Let the whole unfortunate matter come to rest. (Pfui!)

The Socialists reiterated their demand for court action by the Public Prosecutor. They were howled down.

Dr. Bauer rose to ask a vote of censure, and the government squeaked through with a majority of only seven.

Mason and his colleagues left the Chamber. If seven votes had gone differently, they would have had a cabinet crisis to write about, a new Austrian government to describe, a new Chancellor to introduce.

Even so, Mason thought, it was a pretty good little story as it stood. Criminal indictments demanded against A.O.G. directors. Austrian government close to being overthrown. He could see that in the headlines.

"Let's hurry, Otto. Get Paris on the phone."

*

The three roughneck newshawks, Wolfe, Bass, and Clippert, cornered Drew in the café. "Come clean, you son of a bitch," said Bass. "We've been playing tiddlywinks long enough. How much money did you get?"

Drew stammered, "As Christ is my witness, I took nothing for myself!"

"You're a goddamned liar!" snapped Clippert. "We got Bleschke drunk the other night and twisted his arm a little. He says he was with you, right here in this café, when Gmunden slipped him the three thousand and he passed fifteen hundred over to you the minute Gmunden stepped out of sight. He watched you stuff it in your pocket."

*

Mason wrote to Paula:

So the scene in Parliament marks the end of the whole deplorable business, I imagine. I can't tell you now how infinitely disturbed and upset I have been about the case. I felt gripped by forces beyond my own control, quite aside from my own personal involvement and my inability to make up my own mind as between Drew and the organization. As to my being the leader of our end of the investigation, who appointed me to be my brother's keeper? Are we all of us foredestined to be all of our brothers' keepers? Maybe this is one lesson to be derived from the whole mess. But I have hated it that I have had to appear so stuffy.

Mason described the scene involving Drew. Then:

There's some feeling that, in view of what Clippert and company say, we should reinstate proceedings against Drew. Whether we do or not we have to face up to it that we've become Viennese ourselves and are harboring a person guilty of somewhat repellent conduct, to put it mildly, for the sake of our organization. A purist would say that we are thus fatally compromised. How can we be a repository of the public conscience and at the same time protect a crook because he happens to be a friend? Good night, darling. I'll write again by the next mail.

Mason posted the letter at the Westbahn, and then drifted toward the café. He sighed, acutely conscious of his own shortcomings, his self-division, and recalled vividly something she had said earlier in the year: "If you don't know your own mind, you deserve what you don't get."

6

Some 3,900 miles from the Jarrett villa in Vienna a tall room in New York City opened on a granite terrace four hundred feet above the street. The room had casement windows, with a fine fence of steel mesh inside the glass of the windows. From the terrace a person could look across the other skyscraper tops to a glimmering view of hazy water, concrete, and ships. A stocky, youngish man named Ralph Conyers glanced at the afternoon newspapers during a lull in the market and one story made him summon a secretary and ask for a folder of recent clippings from Vienna, which he had been assembling for some weeks.

Conyers dined that night in the Centennial Club, of which, somewhat remarkably, he was already a member. A squall, which dumped out bucketfuls of light June rain, dashed down Forty-third Street, while the traffic chirped and moaned. Thank goodness here was a room without an inch of chromium in it, and no damned nonsense about having to tip headwaiters to get a good table. He spent a pleasant hour in the library, looking forward to dinner— the cuisine of the Centennial was renowned. His colleague Bates dropped in to meet him at 6:45. Bates was second in command of the foreign-loan department of the Amalgamated Continental. They had a leisurely dinner together—clams, rich young duckling with strips of orange, and cherry pie. Conyers liked the duck, but was a little sorry he had not had the Boston scrod instead.

Ralph Conyers: five foot ten, somewhat heavily built, smoothly shaven reddish neck just bulging over a soft white button-down collar; steel-rim spectacles with heavy toric lenses, so that his large gray eyes seemed even larger than they were; deep blue foulard tie with red spots; gray herringbone Cheviot suit, rough, hairy; broad light tan leather belt where his belly was sucked in; brown calf shoes with blunt sewed-over tips; in manner deferential to seniors, agreeable with juniors, clever, alert; conversation intelligent and assured.

With coffee Conyers said to Bates, taking out of his pocket a clipping or two, "I've been interested in a couple of stories from Vienna recently. Wonder if you've seen them."

"About that bank—the A.O.G.? Sure, but I haven't paid too much attention. Those crackpot Europeans never know what's good for them."

"It's not a question of their not knowing what's good for them. There's been a scandal—they've been throwing money around to a lot of newspapermen, that sort of thing."

"Oh yes," Bates said vaguely.

"Look at this from the Chicago *Star*, that's a highly responsible paper, released by their New York outlet here. It's by the chap who broke the story in the first place, and he's been right on top of it."

Bates glanced at the clipping. This was Mason's dispatch about the scene in Parliament.

Conyers then put before Bates several other background reports, agency recapitulations, and interpretive stories from the New York *Sentinel* and papers in Washington and Boston. Bylines included Sandor, Dixon, and Bishopson.

Bates finished reading. "Well, what about it? You're not expecting moral rectitude from a bank in Central Europe, are you?"

"No, but the implications might be interesting. What aroused my curiosity in the first place was why the A.O.G. should be trying to influence opinion in such a clumsy way as bribing journalists just now." He lit a Fatima. "How much money have all of us in that bank on short term?"

Bates shrugged. "I don't know about the others exactly, but as to us, oh, about thirty million, I suppose."

"Dollars or Schillings?"

"Oh, dollars, of course." Bates looked at him sharply. "I see what you're driving at. And thirty million dollars is a lot of money."

The next day Bates sent two cables to Vienna, one to Paris, and two to London. When the replies came back he called Conyers in, and they had a talk with a senior vice president of the bank. He presently summoned two other vice presidents, a lawyer, and an accountant. Conyers still had the clippings in his pocket.

❋

Herr Generaldirektor Dostal stood behind his rosewood desk, irritably slapping a batch of papers against its gilt-embellished top.

"So, Treuwalt, that is your last word?"

"Yes."

"It is preposterous."

"With Behemoth about to liquidate, there is no other solution. Moreover things in Brünn are shaky and in Cracow worse."

Paultraxl snarled, "I never liked that Cracow operation."

"It was mostly your work," put in another director angrily, "Your report persuaded us to go into it."

"That's a lie!"

They were screaming at each other.

"Gentlemen, gentlemen," said Dostal, rapping on the desk. "Enough of personalities. We must decide what we propose to do.

The political situation is not auspicious and I do not like recent reports from London and New York. As to Paris, the French are still so bitter and so megalomaniacal that they make no sense. They will punish us, if they can. Nothing is to be expected from Germany at the moment, because they are in much the same situation as we are. The market is very, very tight. My own proposal evades the issue, but in the circumstances it is perhaps best."

After argument his proposal was adopted. For the first time in fifty-seven years, no balance sheet of the A.O.G. appeared.

The next day Paultraxl accepted as final Dostal's word that he could not get him appointed to Geneva, listened alertly for ten minutes on the telephone to London, called Amsterdam, and flew suddenly to Paris. A little later Dostal began to sell some shares heavily, and Treuwalt took two quick trips, one to Zurich, one to Frankfort. The telephones were busy. The auditors were busy. Dostal forgot all about his sweetheart roses. Treuwalt skipped to Helsingfors, and another director scuttled to New York.

IX. THEN, IT WASN'T OVER

Mason Jarrett did not telephone Erika Falk for several days. He was afraid. There was enough office work to keep him busy, and he spent one languid evening, not very satisfactory, at the Koenigen. But he could not get her out of his thoughts, and his yearning to see her grew beyond bearing. He rationalized his desire to do so by some highly fallacious and transparent reasoning, arguing that it was bad manners on his part not to call her again, that he owed her another meeting, that he must not let her down after her offer to get rid of Stefan, that in a word he would call her out of consideration for her rather than for himself. He ground the butts of his palms against his temples. When at last he did call, her voice in response was attentive, not surprised, and completely natural, without a trace of implied rebuke. He asked her to have dinner with him, and said that he would pick her up after Stefan had left.

But perhaps Stefan had gone to Prague.

He had.

Mason plodded, his step unnaturally heavy, around her studio. His eyes were bloodshot. The curtains were partly drawn and the last tapering shafts of pale sunlight sparkled with agitated motes. Mason said, "Erika, there's something I have to say." He felt like an utter fool. "I really can't . . . go on . . . from where we left off the other day. I'm too bound, too tied up, too close to Paula. You're the most marvelous girl—I've never known anything so exciting. . . . I'm

313

crazy about you. . . ." He became more and more inarticulate as he
saw that her look said clearly, "But what does any of this matter?"
He proceeded, stumbling: "I don't see any . . . any prospect of being
able to go on . . . any solution. I don't want to fall in love with
you. You're marvelous, but I can't afford . . . afford . . ." He didn't
finish the sentence. Perhaps what he intended to add was ". . . to
risk destruction of my marriage." Or perhaps simply "I cannot
commit any act of duplicity, because of bad conscience about Paula
—the tie to her is too strong."

All she did was put her warm hands on his lapels, saying, "Kiss
me."

＊

They explored one another in the soft, warm June darkness. He
had been nervous and hurried at first; a spasm cast him out of himself. She did not appear to mind in the least; she became complete
anyway, and, murmuring "Du . . . du," covered his chest, his
shoulders, with small cool relaxed kisses. He felt reborn, exalted: as
if he had been given a new skin. Now it was an hour later. Half
asleep, he slid his hand down over her hill of hip; then accidentally
his toes touched the curved sole of her foot. She was all of a piece;
her whole body became at once alive; she hugged and jostled him,
shook him, eager, happy. Then she became a pale rosiness limply
stretched out as she tossed her head from side to side with her eyes
closed. They made love again and her response was continuous, a
continuous flow; she crooned and murmured. He put a forearm along
her belly. The elbow lay just atop where he had made love to her;
without moving elbow or arm his fingers stretched out, and with a
thumb he could caress one of her nipples, with his little finger the
other.

He did not know what he was saying: "I hold you like the root
of a tree. A tree grows out of you, and it is me."

＊

Mason reached home very late. He sank down on the big sofa,
dazzled, dazed. He could not quite believe in the reality of the
experience. He had never known anything like it. His emotion was

not merely of delight, but of astounded wonder. He was shattered. He took a series of short deep breaths. Incredulous, he sought to recapture details out of the enthralling blur. Each time it has been different, but constant was the freshness of her climbing young body and the harmonious flowing attunement between them; always too the little ejaculations of satisfaction and release, also the gentleness; and the modesty as well.

Mason's previously known world began to recede: the conventional world of the intellectualized Anglo-Saxon West, so cross-grained, inhibited, confused, suppressed; packed with God knows what impedimenta—hesitations, trepidations, timidities, false pride, resented childhoods, talk-talk-talk-talk, fear, discomfort before the realities of naked emotion, aridity, frigidity, sterility. Compare all this to Erika with her warmth, her spontaneity and sweetness, her sense of unburdened joy.

Perhaps it was odious of him to think of Paula in this connection but Mason did so. Paula too was skilled, loving, delicious, articulate, and, like many puritans, quite capable of being lascivious in the act of love, when aroused. But she was not like Erika. Sex did not mean so much to her; it was more part of a general broad picture than an end in itself. Paula deeply demanded spiritual as well as physical expression. That was all there was to it—Erika was different. She gave a new dimension—not so much a note of passion as of sheer easy fulfillment and delight.

Mason's thoughts, his memories, became more general. So many American girls had, it seemed, all the sex petted or necked out of them before they grew up. Or they promised, and then did not, or could not, deliver. Or, passionless, their reactions were marked by nothing more than a thin sigh, a single squeak or quiver. Once done, they were done. Or, like that girl who had been his first sweetheart in Chicago, all that interested them was dexterity, the technique of performance. Their curiosities, their ardor, came not from the body but the mind.

Mason rushed out of the villa, drove down to an all-night pub in Grinzing, and got roaringly drunk.

✳

A cablegram cut through an enveloping fuzziness the next morning: ROCKS EXBUDAPEST ANTISEMITE FASCIST ORGANIZATION FORMED HUNGARY CUMSECRET GOVERNMENT SUPPORT HOW HILLIARD. "Rocks" was the code word for Mason's principal opposition in Chicago, John Dixon, and "How" meant "Check," "Follow," or, by inference, "Why the hell did you miss this?" Mason, groaning, reached for the telephone. There had been no hint of this story in Vienna, and Dixon, who had been away, must have picked it up in Budapest. Mason decided that he must watch the legations in Vienna more closely, and ought imperatively to go on the road again. Too damned much time spent on the A.O.G. The ideal time for a quick roundup trip would be this week, while Paula was still away. He plowed through the papers groggily and took Bleschke's call. Yes, he ought to set out for Budapest, Bucharest, and Warsaw right now. He telephoned Erika. To hell with going away, he decided.

At lunch Erika said, "Could you get me a copy of the Declaration of Independence?"

"Of course, but why?"

"Words from it would be very amusing if printed on a scarf. I had thought of designing one. Soon there will be much American tourist trade."

"Nice idea!"

Mason thought, Could there possibly be any subconscious symbolism to this? He must not get too Viennese about it, but it was really quite curious that Erika should have "Declaration of Independence" in mind in relation to him. Did she want him to declare his independence of his wife?

"Do the Gettysburg Address instead."

"I do not think I know about the Gettysburg Address."

"It's about unity, indivisibility."

She flushed.

Late that night, very late, after a long close afternoon, they had dinner at the little bar on Bognergasse. She was lustrous, twisting happily in her chair like a child.

Erika said, "About me it does not matter in the least, but I am wondering, is it discreet that you should be seen with me in a place where Americans congregate and are much to be seen?"

He had another drink. "I don't give a damn whether we're seen or not."

Erika said, "In any case I think you should not look so conspicuously happy."

She adored sweets, and they had crêpes suzette for dessert. Extravagant! They were worth it. The pool of blue flame, yellow at the edges, flickered, and Erika, with an expression of appreciation, put her hands close to the flame, as if warming them gently. Her hands, becoming pink, converted the flaming dish into a small campfire, cheerful, homely, their own. With delicate gestures, she seemed almost to be wafting the flames toward her face, and a blue incandescence, soft, luxurious, became reflected in her eyes.

As a matter of fact someone whom Mason knew well did happen to walk in that night—Dr. Ricardo Stein. He bowed slightly, catching it at once that Mason probably did not want to be recognized and wishing to make it clear that if this were so he, Stein, would pretend not to know him. But at once Mason greeted him cordially and asked him to sit down; they chatted, and had a coffee together. Mason told Erika that Stein had his own airplane and what an exhilaration it had been to fly with him. She became interested and asked Stein questions, and he in turn questioned her.

"But of course you must be Viennese," said Stein. "None but the Viennese can be so charming." She talked to him in German and Mason noticed that her accent was softer than his, with such a pleasant slurring of the verbs, beguiling, sweet. Stein finished his coffee, sipped a brandy, and prepared to go. Mason was too relaxed, too much at ease, too proud of Erika, too delighted with himself, to be impatient, and it was some time before Stein left.

＊

The telephone rang with its shrill international signal at about three that morning. For a second Mason didn't know where he was.

"Which is the more important, your country or the truth?" Cairn did not seem drunk, and his voice was pressing.

"Hell-o! Tom! Where are you?"

"London." He repeated his question.

Mason struggled to become fully awake. "That's a hell of a question to throw at a friend at three o'clock in the morning. The truth, I suppose."

"Would you lie for your country?"

"*Cela dépend.* In wartime, yes, maybe."

Cairn said, "Would you conceal the truth out of a patriotic motive?"

"Countries are different things at different times. I think I'd have done anything for my country under Wilson. Under Harding and Coolidge, I'm not so sure."

Cairn appeared to be ruminating. "Listen to the man. What about now?"

"Don't know. What started you on all this big cogitation, anyway?"

"Something I want to broadcast that, if known, could embarrass the hell out of Washington. But it ought to be known—stuff about American policy toward Germany. Can't tell you more just now."

"Go ahead and write it, if it's true and you're sure you want to get it out."

"How's all that A.O.G. business coming along?" Cairn asked.

"Wound up, I think! We've whitewashed our people and I don't think they're after me any more."

"Let me speak to Paula for a moment, the proud beauty."

"Paula? She's in America."

"Where? What?"

"Her mother died."

"Oh, dear! I'm going to New York tomorrow. What's her address, and I'll call her and tell her we had a talk."

*

They held one another securely, comfortably. Mason talked about himself a good deal. Only rarely did he reminisce about his childhood, but now he felt unlocked when Erika asked him a question or two. She wasn't inquisitive, but calmly interested. "My father ran a wheat farm in Montana. It was a quite big place, the kind of farm no one in Western Europe can even imagine, but he died when I was a child. There was a panic that year, and farm prices collapsed around the time of my father's death. We moved to a town called Great Falls, and to support us, my sister and myself, my mother worked in a shop—she was a saleswoman in a general store. In the afternoons after school I'd walk home—of course we didn't have buses in those days—down our main street. It was bitterly cold in winter. We had snow like nothing any Western European knows about. I'd slide through the big drifts and then twist my way through narrow, crooked passages hacked out of solid snow that was shoulder-high and pass my mother's store. Then, stamping my feet, I'd lean against the window, breathing on it to make a little hole through the frost—pressing my nose against the cold pane until I could feel it flatten. There inside, through the frost, I could see my mother standing behind a counter, demonstrating very brightly the things on sale, wrapping packages, and counting change. Her hair was getting thin, and she looked frail. She desperately wanted me to be ambitious, to be a success. But she would never tell me so. Once I overheard her say to her sister, 'It's the worst of mistakes to tell a child to get on in the world, make his mark, get ahead. No one can predict what life holds for any of us, and if a child who's been pushed ahead too much turns out to be a failure, he will blame his parents for it—sure as sin. All we can do is give him as good an education and as much character building as we can. Esther, have some more coffee cake.'"

"Your mother is still alive?"

"No. She died three or four years ago."

"But she lived long enough to know that you were going to be a success?"

"She was proud of me, but I don't know what else she thought."

Mason stirred. It still excited him, but terrified him too, that black hair should be on the pillow next to him, not red-gold.

"And your life with what you love best, your newspaper, how did that begin?"

"Oh! I've earned a living since I was fourteen. Lots of American youngsters do. I had all sorts of jobs, but nothing interested me much but writing. How did I get my job on the *Star*? Well, that's an odd little story. I worked on several newspapers and drifted east as far as Chicago. Youngsters everywhere wanted to work for the

Chicago *Star*, to get their training there. They still do. I managed
to get in to see a marvelous man named McFarland, but he said he
didn't have any openings and then appeared to reconsider. He asked
me, after we talked a while, what books I liked, and it seemed to
startle him when I mentioned writers like Sherwood Anderson and
James Branch Cabell. We got into a big discussion about the
Georgian poets and then Ezra Pound. A distant, almost romantic
look crossed McFarland's face. He said, 'I've been trying to get a
good, bright, unorthodox story about Henry Ford for years, an
interview that tells something—what he's really like. Nobody can get
to him. Here's a hundred dollars. Go to Detroit, and if you can see
Ford and write the kind of story I want I'll give you a job.' Well,
I went to Detroit, and by some absolutely outrageous fluke I did
manage to get an interview with Ford. McFarland liked the way it
was written, and I've been on the *Star* ever since."

This was all most interesting, Erika thought; a European would
not be likely to talk in quite this way. A European would not tell
all. An American wants to share.

Erika said, "There is much that I would like to hear about. You
must inform me. Who is Ezra Pound? Who is Sherwood Anderson?"

Mason made an amused sound, then told her.

"From the hard work of your mother and your own childhood
you have no resentments?" she asked.

"I don't think so."

"It has not made you want to be rich?"

"No, no. On the contrary, I think it gave me a kind of contempt
for money. Maybe that's why I've always been extravagant, or
wanted to be." He kissed her. "Very unwise."

"But if you had had—what is it called—a certain private income,
you would have been freed of the necessity to work for a newspaper
and you could have written your own private stories."

She accepted it as correct and natural that his work was the most
important thing about him.

"Yes, perhaps, but I'd have missed a lot."

"What, for instance?"

"Varied and concrete experience. The sense of being—how shall
I put it—at the ringside of history. The sense of being in the know."

"Is that sufficient recompense?"

He had a sharp memory of Paula—that night around the time of the Customs Union crisis when she told him that if he really in tended to be a serious writer he ought to quit the *Star*.

Now another Chicago memory jabbed him. The *Star's* antique building on the edge of the Loop looked like a pile of cigar boxes partitioned into sections by a madman with a jigsaw; through shelves in these boxes one ancient elevator protruded vertically, like a hollow piston. Its operator, who was also the receptionist on the news floor, was a white-bearded Lithuanian, his head shaped like a thumb, who spoke scarcely a word of English. Mason, a cub reporter, took a taxi back to the office after covering a routine assignment, and discovered that he had exactly fifteen cents in his pocket; as security for the fare, he gave the driver his gold watch, a gift from his father. Next day, he borrowed a couple of dollars from a fellow reporter to hold him till payday, left a dollar with the antique Lithuanian when he went out on an assignment, and instructed him to give this to the taxi man when, as arranged, he delivered the watch. Surprisingly, the taxi man showed up, but the antique Lithuanian had lost—or spent—the dollar. The taxi man was never seen again; nor the watch.

He told this little story to Erika now. "How strange—how sweet!" she murmured. "But you must have been very innocent."

Mason told Erika things about the *Star* that he scarcely ever thought about, because he loved the paper so much that he could not bear to acknowledge its defects. He mentioned a man on the copy desk who was almost certainly embroiled up to the neck with the Capone gangsters, and how Plover and McFarland, his gods, hated each other and were scarcely on speaking terms although they put out the paper together every day. He told her about jealousies in the literary department; how feeble and shoddy the old-timers at the telegraph desk were, half drunk all the time and trying at all costs to carry on; about the atmosphere of the city room, full of dog-eared, scruffy riffraff, and the business office, so starched, impervious, and superior. He talked and talked. Love produces the clean breast.

Love? Erika was marvelous, an utter darling, and certainly not a girl to be regarded lightly, not somebody picked up in a bar, to be dismissed after a brief romantic interval; this was not a mere adventure for the shining of one moon.

But did he love her?

What in the name of heaven was happening to him, since he wanted to see her every day of his life and enjoy her and teach her and make her happy and be happy with her and make her utterly his . . . forever.

Surely he wasn't falling in love with Erika?

Of course not.

2

Carefully, dutifully, Erika wiped the brushes she was using and pulled off her smock. It was a day or two later. Tilting her head abruptly, so that her dark curls spilled on one shoulder, she squinted at the design she had completed. She looked flushed, but also drained, and Mason felt her forehead, which was burning.

"Do you still have a temperature?" he asked.

"A little."

"How much?"

"It goes down now most of the time."

"You ought to take better care of yourself if you're still running a temperature." His voice was anxious, but he was still young enough to be bored by ill health.

"Darling, what's the matter with you, anyway?" he asked her.

"Nothing much." It was obvious that she was not telling the whole truth, but he knew her well enough by this time to be confirmed in his knowledge of how elusive she was if he touched a sensitive spot. He still knew nothing about her, really, except that she was the sweetest girl in the world, although in another sense he knew everything.

"Have you got a doctor?"

"Oh, yes."

"Is he a good doctor? What's his name?"

"He is quite a famous doctor. But he has a certain contempt for me."

"I don't believe it. What kind of doctor could that be?"

"It is quite true." A series of thoughts came to her: This is probably the most interesting man I ever met and I'm wildly in love with him and perhaps I will love him always, but he is still a little naïve, and it is time for him to know more of life. He thinks too much in terms of simple absolutes.

"Get another doctor, then."

"I can't. At least not now. In fact, I have an appointment to see him exactly now, and if you wish you may come along."

They climbed into a taxi. She said, "Trattnerhof, *bitte.*" On the Graben they pushed their way through crowds swarming out of the office buildings and spreading down the street like strands of a mop beaten out. They penetrated into the dimness of the building and Erika explained to him the mechanism of the fantastic elevator, the chain of cubicles on an endless belt.

"Six," Erika called, darting ahead with a vivid smile. She grasped his hand when, coming into view on the sixth floor, he stepped out, and they jogged together down the corridor full of doors with windows made of frosted glass. When had Mason last peered through frosted glass? Montana? What was real, what unreal? What was the present, what was not?

The office of Dr. Kohner, the well-known gynecologist, stood at the far end of the hall. In the reception room two or three women waited anxiously, with the look women have in a doctor's office when the finality that rests in the word "verdict" will come soon. Erika's face, as they sat down, wore an absent, pensive expression; Mason stirred in his chair, restless. A nurse emerged and led Erika into another room.

Twenty minutes later she came out, blushing, with Dr. Kohner at her side, polite but rigid. His expression showed priggishness, aloof satisfaction, and solicitude. Erika introduced him to Mason. It became clear to Mason at once that the doctor assumed that he must be the man involved with whatever had to do with Erika, and he measured him coldly. It even occurred to Mason that Erika had brought him along in order to present to the doctor a man obviously respectable; she was using him to make herself more respectable in the doctor's eyes.

Dr. Kohner took Mason aside. "For some months, as you doubtless know, sexual relations have been, er, explicitly forbidden to the young lady." Mason could not conceal a start. "Now perhaps the

ban can be relaxed, but slowly, with care, prudently! Under no circumstances, *none*, can she afford for some little time to risk becoming
pregnant again."

He bowed stiffly and returned to Erika.

"Thank you, Herr Doktor," Erika said.

"Good-bye," the doctor said in English. "I will hope not to be
seeing you again, except for occasions happier."

Quickly Erika led Mason from the office and down the corridor
with its smell of dust, wet paint, and iodoform, and once more
they entered the crazy elevator. Out on the street, day had changed
into dusk. When they arrived the sky had been a pure transparent
cobalt, but now it was solidly violet and the windows in the office
buildings were lit up and looked like rows of illuminated ice cubes.
They reached a café.

"I wish you'd tell me what all this is about," Mason said.

"Some months ago I had a . . . a friendship. I became in trouble
as a result, and Doctor Kohner made it right, but with much rebuke."
She paused. "But then there came a slight infection. . . . Now at last
I am cured, if I take care!"

"Erika, I have something to tell you—it's quite important, serious."
He proceeded to repeat Doctor Kohner's warning.

Her only reaction was to burst into soft peals of laughter. What
the doctor said was preposterous!

They dined together at a restaurant out near the Danube. A current ruffled the shiny surface of the river, so that it divided into
two types of surface, one smoothly flowing, one dappled, which
continually separated and met again. Mason felt a closeness with
Erika unrivaled in his experience with anybody. Like the water on
the river they flowed into one another. Communication between
them was automatic, instantaneous, and complete. They went back
to her studio and it seemed that, in an hour and a half, he had lived
a whole life. She too was rapt. Nothing could match her accomplished
sweetness. Probably it was on this night that he realized he truly
loved Erika.

*

Every aspect of Mason's life became quickened. For a week he
spent virtually every minute with Erika. He felt altogether burnished,

sparkling, shined up, by delight. Most of all he welcomed the
exultation that came with the awareness that, not only was he in love
with her, but that she was in love with him. The response was what
moved him most—her excitement, her curiosity, her unabashed delight at being with him. All his creative energies were unleashed. To
his astonishment, he found himself waking up in the middle of the
night, saturated with ideas and the impulse for expression. He began
to outline plots and scribble notes for stories. Then too he expanded
in another sphere. He had never thought of himself as much of a
ladies' man. He knew that he was not as graceful as young Stein, not
as bullish as Mark Thorne, not as magnetic as Tom Cairn, not as
good-looking as Karl Tetzel. But now he felt confidence, strength,
and even superiority. The magic wand of her prowess, her proficiency,
communicated itself to him.

A day or two later he looked at the calendar and sought to pull
himself up. Paula would be returning soon. And he must face it
that something terrible as well as extraordinary had happened to
him. He loved one woman, his wife, and had now fallen in love
with another. And he had fallen in love with her after sleeping with
her, not before. That was the sure way, because then you knew
truly what you had; the process was not tied up with hope, despair,
yearning, or illusion. But what was going to *happen*? What, as he
had asked himself with premonition even before he had become
deeply involved with her, was the solution? Because he also loved
Paula, who loved him, and Paula was his wife. How had this shattering development come about? The most fantastic and frightening
factor was that he had not thought about Paula at all. It was as if
she did not even exist. A whole new division of his life had opened up,
a limitless, unexplored domain, with which she had nothing to do.
Nothing whatever that had to do with Paula had led him to the first
irrevocable step with Erika and nothing that Paula could do or say
could change it now.

Mason dropped in at the Weissenhof. He had not been there
for a week. Everybody asked him about Paula. Seeing friends here
who did not know him except as a person always interlocked with
her woke him up to other awkward, damaging realities of his
new situation, and bad conscience began to smite him. When Paula

returned, could he continue to play ball, as the phrase was, on two lots? His worry and distress increased. He had puritan roots as deep as Paula's. He must somehow acknowledge the fact that he was involved in a critical dilemma, and do something about it. He thought of the cheap little adage which says that morals are a matter of geography; even so, what he was doing was called, in simple language, cheating. Out of his bad conscience came self-division. Must he give Erika up? If so, when? Now? No, no! But what about Erika's position? He had to think of her. What would all this do to her?

An additional factor was the extraordinary air she herself continued to give of utter sinlessness. He thought of her warm, sedate, gentle face, the broad brow, and funny, somewhat crooked little nose. She was certainly not innocent, but she gave no faintest trace of any sense of guilt, for the good reason that she felt none. She had no hesitations, no equivocations. She was a giver, not a taker. That was the most wonderful thing about her. Her complete acceptance of the relationship they had set up tended to make him forget or ignore his own scruples; because of her sinlessness, he felt sinless too. She blotted everything else out. What talent a man could have for being disingenuous in order to make things easier for himself! But now he had to face blunt, fearful, imminent realities.

The bank scandal and its shadowy and sinister implications came to Mason's mind. Of course there was no direct analogy, but the A.O.G. business had, after all, presented an ethical issue, an issue based on probity, on which he had adopted a strong point of view. He couldn't take one line on the A.O.G. affair and be the leader of a crusade against dishonesty in the public domain while, at the same time, he was being flagrantly dishonest in his private life. But was there any true similarity? How could he possibly give Erika up in any case? He thought no longer merely in terms of her soaring sweetness and glowing love for him but of their compatibilities and companionship. Must he surrender all of this? Yes! No, no! He felt torn apart.

Erika said the next evening, "The minute your wife returns, all this comes to an end. You know that? It will be hard for me. You have made me want to change my life."

3

Mason picked up the Sandors and the three went together to a party at the Poles'. Because he was a Herr Präsident he was asked to many more diplomatic affairs than before; his social life had expanded considerably. Most of the parties were dull, but he had to confess that it pleased him to be rubbing shoulders with cabinet ministers, clinking glasses with eminent creatures of the theater, or meeting scientists such as the man who had just won a Nobel Prize for theoretical work on the structure of the atom. Certainly it was all a new experience.

The Poles were the most Lucullan hosts in town, and this was their big annual reception. Dr. Wiskiewicz stood near the Minister and his wife and helped with the introductions as the guests waited patiently in line. Today his frizzy ginger hair, a split pyramid towering in large fluffy waves, resembled a sponge rather than a football.

Sandor, omniscient, was a splendid guide at parties.

"Will you now observe—the young woman who stands near Bach-Dengler, the Minister of Finance. She was nothing yesterday, a girl I think from the Grand Bar, or even lower, and is today the mistress of Prince P. Yet those innocent, they wonder how she came to all that fox! And the pearls!"

Erji, giddy with excitement, murmured without a trace of envy, "Ah, those pearls of pearls!"

"In that corner is Marcus Siebenstern, the dramatist, talking to the Regisseur of the Josefstädter. He could be the new Hauptmann, if he does not continue to collapse in alcoholism. Ah, now, there is Maximov, the Soviet Minister. He is of the new school, a Stalin man, to be watched. Behind, the slim woman in the black mantilla, but of course you must recognize her, with all that highly false golden hair—the celebrated new coloratura, Mladek. Approaching her is Prince Starhemberg, and behind him, what a combination, Otto Bauer!" Sandor gave Mason an excited nudge. "Now, ah, we have a true rarity. Enters Freud!"

And indeed Dr. Sigmund Freud, no less, with his gleaming violet eyes, his hard carved beard, his note of tense and even exasperated superiority, was advancing gravely to host and hostess. A hush came over the room as he moved forward like a boat through bulrushes; guests craned to watch, but were bent back by the force of his slow, majestic passage. "Freud!" people whispered. The whole assembly became silent in awe.

Mason had a moment of recessiveness. He felt shy in this galaxy. There might be important news sources here, but he was sick of having to think about news all the time and making use of people. It pleased him, after having participated closely behind the scenes in recent events, to be a purely detached observer. He walked up to the bar alone, and then saw the sunny face and blond curly head of Dr. Ricardo Stein. They greeted one another with a closeness so taken for granted that it needed no physical expression, not even a tap on the sleeve. Stein talked about a projected flight to the Burgenland to see Haydn's tomb, whereupon his face took on a somewhat troubled look. He half grinned. "What an interesting-looking girl that was—the girl you were dining with on Bognergasse the other night."

"Oh." Mason became alert.

Stein continued, dogged. "Her name was Miss Falk, was it not?"

"Yes. Erika Falk."

"I wonder if you would object if I called her up sometime."

Thunderstruck, Mason waited.

"There was something about her. She was most remarkably attractive, I thought, and I cannot seem to get the image of her out of my head. I would like very much indeed to see her sometime. Would you mind, Mason?"

"Gosh, Ricardo, she doesn't belong to me!"

"Yes, but I met her through you, and I couldn't possibly call her unless I . . . I . . . cleared it with you first."

Mason thought fast. He must not, under any circumstances, give away to Stein what Erika meant to him. On the other hand, he certainly did not want Stein cutting in on him and taking her out.

"Hell, Ricardo, it's a free country, isn't it?" Mason was equivocating. He was caught in a box. He fumed inwardly. If he gave voice to resentment at Stein's question, then Stein would know that he and Erika were close. If he did not he ran grave risks, because Stein was a free man and he was not. "What you do is up to you."

"She has a studio, has she not? Did I not hear her say that she has a studio?"

"A sort of studio."

"Anyway I would like extremely to see her again."

Mason shrugged, as if idly. "I'm not her father. Or her manager."

"Her manager?"

"Oh . . . she makes things . . . sells them."

"I would like very much to be able to call on her."

Mason looked black.

"I beg your pardon."

"Don't beg my pardon. What for?"

"I beg your pardon again."

"Oh, Christ, Ricardo, I don't know her very well. She's married and she has a very complicated boy friend, a young sculptor." The words were hardly out of his mouth before he realized that they opened the way for Stein.

The cogs in Ricardo's mind practically became visible as they clicked to a decision. He said, "Thank you very, very much."

Mason, desperate, wandered alone to the bar and had a shot of vodka, following this with champagne. With interest he tasted some caviar, of which large amounts seemed to be available. Dr. Wiskiewicz came up. He had just returned from a trip to Moscow and wanted with relish to tell Mason a story or two about Throckmorton, the *Star* man there.

"What a character. He is as much a problem to the Soviet Union as the Five-Year Plan. They like him for it. Such anecdotes are heard as can scarcely be believed. Throckmorton received an invitation from Ivy Litvinov to tea. It is ten years or longer since any Western correspondent has been asked to tea by the Litvinovs. And what did your magnificent Throckmorton do? He refused the invitation! On the ground that he understood that it was unsafe for Russians to be seen with foreigners!"

Dr. Wiskiewicz almost wept with amused appreciation.

"Throckmorton was summoned on another occasion to the Foreign Office at three o'clock in the morning and given a statement by Bukharin. He began his story: 'In an exclusive statement personally delivered to this correspondent today *by the assistant night elevator man at the Foreign Office*, Nikolai I. Bukharin, the Foreign Minister, said, et cetera, et cetera.' "

Dr. Wiskiewicz was near to rolling on the floor.

The great white-walled room with the deep blue curtains had become packed. Still Mason had little desire to seek anybody out. Erika . . . Erika . . . He must tell her what to say when she got the call from Stein. Stein's intervention could be a serious nuisance. Abruptly then Mason's thoughts swerved to Paula, who was always spectacularly good at parties of this kind; people pointed her out, asked who she was, or clustered around her with admiration. She was a very distinct and tangible asset at a party. She gave him face.

He felt a grip on his elbow.

"Well! Hi, Willi!"

The Archduke's smile enlivened his whole face; so did Mason's.

"I would like to ask you a direct question. When does the *gnädige Frau* return?"

"In about a week."

"A man should not let a beautiful woman of her category out of his sight for so long."

"What's her category?" Mason asked.

"Special."

"I trust her."

"The question of trust is not involved. A woman is weaker than a man. All women are weak. There can be a moment when any woman may become particularly weak, and is therefore lost."

Mason gave him a sideways grin. "And you're waiting for just such a moment, are you, Willi?"

The Archduke made a mock bow. "Of course."

"With confidence?"

"No."

They both laughed.

"It's my turn to ask you a direct question. What makes you so interested in Paula?"

"What could be simpler—I would like to find out what she is."

Sandor, who had been talking to Dr. Wimpassing, rushed up,

sweating. "Now has entered Generaldirektor Dostal . . . of the A.O.G.!"

Mason looked him over, curious, and then Yancey approached. Dostal was the man with chocolate hair who had been at the Koenigen that night! It seemed years ago. Yancey saw Mason and Dostal standing a few yards apart, took in the possibilities of this piquant situation, and with a mischievous gesture pushed Mason forward. He resisted. Yancey, with his easy superior twang, said commandingly, "Come now, Jarrett, really you must meet the fellow. Think of all the trouble you've caused him." "Think of all the trouble he's caused me," Mason replied. Yancey exclaimed, "Quite," and then performed the introduction: "Herr Generaldirektor Dostal, this is Mr. Mason Jarrett, of whom I think you've heard."

Dostal, almost as tall as Mason, bent closer, with a hand funneling an ear.

"Who?" he shouted. The usual party noises made talk almost impossible.

"My name is Jarrett, Mason Jarrett, Mr. Dostal. I work for the Chicago *Star*."

"Ah, Herr *Jarrett* . . . of Chicago . . . So! Ah! It is of great interest for me to meet you."

"I can say the same." But Mason floundered—he felt embarrassed. Dostal, on his side, had the un-American knack of being perfectly at ease, courteous with an adversary. Sandor and Yancey hung close by.

Dostal said evenly, "We have had contact with one another for some time. How did all this come about? Who started it? Eh?"

"As I recall, Mr. Dostal, your bank undertook to . . . to play mischief with certain journalists . . . if that's a way to put it . . . in a way that was sharply resented."

"Eh? But you yourself were not involved. What business was it of yours?"

Mason became nettled. "In some circumstances, a man has to become involved in the affairs of his colleagues whether he wants to or not. There was a very important issue at stake."

"But how did you dare to arrogate to yourself the right to pass moral judgment on us?"

"It wasn't altogether a matter of moral judgment, Mr. Dostal. Nobody likes to be compromised, then left in the dark, then pushed around." Mason paused. "You have a job. But so have I. Yours is to run a bank. Mine is to report the news. Once the bribery story reached a certain pitch, it was *bound* to get written about. The public has a right to be informed, to know the truth."

"Did we interfere with that?"

"Mr. Dostal!" If he had been a child Mason would have crossed a pointed finger at him. "You know perfectly well you did. Moreover you retaliated directly against me. You even sent a man all the way to Chicago to try to get my job."

"Of such a thing I know nothing."

Mason did not know whether he was lying or not, but Dostal became embarrassed.

"The public may have a right to be informed, but institutions as well as people have the right of privacy."

"Not if privacy shields corruption, not if it is contrary to the public interest."

"You use strong words, Mr. Jarrett. One must also reckon in terms of consequences. The price of unwarrantable intrusion, meddling, can be very serious."

Mason took a plunge. "For me or you?"

Dostal's eyes sharpened; he ignored the question. "The whole business . . . purely a local affair . . . petty, petty . . . a matter of three hundred thousand Schillings . . . tips . . . our custom . . . petty!"

"Three hundred thousand Schillings isn't petty."

"I would like to put something to you very frankly. Was it solely the desire to serve your newspaper, to write what you call the news, that impelled you to make public the story, with possible tragic consequences to all? Or was it personal vendetta, because, as you say, you were pushed around?"

The group around them became tensely silent.

"Both. And that is one of the principal lessons of this whole miserable business. Abuse truth, as you did, and the personal element becomes uncontrollable."

Mason and Dostal, neither yielding, faced each other. Dr. Wimpassing, with light flashing from his octagonal glasses, saw what was going on, and rushed up on his spindly, spidery legs. Looking alarmed he broke up the confrontation and, with a cold bow to Mason, led Dostal away.

Gloomy, Mason reached the Döbling villa. A long letter from Paula awaited him. Before this he had had nothing but a brief scrap written on the boat and a cable when she landed. He waited for a moment, nervous, feeling guilt, before opening the letter. There were several pages of family gossip. "Sometimes I think that I didn't come out of a live family at all, but was born of a set of scruples." She had visited lawyers and the family trustee. After seeing her stepfather, the one she particularly detested, she had had an attack of hives. She had had a pleasant visit with Mason's sister Belinda, who was married to an industrial designer. "I've seen my father constantly. He's pretty good, I adore him, and yesterday I stood him quite a splendid lunch at the Ritz. He still thinks I'm six."

Mason proceeded to read:

New York was fascinating, thrilling, although I didn't spend more than a few hours there. Steam blows up through manholes on the hot streets, even in this sweltering June, and the policemen are all fat and carry guns and belts stuffed with bullets. There are noises all the time of a kind we never hear in Europe—sirens, whistles.

People talk about Wall Street incessantly and how terrible the crash was in 1929 and indeed a great many people have suffered badly but at the same time everybody *jokes*. I don't mean nice satirical jokes like our Vienna jokes, but jokes that seem to reflect an utterly childish euphoria, plus masochism. Really, this isn't an altogether grown-up country.

Darling, I care for you more than words, even the sweetest. I love you and miss you and yearn for you and kindly continue to be altogether mine. X X X

Mason flapped the letter down.

P.S. I've bought the most lovely leopard coat, very pale. Not my usual type of thing, but it's glorious, and I found it at a summer sale. I won't forget the corkscrew.

Leopard? Pale leopard? Snow leopard? He became moody. Why had he been so bitterly jealous of Stein over Erika, but not jealous in the least of the Archduke over Paula. Well, Paula was invulnerable, and besides Willi could not be taken seriously; basically he was harmless, not a threat.

But this wasn't the real reason. He knew what the real reason was.

4

Mason, while remaining desperate over his consuming problem, found himself drawn into another passage in the labyrinth of Vienna. The case brought by the Countess against James N. Drew came to court. Mason met with the Sandors. "It is very serious. He could be fined heavily, or even go to jail," Laszlo said. The Countess knew this, Erji went on, but nevertheless remained implacable; but the most extraordinary thing of all was that Drew still continued to live with her. Even in this revolting predicament, he shared her bed and board. Moreover, Erji explained, he insisted that he would make no defense. He refused to engage a lawyer and he said that he would utter no word of explanation or rebuttal in the court. He would not "sully himself" by telling "those crooked lawyers" any personal facts about his "fiancée," whom he loved.

Mason was shocked by Drew's face, not shiny now, but gray and haggard. He was even moved to ask if he, by some wild chance, could, although this was the last moment, act as an intermediary with the Countess.

"My dear sir, I'm quite capable of taking care of my own affairs."

And all of this had happened, Mason now learned from the Sandors, as a direct result of his own visit to the Countess. Drew had slammed that chair at her and knocked her down, as Mason had guessed, because she was about to tell him why Drew had been in such desperate need of that fifteen hundred Schillings and how the A.O.G. had come along at just the right moment and provided it. Drew's whole involvement in the A.O.G. case derived from a relationship between the Countess and a man named Zapp, whom Mason had never even heard of. She had needed the money to settle a scandal involving one of her former husbands, whom none of them had ever seen. That his own involvement in the A.O.G. affair and that of the Anglo-American should have arisen out of such circumstances was grotesque. As Sandor had once said in a different connection, the cause of everything is nothing. The final irony was that the Countess had been about to ask Mason for the same sum, fifteen hundred Schillings, in order to make it possible for Drew to save himself by repaying the bank, as Ritter had. Drew became wild with fury at the thought that she had been on the point of disclosing his guilt to Mason; hence the attack. But he had never given *her* away!

Drew had now entered a religious phase. He talked endlessly about theology. One Sunday at the Weissenhof Mason had been astounded to see him in a black suit, with white shirt and collar.

"Where on earth have you been?" Mason asked.

"To church, man."

Religion aside, Drew had alternated between pompousness and humility since the Anglo-American meeting and the resolution of the A.O.G. scandal. There were times when he deliberately seemed to wish to be treated like a dog. He must feel that the greatest humiliation now might be the greatest victory in the hereafter. At other times he merely talked about "bad luck"; it was always other people who got the breaks.

This morning as they walked over to the court Mason's imagination raced forward. He could envisage the scene that would presently unfold. The grayish mottled walls of the shabby Landesgericht, faintly stinking of disinfectant from the hospital next door. . . . The judge in his three-cornered cap and the crucifix and silver candles on the bench below the bar. . . . The Countess, taut, triumphant, listening to the evidence as Drew sat bent in the defendant's box. . . . The tall, sweating policemen fiddling with their green caps, and the lawyers with their heavy robes and sleek voices. . . . Then would come the sentence. Drew would be acquitted, acquitted of this absurd charge. Then he would spring forward. Masochism is inverted sadism— overcompensation for sadistic impulses. Drew would snap the cords of his bondage finally, leap across the room, seize the Countess by the throat, strangle her. There in the courtroom, freed of this minor charge of assault, he would commit the major crime of murder. . . . He would bear down on the Countess before the horrified eyes of the judge himself, choking her to death.

Nothing remotely of the sort happened.

The judge, a sophisticated man, listened carefully to the Countess, examined Drew briefly, and asked one key question—where each of them was living. On hearing that the two still lived together in the same *Wohnung* he at once dismissed the case, rebuking the Countess for having brought the action and admonishing Drew for his bad behavior. Nothing at all happened then except that Drew and the Countess left the courtroom together arm in arm; the Countess purred with happiness and Drew contentedly fondled her.

*

In Paris Herr Hofrat Paultraxl of the A.O.G. picked up his gloves, his stick, his hat, which was carefully brushed along the grain of the felt, and departed from the inner offices of the private Descaze bank. He scowled, pondered briefly in a taxi, and told the driver to go to the Gare de Lyon instead of the Gare de l'Est. He turned in his ticket for Vienna, inquired for trains to Marseilles and connections with ships to Tunis and beyond, and prepared to wait for the next express.

*

Another letter from Paula came from the Hotel Chatham in New York:

Darling, you'd never guess. Tom Cairn called me in Cambridge and met me here when I came down yesterday. We had dinner, quite glamorous I must say, in a speakeasy which seems to be a private house on East Fifty-second Street. You have to be quite well known to get in and there was anything anybody could want to drink. Dinner was splendid, too. Tonight we're going to a play by Robert E. Sherwood called *Reunion in Vienna*. Yes, yes, of course I chose it because of the title. Anticipatory symbolism.

As I cabled you, I sail on the *Europa* Tuesday. I hate to take a German boat, but it's the quickest.

Otto said to Nella, "I have never seen the Herr Mason in such an atrocious temper. When I forgot to buy postage stamps he used language quite unheard of, extraordinary! I could not possibly tell you the actual words."

5

Fully dressed, Mason lay face down aslant at the foot of the bed, his feet sagging toward the floor on one side, his head hanging down on the other, in a primitive posture of passion and despair. How could he endure life without Erika? He felt an emotion for her now that went far beyond appreciation of her pretty sweet softness and delicious fluency in the act of love. Not only was he madly in love with her still but he found a soothing health and at the same time stimulating quality in her companionship—comfort and encouragement. He was always at his very best with her. There were no superiorities to confront, no competitive instincts to allay, no criticism, no crossnesses, no afflicted vanities to support, no intellectual patnesses to parry. Yet he was not so bereft of his senses as not to know full well that, even remotely, Erika could not compare with Paula. She was no match for her at all. She had nothing of Paula's dash. She liked to laugh, but had little sense of humor; she was intelligent, but not clever, let alone original and brilliant. Nor, he was sure, did she have anything like the love for him that Paula had; in a day, a week, a month, she would pass on to another. Paula might have defects, but, to put it crudely, was better value; she would love him forever, and she was incontestably a very good wife indeed. Besides, to cast her off, throw her out, dismiss her without cause, she who was guiltless, expel her, ruin her life, divorce her, was for him an occlusive impossibility. It was something altogether beyond the realm of the possible.

Moreover he loved her and always would.

But he loved Erika too!

Mason groaned. He bit into the hard wood of the bedpost. Forgetting where he was, he yelled aloud.

There came a knock on the door. Mason stumbled to his feet as Frau Gertrude, looking alarmed, entered. He tapped his head, as if to shake a thought loose, or explain that he was temporarily crazy, and tried to smile.

"You have had no lunch," Frau Gertrude said gravely, "and now it is long past the dinner hour." He thought for a moment that she was going to stroke his forehead as if he were a sick boy.

He had said good-bye to Erika the night before. Hour after hour, through the whole of the gray night, they waited for the daylight that would finish their affair.

Paula would be home tomorrow.

6

The best things in Vienna, Mason liked to say, were outside it. The city was, of course, bounded by the Danube on one side, and on the others by the green wooded hills of the Wienerwald. On the first fringe of slopes leading up to this splendid, romantic forest, scarcely half an hour from the urban grace of St. Stephen's, stood a number of small rustic wine houses known as *Heurigen*. Most of these were half hidden in the forest, with little pebble-speckled terraces and a fox tail of pine boughs over the door to signify that the new wine was ready; they had a dozen rude tables, lanterns attached to the low branches, bursting with green, which overhung the outdoor restaurant and dance floor, and a primitive orchestra. The *Heuriger* wine itself, grown by the vintner on his own premises, served icy cold after a somewhat brief process of maturing, was fresh, straw-colored, and fragrant with grape; it tasted innocently like lemonade, but was wickedly, ferociously intoxicating.

Here, tonight, near a *Heurige* halfway up the hill toward Kahlenberg, there were bluffs and crags, copses under arching trees, and the dank odor of slow, brown water, clotted with leaves, that made a rivulet out of the ditch behind the chicken coops. The establishment reflected the character of its owner, a red-faced man—rough, friendly—in plaid slippers, smoking a pipe well broken in and not too clean. A mild *Föhn*, unusual in June, blew lightly.

John Dixon of the Chicago *Daily News* had just received a magnificent promotion; he was being transferred to London to be chief of bureau there. The party tonight was to celebrate this cardinal event.

"I'm nervous as hell," Dixon said to Mason. "Do you think I'll get any chance to do any writing of my own up there? Vienna's a pushover, but London, that's a tough town, gee, you work all day and night!"

Lieber Gott, how they all adored Vienna; it had imperfections, but these could be ignored. Tonight was perfect. The evening was warm but still had the freshness of a late spring at last budding into summer; the roof of branches over the heads of the guests stirred with a silken creak as the breeze pushed paper lanterns to and fro;

there was sap in the branches, sap in several hearts. The correspondents bought pretzels and *Aufschnitt* from waiters wandering from table to table, and drank out of triangular flasks of wine; some became giddy, and people crossed from one table to the next; everybody became friends, everybody was a little tipsy, but few got drunk; the *Schrammelquartett* (violin, bass viol, melodeon, and guitar) and a *Komiker* kept up an easy flow of dulcet, insinuating Vienna songs:

> *Wien, Wien, nur du allein*
> *Sollst stets die Stadt meiner Träume sein.*
> *Dort wo die alten Häuser steh'n,*
> *Dort wo die lieblichsten Mädchen geh'n.* . . .

The journalists pulled two tables, made of rough planks, together, so that they made a big square, and sat four or five people to a side. Singing, they rocked right to left; shoulders were touching, and people at nearby tables rocked as well. Probably nobody in the entire establishment had a hundred Schillings in his pocket. Who cared?

Mason sat at the middle of one end of the big double table, Paula at the other. Hunched closely together, or moving across the small, primitive dance floor and careening back, were the Bishopsons, the Sandors, Karl Tetzel with Nella Blohr, Hanley the red-cheeked fisherman, the Wheatleys, and two of the three hard-boileds. The third was incapacitated temporarily by a case of gonorrhea.

From every quarter, as new faces appeared, came a chorus of "Küss die Hand." Drew was not there, nor had Ritter come. Clean and unclean; sheep and goats. Mason, sitting next to Helen Bishopson, felt somewhat absent, remote. He was pale, and his talk laconic.

John Dixon cut in from across the table. "In a play the author should make the audience laugh in the first act, cry in the second, and think in the third."

Now, where on earth had he picked that up?

Dauphine Dixon, in a dirndl, looked pretty and relaxed, as if sighing with contentment that a great landmark had been satisfactorily passed. The French took things like promotions very seriously. Mason heard Dixon say something pertinent about a new political crisis building up. The Socialists could find themselves in a critical situation overnight.

"Un-huh."

"You seem dim tonight, Mace. How are you?"

"In slipcovers."

Dauphine whipped out her notebook.

The Komiker came up, bowing. What songs would the esteemed and honorable party of Ausländer like?

And the high liquid refrain began again, with the melodeon moaning:

> I' muss wieder a'mal in Grinzing sein,
> Beim Wein, beim Wein!
> Da sicht ma ja grad' bis in' Himmel 'nein,
> Beim Wein, beim Wein, beim Wein. . . .

Mason had a Viertel, quarter flask, then another. He began to wake up. Suddenly he found himself telling jokes, inventing anecdotes, encouraging others to talk. Halfway through a story he choked with laughter at what he himself was saying and could not finish it because of his own laughter. Paula overheard him putting words together in his odd, original way. He told Mrs. Bishopson that he maintained an office "almost viciously disorganized," and when she asked him where he hoped to take his holiday, he replied, "On the ineluctable Mediterranean, where the sea is bluer than God."

Helen looked puzzled. "Is God blue?"

Mason sighed: "If you see him early enough in the morning."

He's large, Paula thought. He's alive, and his greatest gift is that he has the knack of making other people come alive.

Mason stretched, yawned comfortably, loosened his collar, and let a notch out of his belt. He took a stroll, breathing in the Föhn.

"Mason Jarrett is a slob," he heard a sharp clear voice. It said again, "Mason Jarrett is a slob, slob, SLOB." The voice was his own.

Paula had been back about a week. She had looked luxurious, radiant, but a shade crisp, when she got off the train and hurled herself in his arms. They reached the villa and he felt constrained, almost cool. God willing Paula must never, never find out what he was thinking about. God willing she must never, never find out about

Erika. Curiously enough, after the first tense, biting hug, she hadn't seemed to be particularly curious about what he had been doing. But pleasure in the villa shone all over her. She jumped, danced, from room to room, turned on every light, paraded around, opened doors and closets, skipping, chattering. "Oh, I've missed this so. You too, sweet. But this darling villa, it's heaven, it's delightful. Never in my whole life before have I had the sense that where I lived was permanent, really mine, ours, forever." She peered out of windows, stroked old bits of furniture, and patted curtains. "My, I love it so, I love it!"

More calmly, after a drink, she surveyed him. "I must say you look rather shattered. Is it because you missed me, and are glad I'm back?"

"Of course. How was Tom?"

"Divine. Perfectly divine. He's the most amusing man I ever met, except you. Altogether mad, of course. He saw me off on the boat, and, do you know, can you *believe* it, he missed the signal to get off, and they had to send him back with the pilot from out near the Statue of Liberty! He had to climb down a sort of ladder hitched to the ship's side!" Paula did not mention that at the last minute Tom Cairn had said that he thought he'd sail back to Europe with her, just for the ride. And he didn't have so much as a toothbrush with him. It had been a struggle to get him off. "By the way, did I write you that that play, *Reunion in Vienna*, is about an archduke and a love affair!"

The *Komiker* returned with the melodeon player. He addressed himself to Paula, who seemed to be the most responsible person at that end of the table. "Perhaps the *Gnädige* would now enjoy something with a little pepper in it."

"For shame," the melodeon player rebuked him. "One can see very well that the *Gnädige* has no need of pepper."

"I confess myself misinterpreted. The *Gnädige* obviously has no need of pepper. But perhaps she would like some pepper?"

"I am willing to play songs with pepper. But first I wish the *Gnädige's* unequivocal permission."

Paula said that they could all of them stand as much pepper as the law allowed. So the quartet and the *Komiker* played and sang the "*Kleine Kontesschen*," a forthright Viennese ditty, gay, aromatic, and full of love:

Ich weiss auf der Wieden ein kleines Hotel
In einem verschwiegenen Gässchen;
Der Tag ist so lang und die Nacht ist so kurz
Komm mit mir, Du kleines Kontesschen. . . .

Paula and Helen Bishopson had not met before. Mrs. Bishopson said, "I've heard that you and your husband live the most thrillingly unconventional lives!"

"Not really."

She went on, "I can't understand why we've not met before. Please come to dine with us sometime soon."

Paula: "We'd love to come, Mrs. Bishopson. Let's meet a lot from now on."

Mrs. Bishopson: "May I call you Paula? What about lunch on Tuesday?"

"I'd be delighted, Helen."

The tart new wine smote John Dixon like a mallet on the head. He stumbled away from the table, walked unsteadily to the edge of the garden, and disappeared into the woods. Mason could just see him holding onto a tree, embracing it.

At this moment, when the whole café was exploding with violent, if decorous, commotion, Dr. Ricardo Stein walked in with Erika Falk. Mason's heart was a child's top, whirring, then beginning to wobble. It lay down, and died. He greeted Erika, smiling, and she flushed slightly. "We've just been flying," Erika said. "It was the loveliest experience, as if to float . . . float. . . ." Mason felt an acrid taste of blood; clenching his teeth behind his smile he had bitten himself inside the cheek.

Erika's eye went around the table, and he saw that she recognized instantly who Paula was. Stein introduced her, and Paula, not having the faintest idea who she was, stretched out a hand to shake hers firmly. Erika tossed her curls back, a little breathless, and then the Bishopsons greeted her. Mason made room for her next to him, and, hot and cold, asked her about Stefan, about her work, about the studio.

Stein, after chatting with Paula ("You've been away . . . so nice to have you back"), rose to take Erika to the dance floor. As if casually, Mason watched them. Stein's appearance was remarkable.

The youthful rationalist, the intellectual, had become transformed. His face was set, his eyes glazed; he danced doggedly, clutching Erika, like a man in a dream. The music stopped, and he did a curious thing. Approaching Mason, he dumped from his coat pockets everything that they contained—his wallet, a notebook, his passport, pens and pencils. "Keep these," he murmured. Then as the music resumed he took Erika back to the dance floor. In a flash, Mason understood. Those flat protuberances in his pockets, like packs of cards, kept him half an inch away from her. There must be nothing at all between his breast and hers. Mason had a further perception more subtle. Stein was symbolically giving him everything he had, in exchange for Erika.

No one else danced; everybody watched them; Stein still looked dazed; he was rigid, transfixed, but holding to the rhythm closely—now a waltz. Erika's skirt flowed in a big circle, swirling, swelling, now up, now down, lopsided for a moment, then slanting straight. They returned to the table. Her chin was up, her blue-black eyes were bright.

Mason handed Stein, who wiped his forehead, the things from his pockets, and resumed small talk with Erika. Hestery, Brewster, Sandor danced in turn with Paula. Mason rose, circled an edge of the floor with Erika, and inconspicuously led her into the shadows under the trees. "Ah, your wife is beautiful, beautiful!" she exclaimed in a low, moved whisper. In the darkness she pushed him away when he tried to grasp her. She picked up his fist and bit him hard across the knuckles, very hard, so hard that he cried out. "Du, du," she whispered, "I love you." "I love you," he whispered in reply.

Paula and Erji sat now with the Bishopsons; Mason joined them casually, and Erika danced again with Stein. Paula watched them. She said, "What a lovely girl! She's probably a marshmallow"—Mason started—"but," she smiled at him, "if I were a man, that's the kind of girl I'd go after!"

Marshmallow? Had Paula, as so often happened, hit a nail right on the head? Was she demolishing his image of Erika already? Was she, as usual, right? He replied with the utmost vagueness, "She's very nice. I met her while you were away—ran into her a couple of times."

Paula showed no interest, or perhaps had not heard him clearly, because Bishopson was asking her to dance. Mason felt nervous. Like most people who have been deeply involved in a love affair that must at all costs remain secret, he thought that this stood out all over him and must be instantly recognizable, so that he would be given away by the slightest gesture if only because the love affair was so vital, so important, that it was impossible to conceive that it would not be recognized.

Paula and Bishopson talked as they danced.

Could Bishopson possibly be gossiping about the time he had introduced Erika to him in the Grand Bar?

But she made no mention of Erika when she returned, did not look at her, and seemed to have forgotten her. Mason felt relief. He then illogically thought that it was curious that Paula should be so lacking in intuitive perception as not to show interest in her. But, he knew well, she was sometimes strangely dense, quite dense, in spite of her acute sophistication, in certain spheres having to do with relationships. Partly this arose out of innocence, perhaps out of self-blindness too. It was difficult for her to believe that people she knew and accepted could be illicit, false, or evil. She could not conceive that reprehensibility, disreputableness, could touch her circle. And this denseness, this self-blindness, rose of course out of her superiority. She was too superior to be suspicious. That was the whole key to her character—superiority!

What was the key to Erika? She was serene—above all, serene. She had no vanity. She kept her secret value to herself and had no sense of sin at all.

Now it was late and the party was breaking up. Men and women coupled up informally, taking a last stroll under the trees. Stein and Erika said good-bye; Mason's heart turned over. Dauphine Dixon found John out behind the chicken coops and saw that he had been sick.

The proprietor of the *Heurige*, sweating, pushed his way through the crowd saying that Herr Doktor Laszlo Sandor was wanted on the telephone. Mason accompanied Sandor to the kitchen, where an antique instrument hung on the wall. Two stalwart girls, their faces and thick arms bright red, were furiously washing dishes, and the place stank tremendously of the new wine.

Drew's voice came over the ancient phone, faint and squeaky. Sandor suddenly started to shake, and handed Mason the receiver, as if he himself were helpless to take in such news. Mason listened closely. "What?"

"Come on down, you chumps," Drew called. "Hurry! The A.O.G. has failed!"

BOOK THREE

❧

The Crisis

X. THE CRASH

Seldom had the café known such agitation. Two British correspondents were telephoning intermittently from the A.O.G., while Drew, assisted by Bleschke, translated the long official statement from Dr. Wimpassing. Emil, the junior Zahlkellner, with his sallow cheeks puffed out, hovered over the *Stammtisch* satisfying his curiosity and trying to be useful. *"Das ist aber arg!"* he kept exclaiming, sucking his cheeks in and out.

Mason, Sandor, and a dozen others arrived from the *Heurige* and tumbled out of a pair of taxis eager and tense. Sandor, who had been passionate with excitement, now became so deflated, out of worry, that he appeared to be in a state of collapse. Drew told them what had happened.

"They've been at it for three whole days. Dead secrecy, my dear sir, and a secret that was really kept. Dostal and Bach-Dengler, the Finance Minister, together with someone from the municipality, have been shouting at each other behind closed doors since Tuesday. Two directors have fled. We can't get their names." He gave a scribbled longhand dispatch to the messenger from Radio-Austria. "The biggest bank in Central Europe down! The end of the reign of Diederbach!" Drew clucked with his tongue. His tone was full of admiration. He had appropriated the bank and its failure to be his own. It was hard to tell whether he was admiring the monolithic power of the bank, the events that had brought it down, or the fateful extent of the debacle that might ensue.

"Sit down, Jarrett, here's the official statement, listen. Sandor, you know the British commercial attaché pretty well, ring him up. Oh, it doesn't matter if you get him out of bed. This is something that doesn't happen every day of the week." A waiter ran to call him to the telephone. "*Ja? Augenblick.*" He returned portentous and authoritative. "The terms of the settlement are out. Settlement? My dear sir, of course there has to be a settlement. They can't let a bank like that simply close its doors. If the A.O.G. simply shut down, all of Austria would have to shut down. The bank's insolvent, all right, and how insolvent! But of course they have to save it, like the Donau a couple of years ago. The Austrian government will have to pump in money enough to keep it open even if it's ruined. These seem to be the terms." Eagerly, admiringly, Drew read from his notes. "During the last year the losses of the A.O.G. are estimated at one hundred forty million Schillings. Now, listen, this is how they're going to make up the loss. The bank is to be reorganized from top to bottom. The Diederbachs and the old shareholders will contribute something, and the Austrian government the rest. Where's the Austrian government going to get the money? It will borrow from the public. But the public hasn't any money! Isn't finance marvelous!" He clucked again. "You watch. It'll end up with the Austrian government borrowing from the A.O.G., which hasn't got a bean, so that the A.O.G. can pay back the Austrian government, which hasn't got a bean. O-ho!" He shouted to the radio messenger. "Here *noch ein* dispatch, *schnell, beeilen Sie sich* across the street."

Mason was thankful that he worked for an afternoon newspaper, since he would have all night to work on his dispatch. He slammed Sandor on the back. "Laszlo, isn't this the stuff! We certainly started something with the dear old A.O.G., all right!"

Because of course the A.O.G., secretly terrified about the realities of its position, fumbling, arrogant, Bourbonesque, must have started that bribery business in an attempt to conceal the facts, and, as Yancey had once said, to help produce a "favorable" atmosphere if a crisis came.

But Sandor turned to Mason, his face gray with worry. "It is no cause to rejoice. It is a lot of somber that will happen."

Mason had a thought. Ricardo Stein was, he knew, covering for Allbright, the Boston *Times* man, who was away on holiday. It would be serious for him to be caught short on a story as big as this, but Stein and Erika had left the Heurigo before it broke. Mason didn't know quite what to do. He looked at his watch. It was late. He telephoned Stein at home—no answer. Then, feeling as if his heart were flapping exposed and naked against his shirt, he put in a call for Erika's studio.

She recognized his voice and, shocked, whispered, "*Nein*—no! Please, *du*, you must not—!"

With the gesture of a man waving cigarette smoke from his face he impatiently brushed her aside: "This isn't anything personal, for God's sake! Is Stein there? I have to talk to him."

Stein's voice was sleepy. Even if he had lost Erika to Stein he was his friend and colleague and he must protect him on a story. It was an absolute necessity to protect him on the story.

"Sorry to disturb you, Ricardo," Mason said in a hurry. "Get in touch with your office or hop down here to the Weissenhof right away. You can just catch Boston with a story. The A.O.G. has failed."

Paula helped Dixon, who had been turned cold sober by shock, translate another communiqué from the Finance Ministry. "The A.O.G. . . . Sudden untoward events in the field of international credit . . . Repercussions from the Paris money market . . . No cause for alarm . . . The Austrian government will tomorrow present the necessary regulations to Parliament. . . . Perfect stability of the Schilling guaranteed. . . ."

"Of course the A.O.G. must have known for at least a year that this was coming," said Stein when he arrived. "Even an Austrian bank can't lose one hundred and forty million Schillings overnight."

Mason nodded. He couldn't get over a childish gleeful feeling. That damned impregnable bank! That arrogant, churlish bank, which undertook so lightly its adventures in the world of journalism! "Laszlo, Laszlo," he kept saying to Sandor, "what swell dumb fatheads they were!"

Drew had some new figures. He whistled. The A.O.G.'s debt to banks abroad, in London, Paris, the United States, and elsewhere, was 700,000,000 Schillings—a hundred million dollars. Drew predicted that the international creditors would arrive in Vienna in the next few days like a cloud of grasshoppers. A messenger came in with a telegram for Drew with the red "Urgent" sticker pasted on the envelope. This must be acknowledgment from New York of his first dispatches, possibly with a word of congratulation. Pleased, he slit the envelope open. His face clouded.

"Will you look at this!"

The telegram informed him that a Japanese athlete, by name Kokomu, who had recently set a world's record by running the mile in a little over four minutes, would arrive from the Far East at Trieste the next morning and would proceed at once to Vienna to compete in Central European track meets and to run in the Budapest races in July. Drew's Tokyo paper was subsidizing Kokomu's trip. Drew was to meet him in Vienna, stay close to him, and send every line of news about him even to what he ate for breakfast.

TOKYO RAVING KOKOMU SEND DETAILEDEST, the telegram concluded. It contained no mention of Drew's dispatches on the A.O.G.

2

The next morning Frau Gertrude, estimable cook to the estimable Jarretts, did something unprecedented; she waited till Mason had finished his first cup of coffee, not his second, before addressing herself to him. Then she unfolded the front page of the *Presse* and pointed to the headlines about the A.O.G. She said, "Gnädige Frau . . . Herr Jarrett . . . Was soll ich tun?"

Her entire life's savings were on deposit in the A.O.G. As she spoke, her proud, handsome face showed profound emotion, almost the first emotion unconcerned with *Gedünstetes Bries* or her daughter that Mason and Paula had ever seen her express. It was not a complex emotion. It was the emotion of fear. It was emotion deriving from acute fear that all she had worked for all her life, her security, might vanish. In her terrified eyes, staring out of her milky white face, Mason saw a lifetime of work, frugality, simple pleasure, sacrifice, and hope. And he saw terror in her eyes—terror that all that she had might disappear.

"Ach, entschuldigen Sie, gnädige Frau. In such times, one does not know the proper course to take."

Mason didn't have a moment's hesitation. "Frau Gertrude, go home right away, get your passbook, and take your money out of the A.O.G."

"I have my passbook already with me. But Herr Jarrett perhaps does not understand. *Was für andere Banken gibt es?* What other bank is there? *Es existiert keine andere Bank!*"

Paula listened, shocked and alarmed. Mason said, "Oh come, Frau Gertrude, there are plenty of other banks—several just about as big as the A.O.G.—like the Credit Anstalt or the Wiener Bank-Verein." But he knew that Frau Gertrude was right. If the A.O.G. closed its doors, no bank in Austria could remain open. He understood completely the implications of Frau Gertrude's question. *There was no other bank!*

A great many people followed Mason's advice to Frau Gertrude that morning. He saw them as he passed by the ornate baroque building he had surveyed so often. Looking in, he was mortally shocked. All the glee, the sense of victory, of last night was knocked out of him. Hundreds of people stood in line before the tellers' desks and windows. Here was something grim—a Run. Here and there he saw wealthy stockbrokers, a playwright of international reputation, society women in chic sport coats, students with tattered briefcases, policemen holding their green helmets in trembling hands, nurses, tram conductors, frightened housewives, pushing their way into the building. The bank itself could not hold them all, and a queue formed and spiraled down from Haydnplatz toward the Ring. The bank, determined to meet the Run, stayed open till 8:15 P.M. The tellers did not finish work till midnight. An assistant cashier fainted. By nightfall the A.O.G. was reported to have lost more than 200,000,000 Schillings. It was gutted, a hollow corpse of iron.

3

Of course it would have been nonsense to say that Mason Jarrett and the Anglo-American Press Association caused the downfall of the A.O.G. Mason knew perfectly well that the bribery affair which he and his colleagues had written about was no more than an incident in a long chain of circumstances. American bankers, like Ralph Conyers, who were alarmed by their stories and who thereby felt doubt about the bank's solvency did, it was true, call some of their short-term loans; a pool of New York banks had, in fact, withdrawn about $7,000,000 from the A.O.G. the week before. And although this withdrawal came at a time when the bank could not comfortably afford to lose the money, it did not directly cause the crash.

What caused the crash of the A.O.G. was something more abstract and fundamental. Its insolvency was caused by the peculiar geography of the river Rhine. It was caused by the division of Charlemagne's empire between France and Germany. It was caused by the Protestant Reformation, the Thirty Years' War, the partition of Poland, the wars of Frederick the Great, the Congress of Vienna, the Industrial Revolution, the invention of the technique of international credit transfer, World War I, the principle of nationalism, and men as various as the Emperor Franz Josef, Wilhelm II, David Lloyd George, Woodrow Wilson, and Thomas Garrigue Masaryk.

"Even so, I did have something to do with it," said Mason Jarrett to himself. "I helped bring that bank down."

Another cause of the crash of the A.O.G. was, of course, greed. Then too there were such factors as obscurantism, false pride, sloth, and arrogance in the Austrian ruling class. The monstrous economic techniques that had come to be practiced in the mushroom countries of the Danube Valley also played a role. Nor were American and British financial manipulators, even those most respectable, without their share of responsibility. Mason drew a diagram. It was weird. America lent money to England at three per cent. England lent it to France at four per cent. France lent it to Switzerland at five per cent. Switzerland lent it to Germany at six per cent. Germany lent it to Austria at seven per cent. Austria lent it to Hungary at nine per cent. Hungary lent it to Yugoslavia and Rumania at eleven per cent. The Yugoslav and Rumanian banks then lent it to their local farmers and manufacturers at fifteen, twenty, even forty per cent. It was a beautiful progression while it lasted. Then suddenly the Rumanian, or Yugoslav, or Polish farmers and manufacturers could not earn their keep, could not meet their obligations, could not maintain their interest payments, could not refund their debts. And so the Rumanian bank could not repay the Hungarian bank. And the Hungarian bank could not repay the Austrian bank. And the Austrian bank could not repay the German bank. And the German bank could not repay the French bank. And so on all the way back to the City of London and the cloudy stalagmites of Wall Street. A pack of cards, Mason thought. A pack of cards tipped in one direction, then reversed. The pathetic, miserable Austrians . . . caught in the middle, frozen, helpless . . . trying to liquidate overnight their enormous holdings, now tied up in deserted mine shafts, derelict textile mills, and steel foundries where rats nibbled at old timbers and dust softly obliterated the shining edges of machinery. . . .

Mason filed heavily for a day or two. He got a cable back: ASSUME YOU ABSOLUTELY SURE ALL YOUR FIGURES BANK STORY KINDLY DOUBLE CHECK.

He threw the cable into the wastebacket. And he kept thinking, I helped bring that bank down.

✻

That evening James N. Drew brought Kokomu to the Weissenhof. Drew had to be with him night and day. He was a respectful and attentive little man, with crooked shining teeth and a splendid hiss.

4

During the next week or two Mason and his colleagues learned perforce a good deal about the banking business. The A.O.G. managed to stay open, but only just. The Austrian Parliament approved an emergency credit of 140,000,000 Schillings to succor the stricken monster, to be paid for by the citizen, the taxpayer. Mason grimaced. Drew's prediction about foreign creditors turned out to be correct, and the Orient Express, with its sleek blue flanks, unloaded daily a cargo of foreign financial advisers, French, British, Swiss, Dutch. In London a creditors' committee was duly formed and it was announced that the management of the bank would be "revised" under foreign auspices. Warrants were sworn out for two absconding directors, Treuwalt and Paultraxl, and another director was charged with having lost 25,000,000 Schillings of A.O.G. money speculating privately in Wall Street.

"Now, I ask you, look at." Sandor flourished the financial column of the *Sternblatt*. "Linzmann steel shares are down from 212 to 177.

Mercury Autos are down 67 to 44. Do you not see what this indicates? The A.O.G. owns these companies, which means a paper loss of some twenty-five per cent. *How* will it recover?"

"Bank rate up to six per cent," James N. Drew snapped a few days later. "Jove, that means inflation." A day later it was up to seven per cent. But Drew's agency betrayed only the slightest interest in such details. It wanted full details of Kokomu's new assault on the mile record at Bratislava: KOKOMU STILL HOTTEST TOKYO.

But the A.O.G. was saved, because, as Mason wrote, it had to be. If the A.O.G. collapsed, Austria collapsed, and if Austria collapsed, all of Europe might collapse. The bankers from London and New York, Amsterdam and Paris, found themselves caught in a grave and delicate dilemma. At first, like the Amalgamated Continental in New York, they had drawn out their money or some of it. Now such withdrawals came to a stop, because, obviously, if the foreigners continued to cancel credit and demand foreign exchange in payment, they would wreck the bank even more completely than it was already wrecked. To save the hundred million dollars they still had in the A.O.G. the foreign bankers had to leave it there. If they removed it, the A.O.G. would have no recourse but to close its doors and they would lose their stake altogether.

At the Weissenhof Mason and his colleagues anxiously awaited details of the standstill agreement that was finally hammered out. The Austrian government gave its guarantee for both the domestic losses and the foreign credits, and it was now revealed that the total losses were not a mere 140,000,000 Schillings, as had been first said, but a cool billion. Herr Direktor Dostal was discharged, as were nineteen of the A.O.G.'s twenty-three directors. A Danish financial expert was brought in to replace Dostal, the foreign creditors promised not to withdraw their money for two years, and everybody's face was saved.

Drew filed 125 words on this standstill agreement. He was still chasing Kokomu.

Sandor, bubbling cheerfully, ironically, made caustic reference to the fact that the Austrian government, that is the Austrian citizen, that is the Austrian taxpayer, was required to guarantee fully the A.O.G.'s new position. "To think on it!" Sandor exclaimed. "The

Bank of England, the A.O.G., and the Diederbach family has been in need of my guarantee!"

5

Mason was late coming back from the café and Otto seized the opportunity to write secretly in his diary:

Nella, my cousin, has become in love with the Herr, I think. We tease her about it and she gets angry and flounces out of the room. For the most part he does not notice her. It is just as well, because the gnädige Frau would tear her eyes out. She is fierce as a panther. I admire this very much in her.

Nella says nothing about it, but is seen around the town with the journalist Tetzel, a poor fellow in my opinion. Tetzel is of life embittered, but to her does not show this.

There is a change in the Herr. He appears to be morose and dejected. Perhaps he is taking too seriously the affair of the A.O.G. I have become so fond of both of them it cannot be believed. Never have I seen anything as beautiful as the molding of the G.F.'s lips, though there are people who would perhaps think them too big, somewhat coarse.

In America the woman is the boss, or so it seems. I have even heard the G.F. contradict the Herr aloud, in public. No European wife could ever do such!

The Herr left suddenly the other afternoon saying that he had to meet a visiting fireman. I am extremely puzzled. What can he mean—that he has contact with members of a foreign fire-fighting force?

Nella, for the first time in months, took me to an extent in her confidence today. She described a party held several weeks ago at a Heurige in celebration of the promotion of Mr. Dixon. Nella said that during the whole evening the Herr never addressed a single word to her, not even cast one look in her direction. During the first part of the evening he was so depressed that it almost seemed that he was drugged, and then he became too much exhilarated, even drunk.

I think I was perhaps incorrect in assuming that the Herr had no interest in serious thought. True, he reads no philosophy and has no knowledge of it, but I think he is much disturbed by what is his relation to the universe.

Yesterday both came back from a farewell party for the Archduke Willi and both seemed almost maudlin with sentiment. Why they should have interest in such an anachronism as an archduke I do not know. It seems that the Archduke is leaving for Sofia, where he has been offered a position as steward to the Royal Bulgarian household. What a thing to have to become. *Wie schade!* What for shame!

My father, now that he is retired, broached tonight at dinner the thought that we might all move to Palestine, where much work of medical nature, even research, is waiting. Fie, fie! I would commit suicide.

Otto heard steps down the hall, and snapped the diary shut.

6

They had had a miserable summer. Mason was grumpy, distant, and crackling with strain. Paula could not reach him. What made this more difficult to bear was his carefully contrived politeness and consideration toward her—as if he were seeking to make up for his remoteness by an excess of superficial tender attention, pampering her to compensate for a lack of love, of fundamental desire to share. Never, in fact, had he been more solicitous. But his spirit had fled from her, and they lived in a vacuum. Paula was profoundly worried. Clearly he was worried too and, in his most reasonable and adult manner, sought after a while for some kind of solution, without letting any hint of what was troubling him come to the surface. Let's get the hell out of town for a while, he suggested. Let's take a walking trip. He wanted to do anything, for her sake as well as his, to alleviate the strain.

So they brought rucksacks and set out for a trip in the Semmering country. Paula, as Mason was well aware, loved practically everything in nature. He himself was seldom moved except by things spectacular, but she could locate and appreciate the spectacular in almost anything—the configuration of a seashell or the way a collie yawned, its tongue rolling like a red snake. The fact that it was a glorious day was enough to make her happy. They climbed slowly. Mason puffed. He leaned forward on his stick every hundred yards or so. He knew that this was just the beginning. He was dripping with sweat, while she was still cool, but halfway up he would get a second wind and it was quite likely that he would reach the top stronger than she.

It was September already. How the stormy, agitated summer had slipped by! The morning was very hot. They strode up the yellow-marked trail from the Erzherzog Johann, which twisted through woods with short pines toward the summit of the Sonnwendstein. After a long series of Z-turns tunneled in the woods they reached the bare side of the mountain, exposed flatly to the hard sunlight. Then the trail dipped into the pines again, moist and almost cold. Beyond them steep ravines were dotted with rocks and brown streams flowed slowly over flat brown stones. The mountain, with its bare patches, looked like a buffalo with parts of its hide worn off.

Mason grumbled, shifting the pack from one shoulder to another. "Whew! It's a long way still to the top. Say, I don't think I really do need new walking shoes."

Paula smiled. Whenever Mason, in his mysterious manner, brought up the subject of not needing something, it meant that he would purchase that something promptly.

"We'll pick up a pair in the village. Oh, Mason, it's such a beautiful day, it's such a heavenly, unbelievable, glorious day," she exclaimed.

He wanted extremely to meet her mood, to respond to her happiness, and made a determined effort to put his troubles behind him. "Lord . . . never thought we'd really get away. . . . To think that we aren't going to have to answer that damned telephone for two solid weeks. Paula, stop a second, will you? . . . Stone in my shoe. Ouch . . . And what a couple of months! Those banks popping like corn in a popper. Never heard anything like the sound of those German banks popping. And we started it. Look, Paula, isn't that marvelous—the way the light hits that field, like silk being rubbed the wrong way. Do you suppose we can get any newspapers on the Stuhleck when we get there?"

A group of peasants passed, wearing green hats with cock feathers and leather breeches; their knees were bare, knobby, and the men smoked long pipes adorned with silver.

"Grüss Gott."

"Grüss Gott."

"Are we halfway up?" Paula asked.

A ripe mountain accent made the answer "Yo" for "Ja."

What a summer indeed! Infection spread outward from Austria in concentric circles. Banks crashed in Danzig, Riga, Bucharest, and Lvov. The entire financial structure in Germany broke apart. Inflation reached a serious pitch in Hungary and Greece. The bourses closed; tourists were stranded; nobody could buy foreign goods; the black market spurted up. One item in the news was anticlimactical in the extreme, but it amused Mason to read a self-righteous story from the new directorate of the A.O.G., dragging the bribery affair to the surface once more, defending itself and boasting that the slush fund had, it was finally calculated, produced between five hundred and six hundred articles favorable to the bank in 540 papers scattered throughout the world. These must have been handouts distributed by Wimpassing's office, Mason thought. Fat lot of good they had done.

After Sonnwendstein it was up and down, up and down, along the yellow trail for a while and then the red trail, up the shaggy sunlit slopes where the high fields of rye were the color of stucco in Rome, down into the cool valleys, up, down, up, down, circling the northeast side of the naked mountain, climbing until they reached brushland and open pasture, where the trees stopped at last. They sank into a glade, where the sun was trapped, through long grass, and came to a thicket boiling with butterflies. "Look!" Paula pointed to a lizard darting across the path, its head triangularly marked in black and red. "Like something out of Egypt—no doubt Cleopatra!"

The Semmering, two thousand feet below, looked like a dark green starfish, with five short, turning prongs coming out of the middle. They could see the railway climb over the arms of the starfish where it was not cut off by tunnels. Mason and Paula stood in a rock shelter, gasping. He muttered, "Mustn't overdo it. . . . the Stuhleck a long way off." They were tired, but too exhilarated to want to rest for long. They watched the clouds, white and luminous, break individually from black pods bearing fluffs of cotton. At dusk they reached the stone Alpine hut on the Stuhleck, their destination. The hut was very small atop the mountain's bald scalp. Mason sat down on the bench outside, scarcely able to slip the pack off his back. Paula had wanted so badly to sleep up here instead of in the valley. Well, they had made it! Mason had two beers, they tottered to a bare, squeaky room with a pinewood bed, and sank down exalted, purified.

"Oh . . ." Paula breathed an hour later, "I simply can't move. I smell dinner."

"It's goulash. I smell it too."

"Let's not get up."

"I can't move. But I'm ravenous."

Soon the mountains darkened. The sky became dark but stayed intensely clear; the moon shone like a slice of melon, somewhat pink. Then the first star flickered in pale greenish blue, and the profile of the Schneeberg looked as if it had been drawn in ink. The mountains turned blue-black, then disappeared. The world disappeared. Paula and Mason watched it go. They sat on the terrace of the hut and watched everything disappear beyond the pool of broken light cast by the hut's windows. Illimitable blackness cut off the valley, cut off the mountains too.

That night the barrenness between them that had lasted all summer ended: they sealed themselves close again. Paula had of course sensed through uneasy weeks that something important in her husband's life, perhaps critical, but of which she knew nothing, had happened while she was absent in America; she could guess what it might be; she did not want to guess. She was bitterly hurt, if only because there had never been secrets between them before. She had wanted to say, "Mason, dearest, what kind of change has come over you—aren't you in love with me any more?" but she had withdrawn in terror before the actual step of posing any such drastic question because he might reply that he wasn't—and that would be too much to bear, too much to be endured; it would be the end.

He had grasped perfectly well during those strained weeks the gist of the question she wanted to ask, and was grateful that she didn't ask it—because then he might lose her, and life without her, no matter what emotion he still felt for Erika, would be inconceivable. Not once had he seen Erika all summer. There had been no communication between them at all, not a letter, not a telephone call. Both were holding to the unspoken but durably binding Spartan commitment to give each other up.

One hot August night in Vienna, after a day in which he had scarcely spoken to her, Paula had not been able to keep herself from saying, "Mason, do you love me?" hoping that this would lead into the little litany they had so often spoken together.

Not for a long time had she had such a shock. His forehead

crinkled as if being pressed by a nutcracker; he flung a newspaper down and replied with what was almost a snarl, "For Christ's sake, yes—yes—yes! And I'm proving it as I've never proved it before! But for the love of God don't ask me any questions! Don't pry! Don't plead! Let me alone!" He tossed in the big white chair, turned his face away, and opened his mouth in a gesture that was half a snap, half a yawn.

She recovered. "You're telling me clear as daylight that something did happen while I was away!"

"No, nothing."

Light caught her eyes so that the pupils became flashing circles within the green-brown irises as she looked at him questioningly, almost accusingly.

"All right. But whatever it was, no matter what, don't you know that I would always help you? Can't you tell me? Can't you trust me? Don't you know that I'd forgive you anything?"

"Why should you?"

"Because you're me."

He was too tortured even to make the easy retort that it was much easier to forgive another person than oneself.

Another thought had made him ashamed. There had been moments during the summer when he had actively, passionately yearned to tell Paula everything, because to do so might clear his conscience. Besides it was such an interesting story! Nothing was fun unless Paula knew about it too. Full knowledge of what happened between himself and Erika might very well—how should he put it?—increase and make more tangible to Paula his own masculine value to her, which she often seemed to neglect. But, hating himself, he had said not a word. Fear kept him silent. "I am dishonest," he had muttered to himself, clenching his teeth, "weak, and a coward!"

After the night on the mountain they had an easy day, strolling downhill for the most part, following a long steady slope on the other side of the mountain where the grass hummed with dragonflies and fat big bees. They picked up a narrow mountain bus and jolted through passes in the mountains until they reached a village new to them, Susswein, so typically Austrian that, paradoxically, it did not seem real, with its wooden houses and pink and pale blue stucco cottages. The houses had large Alpine porches with jigsaw scrolls of woodwork. Along the main street, where the imprints of automobile tires were moist and sharp in the red dirt, Mason and Paula cozily visited the Tabak Trafik and the Selcherei, which sold Agfa film, Odol cosmetics, rickety sunglasses, and Alpine walking sticks with silvery bands.

An ancient open taxi, the brown wooden doors of which did not close properly, took them to an inn built under eaves of rock. They dined out of doors, where water from the brook made a hiss and a rush. Waiters tossed bread from the tables right into the stream for the bouncing fish. Then the next day everybody ate the fish.

"Oh . . ." Paula lifted her head the next morning. "Oh . . . I always adore you at breakfast—I wonder why? Do you want to stay married to me all your life? I want to stay married to you all my life! Propose to me again . . . once in a while . . . on bended knee. Oh, darling, I'm talking foolishness. I'm lightheaded. It's the mountain air. I love you, I adore you. I want to make some wonderful gesture to you . . . because you're so marvelous."

"It's I who should make the gesture to you."

"Please do." Her laughter glistened.

This village lay on the other side of the Rax, the precipitous mountain they had visited with Cairn. They could see now that it was not really a mountain at all but a broad plateau almost perfectly oblong, rising straight out of the hills like a catafalque with a flat top and cliffs for sides, from which trails hung down. On top, the plateau was bare, blown smooth. Nothing grew there except bits of pasture scattered on the solid rock. The wind had blown everything else off.

Clouds loved the Rax. There were always small clouds hovering at its corners. The giant Rax intercepted them and held them, so that a warm, drowsy summer shower fell out of them every day late in the afternoon, sprinkling the village clean. The Ober in the hotel was an omniscient host, and saw to it that all the guests who wished to do so had Jause together late each afternoon. Mason and Paula sipped chocolate and nibbled Indianerkrapfen. After they had been there three or four days she wanted to climb the Rax, but he hesitated. "My goodness, Paula, it's two thousand meters—stiff rock climbing!" He had an awe of technical things he had never experienced, like what was called so forbiddingly "rock climbing." ("For steady heads only," the solemn guidebooks said.)

"Silly, the trails are clearly marked. You can see them from here."

"You can also see a lot of snow and ice. Looks to me like a long hard climb!"

They set out the next morning. Mason never knew how he managed to climb the last hundred yards. Paula was exhausted too. They had coffee at the Ottohaus and loafed recuperating in deck chairs sheltered from the calm, sunny winds. The view made them quiver. They seemed to be enormously high, perched in the cushion of a cloud. He was overpowered by his accomplishment. He crept to the edge of a belvedere and peeked over, intensely happy and feeling a proprietary interest in this great mountain he had conquered.

"Mason!" Paula found some snow in a lopsided hollow near a thicket of low fir. "Oh, I'd like to wash my face in it!" They followed patches of snow through a defile, walking precariously, and slid noisily down the banks of a half-frozen stream. The ice was thin and whitish with black water spurting underneath; the water was fighting under the ice, gurgling, like black tadpoles, to get through. He cracked a thin film of ice with his stick, so that the water burst up, exploding, and then disappeared broadly in a gully cutting through high grass.

He felt purified, soothed, and at the same time animated. He became reconciled to his position. The sense of grievance and bewildered loss that had afflicted him diminished. He still thought of Erika constantly, but in a different way. Paula smiled a little timidly, watching him. He took her in his arms, comfortably, possessively, all tensions and resentment gone, saying, "My dear . . . I do love you so." The affirmation long overdue produced other affirmations. "I just can't express what depth of feeling I have for you . . . how I care for you . . . what I owe to you . . . how much I love you." And, kissing her, he led her stumbling out of the gully toward the waving grass, under spruce with short high branches bent into the shape of canoes. They found a bit of scarred meadow behind a rock, veined with black stripes, where the sun was still warm, and became closer, she thought, than they had ever been before. She closed her eyes gratefully. "Oh darling," she breathed, "you're sweet."

An hour later they stumbled back to the Ottohaus, had a drink or two, and took the aerial railway down.

7

At the inn that night they picked up in the bar a copy of a slick American magazine left there by a recent tourist. Mason, yawning, thumbed through the pages and then sat abruptly upright, jolted. Eight or ten photographs, arranged neatly like rows of postage stamps, stood under a caption: "America's Leading Foreign Correspondents— Miscellany of Able Reporters Tell Us About the World." Mason took in the photographs with one quick sweep of his eye, then read the text. Smiling brightly, a bit too brightly, he passed the magazine over to Paula. "Well! Will you have a look at this!"

Included on the page were the chief Hearst man in Europe, a veteran whom Mason despised for the kowtowing nature of his endlessly long interviews; the admirable Bowler brothers, who ran Paris and Berlin for the Chicago *Daily News*; Pat Gavin, a graying youth who had knocked about in Mexico and Brazil, advancing then to passionate grips with life in the Chinese and Russian Revolutions; the hard-working Larson Drex of the Chicago *Tribune*, who, like Stein, had his own airplane; Silas Q. Slim, who had been a Berlin correspondent way back in 1914 and who, before many more years passed, would become a household name in every hamlet in America by reason of his radio programs; Ken Butterbacker, the brilliant, charming redheaded Texan who was so well known in Paris that a musical comedy with a long run had recently been named for him; Philip Hazelwood; and of course Marmaduke Haven, the New York *Times* man in Moscow.

Paula saw a hurt, jealous look on Mason's face, which he sought to suppress. She remembered suddenly their quarrel the night they had talked about quitting the *Star* and branching out. His eyes flashed with anger, but he pretended not to be upset, tossing off his emotion to save his pride before Paula. She was shocked. This was not his customary mode of behavior. She had never seen him humiliated before. She had not comprehended how unreasonably hurt he would be at the slight of being left off that page.

"But, Mason, all these men"—she tapped the magazine as he flung it down—"are much older than you. Think of the records they've established. You have all the time in the world to catch up. Anyway what a magazine says doesn't matter."

"Yes, yes."

He gave a short, rasping half-laugh.

"Darling—"

He rose, patted her absently on the shoulder, and a different expression came to his face, one of resolution. This was the kind of challenge to which there must be response. Give him time! he thought. He'd show them—just as he'd shown that bank!

They walked toward their room. Paula sought to mollify his anger, saying gently, "After all, you can't take fame with you."

He replied, "If that remark had come from somebody a bit older, I would say that it was a sign of acute disappointment with life."

"Perhaps. But I'll repeat what I've just said, you can't take fame with you, any more than money."

"You can leave it on the record."

She looked out from their balcony to the fence of low spiky pines, and was visited by an ominous premonition. Mason would give up anything, even her, for his career—would he not? She became frightened. For years she had thought that life was a kind of ticket. Your passage was clearly marked out from beginning to end, the destination was unalterable, the course fixed, stage by stage. Now she had an intense feeling of apprehension, of baleful foreboding, that even a passenger on a good train might conceivably be forced off at the wrong station, eliminated from the journey in mid-passage, dropped, cast off, discarded without real reason.

She clung to him.

"Mason, don't ever leave me—I'd die!"

❋

They took a bus to Mariazell early the next morning and walked a day in the high meadows there. Then down, down, down on foot a few miles, resting at a Gasthaus until another bus carried them to the Gesäuse. They spent the night at a village where the torrent of the Enns, gray with snow, churning, foaming, spurted like a hose full of ice water through a defile of slaty, shiny rocks.

Paula picked up the newspapers in a café and saw the headlines first. England had left the gold standard—biggest story of its kind in years and years.

She read out the details as Mason, incredulous, looked over her shoulder. Aghast but half chortling, she exclaimed, "Well, you certainly started something, darling!"

XI. COILS IN THE SPRING

Back in town Mason prepared for a busy autumn. The crisis caused by the crash of the A.O.G. continued to spread angrily. The explosion in Vienna, having led to the German collapse and the flight from sterling, now sent out shattering impulses almost everywhere. Pessimists cried, "The dollar will go west next!" Politics began to be affected too; and then, as Mason perceived, there came concurrent disintegrations in personal standards and relationships.

"Ah, I cannot control longer the son," Sandor said in the café one afternoon early in October. "Erji, what is doing now our son?"

Actually young Putzi's activities were harmless; he was demonstrating to Jim Drew how to make successively a hat, a boat, and something called "Heaven and Hell" from a piece of copy paper. He was very clever. Erji nibbled at a chocolate, sipped her *Weisse Ohne*, and read a novel slowly. The boy tumbled from Drew's side and rushed triumphantly to his mother, holding up the elaborate paper box he had made. Drew, like so many men with none, adored children—Putzi in particular.

"*Schau, Mutti, jetzt habe ich es schön gut gemacht. Mutti, schau!*" With shining eyes Putzi demonstrated how the Heaven-Hell paper pulled in and out. Wriggling close to Erji he told her, "*Mutti, der Onkle Jim hat einen Bleistift mit zwei Farben.*" The waiter Josef came with more coffee, sighing, "*Ach, die Kinder . . .*"

"*Papa, darf ich zehn Groschen haben?*" Putzi asked.

He was looking gluttonously at a machine newly installed in the coffeehouse, which dispensed bonbons.

"*Zehn Groschen!*" Sandor pretended to be horrified by this amount, while glancing at Putzi with a benevolent gleam of his eye. "Dear

me, the children have already the manners of their grownups. *Zehn
Groschen!* Now!"

"*Bitte, Papa.*"

"Erji!" Sandor's voice was always pleasantly peremptory when he
addressed his wife over a domestic matter. "Can the son again have
chocolate?"

Erji adored Putzi with such tenderness, with such tumult in her
heart, that sometimes she felt helpless dealing with him. The boy
stuck the ten-Groschen piece into the machine, extracted a confection, and, gobbling it, slid away. He was sensitive, impulsive, light as
a bubble; he slid, flitted from place to place with such swiftness that
he seemed to be somebody who could make himself disappear and
then become visible again at will. That this fey, unearthly creature,
this pure-bodied lad with his clear brown eyes and the little square
wings of shoulder blade, should be hers, all hers, the child of her
body, the product of her womb, was sometimes almost too much for
Erji to bear. Her eyes overflowed with emotion, watching him. And
Putzi loved his mother with fierce, possessive passion. His father was
indulgent enough and very loving, but sometimes confused and irritated by the quick movement of the child, his ethereal quality.
Sandor was often stern with him, in so far as he was capable at all of
being stern, in which case Putzi flew to Erji as to a harbor.

"Well, young fellow," Dennis Shipwright said to Putzi, "my theory
is that an equally matched lion and tiger would put up a good fight,
but the lion would win."

"No, the tiger."

Mason crossed to the other booth to have a word with Shipwright,
a young Englishman who had taken over John Dixon's post. His
manner was languid and he seemed to be bored to death with everybody; he thought that it was rather ill bred to be excited about a job,
and transmitted the impression that he could hardly bother to open
his lips if he were questioned on a story, much less look a person in
the eye, while he said, "Quite . . . oh . . . I daresay."

All that Shipwright did seem to be interested in was skiing in winter
and chasing girls at all seasons. Mason was amused, rather than repelled, by his blasé quality. So worldly—and with so little to be
worldly about! Even his politics were dilettantish—like so many

Oxford boys of that era, he was a pacifist and vaguely leftish, with a romantic, sentimental feeling for the underdog—the perfect example of a parlor pink, a *Popalchiki* or Almost-Fellow-Traveler.

Shipwright's nickname, by which he was universally known, was Hal. Sandor pronounced it "Haul."

"I say, Jarrett, what do you pay for money?"

"What money? Schillings? I get seven to the dollar at the A.O.G. Don't you?"

Shipwright glanced at him, lowered his voice casually, and said in his superior, languid way, "You're an ass. You can get seven sixty or even seven seventy by looking around."

"I don't understand."

Shipwright's lofty, almost supercilious manner may have served to throw some people off, but he had become much sought after in the social life of the town. It had not taken him long to become thoroughly knowledgeable about Vienna, and his German was excellent. Not only was he an acceptable extra man at parties but, except for his teeth, which seemed bluish and softish, almost transparent, his good looks were outstanding. Paula thought he was one of the best-looking men she had ever met. Mason said to himself, What a lot is forgiven people just for being attractive and good company.

"My dear fellow, open your eyes. When the A.O.G. crashed, they had to inflate the Schilling. Then came all those *Devisen* laws to keep gold and foreign exchange from leaving the country. You can't get foreign currency here any more, as you know perfectly well. Only Schillings. Well, some people have to have foreign currency—commercial people. Suppose you're importing iceboxes or cotton or automobiles. You have to pay in dollars in order to get them and sell them to the Viennese, but the Viennese can only pay you in Schillings, which are worthless outside the country. So you'll pay a premium to anybody who can give you pounds or dollars for the Schillings you accumulate from your local sales. Oh, not legally. But on the Black Bourse. Here's where we come in. The businessmen give us extra Schillings in order to get their hands on our foreign currency."

"How do they get the foreign currency, the dollars and pounds, out of the country?"

Shipwright shrugged. "Any way you want. By hiring a messenger. By using a diplomatic pouch. By getting on a railway train."

"You mean I could give one of those people a hundred dollars of my salary and get seven hundred and seventy Schillings for it instead of seven hundred?"

"Quite. I'm surprised you didn't know. Everybody is doing it."

"Are you?"

"Yes. Rather."

"Is it honest?"

"It's Austrian."

Mason made a quick calculation. He and Paula were even harder up than usual. Costs were rising since the A.O.G. failed, and Paula couldn't keep the household going on her allowance any longer. Mason didn't, in fact, know how he was going to pay their rent the next quarter. Their vacation hadn't cost much, but even so they were on the edge again. Where *had* the money gone? To buy Schillings from one of Shipwright's friends would mean a ten per cent increase in their income.

He would have to talk this over with Paula. What would Sandor say? "Do not do!"

Shipwright went on, "Don't let scruples worry you. I tell you, everybody is doing it. Not just chaps like us. The banks do it. The railways do it. I'll wager the A.O.G. itself is doing it this very minute. It's taking your dollars at seven at the window and selling them around the corner at seven seventy. Probably it's how the bloody old bank keeps going. I tell you, everybody is buying cheap Schillings, and you're a blithering ass, really, an ass, to penalize yourself. Don't talk morality to the A.O.G.!"

Mason made a quick decision. "All right. Put me in touch with your friends. I'll have two hundred dollars the first of the month."

2

Stein, a day later, asked Mason to lunch. The *Arbeiter Zeitung* had reprinted Mason's articles about the municipal housing program and was about to republish them in the form of a booklet, for distribution to tourists and local visitors. Later this brochure would appear in French, English, and perhaps other languages. Mason was pleased if only because this would give him prestige within the municipality. Prestige equals news sources.

"We're all very happy about this," said Stein, with his sunny look. He had just finished checking the proofs and wanted to work out details of the format with Mason. "There's practically nothing the Gemeinde Wien won't do for you."

With coffee Stein became obviously ill at ease. He had never mentioned Erika to Mason nor had Mason ever asked about her. Now Stein looked up, his eyes direct and very bright, but anxious, and, gulping, he blurted out, "I do not quite know what to say, but I feel that I should tell you—I am on the point of proposing marriage to Miss Falk—Erika."

Mason felt as if someone had kicked him in the groin, while his friend went on frankly, warmly. "I'd very much like the benefit of your advice. I assume you had a small relationship with Erika yourself. I have never mentioned this to her or to anybody for obvious reasons of discretion. Paula—"

"Leave Paula out of this." (How much softer Paula had become recently, less superior, less inclined to dominate, more tender. . . . How was it possible that she should, in some mysterious way, have acquired some of Erika's quality?)

Stein was taken aback by the sharpness in Mason's voice. But he went on: "If I, coming upon you and Erika that night, and then asking you about her later, deprived you . . ." He looked embarrassed. "I have felt extremities of bad conscience. But, after all . . . I . . ."

Mason knew that what he wanted to say was, "But you were a married man, whereas I was free." How much exactly did Stein know, he wondered. Stein himself thought back swiftly to that morning in the Imperial when they had met for the Yugoslav Ehrengericht and he had been so superior and self-satisfied about his bachelorhood.

"If it's any question about me that's bothering you," said Mason, a shade surly, "that's all down the river—just forget it."

Stein took breath. "So I judged." So he judged, did he! But there were few people he liked better than Ricardo Stein.

Ricardo proceeded: "I'm madly in love with her. I've never been in love before in any serious sense. She's wonderful. I love her so much that it has become altogether impossible to express what I feel. The exultation, the exaltation!" He paused. "But should I marry her?"

Mason tried to keep his voice steady. "Why not? She's a lovely girl. Of course it does happen that she has a husband, and she's a Catholic I suppose."

"She has not taken communion for several years. Even so divorce would of course be difficult here, perhaps impossible, but she could go to Prague and establish temporary residence there, or even Paris."

"Well, why don't you go ahead? Send her to Prague."

Stein seemed desperate. His voice became precise. "She tells me that her husband has made his mistress with child, and if she becomes divorced he, the husband, will perhaps have to marry the mistress, which he doesn't want to do. Hence, out of respect for her husband's wishes, she is hesitant to make the final decision."

Mason looked startled. "It surprises me that she cares much about her husband one way or the other. Anyway it's a neat little Viennese situation." He laughed edgily. "Perhaps she's hesitant for other reasons. How are you going to liquidate our friend Stefan?"

"The sculptor? I scarcely ever see him."

"He'll be around."

"Not if we marry."

"Take my word for it—he'll be around."

Stein said despondently, "All this is what combines to make my own problem so difficult. How can I marry into a circle where . . . where standards are so lax? There has never been in the whole history of my family a divorce. Things such as mistresses . . . illegitimate children . . . sculptors with mysterious relationships . . . all of that is totally outside our milieu, our circle. It would even be the most profound of shocks to my parents that I should marry a divorced woman."

Mason said brutally, "In other words you think you're too good for her."

"No, no! If you know me at all you cannot possibly think that." His eyes became so earnest and appealing that Mason thought for a second that he was going to cry. "To me marriage is a very serious matter; it is inseparably connected with the matter of career. It happens that I am not bohemian, not a person who . . . how shall I put it . . . lives on the fringes. Rationally considered, I am not at all sure that Erika is the proper wife for me."

"I should think she'd be a proper wife for anybody."

Stein looked at him with a gleam of appreciation, but went on: "Not only do I have a family, I have a certain standing in my party and much to look forward to in official life, that is a life based on the conventions. My wife will have to be a lawyer's wife, a journalist's wife, perhaps a politician's wife . . . a hostess. Erika, as you must know yourself, fulfills none of these qualifications. She is an artist. I am proud of her for being an artist. But she has no interest whatever in politics. She scarcely knows the difference between Poland and Czechoslovakia. She has no understanding at all of what the tradition of our family is and of the relationship of my family to our party. Perhaps I sound vain, but it is quite possible that I will be a member of a future Social Democratic government someday. If not, I might be appointed to some embassy abroad."

"Come off it, Ricardo. Surely you're not asking me if I think that Erika is fit to be an ambassador's wife?"

Stein's eyes dropped. "No . . . hardly. No, no, not at all!" But that was exactly what he had meant. He recovered. "You are being too American about this, Mason. There is a serious and entirely legitimate problem here involved. I am not being stuffy and I am most certainly not a snob. Whether or not Erika is or is not what is technically known as a lady is of no interest to me whatever. That is extraneous. The real issue is much larger. It involves intellectual background, also temperament and attributes, not social class."

"There's one thing you haven't mentioned. Does Erika want to marry you?"

Stein hesitated. "I think so—yes."

Late that afternoon Mason called Erika at the studio. They had not seen one another since the night of the *Heurige* party and the crash of the A.O.G. But now he forgot his good resolutions and forgot too how he had thought on the walking trip with Paula that he had recovered from her.

She told him to drop in the next day. Stefan was there. Please God get rid of him, Mason thought. Erika greeted him warmly, modestly, serene, but giving out a secret sense of controlled excitement. He poked about nervously, observing once more the dog-eared coils of photographs, wet clay in a bucket, and designs for scarves on the drawing board. Erika said, "My scarves have been a pleasant small success. Now I want something particularly appealing for the British. Can you think of anything? The Magna Carta, or whatever it was called?"

Mason laughed. "You might give them the income-tax schedule."

"It is serious. Do not make jokes."

"Damn right things are serious!"

She looked up startled by the intensity of his voice, but she did not ask him what he meant. That was one odd thing about Erika. She seldom expressed surprise about anything; she never seemed to be curious about anything. Mason relaxed. "Why not the Communist Manifesto? That would be a sure-fire hit with the rich intelligentsia."

Stefan's hands were dirty with clay, and he pulled a wet cloth from a bust half complete. Mason looked at it and felt stung. He tingled. He could see the life beginning to come out of it. It was a bust of Erika.

Mason admired it and Stefan said, grabbing him by the chin abruptly and tilting his face toward the light, "Next I will make a bust of you, Herr Mason."

"That would be very nice, but I don't think I'd be a good subject."

"Why not?" Stefan grasped his head and turned it this way and that, as if it were an inanimate object separated from the body. "It is a face with some rudiments of interest, do you not think? Not much, but some."

"It's a nice face," Erika said.

"They don't actually frighten children with it," Mason said.

"Do make a head of him, Stefan. Then Mason will come every day instead of once every five months and we can discuss politics." But the jibe was gentle.

Once every five months? So she had counted the time too.

"Politics . . . pfui!" Stefan said.

He was pacing back and forth in the far corner of the room. He walked up to Mason again and squinted at him once more with his heavy brows meeting. His tone changed. "I will make a death mask of your face, Herr Mason," he announced.

Mason did not know quite why this remark bothered him, but he answered, "The hell you will." But he had become fond of Stefan and Stefan was fond of him, if only because he knew that he truly loved Erika.

"A death mask would be very nice," Stefan insisted. "I can make one in twenty minutes and when you die Erika will have something to remember you by."

"Shut up."

"I have made five death masks so far. Two of the subjects died, but the others are still living and next year we will use them as decorative motifs for the C'schnasfest."

Erika said, "Stefan, go home." She nodded the soft black curls back from her forehead. So she still loved him.

"I will make a death mask first of Herr Mason Jarrett's handsome political face."

Erika shooed him out. Now that they were alone Mason felt empty; he wanted to jump up, reach out, shout, spread his arms to the ceiling or grind his face into a wall.

Instead, he blurted out, "Are you going to marry Stein?"

She dropped her chin sharply to the base of her soft throat—a peculiar gesture, almost virginal.

"He told me that he was going to tell you."

The telephone rang. Of course it must be Stein.

"Don't answer it," Mason said.

"Very well."

"How can you marry him? You're still in love with me."

"It would be a very good match. I like him. I told you months ago that you made me feel the necessity to change my life. He is of a quality very special, and devoted to me utterly."

She added calmly, "Besides it would be one way to remain close to your circle."

That was the sentence Mason needed. He felt wild with emotion, almost sick, while her face became pensive. Almost timidly she put her hand on the front of his shoulder; he slipped an arm around her and they kissed and her lips parted. He rocked with her gently and before long he was more moved than he had ever been in his life.

"Du! Forgive me," he heard her whisper. He stirred against her and they kissed again; her responding body was soft and sweet, but in turmoil too.

The telephone rang again. She did not rise to answer.

Mason left very late. Her face was luminous, his was dead white. He searched anxiously for a taxi. How was he going to explain being so late to Paula? When he reached home and Paula said solicitously that he looked tired and asked him what he wanted to drink he felt like a murderer.

Mason and Erika for the course of the next weeks met surreptitiously every other day or so in a shabby small hotel near Prinz Eugenstrasse. They made love with ecstasy. The stolen passionate hours they spent together secretly in this dingy bedroom with the stuffed furniture and octagonally shaped white tile stove were not only of inconceivable physical delight to them both, but the confirmation of a friendship, a relationship, as well as a love affair. Paula never guessed. Nor did Stein. There came times when Mason was irritated with Paula for not guessing. It seemed intolerable to him that she could be so obtuse, so superior, that she did not recognize that his life was, once more, ablaze with a consuming interior excitement. About Stein he did not think at all. Nothing whatever mattered except that he loved Erika and that she loved him. But still he would not offer to give up Paula and marry her. He could not. There came an afternoon when, inexplicably, dumbfoundingly, they both discovered that they were exhausting each other. The strain of a double life was too eviscerating to endure. She evaded fixing a day for their next rendezvous and an emotion that he could not identify overcame him—could it be relief? Erika saw his startled look, kissed him, and said, "*Herzerl*, I think it will be somewhat different with us soon." They met once more and Mason told her that he had to leave town on a story in a day or two. In an hour hardly a word passed between them. They parted on the street, and, smiling wanly, Erika made a small gesture toward the hotel, looking back at it and patting her hand toward it in the air as she had so often patted the tall white stove in their grubby room, which had also been their palace, to feel its warmth. Then she murmured a phrase he would not forget. "Good-bye, *du*. You're so good you're bad."

Mason stopped at a bar. He got drunk very quickly. Probably there would never be a day in his life that he would not think about her; he would love her always, but he had the feeling that he would not make love to her again.

3

Mason went down to the Journalistenzimmer later and Bleschke rose dutifully to greet him. "Herr Yarrett, I would beg you to forgive me if I mention something, but perhaps it will be to your advantage."

"Sure. What is it?"

"I do not wish to intrude. But, if by any chance you should be interested in cheap Schillings, I could arrange to get seven ninety."

Mason, without committing himself, sauntered to the Weissenhof, and was waylaid by old Tinkham as he moved toward the *Stammtisch*. Tinkham caught his sleeve. "Jarrett, my dear fellow, I've just made a contact. Please keep this in confidence, of course. You know what's going on and I've made a big coup, laid my hands on some cheap Schillings. I could give you eight."

"Is that so?"

When Mason reached home he telephoned Shipwright and said, "Hal, I'm sorry, but I've changed my mind. Hope it won't embarrass you, but I'm going to call off that Schilling deal."

He didn't want to overvalue his conceptions, but if people like Bleschke and Tinkham were mixed up in this *valuta* racket there must be something seriously wrong with it and it was not for him.

4

Mason liked to take notes and was forever projecting himself into the future with lists and memoranda, but, largely because of his self-consciousness, he had never been able to keep a diary. He would try for a few days; then give up. Now, however, he had taken a trip to Istanbul, and something compelled him to put on paper a record of events.

November 8, 1931

Klaus, my man at the Hotel Majestic, ineffable Klaus, called me ten days or so ago in Vienna to say that E. Rex Marriott, the publisher, had just arrived in town. I had always wanted to meet him. The Marriott-Hopkins list really holds up. We had an amiable talk and I invited him home for a drink the next afternoon. Paula said, "You're after something —what?" The fact of the matter was that I was crazy to get out of town for a while, but what with this economy wave washing over us I couldn't possibly suggest a trip to Chicago without a good excuse. Well, I had seen in one of the book reviews that Marriott was just about to bring out the first volume of Trotsky's History of the Russian Revolution, and that the book was expected to make a big Christmas splash. Trotsky, chased from one place of exile to another, arrived in Prinkipo, the little island near Constantinople, a couple of months ago. Nobody has seen him. But Marriott would be able to fix up a meeting. So I suggested to Marriott that a resounding interview with Trotsky, appearing in all our papers, might be helpful in relation to publication of the book. And of course it would be a big scoop for me. He fell for this at once, and wired Trotsky saying that it would be useful to give me an appointment. Paula kept looking at me with a sly, amused air of admiration when I told her all this. "Glory," she sighed, "I've never seen anybody with such a wonderful talent for making use of everybody!"

Who should call up later that evening but Tom Cairn. Why the hell he didn't give us a little notice I don't know. Paula was excited to be seeing him. Me too. He came over at once and we talked half the night. I suggested, "Why don't you come with me to Istanbul? Trotsky ought to be on your list of people met and conquered." He said "Sure—why not?"

Tom understood, of course, that the story is mine; he would just be looking in on it.

At about four in the morning Paula made some coffee. Cairn transfixed me with that stare of his: "I think it is now time to ask you seriously why you are inviting me to join you on this insane expedition to Istanbul."

"For the pleasure of your company."

"No. You have a certain slight subconscious fear of me, jealousy of me perhaps, and you don't want to leave Paula alone with me in Vienna where I might be staying several days."

Paula looked shocked. I had never had any such thought, of course, nor —obviously—had she. "Nonsense," I said. "Paula's grown-up, even if you aren't."

Marriott got a wire from Trotsky the next day agreeing to see me and Cairn and I caught the Orient. Paula saw us off, and we were very gay.

The train pulled out slowly. I could hear a click-click as the wheels passed over each separate rail, then cloppetty-clop as we got under way. We had a drink and presently Tom's eyes got that slightly glazed look. We crossed the Hungarian frontier and went into the dining car. He looked at his watch, jumped, and yelled to the waiter, "Champagne, champagne! We must celebrate the coming of a new day!" Actually it was nine o'clock in the evening, but, misreading the figures, he thought it was quarter to twelve. He was ahead of life by about three hours. He ate very little, nibbling at a dish and then pushing it aside. I was hungry and ate in a hurry. Suddenly his talk became sexual. He peered at me, not seeing me. "You eat too fast. Do you make love so fast?" I said something non-committal. "How many sexual experiences did you have last year?" he demanded. I said that I had given up arithmetic in such matters long ago.

We finished dinner. His head bobbed from side to side. He was very, very drunk and was pondering. "Something is blocking me," he muttered. "I am old before my time. No, no, I'm not talking about just sex. You can get sex anywhere—most easily and perhaps in some circumstances most pleasantly out of yourself. What I am talking about is love. *Liebe, Liebe.* What I am seeking is rejuvenation through love. Sex is easy to find, but love, very very difficult."

"But at Edlach six months ago you said that you were tired of love, afraid of it."

"So . . . so . . . Nevertheless, it is only love that can cure, that can heal, that can save the world, save me!"

"I've never heard you be trite before, Tom."

We walked back to our compartment. The train rocked. We tossed for upper or lower berth and I got the upper. I climbed up and got half undressed; my bare foot hung over the side of the bed. Tom grabbed me by the ankle, and began to pull, holding my bare foot tight. I squashed the sole of my other foot down on his head, laughing, and pushed him so hard that he fell over, then I hauled my leg up. Half out of bed, almost rolling on the floor, he looked discomfited, and then he too began to laugh. He made a crazy gesture toward me and then jumped back into bed and laughed and laughed, and then was asleep in two minutes.

Most of the next day he read Dante aloud. Since I don't know a word of Italian, this was a waste of effort so far as I was concerned. Late in the afternoon—we were cutting across Serbia—he began to sing. Honestly, I think he knows every line of every opera by heart. After dinner he asked me to look over a manuscript. He had been working on this, a novel, for several years, he said. Opening the pages at random, he came across a cliché—innocent enough, something like "the roar of the great city"—and, horrified that he could have written such a phrase, he began to tear the whole script up, ripping it in long strips. I stopped him.

At breakfast the second morning—the trip took an eternity—he began to think aloud about Trotsky and this set him off on an hour of talk about China. "To think that we are going to meet Leon Trotsky. If he had been in a position to come to Hankow in 1926, the whole history of the Borodin intervention might have been different."

I had not known that Tom had a fairly extensive experience in China. Apparently he had marched into Shanghai with Chiang's forces. He appeared to know the Chiang family intimately. His talk became festooned with Ai Lings, Ching Lings, Mei Lings—I could not tell them apart. He was erudite, lucid, and articulate, and told me much of great interest about the early days of the Shanghai occupation, also Manchuria. [See longhand notes I made of all of this—I have marked them to go into a separate file.]

Tom had never been in Istanbul before. I went to the Embassy to pay a duty call and, returning to Tokatlian's, found a note. "Am at St. Sophia. Follow." He had bought a kind of pallet, a thin bedroll, and borrowed from the concierge a large pair of binoculars. There he was, flat on his back on the floor of the church, gazing upward through the binoculars at the mosaics. "Only way to appreciate the Byzantine," he muttered. "I do the same at Daphni and Ravenna." He rose, pushed his pallet further along, and lay down on it again near the west wall. He restrained my impatience with the words "In half an hour, we will prepare to deal with Leon." When he had had enough of the mosaics we drove to the Blue Mosque, which of course he called by its correct Arab name—I can't remember what it is—where he went through the same business with pallet and binoculars. People stared like hell. We had lunch at a small Turkish place on the Stamboul side which he apparently had heard about, and roamed through the bazaar. He bought a large ugly rug and I asked him what he planned to do with it; he shrugged. Then, without bargaining, he picked up half a dozen bits of jewelry—a fragment from a Sultanic seal, a cameo ring bearing the profile of Alexander the Great, amber beads and bits of silver. "What's all this for—your various wives?" I asked. "No!" he exclaimed, astonished. "They're for my mother." He saw my jaw drop. "Be civilized, Jarrett. Can't a man have an actual MOTHER?"

Back at the hotel, I put in a call to Paula, but couldn't get through to her. Phone communications terrible. I found that Cairn had bought that

morning every book by Trotsky that existed in Constantinople in any
language. He started to read and would not take time out for dinner. I
went to Abdullah's alone, had one of the best shashliks I ever ate, and
wandered down to Taxim's, which I really think is the most satisfactory
night club in Europe except possibly the Arizona in Budapest. Back at
Tokatlian's after midnight I found another note from Cairn, which also
said nothing but "Follow me," giving an address.

The taxi driver gave me a sly wink, so I knew what was coming. Sure
enough Tom had found a luxurious house of ill fame. He grasped me.
"Have you money? The first lesson to be learned in life is that vice, true
vice, is very, very expensive." We sat around drinking with a splendid
pack of young ladies and after a while Tom disappeared with an enormously fat young woman. When he returned after about an hour he
demanded food and, ravenous, ate a can of tinned beef right out of the
can with his fingers. The fat girl obviously adored him. He talked happily
about his "prowess." "I would now," he said happily, "suggest that we
proceed to cocaine"—he pronounced it in the French way, in three
syllables—"except that we must be fresh for Leon tomorrow morning.
Coh-cah-een is likely to give you a splitting headache the next day, if
you're not used to it."

We didn't get to bed till after 4, but caught the Prinkipo boat at 9.
Prinkipo has starched white walls and purple promontories. The talk with
Trotsky was a remarkable experience. I swear I don't know who impressed me most, Trotsky or Tom Cairn. I suppose we all have pre-
conceived ideas of people that are not always borne out by the facts; I
suppose I have always instinctively associated Trotsky with an image of
somebody inflamed, violent, and crude. He was just the opposite. He was
light as air. He was graceful, courteous, and gay. His eyes twinkled, his
nails had a high polish, and he looked as if he had just stepped out of a
Turkish bath. An aristocrat, of course, in all but the social sense, an
actor too, impulsive, vain. As to Cairn, I had thought that he would be
more dead than alive, considering the shape he was in when we turned
in last night. But he had thrown off every bit of the scuff. He was
altogether keen and alert and talked much better than I. What a delight
it is to see a serious professional seriously at work!

He won Trotsky with his first question: "Do you think that Hitler
is a revolutionary or a counter-revolutionary?" There was a vivid discussion and then I asked him all manner of details about Lenin, his
early career, and the beginnings of the struggle with Stalin. We had been
told that we would not have more than an hour but, largely because he

liked Tom, Trotsky asked us to stay for lunch, and as a matter of fact
we spent practically the entire day with him. At the very end Tom
asked him with a sly smile if he had ever been impressed by the fact that
fascism flourishes only in countries famous for grand opera, like Italy
and Germany. Trotsky, in a flash, topped him at once: "You mean by
that that you don't take fascism seriously?" They both laughed and Tom
said he took some grand opera very seriously indeed, like Wagner. Trotsky
said, "I suppose a lot depends on the conductor—and the orchestration!"
I don't know exactly what he meant by this, but anyway it was a quip
that ended the day. [Full notes in my other file—may be useful some
day for autobiography, etc.]

Mason and Cairn parted the next morning. Cairn wanted to go
to Athens to see Eleutherios, as he called him, to have a talk with
him about Balkan policy and carry a message from him up to Aristide,
It was Cairn's conviction not only that Venizelos was the most
intelligent man in Europe but was the only person who could influence Briand and the French. There was a small Greek boat to
Athens that day and Cairn took it. Mason, seeing him off, gave him
an introduction to Kitty. He himself caught the Orient back to
Vienna that night, and decided on the spur of the moment to make
a stopover in Sofia; he thought that just conceivably he might pick
up an interview with King Boris there, thus killing two birds with
one stone on one trip. Besides Willi would be there—the Archduke.
It was even possible that Willi might be helpful in arranging for
Mason to meet Boris. But Willi alone would be worth the stopover.

The Archduke, still suave, still glossy, gave him a splendid dinner
when he arrived. Mason talked about the sheer comradeship and fun
of being with Cairn and how much Trotsky had impressed him and
what a good story the interview made. The Archduke looked puzzled
after an hour. "But how do you relate all this to yourself? What ideas
do you derive from it? Have any of your convictions changed?"

"Convictions?"

"Just as an example—who do you think was right, Stalin or
Trotsky? Which side are you on?"

Mason pulled himself up sharply. He thought of Paula. It was
striking to hear the Archduke, of all people, say what Paula might

be saying. His thoughts chased back to Cairn. Tom, who loved to be a participant in events, not a mere observer, was about to embroil himself in the affairs of Venizelos and the Quai d'Orsay. But all that he, Mason, seemed able to think about was his own story and how interesting and amusing the junket to Istanbul had been. Now he tried to talk all this out frankly with the Archduke and answer his questions. They had a stimulating hour.

Returning to his hotel he found a telegram forwarded from Istanbul. It was a peremptory order from Chicago to stop the arrangement whereby he paid Jim Drew five dollars a day to cover for him when he was out of Vienna. INTEREST ECONOMY DROP DREW AS FROM TODAY.

5

"May I speak to Mr. Jarrett?" The voice was smooth and cultivated. "This is Ralph Conyers speaking. I'm a banker from New York. I've read some of Mr. Jarrett's stories and I'd like to meet him."

"Mr. Jarrett is away in the Balkans. This is Mrs. Jarrett."

"Oh. Perhaps I could talk to you, then."

"Mr. Jarrett will be back in about a week."

"Perhaps you would give me the pleasure of dining with me, Mrs. Jarrett. I assure you that I am reasonably presentable. I've only just arrived in Vienna and I'm eager to get in touch with several people— particularly your husband and some of his colleagues whom you might help put me on to."

Paula was lonely, awaiting a call from Mason. "We might have a drink toward six. You could drop in here."

"Splendid. Thank you very much."

It was years since some man whom she had never met asked her out to dinner. A blind date—at her age! She was thrilled. She took a good deal of trouble with her hair. Conyers arrived on time to the minute. He must be about Mason's age, but he seemed somewhat older, with a stocky Ivy League look. His eyes were big and gray behind the curved lenses of his steel spectacles. He was reserved in manner, rather commanding, and certainly not unintelligent, she thought. They explored the fringes of each other's world. She was delighted when, after an hour, he insisted that they go out to dine.

"Sit on this side, please." His voice was pleasant, but it had force. "Now, though I don't know Austria well and my German is deplorable, let me order."

This was at Cobenzl, the restaurant on the tip of a Wienerwald hill. It was one of the most expensive establishments in town, and Paula, who had never been there before, enjoyed watching the lights of the city below, a necklace of diamonds and sapphires carelessly interlooped.

Conyers ordered dinner with systematic expertness. He suggested *Fogash* ("I've heard of it all my life but never eaten it," he said, smiling), a schnitzel, pressed cucumber salad, and *Kaiserschmarrn*, a dramatic fantasy, for dessert. He ordered wine, and Paula was both horrified and impressed when, with the sweet, he insisted on a bottle of champagne as well. This meal would pay the rent of an average Viennese for a month. She was wistful for Mason. Conyers was so agreeable that she fell readily enough into his mood. Besides, she discovered almost at once that she liked him, if only because, like Mason, he liked to eat. "Forgive me," Conyers said solicitously, "I can't stand excessive people, and I'd like nothing less than to be thought excessive. But I've never been in Vienna before and this is my first dinner here."

"Some French cognac, please," he said to the waiter. He was authoritative now. Good heavens, was the man trying to buy her favor? No, no, not at all. He was simply proceeding on the assumption that this was a normal way in which to have dinner. There was nothing munificent about him. He was exceptionally casual. Still, it came close to annoying Paula that he was so neatly, so correctly dressed. (Poor Mason, she thought, who looked more and more like a tramp as time went on. . . .)

After coffee he asked her if she would show him the town, and Paula suggested going to one of the political cabarets. It was crowded and noisy, but Conyers, with a wave of his hand, got the best table in the place. He knew German quite well in spite of what he had said about it, and there was no need to translate the jokes, even though most of them were in the vernacular. An early laugh came at the story about the Hungarian lunatic who got out of Steinhof, the insane asylum, and asked about the state of the world after fifteen

years, and was told that Hungary was now a kingdom but didn't have
a king, and was ruled by an admiral although there was no fleet—
whereupon the lunatic decided to go back to the insane asylum.

The Komiker was chortling:

> *Früher ist es uns hier gut gegangen,*
> *Jetzt geht es natürlich viel besser*
> *Es wird uns aber noch viel besser gehen*
> *Wenn es wieder gut geht.*

Conyers missed some of this and Paula whispered an English
version: "Once it was pretty good with us and naturally it's much
better now. It would be better still if it got pretty good again."

Conyers roared with laughter. He liked this crowded, smoky
cabaret as much as he had liked the open beauty of Cobenzl. He
had never thought that the Viennese political shows, so well known,
could be as good as they were touted to be. They sat through two
performances, whereupon he said that to make the evening complete
he would like to hear some gypsy music, and they sauntered to the
Ungarisches Weinhaus. He could not have liked it more, and the
moaning rhythms almost made her swoon. His attentiveness grew.
Then, out on the street at two in the morning, he insisted that they
go to one of the regular cabarets to dance. She hadn't danced for
ages. She hesitated. Mason practically never danced. She submitted
and they found their way to a little place called the Bogner Bar.
Conyers danced very nicely, and bought more champagne. It was
three-thirty in the morning. She hadn't been out so late in months.

"This is, after all, a celebration," Conyers explained, smiling. "I
only wish that your husband could be here. After all, it was he and
I between us who brought the A.O.G. down."

＊

He telephoned again the next day and she suggested that they meet
at the Weissenhof, where they sat till midnight. Paula had had a long
letter from Mason, endorsing a fragment of a diary, and was in the
best of moods.

"I'm in town with Payne of the Home National to get the second
creditors' committee organized," Conyers said. "He's the boss, I'm

the office boy." Sandor and Drew listened attentively. "Oh, I suppose I'll be here a couple of weeks, maybe longer. Then we'll appoint a local representative. No, there's not much news at the moment."

To Paula alone, while they strolled toward Sacher's later, he was much more candid.

Things were in a terrible state at the A.O.G. The accountants had been working all summer and autumn. The waste and extravagance had been unbelievable. Plans for the reorganization were held up by preposterous demands such as that the former directors—even those criminally incompetent—should be bought off with huge pensions. In spite of the *Devisen* laws, the gold cover of the Austrian currency had fallen from eighty to thirty-one per cent. The Austrians still seemed dazed.

"I never saw such a mess," Conyers said. "But you watch, we'll pull it through. We have to. But heaven only knows what's going to happen to the Schilling."

Paula became alert. "Tell me—would you buy illegal Schillings if you got the chance?"

"In my position, no. In yours, yes—of course."

"Men have the nicest way with double standards." Paula laughed. "You'll forgive me, but I don't quite understand your point of view. You seem so casual—almost cynical. You said last night so cheerfully that you and Mason helped pull the A.O.G. down, and now you say that you're going to build it up again. Does that make sense? And having caused the A.O.G. to crash and the collapse of the German banks and the crisis in England, are you happy, are you satisfied?"

"N-no."

"Isn't it your demands that make the Schilling fall?"

"My dear Paula, I see that you are not only a very intelligent but a very misinformed young woman. Without us there'd be no Schilling left at all. If you grant the existence of the capitalist system and the profit motive, all that sort of thing, you might as well make it work efficiently. Besides, there's the question of self-interest. Let the A.O.G. go all the way to pot and what have you—chaos everywhere."

"Maybe there ought to be a different system."

"Different system? Of course, but there are banks in the Soviet

Union which operate precisely as our banks do, yet I daresay not so efficiently. They issue bonds in the Soviet Union that pay seven per cent, and their savings banks are used by millions of depositors and pay higher rates of interest than any in the United States."

"But Russian banks don't make a profit out of businesses which, in turn, profit by the exploitation of labor. They don't make profits out of speculation or by the ownership of land or factories or by buying cheap and selling dear."

"In Russia it's the state that exploits the whole people. It's a kind of state capitalism they have there."

"I don't think that's quite accurate. The people own the state and, in theory at least, benefit from it."

"Do they?" He grinned. "Let's get back to the A.O.G. I agree that it was badly run and to pump life into a corpse isn't exactly edifying, but, I repeat, if we hadn't saved it there would have been a revolution!"

"Well, why not have a revolution? Maybe we need one. Maybe we need several...."

Conyers permitted himself an overt gesture; he slammed his open hand on the table. "Good! I see that I'm in the company of an honest radical, though I don't think you're nearly as radical as you give the impression of being. All right, let's have a revolution. Why not? Well..."

They argued for an hour and crossed the street to a small bar called the Renaissance, where they drank champagne. Conyers got bright red in the face, but he was still suave, graceful, and authoritative. Presently it was two in the morning and then three. She could tell that, the minute they left the place, he would try to make love to her. She felt at once miserable, baffled, and excited. He was attractive and she liked him and the circumstances were piquant, but there was no emotional stimulus at all, no aura of the spirit. Not conceivably could she give way to any physical desire unless she found herself emotionally involved as well.

So she talked about Mason briefly, and to make doubly sure, added, "And you, Mr. Conyers? I suppose you have a nice house in Westchester, a pleasant wife, belong to the best clubs, have three children—"

"No."

Embarrassed, she exclaimed, "Oh, forgive me for what I've just said, please. Rather shoddy, wasn't it?"

"Not at all. As a matter of fact I'm a bachelor. I'd like extremely to find a girl I was crazy about, get married, have children, build a home. Perhaps you'll think it's rather pretentious of me to say so, but I honestly think that I have something to give a woman. However, I haven't found her yet, and that's that."

He paused. "Meantime it's easy to see that you're afraid that I'm going to make advances to you, but believe me, I won't."

"Why not?"

"Because it's as plain as a fish on a stick you're utterly, absolutely, committed to your husband."

But then on another evening—Mason was still away—Conyers became passionate and imploring. She had agreed to meet him in his apartment at the Bristol, where they dined. She resisted him fiercely, got somewhat mauled, and felt ridiculous. She should never have agreed to dine in his rooms. But she could not help liking Conyers. She was flattered by his excitement and she could not help responding a little to his hunger. He was so very nice. He was just the kind of person her mother would have liked her to marry. He gave up after a while and she, exhausted, drove home alone, hoping desperately that there would be some new word from Mason. There was none, and she crept—both sad and lonely—into a lonely bed.

6

Immediately on returning to Vienna from Sofia Mason got in touch with Jim Drew. The five dollars per day he had paid him when he was out of town had always been very important to Drew, as Mason was well aware. Lamely, hating himself, he showed him the telegram he had received terminating his services. "My dear sir, a small matter, forget it," Jim said. Mason explained that the telegram had descended upon him without warning and that there had been no explanation as yet by mail. It was not at all the kind of thing the Star usually did. The pressure for economy must be terrific in Chicago.

"I can't help it, and it's not my fault," Mason said. "I'm not responsible for silly decisions people make four thousand miles away."

"I can take care of myself. Don't give it a thought," Drew said. Then he did something astonishing—gestured toward Herr Julius, saying, "I'd like to buy you a drink, Jarrett. Have a drink."

This must have been the first time in living memory that Drew had ever bought anybody a drink.

Mason said, "Not a very loud one—thanks."

Drew, not comprehending for a second, looked puzzled. "What? Oh. You mean something light. Well, have a beer." Drew had, of course, no sense of humor whatever. Mason had known that for a long time, but much else in Drew still mystified him. What went on in that confused, pompous mind? How did he justify himself? He had never uttered one word of apology about the A.O.G. affair and had, in fact, never mentioned it at all since the vote at the Anglo-American. He assumed that his relationships would proceed exactly as before, he seemed to be oblivious of the fact that any stigma could attach to his name, and he had never said one word of thanks to Bishopson, Stein, or Mason for what they had done for him.

❄

Two or three evenings later Mason noticed a new face at the *Stammtisch*. Miss Birch was a pleasant-looking dark girl with brown eyes dotted with tiny gold flecks. Sitting there, she gave an impression of extreme neatness and orderliness, to which was added a contradictory note of lack of direction. Mason noticed her thin, very white small hands; they were narrow and the blue veins stood out. From time to time she gripped the edge of the table as if she were forcing herself to stay there—physically holding on to the table in order to resist impulses to be far away.

She must have started coming to the café while he had been away in Turkey and Bulgaria. He didn't know much about clothes, but he saw that she was dressed with the most exquisite elegance. Good clothes were so seldom seen in Vienna that he stared. The rich, simple brown jacket with its sharply slanted lapel looked like something out of *Vogue*; she seemed molded into it, and the lines were dashing. Then he saw an enormous, glowing, wine-colored stone on a bluish white small finger. He had never seen a ruby so big before. He grinned with total friendliness and asked simply, "Are you rich?"

He remembered for a long time the way she answered the question. She looked at him with a faint gesture of disapproval; she composed herself, and for a fraction of a second said nothing; then, as if delivering herself of a burden, answered simply, but with a note of distance and formality: "Yes—rather!"

He reached for her hand comfortably to see the ruby better. She wore heavy gold bracelets, but on the underside of her wrist he saw a belt of threadlike silver scars. Dropping her hand at once, he made as if to apologize, then checked himself with the thought that this would make his forwardness seem even more conspicuous. So, saying nothing, he cupped her whole small hand warmly in his large paw. Pressing it, he looked her straight in the eye with an expression that said, "Don't be troubled that I saw. I won't give you away."

Conyers came in with Shipwright. Paula had told Mason a good deal about Conyers, but not all. Now they met for the first time. Mason had no jealousy whatever. He took it for granted that Paula was still sealed, armored, made invulnerable by the power and protection of his love.

The story had got around that Conyers had said that he and Mason, between them, had caused the crash of the A.O.G., and people watched them react to one another.

"Jim," Miss Birch addressed Drew, "what was it you were explaining about the British situation?" Mason was surprised. He had not associated Miss Birch with Drew at all. Now he saw that there was something between them—no mistaking it. You could virtually feel a current join them. Drew talked to the table at large, but the way he was trying to impress Conyers now, pontifically, while darting glances at Miss Birch, showed Mason that every word was meant for her. Then Mason realized that Drew looked better than he had in months. That must be a new suit he was wearing and he had even shaved.

"Well, as I see it," Drew said, "you chaps in New York and London got caught on your short-term money just as the French cleaned up their withdrawals aiming to break the Customs Union. Isn't that correct?" His tongue made the familiar cluck-cluck. "Hard-boiled gents, those French . . . Now, of course it's really convenient for the City of London to be off gold. . . ."

Conyers agreed, and before long the Stammtisch was having one of the best evenings it had had in months. Sandor blossomed with anecdotes, and a visitor from Berlin gave them details about the phenomenal steep rise in Hitler's strength in Germany.

Antonino entered. He was the lean, pale-skinned man from Bolzano who was supposed to be Mussolini's secret agent with the Heimwehr, and his white flexible hairless wrists always reminded Mason of oversized cannelloni. Drew took him aside casually. A few minutes later Von Traum came in. Drew rose abruptly from the booth where he was sitting with Antonino, giving him an airy gesture of dismissal, and joined Von Traum, the Nazi.

Mason was fascinated by this. Drew and Antonino had been intimately close for a long time, but Drew had never known Von Traum well and of course Antonino and the German were bitter enemies. The Heimwehr and the Nazis hated one another. Now Drew was giving up the Heimwehr man for the Nazi, or so it seemed. He affixed himself to Von Traum and was talking volubly, with the expression of a man who expected reward for his words. Mason wondered if Drew could possibly be on Von Traum's secret payroll. That might account for the new suit, at least. Could it be possible?

Presently Drew rejoined the *Stammtisch*, while Antonino and Von Traum, in different booths, glared with hostility at each other. Now the talk became nonpolitical and touched first on the new Molnar comedy and then, as it often did, on psychoanalysis.

"What do you think of psychoanalysis, Mr. Drew?" Conyers asked. "I suppose everybody here takes the orthodox Freudian line."

Drew became embarrassed, reddening. "I think it's bughouse. Those doctors get their hooks into somebody and it's Steinhof for them next. It's a racket and I think that the psychoanalysts are in the pay of the lunatic asylums."

Erji whispered an aside to Mason: "Miss Birch is being now analyzed. She pays ze doctor fifteen dollars per every hower!"

7

And now the men and women of the Weissenhof circle, members of the Anglo-American Press Association and their friends, climbed the wall of winter. Every night Frau Gertrude put over their beds for Mason and Paula a giant puff, or plumeau, in red and gold and green with crisscross stripes. Walking to the café in the crisp afternoons, Mason paused often at the Eislaufverein, which overnight had become a skating place instead of tennis courts, and resembled now two or three acres of frozen milk. He watched the skaters waltzing to the triangular rhythms of Johann Strauss, together with subordinate Strausses, and wondered what other city would use four whole square blocks in the center of town for a skating rink. The winter before this had amused him, but now he became irritated. "Damned Viennese!" he muttered to himself angrily. "No sense of reality at all!"

Mason was trying with grim determination to deal with some serious realities in connection with himself. He wanted to get some writing done. Several factors entered into this resolution. One was that damned *Vanity Fair* article about the foreign correspondents he and Paula had seen on their walking trip, the thought of which still made him bridle with jealousy. The only way to become better known was to write more. Another was a recurrent emotion of acute distress and dissatisfaction—perhaps pointed up by the trip to Istanbul— that he had never worked out firmly the patterns of his own thought on a large variety of subjects. The best way to do this would be to write. Besides, he wanted to branch out. He remembered that fight long ago with Paula. She had been right—as usual. He still could not conceive giving up the *Star*, but he wanted to go beyond it.

One of Mason's virtues was that, vague and indeterminate as he often was, restless and diffused, he had the aptitude for progressing from reverie to action once his mind was made up. His ability to detach himself from any background of emotion and apply himself to the typewriter was, as always, pronounced. It would be an obvious folly for him to write a long article these days without having a definite commission for it. But, disdaining caution, he set out to do something deliberately aimed at some such sober and distinguished magazine as *Foreign Affairs*. He chose ramifications of the A.O.G. disaster as his theme. He did not care in the least what money it might bring. An article written in a popular vein and designed for a mass audience would be easier to write and sell. But Mason wanted to do something deeper. Paula, pleased, typed the article out, and, miracle, *Foreign Affairs* accepted it. Mason purred with other ideas. Then after a severe struggle to overcome his shyness about fiction, he tried his hand at a short story, the first he had written in years. Paula didn't like it much, although several phrases in it moved her. In plain fact she became uneasy when he wrote fiction. Perhaps she feared the power and fluency of his imagination. When his mind opened up all the way and he put concepts down on paper that arose purely out of his inner life, she perhaps felt separated from him and feared that part of her power over him was lost.

8

Drew, rubbing his hands to warm them, entered the café and pulled a clipping out of his pocket and showed it to Mason. It was the report of a recent speech by Sir Devereux Ruwe, the managing director in London of the I.P. and its associated agencies. Sir Devereux Ruwe was addressing a meeting of the Chamber of Commerce in Manchester. He deplored what he called "depression psychology." He urged the creation of new buying power. He appealed for a higher standard of living for white-collar employees. He pleaded with employers, in this time of mounting crisis, to be more liberal with their men.

"That was ten days ago. Now look at this."

The letter from London, signed by Sir Devereux Ruwe himself, notified James N. Drew that, together with all editorial employees of International Press, his salary was cut ten per cent.

"I ask you," Drew said.

Bishopson and Mason drove back from lunch at the country club. Caught in a rudimentary traffic jam, Bishopson turned in the wrong direction outside the Ring, and a policeman stopped them. In the Vienna manner, which did away with all such nuisances as tickets and traffic courts, he fined him five Schillings on the spot. Laboriously the policeman, his cloak flapping, wrote out a receipt as Bishopson reached in his pocket for change.

"Say," Mason said as they drove on, "if you don't mind my asking, where do you get your money from? Are you in on this Schilling business too?"

Bishopson cleared his throat. "Yes. I resisted for a time, and then succumbed."

"How much do you get?"

"Eight fifty."

Mason gaped. "Why, that's twenty-five per cent more for your money!"

"It makes a lot of difference, I can tell you."

"I hate to do it."

"It's silly not to. The authorities wink at it, because some of the exchange comes their way, and they grab their share too."

Mason knew that eight hundred and fifty Schillings instead of seven hundred for a hundred dollars would mean the difference between living on the bare edge and having a little margin. That evening he telephoned Shipwright to ask if he could still arrange to procure black-market Schillings. He replied, "Rather!" Everybody was mad for pounds and dollars. "Drop in any time, and I'll take you over to my man."

Mason put down the receiver. So I'm a crook too, he thought.

*

A few days later the *Star's* London man, Preble, called from England asking Mason to order him half a dozen *Sachertortes* to be shipped up to London as Christmas presents. Preble said, "I say, a couple of new stories have reached here about the manners, if he has any, of that madman of ours in Moscow, Throckmorton. He was having trouble with his bath—his *bath*, mind you—which nobody in his hotel could fix. Pipes wouldn't get unclogged, you know the kind of thing. What does Throckmorton do but write a letter to the G.P.U., can you imagine it, the G.P.U., which starts out: 'Gentlemen, yours is, I understand, the only efficient organization in the whole of the U.S.S.R. If this is true, will you kindly do something about my bathtub?!' The tub was fixed within twenty-four hours, and so far as I can gather, half of the hotel staff fired. Probably they've been shot by this time. Other story hits nearer home. You know the cheap-ruble business in Moscow has gone to the most bizarre lengths. The official rate is still four to the dollar, but you can get as much as twenty on the black market. Well, our saintly auditors in Chicago heard about this and wrote Throckmorton asking him why he did not take advantage of this situation. He's been living rigorously on the four-ruble rate and so of course his expenses are five times, literally five times, those of any other correspondent there. What did Throckmorton do? Gad! He wrote back to Chicago saying that it was inconceivable that the Russian authorities did not know fully about black-market operations by correspondents, which in turn meant that all the other correspondents, namely his competitors, *were in effect being bribed by the Soviet government*, since it was taking no action to stop their illegal operations. I say! Did the *Star*, he went on, also want to be bribed? There's a terrible row going on, but my last report is that Throckmorton is sticking to his guns and continues to insist on living on legal rubles, thus costing the *Star* five thousand dollars extra every month."

Mason felt a jolt.

*

Just before Christmas the Jarretts had to let Otto go. Chicago would not pay his meager salary (Mason had managed to get him on the payroll) any longer. Mason fumed. He would miss Otto very much. But that was not the whole point. Had Chicago lost its head? Why should hysteria, panic, be seizing everybody?

Otto himself did not seem too much upset, because he had been eager to return to England for some months. He confided in Mason that he was thinking of shaking off all of his Vienna heritage and even changing his name, although Wallenstein was not necessarily a Jewish name. Hadn't there been a celebrated German general named Wallenstein?

"Well, so long, Ott, we'll miss you," Mason said. "Some day all these difficulties are going to straighten themselves out and we'll hire you all over again—that is if we're still here and you don't change your name to Jones."

9

Mason and Paula asked Valerie Birch to lunch the next day, and began to see her frequently. Mason told Paula that he had seen from her wrists that she must have once tried to kill herself. Miss Birch mentioned to them that she was the daughter of a Kansas City manufacturer, who obviously must be very rich, and that she had had a spoiled, variegated childhood. From the beginning she continued to make references to her brother who, it seemed, was some years older and who lived in Peru, where he was a mining engineer. After Bryn Mawr she drifted to England, where she studied at the London School of Economics, then crossed to the Continent and spent most of a year "studying," that is, looking at monuments all the way from Bruges to Taormina.

"How old do you suppose she is?" Mason asked Paula.

"Oh, I suppose twenty-six or twenty-seven—maybe younger. It's strange, but to be so very well dressed can make a woman look older than she is."

"What's she being analyzed for?"

"The usual thing, I suppose."

"What's the usual thing, if Old Man Ignorance may ask a question, pet?"

"Something to do with her childhood, I suppose. Maybe she's frigid."

"She might even be a virgin," said Mason.

"No."

Miss Birch came to see Paula again. She was bright and vivid and, much to Paula's surprise, began to talk about her analysis. Very seldom did people being analyzed do this, and Paula listened with sympathetic attention. Miss Birch said that for years she had suffered from periodic blinding headaches that, for a time, almost made her an invalid. She had come to a certain Dr. Voelker in Vienna as a last resort because her doctor in New York had told her that he had had remarkable results in alleviating or even curing insoluble physical disorders by psychotherapy. He was a freak, highly unorthodox, but he did really cure people. "He's simply wonderful," Miss Birch sighed happily. "He frightens me, but he's wonderful."

"And the headaches?" Paula asked.

"They've stopped. Maybe it's only temporary, but the fact that they've stopped at all is such a relief."

Miss Birch, very neat and tidy—her crossed gloves and pocketbook made a symmetrical pattern on the table—told Paula more. "I don't know why I'm chattering on like this. I hope you're not bored." Dr. Voelker had said that she ought to see more people and enjoy to the full the good life of Vienna, and he had given her a note to the first secretary of the American Legation. There at lunch she met Jim Drew. Now she saw Drew every day. Oh, yes, Drew had told her all about the Countess. Oh yes, she understood every bit of that. Of course Drew himself was an exceptionally mixed-up character who had been much hurt by life; he too ought to be analyzed and she had been begging him to start treatment with Dr. Voelker. But, she smiled, Drew had resistances—such resistances! But he was a splendid person underneath his proud, prickly exterior. Everybody misunderstood him, but he had an excellent mind, great kindness of heart, and a deeply religious soul.

"I don't know what's come over me," Miss Birch said happily, "but I want to reclaim him. He should be saved!"

✳

The legend spread. The little pebble of fact dropped in the pool and now the broad ripples were bounding on the shore. Miss Birch was rich. She was the daughter of a millionaire. She was a millionairess herself. She was a multi-millionairess. She had a fortune estimated at two million five hundred thousand dollars. She had a fortune estimated at three million eight hundred thousand dollars. Miss Birch could buy the Belvedere Palace. She could buy the Karlskirche or the ferris wheel in the Prater or the A.O.G. She could buy all of Austria.

And at the Weissenhof, attentive, respectful, watching her as if she were some fabulous animal, sniffing at her like dogs near a bone, hoping by the mere smell of her presence to transmit to themselves some of her invisible power and magic, the wretched poverty-stricken habitués came closer, bowing to the hem of her skirt. They were infinitely correct in manner. They greeted her with respect, even awe. She was a golden mythical creature and they would have died for her.

Soon she heard about the A.O.G. affair. She went straight to Drew in the Journalistenzimmer and said, "Will you please take this three thousand Schillings? Don't protest, please. Give it back to the bank and then the whole business is finished and done with forever."

But Herr Julius, the headwaiter, was cross. Always Miss Birch gave him exactly the proper tip. "She's as rich as Rothschild," he grumbled, "and she doesn't put on airs."

※

Valerie Birch crossed her wrists, putting her knuckles to her eyes. When the tears came she felt relieved. Before her was the letter and she forced herself to read it again.

Mademoiselle:

Your affairs are known. You are being on the edge of danger. Interested parties will not allow it that you intrude on a happy and condended combination. You vixen and little minx. You are watched all the time and have care or you will come to grief. You drag a good man from his work and his home by your spurious entertainments. You who are rich can not so meddle in the affairs of others even though they are poor. We are not poor. Your riches will do you no good. You are a spy with your millions. You are vain and pushing and destroy the happiness of others. Let you beware.

A Friend

The Countess had been in bed, ill, for the past seven weeks. But from somebody she had heard of Jim Drew's infatuation with Valerie Birch.

Miss Birch wrote a letter in reply. It said simply:

Dear Countess:

You are unjust, I do think. I want only Jim's happiness. Could we meet some time and talk? I'd like to come and see you.

Sincerely,
Valerie Birch

But her face took on a stultifying deadness, and the next day her headaches began again.

10

Paula picked up the phone and passed it over to Mason, shocked. She turned pale. Mason took the phone and heard the news that Donald Bishopson had lost his job. Of course this would have to happen— such catastrophes always did, it seemed—in Christmas week.

Bishopson's newspaper, the New York Register, decided that its foreign staff was too expensive a luxury to maintain intact in these hard times and it set out to economize drastically. The second men in London, Paris, and Berlin were dropped, stringers in subordinate capitals were discharged, and two European bureaus were closed down altogether, those that seemed most dispensable—Vienna and Madrid.

There was no complaint about Bishopson's work. His dispatches were careful, steady, not brilliant, but thoroughly dependable. He had done his job well in Vienna for four years, in Buenos Aires for three years before that, in San Francisco for a year before that, and in New York and London during his novitiate. Bishopson's getting fired had nothing whatever to do with Bishopson. The *Register* was closing up Vienna and that was all there was to it; no other jobs were available and out Bishopson went, a cog in a machine no longer needed. He was a casualty, like somebody shot in a war.

It was common knowledge that Helen Bishopson had a little money; this made it easier to think about. That is, it made it easier for everybody to think about except the Bishopsons.

They had dined with the Jarretts amiably a week or two before; now Mason had a drink with Bishopson at the Bristol.

"What am I going to do?" His voice grated harshly. "Go back to school, I think. I see that my education wasn't as useful as it might have been."

"I too have had a naïve belief that virtue is its own reward."

"I don't mind it for myself so much. I can always pick up something, I suppose, even in days like these. But it's damned hard on Helen. She takes it as a repudiation, almost a moral affront, a rejection. Thank God we haven't any kids."

"You'll leave Vienna, I suppose?"

"Aye. Helen wouldn't want to be here any more. In a way she's made this her city and there aren't any Vienna jobs that I can see. . . . This may kill her." He gritted his teeth. This was one of the few times Mason had ever seen anybody do exactly that. "It's always harder for a bureau head to get a new job than for a second man, an assistant. People don't like to hire in a minor capacity someone who has been the boss. And other bosses aren't going to move."

"I've always been taught to understand that there's plenty of room at the top."

Bishopson coughed. "The top is so full of elbows you can't see it six inches away. Well, let's have another drink. What? Don't be a fool. Don't think I can't afford another drink. It may be different next

month or next year. Waiter! God damn it, waiter, pay some attention
to your business! Two more whiskey sodas."

Mason had become deeply fond of Donald Bishopson. In character,
in temperament, they differed widely. Bishopson was a conservative,
a traditionalist, a person who despised agitation and disliked change.
Mason had seldom talked ideas with him, and he probably would find
Mason's ideas as vaguely distasteful as Mason might find his. They had
never exchanged views on the indestructibility of the atom, the theory
of surplus value, or Diaghilev. But Mason liked him profoundly. The
A.O.G. business had brought them together and he knew that they
would always be friends. They had been tested on a real jousting
ground of friendship.

"During the war my boss had a big map with glass-headed pins
scattered about, his correspondents. He loved to look at that map
and see an empty space and pull out a man from Lisbon, say, and
stick him up in Riga," Bishopson said with his gritty voice.

He cleared his throat. "Most of those pins disappeared a long time
ago. Just dropped out or got swept away. Drunks, fakers, illiterates.
What hurts me most about this business is that I will be classified
by implication with that rubbish on the floor—a newspaperman who
lost his job. I've never lost a job before. It's a completely new experience. To anyone who doesn't know me, I'm one of those pins that
got plucked out because I was incompetent or a crook. Well, I suppose I might take up some reasonably honest profession, like counter-
feiting or white slavery."

The Bishopsons left Vienna early in the new year, 1932, and the
colony saw them off. The Sandors were particularly upset. Bishopson's position had been impregnable—supposedly. Now nobody was
safe at all.

11

One of the Sunday newspapers sent a correspondent all the way to
Helsingfors and there procured an interview from Treuwalt, the absconding A.O.G. director, who had been arrested by the Finnish
police. Mason slowly made a rough translation:

Since the breakdown of the A.O.G. I am severely being persecuted.
My name is being dragged through the newspapers and my extradition is

demanded without justification. As under a curse, a branded man, I am
harried through foreign countries. . . .

My enemies assert that I was a leader in the ruin of the A.O.C. But
in what manner can such an accusation be orderly and concrete? In the
fact that I owe the A.O.G. some hundred thousand Schillings out of my
current account?

I mostly paid for A.O.G. shares at high rates and then other A.O.G.
directors sold them short.

Mason glanced at news from other parts of the world. In California
the authorities uprooted and tore out of the earth six hundred thousand peach trees, to compensate for overproduction, but even so the
amount of fruit left in the train sidings to rot was enough to feed a
province in China. In Brazil the authorities burned six million bags
of coffee to raise the price. In Chicago twenty-two thousand school-
teachers were forced to borrow money at thirty per cent week by week
to keep alive because there was no cash in the City Hall with which
to pay their salaries. In Budapest a celebrated aristocrat whose immediate progenitors had used old masters for linings of their robes
sold two hundred horses from his racing stud, one of the best known
in Central Europe, for horsemeat.

A sharp letter from Mr. Knowles, the publisher of the Star, startled
Mason the next day. It shocked him that Knowles should be writing
about something on such a level. Everybody must be watching
everything. Knowles had just seen an article on the Polish Corridor
Mason had written for Harper's; he commended him for writing for
such a worthy magazine and said that he had found the article interesting and instructive, but proceeded to say that, in his opinion,
Mason should do no more writing for anything except the Star in the
future, because to do so meant that he was using his energies for out-
lets other than the Star on the Star's time.

Mason blew up. He yelled for Paula. Was everybody going mad?
How could a man like Knowles conceivably take such a ridiculous
position? Had everybody in Chicago lost all sense of proportion?
Mason wanted to reply to Knowles tartly to the effect that he ought
to be delighted that he had a correspondent in Vienna who did not
spend his evenings in drunkenness and debauchery but instead used
his free time for worthwhile activity. Paula dissuaded him from doing

so. In the end Mason sketched out a careful letter saying no more than that he had written the article in the evenings, not on the *Star's* time, and that unless he heard to the contrary he would continue to consider his nights his own. He wrote three drafts before he was satisfied with the tone. He glared at Paula with a distraught expression.

"Right?"

"Right!"

✳

A day later little old Dr. Ritter entered the café pale as ice. He tottered on the doorstep, spoke an incoherent sentence, and fell down. He had fainted. Emil, the junior headwaiter, lifted him up; Mason, making a mess of it, tried to get some brandy into his mouth, while Sandor went to the phone to call a doctor. Dripping and slobbering, Ritter revived. He had never fainted before, he said. The doctor came, and after examining him said in a harsh voice, "Hunger. The man is starving."

"It's an indignity," Miss Birch exclaimed. "People simply *don't* go hungry any more—not people whom you know."

"Don't they?" said Drew gruffly.

"I can't bear it that people I sit with at the coffeetable haven't enough to eat!"

"It's happened before," Drew said. Miss Birch, not telling anybody what she did, sent Dr. Ritter five hundred Schillings the next day.

12

Winter ended, and they coasted down the long slope of spring. There came a nasty little scandal in Graz when it was discovered that the butchers were selling dog meat for food. The political tug-of-war between Social Democrats and Heimwehr became intensified, with the Nazis snarling at both, as economic pressures increased. The country gave up the financial ghost at last, declared a limited "transfer moratorium," and managed to get a new loan from London, since obviously it could only pay what it owed by borrowing more. So the crash of the A.O.G. continued to haunt the steps of everybody.

The political equilibrium within the government coalition failed and, a year to the day after Mason had picked up Strothness's call

about the Customs Union, came a serious cabinet crisis. Mason heard
Sandor's excited voice over the telephone: "A new Chancellor has
been appointed, someone unheard of. His name is Dollfuss."

13

At the Weissenhof the next evening Mason and Paula were introduced
by Tetzel to a Russian named Vladimir Tomm, who had just arrived
from Moscow to represent *Pravda* in Vienna. Mason greeted him and
they began to drink and talk. After an hour Mason asked him where
he had been born in Russia, and he replied, "A town you have never
heard of, Tver." "What do you mean I've never heard of it?" Mason
replied, "It's a stop about three hours out of Moscow on the railway
to Leningrad, the line that hasn't got a single curve or kink in it the
whole way. It's the northern base for river traffic on the Volga. It's
mentioned several times in Dostoevsky and it was, as everybody
knows, a place famous in the lives of Vronsky and Anna Karenina—
if you've ever heard of Tolstoy, Mr. Tomm!"

Tomm looked up at him with curiosity. Here obviously was a person
of some consequence. Tomm was a squarely built man with wide
heavy shoulders. It became clear soon that he worked well with everybody, had a robust sense of humor, was an invaluable source for
Soviet news, knew a good deal about what was going on elsewhere
in Europe, drank well, and never let a colleague down.

This was the period when almost everybody whom the Jarretts
knew, including Tom Cairn, was still starry-eyed about the Soviet
Union. Here was proceeding "the greatest social experiment in history," *und so weiter.* Well, perhaps it was. But Mason was not among
those starry-eyed. He was friendly and sympathetic to much in the
Soviet system and in Soviet foreign policy but he had never become
an addict and never would. He liked very much most of the Russians
he met, but he had never been in the Soviet Union and he wanted to
reserve judgment. He still thought of the prodigious evolution going
on there in terms of a story. What interested him most was who would
win. At that moment he got a glimpse of the answer, seeing the
wretched tipsy Orlovsky in one booth and then observing the rugged,
positive figure of Vladimir Alexandrovitch Tomm.

Mason and Tomm were talking about everything tonight from Litvinov's new policy of the Popular Front to the theory of class war, when Stein came in. He looked happy. This was the first time Mason had seen him in several weeks. Encountering him unloosed in Mason a torrent of thought about Erika. He felt a frantic urge to be in touch with her again, or, at the least, to get news of her. He burned to ask questions, and could barely keep himself from mentioning her name. But this would obviously lead to nothing, because Stein could not talk about Erika in the company of others, particularly Paula.

Mason drummed impatiently on the table, and Tetzel took him aside. Absently Mason asked, "How are things going with you, Karl? You're all right?"

"Tomm, the *Pravda* man, offers me to go to Moscow for six months, all expenses paid."

Bulges formed on Mason's forehead. "To do what?"

"It will be said that I am a student and indeed enrollment in Moscow University is part of the procedure. Nothing whatever is asked of me except that I study conditions and form impressions. It is a kind of scholarship."

"They want to convert you, make you into an agent. That's the catch."

"Of course. But I am not committed to accept their offer, if any."

"Well, if you want my advice, don't go." Mason's experience was that when people asked you for advice they had as a rule already made up their minds.

"There is another thing." Tetzel's voice became a whisper. "I have the craziest thought. If I go to Moscow it may assist me . . . assist me to accomplish that secret objective of mine . . . the objective above all else."

"What's that?" It was difficult for him to pay attention. He was watching Stein and thinking about Erika.

"I cannot get over Mia. Always surrounding me is a cloud of angriness and hate. I have never told you explicitly, but you must have guessed. Some day I will kill him. Then will come relaxation and relief."

"Kill who?"

"Thorne."

"Nonsense, Karl. Journalists don't go around killing each other these days."

"Even so—"

"As to the Moscow angle, it's a lot of *Kitsch*. For one thing the Communists wouldn't accept you for anything in that realm for years and years. You'd have to be trained. For another . . ." Mason paused. "Listen, Karl. You told me not so long ago that you had killed Mia. Surely you don't want to compound that murder with another."

Tetzel looked glum.

"Drop the whole idea," Mason said urgently. "Turn Tomm down."

Tetzel strolled over to the chess table, where Tomm and Stein were playing. Shipwright and Paula were talking at the *Stammtisch*. Her head was cocked up toward him, amused, guarded. Mason saw that he was not observed and, swiftly, unobtrusively, with his heart beginning to plunge violently, he slipped toward the telephone. He could not help himself. He felt sucked under. He felt completely disintegrated. He did not know what kind of catastrophe he might let loose, or care. Nothing mattered now, not even his marriage. He could not contain himself or suppress his uncontrollable desire to see Erika once more.

Trembling he dialed her number. A servant's voice answered.

"May I speak to Miss Falk, please?"

"Miss Falk left last night for Prague."

XII. MARAUDERS FROM
THE NORTH

Mason and Sandor were delighted to get out of the city even for a day or two, because the atmosphere of Vienna had become unpleasantly oppressive. They breathed in the fresh country air like a luxury, trying to forget the pall of fear that had descended on the city. There had been food shortages and the threat of riots.

The two journalists found their way to the grave in the village cemetery out in the lonely, primitive Waldviertel country near Linz. Mason copied down carefully the inscription on the tombstone:

HIER RUHET IN GOTT HERR
ALOIS HITLER
K.K. Zollamts Oberoffizial I.P.
und Hausbesitzer
Gest. 3. Januar 1903, in 65 Lebensjahre
Dessen Gattin Frau
KLARA HITLER
Gest. 21. Dez. 1907 i. 47 Lebj.
R.I.P.

So this was the tomb of Hitler's father. In the Austrian manner a small photograph of the dead man was attached to the stone. Mason observed the skull big and hairless like a melon, a pair of bicycle-handle mustaches, and cruel, wicked little eyes. Mason and Sandor stood there in the cemetery because everything about Hitler was

a story now. Day by day Nazi strength, Nazi obstreperousness, grew
in Austria. As Mason—or had it been John Dixon?—had predicted
more than a year before, the Nazis had indeed become a third
force. They now claimed twenty per cent of the electorate and noisily
day by day badgered the new Dollfuss government for an election.
The political situation had become irremediably changed.

Mason had had an idea which he broached to Sandor. Why not,
while it was still possible, take an expedition to the countryside that
had produced Hitler, who had, of course, been born in Austria, not
Germany, and interview his surviving relatives, if any. Sandor found
out where the Hitler family had lived for several generations and
calculated that there must be at least half a dozen relatives and others
still alive who had known the *Führer* as a child. So Mason and Sandor
traveled to this remote village in the Waldviertel. They burrowed
deep in the archives, examined old birth certificates, visited the house
—now a village pub—where Hitler had been born, and talked to his
godfather, one of his teachers, an aunt, a cousin, and even the mid-
wife who had hauled his infant body from his mother's womb.

This worthy lady had completely forgotten him.

Hitler's blood relatives were a miserable lot, as Mason promptly
wrote, humble, backward, and heavily inbred, and their wretched
hovels seemed to be separated by a million miles from the smartness
of the Brown House in Munich, which was, as a matter of fact, only
a short distance away. Hitler had never once returned to the Waldviertel since leaving it as a youth and he seemed to be totally
unaware of the existence of his poverty-smitten kin.

"All this proves what?" Mason said to Sandor when they returned
to Vienna on the night express.

"I tell you the truth on it—nothing. But we will be able to say
when comes the *Anschluss* that we have visited Hitler's home circle
and that when the beautiful Adolf returns he will be joining his own
kind—vulgar, ignorant, and miserably poor illiterates, the lowest kind
of peasant!"

His ruddy owlish face gleamed.

Mason asked, with what Paula called his divine primitiveness,
"You *really* think Hitler will come to power and make an *Anschluss?*"

"Certain as earth becoming mud after rain."

*

Mason, defying all convention, invited the Herr Bundeskanzler Dr. Engelbert Dollfuss to an Anglo-American lunch. To everybody's astonishment, the new Chancellor accepted. No Austrian Chancellor had ever met with journalists in this way before. Not only did he accept; he came unescorted by any officials except an interpreter from his own secretariat, and talked with exceptional candor. With his peasant's chunkiness, his broad rough accent, his quality of modest appeal, he did not resemble in the remotest degree any Chancellor in the whole of Austria's past. Obviously he took his responsibilities seriously, and by the time lunch broke up at four in the afternoon he looked mortally tired and his voice had become hoarse. Minute by minute he had given everything he had—and he swore to Mason and the others, summing up, that he would resist Nazi occupation of Austria with his life.

"Paula," declared Mason when he returned home, "the little guy has guts. That's a damned unusual thing in this country. He's going to make a fight and I honestly think he's going to keep the Nazis out."

None of the wiseacres, the cynics, the men in the know, took Dollfuss seriously when he assumed office. He was a stopgap Chancellor, nothing more. Now, a few months later, his wary toughness, his friendly common touch, his cleverness, above all the way he got things done—even in Austria!—vastly augmented his reputation. What really made him popular was, however, something else—his size. He was not a dwarf, since all his features were well formed, but he could not be more than four foot eight or nine. His smallness in stature became an irresistible subject for Viennese humor, and the jokes popped like firecrackers. A plot against him was discovered by the police just in time—a mousetrap had been placed outside his door. Portraits of him were to go on the postage stamps—life-size. He fell off a ladder and broke his leg—picking a dandelion.

But seen as a whole the situation was certainly not a laughing matter. What was significant, as Mason wrote, was not merely the swiftness of the steep rise of the Nazis but the fact that they were willing to use violence to attain their end—that is, reach power. Speeches by effete Heimwehr aristocrats were one thing, but Nazi bombs were quite another. For the Nazis had now begun to toss bombs. Trains, churchyards, dams, government headquarters in provincial towns, were attacked. Most of these Nazi bombs were homemade, virtually harmless. They were not designed to kill, but to make a nuisance, disorganize authority, lower confidence in the government. Even so, bloodshed occurred, and there was no telling what further trouble might be imminent.

Mason's stories on Hitler's birthplace, after being printed in America, were picked up by one of the more sensational Vienna newspapers; Nazi sympathizers considered it an outrage that Hitler's past should be probed, and he and Sandor became marked men.

2

Some six weeks later, after Mason finished his work for the day, he and Paula took a moment's respite from the prevailing atmosphere of panicky gloom and pressed their way into the small gallery near the Kohlmarkt where Erika had once taken him to see the Schiele pictures. Today her friend Stefan was having his first show. Mason looked around, and, tall enough to see over the heads of most of the crowd, he had a glimpse of Erika with Stein at her side at the far end of the room. He hesitated nervously and then advanced with his hand warmly under Paula's arm and wondered if his voice was casual enough. "You remember Miss Falk, don't you, Paula? You met at the *Heurige* party. Erika, my wife."

Erika smiled brightly, and Paula was matter-of-fact and cordial. He sought to be matter-of-fact as well.

A few nights before, the Jarretts had come home late from a movie to find a message from Frau Gertrude—Miss Falk had telephoned Mrs. Jarrett. Mason's pulse rippled. "Who's Miss Falk? I don't think I know anybody named Miss Falk," Paula said. Mason looked vague, saying, "Oh, she's a girl I saw a couple of times when you were in America. I think she's tied up with Ricardo Stein." "Yes, such a pretty girl—I remember," Paula said. "The message must be for you." But Frau Gertrude's handwriting distinctly said "Frau" Jarrett, and Paula telephoned her the next day, while Mason did his best to dissemble his curiosity. Erika was asking them to a party she was giving in honor of an exhibition of sculpture by Stefan

Ramiçek. "Shall we go?" Paula asked dubiously. "Oh, might as well—
we ought to be in touch with more young artists," Mason said. So
here they were.

Mason looked cursorily at examples of Stefan's work and then
found Stefan himself, while Paula, he noticed with some apprehension, still talked to Erika—how lovely they looked together. Stefan
greeted Mason with a grinning scowl.

"You are the ruin of a good artist."

"Who? Erika? What do you mean?"

"Not Erika—me!" Stefan jabbed himself in the chest. "You
introduce her to a species of lawyer-journalist, *Dreck*, and now she
will be lost to us, and how will I be able to find myself supported?"

"She'll keep on supporting you. Stein is rich."

"Yes, there is some use to him at least." He went on: "Do not tell
me that you will not miss her too."

Mason and Stefan had seldom been confidential about Erika
before. "I never see her any more," Mason said.

"What for sadness," Stefan said.

But now Stefan was surveying Paula with admiration. "I can
begin to understand now a little why Erika has mortal fear of her,
also respect. I congratulate you on getting everything so nicely confused."

Still nervous, Mason moved over to inspect carefully Stefan's
portrait of Erika, which was commanding much attention. He observed again the modeling of the level brows, the line of her funny,
enchanting nose, her rich mouth, and the long smoothly swelling
throat. He wanted to touch it. The marble might even be warm, he
thought. He could not tear himself away from it. After a moment
he walked toward Stein, who, greeting friends, seemed to be in-
toxicated with pride and pleasure in Stefan's success because it was
Erika's success as well.

Six or eight guests piled into a pair of taxis and drove to Erika's
studio when the reception was over. Mason wondered if Paula could
possibly sense that he had been in the studio before. The room was
big enough to make it easy for half a dozen couples to have private
talk together. Paula was obviously becoming much interested in
Erika, and Stein came up with the words "Erika, *Häschen*, will you

not show Mrs. Jarrett some of your own work, your decorations and scarves?" Erika demurred. Paula insisted. Erika presented her things in the pleasantest way imaginable. She conveyed an air of gravity, modesty, and then smiled brilliantly, eager like a child but still deprecatory, "Do you really like them . . . ?" She bowed her head a little, as if pleasure at the compliments she was receiving embarrassed her.

Paula encountered an old acquaintance, the artist Hofmeyer, and joined him. Mason, watching himself, advanced toward Erika. He was eager to speak to her, but not in the way he wanted to speak to her that night in the café. That kind of spasm was finished with.

"When did you come back? Have you got your divorce? Are you going to marry Stein?"

"You ask many questions. I am now divorced but I do not know whether I will marry Ricardo or not. Now I am so fond of him I think that perhaps I should not marry him."

"Why not?"

"You may remember what I said the last time I talked about this . . . how if I married him it would serve to keep me in your circle." She looked at him clearly, and did not flush. "But now all that is changed. I cannot marry him for any such reason. He is too good, too nice. Other elements now enter into the question. He should deserve a wife who helps him in his career, helps with his work, his career. He is so correct and proper and I do not feel stable enough, I who never think a moment ahead. I am too disordered, too disturbed."

"About what?"

Erika looked up at him, becoming guarded and elliptical. She went on soberly: "He ought to marry some nice, well-educated girl from a good home in Grinzing, whose father is a doctor and who likes to read newspapers and will care for him always, being a good hostess as well as wife."

"But he's wildly in love with you—"

They were interrupted, because Stefan, preparing to serve the Würstels and little cakes from Demel's, needed help. Mason saw that Paula was glancing at him from across the room. Erika said, "I think perhaps Paula may have an impression about us. Please, I will help Stefan now."

Mason, refusing to leave her abruptly, beckoned to Paula, who joined them. This was taking the bit in the teeth, he thought. "How I envy you your way of life!" Paula sighed to Erika, pointing to the stepladders spotted with paint, the tables with their drawing boards, the heavy pedestals holding moist sculpture shrouded in cloth, all the paraphernalia of a working artist, and giving voice to her admiration of the pleasant slap-dash sense the studio gave of not being ruled by the clock. Erika laughed, "I'll trade you." The words slipped out; she blushed. Paula was astonished, then took it as no more than the merest irrelevant slip of the tongue. "How long have you been married, Mrs. Jarrett?" Erika asked her.

"Oh, forever."

"Forever is only one moment, isn't it, when two people are in love?" The two young women surveyed one another.

"Oh! Why aren't I doing any work?" Paula grumbled bitterly to Mason as they drove home. "I admit it's a good-sized job taking care of you, Mason Jarrett, but it seems an awful waste to do nothing else all my life."

"What?" Mason said. "Getting restless again, sweet? Don't I satisfy you?"

"You don't take me seriously. That strange lovely girl making those exquisite scarves and things. She's one of the nicest girls anybody ever met, isn't she? All I ever do is to tell Frau Gertrude what to cook and do the shopping and take walks and think about your work. It's unnatural. I need a life in my own right. I can't continue just to be a reflection of you. I have to be myself—whatever that may be. I need a job, please find me a job."

"A lot more people need jobs a lot more than you do, pet."

✳

Mason dropped in to see Stefan's exhibition again before it closed. He did not take Paula with him. Stefan was there but not Erika. Mason prowled around and paused a long time before the bust of Erika, gazing at it. He admired it intensely. He put his hand on the cheek and patted it with a queer warm affectionate gesture.

Stefan watched him. He was not sure what Mason's gesture meant. It might mean continuing proprietariness, but it could also be a gesture of farewell.

3

Paula and Mason learned soon enough that Valerie Birch and James N. Drew had resumed their relationship in spite of the interchange of letters with the Countess. The Countess did not answer Miss Birch's letter and presently Jim was seeing Valerie as much as before. The remarkable improvement in his appearance, attitude, and manners continued. He was a new man. Miss Birch met him at the coffeehouse every afternoon at about four and sat with him till six; then in the evening she frequently returned to join him, staying until he finished work. Toward midnight he would see her into a taxi, say good night, and return—presumably—to his habitation with the Countess. No one precisely knew.

The Countess, in dignity and dudgeon, retired; she secluded herself until—as she anticipated—Miss Birch got tired of Drew, or he got tired of her. She and Miss Birch had never met. She never lost her supreme confidence in her power to dominate James N. Drew. Drew never mentioned her to anybody, even Erji Sandor. He behaved as if the Countess von Zwehl had ceased altogether to exist.

Miss Birch came to the Jarretts' for another lunch. They did not ask her about Drew, but, as if totally possessed by him, she began to describe compulsively her emotion about him and her efforts to re-claim him. Mason wondered how, how, she could possibly have fallen in love with Drew. He decided that she probably thought of him as a convenient problem child partly of her own creation, so she could transfer her own conflicts to another; then he concluded that, in spite of her analysis, she still lived in a totally unreal world, and had no sense of the realities of life—including Drew—at all.

"But you have no idea what he has gone through." Miss Birch protested, her eyes shining. "I could tell you story after story. His father was a Methodist preacher, as you probably know, with a parish in Tennessee; he kept asking for a transfer to a new post, partly be-cause his wife, Jim's mother, an invalid, couldn't stand the wetness and the dank mountain air. He must have been a very weak man.

After much delay and false hope the word finally came that the request for a transfer was refused. Drew's father read the letter and put it in his pocket, saying nothing. He summoned Jim's mother and then handed Jim the letter, ordering him to read it aloud to her, breaking the news. Jim had no idea what it contained. He read out the news that the transfer had been refused and his mother toppled over on the spot and died. He's never gotten over it."

Altogether an impossible story, Mason decided. What bill of goods was Drew trying to sell Miss Birch?

Now her headaches were under control again, and her faith in Dr. Voelker remained constant. What a lot this analysis had taught her! She knew so much more about the secret motivations that move human beings; she understood the multifarious little stresses that mysteriously determine conduct in big affairs. She was watchful for the manner in which people compensated for inferiority (the way Jim boasted sometimes!); she was aware of the double-edged nature of most emotions; she knew how twisted fragments of childhood memory could lie buried in the mind, concealed, forgotten, to germinate in seemingly irrational behavior years later. This knowledge gave Miss Birch great satisfaction. "I know why So-and-so is timid of policemen and why So-and-so apologizes too much and why So-and-so is too self-consciously vain about her children. No one knows that I know these things. But I know them, and this helps me to be adjusted and mature."

Paula asked her about Doctor Voelker's technique of dream interpretation. She described a dream she had had some nights before. Strolling through a meadow, she passed a large barn with a sloping red roof. A group of large initials, or monograms, appeared then on the sloping roof, but in the form of skywriting. There was a struggle in this dream, a division of personality, Dr. Voelker said. It was a paradox dream. Skywriting belongs to the sky. But instead it appeared on a roof. What had brought Miss Birch's aspirations, her cloud thoughts, to the ground? Why was something being drawn in the sky? Draw—Drew! The association of names was obvious. And a roof connoted shelter. A roof was the first thing that two people who wanted to be united thought of having. The terrain of the dream shifted, and Miss Birch found herself in, of all places, Bessarabia—

contested territory! Dr. Voelker laughed. The logic of dreams was unassailable. She wanted shelter with Drew, but the terrain was occupied.

*

That evening at the café Drew ripped open a telegram and shook his head slowly, growling, grunting, as if the ultimate in the ridiculous had come. The telegram asked him for a situationer about Austro-German relations in—seventy-five words!

"It's no use." He half laughed. "Everybody has gone crazy—my agency crazier than most, I guess. To describe that Nazi situation in seventy-five words, to save them their precious pennies—what do they think a man is."

"It's not your fault if all the newspapers have gone mad. Let's work it out together and make it a good dispatch," Miss Birch said comfortingly.

"It's ridiculous. I want to do good work!"

"I think you take your responsibility to the I.P. almost too seriously. The thing to do is to forget when they're silly and do what they ask you to do as well as you can."

Drew wrote a story concentrating the recent material on Nazi outrages into the briefest possible space and then shaved it, whittled it, and regrouped the words until he had cut them to eighty-one. Miss Birch helped and they took out six more.

He squeezed her hand across the table and Valerie felt inordinately proud and happy that she was being helpful to him, of use to him, in the disordered fragmentation of their world, when it was given to so few people to be useful.

A few minutes later the Countess sailed in. There had been no warning. The *Stammtisch* was crowded. Valerie, her back to the door, knew that something untoward impended because Drew, facing her, rose, startled. Miss Birch gasped as the Countess bore down on her. Tall, stooped, her face the color of chalk, with the tendons in her throat rigid, she continued to advance, reached the table, made an abrupt bow, and sat down, out of breath, stertorous, tottering. Miss Birch could not keep her eyes from that terrible white face with the pale empty eyes. The Countess gave out an impression of demoniac will, fury, and resolution. Drew said sharply, "Emilie, you should not have gotten out of bed." She glanced at him with blasting contempt and sought to control herself. Miss Birch tried to utter a greeting; her lips were dry, and she held on to the table with her taut, tiny hands. The Countess leaned back without a word to anybody, closing her eyes. Her lids, sharply visible, were greenish purple. A boy came in with the ten o'clock news bulletins. Drew fingered through them. "Oh—oh," his voice seemed to come from a remote distance, "cabinet crisis again in Rumania."

In the next booth Miss Birch heard Sandor chatting with the Jarretts, as if they were far, far away. Shipwright was playing chess with Tetzel.

Still the Countess said not a word. Then she took one of Miss Birch's delicate veined hands in her two gloved hands, pressed it hard, and looked harshly, intently, into her face. Valerie felt that the scene was intolerably vulgar and melodramatic. She could scarcely believe her ears at the Countess' first words, uttered in a slow, savage hiss: "Millionairess—vixen!" The Countess continued to hold her hand tightly as if to imprison her while she said what she had come to say. "I care nothing for Drew! You can haf him to yourself and good riddance!" Drew rose as if to take the Countess away. Brazen, decrepit, heroic, she resisted him. "But I care greatly for my security. Who are you who have taken from me my security?" The Countess relaxed her grasp. Oh, this was too horrible, too undignified. How could Jim ever have exposed her to the infamy of this situation? The poor woman— demented! But Drew must be demented too. "You may buy Drew from me. You may make proffision for my security!" Oh, no, no . . . Miss Birch lifted herself out of her chair looking like a bewildered small animal, covering her eyes with her hands, and Paula rose to shield her. Drew muttered something that nobody could hear, looked helpless, then summoned what resources remained to him, and led the Countess forcibly to the door.

4

By acclamation Mason had been re-elected president of the Anglo-American, and now, in October, 1932, he was well into his second year of office. His devotion to this organization was still prodigious. Hardly a week went by but that he did not conduct laborious negotia-

tions by long-distance telephone to invite some celebrity en route to
Vienna for an appearance at lunch. As a result, the organization had
more than fulfilled its original intentions. No one, Mason remembered, had ever even dreamed that this type of newsy off-the-record
meeting could possibly be successful in Vienna, but the catalogue of
guests now included practically every distinguished personage in the
city to say nothing of the parade of visitors.

Today, undeniably, the atmosphere was lively. Self-satisfaction, not
unmixed with irony, could be seen on several faces. Mason kept people
moving, welcoming colleagues and making small talk. His own guest
was Yancey from the British Legation. Shipwright walked in, a
couple of drinks under his belt, and stood with Wheatley at one
corner of the bar. Drew came; Stein came; and Bishopson was sorely
missed.

"Who's that old chap with the gravy spots on his coat lapel?"
Yancey asked Mason. It was Dr. Heinrich Ritter. "Ah, one of your
criminal associates."

The guest of honor and speaker today, who would be severely
questioned, was strictly eligible to attend a luncheon of the Anglo-
American Press Association. He was a very busy and important
person, but when his secretaries, somewhat doubtful, submitted the
invitation to his attention he looked sharply over his half-moon
glasses and accepted with alacrity. He was none other than Dr. Sven
Jacobmuth, the Danish financial expert, who had been prevailed upon
by the foreign creditors and the Finance Ministry of the Austrian
government to be the new Director-General of the A.O.G. Dr.
Jacobmuth's salary was three hundred dollars per day, gold, a five-year
tenure of office guaranteed. He had demanded this large sum in view
of possible future damage to his reputation, in case he failed in the
almost impossible job of putting the bank back on its feet.

Sandor beamed ironically. "He should be grateful to us, that Dane.
After it all, if it were not for us, he would not be here!"

Dr. Jacobmuth spoke well. He was asked about the bribery case
and replied blandly that he had never known a bank that paid such
close attention to all the appurtenances of publicity as the A.O.G.
Laughter.

Mason left the Majestic in company with Vilmos Hestery, who

had perforce lost his job when Bishopson lost his but who had recently had a miraculous stroke of luck. The Dutch commercial attaché
offered Hestery part-time work, and he grabbed it. The work was dull
and ill-paid, but it meant that he and his wife had a living. But the
fact that Hestery had found a new job served to intensify everybody
else's sense of precariousness; his good luck made his colleagues wary
and even jealous. The next time somebody lost a job there might not
be this comparatively quick relief waiting around the corner. It was
every man for himself when they were all in the street together.
Hestery himself had never betrayed the slightest sign of nerves. Now,
gossiping as they crossed the Ring, he told Mason about a recent
emergency operation for appendicitis undergone by his nine-year-old
son. "The pain came to the boy soon after midnight. There was no
time to waste and the only doctor I could think of was one that
sometimes served the Bishopsons. This doctor said on the phone
that I must at once call Herr Professor Bruckner, the best child's
surgeon in Vienna. Bruckner operated at about six that morning and
the boy came through perfectly well. Entirely a routine procedure,
Bruckner said. Today has come Bruckner's bill. It is one-tenth of
my annual salary." Hestery shrugged, grimaced, and, apparently giving
the matter no further thought, waved good-bye to Mason. No re-
crimination; no request for help; no plea for sympathy. Mason
thought of some of the old jokes about Hungarians. Only a Hungarian
can follow you into a revolving door and get out first. He watched
the huge figure of Hestery, who must weigh three hundred pounds,
exhaling vigor and cheer, disappear down the street. Well, Mason
reflected, when God makes a good Hungarian they're certainly the
best.

✻

Panic. Mason could feel it in the air. Panic—he could hear its
whisper; its cold breath was in his ear. Panic hid behind the wall, cold,
hot, dancing, with flames rising out of ice, waiting to spring. Erji
Sandor, who was sometimes so beautiful, came to the café pale and
haggard, Putzi clinging to her arm. She was frightened. She still
could not get over it that Bishopson, of all people, had lost his job.
Drew became more standoffish, rude, and pompous; Wheatley became more silent, more recessed. Shipwright, whose spendthrift

habits were notorious, said, "I am never going to the Koenigen again
—it's time to save our pennies, lads." Even the waiters felt the
fear, the pressure. Emil, who had elevated Mason to the nobility
some months before, calling him Herr von Jarrett, was curt and even
rude, addressing him now merely as "Herr." The time for gracious
niceties had passed.

More and more Mason's work, like that of his colleagues, had to do
with the crisis. There seemed to be no news except stories about
poverty, disintegration, and collapse. Mason wrote of unemployment,
export deficits, frozen credits, and more shattered banks. The crisis
jabbed at them from every front. Down in Klagenfurt, horses began
to replace trucks: no gasoline. A heavy snowfall came to the Tyrol
ahead of season: no transport, and all the schools had to be shut down.

Life along the Danube, as Mason wrote, took on an unusual atmosphere of torpidity. Instead of struggling against this blight, the bulk of
the people grumbled, pulled in their belts, wondered why God had
deserted them, lost energy, and waited, apathetic, dormant, for the
storm to pass. As they got hungrier they became less active. They
hibernated, burrowing deeper into the drift of their own misery.
But those inflammatory by reason of their position became more
inflammatory. Crackpots in the Heimwehr became more vociferous,
and Nazi agitators became bolder. They hurled their bombs at railway stations, power plants, and important government headquarters.
One thing that worried Mason particularly was that the wearying old
struggle between Christian Socials and Social Democrats had taken
on a new bitterness. Prince Starhemberg, the Heimwehr leader, with
his taut, spoiled, handsome face, he who owned castles all over Austria
and traced his ancestry back seven hundred years, and who had been
a playboy of conspicuous dimension, made violent speeches, using
phrases like "We must tear the poison teeth out of the mouth of the
red beast!"

And did Conyers and I really start all this? Mason asked himself,
agonized. No, no!

*

Mason felt that he was changing. He knew that the case might well
be made that people never change—the end is always the beginning,

the beginning is the end—but this was true only within limits. After all there was such a thing as learning from experience. Experience could not be real unless a person had a capacity to learn from it. Most people picked up the taste, the sniff, the color, the texture, of their time and what they lived through.

He was less given to constraint now, less abstracted. He did not play with words so much; he had to make words work. But he still had a way with them. During a conversational melee at the Weissenhof somebody asked him what he thought the most difficult job in the world was and he replied, "Haul a piano with dental floss." Paula too was changing, Mason thought. The perpetual air of crisis and impending disaster hanging over them sharpened some people and gave them a sense of challenge, but it made others softer, more aware of the infinite complexities of life, more tolerant. Paula had become less contentious, less critical, more malleable.

Mason was still the most generous of colleagues, but he played his cards closer to his chest these days. There was desperation in the air —every-man-for-himself-ism.

Cairn blew into town. Mason hadn't seen him since the trip to Prinkipo. He came to lunch. He seemed to be at once reckless, gay, and troubled. He had been in Madrid, where he had interviewed various leaders of the new government, all of whom he called by their first names. These men were pure, they were noble, they were intellectuals—praise heaven they would last. But what seemed to have interested him most was something he had seen at an important European embassy in Madrid. The Ambassador, well known for his eccentricities, a dilettante, a friend of Proust's, a litterateur, a personage of the most exquisite refinement and cultivation, had become something of an object of scandal to the Madrileños because of his mother. Tom had heard the story but hadn't quite believed it. There she was. In the central hall of the great embassy stood a large jar of alcohol clouded with ferns, in which reposed placidly the body of the Ambassador's mother, pickled.

"Was she dead or alive when he put her in?" asked Mason.

Cairn threw a napkin at him.

He reminisced about Turkey. His voyage from Istanbul to Athens had been one long poker game, he recounted.

"Did you see Kitty in Athens?" Paula asked.

"Kitty who?"

"A pretty girl named Jameson, an archeologist. I gave you a note to her," Mason said.

"No, I forgot. Eleutherios kept me far too busy."

"Well, you missed something."

Cairn brooded. He hated to miss anything.

Mason said, "Will you take Paula out to dinner tonight? I've got a mailer I have to do."

Why was he being tempted to give way to such an inexplicable caprice—to throw Cairn and Paula together, to give them every opportunity to be alone? Cairn was silent, and Paula looked surprised. What, ever so faintly, had taken fugitive possession of him? Surely it could not be possible that he *wanted* Paula to be closer to Cairn than she already was. Could it be possible that he subconsciously wanted her to have an affair with Tom so that he, Mason, could salve his own bad conscience about Erika; or was it something more complicated, having to do with their triune relationship?

Cairn had to go to Moscow next. "Now that I have inspected a Jeffersonian revolution I must refresh myself by observing again the real thing. Spain will go under, but Russia won't. I shall have to have a long, truly *serious* talk with Josef Vissarionovitch. I do not think his information about the external world is all that it ought to be."

"Will Josef Vissarionovitch see you?" Mason's voice was slightly mocking.

"Of course. How could he not? I command the forces of the universe, though not, alas, myself."

He took Paula to Schöner's, and Mason worked. All the bureau heads on the *Star* had been asked by Hilliard to do an article for a roundup series on the foreign policy of their countries. Mason's lead was easy: "The foreign policy of Austria is that of the nut in a nutcracker." Cairn and Paula came back early. Both seemed subdued. Paula brushed nervously at her hair. Cairn put some *Lieder* on the gramophone and made himself coffee in the kitchen, behaving exactly as if the villa were his own. But his ego seemed to be blunted, dented, scratched; and his ego, which was a private ego, not a public ego like Drew's, was what he depended on for everything.

Cairn took them to lunch the next day; he was still depressed. He frowned. "I don't like the way things are going—I'm actually frightened."

"Of what?"

"Of the impending death of our society."

They put him on the train.

❋

Mason and Paula went that night to a big, flowery reception at the Turks'. Paula wore a dress the color of blueberries crushed in cream.

"Mason," she said in the taxi.

"What?"

"Nothing. I just wanted to hear your name aloud."

Dr. Dollfuss was guest of honor at this reception, and Paula was glad to meet him. Ordinarily she did not care about meeting important people, because they made her shy, she felt that she had nothing to contribute to them, and she did not think that it was good manners to be curious about them. But the ubiquitous little Chancellor fascinated her. He had become very social. A peasant at bottom, he wanted to know his way about. Not since the war had any Chancellor been seen at so many parties. Invariably he was agreeable, fresh, and almost naïvely impressionable. He remembered Mason perfectly and advanced to him cordially, mentioning what a good time he had had at the Anglo-American lunch. Soon other guests clamored for his attention, but he held the Jarretts alone for a long moment, chatting, until the protocol officer came up in a formal, agitated manner to say that the Cardinal Archbishop had arrived. Dollfuss, sighing, muttered something about the intersection of the sacred life with the profane and, one of his hands on Mason's shoulder and the other on Paula's arm, asked them if they would come to lunch at the Chancellery some day next week.

"You made a hit," Mason said.

"No, no, he's just interested in you. The American press counts. I was an ornament."

"What did you think of him?"

"I liked the way he looks at people, like an innocent schoolboy. He's cunning, nimble, and about as theoretical as a flea."

Back at the villa, they saw that a large parcel, wrapped carelessly, stood in the hall. Mason lifted it, and made a comedy gesture as if his back was strained; indeed it was very heavy. Curious, he tore the brown paper off. No wonder the object within was heavy. It was a bronze casting of Stefan's bust of Erika.

"But did you buy this, Mason darling?" Paula surveyed the bust carefully, then watched Mason's face. His eyes seemed to be transforming it from metal to life.

"No. But I dropped into that gallery the other day and had a word with Stefan there. He must have sent it as a present."

Paula gave him a puzzled, enigmatic look.

5

She fell into a peculiar kind of tense, light, uneasy sleep—as if she had swallowed a sleeping pill that hadn't taken full effect. It could have been the beating of her own heart that wakened her. She waited till the beat was normal, and then woke Mason.

"Did you ever make love to Erika?"

Mason struggled to wake up. He pawed his face, confused. "No."

Paula said, dreamily, "What's true is good. Tell me the truth."

Mason said, "Yes."

Neither stirred, and the longest moment in his life passed.

Paula asked, "Was she very sweet?"

"Well, yes—I suppose so—I—"

"Were you in love with her?"

It did not escape him that she used the past tense. "No," he lied.

"Why were you in love with her?"

A flash shot through Mason's mind. *If you were really in love, you never knew why.* Mystery was part of the cement.

She sat up; so did he; she turned the light on and said, fumbling, "But, Mason, this is very *serious*—isn't it?" Strangely enough, she was blushing. "You must tell me more. Aren't we supposed to fight, have a scene, shouldn't I threaten to leave you, how do we face the fact that something terrible has happened?"

"It doesn't need to be terrible, necessarily. It's all over." She stared at him intently. His face had changed. There were lines in it she had never seen before. He no longer looked like a young man.

Inwardly, though, he was gasping with relief. The period of double life was over. He was no longer a hypocrite, a cheat, a liar.

On opposite sides of the bed, they continued to face one another. Her eyes were large with hurt, his with fear. Her head was up, his low.

Paula said, "It's rather breath-taking. . . . I feel aswirl. . . ." She looked dazed. "You must tell me all about it—everything."

She was torn open. She thought back suddenly to a time when she was sixteen and had a mad crush on a boy in Cambridge. He came to call for her one evening and she had been so frightened, so incoherently moved, so excited, that she had fainted in the bathroom. And there had been that terrible scene that day with her mother years ago. Something at school—what was it?—made her ask, "Mother, do you think that mere physical infidelity should be reason enough for a divorce?" Her mother, who was getting toward the end of her third marriage then, took unaccountable affront at this question, became confused, said "Fidelity is worthless unless it's involuntary!" and slapped her hard across the face. Never before had Paula been slapped by anyone. She gasped, rushed out of the house, calmly appropriated her stepfather's car, and drove to Kitty's, where she spent the night.

Now . . . Vienna . . . she reflected on men she had resisted. There had been that absurd creature, what was his name, Dichter, whom they had met at the Dozent's. And then Hofmeyer, the artist, who had telephoned her at least twenty times in the past few months; then Willi the Archduke, dear Willi, who in his own particular way really cared for her, really wanted her, and whom she could have by waving a finger; and Tom Cairn, gnawing and picking at her for hour after hour those wild nights in New York; and the supercilious, sensitive young officer on the German boat who threatened to jump overboard if she wouldn't go to bed with him, and almost did; then a man as decent and personable as Conyers, who had asked her to leave Mason and marry him on the last evening they had had in Vienna; soon, too, there could be others, there would be others.

Paula repeated, "She was lovely, wasn't she?"

Mason wanted a glass of water. He passed the tip of his tongue forward against dry lips. Again he nodded.

But whether or not Erika had been lovely was hardly the point. Her husband had betrayed her, slept with another woman. Now the shock she felt became liberated and reached the surface. She became furious as well as hurt. She berated him.

"Now, listen—" he stumbled. "I suppose it's impossible to understand, but there were special circumstances involved. Let me explain—"

"When did all this happen?"

"While you were away in America." Carefully, so as to save her feelings, he did not tell everything.

So *this* was what had been going on when she was away, Paula said to herself. *This* was what had upset him so much all that summer when she returned.

"And you've lived with this . . . this secret . . . ever since? Living an intolerable lie? All this time?"

"Yes."

"And it's really over now?"

"Yes, she's going to marry Stein."

As he talked Paula's emotion took on a different tincture. She felt a love for him of extraordinary depth, breadth, and intensity. Nothing could make her give up Mason; nothing could be permitted to happen that would take him away. She would not banish him. But should she offer to release him? No. Love was never just the present; it was what happened last year and the year before that and what would happen in years to come. She faltered. It was her love that made her forgive him. At last she decided what to say, and her voice became clear. "I don't think you and . . . Erika should do it again . . . do you? That wouldn't be quite fair. It would diminish so much my value to myself. . . . Please!"

Mason said calmly, "It won't happen again."

"You promise?"

"I promise." His voice was low.

She passed a hand over her eyes. How could I have not *known*, she asked herself. How could I have been so complacent, so blind and stupid? I'm supposed to be intelligent, a realist—yet obviously I know nothing, nothing. I know nothing at all about Mason, nothing at all about life. By an extreme effort of will, she sought to adjust herself to this new situation. She recalled vividly an occasion when she had said, "To be superior means not to compete." To hell with that kind of nonsense. If Erika could give Mason something he obviously yearned for, loved, needed, it should not be beyond her powers to do the same. But she felt utterly destroyed. She leaned close to Mason, and touched him for the first time since she awoke. She must overcome her weakness. But she felt completely weak. Her fingers contracted and her nails bit into her palms. Then she found herself intolerably sad; she touched him and her touch acquired the gentleness that comes from despair. When he grasped her she became violently aroused, open, to a degree unique in her experience, and all the power of her mind was unloosed as well.

His chin lodged against her cheek; he kissed her. They made love with passion and then lay together a long time, united, cemented, by the sticky moisture of his seed.

6

"Johnny Dixon asked me to call you." The voice had a slightly Bronxish tone. This was the next day. Mason knew at once that the man on the phone could not possibly know John Dixon well, since no one who did ever called him Johnny. Dixon was one of those Johns perpetually condemned to be just John—not even a Jack. "I'm an agent—Broadway, movies, anything you like. Even my own studio on Long Gisland." Mason became alert. The voice went on as if it had all the time imaginable. "Dixon's got a lot of talent, rewrote that play in my office and I suppose you know it did well—not any smash hit, but a hundred fourteen performances on Broadway, not bad. Next one will do better. They've got me going to the Reinhardt theater tonight." Who "they" were Mason had no idea. "Then, over the weekend, Leopoldskron and the real works." Mason had never been asked to Leopoldskron, the Reinhardt castle in Salzkammergut, where only the most successful of Viennese show-business people were to be seen. "Atmosphere there's going to be a little too rarefied for me, which is why I called you. Want to see a couple of newspaper bums, my own kind." Newspaper bums? "Anyway," the voice concluded, "Johnny Dixon said you were the only guy in all Vienna worth looking up. You got a wife, too, and he says she's a peach."

This was Howland Snyder, one of the most renowned agents in the world. Mason asked him to lunch at once, but at the Meissl und

Schadn, not at home. He wasn't sure that Paula would appreciate the type. The Meissl und Schadn was exactly right. It wasn't too obviously flashy, like the Majestic, but it had style. Besides, Mason was well known at the Meissl und Schadn, and he was not above a desire to impress Mr. Howland Snyder.

They met in the lobby and walked into the restaurant, with its tall crimson curtains looped with gold braid, and roses on every table. Herr Dorfmann, the venerable headwaiter, greeted Mason effusively. "We have not seen you for too long a time, Herr Jarrett!" Mason told Snyder a bit about the history of the Meissl und Schadn, adding several anecdotes about Herr Dorfmann. For many years he had been a major-domo to King Edward VII when he was Prince of Wales, traveling with him from spa to spa throughout Central Europe, and he had preserved carefully the menus commemorating these regal occasions. "I wonder, Herr Dorfmann, if you'd be good enough to show my guest Mr. Snyder some of your treasures," Mason said after lunch. Herr Dorfmann, an adroit, round-faced man with pink cheeks and a silver mustache, beamed; he was the brightest, most amiable little man Mason had ever met. From a cabinet he brought out his collection. Here was the menu of the Olympian feast he had arranged for King Edward on a state visit to Marienbad; here a stiff white card, beveled in gilt, listing the food and drink at an intimate dinner given for Kaiser Wilhelm in Baden-Baden. About each menu there were anecdotes. Amused, impressed, Snyder thanked Herr Dorfmann, and then turned to Mason. "That's a good story, Mason. If you're hard up for a spot of cash, why not write it? I could sell it for you without much trouble. The title should be 'Cabbages for Kings'—get it? Not 'Cabbages and Kings,' but 'Cabbages for Kings' —see?"

"I didn't know you handled anything but theater stuff," Mason said.

"Handle anything if it'll make money for the author and ten per cent for me, especially if the guy has potentialities, you know what I mean, somethingg maybe hot for the future." Already Snyder knew that Mason was a rarity: a man with talent who could use it—produce; a dreamer with his feet on the ground.

"Got an agent?"

"No."

"Try me out. Any time any of us has dissatisfaction with the other, we're quits. Now I want to ask you. Any night life in this here town? Any talent?"

Mason thought a moment. "Pick me up at a café called the Weissenhof after your show tonight, say at eleven, and I'll take you to a place you might like."

So Mason led Howland Snyder that night to the Koenigen. They watched the girls dancing. "Only three have good shoes," Snyder noticed. "Shoes wear out damn fast when you have to hip around like these dames." Mason explained the theory and practice of relationships at the Koenigen, how the girls handled their suitors, which ones were kept by the waiters or the barman, Hugo, which were desperately in love with what middle-aged man in the orchestra, which was married to a law student and had just had a baby, which would go to pieces and be out on the streets first.

"Heard about this sort of thing all my life, but never seen it before," Snyder said. "My wife, too, she's Hungarian by origin, but says she's Viennese." The czardas moaned; the lights went out; and Hilda sang. The muffled voice rose shaking out of her throat, and Mason could see Snyder's interest rise. He made no attempt to be blasé. Mason caught Hilda's eye and she joined them, as did Trudi. "Hi, *Kleines*," Mason said. Tonight he had a feeling that Trudi and Hilda were not as harmonious as usual; maybe they had had a fight. He explained to them both who Snyder was and Hilda coolly gave him a tiny simulacrum of a kiss, as an ironic salute to his eminence, on the top of his bald head. "That's a hell of a voicebox you have, dearie," Snyder complimented her. He ordered champagne. Mason left after an hour; Snyder stayed.

He called him the next day. "I stuck around in that damned Koenigen of yours till five this morning. That girl with the monocle has something, I don't quite know what, but it kept me up till five, and that's a late hour for me. I forgot something, Mace. Johnny Dixon said there was a funny kind of shop here in Vienna, they have art works of a certain kind, a *certain* kind, if you know what I mean, and he said he had taken you there and you knew the address."

Mason led him that afternoon to Herr Abt's establishment. He said something lightly to the effect that pornography was either for the very young or the very old, and Snyder grinned. "That just about includes all of us, depending on where you draw the line." With curiosity he rustled through Herr Abt's photographs, pored over several of his mechanical contrivances, and, Mason saw, began to sweat slightly. Herr Abt took Mason aside and said, "Now I show you a special treasure. Look at these." What were they? Loving cups? They were globular, cast in thin copper, large, almost perfectly round, with a small pit at the bottom. One showed a line, a heavy scar. Mason beckoned to Howland Snyder. "Ever see anything like these?" They were casts made of a woman's breasts. Mason wrinkled his nose, and put them down. Herr Abt whispered to him, "I got them just in time. If I remember correctly you were much interested in certain photographs of the lady. Then she died—committed suicide!" Mia! Mason jumped as if he had stepped on a live wire. These were goblets made from Mia's breasts!

Again the next day Snyder called. "Maybe you won't believe it, but I think I owe you a big lot of thangks. I've signed that girl Hilda. Yes, she'll report to me in California in about a month. She's terrific, she's really got a voice, and now that talkies are here to stay, we need every new voice we can get. And do you know what? She's held me up something fierce. No, no, I don't mean *that!* That kind of thing distragts you. I've given it up. What I mean is that she wouldn't sign without an oblig-gation on my part to give a contract to that other girl too, the little one selling cigarettes. Now, what do you think of that? Hilda says she can't get along without her—she's her hairdresser, manicurist, secretary. Well, I'm off to Salzburg in an hour, and look at the kind of thing you got me into. I ask you for talent and now I got *two* girls on my neck. Now, don't forget that story, 'Cabbages for Kings.'"

The next morning a pair of Herr Abt's loving cups arrived at Mason's door with Howland Snyder's compliments.

✳

That evening Mason felt like going to a movie; Paula didn't. For several days she had been reserved, aloof, mysterious, even touchy. He returned home early and found her in pajamas, staring at herself in the dressing-table mirror, where an image of her pale flawless skin floated. He took her by the shoulders, she wriggled, bent low, held him tightly by the wrists, and began to laugh hysterically.

Mason's voice was mild: "What's going on?"

She knelt on the floor, put her head on his knees, and, crying, laughing, twisting her face upward to his, shaking herself free, laughing, crying, said wildly, "I'm pregnant! Isn't it a scream!"

It must have been the night of the revelation about Erika.

7

Not in living memory had a winter been so chill. Snow fell, froze in the streets, melted, froze again. Lumps of black ice, which took on the shape of squashed seals, lined the curbs; automobiles crashing through the swollen streets sent up whiskers of icy spray along the walks. The gloom outside made Christmas a ceremony even warmer, more intimate, than usual; Vienna was, as always, a great town for Christmas, and the Jarretts hung chimney sweeps on the mantel in the traditional Viennese way, had *Karpfen* and fish cakes, without which no Viennese Christmas could be complete, on Christmas Eve and—of course!—a roast suckling pig for New Year's, with cherries for eyes and an apple in its mouth.

Duly, inexorably, they slipped into the next year, 1933, and Mason often reflected later that its first few months were distinguished by what was surely one of the most remarkable juxtapositions in history —both Adolf Hitler and Franklin D. Roosevelt came to power.

Once more Austria, to be kept alive, had to be given a new international loan, and the Heimwehr now threatened to take over the Austrian state by force if Dollfuss did not adopt a stronger line against the Socialists. The Schutzbund, the military organization of the Social Democrats, met this threat by responding in kind, and one wing of the Heimwehr went over to the Nazis. Conditions in all the Danubian states worsened as the coils of the crisis became tighter, and Mason, with his taste for neat leads, wrote one story that began, "Half the people of the Danubian world are starving because they cannot buy goods produced by the other half, which is starving because it cannot sell."

What exacerbated everything beyond measure was that, as Mason kept pointing out, the Nazi movement within Austria had inevitably taken on a new momentum when Hitler became installed in power in Berlin, and the direct German onslaught on Austria became intensified. A Nazi radio station was set up in Munich which spattered vituperative propaganda over the whole country, and the Germans began to impose economic sanctions on Austrian trade.

At the Weissenhof activity went on much as before. But Jim Drew's portentousness increased, as did the weight of his prejudices. The U.P. hired a man who, Drew said, was partly Jewish; he threatened to resign from the Anglo-American if this person, who clearly had every right to membership, was admitted, although other Jews were members. He talked bitterly of "American journalistic methods," and indeed of almost all things American, with increasing contempt. The reforms of the New Deal began; these outraged him and he became an acrid Roosevelt-hater. Meantime came the great American banking crisis, and presently the United States was forced to devalue the dollar. That evening, glowering, Drew tore open his wallet, took out a dollar bill, and slid it up and down the back of his trousers with an obscene gesture. "Toilet paper!" he grunted.

Miss Birch had left town, presumably for good.

Automatically the dollar lost value in terms of Austrian exchange after the devaluation. Mason, checking against his monthly draft at the A.O.G., wiped his forehead. He said to Paula with consternation, "It's the equivalent of forty per cent off our salary. What do we do next?"

Mason, Wheatley, Shipwright were among the journalists who saw Dr. Engelbert Dollfuss, the Chancellor, off on a trip to Rome. Of course the joke had gone around that he would be dispatched to Rome airmail. He greeted them cordially at the railway station. Mason said that he looked well, which he did, and Dollfuss replied with the intonation of a peasant refusing to accept flattery, "Aw, go on!" Mason returned home to pound out a situationer. Dollfuss had to go to Rome because he needed to clarify his position vis-à-vis Mussolini. He needed help, help, help, against Hitler, and only the Duce could give him help. It was his supposition—and that of the journalists as well—that Mussolini could not refuse him help, because the Duce still desperately wanted Austria to be a buffer state between himself and Germany.

Mason's feeling about the Chancellor was ambivalent. He still found him extraordinarily attractive as a man—modest, decent, bold; and he admired the stubborn adroitness of his fight to keep the Nazis out of Austria. But Mason disliked hotly the whole apparatus of clerical demagogues that surrounded him, his alliance with reactionary forces, and his dependence on the Duce. He was a delightful little man, clever too, amusing; but his fundamental ideas, his associations, were all wrong.

Austria, he wrote in a mail story, had always been a country that took no crisis seriously, which wriggled in its own inimitable slippery way out of any difficulty. Heretofore something of the very softness of Austrian character had been a factor of strength, because the thorns of the crisis were apt to disappear through absorption—the crisis lost its point, melted, deliquesced, in the prevailing solvent of easygoing compromise. Certainly the Social Democrats and Clericals were at swords' points, as usual, but Mason still thought it was almost unimaginable that their struggle could produce really serious disorder. The Austrians were too sophisticated, too civilized, to fight.

But, he conceded, the old two-way tug of war, Social Democrats versus Christian Socials, had now been made infinitely more complicated by the Nazis. The struggle was now irreversibly triangular. Some of the Dollfuss people flirted openly with the Nazis. The Chancellor had to fight secret defection in his own ranks as well as the Nazis on his right, the Socialists on his left. The Socialists, if they had been more sensible, might have cooperated with him against the Nazis, but could not bear to bring themselves to do so, and the Nazis attacked both sides. So the little Chancellor had to accept battle on two fronts. Or was he provoking battle? Mason held his head. The outcome of the conflict was unpredictable.

When Dollfuss returned to Vienna from Rome there came a ridiculous little contretemps. Ridiculous as it was, it ended parliamentary government in Austria. Mason, an eyewitness, marveled. Not even Franz Lehar could have concocted such a fantasy. Dollfuss had a majority of exactly one in the Chamber. Debate began on his new emergency decrees. Just as the balloting began, a Social Democratic deputy went out to the men's room. A colleague voted in his place, but the ballot was incorrectly marked. The vote was eighty-one to eighty against the government. Dollfuss was beaten and would therefore have to resign. But then the high-minded Speaker of the House, a Social Democrat, inexpressibly legalistic even at the expense of his own party, ruled that an irregularity had occurred. So Dollfuss was not overthrown after all. The Chamber became wildly excited, and in the confusion the Speaker so far lost his head as to resign office. The Deputy Speakers similarly walked out and the session ended in pandemonium. Then clever Dr. Dollfuss, pouncing on his opportunity, pointed out that the Parliament could not legally reconstitute itself, since the law said that nobody but the Speaker or a deputy Speaker could convoke it, and since these had resigned, they were powerless to do so. Like a bulldog, Dollfuss held on to his new position. A flood of decrees splashed on Vienna, and citizens discovered that the Chancellor had become a dictator. Parliament was gone.

Protesting violently, the Social Democrats proceeded to call a rump meeting of the Parliament. Mason and Stein covered it. The session lasted exactly ten minutes, whereupon the police moved in and closed the building.

"The victory is ours," Stein said judiciously. "We *did* hold our session, and have thus vindicated ourselves. It was a moral victory." His voice was friendly, trusting, pedantic.

Mason looked at him. "Moral victory? Ricardo, you're crazy—the crisis has gone to your head." For he knew in his bones that Parliament would never meet again.

They walked down the Ring in a buffeting March wind, arguing, and Mason worked out what his first paragraph would be. "Having committed suicide yesterday the Austrian Parliament attempted without success to revive itself today."

Stein, his face bright again, laughed at this, and left him with the words, "Erika sends you her very best regards."

"Give her mine, too."

"I am leaving town for a few days, and we shall hope to see you soon." His smile, sunny but enigmatic now, seemed to conceal a secret.

A week later a telegram came from Stein and Erika in Paris announcing their marriage.

※

Mason picked up a new Dollfuss joke from his colleague Ernst Boericke, the small man on tiptoe with the timid manner and his way of prefacing every remark with "Excuse, please." A tortoise was observed leading a military detachment down the Ringstrasse, which puzzled onlookers until they discovered that it was the Herr Bundeskanzler in a steel helmet.

※

The bedroom was dark, but a little glow crept along the ceiling from the moon which, exactly at the half, looked like an executioner's axe. Paula, who had sought to apply to the whole phenomenon of pregnancy her usual expertness, her direct and realistic view of things, felt unaccountably nervous. Mason was still working. She heard him shut the office door quietly and walk down the corridor to the kitchen.

In the whole world, over Europe, over Vienna, over their own small society, she felt not merely a sense of malaise, of worried uneasiness, of panic around the corner, but of calamity impending—disaster unmitigated. "Darling!" she called, after waiting a long moment.

Mason tumbled into the room, looking alarmed.

"It's nothing . . . but I'm worried. . . . Come to me, please. . . . Oh, Mason, I love you. And you're strong."

"You're the one who's strong. I'm worried too."

He slipped from his clothes and was in bed in an instant, holding her with all of his body.

"I don't know what's the matter."

He listened to her heart thump and his began to thump too.

"Take me away where we can live among healthy people."

"We're healthy people."

"I know. But no one else is. I can't stand it here any longer. Everyone is sick. Everyone is mentally or morally or physically sick. Let's go away." She began to shiver. "Take me away, Mason, please."

"There's no place to go. We'll have to stick it out here for a while longer."

"No place to go . . . Isn't it awful that there should be no place to go?" She was weeping quietly. He kissed her eyes and cheeks and squeezed her with his hands, elbows, and the inside of his knees, to give comfort to her frightened body, and to transfer to her the warmth of his.

8

One thing in Vienna, Mason and Paula Jarrett were delighted to discover, managed to survive the Great Depression. The elaborate *Fasching* balls continued to be given throughout Lent, no doubt because the Viennese simply could not have endured the transition from winter to spring without them. During the season the addict had three or four balls to choose from every week—like the *Schützenkränzchen* (Marksmen's Ball), the *Schwarz-Weiss Ball* (mostly for medical students), the *Wäschermädel Ball* (originally for laundresses and pretty servant girls, so all the old-style aristocrats went), the *Fiaker Ball* (for coachmen in the old days), and above all the *G'schnasfest*, or Nonsense Ball, given in the Künstlerhaus every year by the artists, the bohemians, the sculptors, playwrights, actors, and musicians. Paula thought that she could go safely for an hour or two, although the crush would be great and Dr. Antioch, examining her the week before, had warned her against the danger of a possible miscarriage. Mason grumbled at having to go because he loathed affairs in costume. But he organized a party, inviting Shipwright and the Sandors. It was expensive—very. The *G'schnasfest* was the only public entertainment in Austria not heavily papered. You really had to pay to get in.

Shipwright dressed as a pirate—a conventional enough choice, but it suited him well; the Sandors wore Slovak peasant costumes. Mason became a huntsman, while Paula did not change except to wear a lace-and-tinsel crown. Mason had two or three drinks—straight slivovitz—at the restaurant where they assembled. During dinner he gulped a beer and then slipped away to the bar, where he had slivovitz again. Then more beer.

By the time they left the restaurant he was mildly tight, but he did not feel gay. Paula winked at him. Did she know that he was tight? Was she encouraging him to get tighter? Scrambling from their taxis at the Künstlerhaus they went into the dressing rooms—unheated and freezing cold—to adjust their costumes and put on their masks. The decor was a mixture of art, sex, and politics. One room was the nine month-plan room, and another was hung with odalisques in chastity belts. Because of the crush no one could move more than an inch at a time; they forced their way up one staircase, down another, through halls cut apart by beaver-board partitions, stuck with posters. They encountered fairy queens, Moorish princesses, harlequins, chimney sweeps, and apaches from Montmartre. An astounding number of girls appeared in nothing but pajamas. These were at once cheap, colorful, and an alluring costume.

One of the orchestras played a rumba and Mason's party frayed apart and its members separated.

Shipwright seemed to be slightly remote from the group, superior to it, secretly conspiratorial. What he was saying to himself was: Paula said she didn't ski, because Mason won't—he thinks he's too clumsy now though he skied a lot some years ago. I'll teach her to ski next winter. With that coloring, how marvelous she'd look against the snow. She's about four months pregnant, I should judge, but she doesn't look it. Hardly shows at all. I wonder how it will feel to hold her very close, dancing. She looks so unassailable, virtuous, impregnable. What would she be like cracked open? Lord God, I'd like to be rich. There's something fundamentally bourgeois about me, in spite of everything. What a delight it would be to have four mistresses, say, each in a different city, completely self-sufficient, each installed in a lovely house, with beautiful clothes. . . . Vienna, Paris, St. Moritz, New York. Or four wives. Why don't they have Mormons any more? Why can't a man have four wives? A pack of youngsters in each house—I don't see why it wouldn't be fun if a man were rich enough. . . . I'll ask Paula to dance now. Mason's a good chap, even if he's so muddled.

At the bar on the top floor, which was decorated with drawings of naked Egyptian priestesses, Mason ordered a flask of *Heuriger*. I'm not tight, he thought confidently. What the hell if I am tight, he added. Where was Paula? At what seemed an extreme distance, through a throbbing blur of faces, he saw Karl Tetzel, unmasked, looking lost. A pretty girl tweaked Mason's nose, murmuring,

"*Warum so traurig?*" It stabbed him that anybody, particularly a pretty girl, should think that he looked sad, and he moistened and twisted his lips trying ridiculously to give his face a different and happier expression. He drank another *Viertel* of the tart new wine and felt that he was existing in another layer of time. There was a deep roaring in his ears. He muttered to himself, "What a good party that *G'schnasfest* was!" as if tonight had taken place years before.

He stumbled downstairs, but he could not find any of his friends. The orchestra was swooping into old Viennese songs and he remembered that party in Grinzing so long ago, the night the A.O.G. collapsed.

> *Wien, Wien, nur du allein*
> *Sollst die Stadt meiner Träume sein. . . .*

Shipwright led Paula off the floor to the bar Mason had just left. She looked out for Mason but did not see him. She sat down, out of breath from dancing, on a rough sofa under a canopy, and Shipwright brought her some wine. She felt happy and relaxed.

Shipwright said easily, touching her silver crown, "I don't believe you're a princess. I believe you're making it up." She shook her head, smiling. "Anyway, I don't believe in princesses."

"Why not?"

"Life has so many obstacles as it is."

Paula replied, not realizing how her remark might be interpreted, "But of course you're a pirate, and pirates are always bold, aren't they?"

Quite suddenly and directly Shipwright kissed her.

She withdrew as he whispered, "I adore you. I'm madly in love with you. I have been since the second hour we met."

"Why the second hour?"

"The first hour I was interested only in your mind."

"You're being perfectly absurd," Paula said. "I'm a happily married young woman in a moderately advanced state of pregnancy."

"But what has any of that to do with it? This is the *G'schnasfest!*" he expostulated.

Men! But she couldn't help murmuring, "Is that the only reason?"

Shipwright looked encouraged. He said, "I'm mad about you," and grasped at her hungrily.

Paula said, serious, "It's against the law. You're not mad about me at all, and you know it. This is something you're contriving . . . it's mischief. Now, stop it."

❋

Downstairs in another bar Mason was ready to search for Paula and call it a night when he saw a young girl who, even though masked, seemed familiar. A man in officer's uniform heavy with epaulettes led her to a loge, bowed with a perfunctory gesture, and departed. She was alone. She wore a nymph's costume; her mask was white. Mason noticed that her hands were pretty, that her waist was incredibly slim, and that her hair, what showed of it, cut like a boy's, was sand color. We intersect at odd angles, Mason thought. He walked toward her, trying to keep his gait steady, and greeted her with his voice somewhat thick, "Well—Miss Nella Blohr!"

Surprised, she knew him from his voice and size, and asked brightly, "But how did you recognize me?"

"How could anybody who has ever known you not recognize you? Besides, the freckles show."

But, as a matter of fact, Nella had changed considerably in the past year. She was still very young, her shoulders were still extravagantly youthful, thin; but unmistakably she gave an impression of maturity, of having grown. She fumbled for a cigarette and Mason lit it. She blew the smoke out in a long funnel, and when she tilted her head back her throat, which seemed fuller now, arched out. The lines of her collarbones and the hollows under them were lovely.

Mason, stirred, could think of nothing to say but "How's Tetzel?"

"It is amusing that you should ask, particularly in view of what you just this minute said, that anybody would recognize me. He is here, but cannot find me."

"I found you."

"True. Of course I did tell Tetzel that I would come in the dress of a milkmaid, and then at the last moment changed to dryad. Perhaps he searches only for milkmaids."

"You're rather naughty, aren't you?"

She looked at him with an understanding, slightly self-mocking smile. "Soon I will go out and search for him. I will find him, and all will be made up."

"Is he still in love with you?" His voice was still a little thick.

"Perhaps." She shrugged.

Smoke jutted from her nostrils, and she seemed misty, troubled, not thinking of Tetzel at all, not thinking of Mason either, but trying to fix herself on some object not readily identifiable. Mason remembered the time he had given her that one kiss. He took her hand in his, but she withdrew it coldly. Now the young man in officer's uniform who had left her wandered past the loge, waving, with another girl on his arm.

"Who's that?" Mason asked.

"A spoiled nothing—a prince. He has seven castles in Lower Austria and takes me to St. Stephen's to show me there the tombs of his ancestors. His grandfather is on a horse outside the Hofburg and his brother is deputy leader of the Heimwehr. *Pfui!*"

"But you're a little crazy about him?" Mason asked.

"He is no more than part of a generally disturbing atmosphere."

"He's crazy about you?"

"He pursues, then stops, then pursues again. He thinks it tantalizes."

Making sure that his stance would be steady Mason rose. This was a damned complicated little girl. He would like extremely to know her better, but now, of all times, was not the time. He gave her a rather wan smile, patted her shoulder like an elder brother, and said lightly, "I've got to go."

She rose and kissed him on the cheek. The warm lips rested there a second. Mason remembered suddenly a passage about her in Otto's diary. He looked at her eyes, with the yellow spokes near the pupil and the blue-gray periphery, and made as if to take her aside, but at that moment the young prince returned alone. Nella introduced them, then walked with Mason toward the door, dismissing him. "You're very nice, as I've known for some time now, but you're not very daring, are you?"

9

"Mason!" He had spent five consecutive evenings loafing at the Weissenhof, following a hangover, the result of the *G'schnasfest*, that lasted two whole days. "Darling, I don't think you ought to waste so much time. Weren't you going to get started on that series about Ruthenia—or was it Thrace? Can't you try to work a little more?"

"Lord—it's been your line for years that I work too hard!" He went on: "I have a job to do and nobody in Chicago is complaining about the way I do it. Sitting around in the Weissenhof is part of the job, and besides I need a little relaxation in the evenings."

"You've done nothing but relax for six whole months, it seems to me!"

"Come, Paula, that's unfair."

She did not know what gave her this impulse to be prickly tonight. To blame the pregnancy would be silly. She knew perfectly well that what she had said was unfair. Perhaps she was punishing him for not being attentive enough. She could not keep herself from going on.

"As a matter of fact I've been doing most of your work since Otto left—at least I've spared you all the routine. And it bores me to death, if you want to know!"

"My work bores you, does it? Well, I like that!" He hoisted himself forward in the big chair. "After all, it's what supports you."

"God, give me some money of my own!" she cried, as she had cried once before. "Of all things intolerable it's the spectacle of a man exerting pressure through financial superiority! I asked you to help find me a job. I'll find something to do if I . . . I . . . burst!" She poked at her hard belly.

"You're going to burst soon anyway."

Neither could resist laughing. But she was determined to continue with this little spat, if only to get more reaction out of him. For days he had been totally immersed in himself, out of focus, apathetic, torpid. Once she had even caught him taking a nap before lunch as well as after.

"What do *I* get out of you?" Paula asked.

"Well, now, you're raising an entirely different question—"

But she had got an enormous lot from Mason, as she would in normal circumstances fully acknowledge, even as he had got an enormous lot from her. She had been hollow; he had filled her up. She had had splendid fancy theories about life and he had shown her what was real.

"You're raising an entirely different question," he repeated. "And I might ask on my side—what do I get out of you?"

She stiffened. Briefly she said, "A great deal!"

One of Mason's most conspicuous failings was his tendency to hoard injuries. He hated quarrels and scenes; he loathed the exposures brought by open friction. When she said something that hurt him he would, as a rule, say nothing and attempt to swallow it, suppressing his own injury: whereupon it was apt to burn and fester and burst out days later in unreasonable terms. Now he was determined to have a few things out with her.

"The other day you said that I was frightfully selfish and that I lacked discipline."

"I didn't say that. You said that you admired unselfish disinterestedness in people and thought that a sense of discipline was one of the most valuable qualities a person could possess. Then I replied generally that most people were inclined to admire the qualities they lacked."

"Oh, don't be so damned intellectual."

"What has my being an intellectual got to do with it? Do you want a stupid person around the house? I think you're about ninety per cent disciplined, which is a great deal more than most people, and when you do break down it's only because you're reverting to some kind of childish delight in being impractical."

"But you say I'm selfish. I'm not. I do things for other people all the time."

"Out of a sense of obligation. Or because you hope for something in return." Mason, furious, was about to make a sharp reply when the telephone rang. Bleschke was ill and his brother, who didn't speak English, gave him the news. In hideous German he attempted to maintain his end of the conversation.

"Mason! I appeal to you. Can't you, after all this time, learn to speak one, just one, correct German sentence?" He looked hurt. "It's unendurable that you can't learn the genders of even the simplest nouns."

"I know all about the female gender. Anything's better than a nagging wife."

"You have no right to say that! You're so large, so easygoing ... you *absorb* everything so easily. . . . Just the same you're suppressing a lot. You'd be a better person if you faced up to some of your defects. You don't take the lead enough. A woman needs a leader. The man should set the pace. It's right and proper for a man to be interested in his wife. You lack edge—"

He sulked. "I'm tired of being your intellectual inferior."

"You're not my intellectual inferior a bit!"

"Oh hell, let's not fight." He closed his eyes. "It's bad for your condition."

"My condition is my own business!" She became so incensed that she could not go on, but after a moment they made up and began to giggle. Marriage is like a boat, Paula reflected, fragile, with two people at the oars. One compensates for the other's lack of balance. Then the other, meeting this stress, may tilt too far in the wrong direction.

10

Next day their quarrel was forgotten. After breakfast Mason chucked her under the chin, saying "Well—time for me to go into my sausage, I mean office." Any time that he was flip with words it meant that he was in a good mood. She murmured to herself, "Feed on the future, not the past," and they discussed plans having to do with the baby. There was still a considerable time to wait, but they worked out how to turn the spare bedroom into a nursery and talked about the kind of nurse they wanted and where to get her.

Day by day Paula, having finished her work as Otto's substitute, would rush out and buy equipment—a cradle, scales, infants' furniture, whatnot. Mason's eye grazed over the bills. Day by day, too, what he called their nonbaby life went on. They seemed to be entertaining more than before. Paula gave luncheon parties, tea parties, dinner parties, and it was a rare week when they did not break bread with some minister or other. The Jarretts managed their entertainment in the simplest way—on the cheap—but even so it cost money. Mason was somewhat taken aback when the Yugoslav Minister, surveying their guests at an evening party, pinched him on the arm and grinned. "And who is now bribing you, my dear Jarrett!"

Mason met Sandor at noon at the Imperial the next day. Sandor showed him a story in one of the Nazi sheets.

"Well now, I ask you. Look what has become our friend Von

Traum—grown to twice as his size!"

"Let's go and see him," Mason suggested.

"A worthwhile idea," Sandor replied. "It may be the wisdom to take *Gummiknüppels* for self-defense."

"We could borrow plenty of them there."

Von Traum gave them an appointment for a day later in the week. The Nazi movement in Austria was run from Berlin and Munich, but a Viennese, by name Pfaul, had become the local titular commander. Now it was announced that his chief of staff would be the well-known journalist Herr Gustav von Traum. He certainly moves fast, Mason thought. When Mason and Sandor arrived to keep their appointment at the shiny new Brown House recently set up on Kochstrasse, they were much impressed, as well as repelled, by the orderly bustle and military atmosphere. They had to sign chits to gain admittance, and a brawny storm trooper in a brown shirt and shiny boots looked them over carefully before passing their names upstairs. An orderly with a black and red swastika armband conducted them to Von Traum's office, and Von Traum gave them the Nazi salute and called out "Heil Hitler!" as they entered.

The telephone kept ringing and assistants flitted in and out. Once the Nazi excused himself and left the room for ten minutes. His guests waited patiently.

"If you're too busy to talk to us this morning, we'll be glad to get out," Mason said smoothly. "I hate to interrupt all these affairs of state. Though you aren't quite the state just yet, are you?"

"I'm never too busy to greet old friends and colleagues. I even forgive the fact that you wrote all that silliness about the Führer's family. We will be the state within six months. Perhaps you will be good enough to recall my prediction about the assumption of power by the Führer in Germany. Mark well my new prediction today. Within six months we will rule Austria."

He closed his fists tightly and the delta of red veins stood out on his forehead. He made a triumphant little snort. "I do not speak for publication. Formal interviews are now a matter for our propaganda section. Presently I will introduce you to the director. I greet you simply as former colleagues, who perhaps wish authentic background information."

Von Traum began to expound his views. His contempt for Dollfuss and the Austrian government was what might have been expected, but Mason respected the harsh, formidable vitality of this man, to say nothing of his manifest intelligence and ruthlessness.

Sandor asked a pointed question. Would not Hitler's plans for Anschluss with Austria come to grief because of Mussolini?

Von Traum snapped cheerfully at the thought. "Conceivably there could be trouble if Austria were to be taken over by German Nazis. But if Austrian Nazis do the job, what possible grounds for objection can the Duce have? He would be confronted by a purely domestic fait accompli." Von Traum's voice dropped to an amused, confidential, man-to-man whisper. "Besides, can anybody take the Italians altogether seriously? Can Italy remain isolated from Hitler's Reich? Why should not the two Fascist states confirm their community of interest, take advantage of their identity of aim? Why should not Austria be a third Fascist state, a convenient bridge between the other two? Let Italy and Germany work together! Give the Italians Tunis! Give them Corsica!" His voice rose to an excited shout, but now he lowered it again. "Give them Savoy! We will take Austria and Alsace, let the Italians be satisfied with Corsica and Savoy!"

"What about France?" Mason interjected. "Will France take all this lying down?"

"A degenerate power."

"Britain?"

"Shopkeepers."

Once Von Traum got fairly started, he permitted no further interruptions. Leaning over his desk, his long legs projecting underneath, he talked furiously for an hour. Abruptly then he dismissed the two journalists. "Grüsse an die gnädige Frau," he said to Mason. The words did not ring true. Von Traum was beyond any consideration of amenity now, beyond friendship, beyond humanity. He was a combination of automaton and fanatic, a fanatic with a cold heart whose dreams had at last come true, and it troubled Mason profoundly that he had to take him seriously.

Mason and Sandor, leaving the Brown House, walked in sleepy sunshine toward the Ring. Mason savored the blandness of Vienna, its easygoing air of *Gemütlichkeit*, and felt as if he had been sojourning briefly in an altogether different climate, another land. The Nazis would take Austria in six months, would they? His eyes narrowed. The hell they will, he thought.

*

At nine-thirty that evening Von Traum was still hard at work in the Brown House. Into his room passed a succession of high-strung, lean young men—district leaders, emissaries to the provinces, agents from Bavaria. Twenty-four hours were scarcely enough for the day's minimum tasks. Organization, propaganda. Propaganda, organization.

"A last detail." Von Traum turned briskly to his assistant. "We are so close to success that no detail of the planning should be ignored. You have doubtless observed the nuisance committed in the Reich by foreign journalists. They have been troublesome busybodies from the beginning and we should act at once to forestall a repetition of such a nuisance here. I propose to check off in advance the names of the chief correspondents here. It is a small detail, but it is perhaps wise to determine now what we shall do with them."

He had a list in his hand.

"A good many may remain unmolested. They will easily be brought into line. I propose at first merely a severe inspection of the dispatches of the chief agency correspondents. Of the Germans, all of our known, admitted enemies are, of course, to be arrested at once. Particularly Dolliner. Or perhaps we may find some harsher, more fitting fate for Dolliner. Several others may find brief periods in one of the new concentration camps revealing. For the moment I should recommend careful treatment of the Anglo-Americans. Let a man named Drew alone. But as to Jarrett, the man involved with the Customs Union and the A.O.G. affair, he should be got rid of, but without violence. Sandor is a liberal, let him be thoroughly frightened, then expelled. Of one journalist we might make a serious example. A little *Schrecklichkeit* can do no harm. Who shall it be? Wheatley? No—no? The New York *Times* man? N-no. I must think. Of course as to any Austrian Social Democrats—like Stein and Boericke—I have not quite made up my mind. Perhaps we will have to shoot them."

11

The Roosevelt administration sent a new minister to Vienna, an able, somewhat dry career officer named Heather-Smith. Mason in his capacity as head of the Anglo-American thought that he and Paula should give a party for him. (Could they afford it, though?)

"Let's ask the Bundeskanzler," said Mason.

"He wouldn't possibly come," Paula said. Never had Dr. Dollfuss been to a foreign journalist's home before.

"He might."

The Chancellor accepted the invitation promptly, and this caused much commotion and excitement. Paula could not deny that she was thrilled. On the day of the party the security police explored every cranny of the villa and posted themselves at vantage points in the garden, because the Nazis were now openly threatening Dr. Dollfuss's life day by day. The streets were cleared, and the whole neighborhood put under guard.

It was a calm, pellucid April afternoon. The great tree near Mason's window with the double trunk and heart-shaped leaves foamed with blossoms. Budding hyacinth and iris stood along the walks under the lilacs. The Chancellor arrived on time, greeted Mason and Paula warmly, and took a place next to the Heather-Smiths. The new minister had a schoolmaster's manner—one could almost see a pointer in his hand—and began at once to lecture Dollfuss, the Milli-Metternich, about the position of his government vis-à-vis the Nazis. Dollfuss listened amiably, dutifully, like a clever schoolboy. Heather-Smith had been councilor of embassy in Berlin and knew the Nazi menace well. Mason, who was always a lively and enthusiastic host, did his best to keep the party as fluid and informal as possible, shaking people back and forth. Soon the Chancellor, adroit, smiling, perched on the big squashy sofa under the orange curtains like a bright pygmy, became surrounded by the correspondents' wives, with Erji Sandor next to him. The Heather-Smiths behaved agreeably, in their grave manner, to everybody, and Paula helped Frau Gertrude serve the drinks. Mason heard Karl Tetzel say something to Hal Shipwright in his adhesive, tenacious way, and Shipwright replied in German with a quotation, "Withdraw liberty from France, and you have a revolution. Withdraw it from Germany, and you unite the country." Mason felt a stab of jealousy. He had never quite reconciled himself to the fact that Shipwright, the dilettante, spoke such flawless German.

There came a stir at the door. In walked Randolph Tallent, the novelist. He had drifted into Vienna recently from Berlin with a note from Strothness, and had had dinner with the Jarretts a few nights before. He was one of the most renowned men in the world. He was reputed to drink a lot. He did. Mason and Paula were not at all sure that he would remember their invitation and come to the party today. Now here he was, swarthy, portly, pugnacious, weaving and bobbing from room to room. Mason was terrified. He thought that Tallent, who was notorious for his dislike of officials, might be rude to Dollfuss or the Heather-Smiths. But Mrs. Heather-Smith demonstrated a close knowledge of his books, which pleased him. Dollfuss, learning who he was, took the initiative and walked up to him respectfully. Tallent grimaced. He hustled Paula aside and Mason heard her gasp, but luckily the Chancellor was out of earshot. What Tallent said was, "My s'pposed be impressed by that little runt?"

Shipwright, languid but attentive, hovered close to Paula, and looked pained in a well-bred way when her duties as hostess took her from him. Hestery, out in the hall, was heard to say explosively that, in his opinion, "serious" bloodshed was inevitable soon. Nella Blohr said to Mason, "Entering is the girl who upset you so much at the *Heurige* that night." Mason was shocked that Nella could have remembered that, as well as detected it in the first place. He saw that Stein and Erika had arrived. He had not seen them since their marriage. Erika, advancing into the room, kissed him on the cheek, and searched around for Paula, who pretended not to see her enter. Then Paula shook hands with her with a vigorous friendly smile. I must tell Erika that Paula knows, Mason said to himself. Erika looked happy. Her cheeks had a luminous sheen, the glow instantaneously recognizable in a girl who is having a surfeit of sexual pleasure. Mason felt a small fire lick in his bowels. Paula was now being a model of politeness to Erika. Ironies, ironies, thought Mason. Had it not been for Erika, Paula might very well not be pregnant.

Sandor was saying to Tallent, "But if Hitler indeed now is considered to be a god, that is very bad for him, I mean! Gods have to perform miracles!"

Tetzel and Nella stood alone near the bar. Manifestly she was saying "No—no—no" to him. She looked as if she had to restrain herself physically from some such gesture as stamping a foot. Disconsolately he turned away, and Paula, seeing his stricken face, offered him a drink in a loving cup, the first receptacle to come to her hand, as Nella scampered off. "Isn't it pretty—cast from a girl's breast," she said lightly. Tetzel looked at the cup with curiosity. He noticed a scar on it. He became startled and agitated and scrutinized it again, turning it around against the light from the window. Marching up to Paula he exclaimed, dead white, "What is this cup? From where comes this loving cup? Tell me—I must know."

"I really don't know. A friend gave two of them to Mason a few weeks ago. Actually, not a friend. A man from New York . . . an agent . . ."

Tetzel put the cup down. Even his hands had turned white.

Dr. Dollfuss indicated that it was time for him to go. He had stayed an hour and a half. Mason cast around desperately for Paula, who was staring at Tetzel with a bewildered expression. Together they escorted the Chancellor to the door, and Mason saw him into his car, followed by the Heather-Smiths. The party became noisier, more fluid. Nobody would go home. Mason started to drink and saw his friends flicker before him as if they were figures in a blurred kaleidoscope. He managed to have a few minutes alone with Erika and told her what he wanted to tell her, namely that Paula knew about him and her. "If Paula is not hurt I have no objection," said Erika. Not till midnight did the party wind up. They could not find Randolph Tallent and then discovered him peacefully sleeping on the floor in Mason's office, curled like a contented child. They could not wake him up and he was too heavy to move and so they put a blanket over him lightly and inserted a pillow under his head and left him there.

✻

Late the next afternoon Mason ran into Dozent Dr. Wallenstein in the garden. The Dozent, always the friendliest of men, raised his finger, wagging it angrily in Mason's face, shaking it. Mason, wondering what had happened, was shocked. The Dozent said with an expression he had never seen on him before, "So now you consort with the enemy!"

Mason temporized. "Dollfuss? Well, not actually the enemy . . . At least not yet . . . Isn't he doing his best to keep the Nazis out of Austria?"

Rigidly the Dozent stood there, still wagging his finger. "The Chancellor is the enemy of all decent men, because a man cannot be judged by himself alone. You may consider that Dr. Dollfuss is attractive personally, but he is a prisoner of much larger forces, as all men of politics must be. He represents blackness and reaction and his policy will create evil, and in the end the result of it all will be that the Nazis will find it easier, not more difficult, to get in!"

Mason gaped. Abruptly the Dozent turned his back and walked off. At that moment Randolph Tallent emerged from the villa, weaving unsteadily, muttering incoherently to himself, and in bad need of a shave. The Dozent jumped as if he had seen a wraith.

12

May Day. A bright wind blew hard. The Socialist celebration traditional for May Day had been forbidden by the government, and for the first time since 1919 the Social Democratic leaders were unable to address their followers from the city hall. The crowds, eager to make some kind of march anyway, spread out into the streets, but the police had orders to keep everybody off the Ring. Mason ran down the Gürtel with a mob of demonstrators trying to reach the Ring, but the police pushed them back at every intersection. The crowd was not yet truculent or even out of temper; boys laughed, racing across the cobbles, and the shouts were cheerful. "*Freiheit! Freundschaft!*" they chanted. Everybody was out to see what would happen, to see the fun.

"This way!" a youngster in mechanic's overalls called to Mason. "Hurry—slip in through here!" Somebody asked if the Schutzbunders were going to march. "Are they waiting in formation?"

Mason knew that the Schutzbund leaders, anxious to avoid provocation, had agreed not to march.

"Naw, they ain't going to march," another workman said. "Guess they want to all right, but orders is orders."

"The basic order is to take no action, because if we raise a rumpus nobody will gain from it but the goddamned Nazis."

"Blast the Nazis! We could clean 'em out in ten minutes. There's nothing to worry about except the Heimwehr and the government."

Mason's object was to reach the Ring, and he advanced slowly. A policeman darted out of an alley, grabbed him, and in a broad peasant's accent shouted "Za-roook!" instead of "Zurück!" Then a squad of police on horseback rode hard down the cobbles. Mason saw the great white slimy eyes of the nearest horse as it tossed its head wildly, neighing and bearing down on him.

He ducked down a side street, then gasped. He could see that the Ringstrasse was lined with police and troops shoulder to shoulder. At intervals stood barricades of timber and loose, untidy rolls of barbed wire. Each intersecting street, every street, was cut off with barbed wire. In the center of each barricade, snub-nosed under the wire, were short, olive-green machine guns, with their ugly funnel mouths. Mason could hardly believe his eyes. He could not believe that the government had made such efficient and elaborate preparations. The sidewalks were empty. Nobody stood here but troops and police.

They had barricaded the whole Ring! By God, this was a show of force! Mason knew too that it was a dangerous and wanton folly. Such a display could only defeat its own ends—it was a provocation in itself. Came a commotion at the next corner. Some youngsters in brown shirts—obviously Nazis—were tumbling on the ground, running, yelling. That was it! The Nazis were the troublemakers! They moved swiftly in and out of the crowds, trying to provoke incidents on the traditional Socialist holiday, so that if trouble came it would be the Social Democrats who would be blamed.

Citizens in the mob near the city hall taunted the police good-humoredly. They stood near the police lines and the police did not molest them, so long as they kept back a reasonable distance. Most of the Vienna police were country boys and many, coming from the Ostbahnstrecke, spoke in an outlandish broad argot. People in the crowd tried to make individual policemen lose their tempers.

"Mistelbacher! Spinatwachter!" ("Dolt from Mistelbach! Spinach-watcher!") they called at the police.

The police stood there, sweating in the sun, patient, irritated but silent.

"*Spinatwachter!*" The policemen remained silent, immobile. Their discipline was good. Their job was to keep people off the Ring. That was all, and they were doing it.

Mason saw a youth in a brown shirt dart forward and bend suddenly to the ground, reaching for a rock to throw. Mason was next to him in a second and powerfully dug his heel into the boy's hand. The boy screamed, and a dozen Socialists fell on top of him. Mason heard himself shouting. An officer came up and dragged the Nazi away, together with two of the men who had pommeled him. Another officer grabbed Mason, but, protesting, he showed his journalist's card and tried to explain what had happened. He became the center of a struggling, shouting group. He went up to the officer who had arrested the two Socialists and talked hard. The officer let the two go.

An hour later Mason watched the Socialist leaders, Dr. Otto Bauer and Colonel Julius Deutsch, the commander of the Schutzbund, pass along the streets in open cars appealing to their people to retire quietly and go home. At all costs they did not want to have an explosion, and now they were openly cooperating with the authorities to prevent trouble. So the crowds began to disperse and scatter like those at the end of a performance of the circus; they chatted and laughed and bought raspberry soda, wrestling on the streets and horseplaying as young men do. Some continued to taunt the police and yell friendly insults at their own leaders, as if they did not think that the demonstration of military force, all that barbed wire and those machine guns, had much reality.

Mason reached home deeply troubled. He did not toss off the events of the day like these young men sipping *Himbeersaft*. A man usually so steady, he was filled now with consternation and an emotion akin to panic.

❋

Sandor's voice over the telephone that night seemed broken, strangled: "Mason! I've been fired. I've lost my job!"

XIII. MASON, PAULA, ERIKA

Laszlo Sandor, like Donald Bishopson, did not lose his job by reason of any personal fault or dereliction. The reason was more dramatic than in the case of Bishopson. Bishopson's New York *Register* had decided to lop off several foreign bureaus, but Sandor's Washington *Sun* went further—it disappeared. The *Sun* had been languishing for some time. Its owners operated newspapers in several other cities which were, however, profitable. When a chance came to sell the Washington property and still retain the others, they snapped at it. The Washington *Sun*, after seventy-three years, sank overnight without trace. There were no warnings, no premonitions of trouble. One day the paper existed; the next it vanished. Any newspaper, as Mason well knew, is a living organism, an organism with flesh, skeleton, nerves, glands; it has a life which consists of more than the aggregate of the lives of the people working for it. But the Washington *Sun* was killed by its owners like a clubbed dog. Without a struggle, without a sigh, it died.

Sandor loved the *Sun*. He had a deep intimate attachment for it, like Mason's for the Chicago *Star*. Sandor was one of the spirits who counted most inside the *Sun*'s composite animate existence. He was totally stunned by the catastrophe. The philosophy he had lived on, which, despite his habit of irony, made him see something good in almost everything, could not cope with this disaster. He was like a man suddenly deprived of some integral part of his own structure. His feet no longer trod firm earth. That his job, his livelihood, his security, the security of his family, and even more the work that he loved so passionately, should be so brusquely snatched away from him, without

455

any warning or reason that related to himself in any way, was almost beyond his power to grasp. Dazed, he groped to stand up under the force of the blow.

He was appalled and hurt and he felt betrayed, but, Mason noted, he was not bitter in the sense that Bishopson had been bitter. He was forlorn and anguished, but there was little bitterness in Laszlo Sandor's soul.

After a few days he took stock. He sat down quietly and typed out twenty neat letters, written with restraint, to newspapers in New York, London, Brussels, Zurich, Prague, and Amsterdam. He outlined his experience and qualifications and asked if any job were available, and, if not, would any correspondence from Central Europe be welcomed on a freelance basis. From seventeen of his twenty letters he got no reply at all. The other three told him that nothing was open. One of these misspelled his name.

"Letters seldom do much good," Mason tried to encourage him. "That's not the right way to go about it. See everybody you know here, get them to go after people elsewhere, try to do it through friends."

Mason discovered that Sandor had told few of his Viennese associates about the disaster. He simply could not bear to address himself to cronies in the cafés and confess that he was out of work. He was too proud. And he was ashamed.

"Hell, Laszlo, practically anybody can lose a job in times like these. It may very well be me next. And think what's going on in the United States—millions out of work. Don't have a sense of shame about it. You must see people, absolutely everybody you know, and tell them frankly that you have to get some sort of job."

"I cannot bring to myself the odium. But you are right, soon I must do a roundabout."

He proceeded then to call on all the seventeen daily newspapers in Vienna, the local news agencies, and the foreign legations. No jobs. He tried the Danube Control Commission, the Pan-Europa Union, the various chambers of commerce, Radio-Wien, Radio-Austria, and several institutions devoted to cultural affairs. He applied himself to the tourist administration, the international business houses (after all, he knew seven languages), the banks, the exporters. No openings at all.

He wrote two long articles—exhaustive and discriminating treatments of Danubian political problems—and sent them hopefully by airmail to an agent in London, worrying about the cost because Austrian postage was so inordinately expensive. He waited one week and then another week. The agent refused to handle the first article because, her almost incomprehensible letter said, "it was too technical and too well done," and sold the second to a Sunday newspaper—for three guineas.

Sandor trod the streets. He was cheerful until his shoes began to go.

He saw more people and was buoyed occasionally by false hope. "I write letters to everybody else I can think of it," he told Mason. And he waited for the replies that did not come.

He heard of the possibility of a job in Belgrade, doing confidential translations in the Prime Minister's office. He went to Belgrade. The job had gone. "Soon I will become a desperator," he confessed.

When the *Sun* vanished Sandor calculated that his savings would last six months. After five weeks of searching for a job he made a radical recalculation and decided that what money he and Erji had saved must keep them a whole year. It might take a whole year to find a job. It might take even longer. . . . He scrutinized the expenditure of every Groschen. He bought cigarettes now by twos and threes, and Erji gave up smoking altogether. They began to refuse cocktail and dinner invitations—they who adored people—because they knew that they could not reciprocate any hospitality. They were even loath to accompany the Jarretts to swimming parties in the country. They still came to the coffeehouse almost every evening, but that cost almost nothing. Laszlo confined himself to one small *Nussbraun*, and Erji drank only water.

During this whole period Sandor tried hard to maintain something of his old routine, to keep up his spirit. He read all the newspapers faithfully, he was excited by the news, and he expounded to friends the background of events. He was respected as much as ever at the Weissenhof, and at the Imperial the headwaiter still addressed him as the most distinguished member of the group. What, in fact, hurt

Sandor almost as much as lack of money was his enforced inactivity. It stifled him that he could not be writing news. To be unable to express himself in days as blazing and volatile as these, to be unable to write, unable to describe the swift, implacable unfolding of easily predictable events, became torture.

When Mason left the Imperial at noon to file a story, Sandor almost wept.

"Papa, warum ruftst du nicht Par-ees weiter an?" Putzi asked one afternoon at the Weissenhof.

They hadn't told him yet.

"Bitte, Kind, Papa ist beschäftigt," Erji said.

"Der Ober hat mir gesagt, dein Büro ist nicht mehr da. Ist das wahr, Papa?"

Erji enticed Putzi away. The boy said over her shoulder, "Where did it go, Papa?"

Erji got into the habit of leaving the apartment early in the morning. Sandor suspected that she too was now looking for work but could not bear to tell him so. It revolted him that his wife should have to search for a job; it was unbearable that Erji should have to work to support him, that he would ever have to be dependent upon her, whom it was his love and pride to support. But he said nothing and pretended not to be aware of her absences. He was brief with her, tired, and stricken. If she did have the miraculous luck to find a job, he would have to pretend to be delighted. And, after all, they had Putzi to consider above everything. (And not so long ago . . . their wide, confident plans to send him to an English public school . . . their talks with Shipwright about whether Winchester would be the best . . .)

Soon another emotion tortured Laszlo Sandor. He still felt shame and grief, but these reactions were forced to the background and supplanted by another—fear. The emotion of terror came to Laszlo Sandor—terror that he might not find a job even in a year, terror that their money would give out sooner if times got worse, terror that they might not have enough to eat; literally, terror—sheer, active, violent terror—that they might starve.

He remembered his father—the glowing ease, the comfort, the indulgence of those lost days, the yachting trips in the Adriatic, the

holidays in luxurious hotels in Switzerland. . . . Yet there was not a
trace of self-pity in Laszlo Sandor. Mason, for instance, never once
heard him during this whole period talk with any jealousy or envy
about anybody else, refer in any way to the happy opulence of the
rich, or complain at all about his present status in comparison to
things past.

Erji, discarding her pride, now gave language lessons in the café,
and had half of a promise of a job in a language school. She was
perfectly competent to instruct young people in Slovak, Hungarian,
or German. There was little demand for Hungarian or Slovak, but
there must be plenty of people, temporary visitors to Austria, who
would want German lessons. Erji could ask as much as 3.50 Schillings
per hour. If she taught ten hours a day they could get along. Of course
it might be years before she would do as well as that. She had only
two students now—an hour each—and one of these couldn't afford
all of 3.50 Schillings per hour. Erji sat in an inconspicuous booth in
the café drilling out words. *Der Tisch. Die Lampe. Das Buch.* Over
and over and over. *Der Tisch. Die Lampe. Das Buch.* The drill in
genders, cases, verbs, became mechanical; she felt like a riveter in a
mass-production line, driving in words with hateful, repetitious regu-
larity. *Der Schuh. Die Blume. Das Bild.* She became rapidly worn
out and nervous. If only she could have another cup of coffee. As for
the sweets she loved, those were now out of the question.

2

News came to the correspondents in gusts, and Mason was very busy.
Economic collapse, initiated and symbolized by the crash of the
A.O.G., continued to produce political fragmentation and disorder.
The *Reichspost*, the clerical organ, flatly predicted that a Nazi invasion, launched by formal military action, was imminent, and day
by day Nazi outrages continued to deface Austria. In retaliation
Dollfuss took the courageous and sensational step of outlawing the
Nazi party. Mason grinned. Von Traum's elaborate establishment certainly hadn't lasted long. But what Von Traum represented was far
from liquidated. Underground, the Nazis might become even more
dangerous than before.

Mason took a quick trip, visiting all the Austrian provincial capitals to inspect this new situation. When he returned a story in the *Arbeiter Zeitung* caught his attention, a story about the United States. In America, the paper said, four thousand banks had failed in the past year.

Consider the number 4,000, Mason thought. It was the number of years between, roughly, the reign of Sargon I of Babylonia and that of the first Habsburg. It was the number that could be expressed algebraically as 10×20^2. It was the number of people in a good-sized village or a large factory. If, Mason continued to calculate, you counted to 4,000 with a minute between each count, it was the number you would reach in 66 hours. It was roughly the number of miles between London and Teheran, and if you walked one mile a day the journey would take eleven years. In America in the past year, four thousand banks failed.

He considered the number 2,000,000. In England, that year, two million men were unemployed.

Nevertheless—and Mason thought of it as a kind of miracle—people survived. Not only that—they were happy to be alive. The strong sap of life continued to burst through the crust of misery, men and women made love, husbands and wives cracked jokes at breakfast (even as he and Paula did), and children were being born.

"How feeling, darling?" he asked her. She seemed well, but her eyes were heavy, deeply ringed, secretive, and her cheeks had a thin, transparent look. It wouldn't be long now. Both were counting the presumptive days.

"Simply marvelous—only it's heavier every day getting out of bed."

A postcard came from Tetzel, which Mason inspected with curiosity. The representation of Red Square was amateurish, and the quality of the printing bad. Even so this was a souvenir worth keeping. People did not get postcards from Moscow often.

What a scene that had been with Karl the day following their Dollfuss party! He arrived at the villa, without notice, around noon, and demanded, "You must tell me—I have the right to know the truth—what was the origin of the loving cups in which Paula served drinks yesterday?" Mason hesitated. Tetzel went on: "Of course you would not know, but unless I am under some extraordinary misapprehension, those cups were molded from . . ." his voice did not break, but became lower, angrier ". . . from Mia—it could be no other person—from Mia, my wife!" Mason equivocated. "How did you happen to get them—where?" he continued. Mason decided that he had no choice but to tell the truth, but he did not tell the whole truth. He described Herr Abt's shop, and how he had happened to visit it with Howland Snyder. Tetzel left him.

The next morning Mason read a small item in the *Presse*. A vandal had apparently broken into the premises of an art shop near the Graben and had destroyed several objects; in particular a large file of photographs had been ripped apart. The mess, said the *Presse*, was "hideous" and "indescribable," and police were looking for the miscreant. The proprietor of the shop, Herr Abt, could not be found. Neighbors said that he had left for a holiday on Lake Balaton, with his wife and two teen-age daughters. Mason plopped the paper down. That evening Tetzel telephoned. "I wish only to say good-bye," his strained voice said. "I have much to thank you for. Perhaps I will see you again in some months—perhaps not."

"Where are you going, Karl?"

"I have accepted Tomm's offer—Moscow."

Mason the next day had a letter from Otto Wallenstein at Oxford. He wanted to know if reports about Jews being beaten up in Germany, as reported by the sensationalist press, could possibly be correct. The letter was agitated.

Toward evening that same day a cable arrived from Chicago announcing that Mason's salary was cut fifteen per cent. With a bemused expression, he took it in to Paula. "What do we do now?" He did not seem as much worried as shocked and curious.

"Darling, you might join the army. Or go to the Chancellery and ask Dollfuss for a job."

Hazelwood, Throckmorton, Preble, Strothness, Elliott, were similarly cut. Several of the *Star's* second-line bureaus—Stockholm, Dublin, Rio de Janeiro—were closed down and all stringers were put on space rates, their retainers withdrawn. Mason would have to pass on this calamitous news to his men in Warsaw, Athens, Budapest, and Belgrade. The prospect appalled him. Never in his life had he had to fire anybody. He shook with agony. Hazelwood called from Paris, his voice warmer than at any time Mason could remember. "We're all in the soup together," Hazelwood said. "Honestly, I don't dare to think what may happen next."

So now indeed the Great Depression settled down on the world of the journalists, as well as almost everybody else, in earnest. The broad low walls of their domain cracked and swayed sickeningly. Life became a struggle for existence.

❋

Sandor wrote a careful letter to his brother Heinrich, explaining his predicament in full for the first time. He had not written Heinrich earlier because he knew that he had always thought that Laszlo was worthless—ineffectual, a scribbler. Heinrich still had a bourgeois, complacent contempt for all that Laszlo stood for, and would assume that he had lost his job through incapacity. Besides he would ask him why he had not saved more during all these years. Heinrich was prosperous now, and his wire-netting and fence factory in Czecho-slovakia was doing well. Swallowing his pride, Laszlo wrote and asked his brother for a loan.

Heinrich replied that at the moment he could not see his way to help Laszlo substantially, but that considering the circumstances he was glad to enclose a check for twenty-five dollars. Sandor showed the letter to Mason, groaning, "Only the poor have heart!"

❋

Hilda, the girl with the monocle, telephoned the next afternoon. Her voice was cool as coral. She was going to New York that week, and wanted to say au revoir.

"Have a wonderful time. You must be very much excited," Mason said. She did not thank him except cursorily and he felt hurt. Like so many generous people he loved doing things for others, but he liked to have some acknowledgment of the generosity.

"It is my big chance," Hilda said. "Now I revenge myself on the toothpaste people."

"Yes. Give my best to Snyder. Is Trudi excited too?"

There came a slight hesitation. "There has been a change in plans at the last moment and Trudi is not accompanying me after all."

"Really? Why not?"

Hilda's voice was composed. "She thought that in circumstances new of this sort and so important she might be in the way."

Mason was shocked. Was Hilda telling the truth? All along he had known that Hilda was not only an ambitious but probably a ruthless person. Did she fear that Trudi would be a nuisance in the American expedition, cramp her style? Had she gone so far as to throw Trudi out?

"She must be very upset."

"Perhaps."

Mason could not resist a barbed remark. "Well, well, and I thought you and Trudi were the happiest married couple I ever met."

Hilda talked a moment about nothing and rang off.

Later that evening Paula asked Mason, "Have you seen Erika?"

"No."

"I'm going to call her up and ask her to lunch sometime. I'd like to know her better. Do you mind?"

Mason was surprised, but shook his head.

3

Mason had a letter from McFarland, which had to be taken more seriously than one from Hilliard, asking for mail stories about the two private armies in Austria, the clerical Heimwehr and the Socialist Schutzbund. Mason got to work. He contrived to see Prince Starhemberg, Major Fey, and the other Heimwehr chieftains by the simple expedient of having the whole leadership to an Anglo-American lunch. Major Fey interested him in particular. He was a newcomer to the high ranks of power—a tall man with a jutting chin, cold, saturnine, able. Few liked him, and his loyalty to Dollfuss was questioned, although he had just been promoted to be Minister of State Security. Perhaps he was destined to outdistance his theoretical commander, the handsome youth Prince Starhemberg.

Mason wrote his Heimwehr series and passed on to the Schutzbund. Its leaders, like Bauer and Colonel Deutsch, the military chief, were not easy to meet; they did not like to expose themselves to any journalist, even the friendliest. Mason managed to get permission to visit their barracks largely as a result of intermediation by Dr. Stein, and one afternoon late in May, with a heavy *Föhn* blowing, he reported at a *Turnhalle* in Floridsdorf. This was a worker's district across the Danube.

Almost before he was introduced to the officer in command Mason saw a familiar figure. A Schutzbund company from Döbling was visiting this company today and going through drill at the far end of the long, arched, badly lit hall. Surely this small dark-haired man, who walked on tiptoe, who smiled with such readiness but with timidity, this small man so trim, gracious, and agreeable, was somebody well known to him. Mason peered closer and crossed the room. It was Ernst Boericke, the journalist who worked for the Swiss newspaper. "*Meine Hochachtung! Meine Verehrung!*" Boericke laughed, tilting his head up and appraising Mason with incredulity and pleasure.

"But how did you get in? There is such fear of spies and agents provocateurs!"

"It wasn't easy. But Stein vouched for me and I had a note from Deutsch. All I'm setting out to do is write a story."

"Well, well! But I am quite differently positioned. I write by day, I prepare to fight by night. My rank is captain, although I know literally nothing about military procedures. All of us must learn."

"Comrade Boericke, I beg to be excused, but you are needed now— your company is waiting for exercise with the field telephone."

Then somebody else lumbered up to Mason, grunting a muffled welcome—old Unzicker of the *Sternblatt*.

Mason had scarcely seen him, except casually at the Imperial, since the Yugoslav *Ehrengericht* so long before. Old Unzicker! "Hello!" Why, this was almost a reunion!

Mason spent an hour being briefed, as a youthful, metallic-voiced captain took him around. He became fascinated by these men and their activity. Unzicker returned and asked him if he were getting enough for a story. "Not yet," replied Mason. Unzicker pondered. "You will learn nothing without a minimum of actual experience. I propose something now a liddle strenuous. You will pretend you are a new recruit and go through the routine, stage by stage. *Gut?* Vell then, I give the necessary orders."

Not since childhood had Mason had a rifle in his hands. It amazed him that it should be so heavy. Take up slack, hold your breath, squeeze. Hold your breath, easy on your feet, squeeze. Easy, hold your breath, rock, squeeze. Mustn't let it throw you so. Must learn just to lay the stock on the cheek and hold your breath and squeeze. He returned to the villa that night totally exhausted, as well as exhilarated, and proud of a split lip and a bruise on his cheek.

During the following week Mason became a curiosity to the whole company—the eccentric *Engländer*, or was he *amerikanisch?*—who wanted to help defend the Austrian Republic against the Nazi and Heimwehr interlopers. His own responses were mixed. It was disconcerting to discover that the Schutzbund was a pretty sloppy outfit. It had discipline, yes, but not nearly enough. The men were not well trained, and equipment was pathetically inadequate. What is going to happen to these boys if they have to fight a real army, Mason asked himself. The spirit is good, but can anybody win an armed engagement—or a civil war—on spirit alone? He knew the answer, and didn't like it. Shouts did very little good against armored cars; outmoded rifles didn't have much of a chance against machine guns.

Several times in the past few months, Mason learned, the Social Democrat authorities had volunteered to disband the Schutzbund if the government would similarly disband the Heimwehr. The government refused. In fact it had recently given the Heimwehr renewed blessing as an official auxiliary force. The Schutzbund didn't want to fight. It had been legally constituted by the Peace Treaty in the first place and its function was still held to be nothing more than defense of the rightful privileges of the Vienna municipality. It was willing to eliminate itself if the Heimwehr did. But the others were spoiling for a fight.

Some Socialist leaders still made the tragic error of confusing the issue. They could not grasp that the Nazis had become the serious enemy. If they had cooperated fully with Dollfuss—granted that Dollfuss would be willing to cooperate with them—Austria might still be saved, Mason thought. But the Socialist extremists hated the government too much for that, and were hated in return. As a result, armed collision between Dollfuss and the Social Democrats came closer, and the Nazis—the real enemy of both—prospered. Now a showdown of some ugly sort had become certain. Indeed time was running out.

Mason returned to the *Turnhalle* twice that week, and, early on Sunday morning, made his way to the Wienerwald, where, in a hidden valley near Mayerling, the company held maneuvers. He had more than enough material for his story; it wasn't devotion to the news that kept him interested, but a sense of comradeship with this group, a feeling of thrill and uplift, of community with an organization that had honesty and courage. Then too the men fascinated him as individuals. They differed widely in education, temperament, and jobs. There were bank clerks, a waiter, a dentist, a radio technician, railway workers, an upholstery designer, the proprietor of a delicatessen, and a Ph.D. in economics. Not one got a Schilling for his services with the Schutzbund; every ounce of energy, every hour of time was volunteered.

These Sunday outings cleansed Mason Jarrett's mind. In a state bordering on complete physical exhaustion, when the symptoms of fatigue were so acute that he felt drunk—he hadn't had a drink for days—he felt freer, happier, than he had in years. He was dog-tired, but his mind spun on productively of itself.

Soon he became close to the young doctor of philosophy, Hans Kreer, the sort of youngster who never, in all his days, no matter what, could be turned into a soldier. The officers knew this after his first hour of drill. They sighed. Yet they respected him. Young Kreer reminded Mason of Otto—educated to his fingertips. But he had no job in sight, no place to go. His confusion was marked, and he did not seem able to direct himself. Kreer gave point to Mason's latent worries about the Schutzbund, its diffuseness, lack of gumption, and weakness in organization. These men stood with their backs to the wall, but the leadership seemed altogether ineffectual and remote. Kreer was fascinated by Mason, as Otto had been, and Mason talked to him—often about America—for unending hours.

❋

Sandor had a call from Dr. Wimpassing, who looked at him appraisingly. "Ah! *Lieber Herr Kollege! Setzen Sie sich!*" Dr. Wim-

passing was more than ordinarily circumlocutory. He understood that
his dear friend Dr. Sandor was temporarily—ah!—embarrassed. He
understood that, as the word was, Dr. Sandor was, so to speak, out of
work. He understood perfectly that the fault for this embarrassment
was not Dr. Sandor's own. He was well aware of Dr. Sandor's unique
distinction in the world of journalism, his prestige, his close association with news sources all over Europe, and his aptitude for negotia-
tion in what might be called delicate affairs. It had occurred to him,
Dr. Wimpassing, that, in the somewhat unusual circumstances,
Dr. Sandor might well be able to render useful service to—ah—the
Austrian motherland, their beloved Austria. . . . He might—Dr.
Wimpassing coughed delicately—be willing to undertake certain confidential missions . . . gathering information . . . or conveying it.
Dr. Sandor could circulate among his friends the foreigners, travel
widely, and gather from people all over Europe details of interest
to the Austrian government on certain difficult matters without ever
hinting—ah!—that he was a secret representative of Dr. Wimpassing.
Of course under no circumstances could the nature of this work be
communicated to anyone—even to Frau Sandor. It would have to be
extremely confidential. It would be well paid. Dr. Sandor would, in
effect, be a secret agent . . . a spy . . . he would—

Sandor rose. "I will not do!"

A little later the Sandors began to sell things. They sent some of
the old furniture to the auction rooms on Dorotheergasse and got for
it about twenty per cent of its value. Then some of the pictures
went. Then—Sandor's heart burst—the old books.

4

Mason couldn't keep away from the Schutzbund fighters. He, who
had never had the faintest interest in anything military before, could
not resist dropping in at the *Turnhalle* two or three times a week.
Paula sighed and said, "My dear, it's perfectly all right with me, but
you'll end up by *joining* them!"

Presently he was introduced to machine-gun training. Dear God,
what a weapon! He joined a squad under instruction and found
himself planted behind the gun. He heard Eifelbrunn, the company
captain, say, "Kindly have the intelligence to remember that the

machine gun is not only a weapon, but a target!" while Hollering, his sergeant, with his steady, efficient bark, gave the command: "Lay the Number One Gun . . . Up! Ready! . . . Clear gun!"

"Up!"

"Range seven hundred, windage three o'clock. Number Five Paster —fire!"

This was hard physical work. The tripod weighed forty-five pounds, and when you knocked it down it collapsed in a tricky way. ("Look out for your fingers there—*achtung!*") Mason had biceps, but it was still a wonder to him that military equipment had to be so heavy. The terminology was intricate—*Schwanzstück*, for instance, "trail-leg." If good for nothing else, this experience should certainly improve his German.

He found that the guns—the company had only two—were balky and old-fashioned: recoil-operated, belt-fed, and with a traverse which covered only about fifteen degrees. Such guns might easily be out-flanked, since they could not easily turn a full circle as guns did in the movies. But Mason was struck by the enormous power of this weapon, even when it was fired in the shortest bursts. He learned more about it. He found that the bolt was not a bolt at all. He broke his nails jerking split cartridges out when the gun jammed, which was often. Above all he was amazed at the ease—in comparison with that kicking rifle—with which the gun was fired. The trigger was not squeezed or pulled; it was nothing more than a latch which lifted up as easily as a well-greased latch on an old barn door.

"Comrades!" The captain's voice was irritated and expostulatory. "I would have it deeply impressed upon you, the machine gun works by firepower alone, it operates from a fixed mount, it cannot grab a bayonet and defend itself!"

"Can you beat it!" said Sergeant Hollering, a streetcar conductor by occupation, tossing a newspaper at Mason after a period of drill. "A judge at Innsbruck acquits the Nazis of throwing bombs and five minutes later there's a new bomb in the courtyard!"

"I heard yesterday that some Nazi managed to hide a musicbox in the Chancellery and it played the 'Horst Wessel' song for an hour until they found it." Mason laughed.

"Comrade," Dr. Kreer turned to another man, "if you will take your very large feet out of my hat we would all be more comfortable."

Hollering grumbled not only at the lenience of the government vis-à-vis the Nazis but at their own weak leadership.

"Genossen!" Captain Eifelbrunn's voice could be heard from his position with the nest of guns. "For the last time I tell you there are three classifications of bolt stoppages!"

Mason learned about the *Bestrichene Zone*. A literal translation would be "beaten zone." The gun fired bullets like water from a hose and a pattern called the "shot-group" varied according to the trajectory. The bullets pelting at their target formed a cone the width and length of which changed with the range. The object of machine-gun fire was not primarily to shoot down columns of men but to deny territory to an enemy. Set up a group of guns with overlapping beaten zones and any person entering that area was bound to be hit.

Mason left the *Turnhalle* late one afternoon for the last time. It was high time for him to write his story now. He would have to be very careful not to give too much away. As it turned out his timing was, once again, lucky. Never again would a journalist be able to write a firsthand account of the Schutzbund and its maneuvers; no longer would Mason, or anybody else, be able to visit the *Turnhalle*. The government, yielding to Heimwehr pressure, bore down on the Schutzbund at last and dissolved it by decree. Legally it ceased to exist. Its formations were disbanded and its men dismissed. But Mason learned soon that the cadres were secretly maintained and that fugitive leaders continued to do their work underground.

＊

Mason and Sandor walked back from the last Anglo-American lunch of the season—soon it would be full summer—through the old Fleischmarkt quarter. Mason had heard of an antiquarian book-shop here he wanted to visit. He noticed a solid, square, inconspicuous building, with its windows barred and frosted, which gave an impression of power and secrecy. The inscription on the nameplate said "S. M. Diederbach et Fils."

"You do not know what this building is? I am exoctly surprised. It is the Diederbach *private* bank, as distinct from their public properties and the A.O.G." Sandor's voice became a groan. "They keep the *safe* business here!"

They reached the café and, as had happened a hundred times before, found Jim Drew there. He flourished a copy of the *Reichspost* with a long story about events in Washington under the New Deal and announced that F.D.R. must be Jewish. "That damned Jew Rosenfeld—thinks he can get away with that kind of stuff!" Drew snapped. He spat out the words again. "Damned Jew!" Mason turned away, disgusted. At this period even the *Völkischer Beobachter* did not call Franklin D. Roosevelt a Jew.

Erji and Paula drifted in. The handkerchief of gray lace in Erji's hair had spread further, and her eyes looked burning, as if from lack of sleep. After an hour Sandor said that it was time to go. Go to what, Mason wondered. Erji rose, opened her bag on the side of the café table, and with an inconspicuous gesture swept half a dozen lumps of sugar into it. Casually crossing over to Drew's table she murmured, "In spite of everzing you are good boy, we love you," and sat down a moment. When Drew rose she brushed against him, and Mason saw that at this table, too, she unobtrusively picked up half a dozen lumps of sugar and slipped them into her bag.

The Jarretts reached home.

"Did you see that about the sugar?"

"Yes. For Putzi, isn't it too ghastly?"

Mason shivered.

5

Luncheon party at the X—— Legation. Multilingual, polished, dull. Mason looked down the long table, ornate with flowers, the silver glittering and the glasses giving forth highlights, and listened to the carefully modulated shuttling of polite talk. The hostess turned eyes; everybody turned eyes. All these people were so well dressed, with the trousers of the men pressed to such a knifelike edge, their collars knifelike too; all the women so ugly, so conventional, in their flowered prints, and yet so confident as well. All the talk was stamped with the same fashionable pattern. *Meistersinger* at the Opera last night a little under par ... The new program at the Spanish Riding School ... How wonderful Dr. Dollfuss was, how unselfish, how courageous and heroic. ...

"I am so sorry your wife shose not to come," the hostess said as Mason entered. "You will remember—we had such a good time at the Yugoslav dance in Zhanuary."

Mason said politely, "She's sorry too, but she's having a baby practically any minute."

On his left was Vera Yancey, who was, as always, animated in a way typical of Mediterranean women brought up on sunshine. The lady on his right was unknown to him, but he identified her from her place card—the wife of one of the Balkan ministers. She asked him if he liked Vienna, averred that it was not what it once was, complained of the high cost of servants, described her *Schloss* in Carinthia, and observed that the people that one saw on the streets nowadays behaved like pigs.

"I have heard a new Dollfuss joke," said Mrs. Yancey. "When he cannot sleep at night the Chancellor either walks up and down under the bed for exercise, or, in winter, skates on the frozen surface of his pot."

After lunch the host took Mason aside. He had aggressively tilted pince-nez and a blond-fringed bald skull.

"Ah ... my friend Jarrett ..." Purring, he cleared his throat. He talked amenities for a moment. Then, "What in your opinion was the armed strength of the Republican Schutzbund before it was outlawed?"

What was this? Was this why he had been asked to lunch?

"It's very hard to estimate, Your Excellency. One guess is as good as another."

The minister drew him into a corner. His voice was smooth, inviting, confidential. "I am told, in all the confusing admixtures of information, that the Schutzbund retains its organization, it still drills secretly, its armed strength has not diminished."

He looked at Mason ingratiatingly. "What do you think?"

Was it generally known that he, Mason Jarrett, had been in close daily contact with the Schutzbund? Was the minister trying to force him to admit that he knew a good deal about the Schutzbund?

"I don't know, I'm sure." Mason shrugged.

"I daresay the positions for emergency rendezvous remain the same?" Mason did not reply. The minister inspected him keenly, and then his tone changed. "A little dangerous, I presume, a little risky, to be close to that organization now! Ha! Well, I am not unsympathetic. I too have strong democratic sympathies. . . . Have not you?"

Mason said a casual, "You bet," as he joined the other guests for coffee.

How had the minister found out? Who else knew? Was the minister doing him a favor, or trying to pump him? What spies could there be in the heart of the Schutzbund?

Mason stood between a sleek, pretentious textile manufacturer from Klagenfurt ("Must be mixed up with the A.O.G.") and a woman glacially supercilious, who, it seemed, took in paying guests, of the right kind, on her hunting properties near Eisenstadt. Repugnance, revolt, overcame Mason. This was not his world, not Paula's world. He must get out of it. These people were not his people. They were commercial, shallow, privileged, and false. Their only standards were money and success. But their worst quality was unawareness. They were not only smug, ignorant, unfeeling, but blind. They had no conception of what was going on, what might be coming. They did not even have the wit to be interested in their own preservation. Vienna was lost, lost, their society was lost, their way of life was lost—could they not see?

The beaten zone, the *Bestrichene Zone*, is shortened on rising ground, lengthened on falling ground, Mason recollected.

Mason said good-bye to his host and hostess and hiked to the Majestic, where he saluted Klaus, the concierge, and slipped him his monthly retainer. "Only eighty-five, not a hundred," Mason said cheerfully, "I got a salary cut, you get the same." Klaus laughed, saying, "*Macht nichts*, I work for you for the pleasure." Why didn't they make Klaus the Bundeskanzler, Mason thought. Or at least mayor of Vienna, or leader of the Social Democrats. This was a man of heart, of robust cheer, efficient and alive, a realist too, who would put everything in order. Of course it could not be denied that he, like the people at lunch, liked money and had certain commercial values. How rich was Klaus? Mason wondered. But his attitude toward money was different. He liked money for fun, It did not consume him.

Klaus said, "I've just heard a new Dollfuss joke. When he cannot sleep at night the Chancellor—"

"Yes, yes," said Mason impatiently.

"—either walks up and down under the bed for exercise or, in winter, skates on the frozen surface of his pot."

Mason had an appointment with Stein in the bar.

"Well, Herr Doktor," Mason began easily, "what are your leading philosophical ideas, if any, on this pleasant afternoon?"

"I have decided that for the moment I believe in teleological causation."

"What's that?"

"The theory that the goal determines conduct and action, not causations out of the past."

"In other words you're an idealist."

"Is that news?"

The Steins had just moved into a splendid modern apartment on Modena Park, in the heart of the legation quarter. They talked about Paula and Erika for a moment.

"It's difficult for me to be an idealist because there's not much moral indignation in my character," Mason said.

"I think you're more of an idealist than you're willing to admit. It's because I'm an idealist that I believe in socialism."

"But you're not even a Schutzbunder, are you?"

"Of course not. I detest machine guns and hand grenades and poison gas. I detest *radikalskis* and the hotheads in our party. It's abysmally useless to try to fight the present government with force. If we wanted to use force we should have used it last year when Dollfuss ousted the Parliament. By the way, you were certainly right about that, Mason. That was our chance to make a general strike and we missed it. But now we would be exterminated if we sought to rise."

"What's your solution, then?"

"Hold on to what we have. I've said it all before. Educate the masses. Wait."

"Suppose the government should occupy Vienna and abolish the party by force?" Mason asked.

"The government will not dare do that. They fear too much the Nazis in the event of disorder."

"Well, I'm not so sure."

"Incidentally," Stein said, "do you carry cyanide?"

"What?"

"You know all that goes on in Germany—people dragged out of their beds in the middle of the night, beaten, tortured. If there should be a Nazi *Putsch*, I should certainly be arrested. Well, I'm not going to let anybody in one of those brown shirts torture me!"

"I might be arrested too."

"No. You are an American."

"I agree with you that something unpleasant may be coming."

"Yes. And soon." Stein's face did not look sunny now. "I'm quite serious about the cyanide. In the event of my arrest it is probable that you, as a foreign journalist, would be able to visit the prisons. You would be able to see me. At least at the beginning. What I wish is that you would come to me in prison and smuggle me poison."

"I could try."

"I do not fear death," Stein said calmly. "I do fear torture. Rather than be tortured, I will kill myself."

"Why not fix up some secret little pocket in your suit and carry poison with you now?"

"It would be found. Besides"—he laughed—"how do I know what suit I will have on when I am arrested?"

Mason laughed too—somewhat hollowly.

Stein asked, "Do you think there is anything we journalists could do, right now, anything positive we could do in the proper sphere of our work, or otherwise, to help stave off a Nazi *Putsch*? Any way to break up their organization or cripple the new leadership?"

Mason had a thought, but hesitated.

"Have they arrested all the Nazi leaders?"

"By no means. There have been few arrests. You know the reason as well as I. The government wants to leave some loophole open for negotiations with Germany."

"Have they arrested our friend Von Traum?"

Stein looked up.

"I don't think so. Certainly no announcement of such an arrest has been made."

"I think if trouble comes Von Traum will be connected with it. He's the best organizer the Nazis have. I don't like the idea of turning anybody in, but he'd certainly do the same to us."

"Ah! You suggest that we contrive somehow to cause the arrest of Von Traum?"

"I didn't quite say that—"

Stein rose. "My scruples are perhaps not so great as yours. It is very difficult for us to communicate with the government. I do not think any of our emissaries have been received at the Chancellery for weeks. However, I will do my best."

6

Arriving home, Mason had once more the sense that time was running out, that all of them were irrevocably headed for some kind of dissolution. He was astonished to find Erika with Paula. If Stein knew this, he certainly hadn't mentioned it. Paula gave Mason an amused look, as if to convey a note of triumph, naughtiness, and mild perversity. It was as if she were saying, "Aren't women the devil? Observe the spectacle of your wife spending a cozy afternoon with your former mistress!"

Mason crossed the room as Erika rose, and he kissed her on the cheek, aiming at a distance as if his mouth were at the end of his arm. He smiled, "Good afternoon, my friend Frau Doktor Ricardo Stein," adding, "To what do we owe this honor?"

Erika said, "I've overstayed my leave. Paula asked me to lunch—"

"And," Paula put in, her eyes bright, "we've been chatting ever since. And do you know, Erika has just offered to do what I think is just about the nicest thing I've ever heard of. She's going to give Erji Sandor a job."

Mason sat down. He was patting Paula's knee. Apparently Erika's work was going extremely well. She continued to collaborate with Stefan much as in the days before her marriage. There had been considerable success with charm bracelets in letters that spelled out "Glück in Wien" and other greetings, together with intricate little gadgets made of gold and leather. Also Erika had devised a method of painting, not printing, designs on fabrics, which could be made into skirts. The studio was going to be transformed into a shop and they could use a sales person if, Erika had suggested delicately, Mrs. Sandor would not think such work beneath her. "The pay isn't much . . ." she explained, almost apologetically, surrounding the whole conception with something of her own considerateness and modesty, making it seem that it would be Erji who would be doing her a favor, not the reverse. "It's not to be thought of as something important, but perhaps to tide them over . . ." she went on hesitantly. "I know how fond of them you are. You are sure she would not object?"

"Object?" interposed Mason heartily. "Why, you'll be saving their lives!"

Paula went to the kitchen to make Mason a drink, while he sought to collect himself. Erika, tossing the soft black hair back from her forehead, smiled. She sat primly with her hands clasped in her lap. Mason looked at her crinkled little nose and the wonderful blue-black eyes. He remembered her sweet tender softness, her magical capacity for continuous response, her vigorous femininity. He wanted to put his arms around her. He could not do so. He wanted to cry out. This girl was the life of his heart, the heart of his life, and, seeing her now, projecting this slight precious glimpse of her far into the future, he knew he would love her his whole life long.

Yet he would never pursue her again. Never again would he telephone her surreptitiously. All that was over. He would never, never try to win her back. Why not?

There were girls whom a man wanted to marry and girls who, no matter how crazy about them he might be, he did not want to marry.

This was a peculiar truth, but it was a truth.

His wife was Paula.

"Are you happy with Ricardo?" Mason asked.

"Extremely. He is the nicest man I ever met, except you."

"I have you with me every day," Mason said. "You're in my office."

"Oh—the statue."

"Yes, but not only that."

She smiled. "Stefan sent the statue, not I."

"I know. The damnedest things keep dropping on my doorstep." He told her about Mia's breasts. "Why did Stefan send me the statue?"

"I was puzzled too at first. Then occurred to me the answer. Stefan is fond of you, but he hates Ricardo. It was a beau geste to you and I think he hoped that it would keep me in your mind."

"I don't need any reminder," Mason said.

"Perhaps in the course of years you may." Her glance was still calm, level.

Paula said brightly, re-entering the room, "Erika and I are going to the Philharmonic on Saturday." To Mason: "Want to come along?"

"Thanks, no, I'll probably be working."

Erika left presently; they both walked her to the door.

Mason asked Paula why she had asked her to lunch. She smiled, "I think you ought to be able to work that out for yourself, darling."

"You're appropriating Erika yourself to keep her away from me—is that it? By making her your friend you establish a new taboo?"

"Perhaps."

"You don't need to go through such a lot of artifice," Mason said.

"It wasn't just that," Paula said. "I think I like her very much, but of course I resent her too. I have a lot of curiosity about anybody who loves you. Oh yes she does. But please don't think that this is establishing a pattern. I'm not going to take in any other girls, just because you may have had a little flutter with them—if you ever do again. Have another girl and I'll promise faithfully to hate her, hate her to the death."

Soon Paula and Erika became friends. Erika knew that she had to obey only one rule—never, never, to show to Paula any knowledge of Mason superior to her own.

7

They had a new game at the café these days—chasing bombs. Nazi activity throughout Austria had been stepped up again. The Germans, applying their powerful shoulders to the whole frontier, made it bulge and quiver. Border raids took place more frequently, and the correspondents listened night by night to the topsy-turvy lies of the Munich radio. Poor, helpless little Germany was under fierce attack by the uncivilized aggressive Austrians! Nazi hooligans tossed rocks through the windows of Viennese shops owned by Jews, and Nazi farm boys set bonfires in the shape of swastikas on hills out in the countryside. More important was the heavy increase in bombings. The bombs were no longer amateurish homemade weapons; they were expertly designed to hurt and kill. Nor were government installations the principal targets any longer; no place was safe. When news of a bombing in Vienna came, the correspondents jumped into taxis, drove swiftly to the scene, collected eyewitness stories, and surveyed what damage had been done.

Mason sent off a long cable. The situation had reached a point, he wrote, where Dr. Dollfuss would be forced to choose—liquidate once for all, really liquidate, either the Nazis or the Socialists, because he was no longer strong enough to fight both. He could no longer maintain a simultaneous struggle on both fronts.

Drew came back from the telephone in the Weissenhof. "Bomb outside the police station, Tenth Bezirk—two killed."

Mason, Shipwright, and Sandor grabbed a taxi; Sandor still sought passionately to be a participant in everything, even though he had no paper to write for. When his colleagues chased after a story, he tagged along. Shipwright was in one of his bored, languid moods.

The taxi bumped through territory unknown to Mason.

"How's Paula?" Shipwright asked, yawning.

"Just about as well as could be expected," Mason said. "Fine, in fact."

"It must be hell," Shipwright sighed, "not just for her—you too."

Mason peered out of the taxi window. The streets were dark out here.

"Do you know how to make love to your wife's servants?" Shipwright asked nobody in particular.

Just get into bed with them, Mason thought.

"Just get into bed with them," Shipwright said.

The taxi stopped at their destination, the police station, and they got out. There came without warning a white exploding flash, then a blurred, hot, fanning sheet of light. Another bomb! The façade of the houses facing Mason tilted sharply, the street abruptly tipped up, and he found himself skidding and sliding down the street on his face. Whoosh! and another explosion sucked the breath out of him. His legs went and he felt a fierce pain in his mouth and seemed to be slapping his jaw hard against the curb.

A policeman, staggering, sought to run, while uttering a piercing, continuous scream. He ran like a blindfolded child in the parlor game in which youngsters rotate their foreheads on a cane; all his weight rested on one leg, he veered sideways in broad eccentric circles, then piled up on himself wildly against a doorway, bent, crushed; and still in broken unrecognizable language he was screaming.

Another policeman, running up, bending over him, shouted angrily at nobody, "Quiet, quiet!"

Shipwright reached Mason, leaning over him anxiously. He turned him over and propped him against the curb. A young policeman with a white face and his mouth stretched open ran up, unloosing his Gummiknüppel, as if he were confused and was about to assault those assaulted. Sandor tried to help Shipwright. His hands flapped at the wrists. Crowds gathered. More heads poked out of windows and men in shirt sleeves and women in cheap dressing gowns ran down the stairways agape and muttering, and accumulated in the street. An ambulance whished up, and the doctor, looking indignant, saying to himself "Also, also" ("So, so"), then called out to another policeman, "Was ist denn passiert?" A second doctor stepped toward Mason, who was being supported by Sandor and Shipwright. "Was sind denn das für Geschichten?"

Shipwright walked over to the policeman who had run like a child in circles. His leg had been mangled. He was dead. Mason, groggy, tried to stand; the doctor led him into the ambulance. There was a long wait before it got under way. Then in the emergency division of a nearby hospital came half an hour of confused inquiry. Mason could not stop panting. He tried to give his picture of what had happened.

"Sandor," Mason said, "take a taxi out to Döbling just as fast as you can, tell Paula I'm all right, don't upset her, don't alarm her, just tell her that I'm all right. I'll be home just as soon as they let me out of here."

"Sandor's in no shape to do that," Shipwright said severely. "Let me take charge." He went to the telephone.

Mason was not badly hurt. He had a wrenched knee, a skinned elbow, and a large purplish bruise along a cheek. He felt his jaw. The doctor bandaged him, and he yelled with pain. "You have a couple of teeth jarred loose," the doctor said. "One has been pushed upward into the bone of your jaw, pushed straight up into it. Here are pills to assist you in sleep. Go home now, and call your dentist first thing in the morning."

Sandor and Shipwright led him out to the street and they found a taxi and set out for Döbling. Shaken and bewildered, Mason could not obtain his bearings. He could not get over the thought, *So they've bombed me!*

It was an accident of course; nobody could have known that he would be there. But he continued to mutter to himself, "What a hell of a strange thing to happen. . . . I've been bombed . . . by the Nazis! . . . *me!*"

❊

Mason recovered quickly, but the dental work was painful and expensive. To a degree Paula suffered more shock than he did. To her, an intellectual and a rationalist, it was utterly inexplicable that her husband had been hurt by any such wicked, monstrous irrelevancy as a bomb. It was the irrelevancy that shook her most. Such an irrelevancy was an insult to the orderly mind. Mason tried to cheer her up, mollify her anger and appease her resentment. "Don't take it so personally. All it proves is something that we ought to know anyway—there's no security for bystanders any more."

But, Mason thought, could Paula be right? *Had* the bombing been nothing but an accident? If life were no more than a meaningless series of accidents, then a person could no longer believe logically in the inevitability of progress, in the healthy development of man. But to be categorical about such matters was impossible. Life consisted of fate and accidents both. There was no possible way to determine within the range of one human brain *all* the circumstances that gave rise to an event, or all the consequences the event or accident might produce.

Nevertheless the train of thought induced in Mason by the bombing was important, because almost for the first time he saw his life in terms of a pattern that might be capriciously, fortuitously, destroyed by an external force. He became aware in a direct personal way that the continuity of his own existence depended on factors totally outside his own control. And Mason Jarrett, the dreamer, the man of little practicality, took out life insurance for the first time in his life.

❋

Some days later Mason sat around the café early in the evening and then, bored, sauntered down the street. Paula was resting at home. He thought that he might go to a late movie, have a drink by himself in the Grand, or even go out to the Prater—anything. He still had a double nature. He still liked to prowl.

In the shadows off Kärntnerstrasse he saw the figure of a young woman who seemed familiar. A dozen yards ahead of him she stopped once or twice, rather longer than necessary, before the shopwindows. Something in her walk, in the half profile that he was just able to discern, made him wonder. Now she was buttonholing a man at the corner of an alley. The man asked a question and then shook his head at her reply. Mason drew back, and the young woman turned a corner. He could not be absolutely sure, but he thought that this girl might be Trudi. Had she left the Koenigen? Had the break with Hilda sent her into the streets?

Christ! Mason thought.

He liked Trudi, liked her intensely, and once—if indeed it were Trudi—she had done him an important favor. She was a loyal friend. He remembered too how she danced, with her solid fluid pretty grace. Hurrying forward, he tried to catch up to her where she had turned at the corner of Johannesgasse, but she had disappeared. The man she had accosted still paced the dimly lit street. Another girl—tall, with a white face caked with powder—approached this man, but Mason did not wait to observe the result. He must find Trudi. She could not be far away. The obvious places to look were Annagasse or the Seilerstätte. Desperately, Mason chased down Annagasse first. He shook his head impatiently at several girls who blocked his way. He must find Trudi, help her, rescue her. But perhaps all this was no more than a seizure of his imagination. He had no real reason for thinking that it could indeed be she.

Nevertheless, outraged, Mason continued his desperate search. Crisscrossing through the whole Kärntnerstrasse district, up one street and down another, he raced back and forth. She could not be far away unless she had picked up some man. He passed girls who paused on hearing his rapid footsteps, and, two or three times, when a girl stopped under a streetlamp, he thought that he had found her, but it wasn't she. *"Kleines!"* he yelled loudly. A girl gave him a look. He muttered an apology, then continued to pass rapidly up and down, back and forth. He could not find Trudi. She was nowhere. She had disappeared. He searched for almost an hour, then gave up.

Back at the Kärntnerstrasse he was seized suddenly by the tall chalk-faced girl. She had big eyes heavily daubed with mascara. He shook his head, but she clasped him with both hands on his shoulders. He broke away as he heard her hiss, "I'll lick your Popoloch for ten Schillings!"

Mason fled.

What kind of muddled pudding had he become, he asked himself the next morning. How the hell could a man let himself become so hysterical? Why had he not simply gone to the Koenigen to see for himself if Trudi were still there?

He contrived to get out of the villa that evening and dropped in at the Koenigen.

Trudi was not there. His heart sank. Her place at the *Garderobe* had been taken by a tall redhead.

Mason advanced to the bar. Hugo said, "Trudi? *Ach,* such troubles she had with Hilda, such troubles she gave us all. Some weeks ago she became courted by a munitions manufacturer from Pilsen and now hass run off with him."

8

Eight days later. It was Frau Gertrude's night off, and Mason and Paula had dinner at the café on Döblinger Hauptstrasse that had the nasturtiums streaming from the windowboxes. This was midsummer now, and the night was hot. Paula felt well, but they walked slowly. Crossing each intersection, before each curb, she paused and tried not to breathe too heavily. She was quite big. Her eyes were lustrous still, secretive, heavy, as if she had a little fever.

They dawdled over coffee, then went to the movies next door. The picture was a brightly shellacked American comedy; its pace was brisk and the Viennese audience followed carefully the bits of dialogue flashed on the bottom of the screen. You could tell who in the audience knew English and who did not by the tempo of the laughs—those who didn't have to read the dialogue laughed first. In the darkness Mason's hand slipped toward Paula, and he squeezed the inside of her arm.

He whispered, "Well, how's that football player in there? Kicking tonight? Getting along all right?"

(He thought, Paula's been marvelous so far. But I hope it's soon.)

Paula answered, "We're both splendid, thank you kindly."

(She thought, My, Mason will break down if this lasts another day.)

She shifted suddenly in her seat, and he tilted his head toward her, still with one eye on the screen. She put a hand over her mouth, as if she were about to faint, and leaned sharply forward.

"Mason! I think it's happening. . . ."

He slid out of the seat. Over his shoulder he got a last glimpse of a man in a top hat outside a night club in Florida flirting with a pretty girl in a bus. He led Paula down the aisle and in a moment they were out in the street and in a taxi. He would not risk the time necessary to go home for a suitcase. She was holding herself together, clasping herself, bent over. Mason gave the driver the address of Dr. Antioch's sanitarium, saying, "Carefully—but hurry!" Paula gasped, "Oh . . . it's a wonderful sort of pain . . . only . . . only . . . let's get going!"

Mason happened to have no change, only a fifty-Schilling note. The driver started to grumble, pawing in his wallet. "Hurry up!" Mason snapped. He almost hit him. A porter ran out from the sanitarium door, and Paula started to climb the broad steps, panting. "No hurry, gnädige Frau, there is never as much hurry as one naturally is given to think, do not exercise yourself," the porter said. They reached a room and presently a nurse, busy, bustling, with a broad peasant's face, helped her undress. Mason set about trying to get Dr. Antioch on the phone, while another doctor, sticking an arm through the sleeve of his starched white coat as he ran up, greeted them. This young doctor seemed nervous and alarmed and Mason became violent with anxiety when it seemed that Antioch was not at home and could not be reached.

The nurse sent Mason out of the room. He waited in the corridor, hearing Paula's gasps. Another nurse entered, carrying a hospital gown and other paraphernalia, and in a moment Paula was being trundled toward the elevator. Her stomach rose like a hill under a white blanket and her head was flung back, so that a mass of pale flame lay twisting on the pillowless cot. Her face, dead white, had become small. "Darling," she breathed as she passed him. "Ah . . . oh! Don't leave me. Don't let them take me away. Yes, go—ah!"

Dr. Antioch arrived shortly before midnight. He took one look at Mason, whose eyes were bloodshot, and laughed, "For husbands like you we usually prescribe the bar around the corner. Now, let me be."

At four in the morning he emerged from the delivery room rubbing his hands. Mason was dozing in a chair in Paula's room. "You have a splendid son. Felicitations." He added, "The birth was unusual and interesting—présentation par nez!"

"Paula's all right?"

"Yes. But it was not an easy delivery. Your son came out nose first. He will be a journalist, he wanted to see his way, so he came out nose first. But I had very much to help him along."

"What do you mean?"

Antioch shrugged. "Forceps. We shall have to have a talk one of these days. Her hip structure is too narrow. Come now. Your son . . ."

When Mason saw Paula a minute or two later he could hardly believe that it was she, with her body so flat under the sheet. She moaned and made unintelligible sounds. Then, mumbling, she said, "I am of use to you—of use—at last!" But perhaps he did not hear correctly. An hour later she looked intently at the child when it took her breast for the first time. She burst into laughter, with the words "Why, isn't he ridiculous! Isn't he enchanting?" Mason had hardly noticed the baby except to see how fantastically small he seemed to be. His eyes were pasted shut. Now they opened and the lids looked like shells being peeled upward off black almonds. Mason, who scarcely dared touch this tiny, fragile object, saw Paula's hand roam lovingly around the child's body. "How little one is born with!" she exclaimed. "But look!" The baby had a good deal of very black hair, and, smiling, Paula touched a spot proudly on the top of the skull where it clearly grew in a whorl, as Mason's did. The stamp, the signature, was there.

✻

Mason called Antioch the next day asking when he could see him.

"Gegen fünf."

Why the Viennese should say "against five" instead of "around five" was a mystery to Mason, but never mind.

Just as he was about to leave the villa a cablegram arrived from Chicago. He was notified that the Star's bureaus in Madrid, Hong Kong, and Manila were being closed down, and that the salaries of all surviving correspondents were now cut ten per cent on top of the previous cut of fifteen per cent. Mason calculated soberly. This would mean that more than half his salary was gone if he included the loss caused by devaluation of the dollar. Even black-market Schillings could not make up a loss so grave as this. For the first time since the crisis began he became frightened. He felt icy. He did not know what to do. He did not see how he and Paula could in any way continue their present mode of life. So the crash of the A.O.G., which he had caused in part, continued to pursue him.

XIV. ON THE EDGE

Now, incredibly, the calendar said that they had reached October, 1933. Mason and Paula, happy, without a tiff or tussle, living as cheaply as they could, had spent a quiet summer, and the youthful Richard Mason Jarrett, named for Mason's father, grew lustily. Mason and Paula saw changes in the colony become solidified. Nobody ever saw little old Dr. Heinrich Ritter any more, and nobody heard much from Dr. Karl Tetzel, still in Moscow. Young Dr. Ricardo Stein and his bride left for a two months' trip around the world. Bishopson, they heard indirectly, was still looking for a job in New York. The three hard-boiled colleagues had disappeared without trace—Wolfe transferred to Buenos Aires, Bass fired, Clippert back on the New York cable desk—and had been replaced by three agency men even leaner, more newshawky, and harder-boiled, by name, Cobb, Hirsch, and Callister. They were so much the same type that Mason could hardly tell the difference.

Jim Drew stayed. He had become fatter, grayer, more buttery of face, and his surliness increased. One evening at a party, when a colleague asked him—quite politely—to step aside at the buffet table, he snapped in reply, "I don't need lessons in courtesy from you, you *Schumpf!*" When he telephoned the Rumanian chargé d'affaires to ask for a brief interview with Queen Marie when she passed through the city and was refused, he shouted into the telephone, "Isn't it too bad I'm not a cosmetics salesman!" He never referred to Miss Birch any more, and the Countess was never seen.

Hotchkiss, the New York *Herald Tribune* man who had never fully recovered from his skiing accident, had gone to Johns Hopkins for a series of operations, and Allbright of the Boston *Times* took his avant-garde magazine all the way to Jamaica, gallantly, stubbornly, when his bureau was closed down. Wheatley stayed; Shipwright stayed; so did Simms, the Nazi now on the top of the wave; and Sandor was still out of work. The Depression marked lines in the faces of them all, but in Laszlo and Erji most deeply, most irreparably—even though Erji had the job in Erika's studio.

Night by night those in the colony who survived still met at the Weissenhof, bantered, and traded stories about their friends. Old chestnuts, which had rolled from café table to café table all over Europe for years, rolled again. There was the story of the copy reader in Paris who had been fired for the outrage of making love to his fiancée on the very desk of his boss, of the cook in Moscow who mistook a can of tennis balls for dumplings, and could not get them tender no matter how long she boiled them, and of the former New York *Superior* man who, consumed by drink and disappointment, left a scribbled memo with his will: "Don't put R.I.P. on my tombstone!"

Mason had to travel a good deal as autumn began. The *Star* was shorthanded, and aside from his customary Balkan rounds he had to fill in at Geneva and Berlin, even Madrid. He and Paula seemed always to be saying good-bye or hello at the Westbahn or the Ostbahn. They corresponded mostly by scribbled postcards or the long-distance telephone. Paula continued to miss him desperately when he was away, but now she had the baby to keep her pleased and occupied.

Two and a half years had now passed since the A.O.G. scandal first became known, and the shadow of economic crisis still lay heavily on the city. Nazi bombs continued to explode. There was terrorism in the provinces, hunger on the city streets. The long autumn passing inch by inch was distinguished by adjustment to bitingly altered circumstances, alarm, disappointment, unbearable uncertainty, warped values, hope, frugality, and recklessness.

The community of journalists became more than ever distinguished by ebb and flow. There were comings and goings among colleagues all over Europe. Mason in later years often wondered what had become of several close companions. The drifters, the failures, the drunks and fakers petered out and disappeared. But others who had seemed certain of prolonged good careers also fell by the side of the road and mysteriously vanished. Perhaps they lacked durability, but surely that could not be the only reason. What ever happened to Youmans, the sober, able, conscientious second man in the I.P. bureau in Berlin? Why did Severance (London *Merchant*, Istanbul) lose his job? What fate overcame the crazy youngster sparkling with dash who had been Bishopson's stringer in Budapest, who once stripped off all his clothes in the middle of a game of tennis on a hot day and played out a set stark naked, then crawled the whole length of the Dunapalota bar barking like a dog? What had happened to Larned (*Daily Compass*), who had been assigned to Warsaw and wanted so desperately to fall in love with a Polish princess and never did? What to Hamrick, the grave, utterly decent executive-looking man, who was fired by his Scottish paper because he fell in love with a girl in Athens and his wife made a witless, useless scandal? Why had Luke Ivery blown up? Surely not just because of alcohol or even that Rumanian floozy with the tic.

Despite all the turbulence, the commotion of change, despite the topsy-turviness, drift, and confusion, echoing all the way back to the A.O.G. affair, even despite being so hard up, Mason and Paula continued to live their daily existences much as before, as did their colleagues. They still gave intense value to their camaraderie, took Sunday walks in the Wienerwald, continued to wonder about such local phenomena as that, even when in love, the Viennese were sad, and admired the graceful, stately fenestration of the Hofburg. Much that happened all around Mason was hateful and his sensitiveness to the plight of others was indisputably genuine, but he himself still had a strong, positive attitude toward life, which meant that he still thought that it had meaning. The stream of challenges, the atmosphere of tension and conflict, stirred and exhilarated him. In spite of everything, he was happy. His vitality was based not merely on his inner resources, but on his love for people. He took, but he gave in greater measure. Perhaps his capacity for happiness, his knack for absorbing tumult, his fresh pleasure in satisfying curiosities, his appreciation to the full of the concept that life, such as it was, must go on were what gave him his special quality.

2

Soon the Jarretts moved. They had to. It was the worst wrench of
their lives. They spent an evening arguing, gesticulating, brooding
about the new salary cut, soon after Paula came back from the sanitarium. He knew from the beginning what would have to be done, but
he wanted her to give voice to the same conclusion independently.
Scribbled bits of paper littered the floor near the big sofa—their
calculations. They went over the figures again and again and no
legerdemain or wishful thinking could make them different. They
simply could not afford to pay any longer the rent they were paying;
therefore they had to give up this villa they loved with such comfortable and intimate love; they had to move.

What would this do to the Wallensteins? Mason shrugged. "I
think they'll miss us just as much as we'll miss them. But they'll have
no trouble renting. In fact they should have raised our rent. They'll
get more from almost anybody, probably some diplomat."

Darkness lay heavily on Paula.

"Where do you think we can find something decent for, say, half
what we're paying now?" Mason asked her. "That's all we'll be able to
pay, I'm afraid. Well, I'll sound out people, and you'd better scratch
around."

She grasped him. "Mason—I have it. Why not a *Gemeinde* house?
You have a lot of influence with the municipality—remember that
pamphlet. They'll find a place for us somewhere, I'm sure."

"That's just the kind of nutty, wonderful idea you would have!"

He remembered that day he had first seen the great fortress-tene-
ments with Stein. He telephoned Stein's assistant. Wheels moved. A
few days later the Jarretts were shown an apartment that had become
free at the Goethe-Hof, and, practically on the instant, took it. The
apartment did not have a direct river view even though it faced the
Reichsbrücke, the great bridge over the Danube, but it was airy and
had a balcony. The neighborhood had utterly nothing of the charm
of Döbling, but, from some points of view, it was more convenient;
the bus brought them to the Ringstrasse in six minutes. Rent: $11.35
a month!

Mason observed carefully the clean, compact rooms, shining with neatness, easy to run. The courtyard would be lovely in the summer and the nursery-kindergarten on the premises would be a great con· venience for the nurse they had hired, Fräulein Hedy. Certainly they would not have space enough for big parties, but nowadays big parties were out of the picture anyway. How odd it would be to be living in a building named for Goethe! His thoughts went back to that night at the villa when he had talked to Rob Elliott in Rome and quoted Goethe in connection with the expansionist habits of the German people. They were certainly still expanding.

Every night at nine Herr Michaelis, the porter in charge of their wing of the giant tenement, locked the door at the bottom of the stairway. They had to use a key to get out as well as in. Living here was almost like living in a dormitory. Another key was necessary for using the elevator, which stood inside a white shaft of iceboxlike material, smart, moderately efficient, and not much bigger than a big dumbwaiter. With passengers it traveled only up, not down. Day and night, through their somewhat flimsy walls, Mason and Paula could measure the activity of their division of the building by the wheezy sound of this elevator in its smooth-shiny, satiny shaft.

Herr Michaelis, that grave and competent man—Paula and Mason had never seen him smile—came up to take measurements for the bookshelves. Soon they would be tidy, settled. But Paula's heart remained black. The Döbling villa meant something to her above and beyond reason. Contained there, represented there, was the total embodiment of the life she and Mason had made together; it bound them, nurtured them; it was the first home of her own she had ever had, and they had passed together there nearly three years of rich, crowded life. To have had to move was a bad omen, Paula thought. But not for the world would she have said this aloud to Mason, because briskly he was trying to see nothing but the best in the new arrangement. Her job, in this period of crisis, was to protect Mason, lift him up, not bicker or haggle or give him reason to feel misery. "You really do like it, don't you?" he asked her anxiously after a week. "Yes," she lied.

Mason picked up the phone—the Dozent. They were full friends again. "I think you will be amused by the identity of your successor in our villa—we have today signed the lease with Herr Rechnungsdirektor Dr. Jacobmuth of the A.O.G.!"

❋

Almost from birth Richard Mason Jarrett showed a definite temperament. He was tense, willful, and responsive. For an infant so young his strength of personality was unusual. Paula fell madly in love with him. Her habit of realism and good sense made her want to be efficient with him, casual, not possessive, but when she watched him reach happily for a toy or turn crimson with anger at some affront she could not control expression of her delight or conceal the powerful, elemental love she felt for this husky small creature. Her passion for him became fixed and insatiable. She knew that she would gladly go through fire and water for this child. Mason's emotion was more remote, and he thought of Richard mostly in futurity; when he would pick up his first tennis ball, learn to read, ask questions about trees and snow. But Paula thought of him in a blindly concentrated and pervasive present.

❋

Mason didn't recognize the voice—German—on the telephone. "Herr Jarrett," the woman said urgently. "Yes?" "This is Frau von Traum. My husband was this afternoon arrested. Can you do something for him?" Mason thought quickly. "I can write a story about it. It's a story, I suppose." "But cannot you actively *help* him? Cannot you go to the authorities, render him assistance, help to make him free?" Mason made his voice strong. "I'm afraid I can't, Frau von Traum."

The Sandors dropped in for drinks on a slaty, windy November afternoon—the Jarretts' first guests in the Goethe-Hof. Laszlo looked terrible—he must have lost thirty pounds—but he had not surrendered his habit of irony, his levity.

"I would point out to your attention something of novelty. The great country of the United States of America possesses still the largest reserve of gold in the world and the gold coverage is fifty-seven per cent. Germany, a great country too, if you would be so kind as to believe our friends on the northward, has almost no gold at all—a coverage of 2.07 per cent. But America is 'off' gold and Germany is 'on' gold. I see that finance even not in Owstria is still containing many strange problems and I look forward to elucidation on them."

The next day Dr. Karl Tetzel came to see them. He had just returned from Moscow. That the Jarretts had moved into a *Gemeinde* house startled and impressed him. Within ten minutes both Mason and Paula knew from his talk and manner that he had become a Communist.

3

Paula listened to Mason fume. He had had a couple of bad days. Hilliard was on holiday, and his assistant, Logan, whom Mason detested, kept pestering him with service messages. One was a complaint about allegedly inaccurate figures in a story about the land reform in Poland. Then came a telegram ordering him to go to Macedonia to investigate what he knew to be nothing more than an insignificant blow-up in the struggle between the Macedonian *comitadjes* and the Bulgar government. "By God," Mason blew up to Paula, "if I ever have to rush down to any more God-damned Balkan stinkholes for stories that aren't stories, I quit!"

At this moment arrived the morning's mail. In it was a large, square envelope from the Krankenkasse covered with seals and stamps. Mason had to sign a slip for the postman as proof that he had received it. He tore the envelope open roughly and spelled out the difficult, technical German.

"Fined one hundred Schillings! Or twelve hours in jail!"

"What? Let's see."

"My God!" Mason howled. "This is going to be a real showdown. Arrest me, will they? Well, by God, they will! Call the police! Paula, give me the phone, I'm going to call the police right now, make them arrest me! Yes, I want to go to jail! Catch me paying one hundred Schillings again for all that confounded, infernal nuisance—Frau Gertrude, Frau Gertrude!" he shouted toward the kitchen. Frightened, she joined them. "I just want to tell you, Frau Gertrude, that I'm going to jail for you, to *jail!* I'm going to call the police right now and have them arrest me here on the spot with

you as a witness and I am going to spend those twelve hours in jail
for you and what a story that will be!"

"*Heiliger Gott*," muttered Frau Gertrude.

"Is it the Krankenkasse again?" Paula asked. "Oh, mercy."

Nobody ever obeyed the law in Vienna any more. This was one
of the symptoms of dissolution that had come over the city since
the A.O.G. affair. Vienna had always been a place notable for
financial slipperiness, but now the ramifying net of petty corruption
had become limitless. Life had always been complicated here by an
infinity of minor financial obligations on the part of citizens, to
evade which was the greatest of all Viennese pastimes. No day in
the life of the average Viennese was complete without at least one
small adventure in trying to cheat the government, and usually
succeeding. And now things were worse.

The profusion of taxes Mason and Paula, along with theoretically
everybody, had to pay were monstrous and irritating. At the villa
they had paid a tax on the rent. They paid a tax on the number of
windows. They paid a tax on the number of staircases they used.
Now in a *Gemeinde* house they had still other taxes. They paid taxes,
directly or indirectly, on coffee, the telephone, telegrams, restaurant
bills, opera tickets, railway fares, bank balances and beer. And above all
they paid the Krankenkasse, which was the combined fee for social
security services including health, old age, pensions, insurance and
unemployment.

Frau Gertrude, white and suffering, stood waiting by the table as
Mason continued to shout. A statement of her Krankenkasse sched-
ule, with bill and *Erlagschein* attached, had arrived as usual on the
quarter date a few months before, and Mason had duly paid it.
Then he discovered that he had neglected to fill out the correct
forms for her income tax, and this produced fantastic complications.
His own income tax situation was opened up and coldly surveyed.
The upshot was that he was fined by the government. Then came
another bill apparently to cover the interest that had accrued.
Naturally Mason forgot all about this and discovered it later in
the pocket of an old suit (the oldest suit he had, and the one he
always wore, so that he would look poorer than he was, when he
confronted the income tax authorities), tucked inside a *Fidelio*

program and scribbled over with notes from Sandor on the private life of the Empress Zita, the precise amount of the budget deficit in Rumania, and notations of train times to the Semmering.

So Mason was fined again. He paid the fine. He was then fined once more by the Krankenkasse for having delayed payment of the other fine. Now came this bewildering new fine and the threat of jail.

He flung the document across the table. His voice was sardonic. "Now I have it. We're fined now for having paid the last fine on time!"

Frau Gertrude tiptoed out of the room.

❋

Paula thought hard. At lunch she turned to Mason and brought up a subject she had brought up before. But she was calm and detached about it now.

"I'm not taking advantage of your being cross with Vienna for the moment, but let's get out."

Startled, he surveyed her.

"I feel fed up too, but—"

"We have the baby now. Things are going to pieces here. I'm frightened. It's not so much the possibility of violence, oh, you know, fighting in the streets, that upsets me, because that wouldn't touch us, but the general atmosphere of impending doom. I don't like it. It's frightening and I'm scared. It's ghastly. Let's move. I'd be willing to take a chance on getting along somehow in New York or California. Let's go home."

"We can't."

"Why not? You could write."

"We can't." He groaned. "It's the code. You're a newspaper wife, and you know what I mean. I can't quit a job under fire."

4

For months Mason had been trying to discipline himself into keeping a formal diary; he succeeded now in doing this for no fewer than twelve whole days.

December 5. Willi, our private archduke, is back from Bulgaria at last. He took us out to dinner. Appalled that we have had to move. His glossiness, his imperturbable suavity, are unchanged. He was comical about the Bulgarians. They are the Prussians of the Balkans, and the court has the stiffest protocol in Europe, even stiffer than that of Sweden. "I am a cripple," Willi laughed, "from the exercise of so much bowing." He has been trying to get out for months—no luck. Then came along this offer to be manager of the Austrian Davis Cup tennis team, which he accepted at once.

He is still crazy about Paula and she is very, very fond of him, but he defeats himself by always giving the impression that he can have any woman by the mere exercise of lifting a finger. Yet, at bottom, he is not really conceited—just can't help giving out that wonderful air of effortless superiority.

During dinner I had a mad idea, namely that Willi and I might start a restaurant together. We both love food and any decent restaurant would be almost bound to succeed here—after all, the Viennese eat five sound meals a day. I expounded the suggestion. Paula was aghast, but we shushed her. Willi began to think out loud in terms of a place like Horcher's in Berlin, with its special luxury and refinement—ham stuffed with pistachio nuts, caviar inside a baked potato, et cetera. But I had in mind something simpler that would really fill a need—a place where visitors could get a simple, quick lunch if they were in a hurry. There's no good restaurant in town now where you can eat lunch in under two hours. There would be one good Viennese specialty on the menu every day—say *gebackenes Huhn,* and one good dessert, like that dumpling thing with the hot plums inside. Herr Dorfmann of the Meissl und Schadn could be headwaiter.

At last Paula quenched us with "But where would you get the money—who'd finance you?" Our faces fell.

All such wildness aside, I ought to keep thinking of some kind of work on an emergency basis if the worst comes to the worst. Strothness said over the phone yesterday that after all Vienna—with the possible exception of Peking—was the most dispensable of all our remaining bureaus. And I don't want to leave Vienna, if the *Star* is forced to close me down. We've just got settled in this new place and Richard is too young to travel.

December 6. The Nazis have imposed a steep tax on German citizens visiting Austria. Of course the Tyrol and Salzkammergut practically live on the German tourist trade, and this could be a deadly blow to the Austrian economy.

Paula said sweetly at breakfast, "If you own a restaurant, does it mean that we'll get food free?"

Speaking of food I am up ten pounds. It'll come off again when tennis starts. Some weird character told me about an infallible way to reduce, keep in shape. You buy a pack of playing cards and, with a violent gesture, hurl all fifty-two cards against a wall, scattering them over a room. Then you pick them up one by one. Repeat this performance for each room in the house, twice a day. Promptly I bought a pack of cards, and, of course, Paula walked in while I was midway through my first pack. She thought that I had gone absolutely mad.

December 7. A letter came from Kitty Jameson this morning, explaining a lot that has been puzzling us. It took Thorne, it seems, a solid year to persuade his wife to give him a divorce, but he finally managed it. But he would have to wait until the decree is final—the usual technicality under British law—before he and Kitty could marry. Apparently they have been very happy together, though occasionally tearing one another apart in the usual banal way. But she made the great mistake of telling that damned professor back home that she was going to marry Thorne in the spring. The professor's bleats and howls could be heard across the Atlantic. Finally convinced that Kitty meant what she said, what should happen but that the professor popped off to Reno and at last got a divorce himself. Kitty didn't sleep for three weeks. Finally she decided to go back to the United States and marry the professor. Thorne is very, very sore. However, Kitty says that he behaved well. This is not a particularly edifying story. I feel sympathy for Thorne, and Kitty points out strongly that we have always misunderstood him and never grasped his true quality.

Tetzel, among others, will be pleased at Thorne's discomfiture. But Thorne will cast off the shock and disappointment, real as they may be: a seal shaking away bubbles. Tetzel's hatred of him remains relentless.

I asked Tetzel the other day what communism gave him. He replied with one word, "Fixity." He still hangs around us a good deal. Paula explains this by saying that people who have lost everything are always touched by the happiness of others.

Paula did a complete about-face on digesting Kitty's letter. "What a thing!" she exclaimed, and is horrified that Kitty should have treated Thorne so badly.

Otto Wallenstein is in town for a few days. He came to lunch. He has changed much—not so gawky. I should refine this to give voice to a paradox: his smoothness no longer betrays the gawkiness within. Otto intends to become a naturalized British citizen. He talked through lunch about how he had "changed." Paula asked him what he meant. His reply was that the metamorphosis he had undergone was too shattering, also too ennobling, to describe. "Never must I confuse the I that I am with that unfortunate being that I was!"

He slipped his wristwatch off; there on his wrist, tattooed, shone the Star of David.

"Hitler has turned me into a Jew!"

We took him in to see Richard, of course. More than anything on his limited earth Richard loves to lie on his back and balance a big light rubber ball between his belly and extended knees. His mouth will be like Paula's. The upper lip cants forward and is defined by an infinitesimally thin white line. Richard does not complicate our financial life as much as we anticipated—at least not yet. The nurse's salary is minimal.

Tonight I worked fairly well on the article on the Kemalist reforms in Turkey, which Howland Snyder thinks he can sell. I am loading it with curiosities such as the way Turkish names are spelled since westernization of the alphabet. "Amerikan Ekspres Ko, Ink" is an example, as are "or duvr," "waytaus," "Dizl enjn," and "Moris Sovaliye" (Maurice Chevalier).

December 9.   An American banker coming up from Belgrade told me that a couple of sixteen-year-old boys in Zagreb were caught cutting the eyes out of a portrait of King Alexander on the schoolroom wall. They was sentenced to life imprisonment. Good story, if I can confirm it.

December 10.   I scuttled over to Erika's studio in the afternoon after finishing a short mailer on the Dobruja. This was about my fourth session with Stefan, and he can't get me right. He says that I am a totally impossible subject, largely because of my mouth, which won't stay still; also that I have "volcanic" eyes. Nobody would guess it but in reality I am a very unstable character, Stefan says. He can't keep a "wild" look from coming out.

Stein's plane ran into a sudden squall in Singapore, crashed, and was wrecked. By some miracle neither Ricardo nor Erika was badly hurt. They're coming home by boat.

Paula is upset because I have a cold again which seems to be running into a mild bronchitis. Antioch came over.

December 13.   There has been some tension with Paula, which is my fault entirely. We ran into Nella Blohr at a dinner party and it seems that I flirted with her. I wonder if there is some kind of Gresham's law which applies to love. Does inferior love, the less valid love, tend to drive out the superior? In any case there are certain desires, instincts, which are essential to the expression of my own being—to the harmony of my own nature. Everybody has his own natural laws, which he must discover and obey. But what are mine? Am I merely saying something so banal as that a man has to be what he is? I asked Paula this and she replied, "As a matter of fact, he doesn't."

December 15. Dollfuss is making ready for the formation of his corporative state and Fatherland Front. I haven't seen D. since he was pinked by that lunatic Nazi a couple of months ago. His being shot made him the world's favorite convalescent. I still can't help liking him. He was very cordial when I called on him in the hospital, saying that he and I were obviously twins—I had been blown up by the Nazis, and he was shot.

December 16. Paula and I had a talk which degenerated into a mild fight which was comical as well. I have been neglecting her. I found her leaning over the dressing table and pressing her forehead right down against the glass—a true picture of despair. But nothing was wrong at all—she had merely given way to one of those moods in which quite sincerely she thinks that she's no good. She paraded all her deficiencies, and then crossed all the way over to the other side and said that the real reason for her habit of self-depreciation is her overwhelming vanity, which she described as "frightful." Then we got into a fight about my alleged instinct to look out for what is useful, my compulsion (as she put it) to make use of people. She said that the only reason I loved her and stayed with her was that she was useful. Naturally I denied this. She even brought up Erika and said that the real reason I had not given her up for Erika was that she, Paula, had a greater utilitarian value. "You chose to stay with me and gave up your *heart* to get ahead," she said. "You make use of everybody in the most outrageous, appalling way. If having an infinite capacity to use people for your own ends is a mark of genius you're the greatest genius who ever lived!" Well, I could only laugh at that. She tittered too. Then I became just a bit angry and told her off for some of her own obvious faults—that she's priggish for example. This made her furious. Her reply was that I had faults much worse, mostly the same old story that I was incapable of sharing myself fully. "You don't deserve a wife. What you need is a secretary, a nurse, a cook, a manager, and an *occasional* bedfellow!" I got mad at that and criticized her for being spoiled and bossy and masculine and said that in reality I gave a great deal to everybody, more than I get, and she said, "Oh yes, you're the life of the party outside, but a dead fish at home!" Then I accused her of being a filthy snob as well as patronizing and stuffy, and she ended the whole weird fracas by reverting to my alleged desire for utility in people and said, "*You'd skin your own sister alive for a story!*"

❋

A call came the next morning from the American Legation in Budapest. An interview Mason had sought for years with Admiral Horthy, the Regent, had at last been set up. This could be a very important story. Mason forgot his bronchitis, forgot his diary, forgot the tiff with Paula, asked her to pack for him, and caught the noon train.

5

Mason liked Budapest, if only because it always gave him a feeling of freedom, of relaxation. He took a Hungarian friend, the foreign editor of the *Pester Lloyd*, out to dinner on the island. A great smeary orange lollipop of a moon hung over one of the bridges. One thing that made Budapest, with its gloss, its sheen, so different from Vienna was the river. It was a city of the river, on the river, by the river. The casual visitor practically never saw the Danube in Vienna, but in Budapest nobody could get away from it for a moment. It flowed right through the heart of the city. Then too most Hungarians, romantic as they were, had much more solid stuff in them than the Viennese. They were a curious mixture of the sacred and the profane.

Mason drove his friend home and returned to his hotel, the Dunapalota. He called Paula and had a long close talk with her and told her that his appointment with the Regent was established for the next day after lunch at the Legation. She said, "The next time I talk the way I did yesterday, conk me on the head. Hold me under a water tap until I *drown!*"

Restless, Mason descended from his room to the flamboyant lobby and had a drink alone in the bar. He thought that he might go out and have a nightcap at the Arizona, but decided against it. Better nurse his bronchial cough, go through the Horthy clips again, and turn in early.

Walking over to the porter's desk to pick up his key he ran into Nella Blohr.

He greeted her with pleased surprise. "Nella! How nice to see you! You look charming. What are you doing here?"

"I drove down with Otto. He is courting a rich girl who lives in the country. Tonight I am alone."

"Let's go out and have a drink."

The Arizona, which was as flashy a cabaret as Central Europe could provide, put on a lively show, and the *Animierdamen* in the loges looked sumptuous. A team of acrobats appeared with a greyhound, which was tossed around with great abandon, eventually being flung in huge circles between the legs of the acrobats. A magician (no cabaret like this was complete without a magician) performed arcane miracles with roses and an elephant's tusk, and the performance of the cimbalom player was exemplary. One of his fellows in the orchestra had an unusual instrument, a guitarlike box with thirteen strings.

Nella appeared to be guarded, somewhat aloof, and Mason asked her about her work. He had heard that she now had a part-time job in a metallurgical laboratory. He remembered that evening they had met outside the villa with the *Föhn* blowing so long ago.

"To talk about my work gives me an ulcer!"

He was taken aback. "If you hate your job that much you ought to give it up. You're too young for ulcers."

"I don't hate my *job*, what I hate is *talking* about it."

He tried a different tack, mildly flirtatious. "When two people meet by accident in a strange city, do you think it means that fate is giving them a nudge?"

She cocked an eye at him. Mason had not meant his question to be taken seriously and he was surprised when she replied, "In this case, I hope so!" He knew that she had had a crush on him, but he thought that it had disappeared. Young girls are fickle, volatile. What a strange, difficult, pretty creature she was, he thought, kittenish but something else as well. He admired her freshness, the silky elastic texture of her hair, her eyes now staring at him with deliberation. He said lightly, "You're one of the few girls I know who can turn their eyes on or off." She replied, "You talk with your eyes too. But your eyes don't always smile when your mouth does." This caused him to take stock abruptly, and he made absurd grimaces to demonstrate that his eyes did smile. Now they were both laughing as the orchestra beat into a rumba.

Nella was provocative, arrogant, and appealing all at once. The long tendons with the hollows stood out on her youthful throat. She was a difficult girl and difficult girls showed signs of strain easily. Mason had a coughing fit. "I've had a cold in my chest—sorry," he apologized. "It's two in the morning, and I have to be up early. I'll take you home."

Obediently she rose. She tidied herself and they walked out of the establishment. He held her arm close above the elbow. Mason became somewhat alarmed when, back at the hotel, he discovered that her room was on the same floor as his. He was now almost certain that if he suggested it and took the time to press her and paid court to her he could make love to her, but he did not want to do so. Think of Paula. He took her dutifully to her door.

"Good night, Nella. You're a darling. Rather, you're not a darling at all, but you're attractive. You're a little crazy, quite complex"—he smiled—"and a tough little nut as well." He kissed her on the cheek. "Well, good night."

"Good night."

He could not get to sleep. He felt a lack of ease, and his large body tossed. He could not control his coughing. His opening question to Horthy ought to be about Hungarian revisionism . . . then something on the Nazis. . . . Mason heard a curious sound. It was not a knock, not a tap, but a scratch. He listened carefully, then became rigid. Somebody was scratching very lightly on the door of his room with a fingernail. It could not be a key or other implement. It must be a fingernail. The sound was that of a spoon grazing the inside of an eggshell. He switched on the light, levered himself out of bed hastily, and strode to the door, pulling it open. There stood Nella. She looked wan. She put her fingers across her lips saying "Sssh," and he led her into the room with an arm protectively around her shoulder. He turned her around in his arms. Now her little hard ball of chin was low and he lifted it. From her eyes came a message at once questioning, bold, and shy. Her breathing was sweet and she seemed embarrassed, even frightened. Mason held her closer and when he kissed her he felt her lips respond, quivering softly. My God, she kissed like Erika! With that peculiar Viennese lusciousness, her lips widened, quivered, they grew warm, they became soft and hungry, they searched him. He crushed her thin shoulders in his hands and sat her down on the bed almost roughly. Like Erika! But no, there was a difference. This girl kissed him with her lips, but her soul was not exposed.

Neither had said a word.

A thought came to him; his eyes pried.

"Did you know that I was here in Budapest when we met tonight?"

"Yes. I was lying. Otto is not here at all. He called your *Wohnung* to say good-bye, and Paula told him that you had gone to Budapest. I followed you on the next train. I have pursued you here."

He reached for the buttons on her blouse.

"No, no. It is ridiculous after all this, but I cannot."

He kissed her again. "Why not?" His scruples, his fear, had vanished.

She bolted for the bathroom, and came out a moment later naked. He had never seen a slimmer, whiter body. He had forgotten that there could be breasts like these. But across her hips—Mason stared— he saw a white bandage, a light menstrual harness.

He understood. "Oh!" Disappointment overcame him.

She bent her head in what seemed to be abject apology, and pressed her breasts, so firm and round, so youthful, against his chest. The nipples stood out like pink raspberries. Her face took on an extraordinarily enigmatic look—tender, daring, ashamed. He kissed her again. She seemed to become more frightened and twisted suddenly away. Then, as if all the strength had been sucked out of her, she bent her head.

"I . . . I feel like such a fool. . . . I don't know what to do."

"I don't see any reason why you shouldn't sleep here anyway."

She climbed into the bed, smiling now. Cautiously he held her. She pressed her hands against his temples and with swift friction rubbed her hands hard against his hair, then lay there tensely. Mason fell asleep, but he woke up an hour later with a burst of intuition. But to put on such a charade—why? To test him, try him? Perversity? Timidity? Sheer naughtiness and trickery? To determine once for all how daring he was? To symbolize a *ceinture de chasteté?* He reached toward her, turning her over, and cautiously undid the strap of the white harness-bandage. It was as he had guessed—of course. The harness was a fraud, a fake.

She wakened but said nothing. He could hear her breathing. They made love, and Mason had a second surprise. He discovered that she had never been with Tetzel, or anybody else, and was glad.

＊

Mason was late for lunch at the Legation the next day and did not seem totally in focus during his interview with Admiral Miklos Horthy von Nagybanya, Regent of Hungary. The Regent said testily to an aide after he left, "Very absent-minded fellow, that American! Confound him, I had a sense he wasn't paying the slightest attention to what I said."

6

Mason was back in Vienna. Journalists from the four press associations met at the Chancellery at eleven and got into three official cars, escorted by Dr. Hohnstedt. The trip took an hour through slush and rain. It had taken weeks to get permission for the visit and Mason said cynically that the authorities certainly had had plenty of time to get the place nicely cleaned up. "Quite," Wheatley, who was also representing the Anglo-American, agreed. Their destination was Wöllersdorf, the first—and only—concentration camp in Austria. The Colonel in command was an apologetic, fussy little man who looked worn out. The journalists' delegation walked into the barracks and a salvo of boos, mock cheers, whistles, and stamping of boots came from the imprisoned Nazis. About four hundred political prisoners, mostly Nazis, were in Wöllersdorf now, charged with sabotage, incitement to riot, or conspiracy. The Austrian government, taking the hint from Germany, found it more convenient to intern them without trial than to give them a public hearing.

The Nazis continued to boo, shout, stamp, and bang with their tin cups and plates. "No discipline . . . no discipline. I am not supported from above," muttered the Colonel. "My predecessor was transferred after three months with a nervous breakdown."

A prisoner shouted at the Colonel, "Imbecile! Scoundrel!"

About twenty men stood defiantly. It was impossible to tell who had called out.

"Bravo, bravo!" shouted the others, backing up the leader. "Bread and water for a week for the man who said that!" screamed the Colonel. "Find him!" he said desperately to one of his lieutenants. The lieutenant looked helpless.

"Very well," the Colonel said. "Bread and water for two days for every man of you, the whole lot!"

The Nazis looked picturesque, because, although they could smoke, read, and play games, they were not permitted razors. One could tell how long each man had been in prison by the length of his beard. Mason kept his eyes open. He was looking for somebody. Bedraggled Heimwehr guards, who seemed to be less fit than the prisoners, carelessly watched a group of Nazis playing football. At the corner of the compound, Mason noticed, a stack of rifles stood unguarded. Wheatley prowled inside, and saw that the cell doors were not even locked. "It's certainly an Austrian kind of concentration camp," Mason said.

On being questioned by the journalists the Nazis wailed and roared. Mason and Wheatley found themselves in the center of a circle of waving arms. The prisoners wanted desperately to communicate with the outer world; they wanted to transmit messages to their wives, their sweethearts. Complaints were loud, but it became clear that there had been no beatings, no wanton cruelties, no punishments out of the ordinary. Obviously the Nazis were well fed, and the place was decently kept up—even the toilets were reasonably clean.

"Think by comparison what a German camp is like. Oranienburg or Dachau," Wheatley whispered. "This is roses and honey by comparison."

But one of the German correspondents, a member of the journalists' delegation, protested violently that this concentration camp was an infamy, a disgrace. He kept muttering in a high monotone, as if he were witnessing the most ghastly spectacle in the world, "Shame . . . agony . . . disgraceful maltreatment . . . the shame of it!" He became hysterical. "God deliver me from Germans even if they're not Nazis," Mason mused.

He found the man he sought. Von Traum sat alone in the machine shop. His beard, probably six weeks old, was raw and yellowish. Mason could not forget that he and Stein had put him in this place.

"Von Traum! Hello!"

The German dropped his tools, and the expression on his face was one of the most terrible Mason had ever seen. He looked strangled. He looked as if his brain were boiling inside the skull. His words seemed to emerge in a spatter of steam.

He gasped: "Jarrett!" For a moment he was unable to utter more. Then, hoarsely, "Give me information—quick! We know nothing here. There are no newspapers and only music on the radio. How is it with the *Bewegung*? Tell me who is now in charge underground? How has the organization been maintained? Oh, don't be a fool. I know you're nothing but a journalist, you have no inner knowledge of our doings, but you should have some information about such matters. It's your business. What is the situation in regard to propaganda? Has the ban on tourist traffic hurt? Quick! Tell me."

The vision came to Mason's mind of the thousands of absolutely innocent men and women, tens of thousands, whom Von Traum's own people had put into jails and concentration camps.

"I don't know anything, Von Traum."

He grasped Mason.

"Get me out. We have been friends. Get me information if you can, but above all *help me to get out!*" There was desperation in his voice, a hysteria of terror.

"I can't do anything. I'm sorry you're stuck here, but there's nothing I can do about it."

Mason thought, And if you Nazis take power in Austria it'll be Stein and Tetzel and Boericke inside this wire, perhaps me too, and a fat lot of help we'd get from you!

Who could know indeed? . . . Gustav von Traum might very well be a member of a Nazi government in Austria some day.

❊

Mason arrived back at the Goethe-Hof at dusk. He noticed how the great building commanded the Reichsbrücke on a bias. Here the river was much less fresh than in Budapest. It looked like flat floating intersecting turtles.

Herr Michaelis, in blue overalls, was scrubbing the front steps and cleaning up for the evening. Mason felt friendly. "Not such a bad day considering it's December," Mason said.

The Hausbesorger straightened, leaning on his mop. He nodded.

The conversation seemed to be running down.

Mason proceeded: "I'll bc glad when winter is over. Of course there's still quite some time to wait."

When winter was really over. For some people winter was never over. What was Herr Michaelis's private winter?

He had a sudden thought of young Richard upstairs. "You and Frau Michaelis don't have any children, do you?"

Michaelis answered in the negative, and Mason went on doggedly, "Well, that's too bad."

Michaelis replied surprisingly, "Birth control is the first defense of the proletariat."

7

"Prosit Neujahr!" The words rang through the tense, stricken city as 1933 became 1934. The first January days were harsh, and not merely in the realm of climate. The government and the Socialists continued to snap at each other, and the Nazis made new troubles. Then Mason was delivered for a moment from the Vienna scene, because the *Star* assigned him to cover the League Council in Geneva. This was normally Hazelwood's beat, but Hazelwood had influenza. Mason made plans to go.

"I think I'll come with you," Paula said.

He hesitated. He wanted very much to get away. "No, sweet. I'll only be away for a week and it's hardly worth the effort. Besides, we can't afford it."

"I'd love to see Mont Blanc again and have a bit of winter sun."

"Lord God, there's never any sun in Geneva!"

Mason had just returned from a rendezvous with Nella. He wondered if anything in his face or talk could give him away. To see Nella in secrecy required careful maneuvering. He went into the bathroom and scrubbed his face hard.

"Dinner ready soon?"

"Yes." Her voice was hurt, even cold.

Mason was not in love with Nella in the least, but he found her delectable and exciting. Every time he left her he thought he would not see her again, but then could not resist telephoning her the next day. He got into the habit, which delighted him, of buying her little gifts—objects on the level of a mechanical pencil. She was unbelievably fresh. She had a strong will and pretended complete independence of him and anybody else, but the simplest thing could melt her. He sent her some yellow roses one day and she was completely bowled over, ravished with pleasure. One of the nicest, most rewarding things about being in love, if you really were, was that it gave you such illimitable and marvelous power to bestow happiness on another. And how splendid the refreshment that came to oneself, the creative delight, the spur to the imagination, the lift to the expanding ego! Then too Nella was original. She was fascinating to explore.

But Mason did his best not to think of her in connection with the normal level of his life. He hated deception but, as a matter of fact, he felt little of the gnawing, corroding guilt he had felt about Erika. But of course he had been madly in love with Erika. This was nothing more than a brief romantic companionship. He compartmentalized himself. Nella filled a sliver of an enormous space otherwise occupied by Paula, and was altogether separated from her, dissociated, not a problem connected with her at all.

Mason scowled. Am I telling the truth to myself, he asked himself. The plain fact of the matter was that he had become much more deeply involved with Nella than he admitted. She excited him beyond measure. He could not forget even the most trivial or outlandish of her remarks. Once she had whispered, "I love to get lipstick on your teeth!" He could not get her out of his mind. But it had to stop. He muttered to himself, "What has happened to me? What kind of person am I? Now I too have become corrupt!" He began to think of Paula more directly. He shook his head angrily at himself. "What is worse than betraying Paula is the reason for it. In some monstrous way I seem to be taking some perverse pleasure in betraying her. I think secretly in such odious terms as 'Serves her right!' I am paying her out—but for what? I am revenging myself on her—but why? She is a completely, utterly virtuous woman. That has always been her principal hallmark, the epitome of her value. Do I resent this? No, no! I'm proud of it. It relieves me of the most vexing burden that can come to a relationship—jealousy. What then is my subconscious motive? Ah! I resent her superiority, that she is superior to me and dominates me. What I am punishing her for is my dependence on her!" He grunted with displeasure at himself.

Paula, when Mason left, felt more than ordinarily depressed. She stared into the darkness. Erika, who had arrived back in town with Stein on Christmas, called and suggested lunch the next day and she accepted willingly. They took Erji Sandor with them. It gave Paula a pleasant sense of satisfaction to be with Erika. After all she, Paula, had Mason; Erika didn't. Erika asked how Mason was and Paula thought, She's still in love with him, but will never move an inch.

What was it Erika had just said? "Women are so vulnerable when they're unhappy, aren't they?"

Paula looked up at her. Mason had said that once in reference to Kitty. But she, Erika, could not be unhappy; she was radiant, purring, glowing. Could she be making a veiled reference to herself—Paula? Hardly—because Erika with infinite delicacy never intruded upon the personal. Paula observed her with increasing interest. Once she had called her a marshmallow. Well, she certainly wasn't that. She gave out without effort, perhaps without even knowing it, an insinuating scent of subtle eroticism. She sat there with her eyes down, as demure as a milkmaid, but every man in the restaurant— even the waiters—caught it. It was like a perfume. Paula sighed. How she envied it.

Back at the Goethe-Hof Paula, alone, had a poignant memory of the Döbling villa. Sternly, she cast it aside. She put some Vivaldi on the gramophone; the precise metrical rise and fall of the notes, like lines on a chart, made her quiver with delight. Guiltily she rushed to the machine, making its voice lower. It seemed impossible to remember that she could no longer play music loud; the Goethe-Hof walls were far too thin.

Her mind flitted to Mason. Why was he being so recessed these days, and also so affectionate, so protective, as if to make up for some other lack? Why had he retreated into one of his old spells of private distance? Why was he both attentive and remote? That was the way he had been when Erika was still a secret. What did the mad, troubled creature really want? What caused his self-division? Well, that was easy. He was an artist, but not an artist enough. No, no, she reconsidered, that wasn't quite the way to put it. As a matter of fact from one point of view he wasn't self-divided at all, although he liked to think he was. He was simply a man doing a job he liked, who wanted

to do other work and have another life as well. But why was he so
hard to reach? Well, she had often called him "romantic"—which
meant that a person held close to his illusions and did not want to
have them touched for fear of losing them. But as a matter of fact
Mason wasn't so darned romantic most of the time. He was often curt
and coolish and he had a very lively sense of most realities. "Oh glory,
I give up!" Paula said.

It was time for Richard's bath. She observed the baby's fat, smooth,
round legs and small grasping hands, which were very strong. His
fingernails were triangular tiny spades; the fists still showed no
knuckles. He began to wail, and she kissed him. The telephone rang
and she turned him over to Fräulein Hedy, drying her hands on
her skirt and skidding out of the room to answer the telephone. This
must be Mason calling from Geneva. No—Hal Shipwright.

The Vienna grapevine carried news swiftly; already Shipwright knew
that Mason was away. He talked about what was going on for a moment and then asked her to dinner; she declined. A long, lonely evening followed. Silently she sought to draw sleep out of the night.

Shipwright telephoned again soon after breakfast, saying that the
snow wasn't too bad on Kahlenberg and would she ski with him that
afternoon and then dine? Temptation stirred her. Paula, Mason, Shipwright, and other friends had had several skiing expeditions recently
and she had just reached the point of being able to get herself up—
and down—a modest hill. Today, however, she didn't feel like skiing.
Not often had she met a man as good-looking as Shipwright who was
also well mannered, graceful, and not unamusing, but she was not sure
she really liked him. Not since their passage together at the
G'schnasfest had he made the slightest advance to her. No doubt his
vanity made him fear a rebuff. But the frankness with which he
looked at her or sat himself close beside her in the café, as if they
had a secret that needed no discussion, disconcerted her. What an
idiot she was, she thought. She regretted her decision. She might have
had the most amiable of dinners with him; it would have been perfectly innocent and Mason (so sure of her!) would not have minded
in the least. A little skiing could have been distinctly pleasant, with
Jause afterward in the Kahlenberg inn, full of the clatter of young
people knocking snow from their shoes and bending over to rub their

pants free of hairy ice. Shipwright would take off his huge red mittens and order a *gemütlich* tea. Idiot! she said to herself again.

It really was strange that Mason hadn't telephoned. Swallowing her pride, she put in a call for the Beau Rivage in Geneva. The operator said that Monsieur Jarrett had left a message that he was not to be disturbed. Paula thought, Well, he had a big night in the Bavaria or somewhere, maybe with the Cookes if Cooke has come up from Madrid, and he's sleeping it off. But when is he going to file his story? Funny!

Frau Gertrude made her scrambled eggs for lunch; she pecked at them. Shipwright telephoned again at three, as Fräulein Hedy bundled Richard up for his afternoon expedition in the nearby park. "Please meet me in the Renaissance Bar tonight, half past six," Shipwright said in his best languid voice.

"I'm just not in the mood. I'd love to see you, but I don't feel like going out—laziness, I guess."

He persisted. "We haven't had a moment together for months." Nettled, she retreated into a coil of reserve, disliking the intimacy implicit in this remark—why should he assume that they should have a moment together, ever? Oh, bosh, I'm being too touchy, Paula thought. After all they had been friends for several years.

"I want so much to see you for a special reason—please."

"I hate to seem so negative, but—"

Shipwright said with decision, "I can't force you to come, but I'll tell you what I'm going to do. I'll go to the Renaissance at six-thirty sharp and I'll simply wait there. Six-thirty, seven-thirty, eight-thirty, midnight—till you come."

He rang off.

Damned impertinence, Paula thought. But she was flattered. Nobody had ever made quite such an approach to her before. It was extremely obvious, old-fashioned, and Viennese, but somehow it carried a festive thrill with it. Of course he didn't mean it. Hal Shipwright was an exceptionally egocentric young man with a hundred fish in his net; he wouldn't wait ten minutes. Six-thirty came, and still there had been no call from Mason. At seven Paula began to wonder uneasily if Shipwright could really have turned up at the Renaissance and was still waiting. She telephoned his flat; no answer. Should she call him at the bar, tell him to make himself scarce, say that she was not, under any circumstances, coming? But how childish it would be for her to go through any such performance. What was she afraid of? Seven-thirty came and Paula, on edge, became desperate. After all, Ship-wright was a close member of their community. Certainly he was taking advantage of her good nature, but there was no reason for her to be so stubbornly disobliging. The phone rang; she jumped; Sandor asked what news she had had from Mason in Geneva. "Nothing much," she evaded. Eight o'clock. Eighty-thirty. She changed clothes swiftly and took a taxi to the Renaissance. Calmly, Shipwright was waiting there.

✳

How the devil had he got her up to his flat? Good God! There had been a luxurious dinner at the Three Hussars, with dry martinis, a couple of bottles of wine, brandy, Scotch and soda. He had been the quintessence of amused, calm gentility; not a word to make her think that she had anything to fear, not the slightest advance by word or hand. His eyes burned, though. Then they had taken a taxi to an ill-lit boîte with charming Hungarian music where the guests could, if they wished, sit in hammocks. And they did. But what had hap-pened then? They had more wine. Yes—but what else? How was it possible that she could be lying now in Shipwright's bed? She jumped up, incredulous, agape, wildly staring; she discovered that she was stark naked and that her clothes lay in a disordered heap on the floor. She remembered saying, "But I can't . . . I can't. It's impossible for me unless I'm in love. . . . I can't possibly. Hal, you just must not."

She sat shaking on the edge of the bed, wild with astonishment. He woke up, kissed her, and pulled her back into the warm bed, and they made love again. Who had ever called him languid? He was tumultuous, expert, and voracious. "Now sleep a while," Shipwright said.

But this man meant nothing to her, nothing! She thought of Tom Cairn, even of Ralph Conyers, who cared for her, really cared. But perhaps the fact that Shipwright meant nothing made it all right.

Now she too was asleep again.

8

Enormously chic, tidy, much relaxed, Valerie Birch left the hotel to stroll around Schwarzenbergplatz. She had half an hour free before lunch. A walk, any kind of walk, was always an adventure for her. First this turn, then the next turn, first to the right, second to the left. This morning's half an hour was nothing more than a bit of exercise to kill time, but she seldom walked carelessly, casually, as other people did, without thought of purpose or direction. Almost always she marked out her path in advance, worked out her route with care, then tuned her mind to a certain pitch to follow it and reach her end.

Miss Birch jumped back as a taxi almost hit her. Resentful, she frowned at the driver. This was an affront. This reminded her that accidents could disturb the best-laid plans. Sometimes her friends thought that she seemed to be almost simple-minded about the realities of the external world. She would not believe that a rock really had weight until she tried to lift it; she could not realize that a car might topple over if it turned too quickly.

Valerie was much better. Only seldom did she have those searing periodic headaches. She had, however, returned to Vienna briefly for a final brushup with Dr. Voelker, and his resumption of her analysis now reached down into the very bowels of her past. Not once had she visited the café, and she had not even telephoned Jim Drew. Paula and Mason—he had just returned from Geneva—ran into her by chance at a cocktail party at the Heather-Smiths'. They were warm and protective and expressed hurt that she had not called them and at once asked her for lunch later in the week. This would be the first lunch party they had had at the Goethe-Hof; they would just be able to squeeze in six guests and they decided to ask the Yanceys and the Steins. What about a man for Valerie?

"Shipwright," suggested Mason.

"N-no," Paula said.

"Well . . ." Mason fished around. "Why not Tomm, the *Pravda* man? He's probably never met a pretty millionaire."

Tomm was out of town.

"Willi," Paula suggested.

"Good!" And at once Mason became possessed of an idea. The Archduke had done him an important favor once, and Mason was a man notably punctilious about paying debts.

Miss Birch glanced at her watch and hailed a taxi. Paula had said that lunch would be prompt. Miss Birch felt that it was very dashing for the Jarretts to live in a *Gemeindehaus*, but it disconcerted her to find that their new quarters were so small. Introductions were performed. What a delightful-looking girl Mrs. Stein was, Valerie thought. Clearly Yancey thought so too. He was falling all over her. She's tentative, she's proper, Miss Birch said to herself, but something else as well. Erika's laugh tinkled as she fended Yancey off.

The Archduke's smile as he sat down next to Miss Birch was that of a man rubbing his hands secretly. He glowed all over, lustrous. Mason had not said a word to him about her except that she would be somebody moderately decorative and pleasant to meet, but Willi had an experienced, accurate eye. From the first second, he knew that she was rich.

His conversation was bland, effortless.

"I know exactly what you think of me, Miss Birch. I am old, I am corrupt, I am useless. You with your democratic background have a deep prejudice about persons with my inheritance. We are anachronisms of no value, haughty, brittle, disgracefully inbred, and perhaps stupid as well." He paused. The russet mustaches quivered. "And do you know, *gnädiges Fräulein*, every word of what you think is true!"

She replied seriously, eyes bright, "No, that's not what I think at all."

"What do you think?"

"That you're trying to impress me by giving a bad account of yourself, and I find this rather amusing."

Willi totally neglected Paula on his other side.

"What line do you take in politics?" Miss Birch asked.

"Politics, a lot of *Quatsch*!"

"But you mustn't say that about politics, or I'll think you're irresponsible."

His small brown-red eyes, crinkling within their pouches, sought the ceiling. "Very well. First, I hate the Nazis."

"Good."

"Second, I think that on the whole you would have to call me a conservative, if only because on several levels I believe in conserving things."

"So do I. *Certain* things. But don't you belong to a world that's lost? Aren't you conserving feudalism, privilege, exploitation, poverty?"

"I do not think it fair that we who created Austria, who are its former brains and blood, who made the nation, should be ground out of existence so that people who aren't capable of earning a living should be kept alive by state charity!"

Talk became general, and several crosscurrents were apparent. The Archduke told stories about Bulgaria, mentioning that King Boris drove a locomotive for exercise and how the people were so frugal that they carried their shoes in their hands to save wear on the leather. The table rocked with badinage and laughter, and nobody rose till after four. Mason heard Erika offer an opinion to Yancey about Kandinsky and Kokoschka, and the Englishman's reply was emphatic: "You cannot be such a child as to think that! My God, girl, art has to have reality—face it!"

Mason managed to have a word with Erika alone. There was no tension at all between them now, nothing binding them. No longer did he see her face, so serene, so sweet, swimming before his eyes the first thing every morning. He told her that he had been having a "problem." Erika, with the intense sexual sophistication of the Viennese, guessed at once what he meant, and her voice in reply carried a note he had never heard in it before, a note of warning and appeal. Then she scolded him when it appeared that his problem might be serious. Erika said, "Mason, please do not do any foolishness, please! Paula is worth ten of anything. Be very careful, and do not do anything foolish at all that will last. If you should ever part from Paula you would make the greatest mistake in the world. You would be utterly lost without her. Without Paula you are nothing."

Mason was disconcerted. He sought to protest.

The Archduke and Miss Birch left together, following Stein and Erika. It was five o'clock. At last the room was free of their guests; Mason sprawled in a chair, and Paula said, "I knew right away that you had a bright idea when I thought of asking Willi. Do you think it could possibly work out?"

"They seemed to fasten on one another." He was fighting in his mind what Erika had said. *Would* he be lost? Would he be nothing?

"What if it goes on? Will she have reason to be grateful to us in the long run?"

"Neurotics are never grateful. Anyway I'm a great believer in masculine solidarity and I'm on his side more than hers."

Since his return from Geneva Mason had seemed even more abstracted and remote than before, Paula thought. Obviously he was much upset by something. She gave a thought to her own secret life, which still gave her a sharp tingling sense of guilt. She was still amazed at herself. What if Mason should find out about Shipwright? She had been seeing Shipwright secretly all the time and now this made her extremely nervous. In thinking about Mason and whether he had possibly become involved in some new love affair she must keep steadily in mind her own sensationally new position. Now she had a lover. But she yearned ardently for Mason. The lunch had excited her and she felt exposed and generous, impulsive and aroused. With all her heart she wanted Mason to make love to her, right there, that minute. But he hoisted himself heavily out of his chair, groaned, said that he had work to do, and walked out of the room without so much as the pat of a hand on her shoulder or a kiss on her hair.

*

That evening, Miss Birch said to Willi, "Are you going to marry me for my money?"

"Yes. But I rather like you, too." His laugh was amiable.

"Why?" she asked.

"It will be a challenge to control, assist, and perhaps love a slightly crazy woman."

Later she whispered, "Don't make me pregnant. I'm sensitive about it."

"Who isn't?"

"When I was nine years old my older brother, Robert, fondled me —you know, ugh—and I thought I was pregnant for three solid years."

They went to Switzerland a fortnight later and got married. And so, with her earnest groping walk, her taut prettiness, her marvelous clothes and the great glowing ruby on her finger, Miss Birch became an archduchess, and as such was automatically a cousin to the kings and queens of Rumania, Yugoslavia, Sweden, Denmark, Norway, Belgium, and Great Britain.

*

News of the wedding swept through the café. Erji Sandor murmured, "What for happiness!" but Sandor gave out the opinion that the marriage could not possibly last. Drew, looking glum, exclaimed "Humpf!" and hid his eyes, pretending to work on a dispatch.

Three days later Drew's Countess died in her sleep. It was as if the gnarled, thorny old woman had willed herself to keep alive until Miss Birch was safely out of the way. Even though Drew had not seen her, the Countess knew that she was in town and she had been alert as a tigress. Now she relaxed—all the way into death. She could not wind herself up again, and the worn old clock of her heart stopped at last.

9

News, news. Mason got to his desk early. Austria appeared to be on the brink of civil war. He had hoped amiably to steal some more of Mr. Knowles's time, and finish an article for *Fortune* on the Skoda arms works in Pilsen and how the international munitions makers influenced policy. But his cup was full with work for the *Star*. For weeks there had been stories to write almost every day about Nazi activity and today was no exception. Border raids in the Alps west of Salzburg. Formation of a so-called Austrian Legion on German soil just across the frontier, composed of Austrian Nazis who had decamped to Germany, and were being trained for offensive action against their mother country. Air raids. Half a dozen times Nazi planes soared along the frontier, dropping pamphlets attacking the Dollfuss government. Bombs everywhere. Kidnapings of Tyrolese officials by Nazis disguised as tourists. Boycott by Germany on Austrian exports of timber. A swastika found painted over the figure of Christ in the shrine at Mittenwald. These were no longer mere episodes in terrorism; what had come was guerrilla warfare.

Mason kept his head. The Nazis might well take Austria any

minute, but, he still felt, some sort of tremendous crisis between Dr. Dollfuss, the Milli-Metternich, and the Social Democrats would come first, if only because the Socialists were the enemy easiest to liquidate. Not all his colleagues agreed. "Let the government act against the Nazis," Sandor said. "If the government and the Nazis destroy each other, it is the Social Democrats who gain." Mason said, "No. The government won't take serious action against the Nazis because, after all, Austrians are German."

Mason wrote his dispatch for the day and Paula typed and filed it. It described a clever appeal by the Munich radio to Austrians to stop smoking and thus weaken the Austrian tobacco monopoly, which was an indispensable source of income for the Dollfuss government.

They went in to lunch and Frau Gertrude announced, "All the fat is drawn most carefully out of the stuffing in the chicken, it will not add to the weight." Paula told Mason casually, "You seemed so busy that I didn't want to interrupt you—Nella Blohr called twice. Wants you to call her back." Mason felt a tickle of apprehension. Paula looked at him. He slipped out after lunch. In the villa they had had several telephones with different numbers but not here and he could not risk telephoning Nella with Paula in the flat. Mason was violently worried about Nella. He hadn't seen her for about a week. He didn't want to see her. Maybe she was the most fascinating, if tricky, girl of twenty in the whole wide world, but he didn't feel that he could keep up an affair with her any longer. It was too difficult and dangerous. He could not bear the thought of wounding Paula. But what was he going to do about Nella? She was wildly in love with him and said that she had been in love with him since that moment they had talked on the misty street near the Döbling villa years before. And there was no doubt about his continuing delight in her and desire for her. But the whole business had to stop. Meantime she was a full week late, and what in hell was he going to do if she really was pregnant?

He could not reach Nella on the phone, and he returned to the flat. It had begun to snow, and Mason watched a steady pattern of snow fall outside his window, like a curtain of carnations. The snow carried him back to Montana, and he closed his eyes. The smell of fresh birchbark—was there anything like it anywhere? Bees industriously, professionally, sucking at the heads of a clump of devil's paintbrush, so that each long stem swayed, bending almost double— how much did a bee weigh? He remembered the clang when the milk- man deposited bottles on the back porch early in the morning, and then the frozen shafts of cream thrusting their way out of each bottle, pushing up the cardboard tops. Mason dozed, woke up, and trans- posed himself into the future, reaching for a pad of scratchpaper. As he had done a hundred, a thousand times before, he scribbled out a calendar, an agenda, not merely for weeks and months to come, but for years:

1934. Clean up what I've not seen of this territory. Not yet been to Slovenia, the Sudeten country in northern Czechoslovakia, or the Banat.

1935. Should be about time to leave Vienna—we'll have had five years here. Apply for transfer.

1936. Maybe try my hand at a kind of political book on what's really going on in Europe. (Paula's idea.) Don't know where I will be stationed, but I could use holidays for quick visits to capitals I don't know, like Moscow.

1938. Home leave. See places I've not seen yet, like the Arizona desert, the California coast near Monterey, etc., etc. Write stories.

1939. I'd like to try my hand at something autobiographical. Too early?

Mason stopped scribbling for a moment. Then he added idly in purely impersonal fantasy:

19—. Second marriage?

The telephone rang with its shrill long-distance bleat—Strothness. His voice, his manner, were still the same: taut, tense, articulate. "Heard from Chicago yet, Mason? You'll be getting a wire any minute. Hop up here right away—better take a plane. I've been expelled from Germany and you're to cover."

He managed to meet Nella on the way to the airport in a bookstore near St. Stephen's. There wasn't time to go to a café. He found her in a dark room stuffed with books in old bindings at the back of the shop. She wore a shaggy sheepskin coat and as he entered his eye caught her in the gesture of reaching upward to take a book from a high shelf—on tiptoe, stretched to her full height, her head bent sharply back, and a scowling look of concentration, which was totally fabricated, on her face. She turned around, and Mason thought that he would never forget her expression. Now her soul was exposed. "I've got my period," Nella said, eyes low.

*

An hour after Mason left, Tom Cairn called up. He was in town overnight, en route from London to Belgrade, where King Alexander, something unprecedented, had promised him an interview. Was that a start of disappointment in Cairn's voice when Paula told him that Mason had just left town—or what? He asked her out to dinner and said that he'd be right over.

10

Strothness met Mason at Templehof and they drove together to the Adlon. He was tense. The veins on the backs of his thin, brown hands would, Mason thought, twang like cello strings if he touched them; his brilliant blue eyes flashed with scorn. It wasn't quite accurate to say that he had been formally expelled from Germany. The position was more subtle and complicated. "They're squeezing me out," Strothness explained. "Incidentally, the S.A. man you'll see stationed outside our office isn't there to threaten us but probably for the opposite reason —to protect me from the S.S.!"

Mason listened. At this time several groups close to Hitler competed hotly for his approval. Hitler was known to have expressed hysterical resentment at Strothness's stories exposing outrages committed by Nazis against the Jews. One group of Elite Guarde extremists, hoping to take advantage of this situation and thus gain Hitler's favor, conceived the idea of murdering Strothness. This, they thought, would not only please the Führer but strengthen their position with him. But news of the plot leaked out. The more respectable members of Hitler's entourage did not at all like the prospect of a political assassination which would certainly make an ugly scandal. The German Foreign Office sent a confidential message to its embassy in Washington saying that Strothness's life was in danger and that, for his own safety, Chicago should remove him at once from Berlin. This put Plover, Hilliard, and McFarland into a quandary. They did not relish yielding to pressure from the Wilhelmstrasse, but in the end they decided that Strothness must be withdrawn to save his life. But when Strothness heard from Chicago that he must leave Berlin he refused to go! Chicago broke the stalemate by saying that if he did not obey orders he would be fired. Strothness said to Mason wryly, "I wouldn't mind being killed for a worthy cause, but to lose my job—a job on the *Star*—that's a different matter!" So he would be off to Paris the next evening on the Nord Express.

"Am I in any danger?" Mason asked.

"I shouldn't think so. Of course they know perfectly well who you are and what your record is, but they won't try anything fancy with a newcomer here on a temporary basis."

"Well, well, let's have dinner," Mason said.

Mason, going to work on the Unter den Linden the next morning, was suddenly eaten up by fear that he might be transferred to Berlin as Strothness's permanent successor. The idea appalled him. He didn't fear the Nazis, but he loathed Berlin, and so would Paula. After a week Hilliard informed him that it had been decided to give Berlin to Throckmorton, whose position in Moscow had become untenable, and that he, Mason, would return to Vienna and continue to hold the Vienna post, where the political situation he had watched for so long was obviously coming to a head. Strothness was appointed to Tokyo and the Tokyo man would in turn succeed Throckmorton in Moscow. Musical chairs, Mason thought.

He met Throckmorton, a man with iron-gray hair cropped to the skull who smoked a corncob pipe and wore a perpetual sardonic smile, when his train came in. He was tough as Brazil nuts, humorous, and mercilessly detached. They sat up most of the night, and liked each other. Mason filled him in on Berlin and talked about the Nazi terror, which was daily becoming more outrageous. He, Mason, had firsthand knowledge of a Jewish doctor in Berlin whose eyes had been ground out with a broken billiard cue by Nazi gangsters and of the Socialist foreman in a metal workshop in Pankow who had been stuffed into his own furnace and burned alive.

"Tiddlywinks, tiddlywinks!" Throckmorton snorted. "Heard about what's going on down in the Ukraine? There's a purge of kulaks there. Where I come from we murder millions!"

＊

Paula had lunch at the Wallensteins' while Mason was still away. Entering the grounds of the villa, she looked enviously up at what had been her own windows only a few months before. The Dozent greeted her with hearty, nervous courtliness, and the Frau Dozent, with her distinguished bearing, chirped and chattered. Nella sauntered into the room when coffee was being served, gave Paula the brightest of smiles, and sauntered out again.

"Nella presents problems," murmured the Frau Dozent. "A few weeks ago she flits off to Budapest on some mysterious business— oh, by the way, she told us that she ran into your Mason there—and then goes to Switzerland for a week of skiing. Where in Switzerland? Geneva. Then, last week, she insisted that she must fly for the week- end to Berlin—of all places at this particular time, Berlin!" The Frau Dozent wrinkled her nose in distaste. "However, she didn't go. She is moody, cross-grained, and secretive—not an unusual phase, I daresay. Thank God at least she seems to be finished with your friend Tetzel. A most persistent young man—but dull, dull, *nicht wahr?* Meantime, you will forgive me for being pleased, what could be more satisfying than the success of our Otto—he has a job on the *Daily Mail!*"

But Paula wasn't listening.

Rising, she felt utterly confused. Mason would be home tomorrow. Obviously he must be having an affair with Nella. It was clear as daylight. First in Budapest and then Geneva. This would account for all of his queer behavior lately. Oh, how awful! How ghastly—dis- gusting and revolting! She trembled violently, so violently that the Frau Dozent thought that she must suddenly have been taken ill. Paula tripped down the stairs, crossed the garden she knew so well, and hailed a taxi. But what about her own affair with Dennis Ship- wright? How could she tax Mason for having an illicit affair if she was having one herself? This really was a bit awkward! Things had become terribly mixed up! In fact she was supposed to be en route now, this very minute, to visit Shipwright for what was to be their last rendezvous—their last because Mason was coming home.

She had little room in her mind now for anything but Mason, but she kept the rendezvous with Dennis Shipwright, known as Hal.

❋

Mason, crossing the barrier at the Vienna airport the next afternoon, thought that Paula had never looked lovelier. The whites of her eyes shone around the green-brown core, her skin was radiant, and her hair had a cinnamon sheen. It had in fact occurred to him several times in the past few months that there had come a subtle change in Paula's looks, ever since the baby. She had always been a pretty girl, but now she took on a new and different quality, a new dimension; she had become a beauty. There was a new quality of elevation and an aura of mystery as well, although she could still be the most explicit creature alive. But she was calmer; her face had a luster that indicated repose as well as power; her face had meaning beyond its skin and structure. Willi too had noticed this that day at lunch and pointed it out. She had become a beauty. A great beauty, Willi said.

Mason put his arm around her; she evaded him.

After dinner she asked, without any preliminaries, "Mason, what's going on between you and Nella Blohr?"

Startled in the extreme, he looked up. "Nothing."

"I'm not prying, I hate to pry, but I'd like to know. Don't lie."

"Well-l-l-l," he began elaborately, "I think she had a kind of crush on me and I walked into her in Budapest—"

"And you had an affair with her. That little cat! Oh, Mason, how could you! It's ugly, cheap."

"Well—"

"And then she joined you in Geneva for a week and then she was going to meet you in Berlin. Perhaps she did for a day, yesterday. You brought her back with you. Where did you hide her when you got off the plane?"

"Berlin, no. I refused—I broke off—"

"Erika was quite different, because you loved her." Paula's eyes blazed. "But you can't be in love with Nella Blohr, can you?"

She had been able to forgive Erika because she had really meant something to Mason. She had been frightfully hurt and wounded by Erika, but Erika could be understood. To forgive Mason for Erika had been her triumph. But this was nothing more than a furtive cheap affair.

"Lord, no—she's a fascinating little girl, but it was just a kind of thing." He stumbled. "Pure accident—I got involved, I wanted to tell you, but I knew how angry and hurt you'd be—"

"Angry and hurt?" She was outraged. "You're the weakest man alive!"

"Incidentally, how did you find out about all this?"

"Never mind."

"I suppose you've been spying on me!"

She reached forward and with a swift gesture drew her nails down his cheek. They tore into the cheek deeply. He dabbed at the blood with a handkerchief. Snow leopard, he said to himself.

"Oh, I've hurt you!" She became contrite.

Blood was dripping down his collar and shirt and fell on the chair.

"That'll leave a scar, damn it! I'll have to be sewn up! Call Antioch."

She rushed to the phone.

"No, better not call him."

His face became so contorted with rage and pain that it looked funny. She could not help it but, hysterical, began to laugh.

"Now you laugh!" Mason yelled indignantly. He mopped up the blood. "Stop laughing, for God's sake!"

But surely he must understand that she was sad, sadder than she had ever been in her life. The sadness welled out of her. She bandaged him.

"I've had an affair too," Paula said.

"What?" He stared at her. Was this what had given a new quality to her looks?

"Yes."

"Nonsense. I don't believe it."

"And if it's of any interest to you, I spent one splendid evening last week fighting off your best friend, Tom Cairn."

❋

Wearily, mechanically, they walked toward the bedroom. He daubed at his torn cheek. As usual, she unpacked his bag. How many hundreds of times had she packed it? Would she ever pack and unpack it again? What stunned and wounded Paula most was Mason's deception. How could a relationship be maintained if its essential glue—trust—was gone? How could she ever trust him again? How could she continue to love him, adore him, live with him, if he was capable of such a betrayal? How could he be so false? Later came a burning sense of dissatisfaction with herself. What was the failure in her? Had he felt the necessity to have another love affair because of her? What lack in her shunted him off to vile, secret, cheap adventures? What did other girls give him that she did not give? Was it possible that she was no longer loved? Or did this sort of thing just happen in a man with Mason's temperament? But Mason was not these days a particularly urgent person physically. He liked fondness, warmth, companionship. Still he had that damned wandering eye. And how, she went back on her tracks, could she be blamed and be held responsible if it was he who could not control his infantile impulses to roam? Nevertheless the ghastly, miserable consequence was that he had once more destroyed her own faith in herself. She had had enough trouble in her life because of underconfidence, and now she could never be confident about anything again.

One major reason for his infidelity, now as before, did not occur to her. Perhaps it was just as well that it did not. He loved her, but several of her qualities and characteristics bored him.

In bed, Mason sought to embrace her, but she pushed him away. "No, no, you can't buy me off with just sex."

Confused, he said nothing.

After a while: "What was that you said about Tom?"

"He made frantic love to me, saying that only I could save him. But of course it's you he wants—subconsciously at least."

"Me?"

"Hasn't it dawned on you yet what his basic problem is?"

"Yes, but drop it." He turned. "Now—what's this business of your having had an affair?" The blood started to leak from his cheek again.

"Really, I prefer not to talk about it."

"Who was it?"

"Nobody you know." She shivered inwardly. It was a frightful thing to lie. Now she, she, had become corrupt like everybody else in Vienna. But she had to lie. "Nobody of any interest whatever, and, besides, it's over."

"How long did it go on?"

"Not for very long."

"What started it?"

She shrugged and lied again. "I don't really know."

"Was it important to you?"

"In a way, yes."

"And you enjoyed it?"

"Yes."

Mason never asked her again about her lover. He would not give her the satisfaction of being curious, and he knew that the way to win her back was not to make a fuss. Or perhaps her revelation was so unutterably painful that he could not face it, could not open his mind to it at all. Or perhaps he was determined to demonstrate to her *his* superiority, by rising above the coarseness, the vulgarity, that would develop out of prolonged inquiry. Or perhaps he was a coward. Or perhaps he didn't care. At this last he pulled himself up abruptly. No, that was certainly wrong. The one thing certain above and beyond all certainties was that he cared for her. Oh, he cared for her, all right!

In the morning Paula remembered something that her mother had told her years before. "No matter what, never be dreary!" Going through the mail and papers with Mason she was as bright as bright could be.

❋

Luck came to them, releasing them from intolerable strain, in the form of a wave of visitation. It happened by chance, and exceeded anything they had known in Vienna. In one remarkable week they had to entertain a British M.P., a professor of neurology from San Francisco (to be analyzed by Freud himself), a soprano from the Chicago Opera, and a well-known American playwright. To all, Mason gave fully. If only he could give so fully and easily to me, Paula thought. If only *I* could give him back the vitality he spends. Oh, the devil with it. You can't have everything. (But I used to think I could.)

At last they had five minutes alone. Paula said, "Have you seen Nella—been in touch with her again?"

"No."

"If you say it's over I'll take your word for it."

"It's over. Let's not talk about it again. Or your lover either."

❋

Regierungsrat Dr. Hohnstedt, Wimpassing's assistant, telephoned. He sounded intensely formal, as if a matter of grave importance had come up. The Herr Bundeskanzler, he explained, had been invited by the largest American radio network to make a half-hour talk next Sunday to the people of the United States. A big thing for Austria— never before had an Austrian Chancellor received such an invitation. Millions of people would hear at first hand the heroic little Chancellor's own voice, hear him describe the gallant fight he was putting up against the Nazis—David against Goliath. Dr. Dollfuss had accepted the invitation promptly and had, moreover, suggested that it would be appropriate to be introduced—across the Atlantic— by one of the American correspondents resident in Vienna. Dr. Hohnstedt concluded impressively: "The Herr Bundeskanzler indicates that his choice for this person is you, and I am empowered to ask if you will accept."

Mason gulped. "I'll call you back in twenty minutes, Hans."

He grabbed Paula out of her bath. She shook her head.

"It's a shame to have to say no, because it would give you a whole lot of prestige back home, the *Star* would be pleased, and you'd get all sorts of kudos. But I wouldn't do it. It puts you too much officially on the government side, and besides, you're not at all sure these days that the Dollfuss policy is right."

He disagreed with her.

"No, I'm going to do it."

He called Hohnstedt to accept and then took the bus into town to do his daily rounds. A harsh February wind swept grayish snow down the streets. Patties of ice clung to the cobbles, eaten away at the edges and drilled with holes filled with gray water. The water whistled along the gutters and he felt sprays of cold water bounce on his socks.

Sandor, to his surprise, awaited him outside the Imperial, as if he were too impatient to stay inside. He did not comment on the bandage on Mason's cheek.

"Hell has burst loose," Sandor said. "Even now police are at raid at the building of the *Arbeiter Zeitung!*"

They took a taxi there. Apparently the raid had been ordered by Dollfuss's own security service, and the *Arbeiter Zeitung*, organ of the Social Democrats for fifty years, would be suppressed, shut down. Squads of police went through the building and kept in control the crowds gathering on the streets.

Mason rushed back to the Goethe-Hof to write his story. It presaged much. As he pushed open his office door Bleschke telephoned.

"The government has now decreed the redistribution of the Vienna taxes, the government now takes a share of the municipality's housing money, and soon the *Gemeinde* houses themselves will be taken over!"

"What?"

"Also comes now on the radio, you must listen, word by word, a speech by Major Fey. He has said so far, 'The time has come to exterminate the Reds once for all. . . . In the last days we have made certain that the Chancellor is with us. . . . Tomorrow we are going to clean up Austria!' "

Mason thought a moment. Paula slipped into the room and was watching him. He picked up the phone.

"Dr. Hohnstedt? Hans? Listen, I hope this isn't going to embarrass you too much. I've changed my mind. I've decided not to introduce the Chancellor Sunday. . . . Yes, that's what I said. Give him my excuses, but tell him that I won't have a thing to do with it. . . . As a result of today's events? Yes . . . What's that? *What?*"

He turned to Paula, excited. "Do you know what Hohnstedt whispered into the phone? 'Congratulations! I am with you!' "

*

They slept late the next morning, February twelfth. They were warm and close. They were once more united. Mason pulled back the curtains—mist and fog outside. He twiddled the electric light button. No light. He tried another switch. Still no light. Paula peered out of the window and saw a line of streetcars stranded near the bridge, immobile. No power. "What? It must be a general strike!" They stared at one another.

XV. THE BARRICADES

Mason dressed in a hurry. He said to Paula over his shoulder, "Stick here, I'll telephone in an hour—you relay the stuff to Paris. If the phone's cut, sit tight. Safe? What could knock over a building like this? Who would ever dream of attacking it? Kiss Richard." He grabbed a taxi. A policeman hailed him at the corner and stopped the taxi. Mason asked, "What's up?" and the policeman replied, "Don't know. General alarm. Drive me into town."

Mason had little money in his pocket; the banks would probably close, as would the tourist bureaus, and he might need quite a lot, particularly if censorship was clamped down and he would have to take a car to Bratislava, across the Czechoslovak frontier, to file. He drove in to the Majestic, leaped at Klaus, and said, "Give me all the money you have." The concierge emptied his wallet with the words "*Geht in Ordnung!*"

It was a few minutes before twelve. Mason gave his driver an address in Floridsdorf. Curious crowds on the main streets surrounded the streetcars still stalled by the lack of power. He didn't want to drive all the way to his destination, and told the driver, "*Bitte,*—drop me here," a block away from the address he had given. He wondered if the driver could be a Social Democrat. No way of identifying your friends these days, unless you were willing to risk giving yourself away.

He paid the driver. "*Freundschaft,*" the driver said. So he was a Social Democrat. Well, no matter.

Mason sauntered up the street, trying not to appear in a hurry, with his eyes open. There definitely should not be a crowd around this building. There was—quite a large crowd. Closer, he almost bumped into two Heimwehr men with rifles slung over their shoulders—not in uniform, but wearing green badges. The Heimwehr were openly on the streets with rifles—a bad sign! Mason pressed between them with deliberate rudeness; he knew that he was almost invulnerable in positions like this, because he could prove that he was a journalist, and had a right to be almost anywhere, by the legitimation card safely in his pocket.

The building was filled with police.

This was the *Turnhalle* where Mason had watched the Schutz-bunders train and drill. He had learned from Unzicker that, in the event of trouble, a certain group was to make a rendezvous here. The group was to act as a liaison staff if the Social Democrats were attacked, insuring communication among the trade-union staff, the *Arbeiter Zeitung*, and the fighters out in the field. Only about twenty men, Mason knew, were assigned to service with this special group. It horrified him to see this place of rendezvous occupied. The police had taken possession of an underground secret headquarters—within an hour of the outbreak. Yet the location and function of this special headquarters were known only to a chosen few. He was shattered. Treachery?

There must be comrades in the vicinity seeking to report for duty who, like himself, were stunned to find the police already there. A prison van, its siren shrieking, whistled up. Out of the building came half a dozen police, shoving prisoners roughly ahead of them. Mason recognized two men among the prisoners—Schutzbund officers. Quietly he slipped back, mixing with the crowd on the street. This was a working-class quarter, but the people were still good-humored; they did not know what had happened. Men and women chattered. Mason overheard a shopkeeper, standing poised in his doorway, say to his wife, "Just another raid. If there's going to be shooting, let's go to the movies."

He hung around. Somewhere he was almost bound to see someone whom he knew and with whom he could talk. He turned the corner as the police, their batons up, pushed the crowd along. On the next street he reached a Tabak-Trafik, and there, pretending to fumble through the newspapers, stood Dr. Ricardo Stein.

They looked at one another. Mason said to the woman who ran the ohop, "*Schachtel Memphis, bitte.*" He took his time counting out the exact change, while signaling to Stein. Then, still dawdling, he picked up a newspaper, tapped it, and left the shop. Five feet behind, Stein followed. They turned a corner and walked swiftly to the embankment of the Alte Donau, where they found a café.

"What's happened?"

"I don't know." Stein was breathing hard. "I got to headquarters just as the police came, and managed to slip out. They arrested almost everybody else."

"What's going on in town? Are the Nazis rising?"

"I think not."

"Is it a general strike?"

"I don't know. I came from Kolowratring on the tram, and it stopped. The motorman had no idea what was wrong. I got a taxi, after a lot of delay, and drove here, which was the rendezvous for crisis."

"Certainly the electrical workers must have struck."

"I fear so."

"What should we do next?"

"Something has obviously gone wrong. The strike of the electrical workers must have been premature. It could not possibly have been ordered without other strike orders." Stein was bewildered. He talked as if he could not believe in the words coming out of his own mouth. "Something went terribly wrong. The Ring is being barricaded. It is full of armored cars." He lowered his voice. "Look—the police outside." A line of police marched past, and they were wearing steel helmets and carried rifles, not *Gummiknüppels.* "Perhaps there were saboteurs in the electric works. The government took advantage of the stoppage of lights as a signal, and are attacking us in full force. . . ."

"Don't be so pessimistic. It isn't over yet."

Stein talked as if circling each word with a finger. "Now where to go? *Arbeiter Zeitung?* Obviously impossible—it has been shut down. Trade-union headquarters? Perhaps already too late. Where would the nearest Schutzbund group be—we must try to find out and join them."

"I know where I'm going. Let's get out to the electrical works—somebody will know something there."

"Very well."

Crack-wheeeesh! Rifle fire—not far away either. A knowing look came into the face of each.

The noise stopped as men and women dove for shelter. Mason remembered the Kohler *Putsch* a couple of years before. All the people out to see the fun! Indeed, waiters were now passing trays of beer on the terrace of the café. He and Stein rose and walked swiftly until they reached a kiosk. Mason picked up the phone inside. It was still working—what a relief! But of course the phone system did not depend on power from the electrical works and the government needed the telephone. Later it might be different.

His fingers trembled, dialing. "Paula . . . listen, I don't know how long I'll be able to keep phoning. I'll try to dictate a story now, very rough—you fix it up." He described what he had seen and mentioned that shooting had started. "Stick it all on the phone to Paris, urgent, *dringend.*" He paused to try to recollect all the things he must tell her and to dictate a concise, coherent story. He had two duties. He had to do something toward covering a story—by far the biggest story of his years in Central Europe. And he had to do something to help his friends. "Try to follow that lead of mine carefully. I don't think this is a Socialist revolution at all, but a government action against the Socialists. Apparently the Socialists did *not* call a general strike, at least not officially. Try to get Sandor on the phone and I think he will confirm what I'm guessing at. Oh, sure, I'm taking care of myself—no danger at all. All right, I'll keep phoning you, if I can. File till four-thirty or five—later if they want it. So long, darling."

With Stein he reached the electricity works. A group of police stood by the closed gates, together with a troop of Heimwehr. Whatever had happened was over. No crowds, no commotion. Mason showed his credentials, asking to get in. The policeman was courteous but adamant. Nobody was allowed inside the plant. Nobody—no matter with what credentials. And Mason, his temper rising, in spite of the policeman's perfectly respectful attitude and courtesy, felt himself *hating* that policeman. The policeman said that the government was issuing special passes to supersede ordinary press cards, in view of this emergency. He was immovable. He would give no information whatever and he would not let them in.

Mason decided to go to the Journalistenzimmer and get the new press card. Stein said, "I shall leave you here."

Mason looked astonished. "But you will need the new card just as much as I."

"No."

"Where are you going?"

Stein had, of course, never belonged to the Schutzbund; he was an intellectual, not one of the fighters. A slow smile crossed his face.

"Good-bye," Stein said. "I have no need of press cards now."

Mason reached the Journalistenzimmer, got the new press card, picked up all the official information he could get, and gave it to Paula on the phone. This might be the last time he would have access to official information. Not that much information was available. Somebody told him that hot fighting was taking place in Floridsdorf. "It's a regular war over there," a telegraph clerk ejaculated cheerfully. Shipwright called out from a nearby phone booth, "There's a rumor that they're going to bomb the George Washington-Hof. We might go over and have a look."

A big, open motor truck full of police, with their rifles on racks, blocked the entrance to the Ring. Mason, in a taxi, showed his new pass to an officer. The officer inspected it. "What's happened?" Mason asked for the sixth or seventh time that morning. "Socialist revolt," the officer said shortly. Mason replied, "The hell you say." The officer said, "We're doing well. All the Schutzbund nests have been cleaned out. We have caught practically everybody. All the leading Schutzbund officers were rounded up last night."

Last night? Then that boast of Major Fey's on the radio hadn't been vain talk. The government had deliberately planned all of this for today.

Now Mason became dispirited. Such unexpected acumen and energy on the part of the government! "We'll get 'em yet," he muttered through biting teeth.

He told the driver to keep going, but the driver looked dubious. Mason shouted, "God damn it, man, can't you understand language! George Washington-Hof! *Schnell!*"

2

Two Heimwehr guards sat at a barricade by the Westbahn. Their duty was to keep the Orient Express from being blown up by the Socialists, in other words to do nothing.

They wore green and white armbands, since uniforms had not yet been issued, and handled their rifles awkwardly. One was a farmhand from the Mistelbach area with a bobbing turtle's head of cartilage showing at his throat. The other, a clerk in a department store, had a mouthful of bad teeth.

"Any of those dirty red *Schweine* come around here, we'll get 'em," said the farmhand, spitting.

"Ya-a-aw! Those dirty Reds! They teach the children the Virgin Mary was a whore."

"They say they're goin' to try to blow up the gasworks tonight. D'like to see any of 'em 'round here!"

"We'll fix 'em!"

The two men decided to sneak off duty, push into the dining room of the Bahnhof, and shake down the headwaiter for a drink.

"It's sure nice here," said the farmhand. "Imagine it—gettin' two Schillings a day and all you can eat for nothin'!"

To be able to shoot Socialists on sight and get paid for it was too much happiness to bear.

3

Mason reached the George Washington-Hof at last. People were astir, but he had no trouble getting into the building. He found the chairman of the house committee and asked him if a proper defense was being organized. "No orders have come through," the chairman said. Mason said, "Orders? Act on your own, comrade! Listen, I've been around. Don't you understand? The Heimwehr is going to be sacking this building in about five minutes!"

"I can do nothing without orders. I will attempt to communicate with headquarters."

"You can't communicate with headquarters. There aren't any headquarters!"

The committeeman looked incredulous.

"Get out your guns," cried Mason. "It's time to defend yourselves! Don't die here like rats! Get the guns!"

The committeeman did not know where the guns were. They must be hidden in the building somewhere but he did not know where. The Schutzbund had not kept him informed.

It was Mason's turn to look incredulous. He was bewildered. This was insufferable. "You don't know where your own guns are?" He felt his fists swelling.

Another man spoke up: "If we make no resistance, we will not be harmed."

"Harmed? You'll cease to exist!"

"They will not shoot at a residential building with women and children. Let us make no resistance."

Mason said, "Don't you realize that all over the city people on your side are dying, being *killed?*"

Stiffly, "We have no orders." And a third member of the committee said, "So far as I know we have no armament of any kind."

A Schutzbund man rushed in. There was heavy fighting at the Karl Marx-Hof, he reported. He wanted to fight, but could not make contact with his detachment.

Mason got to the Karl Marx-Hof riding on the back of this man's motorcycle. It was now late in the afternoon and quite dark. He continued to be mortally shocked. It seemed almost inconceivable that the Schutzbund had not arrived at the George Washington-Hof, as planned, and that the authorities there did not even know about their own guns. As they drove along bumpily he saw that women formed long queues on the streets outside shops, buying flour, candles, sugar, matches. Now dozens of small mobs, running ahead of Heimwehr charges, spilled down the boulevard, as teams of horses drew the dead streetcars to the barns. More police, more Heimwehr; and then, in an interminable clattering line along the *Gürtel*, trucks ground past with men in quite a different uniform—troops!

At the Karl Marx-Hof, long and low at the dank edge of the river, Mason and his companion encountered sharp rifle fire. Police with rifles were climbing a garden wall. "Get back," an officer shouted to Mason. "You're under fire!" He dodged, taking shelter near a machine-gun post set up in front of a grocery store. "Can I go ahead?" he asked. "If you're crazy," the sergeant in command replied.

"I want to go ahead," Mason said. He noticed that his Schutz-bunder had disappeared.

"At your own risk. *Auf eigene Gefahr!*"

Then, perceiving that he could only penetrate into the Karl Marx-Hof to join the defenders by crossing the line of fire, he realized he must be out of his mind. Am I drunk, he thought. Am I demented? This was impossible—an absurdity. He couldn't cross the garden without being fired on by his own friends. There was no point to getting killed in any case, but to be killed by his own side would be silly.

Wie schade! What a shame! What a wonderful story it would have made if he had been able to gain entrance to the building and describe the defense of the beleaguered Karl Marx-Hof while it was being attacked.

Pi-nnnnnnnnngg-whee!

Mason looked about him. Good Lord, the government troops were bringing up artillery, setting howitzers in place. They were going to fire on the Karl Marx-Hof with *artillery!*

He felt hollowness in his bowels. This was something too unutterably appalling. The government was making ready to attack a residential house with artillery! It was scarcely credible. They were going to commit the unspeakable infamy of killing fellow citizens actually in their *houses*—by artillery fire!

If that Schutzbunder who had driven him here had been able to get in he could get in.

No.

He had Paula and Richard to think about now. If the government was preparing to use artillery against the Karl Marx-Hof it might well use it against the Goethe-Hof. His wife and son could be in mortal danger. What to do?

But to traverse the city and get to the Goethe-Hof from here was utterly impossible, out of the question, in the darkness, without transport or even with it. Every street would be blocked off. He would have to wait till morning.

Now the pattern of the struggle became clear to him. The great sunshine tenements, the *Gemeinde* houses, had perforce become the centers of Socialist resistance. Here the Schutzbund defenders would seek to gather. So the government-cum-Heimwehr took the decision to attack them. So far the Dollfuss forces had used nothing but machine-gun and rifle fire, to which the Socialists in those houses which had arms available and where there was any will to fight had replied in kind. But now the government was bringing up big guns— field pieces, howitzers, artillery. Mason glanced at his watch—just before six in the evening. He decided to try to get back to the Journalistenzimmer, his center for communications. He walked rapidly along the river. Rifle fire spat out again. He was turned back by a sentry, who told him curtly that the whole area was now closed. Mason was frantic. He flourished his pass. The streets were almost empty now, people were scampering into their houses, waiters pulled down the iron shutters over restaurant windows, and shopkeepers slammed their doors. Hurry, hurry. From one closed building, all its lights out, doors locked, he heard a gramophone grinding out dance music. Radio-Wien announced curfew at eight o'clock. All cars must be off the streets, no traffic, no people, movies closed, coffeehouses closed. He had had nothing to eat since breakfast and stopped at a shop still open, and bought all the chocolate and crackers he could stuff in his pocket.

Mason began to run. The streets were black. Near the Nordbahn he came upon a youngster stranded in a ramshackle Steyr. "Twenty Schillings to get me to the Central Telegraph Office," Mason shouted. The lad started the motor. Theirs was the only car in the street. Half a dozen times they were stopped with rough cries of "*Halt! Zurück!*" Once at least a patrol advanced with their rifles nervously level, aimed at the driver's head. "*Halt!* Or we shoot! . . . Show your papers!" Each time Mason flourished his pass and was permitted to drive on. Odd to be challenged by a man carrying an automatic rifle but wearing a derby hat. Finally he reached the Journalistenzimmer.

❋

Sandor, Shipwright, Drew sat at a corner table lit by a bouquet of candles. They jumped up to greet Mason. He waved them off and stumbled to the rank of telephones to call Paula. They watched him; Drew's face had a mildly malicious, superior expression. Mason lifted the receiver off the hook, but nothing happened. No click, no dial tone. Drew called across the room, "All phones cut off about an hour ago."

They compared notes. Sandor said, "This is the first act of the second world war, but who will inherit from it I do not know."

Tomm, the *Pravda* man, looked up at him with interest. His face gleamed with confidence.

4

Two high officials of the government bent on their knees before the high altar in St. Stephen's.

"Holy God, deliver us victory tomorrow. Deliver us victory to save Vienna from the Marxist criminals."

5

Mason went into the main body of the telegraph office, where most of the staff were Social Democrats.

What had happened?

Nobody knew precisely. There had been a general strike. There had not been a general strike.

The railway men hadn't moved an inch. No one had informed the railway men.

The electrical workers struck spontaneously.

The electrical workers had not struck spontaneously.

Bauer, the Socialist leader, was out in the field somewhere, probably behind Floridsdorf. Deutsch, his second in command, was with him.

Bauer was not out in the field. He was a poltroon, incompetent, a coward. So was Deutsch.

What had happened to all the other leaders?

No one knew.

Where was the main body of the Schutzbund? Why hadn't the Schutzbund gone into action in an organized manner?

No one knew.

The city hall had fallen, and the green flag of the Heimwehr was flying there.

It was not flying there.

There were hundreds of men and women killed in the Karl Marx-Hof alone, and at least a thousand more in Floridsdorf and Ottakring.

Such figures were ridiculously exaggerated.

No one knew.

Could they win? Was there any hope?

No one knew.

6

The journalists tried to get out of the telegraph building and were pushed back. Shipwright defied an armed sentry and walked in the darkness until he found a colonel from the regular army. He put on his best supercilious manner. "But this is perfect nonsense, my man," he said. "A group of journalists representing the press of the entire world is stranded here and these ill-informed louts in your militia won't let us out. Don't let them make fools of themselves any longer. The honor of your beloved Austria is at stake. Find cars and an escort, please, and take us to the Hotel Bristol at once. We need food and must have a place to sleep."

Amazingly, the Colonel complied.

Shipwright said to Mason casually when they reached the Bristol, "Is Paula all right? When did you last get through to her?"

"At about four this afternoon. She was okay then."

Mason felt passionately lonely for her, passionately loving her, and passionately worried about her.

"They'll attack the Goethe-Hof tomorrow morning, sure," Shipwright said. "We'd better be there." They looked at one another.

Muted, a radio set in the Bristol bar was working. "Criminal strike at the electric works . . . followed by a general strike not fully operative . . . Mass arrests, prompt action, military measures by the government. The Socialist leaders all arrested. The Schutzbund leaders all arrested. . . . The population should remain calm. . . . Casualties—seventeen police dead, seven Heimwehr. Troops in action in Klagenfurt, Linz . . . No rising by the Nazis . . . The population to remain calm . . . The curfew strictly to be enforced till further notice . . . Loyal citizens to go about their work quietly tomorrow . . . The misguided Socialists urged to give up their arms . . ."

At midnight came further news bulletins and then, after repeated announcements that a major statement would come soon, the voice out of the box said, "Radio-Wien. Radio-Wien. Important declaration by the government. Important declaration by the government. The Social Democratic party is dissolved. The Social Democratic party is dissolved. The Vienna government is disbanded. The Vienna government is disbanded. The illegal Schutzbund is dissolved. The illegal Schutzbund is dissolved. The trade unions are disbanded. The trade unions are disbanded. . . ."

Tom Cairn, wearing a magenta waistcoat, calm, shiny, neat, walked in. He embraced Mason. "I must say I had a hell of a time getting here! Got the news in Belgrade late this afternoon, and had to charter a plane. A pack of bloody idiots, positive cretins, started shooting as we came in to Aspern. Clods! Wretched peasantry!" He ordered a drink. "Where's Paula?" he asked, taking in the faces of the group. Mason explained. Tom looked worried but said merely, "Well, tomorrow morning we'll have to get her out, if she hasn't managed to get out already." He reverted to his troubles reaching the Bristol. "Streets full of bloody clods!" They discussed the story. "Oh, don't tell me what the story is about." He cast off the words to Shipwright. "This old cock knows. End of the established order, end of the bourgeois world."

7

Mason, Cairn, Shipwright, and their fellows gathered the next morning on the Vienna side of the Reichsbrücke. The bombardment of the Karl Marx-Hof up the river had already begun, they could hear the gruff boom of the guns, and now it was the turn of the Goethe-Hof. Mason peered across the bridge and saw the buff stucco tenement six hundred yards away which housed his own family, where he lived. He was frantic. There was no possible way to get Paula and Richard out. "She's a levelheaded girl, she'll have gotten out by this time, but doesn't know how to get in touch with you," Cairn sought to reassure him. At 9:05 an army officer, trim in his grayish-green uniform and with a cap with a patent-leather peak, marched forward on the bridge accompanied by a sergeant who held aloft a white flag. The brown swirling stream of the Danube coursed below, like swiftly

floating olives. A Schutzbunder also carrying a white flag emerged
from the Goethe-Hof on the other side and met the officer halfway
across the bridge. The parley lasted a few minutes. The officer was
demanding the surrender of the Goethe-Hof. No. If the Goethe-Hof
surrendered, useless bloodshed might be avoided. No. Very well. Half
an hour to evacuate the women and children. At ten sharp the attack
would begin. Ultimatum.

Mason watched closely. His heart was pounding. Were Paula and
his child still inside the beleaguered building? What could he possibly do about it?

This was war in the ancient manner. It was antique. You actually
saw, with naked eye, the people you were going to shoot.

Twice, three times, the time limit for the ultimatum was extended. Methodically government troops continued to pull into
position the howitzers to be used in the bombardment, protecting
them with raw earthworks dug out then and there from the streets.

Mason, watching, boiled over. He felt a prickle in his eyes as they
became bloodshot. An officer gave a command, and a squad of
troops took positions in front of the line of guns. The last ultimatum
must have expired, because machine guns now began to bark and a
detachment of Heimwehr formed ranks and began slowly, very slowly,
to cross the beginning of the bridge. This was not merely wicked,
but demented, Mason thought. Somebody had to stop it. *Somebody
had to stop it.* Without knowing what he did he hurled himself
forward and found himself standing athwart the line of march on
the bridge, calling out hoarsely, making a pushing gesture with his
hands high up, then waving his arms wildly to force the Heimwehr
back. Huge, crazed, bellowing, his shoulders hunched forward, he
lowered himself into position like a football player, and began to advance menacingly toward the troops. He was taking on the entire
Austrian army!

A bang—a skid—a slide—and he found himself rolling on the hard
pavement of the bridge, as somebody, panting, yelling, grabbed at
him, covering him with his body. Rolling to the side of the pavement,
the wind knocked out of him, shaking himself loose, Mason struggled
to rise. Now several people yanked at him, pulling and pushing him
to safety, but the man who made the first dive, the first wild tackle,

and who had saved his life, was Tom Cairn.

One second more, and the Heimwehr men would have started to shoot.

"Now really, Mason," Cairn said, dusting his knees, "people can get hurt doing silly things like that."

Mason glared at him. He was just as astonished as Cairn at the words that came out of his mouth: "Thanks. By the way what the hell do you mean by trying to make love to my wife?"

"Shut up, don't be so provincial. Come along now. What if I have? Love is good."

"Listen, Tom."

"Don't talk nonsense, don't talk irrelevancies. You're witnessing something unique—observe it. Citizens destroying their own city!"

"You damn well lay off Paula, Tom!"

They trotted down the pavement to rejoin Shipwright and the others.

❊

Mason never quite knew how he managed to get to the Goethe-Hof. His motive had nothing to do with journalism now. Yesterday at the Karl Marx-Hof he had hoped desperately to be with the defenders for the sake of the story; today his only thought was to be with Paula, to find her, rescue her. If the government did actually dare to open fire on the Goethe-Hof with heavy guns, he had to be at Paula's side.

Calculating carefully he left his companions. He had to work out the route. A press card would get him up to the ferry, or, with luck, the bridge beyond. It was a gray day overhung with sticky clouds, and visibility would soon be bad. He must bear north in a wide swoop and pray that he did not meet a patrol. It was cold. Where had he lost his hat? Mason found himself presently in a kind of rural slum, a checkerboard of small sheds, truck gardens, and dilapidated houses, near the Nordbahn. Once across the river he ought to be able to get right out in the fields and approach the Goethe-Hof from behind, even if it took hours of walking. He might get shot. Don't be absurd, he told himself. What was happening to his nerves? He wasn't in the faintest danger of being shot, except by accident or some crazy sniper. He was a newspaperman working on a story—perfectly legitimate business. A patrol. He stopped. They must be able to hear his heart pounding a quarter of a mile away. He slipped into the shadow of a barn, and the patrol passed. He heard shots, not very far off, rifle fire, and then the boom of shellfire from the bombardment of some other house. Of course he was *not* a journalist working on a story any longer, because, if he actually managed to get into the Goethe-Hof, he would almost certainly be stuck there with no chance whatever of writing anything for days. With chagrin he realized that it wasn't easy to cut himself off from the tradition of his trade, its bondage and excitement. More shooting now—a whishing crackle came from the left. He got lost twice, ran into a blind alley, and at last came to the foot of the ferry station and managed to talk—and bribe—the boatman into taking him across with a cargo of vegetables. Thank goodness Austria was still full of *Schlamperei.* On the other bank, crawling up, he fell into a loop of barbed wire and was sharply challenged by a sentry in workers' clothes. Rigid, Mason whispered, *"Freundschaft."* He identified himself and asked to be taken to an officer. "There aren't any left," the Schutzbund sentry replied. Mason walked toward a suburban railway station, where the defenders had barricaded themselves in the café. The whole place stank of spilled beer and wine. Mason started. Two bodies lay on the floor. They were covered by heavy strips of cardboard torn from a nearby kiosk—advertisements of movies in the neighborhood. Nothing else had been available to cover them with. Mason asked the way to the Goethe-Hof and walked down a wide empty street, slipping on broken glass, tripping on telephone wires torn from their posts. *Piinnnngg!*—he heard a shot, very close. *"Freundschaft,"* he shouted as loud as he could, and somebody dragged him into the doorway of a house. Police had just finished combing through this district, taking off anybody they suspected of having fought.

Mason reached the Schiller-Hof, which was the first *Gemeindehaus* he had ever visited, near the Goethe-Hof. A Schutzbunder told him, "We had seven dead. They're still here." Mason looked at the bodies and saw that one of them, broken and stiff, was that of the young democrat who believed in reason, Dr. Ricardo Stein.

*

Mason arrived at the Goethe-Hof at last at about three-thirty in the afternoon. A porter recognized him, and led him through a passageway toward his own quarters. "No bombardment yet," said the porter. "Parlays are still going on." Mason bounded up the stairs, opened his door, and saw that his clean, compact little apartment looked as it always had—sterile, sensible, completely undisturbed. But Paula and Richard were not there.

8

After interminable plungings down crowded corridors Mason found Herr Michaelis, their concierge, and grasped him, panting, "Where is the gnädige Frau? Is the baby safe? Flat empty upstairs! Where are they—where?" Apparently Michaelis was a Schutzbund captain; Mason might have known. He was busy. He replied, "Women with children were evacuated about two hours ago." His voice was maddeningly slow. "The Gnädige did not wish to go. . . . Other women have remained—they are working in the kitchen and otherwise assisting. But because of the child she was compelled by us to leave. She resisted. But she went." "Where is she now?" Mason asked desperately. Michaelis shrugged. "I do not know. Some village back in the fields, I believe." He sighed. "She will be safe, the baby also, unless there comes complete disorganization and the fighting spreads."

Mason asked, "What can I do to help you?"

"If you wish to remain secure, go down to the basement. If you wish to observe, climb to the roof."

His voice held a faint note of contempt—that of the fighter for the onlooker.

Mason climbed to the roof. Here he encountered Hollering, the noncommissioned officer whom he had known at the Turnhalle. Hollering said that everything was ready now to meet the assault, which would probably come at any moment now—before dark, certainly. February days were short, and not more than an hour or two of light remained.

With intense curiosity Mason peered across the river. Here he had left his colleagues—it seemed a thousand years ago—that morning.

Where were Cairn, Shipwright, and Wheatley now? Probably watching the Karl Marx-Hof being blown up, since fighting hadn't started here as yet and they couldn't wait for it all day.

Mason inspected the ledge where he stood. More than once he had been guilty of calling these municipal tenements fortresses. Absurd! Any building is a fortress if it conceals men who answer gunfire. But to assert that the Goethe-Hof—or any of the other houses —had been *built* as a fortress was an ignorant or willful lie. Mason knew now. He could see that those slits in the corner towers, which looked so much like machine-gun loopholes, were five feet from the floor—ventilation slits for the laundry—and that to work a gun from them was impossible. He saw that the wall protecting him was made of plaster and stucco, not more than a few inches thick.

Even so—even though the defenders were vulnerable to being trapped if the walls collapsed, and had to expose themselves unduly in order to shoot—defense should be comparatively easy. The Schutzbund machine guns commanded the full length of the bridge. (True, there ought to be more guns, bearing on the same position from above.) But defense should not be difficult. The beaten zone covered the upper end of the Reichsbrücke without a possibility of failure. Just wait. Wait till they got in sight. Hold fire until they reached three hundred meters, where that officer had stood early in the morning. Then lift the latch. Then let her go.

There were two more ultimatums, very Viennese.

Not till five did the attack begin.

"They're coming now. . . . Watch!"

"Wait . . . not yet. Head low, comrade."

"Comrade, do you know what I'd like most in the world—a glass of beer."

"Jawohl."

"By heaven, they are coming now."

Two armored cars, *Panzerwagen*, slowly began to advance across the bridge.

"Ready . . . Wait. Now!"

The Schutzbunder next to Mason lifted the latch on his gun like the old-fashioned latch on a closet door. The gun shook. The noise stunned Mason and then the cartridge cases sprang out like beans bouncing. The two armored cars were almost at the middle of the bridge. They were not hit. Aim too high. Then Mason heard a rattling and cracking and he realized that enemy bullets were striking the wall beside him. Dust sprinkled down from holes torn out of plaster. The Schutzbund gunner applied himself to his target again when the cars weren't two hundred meters off. Was he hitting them? Gun jammed. The gunner tore open the bolt. He could not get it back on again, and Mason helped him. The gunner fired again and now Mason could see that he was hitting the forward car. Like hammering on a metal roof. Could machine-gun bullets penetrate steel armor? He did not know. Gun jammed again. Oh, dear God! Then the two cars went into reverse, chugged backward and disappeared.

Troops followed the cars. Warily, they approached the bridgehead. Mason's companion opened fire; nervous, hasty, he fired too soon, but the troops retreated. Mason found himself shivering all over.

A long wait.

At considerable range, across the river, he detected movement, although the light was bad. The government forces were screened by the embankment, and only occasionally could he see men crawl, dodge, or jump. Then Mason realized that probably the bridge was not going to be a vital factor. The government would not waste men by trying to cross the bridge until after a bombardment. A storming party might attempt it but only at the last moment. Those first armored cars and troops were doing nothing more than test the strength of the defenders. The real focus of battle would be across the river. Mason, dismayed, saw why. A beaten zone on a river was something impossible to exploit, because no troops were going to cross that river until it was safe to do so. There was no point in denying them that area. In safety behind the embankment the government was going to blow them up at leisure with field artillery. Curse and blast that river! Of course the embankment was within machine-gun range; Mason could see men plainly if any exposed themselves. His gunner fired a preliminary spurt, searching. But what good was machine-gun fire against artillery, when no enemy needed to advance?

"Save it for the bridge," Mason muttered. "Sooner or later they'll have to come over that bridge!"

But would they?

The Goethe-Hof could be blown to pieces first.

Curse that river!

The artillery bombardment began at five thirty. Mason's jaw hung open. The first shell hit forty meters down the façade of the building, he felt a heavy muffled thud, the floor groaned and shook, and pouring out of the hole in the building came a yellow, thick cloud of acrid dust. From the quick puff of smoke across the river he tried to sight the battery that had fired, and his gunner opened fire carefully, traversing the area. At all costs keep them under fire. Keep on shooting till the end. Then another shell came screaming; you could almost see it. But there was no crash—a miss. Then another. A queer smacking sound, not ten feet under Mason, shook him; he bit his lips. Bits of lath and plaster disengaged themselves from the stucco wall, crashing down. The wall shook, but there was no explosion. A dud. Or perhaps they weren't daring to use high explosive. Then, like a lump of dough dropped heavily on a shiny floor, crushing, sickening, a new crash came, hollow, heavy, wet-sounding, and he knew that another shell had struck—live. Screams came, a shower of plaster fell, and the building shook.

The gunner, reckless of orders, fired madly at the embankment.

"*Achtung!* Sortie across the bridge again!"

But the armored cars, with their ugly metal noses projecting, chugged backward when fire met them.

With glasses Mason explored the embankment scrupulously. He caught sight of a group of men not in uniform, who seemed undisciplined, who exposed themselves carelessly, and who were—somehow—familiar. Mason was about to tell his gunner to train his gun on them, when he discerned near them a big automobile with a foreign flag. He brushed sweat from his forehead. These must be observers—journalists. Refocusing the glasses carefully he looked again and clearly identified two figures, James N. Drew and Dr. Heinrich Ritter.

If Drew and Ritter were there, other correspondents must be there. All his blasted colleagues were watching him get blown up. This was a blasted Roman holiday, and all his friends had come out to see the blasted fun.

He trembled.

It struck Mason sharply that, of all members of the journalists' colony, it should be Drew and Ritter whom he saw first at the side of those enemy guns—Drew so enigmatic, so spotted and bumpy with false pride, and little old Dr. Ritter, aged, brittle, chirping like a sparrow, spitting, drinking his garlic water. Mason's memory went back swiftly to the beginnings of the A.O.G. affair. . . . Drew and Ritter, symbols of corruption . . . Really all this had started with the A.O.G.

Mason saw one short, stout man in the group point at the Goethe-Hof, gesticulating. Could it be Sandor—pointing toward him?

Brrbrfff! Mason hurled himself flat. He slid along the parapet. The pillars started to quiver, and the wall bulged, then cracked. Smoking wreckage poured over the gun, and, turning for help, he saw that his gunner, flattened by the explosion and trapped by a beam, could not move. One end of the terrace now disappeared in a shaking upheaval. Mason heard a gasping sigh, "Ggah! Oooooooooh!" and saw that the gunner's leg was smashed—wet white bone protruded from torn trousers wet with blood. "Ooooh-ggg!" Men, shouting, ran up. They were seeking to rescue the gun as well as help the gunner. Mason tried to assist the gunner as a man yanked at the heavy tripod of the gun, hoping to remount it. Another shell came, exploding just underneath the window; the terrace, slowly, what was left of it, turned on its side, swiveled, toppled, and collapsed.

"Comrades! Up to the tower!"

Three of them wrestled with the heavy gun and started up the stairs with it.

Mason remembered how, years ago when they first moved into the Döbling villa, he had said in reference to something or other that if you hated you lost.

He did not think this now.

The gunner lay there propped against the door, unconscious, bleeding, as a spray of dust, plaster, brick, bits of lath, nails, glass showered violently down.

Mason couldn't believe it. Three bodies lay together on a corner of the staircase. He could not tell which torn fragments of leg and shoulder belonged to which. Nobody knew where the doctor was. The moaning gunner was still alive, and they fumbled trying to make a tourniquet out of a shirt.

"Up to the tower. Quick! North *Stiege!*"

When the gun was ready to fire, Hollering stepped down from the roof and, without a word, tapped Mason on the shoulder. Mason knew exactly what he meant. He was to take the place of the dying gunner. From here he could see along the whole façade of the Goethe-Hof. It was badly damaged. He looked down into the central court and there was a child playing with a broken hoop, although children were supposed to have been evacuated. A woman leaped from a basement door and picked the child up, the child wriggling and screaming. One body lay down there, that of an old man. Someone explained, "He tried to run out and get some food—shot with sandwiches in his hand." Mason, taking orders from an officer he had not seen before, trained the gun on the bridge. No use firing on that embankment any more. Wait for the bridge. Sooner or later they would have to come across. He smelled goulash from a kitchen below, and discovered that he was ravenously hungry. Life went on. But did it? How about his gunner? A long throaty scream burst out from an apartment further down the terrace; a civilian lay there writhing, but they could find no wound.

Now the enemy advanced slowly across the bridge—at last! Mason aimed carefully, lifted the latch of his gun, and opened fire. He was stone cold, but all that suppressed capacity for violence he was supposed to have became released.

9

Two exhausted Schutzbunders managed to penetrate the dark lanes back of the Goethe-Hof that night and gave the defenders news of the town. Fighting still took place in Ottakring, but it couldn't be decisive out that way; fighting still in Hernals, bloody, vicious, in the factories, on the streets; and Floridsdorf might hold out another day. They were sending no fewer than five thousand men to attack the handful of Schutzbunders dug in there. The other Gemeinde houses? Ah!—it was too terrible to be believed. Only nine had resisted in all. The Karl Marx-Hof, blown to bits, had surrendered. The Goethe-Hof was the only important house still holding out. *Wirklich? Ja*—even so! Another fighter, hoarse, trembling, crawled into the Goethe-Hof

from the swamps near Stadlau. He had been in the Karl Marx-Hof—
the last man to get out. Mason and his companions listened, hushed,
to the story of a youthful soldier who had been caught when the
building was evacuated. The authorities chose to make an example
of him when the fight was over. What? No! Oh no! This man, an
intellectual, did not hold great importance in the organization; few·
had ever heard of him. He was quite young, a Doctor of Philosophy,
some reports said. He performed prodigies in the defense of Karl
Marx-Hof, he inflamed the defenders, he led one fighting group. Few
had known him before, but at the end of the day everyone knew him
for the spirit that had seized him. At the trial—trial?—he had refused to make any defense except to say that he was defending what
he thought to be the rightful and lawful prerogatives of the Vienna
municipality. Trial? Oh, yes. Seven men on trial so far. Summary
martial law—no appeal, sentences to be carried out within three hours.
For all Schutzbunders? No—hardly—only for men who confessed to
leadership. Still, one could never tell. What had happened to the
heroic young man? What? Hanged. *Hingerichtet!* Hanged. He had
been sentenced to death at five P.M. and would now be dead.

"What was his name?"

"We think Kreer, or something like Kreer."

"Of what detachment?"

They named it. Mason's group. Mason's friend.

He closed his eyes.

They had been talking in complete darkness; they could not risk
snipers' fire. A woman left the room and presently returned, bearing
three candles, all that she could find. She walked to the window and
slowly, defiantly, lit them one after another.

*

Radio-Wien. Radio-Wien. They crouched listening.

"Complete rout of all the dissident forces . . . The city quiet except for the outskirts and along the river . . . A successful minor action
took place at Goethe-Hof. . . ."

Grunts.

"The leaders of the government detachments distinguished themselves. . . . Prince Starhemberg, out in the field near Linz . . . returned to escort the Chancellor to Floridsdorf. . . . Major Fey . . . leading the regular army forces at the Goethe-Hof . . .

"The population urged to obey the law, to have confidence and faith. . . . The deluded insurrectionists to give up their arms . . ."

❋

Mason and Hollering slid downstairs as sentries went on watch. On the corner rampart they saw one pair of machine guns, and fifty feet along another pair. Four? No more? Good God! "Well, we have six on the roof," Hollering said. Ten in all? No more? "Even now a search party will attempt to find more. We know more guns are here. We know it. But the district leader who has the information of the hiding place—gone! Arrested!" What good were the secret depots if their location was secret even to the fighters? Muddle. Muddle. Mason asked about grenades. None. Rifles? About two hundred, old, rickety, some of them with strips of cord instead of straps. Ammunition? Well, not so bad, at least four thousand rounds.

Mason remembered from the *Turnhalle* that one pair of machine guns could easily use four thousand rounds of ammunition in two hours.

All the wounded had now been picked up and lay together in the shattered clinic. The doctor, hysterical with fatigue—there was only one doctor—tried to snatch a little sleep.

They didn't know what to do with the dead. Sixteen so far. They put the bodies side by side in one corner of the courtyard, and tore down an awning to cover them with.

Toward midnight Mason climbed up to the north tower and took his place beside his gun. It was very cold, and his teeth were chattering.

❋

Hollering and Michaelis sat below. From one of the flats the sound of moaning came.

"There's nothing else to do," Hollering said.

"If we get out of this, you mean."

"Oh, we'll get out of it all right."

"I'm not so sure."

"It's open country behind us, man. Maybe five hours' walk to the Czech frontier."

"You don't think they've got patrols out in Kaisermühlen?"

"Not yet. Too busy in front of us."

"Well, five hours is a long walk. If we get there."

"There's nothing else to do," Hollering repeated.

"I guess not."

Hollering sighed. "And I've been a party member for twenty-four solid years."

He had told Michaelis that they must start over again, join the Communists.

Social democracy was not enough. The Fabian approach had failed utterly. There was nothing else to do.

*

Mason, startled, sensed some kind of movement. Across the river—slaty, shiny—he could see nothing, but on the far end of the bridge itself two small lights advanced slowly—an automobile. Mason recalled the car he had seen earlier in the day with Drew, Ritter, and the other journalists around it—could it be the same car? It continued to poke its way forward cautiously, and he could even hear its motor purring. He moved beside his gun. The car stopped halfway across the bridge, as if its occupants were making a last-minute decision. Its parking lights went off.

Mason had a powerful, an overwhelming sense, not merely that this was indeed the same journalists' car that he had seen that morning, but that good friends of his were in it. Cairn and the other correspondents must have guessed that he was trapped in the Goethe-Hof, and were attempting to reach him, rescue him—or at least inspect the situation. It was just what a crazy man like Cairn would attempt to do. Mason throbbed. Then he had a further thought. Paula might well be in that car too. He knew Paula. She would never be content to sit out events like these among women and children in an evacuation center. She must have contrived to join the correspondents somehow. He had no positive, rational reason for his belief, but he knew absolutely that it was so.

The car—the sound of the motor more clearly audible now—slipped forward.

Mason became alarmed. If the Schutzbunders in the other tower should also see the car, they might fire on it.

If only he could call out!

The car crept closer still. Fools! It was crawling right under the nose of the near embankment now. What were the idiots trying to do?

Mason's companion at the gun stirred. "What's that?"

In another minute the other tower would start shooting.

Mason said, "Ssshhh!"

He grasped his gun, aimed a good two hundred feet to the side of the car, and lifted the latch.

The sound split the grayish-black heavens.

The car ground into reverse, and, heeding this warning, lurched safely back.

10

Mason woke toward dawn, stiff and cramped. The early morning sky was yellowish, as if faintly irradiated by some forgotten sun on the far side of a darkened world. He looked around him. The parapet had been hit just below him by a dud, and craning down he saw the shell protruding from the plaster, half imbedded. He hadn't noticed it before. If another shell should hit that shell!

What the hell am I doing here, Mason thought. At his feet, a gunner breathed loudly. This was service to the Chicago *Star* above and beyond the call of duty, but it wasn't for the sake of his newspaper that he was manning this gun, he knew. Well, anyway, here he was—make the best of it. He became almost cheerful. Who cared? The noise of shots, like paper bags being crushed, came from far away. Luckaday, lackaday, lickaday, his mind said, *pum-pum-bing-BAM!*

Mason, before that day was over, had most of his habit of not taking sides, his tendency to avoid commitment—that is to say his predisposition to avoid reality—blasted out of him. A creature much given to tangents, glimpses, wings, waywardnesses, he was brought heavily to earth. It had always been extraordinarily difficult for him to stand up and be counted. Well, he was deep in the slot, fully counted, now. His self-division, which had been the root reason for his self-consciousness, became welded over, the chasm sealed. Now all the muddle, the groping for illusion, was blasted out. But surely this was the most violent of contradictions! He, a man of reason, a man of peace, was being shot at, and was grimly doing his almighty best to shoot people in return. Where was the logic? Why should it be violence—crude, coarse, raw violence—that should solidify him into reality? He was being brought to the clarity of affirmation by something as monstrously irrelevant as gunfire. Well, what made character was action. Life consisted of reason and un-reason both.

Renewal of the bombardment came at eleven in the morning after more vain bargaining and another ultimatum, and continued without abatement till almost four. At point-blank range, with mathematical precision, the government forces poured shellfire into the Goethe-Hof. The façade crumbled; all the flats on the front became a smashed powdery wreckage. Two Schutzbunders were killed at their gun by a direct hit within ten feet of Mason. The damage would have been much greater had not the military used half-charged shells. Even so walls fell in, floors buckled, inner beams snapped, pipes broke, one stairway crashed. A child was killed when, following the artillery bombardment, machine-gun fire swept the building. Now the Dollfuss infantry was ready, and the armored cars were on the bridge again.

Mason fired at the attackers until his gun ran out of ammunition. The doctor had no more morphine, and was tearing up sheets for bandages. A massacre. They couldn't fight with their bare hands. Men scattered. Senior members of the Party command, those who remained, held a meeting in the wrecked kindergarten, powdery with broken laths and plaster, and came to a decision—surrender. Orders went out for residents of the building to return to their flats and wait peaceably until the military came. The active Schutz-bunders, since they might be shot or hanged if caught, were in-structed to flee at once; they ducked out of the back of the building into the grassy Danube marshes and made for the Czech frontier.

Paula, Shipwright, and Cairn were among the first to enter the

shattered building. The wounded were being evacuated, the premises searched, a guard set up. The confusion was harrowing. Where
was Mason?

A portly, kindly, unshaven police officer led the journalists
around.

"Ach, ach!" he kept muttering. "Cruelty, wickedness . . . Cruelty!
And what's it all for? What good's to come of this?"

The police officer patted a boy's head. He pointed up, with one
hand still on the child. "Up there . . . those towers . . . the Schutzbund up there, shooting at us. I lost my best lieutenant, machine-
gunned through the throat. Why did all this have to happen? Why
did they have to resist? Why, why?"

A lieutenant from the military came up and saluted a tall colonel.
"Seven machine guns captured. No ammunition."

Another officer was ordering the extraction of unexploded shells
stuck in the walls.

A wounded woman was the first to be evacuated. She had been
hit in the stomach by a fragment of shell the afternoon before, and
had had no proper medical attention for almost twenty hours. She
was still alive. A man shrugged, muttering, "Soon she'll be pushing
up the radishes from underneath."

A crew of Heimwehr men—laborers—set about glumly to make
order out of wreckage in the corridors.

"Schweine!" The portly, kindly police officer lost his temper and
screamed at them. "Heimwehrschweine! You caused most of this!
Get to work! Hurry up!"

Women tenants, wives of workers, surrounded the police officer.

"Why, why," they said to him, mournfully, almost without
rancor, "why did you shoot at us?" Mournfully, as if forgiving
him, with swollen eyes, they muttered, "At us! Why?"

Paula set out to find Mason. Near their own flat she saw him
come tottering down the stairs.

11

Mason, Paula, and Erika went to Stein's funeral with his parents
and other members of his family. Paula sat next to Erika in the
first car with her hand on her forearm. The drive seemed endless.

Erika's face was composed except for a twitching of her eyelids. Mason looked at her closely, and thought that her face seemed dry. All the sap was out of it, her face was drawn, the life had departed, it was dry.

There had been a light snowfall and they bumped through half-frozen slush. Mason lifted his coat collar. It was cold, with a heavy whimpering wind, although the snow and mud on the streets had not quite hardened into ice. They arrived at the cemetery at last and police shoved them along. The crowd was not big, and people resembled figures in a Brueghel, in black clothes set against the whitish snow; old women shivered, and everybody, men and women alike, looked curiously stunted, small.

The Socialist dead were being buried together in a mass ceremony, expeditiously and almost surreptitiously. Even for a man of Stein's position private services were forbidden. Tomorrow would come the state funeral for the army, the Heimwehr, the police, with a service at Stephansdom to be celebrated by the Cardinal Archbishop himself, with flag-draped gun carriages, pompous music, the roll of drums, and martial speeches interrupted by the stately boom of guns. Today the police clumsily pushed the Socialist mourners in their rough clothes through muddy passageways in a deserted cemetery while snow fell like wet peonies.

The police shoved the mourners ahead, kept them moving. "Auseinandergehen!"

Planks, rough pine planks, new and wet and yellowish, were laid across muddy paths. Not everyone could keep balance on the springing planks and women floundered in the mud. Mason supported Erika and Paula. No music, no speeches, no service was permitted. One by one the rough pine coffins, shaped like lozenges, disappeared into the yellow mud, each ticketed with a red card. Soon the pits were covered. There came a long wait, and the crowd began to scatter. But some mourners refused to go.

On the horizon the profile of the Wienerwald hills could be seen in rough, shadowy outline. The sun had turned an angry red. Clouds whipped across the sun, driven by the fierce wind, and the red ball of the sun sank slowly, as if igniting these rushing clouds, setting the cold clouds alight. The clouds burst into flame and smoke shot

out of the sun as it dipped down and finally disappeared behind the
trees. The clouds remained pink a long time, even after the sun had
gone out.

"Weiter! Auseinandergehen!"

Wallowing through the mud, Mason helped Paula and Erika
along the planking to the wet street. Erika began to cry. She cried
silently at first, shaking, trembling, and then the real tears came, her
face became distorted, and she sobbed with the anguish of total loss.
For a long time Mason and Paula listened to her cry, hoping that
she would stop, but she didn't stop. She kept on crying, sobbing, her
lashes wet and twisted, as they drove back, until no more tears
would come, and, silent, they penetrated the deadness of the barricades and entered the lost city.

12

It was ten o'clock that evening at Erika's studio. She had given
them shelter there until they could move back to the Goethe-Hof.
She herself stayed with Stein's parents. The Jarrett baby had been
taken in by the Wallensteins, where Paula had managed to deliver
him when she left the evacuation center.

Mason carried on with his eyewitness stories of the fighting. He
wearily slipped another sheet of paper into the machine. Silence
outside, total darkness. Street lights not on yet. Suddenly they heard
the ugly snapping crackle of rifle fire. It was very close, seeming to
come from just outside their window. That ugly snapping crackle
once more, snapping, crackling. Mason jumped up and peered outside; Paula had a hand over her open mouth. Schutzbund men
were emerging from the sewers. A last desperate remnant of Schutzbund fighters, half drowned, half dead, starving, leaped out of the
sewers near the Belvedere and popped to the surface two hundred
yards away. One by one, as they emerged, the police, who had been
alerted, shot them down. Paula screamed.

Later that night Paula had the look of somebody who had taken
a large decision.

She said calmly, "Darling, do you want to marry Erika?"

Mason was staggered. "No," he said. He began to feel strong
emotion. The emotion was about Paula, not Erika.

"I'll hate it, but I'll give you a divorce if you want it and want to marry her."

He looked at her face, trying to read it. "No—no—"

"She's a marvelous girl and you love her, don't you? She loves you. She'd make a much better wife than me in several ways."

"Perhaps, but I'm staying on with you right to the end." He smiled. "Not necessarily the bitter end, either."

She could not suppress a flush of pleasure, but proceeded: "Out of a sense of duty?"

"Oh, shucks, Paula—no!"

"I came across a memo on your desk a couple of weeks ago. You wrote down a date for your second marriage."

His forehead wrinkled. "That was fantasy—pure, unadulterated fantasy. I'd completely forgotten it—silly nonsense!"

"Why do you want to stay with me?"

"Because we're married."

"That's a rather unsatisfactory answer."

"No, it isn't. And because I love you."

Mason had a glowing moment of revelation. He truly did love her as she loved him and that was the basic reason why their marriage was indissoluble, but something else came into play on his side beyond this, namely that he responded to her instinct for domination. He struggled often against her strength, her power, and it was a joy to overcome her on occasion, to conquer her pat, willful certitudes. But he loved her because he wanted— and was now conscious that he needed—a strong woman. Her strength was both a satisfaction and a challenge, and that was one reason why he would stay with her forever. This was not to say that he was weak. He too was strong in his own domain. That was why they clashed and tussled. The question of who was master, a stupid and unnecessary question anyway, since they were both adults, but each dependent on the other, needed no answer.

He telephoned Erika after Paula had gone to bed.

"What can I do?"

"At the moment, nothing."

"Do you want to see me?"

"Yes, but not now."

"Erika, I'll do anything you want, always, but it's over. Even now it's over, isn't it?"

"Yes. Love to Paula."

❋

Paula awoke very early the next morning. One of the things she could not forget was the shattered kindergarten in the Goethe-Hof, where Cairn and Shipwright had taken her. Desks, blackboards, schoolbooks, paintboxes, toys, were smashed together under a cloud of broken ugly debris. On one wall stood a colored-paper design inscribed with the printed name of its author, aged six. A fragment of shell had ripped through it. They had shot at babies, they had murdered *babies!* Paula had long since passed beyond her ancient concept that life was a kind of endless booklet of tickets, to be picked off in neat succession one by one—clean tickets for the most part, carried by people of good will, decent tickets, toward conventional, decent destinations. She had had little room in her mind for the recognition of anarchy, brute force, or evil. Once people were educated (she liked to think) evil would be liquidated, eradicated. Once people were knowledgeable enough, they would acquire good intentions. Give people a chance, give them equality of opportunity, even if they were not equal by right, and they would eventually become decent, sentient human beings. Paula shuddered. She felt that the very bedrock of her existence had been shattered, pried apart, wrenched loose, ground up, by these recent events. Now nobody could feel safe from the cold, stinking breath of evil. Not only this—evil might turn out to be more powerful than good. Chaos, anarchy, unreasonable disaster could destroy them all.

Mason had a thought at breakfast, addressing himself to Paula. "Do you remember, you wrote me a couple of years ago from Boston or New York, about how appalling the noises were in America— people fixing the streets and all that. Well, Americans don't make quite the same kind of noises that we've been having here!"

And Paula thought: It isn't just his vitality, his earnestness, that make him what he is—not even his capacity for detachment and for finishing things. What gives him his strength is his simplicity, his wonderful primitive faculty of innocence.

13

Methodically, conscientiously, Mason tried to find out exactly what had happened to cause the February tragedy. Not what the government said. A third of that could be discounted. But what had *really* happened. He talked to diplomats and politicians, he spent half a day with Hohnstedt in the news bureau of the Chancellery, and he traveled to Bratislava to see Bauer and Deutsch, who had escaped there and were now refugees. It was a complicated, tragic story.

Until the actual outbreak on the twelfth Bauer still thought that negotiations toward a settlement with Dollfuss were possible. The government informed him that it was using all its energies against the Nazis. If the Socialists behaved themselves, nothing would happen to them. Bauer then told Dollfuss that the Socialist party would declare a general strike if any one of four things happened: imposition of a Fascist constitution on Austria, change in the semi-autonomous status of Vienna, dissolution of the Social Democratic party, or dissolution of the trade unions. This was the Socialist ultimatum. Neatly—too neatly—Bauer announced it. And all that the nimble Dollfuss had to do was keep Bauer dangling, whittle his support away, and avoid these major provocations.

Meantime Mussolini told the Chancellor that he must liquidate the Socialists or lose *his* support, and the Heimwehr threatened to join the Nazis if Dollfuss did not take a "final" action against the municipality. All this Mason found out and wrote.

Bauer tried to calm down his own followers. On the late afternoon of the eleventh he took his wife to see Greta Garbo in *Grand Hotel.* Thus the "red criminal" was preparing for revolution! He returned home to find out that Major Fey had announced a "clean-up" for the morning, the same radio message that had so alarmed Mason. Then came a code message from Linz that the Schutzbund there intended to resist by force if the Heimwehr, following a series of coups in the other provincial towns, attacked them. Bauer sent messages urging restraint.

But the Schutzbunders in Linz disregarded him and when the Heimwehr did attack in Linz the Socialists resisted. News of fighting there reached headquarters in Vienna at about eight-thirty on the morning of the twelfth. Bauer, distraught, summoned a meeting of the Aktions-Ausschuss, executive committee, of the Party. While they were discussing what to do news came that the electrical workers in Vienna had, on their own initiative, without orders, struck. Bauer was horrified. It was too late to save the situation now. A call for a general strike was voted, but only by a majority of one. The general strike manifesto was hurriedly prepared and the strike set for five P.M. Perhaps the idea was to try to bluff the government, but what it did was give the government seven precious hours of warning. Then occurred something outlandish even for Vienna. The manifesto was rushed to a special plant to be printed, since the *Arbeiter Zeitung* had been shut down, but no contact had been established between the electrical workers and the printers and at the very minute that printing of the manifesto was to begin the presses stopped. The electrical workers had shut off the power! So the call for a general strike was never sounded, because of a weird fault by the electrical workers, who wanted it most!

Then, Mason found out, several Socialist leaders hurriedly called on the President of the Republic in a last desperate attempt to stave off bloodshed. At this, hard-boiled men like Fey simply laughed. It was pitiable. The government waited until almost every Socialist leader of consequence was conveniently at its disposal in the Hofburg and then placidly threw the lot in jail. Several were arrested while they waited like lambs in the chambers of the President of the Republic himself. Then Major Fey and his men launched the attack by seizing installations like the *Turnhalle* in Floridsdorf and attacking the *Gemeinde* houses.

Journalists asked Dollfuss why he had neglected to accept the Socialist effort to make a last-minute settlement and avoid fighting. The Chancellor replied smoothly that he was in St. Stephen's at Mass and could not be reached and then the lights went out and it was too late.

14

Mason and Paula listened with horrified fascination to the radio.

Now the authorities said that Bauer and Deutsch had run off

with the trade-union funds.

Lies, lies.

Now the announcer said that all Schutzbunders who had given up their arms by twelve noon on the sixteenth had been freed.

And Mason knew very well that they were not freed.

The next day the police cleaned all the foreign newspapers off the kiosks. Some of the foreign papers told the truth.

*

Laszlo Sandor was almost out of his mind with excitement and frustration.

Here he was, one of the best journalists in Central Europe, and during all this chaotic tragedy he had nothing to do, no story to write, because he had no paper to write for.

About a thousand dead in all, he summed up. Twenty-one women killed, seven children. So far nine Schutzbunders had been hanged.

Now they got Wallisch and his men down in Styria. It was all over now. . . .

But it had taken a modern army of nineteen thousand men, with artillery, with armored cars, with every new technical device, seven whole days to clean out perhaps four thousand ill-armed hungry Schutzbunders.

Sandor muttered, "Not so bad . . ."

Mason worked hard on one story that, for some reason, most of his colleagues neglected. The spoils of victory for Dollfuss and the Clericals were tremendous. The Socialist municipality owned about thirty-five per cent of the land of Vienna; it employed fifty-four thousand people and was by far the largest enterprise in Central Europe; it collected taxes of about twenty-five million dollars a year, and its funds in the municipal savings banks alone stood at seventy million. It owned the gasworks, the streetcars and buses and subways, the slaughterhouses and the public baths, and a department store. All of this went into the hands of the Clerical minority in Vienna. "It's sinful," Paula said.

Mason and Cairn forced their way a few days later into a long narrow room in the Chancellery. One of Fey's men spoke. Above them, glossy on the walls, hung portraits of the ancient chieftains, the old emperors; the ceiling was very high, monstrously high, and the chandelier glittered. No room to sit down. The correspondents perched on window sills, on gilt-and-marble tables, on the floor. Not another person could squeeze into the noble, graceful room. It was hot. Someone attempted to open a window. Now some diplomats tried to insert themselves into the room. They had no business here. Throw them out. Fey's man finished his indictment and sat down, and a long wait followed. A young woman journalist, whom Mason had never seen before, asked for some water, but no water was to be found. Mason gave her a quick smile. Even at a passage of time like this he could not help taking out the flash of a second to think about her. He wondered vividly what she would be like. His whole thought centered on her. Incorrigible! Outrageous! There came a flurry at the door, heels scraped, and Dr. Dollfuss entered. He sat down at a table covered with a maroon cloth and all through the room listeners could hear him sigh. His staff waited for him to speak, but he did not rise. Dr. Wimpassing, nervous, subserviently beckoned to him. Still he did not move, but sighed again. Finally he lifted himself from the chair, his face gray. The exophthalmic blue eyes bulged, and his hands shook. He did not speak at once. He was waiting. Then he spoke rapidly for almost an hour, and Mason never heard a more tortured voice. The little Chancellor, who was a great judge of occasion, made no recriminations; he rebuked nobody, nor did he blame the Socialists for anything. He talked in a dead imploring voice, trying to explain—in slow, grim, painful detail—what the government had done, why it had done it, trying to justify himself, to excuse himself, to excuse the bloodshed that had occurred. He talked like a man transfixed with remorse and guilt. Then abruptly at the end his tone changed. He outlined the future. He became aggressive and emotional. He screeched. Mason felt he would never finish. Finally he sat down.

There was no applause. And Mason thought that he saw doom written on the face of this little man.

BOOK FOUR

Afterwards

XVI.   THE UNWINDING

The holocaust was over, and the Jarretts moved back to the Goethe-Hof. Their flat was not too badly damaged; clearly it was a matter of good luck that they had not taken quarters on the river side. Cracked plaster; broken windows; a wall near the kitchen warped, and a thick carpet of dust over furniture—that was all.

The telephone rang late one evening.

"This is Smith."

Mason was slow. "Who?"

"This is Smith." The voice became measured and distinct. "S-m-i-t-h. Your friend Smith."

"Oh." Pause. "Where are you?"

Mason turned to Paula with a hand over the mouthpiece. "Tetzel."

Paula rose.

"I'm in the Eighth Bezirk. Pick me up near the Café Donnerhof. I have a new job. *Herzliche Grüsse an die gnädige Frau.*"

They went rapidly to the Donnerhof, where they saw Tetzel waiting a hundred feet away. He paused until he was sure that they recognized him and then turned a corner, motioning them to keep back a discreet distance. Entering the hallway of an old apartment building he waited till they caught up with him, then led them around another corner into a tailor's shop; they penetrated this and climbed worn stone stairs to a flat facing a deserted dark garden. Here they fell on each other's necks.

Tetzel told them what had happened to him on February twelfth. He had gone first to the office of the President of the Republic in the Hofburg, having heard that the Socialist leaders would be there, but they had already been arrested. Deciding to report to his Party cell to see what action, if any, was expected of him, he reached its headquarters and fell instantly into the hands of the police, who had just raided the place. He watched his fellows being led toward a prison van down the street. Then—incredible detail—he walked off scot-free. Nobody had pinioned or handcuffed him, and the police forgot him in the hurly-burly of getting the others into the van. He disappeared into the crowd and raced to the *Arbeiter Zeitung*, where another exceptional circumstance saved him. The police there said that the paper was shut down but let him into the building when he said that he was a foreign correspondent and wanted to pick up his mail. On the way out, having found that all of his friends were gone, he was stopped by an officer who asked, "Do you know the Herr Redakteur Dr. Karl Tetzel? What does he look like?" Tetzel said he had never heard of the man and skipped away.

Ever since, he had been hiding, since the order had gone out to arrest all known Communists. He hadn't dared risk calling the Jarretts —or anybody else—until today. In this new place of residence he felt fairly safe.

Yes, he could easily slip out of the country on a false passport— easily!—but he preferred to stay.

"There will now come a long period of readjustment," Tetzel explained. "All will have to be done with a new beginning. I have the function to take care of certain secret details in recruiting and administration. Not for anything would I desert this task."

Tetzel looked happier than at any time since he had helped Mason on the A.O.G. affair. Work—a task, a cause—saved him. What he had chosen to do might mean years of conspiratorial activity underground, years of loss of identity and a life totally surreptitious, years of deprivation, anonymous sacrifice, hardship, struggle. And if he were caught, he would be hanged.

But Mason, in a moment of clairvoyance, did not think that Tetzel would be caught and hanged. Always he would manage to glide prudently out of trouble. He thought that he could foresee clearly Tetzel's future in the party. He would climb adhesively and become a dutiful, vigilant office worker and be put into dry dock somewhere in the files. Eventually he would rise to be an assistant in the propaganda department, or a subchief in the political administration. The romantic days were over. And never would Dr. Karl Tetzel attempt to contrive the assassination of Marcus Aurelius Thorne.

There came a cautious signal on the door—three short taps, one long. Tetzel opened the door with care. Paula and Mason jumped, astonished to see Shipwright enter. Had Tetzel established contact with him, as with Mason and Paula, out of irresistible yearning to see his old friends, or what? How did Shipwright know the tap-tap signal at the door? He told them what he had been doing—helping smuggle Schutzbund fighters out of the country. He had been to Bratislava, just across the Czechoslovak border, twice, and to Yugoslavia once. Mason was surprised. He knew that Shipwright had always taken a sentimental leftist position, but he had never thought of him as a person of deep convictions or as a man of action. What had happened now? Obviously he and Tetzel had a close association. Could Shipwright be a Communist? Had he been a Communist all along?

Seeing Shipwright and Mason together made Paula nervous. She fished in her bag for a handkerchief and sniffed, her eyes down. Shipwright was calm, and Mason obviously had no inkling of suspicion about them. What a cheat I am, Paula thought.

They talked till midnight, when Wheatley, the Englishman who never spoke, joined them, also signaling with his knuckles on the door. Strangely he was voluble tonight, as if the excitement of recent events had loosened his tongue at last. He gave nothing away, but it was clear to Mason that he too, like Shipwright, must be leading a surreptitious political life.

When the Jarretts rose to go Shipwright and Wheatley stayed.

*

Soon word got around that Mason had taken part in the actual fighting in February, although he himself said little about it. Certain colleagues were avoiding him and a good many officials became hostile. People he did not know well stared at him with cold curiosity. A man with blood on his hands! A man who had used a machine gun against Austrian citizens, and perhaps killed several!

Julius, the headwaiter at the Weissenhof, took a considerable time to get around to serving him when he appeared for the first time after the fighting, and saluted him, not with the usual florescent "Was ist gefällig, Herr Präsident," but with the much less courteous "Kompliment." And the Heimwehr waiter, the one alleged to be Somebody's Nephew, didn't greet him at all. But Leo, the woozy little Communist, the doorman, was friendlier than ever. He positively gushed. Orlovsky, however, cut him dead. To hell with all of them, Mason thought. I am what I am.

On one of these post-February days Mason went through a communiqué that appeared in all the newspapers:

The balance sheet of the A.O.G. is in process of final compilation, and reorganization of the bank is now effective. [Nice word, "reorganization," Mason thought.] Various sums will be written off at the expense of the foreign creditors, the Austrian government [that is, the Austrian people], and the Austrian National Bank. Total losses to Austria are now calculated at 1,236 million Schillings. . . .

A few days later came another communiqué, stating that the labors of the Austrian delegation in London had been interrupted by the civil war, and as a result the terms now demanded by the foreign creditors were altered, that is, made stiffer. There followed a series of announcements about personnel. *Herrgott*, if they could only learn to do some paragraphing in the newspapers, Mason sighed . . . Herr Generaldirektor Dostal had been rehired by the new administration "in an important capacity," and Herr Hofrat Paultraxl was appointed to be Austrian representative on the Finance Committee of the League of Nations.

＊

The Archduchess drove Paula and Erika to the Wachau (the cherries and apricots were in blossom now) for a day's outing. They would not be back till late, because they were having dinner at the *Schloss* near Dürnstein, where Richard Coeur de Lion had been imprisoned. Miss Birch and the Archduke lived near it now, in a magnificent *Schloss* of their own. Mason finished work early, and gave way to a sudden impulse. He telephoned Nella Blohr. Apologizing for the short notice he asked her to dine with him that night. He had never had a dinner with Nella in Vienna. Budapest and Geneva yes, but Vienna no. Only seldom did he have an opportunity to be alone for dinner in Vienna. He picked her up in the Grand Bar and after a drink or two took her to the place in the old city where they had the *Backhendl*. Nella was happy. She ate greedily, speedily, as young people do who have not had enough to eat in childhood. She had grown up during the privations enforced by World War I and its aftermath.

Mason did not think in terms of moral issues. Paula would certainly be hurt and angry if she ever found out that he had seen Nella alone again, but he overcame his scruples. All he knew was that he yearned to be close to her once more and tell her about himself and listen to her talk and admire her youth and freshness and enjoy her regard for him. It was nobody's business but his own. He had acted on irresistible impulse and if penalties were going to be attached as a result he was prepared to face them.

They passed an exciting evening. She still had a capacity to amuse him, as she did when, burrowing against his chest, she said, "You have a squeak in your chest, it sounds like a clock going backward." But Mason was alarmed when Nella called him the next day. He didn't like this a bit. Paula might pick up the telephone extension or come into the room at any moment. Nella brought up with intensity something she had alluded to the night before—the impossibility of having a decent, normal future in Vienna with its obvious fragmentations and social decomposition. "Get me out!" she asked him. "Even if it means that I'll never see you again, help me to get out!" "Out of what?" "This country." Mason promised to call up the American Consulate and do his best.

Sandor's voice was almost unintelligible on the phone an hour later. He gasped, "Mason, I've got a job again!" The February tragedy had made American editors acutely conscious of Central Europe once more, and the New York *Register* decided that it had better expand its shrunken foreign service. It would be cheaper to hire somebody already on the spot than to send a staffer all the way to Vienna from New York. Somebody thought of Sandor. Oh yes—Sandor—first-class man . . . correspondent of the Washington *Sun* before it folded. Yes, Laszlo Sandor, get on to him at once. . . .

So Sandor had Bishopson's old job! Sandor had the best job in town! And where was Bishopson now, Mason wondered, his old master of *Schwierigkeiten*, of whom he had been so fond? People said vaguely that he had a job in Manitoba . . . assistant managing editor of a paper there. . . .

Promptly Mason and Paula met Laszlo and Erji at the coffeehouse. Pale, Erji said, "Give me a drink of drink!" She was struck by the intolerable exhaustion that may come abruptly when intolerable strain is lifted. Unsteady, she rose and rushed to the ladies' room, where, out of pure blessed relief, out of joy and pride now fulfilled, she was sick.

✳

Some of the boulevard sheets made big headlines with the news, but the more respectable newspapers tucked it discreetly on their inner pages. Jail break at Wöllersdorf. A neat one too. In an official car, bearing what seemed to be authentic papers, two "government officials" arrived to take three Nazi prisoners to Vienna for "re-examination." The timid blustering governor, completely taken in, escorted the bearded Nazis to the outer gate. "That for you!" said one of the "officials," hitting him across the teeth with a heavy wrench. The car sped defiantly off. Wide search disclosed trace neither of the car, the "officials," nor the prisoners. Frontier authorities had been warned, but probably the miscreants were already safely across the German border.

The leading Nazi who made good his escape was the former journalist and sub-*Stabschef* at the Brown House, Herr von Traub.

Mason grunted. Just like the Austrians. They would even have to get his name wrong.

Bleschke's voice was as cringing, bland and monotonous as ever the next morning, but it disclosed a faint glimmer of irony, of *Schadenfreude*.

"I have news that will perhaps make interest for you personally. The name of Goethe-Hof is to be changed to Engelbert Dollfuss-Hof."

Mason walked in to tell Paula. "Guess we'll have to move."

✳

Politically Mason still felt shaken. He had often warned Stein that the Social Democrats would someday be outmaneuvered and beaten down, and he had never been such a fool as to think that esprit and bare hands could withstand machine-gun or artillery fire. Reason could not sustain itself against force by the power of intellect alone. Even so the events of February had been a telling shock. Where was a man of good will to turn? He himself could never be a Socialist, much less a Communist—he disliked too much the circumscription of any kind of dogma, he believed too firmly in the free mind, the availability of choice, in liberty. He had worked for a living since he was a boy, but he could not possibly identify himself with any concept based on class. He was an American, a democrat, a liberal, who believed in justice, progress, and education, a man who tried to see both sides, who believed in the rights of the minority against the majority, all of whose instincts tended to be toward moderation, toward social amity, toward the free critical appreciation of decency and truth.

But was this enough? What truth? Whose truth? How was brute reaction, smash-and-grabbism, to be met and fought?

It was abundantly clear now that potent and aggressive reactionary force, far from being an isolated or peripheral phenomenon, typified the entire epoch. The old bourgeois world was gone, irrevocably lost. It died on the February barricades. The contemporary dictators were not only unscrupulous, voracious, and expansionist, but extraordinarily powerful. Even so Mason did not lose his sense of balance, his optimism and idealism. He refused to be deprived of his innate conviction that man, no matter how feeble, is perfectible; and he still believed that life brought rewards as well as penalties and that it was worth living. But of course the circumstances of life for the vast majority of people ought to be improved.

In any case he knew that his hope for the future, his belief in progress, did not rise out of any facile optimism. If he chose to be an optimist he had at least earned the right to be one. Mason thought back to something he didn't like to think about. Manning that machine gun he had killed people for his beliefs.

The afternoon papers came in; he glanced at the headlines, which had lost all flavor through ceaseless repetition. The little Chancellor, whom he had not seen since the press conference, was elaborating on his adumbration of a corporative state. But it was obvious now that he had been gravely weakened by the events of February, not made stronger, because the murder of the Social Democrats had destroyed the political morale of the country. Confusing inner rivalries abounded. Mason made a small news story out of a joke. Two Heimwehr men met two others; they separated, and the first two said, "I wonder if that pair of Nazis know that we are Communists."

The Nazis became the chief beneficiaries of February, because Dollfuss had unwittingly done their own job for them—annihilated the democratic working class. Now, after a period of cleverly lying low, they inaugurated a new, vicious tempest of violence; bombs came everywhere once more. The Dollfuss response was, strangely enough, to treat the Nazis more gently. Time and time again he threatened to hang a Nazi terrorist, but never did. After a bomb exploded in St. Stephen's early in April Mason wrote a dispatch which began, "The major political factor in Austria today is still the circumstance that the two parties pledged to keep the Nazis out slaughtered themselves to make it easier for them to come in."

Sandor now predicted another civil war within three months.

❋

Paula fingered idly through the magazines one lazy spring afternoon and saw something about a new medical discovery—isolation of vitamin ZZ. She became inquisitive. "Mason, what's the greatest of man's inventions? Printing press? Microscope?"

He laughed. "The mirror."

"Why?"

"So that man may see himself."

That was a very Paulaesque remark. It was extraordinary how married people came in time to acquire each other's characteristics. Two people lived together for a while and liked each other and loved each other and inevitably came to resemble each other in their habits and characteristics.

She slipped out of the room for a moment because Richard was crying, and he noticed a couple of envelopes on her desk that she had addressed but not yet mailed. Even their handwriting had become alike.

He was the stronger, in spite of his dependence on her, because he was indissolubly conjoined with work, with the process of creation, which continually gave him force, flavor, and refreshment; yet it was he, not she, who now became worried and helpless when she left the flat even for a brief interval; it was he, not she, who hated desperately to be alone and suffered torments of despair when she took a walk without him.

Nella? He learned from her that no woman will believe that a man has given her up merely because he says so; he must stop seeing her. But she was going to America in the autumn, and she would forget him there. . . .

Mason joined Paula in Richard's room. The child pawed at them gustily through the bars of the *Gehschule*. They thought, in the manner of all doting parents, that he was remarkably advanced. He could say "Tick-tock" for clock and "Bim-bim" for streetcar and would be walking without support very soon.

Summer came, their fifth summer in Vienna. The warm insidious *Föhn* was blowing and they skipped off to the Salzkammergut for a brief holiday and were tender and warm together, as they always seemed to be when they left the turmoil of the city. Again they saw and savored the green velvety mountains, the poppy fields, lads with cock feathers and leather pants, peasants stumbling sleepily along creamy dusty roads, and the scarecrows flashing blue and crimson out in the wheat.

And, once more, they devoured the beauty of the lakes; they had never seen anything so radiant as these mountain lakes. They really did resemble jewels—the surface clean, the color deep, and the banks straight, so that each lake seemed to be cut out of the rock and set, rather than filled, with solid water. And the trees were marvelous. . . . One afternoon the stumps of a rainbow rose iridescent on each side of them in a field while the arc disappeared above; at their feet were flowers—pansies—with Rorschach ink blots painted on their faces. That night the moon looked like the head of a golden bollard in a Venice lagoon—a somewhat phallic moon; maybe it would bless them. It was a pity to have to return to town. But they had had a call from Cairn, who was passing through Vienna once more, and both of them would still give up almost anything to have an evening with Tom Cairn.

Back in Vienna Paula said, "Frau Gertrude says that Sandor phoned and will we come down to the Weissenhof this evening."

(She thought, Mason's up to something. Look at him—like a terrier sniffing. He's got an idea for a story.)

Mason said, "No, I'm going to clear up some nuisances tonight, if I can. Tend to that mail, will you? Thanks."

(He thought, I'm going to start serious writing on a book tomorrow.)

2

Having finished his morning's work Mason wanted to go swimming. This was July 25, 1934, and it was a steamingly hot day for Vienna, although not sunny. At a little after one the telephone rang, and he heard Sandor's voice. "You have heard the radio? Radio-Wien has this minute made the announcement. 'The government of Dr. Dollfuss has resigned. Another government has assumed power.' It may be a joke. I don't know what."

In later years Mason read a good many accounts of the events that followed, just as he read many accounts of the February tragedy; since he had witnessed both these spectacles himself and had even taken part in one of them, the words he saw in print seemed somewhat pale. He rushed to Ravag, the radio station, in the Innere Stadt. Armored cars already surrounded the building, and he heard once more the harsh angry rattle of machine-gun fire. Nazi conspirators had, it seemed, gained entrance to Ravag, seized the transmitting apparatus, and broadcast the false news that Dollfuss was deposed. A coup by radio! This was to have been the signal for a general Nazi revolt throughout the country, but the plot miscarried. Now the police were attempting to blast the Nazi conspirators out of Ravag. An actor who had been rehearsing a skit became hysterical, started to scream, and was shot ten yards away from Mason as he was maneuvering his way out of the building. Mason got the gist of the story, telephoned it to Paula for transmission to Paris before censorship was imposed, and hitched a ride in a police car to the Chancellery, where a crowd had already gathered.

IIe stood there out on the street next to the graceful Bundeskanzleramt, with its walls the color of whipped cream and its two-and-a-half layers of windows so well-proportioned and dignified, until late in the afternoon. A band of one hundred and forty Nazis, disguised as Austrian police, had gained entrance to the building by means of a daring ruse, arrested those members of the government who were within, including Major Fey, and murdered Dollfuss in cold blood. The Nazis had organized their coup with such confidence and precision that a German photographer, who had arrived from Berlin that very morning, was able to set up his tripod calmly outside the Chancellery and wait to take pictures of the raising of the swastika. But the swastika was never raised. The conspiracy went to pieces because the Nazis in the Bundeskanzleramt lost their nerve once they got inside. Orders that they had expected never came. Without these they were helpless. They did not know what to do. To avoid being blasted out of the building by force they opened negotiations, and, using Major Fey as a hostage, asked for terms.

Mason never forgot the unprecedented scenes that followed. With the Nazi ringleader at his side Fey stepped out on the shallow stone balcony on the front of the Chancellery, twenty feet above the sidewalk, and without success sought to establish contact with those members of the government who, luckily, had not been inside the building when the Putschists struck, and who had now gathered, aghast, in the street below.

Mason, Sandor, Shipwright, took positions with them. Little was known to them—or anybody. They thought, as troops arrived, that shooting would start at any moment. First it was assumed that Fey, ambitious and insubordinate, had made a coup of his own against the Chancellor. At about four a loyal police officer gained entrance into the building through a rear door, and then emerged, screaming; he grabbed a portable telephone that had been set up and, communicating with headquarters, cried out in the open, so that everybody could hear him, "The Herr Bundeskanzler is dead!" Major Fey, with a Nazi in civilian clothes at his side, guarding him, came out on the balcony for a second time, pale, with his chin lifted. A stout Heimwehr officer crossed his hands to make a seat, and invited Fey to jump to safety from the balcony. He refused. So a grotesque series of conversations began—between Fey up there on the balcony and the ministers assembled in a tight gesticulating circle on the street below.

Heimwehr men shouted to the Nazis, who could be seen in the room behind Fey, "Woe to you if you harm our Fey! Touch our Fey, and we will hang every one of you on these trees."

Somebody in uniform near Mason gave a strident shout: "Storm the building!"

Fey protested, "*Nichts unternehmen!* Nothing may be done until I give the orders. I am in command." But obviously this was not true, since the Nazi leader next to him on the balcony gave him his orders minute by minute and controlled his every word.

A cabinet minister named Neustädter-Stürmer, who had been close to Dollfuss, arrived out of breath. The crowd made way for him. Again a Heimwehr lieutenant yelled up to the balcony, "Shall we storm the building?"

Fey shouted down, "No, nothing is to be done. Take no action without my orders."

Neustädter-Stürmer answered, "A new government has been formed and I represent it. If the rebels do not surrender within twenty minutes we will storm the building."

Fey called, "No. You will not storm the building. I am State Secretary for Public Security and you are to take no action without my authority."

"You are mistaken, Herr Fey! Members of the government who are prisoners are under duress and are not competent to give orders. It is now 5:28. At 5:48 the building will be stormed!"

Armored cars ground into place.

Mason, chafing with suspense, did not know whether to wait to see the denouement or try to get through to a telegraph office and send the news that the Chancellor was dead.

A few minutes later the German Ambassador to Austria arrived and was smuggled secretly into the Chancellery. Pourparlers began, and the building was not stormed. In the end the Nazi Putschists agreed to surrender on the promise of being given a safe conduct to the German frontier. They were then neatly double-crossed and arrested, while the government took over the Bundeskanzleramt and sought to restore order.

Mason tried stubbornly to disentangle fact from rumor—hopeless!—and to piece together later a coherent account of what had happened. Dollfuss was given no chance whatever to escape, he learned. The Chancellor might easily have been captured alive, like Fey; but the Nazis had one paramount aim, to kill him. They entered the building at 12:55 and at two minutes past one at the latest he was shot. Mason reconstructed the story. When the Chancellor heard the news from Ravag and learned that a Nazi revolt was in progress he retired to his private study, a small room bound in yellow silk, to take charge of the situation and conduct operations. A minute later the Nazi plotters disguised in police uniforms entered the building. Dollfuss saw the trucks unloading in the courtyard, grasped what was happening although he did not know that the men were Nazis, and, leaving the yellow study, advanced across another room toward the great Congress Hall, planning to escape through the narrow passages that led to the archive rooms above, then organize a new command post and fight to the end. The door to the Congress Hall was locked; his secretary fumbled for a key. Dollfuss reached upward to wrench the door open and one of the disguised Nazis, bursting into the room, shot him in the armpit. The Chancellor reeled and the Nazi assassin fired again, aiming at the throat. Dollfuss fell; his head made a loud crack when it hit the floor.

"*Hilfe, Hilfe,*" Dollfuss muttered.

His murderer snarled, "Stand up."

"I cannot," Dollfuss whispered.

His companions picked him up and laid him on a divan. When Mason saw it the next day three large bloodstains, the shape and color of oak leaves, were still conspicuous. Major Fey was permitted to enter. He was sweating heavily. Dollfuss said to Fey, "I charge you to take care of my family if I die." Fey pleaded with the rebels, who stood in an untidy circle gawking at the dying man, to summon a doctor or at least a priest; they refused. Dollfuss thought that he had been betrayed by his own forces—not only that the *Putsch* had succeeded, but that his own men had shot him down. Later, dying, he apparently believed that these were loyal troops, not rebels, who sur-

rounded him, surveying his shrunken body, watching the blood dribble
out and spill down to the floor, because he whispered, "Kinder, you
are so good to me. Why are the others not as you are? I wanted only
peace. May God forgive the others."

All that Mason knew indubitably that day was that the Chancellor
was dead. He decided to try to file a story after the loyal ministers,
in a circle on the green lawn of the Heldenplatz, held their first cabinet meeting standing up under the trees, surely one of the most unusual cabinet meetings in history. He broke through the crowd, which
was now yelling for vengeance, and ran to the Majestic. Phones were
cut; full censorship had been imposed. Panting, he filled out a telegraph form and gave it to Klaus. "Klaus, listen carefully. Give this to
one of your boys in an absolutely normal way, and have him take it,
not to the central telegraph office, where everything will be stopped,
but to some small branch office. Try to have it sent from some small
office in the outskirts where the news that censorship is in force
hasn't percolated down, or where the clerk won't understand what
this message means."

The telegram was addressed to Hilliard at 1000 West Wabash, the
street address of the newspaper, not to the Star itself or its telegraphic
address, and it said simply, LITTLE FELLOW KICKED BUCKET SAFTERNOON.
Klaus said, "Self understood!" and leaped swiftly into action.

The message did not get through.

3

That autumn Mason and Paula became impatient to leave Vienna.
They had, they thought, had their fair share of Gemütlichkeit. They
had exhausted what Vienna, as a spiritual and corporate entity, had
to offer. They would miss the Sandors grievously, they would miss
Erika, they would miss all their friends, but they would go away now;
after five years they had had enough. Vienna, so much part of them,
would be behind them. They would say good-bye to Mozart in the
Musikvereinssall and Schlagobers in the cafés, they would say good-
bye to the Goethe-Hof, Frau Gertrude, and the palaces with butter-
scotch coloring on lovely squares like the Josefsplatz, to all the things
they loved in Vienna, all the things their hearts remembered. Mason
thought that he would ask for a transfer, when an opening came, either

to Moscow, so that he could have opportunity to see something of the Other World, or Shanghai, so that he could learn a little about the Far East. In November an unexpected message came from Mr. Plover. Hazelwood had decided to retire on the first of the year to devote himself for the rest of his life to his history of the Merovingian kings, and Mason, in reward for his work in Vienna, was promoted to be his successor. Paris! Paula was jubilant (neither Moscow nor the China coast would be quite the place for Richard) and Mason not displeased. Paris correspondent of the Chicago *Star*—best newspaper job in the world!

4

So the Jarretts missed the unwinding of the Vienna story, the painful vicissitudes of the Schuschnigg government that followed Dollfuss, the remorseless increase of Nazi pressure, and vicious intolerance by the government against the Socialists; they were not witnesses to the last acts in sabotage, betrayal, disintegration, dissolution; they were taking a holiday in America when the bizarre climax of *Anschluss* came, and Austria disappeared, gobbled whole by Hitler. Even so, Mason was not finally quits of Vienna. This city extracted a permanent toll from its lovers.

Came World War II, both the phony phase and the real; civilization tottered; countries crashed; Paris fell; good-bye to their orderly big apartment near the Champs de Mars. The Jarretts made their way to London, and for several years he worked all over the place—Norway, Egypt, Turkey, Russia. Paula and Richard stayed on in England. He decided one bitter day in Kuibyshev, when the icicles started to form again after a thaw, to quit journalism forever when the war was over, as Paula had been so bold as to suggest so many years before, even if they starved. The book he had started in Vienna, and had been trying to work on intermittently, was still little more than a mass of discordant notes, experimental passages, false starts. The giant, blazing world of actuality during wartime made it utterly impossible to concentrate on any mere work of art. And Mason wanted to quit the *Star* because its character was changing, and after the war no question of duty would be involved. He always thought of institutions in terms of people. Hilliard left the paper to become assistant to the president of a midwestern university, and then, when America entered the war, went into the Marines; McFarland died of a chicken bone stuck in his throat, the most glaringly absurd of accidents.

London, London, blitzed, an inferno, resolute, magnificent; Mason's memory recaptured episodes odious, ludicrous, sublime. Grotesque small recollections stayed with him: the way burglar alarms rang far into the morning from the deserted empty bowels of shops bombed during the night; of pavements covered solidly with broken sheets of plate glass, so that walking was like sliding on ice; of the man whose head was blown right through the windshield of his car, severed but undamaged, with fragments of bloody glass stuck to it like a halo.

Paula, Paula . . . who would ever have dreamed that any such catastrophe could happen? Who could have conceived, even in the wildest, most flaming expansion of the imagination, that Paula would fall in love, through some mysterious permutation of the physical, and have an affair with, of all men, Mark Thorne? Of course it had been partly his, Mason's, fault, the penalty of his neglect of her—to say nothing of the long absences imposed on them by the war. Moreover he himself had behaved badly. Aimlessly, thinking of that fight with Paula before the world collapsed in February, he fingered the scar made by her nails, which, shaped like a jab of lightning, was still faintly visible on his cheek. But Paula had actually fallen in love with Thorne. It was almost inconceivable. She had *left* him, Mason, after that shabby business of his with the Greek princess. Served him right. But for months he refused to concede that any such disaster could have happened; he literally could not endure that it had happened, and therefore could not believe it; he refused altogether to admit it to the precincts of his mind. He denied it. There was no use denying it. "You have murdered a marriage," he said to Paula. "You murdered it long ago," she replied.

Erika, Erika . . . His thoughts still surged backward. Would the lives of all three have been happier, more fruitful, if he had had the courage, the will, to leave Paula, marry Erika, years before in the early days, the green-lit silken days of old Vienna? Paula would certainly have married again, and might have married extremely well and established a splendid life for herself. He himself loved Erika, adored her, and she loved him. But it had not worked out—on account of Paula—as well as because of his sense of morals, cowardice, and indecision. Who would have ever thought that Erika would marry Yancey, whom she had met at lunch with the Jarretts that day shortly before the February bombardment—Yancey, with his purple shirts and shiny nose, Yancey so crisp, competent, and rude. But what an exemplary ambassador's wife Erika had made! And with what demure sweet serenity (serenity was her secret) she would grace the house in Surrey—or was it Kent?—that would be hers when Yancey came into his father's title.

Mason had not so much as seen Paula for a year.

He did not know whether he would ever see her again.

What about Richard?

His memory continued to search back, flickering, sultry. Vienna had been the whirling center of their universe, it had given them a complex and abundant life; but now it was clear that, rich and varied as it was, it had been no more than the merest prelude to what came later. It was astonishing that the Vienna years, so seemingly crowded and glowing with every element that life held, could seem so placid, so pallid now. But they had copious importance still. They held people, scenes, interludes, that Mason would never forget. It was simply that events had moved to a larger stage. Again Vienna seized him. Otto! Passages in Otto's diary! Otto's youthful eyebrows with their herringbone pattern! Otto a Spitfire pilot killed on his second combat flight! Mason closed his eyes. Wheatley! A secret agent of British intelligence all along, caught in the end by the Gestapo, hanged through the throat on a meat hook. Dr. Antioch! Made, barefoot, to carry stones out of a pit endlessly at Buchenwald.

Mason peeled another recollection off his memory as if it were a palimpsest. Just before that trip to Budapest he had made some sort of note or other in a diary wondering if Gresham's law, the law taught to economic students about bad money driving out good, could be applied in other spheres—to the realm of human relationships in general, to the coinage not merely of money but of love. A debased coin drives out of circulation a good coin. Could this be so with other values? Mason did not like to have his basic optimism warped or dented, but these were not times given to freshness or optimism and had not been since the fall of Vienna. Bad values did drive out good in a world corrupt, a bastion fallen, a city lost. Honesty does not pay off. The bad drives out the good.

Mason was an old hand, a bored veteran, around the base near Foggia now. They had reached 1945. He watched the line of Liberators waddling along the runway, their swollen bellies hugging the earth and their fat tails high. A damned uncomfortable ship to fly in, but you could bail out through the bomb bay even if the bombs had not been discharged, and this could be a great convenience. The commanding officer at Cerignola had spent a long interval at Fort Sheridan in Illinois and had read Mason's dispatches in the *Star* and liked and favored him. Two weeks more and Mason would be finished with this particular assignment with the Fifteenth Air Force, and glad of it. His loneliness here was insupportable. Perhaps it would be insupportable anywhere. He had spun himself into a cocoon. The threads were not strong enough to keep thoughts of Paula out. Already he had flown three missions—Athens, Lyons, Sarajevo—and each had been about as exciting as a visit to the Cowes Regatta on a sea becalmed. But he became alert and attentive, prickling, when Colonel Hawkes, not a bad type, not a bad type at all, but limited, provincial, asked him if he wanted to go out again tonight and see his old home town. "You don't mean Chicago, do you?" Mason bantered. "No—for Crise sake. I mean 'Wien, Wien, nur du allein.'" Mason's pulse shot up. He remembered with sudden fresh vividness the flights over Vienna, up and down and all around Vienna, that he had taken fourteen years before with Dr. Ricardo Stein. He knew Vienna like a book—moreover he knew it from the air. Not that this could conceivably be relevant to the night's adventure. His would not be the lead plane, and pattern bombing went by rote; you simply followed the ship ahead and waited to see its bomb doors open and then let go, hoping the platform would be steady. Ships in tight squadron formation, their wingtips seldom more than six or seven feet apart, so that they sometimes seemed to be actually overlapping, always followed this procedure. Even so it would be an undeniable thrill to cross Vienna from the air, see it again from the clouds after all these years, drill a long invisible tunnel over Vienna in an American Air Force B-24.

Mason listened carefully to the briefing. The flight would occupy 7 hours 39 minutes mostly at 24,000 feet at something like 185 miles per hour. Fighter escort of P-51s would be provided till the flight veered off from the Apennines across the Adriatic. The mission would include six groups of the Ninth wing, three of the Forty-third, four of the Forty-ninth, 85 planes in all, carrying 110 tons of bombs. "At 12:05 you will destroy the Südbahnhof." How well he knew that sprawling gray railroad station from which went the trains to Edlach, Semmering, and Bruck! Other primary targets were the Floridsdorf locomotive works (Floridsdorf—where the fighting had been hottest during February!) and a large building that had once housed a well-known bank, the Allgemeine Österreichische Gesellschaft, known as the A.O.G., which was now being used as the headquarters of Goering's Air Ministry and the Luftwaffe.

Now Mason did really tingle. The briefing proceeded. Alternate targets Graz (marshaling yards) and Pola (shipping). Chaff will be dispensed at the rate of 3 small bundles every 20 seconds. Axis of attack 229 M, bombing altitude 1,000 for primary target, change to 9 ship-front formation. Leaders call Button on Channel C, all groups load 500 RDX bombs fused one second nose and tail fuses. Call sign for fighters AMPISH SEVEN, recall signal UNDERTAKER. Mason continued to take it all in. Do not crash-land in the area north of the Drava. Personnel taking to parachutes in Croatia should keep to hill country; most of enemy region is under Partisan control. In Hungary make for heavy forest west of Balaton. If bail out or crash-land immediately behind Russian infantry use the word "Amerikanski," and do not make suspicious moves, as the Russians are quite trigger-happy. Hide chute and stay under cover 48 hours, try make contact with poorer classes of people only, do not smoke. Avoid the Ustashi. Hungarian peasants will try to pitchfork you in the stomach.

Bulky, clumsy, Mason swung himself up through the bomb bay and squeezed himself into the seat customarily reserved in B-24s for an eleventh man—war correspondents, armament inspectors, or perhaps a flight surgeon coming along for the ride. Space was cramped

He could not see the pilot but could reach back up and touch his foot. Next to him sat the bombardier. The plane's engines spat and grumbled into a roar, and the Gay Marietta rolled down the gravel strip, rocking, snorting. At ten thousand feet they prodded up through a cloud bank that Mason thought would never end. It was as if they were lolling through a long shallow trough of snow, and he heard the engineer-gunner in the top turret mutter over the intercom, "Hey, isn't that some hunk of cloud!" A reply came: "Put on your snowshoes, boys."

The nose gunner said, "Seven missions so far, and I still haven't heard a shot fired in anger."

But this flight tonight might, it seemed now, produce excitement. Dirty little black balls of smoke pop-popped at them, and the ship began to rock and pitch. The sound was that of gravel hitting a tin door—clonk, clink, clonk. They lurched, turned, and more flak followed them. Mason's stomach hit his ribs. This was very bumpy flying now; the Gay Marietta groaned and reeled, shaking like a dog trying to get water off its skin. They must be close to Wiener Neustadt now. Vienna lay straight ahead.

Mason exploded into fantasy. Bombardier wounded, bleeding; the pilot kicked him in the back of the neck; the intercom said, "You know Vienna—up to you, Jarrett." Nothing could be easier than to push down that plastic toggle, watching the ship ahead closely and taking the let-go signal from it. All of Mason's energies became concentrated and aroused in a supreme moment of fixed, fierce attention. The pilot brought the quivering aircraft unerringly along the correct line of approach, quieted it down, made the platform solid, and, flying firm, passed in a second over the Ringstrasse and the green velvet carpet of the Volksgarten. Mason dreamed that he could see St. Stephen's and the Burg, and the great baroque building of the A.O.G. came into the line. His hands clenched. Blast that damned bank to bits! Crack it and demolish it and smash it and spill it all over the street! He pressed the toggle. Not merely the A.O.G. but all of Vienna filled his mind now. The bombs sailed down. "That for Stein!" he shouted in demoniac fury. "That for Otto! That for the Goethe-Hof!"

He woke up.

"What are you yelling about, kid?" the bombardier asked mildly. "Don't be scairt. We're just about out of it now, I'm going to sleep till we get home."

Nothing of serious military consequence resulted from this raid, but details about it became well known in restricted circles later, in spite of an attempt to suppress the shameful news. The leading plane of Group Two made what was called "a very erratic run" and the bombardier was unable to kill his target. His box dropped off to the right—and knocked off the Vienna Opera! In fact this raid in which Mason participated was distinguished by several picturesque mishaps. Bombs aimed at the primary target fell short by a quarter of a mile, but the district near the Bourse and telegraph office was hit by accident, as was an area in Döbling near the Grinzinger Viaduct. Mason lifted his eyebrows when, a few days later, intelligence reports supplied by secret agents in Vienna noted that among the buildings obliterated was a well-known café, the Weissenhof. The A.O.G. building was untouched.

5

With James N. Drew Mason had no contact at all throughout the whole course of the war—for the best of reasons—but the general outline of his activity became well known. He went to Berlin after *Anschluss*, became a Nazi, and worked for the Reich in such realms as counter-intelligence, propaganda, and sabotage. He assisted the Germans in ruthlessly interrogating United States agents who were unfortunate enough to be caught on Axis territory, and was certainly implicated in an espionage affair in Switzerland—a trap that cost the lives of two Americans. Drew hid in a hamlet in the Tyrol after the war, and then sought to conceal himself in a students' hospice (the end is the beginning) in Vienna, and was not caught by the American authorities until 1946.

Mason received the following letter from him the next year:

In a jail cell with Christ our Lord.

Dear Jarrett:

In every affliction which comes our way in this life there is contained a message from On High; namely from the Triune God, at whose very existence you, of course, have always seen fit to scoff derisively on your way to fame and fortune.

In view of the many harsh, unjust, and even obscene things which you have said about me in the past years of our so-called comradeship, you will be surprised, no doubt, by a message of any kind from me while you are rejoicing with the gains of your ill-led life. I, however, stand in the shadow of the gallows with a sign bearing the word "traitor" in Yiddish letters around my neck. But I have busied myself with forgiving you and various mutual acquaintances for your various crimes against me, against America, against civilization, and against Christianity. At the same time, however, I must confess, I wish to repeat the slogan, "What the U.S.A. needs is to have a bomb placed under it and the whole country blown to hell."

Is there a connection between the work of American correspondents for "Stalin and Co." and yourself? The answer to this question you can only obtain from God Himself, God the Father, God the Son, and God the Holy Ghost.

If you will pardon a bit of journalistic gossip, I take the liberty to inform you, and anyone else who may be interested, that the "insanity" plea offered at my "treason" trial was not originated or tolerated by me. After almost fourteen months of incarceration awaiting a constitutionally guaranteed "speedy" trial, the prosecution attorneys have submitted me to psychiatry examinations in a vain attempt to have me judged insane; but each time, of course, I emerged with flying colors. The trial judge, as you doubtless know, *refused to accept God as my defense counsel*, and forced upon me a court-appointed lawyer. Even so, I managed to have a few words said about the conspiracy of the Comintern against the U.S. and the Yiddish terror.

Pardon the use of pencil; no other writing equipment is available in my present quarters.

Sincerely,

James N. Drew

Three days later he was sentenced to life imprisonment in an American asylum.

Mason might have felt more emotion about Drew's fate had he not received confirmation that same week of the news, which he had been trying to check for a long time, that Dozent Dr. Wallenstein and the Frau Dozent had both been fed into the gas chambers at Auschwitz.

6

After leaving the *Star* Mason returned to the United States, wrote
a good many books, both on politics and works of the imagination,
and became moderately successful. He had a good deal of pulmonary
illness and, partly for this reason, moved to California, where he set
up residence near Point Lobos when this was still mostly a wilderness, long before the day of electric lawn mowers, power saws,
and other appurtenances of so-called civilized life. Here he lived
quietly for fruitful years in a house built of redwood on a rocky
ledge covered by cypress, and overlooking the broad oval bib of the
Pacific. This July evening he strolled toward the beach at sunset,
through a grove of pine and scrub oak, and stood for a moment by
a tidewater pool covered with foam like white of egg. It was warm,
and soon the pallid, yellowish fog would creep in. Often he saw
pelicans, and occasionally cormorants with their long black necks.
Wet seals barked from wet rocks, and he wondered what human
beings, as well as animals, would do without the phenomenon known
as protective coloration. Conventions were dull, but helped to make
life safer. It was hateful to conform, but convenient.

Mason had intense love for this California neighborhood. Along
the road stood tall spears of straw-colored pampas grass held back
by plantings of red cactus and then the artichoke fields beyond.
Before him spread a carpet made of a bright orange succulent, and
the ground cover near the garage was purple. Here too his wife had
for years lovingly, expertly, tended camellias in big adobe pots.

For no particular reason Mason Jarrett's thoughts this afternoon
were occupied by Vienna. The clement beauty of this niche of California, particularly some of its flowers, occasionally reminded him
of the Vienna countryside. He had not been in Vienna since a
holiday in 1950. At once, arriving, he had taken a taxi from the
Majestic (Klaus retired—a rich burgher out in Hietzing) to the
Döbling villa. It had vanished—disappeared! Nothing whatever survived of it except a few lumps of stone on an empty square of
rubble, on which sparse weeds struggled to stay alive. Walls, garden, crisp walks, shrubbery, the fruit tree with its twisted trunk
and heart-shaped leaves had all been wiped out. Mason was pro-

foundly shocked. Could this destruction have possibly been caused by the raid in which he himself had taken part, when the Grinzinger Viaduct nearby had been hit by accident? It was possible, but not likely. After all Vienna had been bombed a score of times, and there had been plenty of accidents. His shock increased, however, as he stood there silently, a very large graying man, with bright, liquid, big brown eyes, staring at this derelict square of squalid emptiness. That this villa, where he and Paula had spent such crowded happy years, should simply have vanished without trace—obliterated without leaving anything even so sizeable as a bit of ruined masonry— was a kind of insult. He felt as if part of his own life had been destroyed, and that what remained of it was mocking him, with the derision that can be flung at a man by the spectacle of total emptiness in a place once throbbing with life. This was indeed a sinister augury: it meant that nothing was permanent, that nothing of himself would be remembered. He too could be obliterated by a whim.

Probably, Mason thought now in California, he would never see Vienna again. He had lost most of his taste for travel. But Vienna would always be part of him, even if he was not part of it, because it was the city where the forces that made him had been fused into mature, permanent form. A man does not forget the environment which completes his education, makes him what he is, anneals him into the final frame. Mason had changed little since the nineteen-thirties, except for such externals as that he no longer had much interest in politics, beyond the minimum demanded of a good citizen. He seldom looked at TV or listened to the radio, and did not even read the newspapers carefully. He was old, but did not feel so. It certainly marks a watershed when you say, "I'm only sixty," he reflected. The word "only" was the significant word in this brief sentence. Just when you learn how to live, it comes time to die. God, give me another inch.

He flipped a stone across the pool. A gull circled down and landed near an otter cracking open an abalone shell. Well, they hadn't had otters in Vienna! Vienna itself, he had found out to his surprise on that last visit ten years before, was well on the way to achieving a happy ending. The Socialists had regained their fair share of control of the municipal administration, and the *Gemeinde Wien* became once more incontestably one of the best-run cities in the world. A coalition governed the country under a bizarre and characteristically Viennese system known as Proporz. The Clericals and Social Democrats, who had so fiercely torn at each other's throats for so many gnawing years, now had new names and worked together with co-operative amity. Jobs alternated between the parties. Both shared equally in power. Back in America, Mason sometimes repeated the little joke—if anybody was interested enough in Vienna to listen—that Austria was the only country in the world where the two opposing parties did their best to lose, not win, an election. Victory by either might imperil the newly formed and zealously guarded balance of power. So long as both parties ran neck and neck and stayed equal, the political equilibrium was secure.

Maybe it was unwise to think so, but apparently some countries did actually learn from experience, like some men—a few. In a world of no solutions, the Austrians had found one. Everywhere the solution nowadays was that there was no solution, except in Austria—the most slipshod country, the most helpless of them all. What an irony, Mason mused. In contrast he thought of the succession states which had been the field for so much of his endeavor in the Vienna days. After a pitiable scant twenty years of freedom—only twenty years!—they had become slaves again. Austria survived and recovered, but the others went down the Soviet abyss. Where was the logic?

Mason, glancing upward, saw his wife stroll across their terrace bound by chalk-rock walls. The fog was closing in, but he could see her slim shoulders and sharp waistline, and good graceful legs held tightly in a chic skirt, in a last long roll of slanting sunshine. With her dogs—two noisy snapping little spaniels—she walked toward the barbecue. She gave the impression of being cut in cameo: elevated above the surface. She waved; he waved back. Mason started to clamber up the hill, puffing. His son Richard was arriving tomorrow with his wife and children to spend a brief holiday with them, and there were preparations to be made. Richard was still tense, defiant, attractive, unpredictable. In a sudden flash Mason remembered a bit of his conversation at the age of five, when they had been driving down a country road near the sea in France and a new moon shone between the trees. "Look, Poppa, look, somebody has flung a boomerang into the sky and the boomerang has not come back. Poppa, Poppa, the boomerang is waiting in the sky. Who will bring it back?" Today, if Richard chose to discuss technicalities associated with his profession, his talk was totally unintelligible to his father, even if it was still about outer space; he was an aeronautical physicist, and Mason understood that he was presently busy on secret work on missiles.

*

"Moderately" successful? Wouldn't he put his score a shade higher than that? There was the small Picasso (picked up in London during the blitz) and all that china and silver. On a more interesting level of attainment his major books, including in particular the two big novels, were still healthily in print. Who had been more successful? Cairn? No, because Tom's particular style of broadcasting had gone out after the war. Mason had seen Cairn in New York a month or two before; they were still devoted friends. He had aged more than Mason, perhaps because he, Cairn, had stopped drinking. Up to a point, a predisposition to quixoticism makes a man seem younger than his years; after an invisible line, older. Part of Cairn's charm, his power, had been lost through childishness—that is, too much ego. But he seemed to be getting on well with his new job—foreign affairs adviser to a grubby but vastly rich Arab potentate on the Persian Gulf. And he had obviously enjoyed greatly his recent European trip, getting in touch again with Konrad, Harold, and Nikita. He had not seen Charles, however, which nettled him.

Mason reached the rock garden packed with trays of Vallauris tile and carefully inspected the fuchsia with their lavender bells hanging out. John Dixon? Well, one of Dixon's plays had just finished a long run on Broadway, and the travelogues he did for TV had a certain quality and must be lucrative, but he wondered if he were truly happy. Sandor? Still, no doubt, sitting in that new café, the Schwarzenhof, with Erji warmly by his side; still surveying both past and future with affectionate irony through his owl-like eyes. He had no income aside from a modest pension, not a nickel, but Mason felt that he was probably happier, more fulfilled, than Dixon. Climbing further up the hill, Mason passed the bower of tuberoses, sniffing them, and was pleased by an idea that now came to him. Do it in the third person, he said to himself. He was working on a book about his experiences in the war and to write it in the third person, almost as if it were a novel, not a reminiscence, might resolve some difficulties in technique that had been perplexing him. That was it! Third person! It would at least prove to her that he was still objective! Of course he knew perfectly well now that no writing could ever be objective, not even the best of journalism. There was no such thing as objectivity. All a man could do was try to tell the truth.

Paula, brisk, adoring, commanding, fondling a small tawny cat, poking efficiently around the barbecue, called that dinner would be ready around seven, and that he should hurry if they were going to the movies in Monterey. He never worked at night these days. She forbade it. He reached the terrace, kissed her on the cheek, and surveyed the preparations they had made for Richard. She had even brought out the Lowestoft. "Oh, if only I liked her better." Paula murmured, referring to Richard's wife. "All that eye shadow and wearing blue jeans too!" "Well, never mind," Mason said firmly. But he too had been startled when he first learned, a year or so before, that Elaine had had two marriages, two children, and two divorces before she was twenty-five. But Richard was happy with her. Mason poured himself a sound drink, and Paula expertly mixed the salad dressing. Like Mason, she had not changed much except in a few characteristics. She no longer took it for granted that if she spoke inaudibly in a closed room her words would pierce walls and be heard all over the house, and she had gained a certain modicum of confidence if only because, all things considered, her life had turned out well, not badly. She had lost her fear of animals, never had hives, gave less expression to her superiorities, seldom worried about the color of her hair, since it was now white, and had learned how to grill a steak.

Once more Mason's mind touched lightly on Vienna, and nostalgia swept him. Nothing could ever take away from them the years they had had there, and perhaps those years were what in the long run cemented their relationship beyond any possibility of its being eroded or chipped away. Those were the years that bound them without peril of further separation, and it was even possible that

Paula might not have come back to him except for the wry, glowing spell of their commingled Vienna past. Yes—yes—it was a city which took a large toll of its lovers, but it gave returns, satisfactions—ah, more than that!—as well. Mason sat down to dinner with her, and both said "*Mahlzeit*." They drove along the sea and he felt such unbounded tender emotion for her that, for a full three minutes, he forgot about his book.